McArthur & Company

JESSICA

Bryce Courtenay, bestselling author of *The Power of One*, *Tandia*, *April Fool's Day*, *The Potato Factory*, *Tommo & Hawk*, *The Night Country* and *Solomon's Song*, has lived in Australia for most of his adult life.

BRYCE COURTENAY

JESSICA

McArthur & Company

Toronto

First published in Canada by McArthur & Company, 1999
This first Canadian paperback edition published
by McArthur & Company, 2000

Cover design by Guy Mirabella and Tony Palmer, Penguin Design Studio
Cover photography by International Photographic Library
Digital imaging by Paul Fenton
Text design by Ellie Exarchos, Penguin Design Studio
Typeset in 9.6/11.7 pt Sabon by Post Pre-press Group, Brisbane, Queensland

Canadian Cataloguing in Publication Data
Courtenay, Bryce, 1933-
    Jessica

ISBN 1-55278-088-0 (bound) ISBN 1-55278-157-7 (pbk.)
I. Title.
PR9619.3.C598J48 1999   823   C99-931750-4

Printed in Canada by Transcontinental Printing Inc.

The Publisher would like to acknowledge the financial support of the
Government of Canada through the Book Publishing Industry Development
Program (BPIDP) for our publishing activities.

10 9 8 7 6 5 4 3 2 1

To the memory of Jessica
and for Margaret

ACKNOWLEDGEMENTS

I sometimes think my books are made up of all the things my friends know. I never cease to be amazed at how generously they share their considerable knowledge for my benefit. I thank you all.

But firstly, I thank Benita Courtenay who has been with me throughout the making of this book. It is never easy living with an author and once again we have survived the experience.

Margaret and Ian Duff, who brought me the story of Jessica in the first instance and gave generously of their time and hospitality in helping with the research. Without you, Margaret, there would have been no story to tell. The gracious assistance of your family is also appreciated.

Margaret Gee, for the countless hours she put into making sure the manuscript was clean and for so many other ways that made my writing life easier. Bruce Gee, my researcher with his eye for detail and his clever mind. Essie Moses, who helped in a dozen ways. Dr Brent Waters, for medical advice. Denis Savill, who always seems to come to the rescue with the cover art. The Bundanon Trust, for permission to use the Arthur Boyd painting featured on the original hardback jacket, and to the Art Gallery of New South Wales. Robbee Spadafora, for her cover design and production supervision of the original jacket. Alan Jacobs of Consensus Research, for his insights and knowledge.

Susan Killham of the Narrandera Shire Library was very helpful. Leslie Niewodowski for the Yiddish translation. Dr Ken Winkel of the Australian Venom Research Unit. Kathryn Everett, Sylvia Manning, Polly Zack, Peter and Victoria Thompson, Christine Gee and Margaret Merrylees. The wonderfully co-operative people at the New South Wales State Library – a resource it is not possible to replace.

At Penguin Books, Peter Field, Peter Blake, my publishers Bob Sessions and Julie Gibbs for their constant encouragement and help, and finally, Clare Forster, quite the best editor it has been my good fortune to have working with me.

*'If you lose your pluck, you lose the
most there is in you – all you've got
to live with.'*

Eighty-year-old grandmother of twenty-two children,
forced to leave her Oklahoma farm during the
Great Depression, 1936.

(from the exhibition,
The Photographs of Dorothea Lange)

BOOK ONE

CHAPTER ONE

Out in the south-west along the banks of the Murrumbidgee the snakes come out at sundown to dance. The mulga, gwardar and the Eastern brown, the clumsy death adder, black-headed python and the harmless carpet snake. They sway and twist in streaks of twirling ribbon, loops of gunmetal grey and whips of bronze catching the late afternoon sun, reptilian lightning that sends puffs of grey dust into the baking air.

This is country to make hard men whimper and bite their knuckles in their sleep. Old man saltbush tethers the black soil to an endless horizon. By sunrise the day is already grown hazy from the heat. Dark pre-Cambrian rock and mulga scrub tremble in an illusion of moisture. Men see for the most part through squinting eyes plagued by a constant vexation of black flies that suck the moisture from creased skin and feed on the salty sweat stains on their flannel shirts. It is a place where the heat is so severe birds lose their strength to fly and drop like stones from the breathless air.

The women, their hips wide and slack from too many pregnancies, walk with a slow gait. It is as though their shadows contain the weight of their weariness, dark sacks dragging along the ground behind them. Their faces are hidden in the interior of deep bonnets, but it is their hands which first betray them, blunt, calloused fingers and broken nails, skin raw and puffy from the constant use of lye soap and slap of wet flannel against a corrugated washboard.

This is a place to break your heart and leave no sentiment to alleviate a life of bitterness and struggle. Three hundred days a year a hard-faced sky mocks any hope of rain and every miserable dog's day dawn is much the same as the one before it. Monotony and stoicism are constant companions, imagination a bad habit to be quickly stamped out of young children so that they may be made useful and compliant. It is here where, at dusk, the snakes dance on the banks of the Murrumbidgee.

Jessica waits quietly with a shotgun cradled in her arm, her green eyes intent on the scene before her. In the pocket of her pinny are three cartridges, their faded red cases having been used and re-filled half a dozen times with birdshot, and tamped with wadding and cordite with a little black powder added to save money. Joe has shown her how and Jessica can now do it in her sleep: head-wadding, charge, mid-wadding, birdshot, cap and wadding and crimping. The worn cardboard casings with their reseated copper crowns are filled so that the birdshot will effectively spray in a three-foot arc at a distance of twenty feet, well, sometimes, anyway.

At first light when Jessica ventured out of the homestead to the chookhouse she saw that six chicks had gone missing from under the black hen, all taken by snakes, their serpentine slicks plain to see in patches of yard dust leading to the chicken run.

She'd vowed to get the bastards at sundown. Six of them for six chicks. Now, watching the dancing snakes, Jessica repeats her promise silently, 'Six of you mongrels are gunna pay tonight.' She knows she'd be safe cursing them out loud, warning them of the revenge that's coming to them. Snakes are deaf and can't see too well either, so they're not likely to hear you coming except for the vibrations you make as you walk. They can smell, though – with their trembling forked tongues they pick up tiny particles on the ground and transfer them to the roof of their mouths where they have their smelling organs. 'Like having your nose inside your mouth,' Joe says. Jessica doesn't know how he knows stuff like this, he's not a book reader and claims he's never had any proper learning. He can read all right when he's got a newspaper, but like lots of folk his lips move and sometimes you can hear him whispering, struggling with a word, trying to hear its sound, make sense of it.

Jessica has taken care to stand downwind so the snakes won't smell her and cop her presence. When they've come together to dance like this, on the banks of the river, though, they don't seem to take the same notice of approaching danger.

High up in the dark foliage of the river gums the cockatoos and galahs are carrying on a treat, while the cicadas, ready for nightfall, singe the air with their humming. It's all noise and mayhem at sunset, the bush doves kookarooing, crows cawing, grey herons calling out across the river and the kookas adding a good bit of laughing to the night anthem. Meanwhile, below the gum trees in the dust on the river bank the snakes are lost in silence.

Jessica feels, rather than hears, the smooth metallic click as she breaks the twelve-bore, then reaches into the pocket of her pinny for a cartridge and punches the cardboard cylinder into the left-hand barrel, pushing it firmly home. It feels solid and reassuring, the flat metal detonation cap warm against the pad of her small thumb. She charges the second barrel and then snaps the shotgun back into place, keeping her thumb well clear. Now she hears the well-oiled click as the breech closes back onto the stock. Two barrels, won't get away with just the one, she thinks, resenting the extra shot.

Ideally Jessica wants one always ready up the spout in case of an emergency. What she's about to do is not good practice and she knows it. But she's only got one chance and is going to need both barrels if she wants six of the bastards. She can almost hear her father's voice: 'Snakes are risky bastards. Browns have a bad temper, come after you soon as sniff, follow you home, hunt you down. They strike high so the poison gets to yer heart sooner. Always keep one up the spout, girlie.

'You're too bloody cocky with that shotgun,' Joe would say when she was ten years old and allowed to use the four-ten. 'One day you'll come undone, girlie. What then, hey?'

The bite from a six-foot mulga can kill a child,

paralyse it in twenty minutes, and a healthy-sized Eastern brown will do a grown man in good and proper if the poison has an hour to work its way up to the heart. Jessica is eighteen and a bit over five feet tall, with her best Sunday button-up boots adding a further inch if she's lucky. With her short fair hair, narrow hips and flat chest, she could pass for a small lad if it weren't for her pinny. Last time she went into Narrandera she weighed in at a hundred and two pounds on the chemist's scale. A bite from an Eastern brown and she's dead as a doorknob in less than an hour, no risk.

But she's got pluck. 'If I can't take six of the buggers with two barrels, might as well give the game away,' she mutters.

Jessica knows she shouldn't be down here by the river side. If Joe found out he'd be mad as hell. In his book there's enough trouble out there looking for you, without you going looking for it. Jessica has a third cartridge in her pocket but doubts she'll have time to use it if things go really crook. It doesn't occur to her to try for as many snakes as she can kill with one shot and keep one up the spout for an emergency. Six chicks, six snakes, an eye for an eye, that's how her stubborn mind works. 'Too stubborn for your own good,' Joe always says to her.

Jessica is her father's girl, from her stockman's hat to the tips of her sturdy work boots. A small farm needs a boy and Joe being landed with two girls instead was a big disappointment. Joe brought up Jessica to be that son he'd never had. So it's Jessica's older sister, Meg, who takes the role of the girl – their mother, Hester, says Meg is a born lady.

Jessica has always been different, though half of her difference came about because Joe needed someone to help around the place. The other half, her love of the land, her understanding of it, seems to have been born in her.

That is how it was in the Bergman family, then. Hester and Meg indoors, baking, doing needlework, cooking, putting up preserves, churning butter, separating cream and collecting gossip. Jessica and Joe outdoors, doing all the things needed to keep a farm going.

Joe, who knew nothing about bringing up girls anyway, left Meg to his wife and took Jessica under his wing. He didn't think about what it might mean to Jessica's future; all he knew was that the little brat was always hanging around his knees, clutching at his moleskins, wanting to know things. So he just let her get on with it.

Jessica reckons she's as good on the property as any boy her age. Maybe, now she's eighteen, she can't run as fast as a young bloke, but she can shoot as straight, ride as well as any of the young jackaroos in a muster, slaughter and dress a beast, crutch a sheep, brand a calf, build or fix a fence or plough and sow a paddock with winter oats. She's a fair bushman, too. Since she was seven years old, Jessica has been Joe's right-hand man.

This is fine by Jessica. Joe is a tough bastard but fair and you can't ask for much more than that if you love someone as much as Jessica loves Joe. Joe's not one to show his feelings, even to his daughter. Tough bugger, other blokes said so too.

As a young 'un, just twelve years old, Joe Bergman had come out to Australia from Denmark. He was a cabin boy on a tramp steamer, and jumped ship in Sydney. He headed west where they wouldn't bother to come after him. Joe had wanted to work as a jackaroo, having heard wild tales of bush life on the voyage, but he started as a rouseabout, a general dogsbody, until he learned to ride a horse well enough not to come off in the scrub. At sixteen he became a boundary rider, the loneliest job in the world, and stayed at it until he was nearly thirty-five, by which time he'd lost all of his foreigner's voice. The soft singsong cadence of Joe's native tongue was replaced with the lazy vernacular, the slow, harsh twang of the Australian bush, punctuated with expletives, the plain talk of men who seldom see a woman and when they do, can't find words beyond, 'Mornin', missus.' Though most could do you a ballad or two if they were pissed enough and in a mellow mood.

Joe had taught Jessica one such poem, a favourite of his, when she was younger. She had recited it proudly to her class on the first day she'd attended the small bush school for the children of the farmers, shearers, drovers and stockmen.

'Do any of you children know a nice rhyme to recite to the class?' the teacher had asked on the very first morning.

Jessica, not backward even at that age, stuck up her hand. 'Yes, Miss!'

'Jessica, isn't it?' the teacher asked.

She nodded. 'Yes, Miss.'

'Well then, Jessica, would you like to tell the class your rhyme?'

'Yes, Miss. My dad taught it to me and it's by Mr Lawson!' she said.

That first day at school had set the pattern for Jessica's doubtful career as a student, for she'd been the first child ever to be made to stand in the corner in the first hour of her first day at school. Even now, with the snakes swaying before her, she can remember the poem.

Oh, I dreamt I shore in a shearin'-shed, and it was a
    dream of joy,
For every one of the rouseabouts was a girl dressed up
    as a boy –
Dressed up like a page in a pantomime, and the
    prettiest ever seen –
They had flaxen hair, they had coal-black hair – and
    every shade between.

CHORUS

There was short, plump girls, there was tall, slim girls,
    and the handsomest ever seen –
They was four-foot-five, they were six foot tall and
    every height between.

The shed was cooled by electric fans that was over
    every chute;

*The pens was of polished mahogany, and everything
    else to suit;*
*The huts had springs to the mattresses, and the tucker
    was simply grand,*
*And every night by the billabong we danced to a
    German band.*

*Our pay was the wool on the jumbucks' back, so we
    shore 'til all was blue –*
*The sheep was washed before they was shore (and the
    rams was scented too);*
*And all of us wept when the shed cut out, in spite of
    the long, hot days,*
*For every hour them girls waltzed in with whisky and
    beer on trays!*

*There was three of them girls to every chap, and six of
    them picked on me;*
*We was draftin' them out for the homeward track and
    sharin' them round like steam,*
*When I woke with my head in the blazin' sun to find
    'twas a shearer's dream.*

Joe never really went to the trouble of cleaning up his
language when he took up land of his own and came
into regular contact with womenfolk. At home, with a
wife and two daughters, he still talks the same rough
bush lingo. On those rare occasions when the family
goes into town for a wedding or some such, or when
there's ladies and strangers about, Joe says nothing

until he's forced, then chooses words that won't get him into trouble.

'Best keep me flamin' mouth shut, eh girlie, 'case yer sister can't get herself a rich bloke on account of me openin' me trap,' he'd chaff Jessica in front of Hester and Meg, coming home in the sulky from a wedding, or one of their get-togethers with Ada Thomas and her two ugly daughters, Winifred and Gwen.

Joe's wife Hester has got her beady eye on the Thomas boy for Meg. Hester put a lot of work into her oldest daughter, doing the best she knows how. She comes from good stock herself, with her respectable shopkeeper relatives the Heathwoods, but she doesn't have the education to take it too far, though she reads and writes well enough and speaks nicely too when she likes. She's a sensible woman, though, who knows what she wants and has the determination needed to get it. What she wants is a way out of poverty and being ordinary, and a good marriage for Meg would do the trick. Meg took to her encouragement right away, reading and speaking properly, with her rounded vowels and fancy ways.

Right from the word go, Jessica never seemed to get the hang of being anybody but herself. Like Joe, Jessica makes her mind known the moment she opens her mouth, not much of an asset if you're going to be a lady. But Jessica watches her own language around Joe – she'd never call him 'Joe' to his face! – and if she says even one of Joe's bad words half under her breath he's got hearing like a bloody fox and she'll cop an earful to keep her quiet for the rest of the day.

Now Jessica rests the stock of the shotgun on the ground between her feet, gripping either side of the worn butt with the insteps of her boots. Then, bending down so that the twin barrels rest against her right shoulder, she uses both thumbs to force the first of the firing hammers back and then the second.

All this is done by feel – not once does she look down at the shotgun. Instead, her wide green eyes never leave the reptiles less than fifteen feet away. Jessica knows she isn't being cocky like Joe often said she was when she was a brat. She remembers how he'd hit her once for this and she's never forgotten the lesson.

When Jessica was eleven a school inspector had come all the way up from Sydney to visit their little school. In her excitement, she'd foolishly boasted to the inspector that her father wasn't scared of snakes. That when Joe saw a snake he'd bend down and grab it behind the head, his thumb and finger pressing behind the jaws so they'd be open wide showing the terrible poisonous fangs. Then he'd hold it up and kiss it on the head, with the tip of its tail hanging free off the ground, squiggling and squirming. Meg, sly and superior even then, gleefully carried this exaggeration home and Jessica had gotten into terrible trouble with her old man at tea that night.

All of them were sitting at the table, she and Joe glaring at each other, Meg proud as punch at having just spilled the beans, Hester looking on, her nerves on edge.

'But I seen it!' young Jessica protests, turning to Joe for confirmation. 'You done it! I seen it, remember?'

'Bullshit. That were a bloody carpet snake and you know it,' Joe replies. 'Big harmless buggers.'

'Well how was I supposed to know it was harmless?' Jessica shouts at her sister. 'He picked it up, didn't he? He kissed it! That's all I said to the government man!'

'Who's "he", the cat's father?' Hester chides in her tired and exasperated voice.

'Father!' Jessica points to Joe at the head of the table. 'I seen Father do it!'

Joe's voice cuts in quietly. 'You *did* know it was harmless, girlie. 'Cause I told both of yiz meself.' He turns to Meg. 'What's a carpet snake look like, Meg?'

Meg smiles. 'Black and brown mottled patches against a sort of creamy background, Father. They can get to be nine feet long,' she adds gratuitously.

'Good.' Joe faces Jessica again. 'You bragging to that bloke from the government has made a bloody fool outa me, girlie,' he says.

Jessica flushes deeply, biting her bottom lip, looking down into her lap. Meg is a real bitch. But worse, she, Jessica, has made Joe look stupid and that is more than she can bear to think about.

'Country folk don't get cocky with snakes, ya hear? They fear 'em something terrible,' Joe continues, still in a low voice. 'City folk think snakes are evil, it's something that they've taken out of the Bible.' He pauses, then adds, 'But we know different, don't we? Snakes is just another sort of vermin. Crows, rats, mice and feral cats, dingoes and foxes, they're vermin too, all of them meat-eaters. They'll have a go at chooks and take a newborn lamb once in a while, but they won't go humans, they don't kill people. Snakes do. Snakes kill. Nobody fools around with Joe Blakes, girlie. Bloke who fools around with snakes is a flamin' idiot.'

Suddenly he swings his arm across the table and back-hands Jessica hard across the cheek, his knuckles making her skull ring and the teeth rattle in her head. 'You *knew* it were a carpet. Don't ever brag about me to no bastard, you hear? I don't want no flamin' school inspector from Sydney thinking your old man's a bloody fool! Some sort of Injun snake charmer!'

It feels as though she's been hit by a rock. Jessica gasps, shocked by the unexpected attack and the sudden, fearful pain. The blow almost knocks her from her stool and she has to grab hold of the table's edge in order to retain her balance. Joe never hits her indoors, the house is Hester's territory and her head is ringing as she looks to her mother for help.

Hester jumps up from the table, her chair skidding backwards in her haste. Jessica thinks she is going to have a go at her father for hitting her, but Hester only looks down at her, wiping her mouth with the back of her puffy hand. Jessica can see from her mother's expression that she isn't going to come to her rescue. Hester, she realises, wants no part of what's going on between her and Joe. All this has happened in a few moments – it is as if the blow to her head has given Jessica a sudden clarity of vision, an insight into her mother's heart where there is no longer any room for her younger daughter.

Jessica knows her mother thinks she's becoming a

handful, too headstrong. 'Can't tell you anything you don't already know and you've got no manners, just like your father.' She says it often enough and there it is again in her eyes as she turns and leaves the table. Jessica knows her mother has finally given up on her. From now on Jessica must stick with Joe, and Hester gives all her affection to Meg.

Jessica recalls how Meg rose from her stool to follow Hester into the kitchen.

'Stay! You bloody started this,' Joe commands.

Meg lowers herself slowly back on her stool, not looking at her father.

Jessica, not daring to touch her face, turns and nods dumbly to Joe, accepting her punishment. Then she looks down into her lap, fighting back her tears, determined not to show Meg how she feels.

The room is silent. She can hear her mother in the kitchen, angrily scraping the bottom of the meat pan with the metal gravy spoon. Then the clank of Joe's knife and fork on his tin plate as he resumes eating his tea. Joe won't eat his tucker off proper plates, he says tin makes food seem hard-earned by decent folk.

Jessica waits until she can be certain her voice has recovered enough before turning to her sister. 'Fuck you,' she whispers from the side of her mouth.

'Jessie just swore at me, Father! She used a terrible word, too!' Meg howls.

Joe looks up from his dinner plate at Meg. His mind is already elsewhere, his temper cooled down. In his opinion the matter is settled, Jessica has took her punishment fair and square. He plants both elbows on the table, still chewing. His massive sun-bronzed arms give the appearance of two hocks of well-cooked meat with a knife protruding from the end of one and a fork from the end of the other. Swallowing, he asks mildly, 'What'd she say?'

'I can't say it!' Meg looks directly down into her plate as though she's addressing the potatoes.

Joe picks at a tooth with his pinkie nail and turns to Jessica. 'What'd you say to your sister, girlie?'

Jessica, even more furious at Meg, no longer cares if she ends up copping another backhander from her father. She grips the sides of the table with both hands and glares defiantly at Meg, angry tears welling. 'I said, Fuck *you*!'

She shouts out the words in such a bold manner that Joe is left in no doubt that they are now meant to include him as well.

Jessica closes her eyes and pulls her head back so that her neck is held rigid, her jaw exposed to take the clout she expects from her father. Her cheek still burns and the left side of her mouth is numb from his previous blow. She can feel her eye starting to close.

Joe smiles to himself. He likes the courage he's seen in the eyes of his youngest daughter. She's game, all right, he thinks. He turns his gaze on Meg who sits with downcast eyes, straight-backed, chin tucked in, her hands folded in her lap. A man would need a bloody pickaxe to crack open that one's heart, he thinks to himself. Pity the poor bastard who gets her.

How could two girls be so different? Meg, cunning as a shithouse rat, the perfect little lady, at fourteen already a woman with all the looks and tricks that turn men's eyes soft with longing. But what's between her legs you can be sure she'll keep locked up tight until the exact right moment. That one's got her mind firmly set on a better life than most of the men in the district could offer a lass. Good on her, he doesn't mind that, she's got bugger-all inheritance coming from him. The property's mortgaged to the hilt and the bank'll get the bloody lot when he's gone, unless Jessica can keep it going. Meg'll marry the Thomas boy and have babies dressed in ribbons and booties – it's written all over her sulky little face.

Joe thinks of young Jack Thomas, just two years older than his daughter with five thousand acres coming to him when George Thomas finally carks it. A thousand already under the plough and most of that fronting the river. Meg is putting in a lot of groundwork with the two Thomas girls these days. She's gone over to the Anglicans and got Hester to do the same. It's good tactics – the Thomases wouldn't marry a Lutheran or a Catholic for that matter, strictly C of E that lot. If Meg wins over Ada Thomas and the two girls, you can put down your glasses, George Thomas and his boy Jack don't stand a chance. Joe can see it all, the future rolling out like a Sunday church carpet, the same red carpet they use for weddings at St Stephen's: his eldest daughter emerging from the church, Mrs Meg Thomas of Riverview homestead, soon to take to squatters' ways as though she's bloody born to them. Hester will die happy as a pig in mud, she's put that much into the girl.

But what of young Jessie here, waiting, expecting him to clout her again? He sighs and shakes his head sadly as he thinks of what lies ahead for Jessica. The bush ain't the kind of place where defiance gets anyone very far, least-ways a woman without a dowry looking for a husband. And Jessie's having real trouble knowing she's a girl. Maybe he should put her back in her mother's charge. Maybe she'll grow out of it, he thinks. After all, she's only eleven years old. Though Joe knows his youngest daugh-ter pretty well by now and he doesn't much like her chances of losing that stubborn streak. But most of all Joe knows he can't manage without Jessica, he needs her around the place. He decides this time he'll let it pass, leave her be. She's copped enough for one day. He forgets how little she is – the blow he give her, meant to be no more than a reminder not to be cheeky, bloody near knocked her head off. She hasn't blubbed, though. You've got to admire the little bugger for that. She took her medicine like a man. That's the whole trouble, though, if she'd been a real girl she'd be holding her cheek and bawl-ing her eyes out, sniffing and howling and burying her face in her mother's apron.

Joe sighs again and looks directly at Meg. 'What Jessie just said, that's not swearin'. Swearin's only when you *don't* mean it.'

Jessica grins to herself as she recalls this incident. She remembers how Meg burst into tears at Joe's clever remark and fled howling from the table. The back-hander from her father and the black eye that followed were worth it just to see the look on her sister's face. Maybe Joe can't say it out aloud, but she knew then, at that moment, that he loved her.

Now, as she watches the dancing serpents, Jessica wonders why the different kinds of snakes don't seem to need to dance separately, each species in some sort of poison pecking order. They all look to mix happily enough on the river bank, mulga, Eastern brown and gwardar. Even the harmless carpet snakes play with their deadly neighbours, the whole tangle of them moving like they are listening to some kind of secret bush orchestra that humans can't hear. Then she remembers snakes are deaf – it must be the vibrations they make among themselves, she reckons.

Some snakes sway and arch in lazy loops, some spiral in a ribbon of silver light, while others rise to balance momentarily on the tips of their tails and then whip downwards, striking the earth with a thud to send a small explosion of ochre dust into the air.

The thumping and writhing of the reptiles soon causes the dust, lit from behind by the setting sun, to form a translucent curtain in the surrounding air. The snakes now seem to be shadows moving in rippling patterns across a screen of light.

Jessica squints and judges the distance at roughly fifteen feet then waits, holding the gun in both hands below her waist, ready for the pattern she thinks she needs.

'Those two on the right first,' she murmurs. 'The mulgas.' Joe says they're to be called mulgas, though most people round here call them king browns. Joe likes to be right about things, even though king brown sounds better, more deadly. Jessica must wait until the two snakes are at the highest point of their dance when their heads are thrown back, flicking tongues testing the air. That's when they show the soft underside of the jaw where the scales are the colour of putty.

She must make head shots all, her first shot a deadly conclusion of blood, mashed vertebrae, scales and fang. Snakes have their brains encased in hard bone, so she's got to smash the jaws when she fires, make them harmless. She sees them dead already, mangled heads and necks thickened with black flies.

To bag her haul, she must kill four more with her second shot. It's tricky stuff, she must judge it finely, so that when she fires the first shot at the two mulgas, the four snakes three feet to the left must already be in the process of rising. The blast from the second barrel must reach them at the height of their dance with their underjaws exposed to the birdshot.

Jessica knows she will have to shoot fast, empty the two barrels almost as if a single explosion. Six snakes must be left writhing in the grey river dust, too stupid to know they are already dead, taken care of in the name of the black hen and her stolen chicks.

She now sees the pattern she needs, sees it forming, the two large mulgas swaying high, then four more snakes to her left beginning to rise. Two Eastern browns and another mulga and a carpet snake, all of them hopefully contained within the sweep of a double-barrel shot.

In the one sure movement she swings the heavy shotgun up to her shoulder and fires, the second blast following almost instantly. The kick from the double explosion knocks her backwards into a large clump of scrub.

'Bloody hell!' she yells, still holding onto the shotgun with its barrel now pointed into the heavens above. The galahs and cockatoos take to the air in a raucous pink and white mass. The cicadas go silent, their collective hum cut as though sliced cleanly with a sharp knife. The twin echoes of the shotgun blasts race across the river and over the flat country beyond to disappear over the horizon, sucked up into the dark maw of the approaching twilight.

Jessica reaches frantically into the pocket of her pinny for the spare cartridge. She grabs at it and grips it between her teeth, at the same time scrambling from the bush into clear ground, though she's still up to her knees in scrub. Panting with fear, she breaks the shotgun and expels the casings. A curl of gunsmoke still issues from the hot breech. She drops the spent cartridges into her pocket, then takes the live cartridge from between her teeth and pushes it home, snapping the breech shut. Trying to stay calm she positions the butt of the shotgun between her feet and with both thumbs again pulls the hammer back. Her heart beats furiously, she can barely hear for the drumming sound it makes in her chest.

She knows what she's doing is almost useless. If she's killed the partner of one of the mulgas or Eastern browns now fleeing from the vibrations of the blast, it will come back for her. Or if she's in the way of a fleeing snake she'll be long bitten before she's got the bloody shotgun in place. She can hear Joe's words in her head: 'A brown will hunt you down, stalk you all the way home. If it's cranky there'll be no stopping it. If you've shot one of them mongrels, always keep a fresh shot up the spout for its mate, girlie.'

Jessica forces back her fear and makes herself face the river bank, knowing there must be snakes all about her, expecting one to rear up at any moment. An Eastern brown strikes high in an S shape, and could come up out of the scrub to her left or right any second. She waits a few seconds longer, holding the shotgun at the ready, then she runs for the path up from the river. Reaching the path she begins the half-mile walk back to the homestead, trying to keep a steady pace, looking back over her shoulder every few moments. It is only when she is well away from the river and clear of the scrub, with open country about her, that Jessica slows down and she releases the hammer from the firing position so that it seats back into safety. Then she carefully lowers the shotgun, and brings her hand up to rub her painful right shoulder.

Jessica knows only too well what the kick from a twelve-bore feels like. She's padded her right shoulder with a cunningly fashioned pin-cushion contraption which has a looped tape sewn to one end and two tapes

24 BRYCE COURTENAY

to the corners of the other. The loop fits around her neck
with the two further tapes, one pulled under her armpit
and tied to the other at the top of her shoulder. Tied in
this manner the cushion fits snugly into the curve of her
shoulder to protect her right breast and collarbone.

The kick from the first barrel must have pushed the
padding up above her collarbone and she's received the
second blast fair and square in her chest. In a week's
time a purple patch of broken blood vessels the size of
a man's hand will have spread across her right shoulder
and breast.

'Milking's gunna be a bugger,' she sighs ruefully, gingerly rubbing her damaged shoulder with the tips of her
fingers. It could be worse, though, she could've broken
her collarbone. If she had, Joe would call her a useless
bludger trying to get out of her fair share. He'd want to
know what she was doing with the shotgun. She
couldn't lie to him. Couldn't lie anyway. Then he'd go
mad about her going down to the river at sunset.
'Revenge? What for? Six flamin' new-hatched chicks?
Jesus Christ, girlie, you got pig shit for brains, eh?' He
doesn't hit her now she's grown up, but Jessica knows
he'd be well within his rights to do so if she told him
about hunting the snakes with both barrels.

Anyway, Jessica's done what she said she would. For
the moment she doesn't care what Joe thinks, or even
about her bruised shoulder. 'Gotcha, you slimy bastards!' she yells back in the direction of the river bank,
where, in her mind's eye, the serpents lie twisting and
writhing in their last dance by the river.

CHAPTER TWO

The six dead snakes will be easy pickings for the crows and the kookaburras in the morning. In country where snake eats bird and bird eats snake, and snake eats snake and bird eats bird, nothing that hunts gets a free feed too often.

Jessica remembers how, when she was little and Joe killed a snake or a fox, or some other vermin, mostly rabbits, he'd call it a shotgun feed. 'Everything lives off everything else, girlie. That's the way of the world. It's you or them. It's damned hard work getting enough tucker to feed your family.' He grinned and then continued, 'So I give mother nature a bit of a helping hand, see, give 'em a shotgun feed every once in a while and I reckon, in their own way, they're grateful to me.'

'Not if you're the free feed!' Jessica remembers replying, pleased that she'd made her father laugh.

Joe's made regular attempts to tell Jessica about the dog-eat-dog world she lives in, to prepare her for a life which he describes as 'a bloody nightmare most of the time'. She isn't too worried, though, despite his dire warnings. Joe has trained her well, teaching her everything he knows. Isn't that how things are measured? You can or you can't. If you can't you're a useless bastard. If you can, you'll just about do. That's how men judge things. You have to be their equal. Men always look to see if you're their equal. The only thing they fear is if you are better than they are. On the other hand, in her experience, nobody thinks you're much chop if you're the equal of any other woman.

But Jessica thinks she can see why life is tough for these men, for Joe. Her father is stubborn and set in his ways and she's beginning to think the mighty Joe Bergman might not be a very good farmer. He is seldom willing to listen to advice and always knows better than the experts. Mind you, that goes for most of the blokes who farm land settlements in the Riverina. Men in the bush are so busy playing at being God, at having dominion over all they see and touch, that they never listen to the natural voice of the land. Or anyone else's voice, for that matter.

The government agricultural officer gives talks up at the experimental station about soil erosion and the need to keep hedges of box-leaf wattle or desert cassia as windbreaks on the margins of the paddocks and to leave some mulga scrub for the wildlife and to fertilise the soil. He talks about crop rotation and water conservation and other things Jessica thinks Joe ought to know about.

'It's cattle and sheep with us, girlie. Land was always here, always will be. Don't need to bother yer head with them things,' Joe says stubbornly.

Jessica goes with Jack Thomas and some of the young blokes with half a brain in their heads to listen to the lectures. Now she's beginning to think there might be other, better ways of treating the land and using the river than just waging constant war against it, stripping it bare, ripping open its guts, hoping like hell the rains will come in time to save the winter wheat or the paddock of oats. But still Joe says those government bastards wouldn't know how to grow a cabbage in a bucket full of wet cow shit.

Jack Thomas has talked to her about irrigation, about the big canal at Yanco they've built that's going to change everything in the Riverina.

'Imagine, Jessie,' Jack says, his blue eyes lighting up his sun-hardened face, 'you're no longer dependent on the rain that never bloody comes. The soil's good, we know that from the land below the river – give it water and the desert blooms.'

Jessica likes that, the idea of the desert blooming, the black soil plains green as far as the eye can see. If Meg manages to snare Jack Thomas she'll have a good one, all right. Pity Jessica can't warn him about her cow-faced sister.

Jessica turns to take a last look back towards the deserted river bank. A soft haze of grey river dust still hangs in the air where the snakes danced. The orchestra of fowl and insect is back, the birds squabbling away in the river gums, each one trying to have the last word, using up the last rays of the sun to drive home their noisy arguments before darkness comes.

Jessica swings the shotgun up, holding it halfway down the barrel so that the weight of the stock rests on her good shoulder, and continues her walk home in the approaching dark, happy because there's no hurry tonight. No tea to endure with Hester and Meg looking on sour-faced and disapproving as she and Joe scoff down their dinner, too exhausted to talk. 'Like pigs in a trough, those two!' Her mother says it so often that Joe now faithfully responds, 'Oink, oink!'

Hester's Auntie Agnes died recently, and Joe has taken Hester and Meg into Whitton for the reading of her last will and testament. Jessica doesn't expect them back for four days. Hester hopes to benefit in terms of two Irish linen tablecloths and a few pieces of silver, this booty comprising Auntie Agnes's famous silver tea service which, Hester declares, will be the centrepiece of Meg's glory box when she marries young Jack.

Jessica laughs to herself. She's been mates with Jack for four years now, and all this time Hester and Meg have been plotting the marriage. She can't really see that they're any closer to it, though, tea set or no tea set.

Jessica first became friends with Jack Thomas at the age of fourteen, when Joe took her to Riverview Station at the start of the shearing season in early July of 1910.

Most of the small settlers who can manage the work head for the shearing shed at Riverview during the season. George Thomas's big sheep station carries eleven thousand merinos not counting the two thousand lambs towards the end of the season and the burly squatter takes on fourteen shearers to do the job. He'll give every local man who applies an hour without pay on the shearing board, each going full swing, to see if he's up to the tally the foreman's set for the season.

George Thomas doesn't believe in charity and if a local man can't reach a daily tally expected from a top contract shearer he's weeded out and sent packing. It's a popular laugh that by the end of the local trials Thomas has a couple of days' worth of free shearing to his credit. George Thomas has never been known to do anything where there wasn't a solid quid in it for him.

Joe's taken young Jessica along with him to the cut, hoping that Mike Malloy the foreman will accept her to be trained as a rouseabout. If she gets the work, it's another income they'll be able to rely upon for eight weeks every year.

The start of the shearing season is always an anxious time for the small farmers who depend on those two months in the big shed to get them through. If George Thomas throws one of them out it'll mean a lean year for the family. Joe's never missed the cut, even though he is a good bit older than most of the local men. Now he's depending on his past record to persuade Mike Malloy to take Jessica on as a tar boy and sweeper, the first job a boy learns coming into a big shed.

Even though it was four years ago, Jessica can still recall almost everything about that first day. Big, tough old Joe, trying to look at ease, his taut muscles and awkward stance giving away how tense he was, how much he wanted her to succeed, but without him having to beg to get her the job. Standing in front of them was the foreman, a hard-looking man, though a little soft in the stomach and with a complexion scarred from childhood smallpox. His cheeks look purple and pink and raw and sore as he frowns slightly, listening to what Joe has to say.

Then his first words: 'Joe, I dunno, mate, it's pretty unusual.' Rubbing the side of his nose with his fore-finger, 'Shearin' shed ain't no place for a young girl, the men swearing an' all.'

Joe gives a little nervous laugh, at the same time wip-ing the palms of his sweaty hands down the side of his moleskins. 'Won't be nothing she ain't heard from her old man.'

The foreman scratches his forehead just under the rim of his hat. 'It ain't just her, the men ain't gunna feel, y'know, free to express themselves. Jeez mate, I dunno,' he repeats and then glances down at Jessica. 'She ain't too big neither.'

Joe pushes Jessica forward. 'She's just a brat yet. She can start as a tar boy, learn the trade. Don't need size for that, do you? She don't look no different to a boy and I'll wager she'll work harder than all of them little buggers.'

'Yeah, but –'

'Mr Malloy, what with the Wolseley engine and the wool press, there's such a racket going on she won't hear a flaming word unless they cup their hands and shout it down her earhole. It's just noise in there. If she does a good job they'll soon enough forget she's a girl and if she don't measure up she'll get the flick same as anyone else.' Jessica can sense Joe trying to keep calm, trying not to plead with the foreman. 'Just give the girlie a chance to prove herself, Mr Malloy.'

Mike Malloy looks at Joe. 'Mate, I'd like to, we've worked together a long time, but I don't think it's within me authority t'hire a sheila. I'll need to ask Mr Thomas.' He frowns, thinking of something else. 'What about when she's taking her dinner with the men?'

'She'll manage, Mr Malloy, she'll be sitting right next to her daddy.'

The foreman laughs – it's a fair enough answer. Joe Bergman is still a big man and has earned a lot of respect with his fists in the past. There's not too many in the shed will truck with him even now he's getting to be an old bastard. Mike Malloy sighs. 'I'll speak to the owner, Joe. That's all I can promise. Fair enough?'

Joe nods, though he's not too happy. Jessica knows that he didn't want to involve George Thomas.

They are kept waiting outside the tally clerk's office for two hours before the owner finally appears, Mike Malloy beside him. George Thomas is a smallish barrel of a man with a big gut and a very red face, and even with him wearing a hat you know he must be bald on top. He's dressed up to the nines, wearing riding boots, jodhpurs, a tweed jacket and tie. Jessica wonders if he's off to a meeting or the races or something until Joe tells her later that's how owners dress in the shearing season.

'This your girl, Joe?' he asks, pointing a stubby finger at Jessica.

Joe touches the brim of his hat, too proud to lift it off his head altogether. 'Afternoon Mr Thomas, sir,' he says and puts his big hand on Jessica's shoulder. 'Jessica, this is Mr Thomas.'

George Thomas grunts, ignoring the greeting. 'This isn't girl's work, Joe.' He turns to Jessica. 'What do you know about sheep, eh?'

Jessica keeps her eyes on her boots, and answers shyly, 'A bit, sir.'

'A bit? A bit isn't enough, lass. Can you shear?'

It's a cruel question, Jessica is plainly too small to handle a fully grown ewe. 'If it's a lamb, sir,' she replies, looking up at George Thomas for the first time.

'Hmm. Can you crutch? Tar? Sweep? Pick up and throw a fleece?'

'The first three, sir. I reckon I'll be able to do the other when I've grow'd a bit and they've learned me.' Jessica holds George Thomas's eyes for a moment then looks down at her boots again.

'She's a good worker,' Joe mumbles.

'She's a cheeky young bugger,' the boss of Riverview Station replies. 'Got all the answers. If you ask me, she's too clever for her own good.'

Joe stiffens, not knowing how to take the remark, but Thomas doesn't seem to notice. 'Joe Bergman, you've been shearing in my shed for fifteen years and I've no quarrel with your work. I know you haven't a boy of your own to help, but . . .'

Joe cuts in quickly, 'I wouldn't take a boy in her place, sir. The girl's a damn sight better than any lad her age.'

George Thomas is unimpressed. He's not the sort to take notice of other folks' opinions. 'It's putting temptation in the way of the men, I don't like it.'

Joe looks surprised – the idea that Jessica might be a temptation to men hasn't entered his head. 'I'll be in the shed meself, Mr Thomas, keeping a sharp eye on her.'

'Hummph!' George Thomas thinks a moment and then seems to make up his mind. 'We'll put her in with Jack and young William Simon, it's their first full season on the shears.'

Joe smiles. 'She'll do you proud, sir.'

The owner of Riverview now turns to Jessica. 'You'll be the tar boy and sweep for the two lads. Jack's my son and he'll probably make a mess of things, always does, but young Billy's a good boy and he'll teach you or throw you out, one or the other, I don't much care which. I hope you know what you're doing, Joe,' he says, prodding him in the chest with his forefinger. 'She'll get no special treatment, mind.'

'Don't expect none, do we, Jessie?' Joe says, gripping her shoulder and trying to hide his pleasure.

'Well, there's one you'll get right off, girl. You'll take your dinner at the big house with my girls, though I don't know that it's much of a favour at that.' He turns to Joe. 'I don't want her eating with the men in the shearers' quarters.'

'There's no need, Mr Thomas, we couldn't put your missus out. She can sit with me, we'll bring our own tucker,' Joe protests.

'Like hell you will, Joe. The shearing shed's one thing, the shearers' quarters another. I don't want her eating there, it'll make the men jumpy.'

'Too right,' Mike Malloy adds, 'I said that meself.'

Joe shrugs, none too happy. 'If you say so, Mr Thomas.'

George Thomas turns to his foreman and scratches his head under his hat, the posh city hat bobbing under his fingers. 'I must be out of my flaming mind, but sign her up, Malloy.' He pauses a moment and gazes at Joe. 'First sign of trouble out she goes, and it doesn't matter who starts it, you hear me, Malloy?'

'Right, Mr Thomas,' Mike Malloy replies.

'Thank you, sir,' Jessica says shyly.

George Thomas spins around at this. 'Look girl, you're just another tar boy. That's the lowest there is around here. From now on you won't talk until you're spoken to and you *never* speak to me. You hear me?'

Jessica bites her bottom lip, saying nothing, not sure now whether she's got permission to answer this.

'Do – you – hear – me?' he thunders.

Jessica jumps. 'Yes, sir, thank you Mr Thomas.'

George Thomas shakes his head. 'Christ, I must be bloody mad.' He turns back and looks at Joe, placing his hands on his hips. 'She won't get the same wages as a tar boy.'

'What? Even if she's as good?' Joe asks.

'She's a girl, Joe.'

'So?' Joe's face darkens.

'So she'll take sixpence less a day, one shilling a day, no arguments, six bob a week, take it or leave it.'

Now Joe looks down at his boots and the silence grows.

'Well, what's it to be?' George Thomas demands, jutting out his chin.

Jessica can see that Joe's temper is going to get the better of him, and she clutches his arm. They need the money too much to lose this job now. Getting up her courage, she draws George Thomas's attention to herself, giving Joe time to calm himself down.

'Mr Thomas,' she stammers, 'we're more than happy with the pay, it's real generous of you, I'm sure.' She tries to say it in the voice she's heard Hester use when she's talking to Ada Thomas.

'You!' George Thomas shouts, pointing his finger at Jessica. 'Keep your trap shut! Don't you ever listen, girl?'

Jessica cringes against Joe's arm. Joe has regained his composure now, though his lips are drawn tight. He looks straight at George Thomas, his eyes weary and beaten. 'Righto, Mr Thomas,' he says, and the two of them turn to leave.

But George Thomas must have the last word. 'Joe Bergman, I've had no trouble with you and I don't want any with your daughter, you hear me?' he calls to their departing backs. 'Any muck-up with her in the shed, your girlie's out on her ear!'

'You already said that,' Joe replies quietly, but only Jessica can hear him.

Jessica knows George Thomas has made her father eat humble pie and she can feel the shame burning in him. She's never seen it done to him before and she hates the boss of Riverview with all her heart. You're a right bastard, Mr Thomas, she thinks to herself, Joe's a hundred times better a man than you'll ever be. She feels her father's big hand rest on her shoulder, as they walk to where their horses are tethered under a lone kurrajong tree.

Jessica now remembers how unhappy she was at the prospect of eating at the big house. Riding home that day she'd questioned Joe, 'What's Mr Thomas mean about the men being jumpy, Father?'

'He don't want no females eating in the shearers' quarters, the men are liable to get . . .' Joe thinks for a moment, scratching his head, searching for a word, 'you know, ah . . . well . . . jumpy!' he says, lost for a better word that seems fit to use in front of his little daughter.

'The shearers' cook's a lady. Don't she make them jumpy?' Jessica asks again, still not sure what jumpy means, other than it isn't something that's good for shearers when they eat.

Joe looks surprised at the question. 'Molly Gibbons? Holy smoke! For a start she's a missus, not a miss. She's twenty stone and fifty years old if she's a day.' He gives a short laugh. 'She's well past giving men the jitters, more like the fritters now, eh!'

It's a poor joke but Jessica is pleased Joe hasn't gone into one of his dark moods because of George Thomas. 'Anyway, it ain't no use arguing, girlie,' he now says. 'If George Thomas says you're takin' yer tucker at the homestead, that's about it.'

'You don't like Mr Thomas, do you, Father?'

'Like doesn't come into it, girlie. He's got the shed and the work and we need it. Out here it's them what pays says, and the ones who get paid shut their gobs.'

Then he adds, 'We were damn lucky today, he was in a good mood.'

'You could've fooled me,' Jessica says, feeling bold.

Now Joe pulls his horse a little closer to her pony and holds her arm. 'Keep your gob shut, do as you're told, don't muck about and when you see Mr Thomas coming in your direction make yerself scarce, otherwise keep your head down and keep working, ya hear me now, Jessie?'

'Yes, Father.' Jessica knows Joe's giving her sound advice. 'I won't let you down.'

'Never have, never will,' Joe says. Jessica looks up at him in surprise and catches just the hint of a smile. Joe's proud she's got the job and didn't lose her pluck in front of George Thomas, she thinks to herself.

The shearing season at Riverview Station begins the first week in July, with the early mornings freezing cold and the frost white on the ground. The shearing starts at six-thirty in the morning unless it's rained during the night, when it starts at ten, after the sheep have dried in the sun.

Half of what little rain comes in the south-west falls in the winter, the best eight inches of the year, God's half. The other half comes in the heat and is pulled out of the soil by the remorseless sun before it can do any good, that's the Devil's half. God's half falls when the fleeces are at their thickest, so what grows the grass for the lambing season interferes with the shearing season, which goes to show that not even God thinks to help folk around here.

Jessica and Joe rise at three-thirty in the morning to

do the work around the farm before leaving just after five to ride to Riverview on their horses. They return home an hour before sunset and Jessica milks the cow, then mixes mash for the pigs and gives them fresh water. Joe checks on the sheep and cattle. It's no more than maintenance work, and if anything should go wrong Joe and Jessica try to fix it on the Sabbath or on the occasional day when it rains.

Meg and Hester look after the chooks and do a bit of gardening, the only farm work they do outside the homestead. Hester keeps a small rose garden as well as a vegetable patch, both wire-netted, the wire dug in three feet underground so the rabbits can't burrow under it. Hester has the gift of a green thumb and there are always plenty of fresh vegetables in the kitchen. Joe and Jessica do the heavy digging, but she and Meg will carry water from the windlass tank and they take some pride in what they produce for the table.

By eight o'clock at night Jessica and Joe are sleeping the sleep of the dead until Joe's old Wesclock goes and he calls her again an hour and a half before dawn.

It's a hard slog, but Jessica is used to hard work. Sweeping the boards and tarring the nicks on the newly shorn sheep keeps her busy enough, but she can still find time to boil a billy for Jack Thomas and William Simon.

Billy Simon is a strict Roman Catholic and some call him 'The Mary Boy'. He is often seen at night in the shearers' quarters holding a set of rosary beads, quietly reciting Hail Marys.

'Hail Mary, full of grace, the Lord is with thee;
blessed art thou among women, and blessed
is the fruit of thy womb, Jesus.
Holy Mary, mother of God, pray for us sinners,
now and at the hour of our death. Amen.'

The Mary Boy is not a name too many are game to call him to his face, though – at only eighteen years old Billy Simon is six feet four inches tall, hard as an ironbark and still growing. He has a mass of black hair, wide blue eyes, a well-muscled body and the constitution of an ox. He's no fool either and is known to have a bit of a temper when provoked. He's a good man with his fists – all in all, not someone to be picked on rashly.

He and Jack, who's not as big as Billy, are friendly enough, but Jack, who's just out of the King's School in Sydney, doesn't want to be shown up by Billy Simon. George Thomas hasn't brought his son up soft. Both lads have been rouseabouts to two of the gun shearers in previous seasons and there's been competition between Billy and Jack since they were tar boys together.

Jessica soon sees that Jack Thomas has a lot of pride, but Billy is the better shearer. Jack is using his blade, making his blows carelessly while he tries to keep up with Billy. His sheep carry twice the number of nicks as those of his mate. Some of them are pretty bad, needing a whole pot of tar to stop the bleeding.

She senses that Jack knows Billy is the better shearer, but as the boss's son, he has to keep his pride intact. He can't be thought to be soft or lazy. But he's trying too hard and slowly losing out.

Jessica wishes she could tell him what Joe always says to her, 'Do the job well first up, in the end that's the fastest way to get it done.' As their tar boy it's not her place to say anything. She's at the bottom of the ladder and, besides, there's no one but her who knows which sheep are Jack's or Billy's when she sends them down the race into the pen. She knows enough to keep her trap well shut if someone should ask.

But while the competition between these two is fierce, it is always good-natured and they remain firm friends. They make an impressive pair, the dark and the fair, and they're the heroes of all the young tar boys in the shed. Jack is no bad sport nor a poor loser, not like his old man, and Jessica likes working with both the lads. They laugh and chaff each other and tease her when they stop for a smoko.

They don't seem to mind in the least that she's a girl and take some pride in the fact that she's a better worker than any of the tar boys on the board. Besides, she can make a damn good mug of tea and a corned beef sandwich if needed. After a few days, at the morning smoko, Billy christens her 'Tea Leaf'.

'What's that for?' Jessica asks him. Once she had heard someone use that name for a thief, and she doesn't want to be called a thief.

Jack laughs. 'Don't you know?'

'No. Is it because you don't like my tea?' Jessica looks worried. 'What's wrong with it?'

'No, the tea's good,' Billy laughs, 'it's just that you're the dregs!'

Jessica is puzzled and looks to Jack.

'The tar boy is the dregs of society, see,' Jack explains, 'except that you're not even a boy.'

Both of them chuckle, pleased with themselves until Jessica, on a sudden impulse, picks up the billy and pours what's left of the cold tea over their hats. It's all done in a flash before she realises she may have gone too far.

They both look surprised and Billy shakes his head then takes his hat off and turns it upside down, watching the dark mess dripping from it. For a moment Jessica is really scared, then Jack grins and slaps Billy on the shoulder. 'She gotcha!' he yells in delight, and Billy smiles up at Jessica.

From that moment a deep friendship grows between the three of them. Billy and Jack only call her Tea Leaf among themselves, they're a team now and it's her special name. Soon Jessica feels confident enough to talk to Jack about his shearing.

'Billy's your mate, Jack,' she says. 'It don't matter if he throws a few more than you. Joe always reckons that if you do things right in the first place you get faster, it's just natural. He says the real gun shearers don't waste blows and seem to have plenty of time to make them clean. You can tell the quality of a shearer by the number of nicks he leaves behind him.'

Jack is silent a while, then looks up at Jessica, his eyes narrowed. 'If you were a bloke I'd probably have to fight you, Tea Leaf. Or leastways tell you to mind your own business. Cheeky little bugger, aren't you?' He grins and then says, 'But you're right, a man's stupid, I should know better.'

Jessica grins. 'Jack Thomas, there's a lot of sheep out there are gunna be grateful!'

Jack laughs. 'I dunno about that, being thanked by a mob of sheep ain't the biggest compliment in the world.'

Right from the start the other tar boys have resented having a girl in their group, especially one who works faster and better than they do. Being a tar boy is a shit job, the shearers give them a hard time, and most are lucky to come out of the day without a thick ear for doing something one of their shearers doesn't like.

Mr Malloy buggers things up even more by singling Jessica out and calling her the gun tar and best broom on the board. Jessica can see from the looks she gets that the other tar boys don't like it much.

The young lads can see how Jack and Billy have taken to Jessica, the three of them getting on like a house on fire. It doesn't seem fair to them and Jessica can well understand their gripes – all they get all day is kicks and curses and meanwhile she's jake with her two shearers. At every opportunity they get, the tar boys are at her. Teasing, jostling and pushing her, calling out insults, and very little real good humour behind it all.

At first Jessica cops it sweet. Then she decides to give as good as she gets and soon they're no match for her sharp tongue. Joe says a fourteen-year-old girl is near grown, ready to have brats, while a boy the same age hasn't got his wits about him yet and can only think about tossing off. Jessica doesn't know yet, though, that you can't make fools of folk without them wanting to teach you a lesson.

George Thomas demands that his foreman work the tar boys hard. Ten minutes before a smoko they have to leave the shed and prepare the billy tea and biscuits for their shearers. One afternoon, a day Joe's gone to the land office and isn't with her in the shed, Jessica leaves to make tea for Jack and Billy. When she gets outside the six tar boys come at her, grabbing her and pushing her into the nearby sheep pen where they knock her down and turn her on her back. Two of them jump astride her body, one on her chest, pinning her wrists to the ground, the other sitting on her legs. There's sheep milling about and bleating and dogs yapping but the other four keep them away so there's a clearing in the middle of the pen.

'Let me go, you bastards!' Jessica yells. 'Let go of me!' The sheep are panicking and one comes flying down the race and crashes into Jessica and the two boys, sending them flying. Jessica rolls free and tries to get to her feet but another of the young blokes falls onto her and pins her down again while a second takes hold of her feet.

'You'll take what's comin' to you, Jessie Bergman!' the boy sitting on her chest shouts. 'Yer too bloody cocky.'

'Yeah, bloody oath!' the one who's holding her legs shouts. 'Here, gi's a hand!' he shouts at one of the others, who immediately sits astride her stomach.

'You think you're better than us, don't yiz?' says the

tar boy on her chest, the biggest among them. 'Well, you bloody ain't, see!' he grunts. 'Yer just a fuckin' sheila!'

With the sound of the donkey engine, the yapping of the dogs, bleating of sheep and the clanking of the wool presses they have to shout to be heard and Jessica knows it's pointless to yell for help – the men in the shearing shed won't hear her. So she saves her strength to curse them with every obscenity she's ever heard Joe use and some private ones of her own as well. But the three of them on top of her are too strong. 'Bastards! Let me go!' she cries.

The three remaining tar boys now get to work, rubbing a preparation of Stockholm tar into her scalp with their tar sticks. It's all over in a matter of moments and the boys are up and away, leaving her lying on the ground in the sheep pen with the newly shorn sheep closing in, pissing and shitting and milling about her.

Jessica jumps to her feet, panicking the sheep around her legs. 'You'll pay for this, you miserable bastards!' she screams after them as a wether bumps hard into the back of her knees and she falls down again, the hot tar burning and stinging her scalp.

She is shaking with anger and humiliation and wants to cry, but wouldn't give them the satisfaction. She chokes back the tears and, still on her knees among the sheep, searches for her hat, which fell off her head when she was knocked down. Jessica is still snorting and swearing when she finds it trampled in the dirt and smelling of sheep shit. She rises again, bleating sheep up to her waist, and slaps her misshapen hat against the rump of the nearest ewe to dust it off. The slapping gets rid of some of her rage, and she gathers her wits. Jessica pushes her hat roughly into shape and pulls it over her head as far down as she can to cover her tarred hair.

She's got no time to feel sorry for herself. Smoko's only a few minutes away and she still needs to boil the billy for the lads, catch up on the sheep she's missed tarring and then sweep the second cuts and bellies away so her section of the shearing board is clean.

Jessica doesn't know how she's going to hide what's happened from Joe when she gets home. He'd be just as likely to come looking for the tar boys who worked her over and all hell would break loose. Then, like George Thomas said, any trouble in the shed because of her and Jessica gets the chop, no questions asked.

She's still cranky as hell because the only thing she's done wrong was to be a girl, but she can't do anything about it. She knows Joe needs her six shillings to help pay the bank interest on the mortgage. The man from the bank has been around twice in the last month and after he'd left the last time Joe went quiet and didn't speak a word to her for two whole days, so Jessica knows things must be real bad.

While Jessica shares most of Joe's problems around the place, money is the one thing he never speaks to her about, nor to Hester and Meg. But she sees how things are, and she knows money is what's going to finally drive Joe mad or kill him.

Jessica just manages to make tea for her boys and

cut two corned beef sandwiches for them when the hooter sounds in the shearing shed for their afternoon smoko. Jack's and Billy's shearing stands are the last on the board, so they're first to come outside to take their mug of tea, sheltering from the sun under a bit of tarpaulin Jessica's rigged up as their spot.

The boys are all but spent, their shirts clinging wetly to their chests, their necks and faces shiny with perspiration. They sit on the apple crates she's put out for them and gulp gratefully at the hot, sweet tea in silence. After a while Jack notices that Jessica isn't yacking away like she usually does. Without looking up from his mug he says, 'Cat got your tongue then, Tea Leaf?'

Billy glances up at Jessica, and his eyes grow wide with surprise. 'Shit, what happened to yer neck?'

'Nothing. It's nothing,' she mumbles.

'It's bloody tar! There's flamin' tar running down yer neck!'

Jack now looks up. 'Hell, what's happened?' he exclaims.

But by this time Billy has put down his tin mug. Jumping to his feet, he reaches down and pulls at Jessica's hat.

'Ouch!' she yells. Billy has lifted her hat and her blonde hair sticks to the rim, glued to it by the tar.

'Who's done this?' he demands.

'Ouch, Billy, let go!' Jessica yells again as Billy tries to unglue her hat by pulling still further, but more gently, finally yanking it free.

Jessica snatches at the hat and with both hands

plants it firmly back on her head, then she pushes Billy away. 'Leave off, will ya, I'm all right!'

'No you bloody ain't,' Jack says. 'What happened, Jessie?'

'It's none of your business,' Jessica says, trying to sound tough.

'Like hell it's not,' Billy exclaims. 'Who's done this to you, Tea Leaf? You tell me and I'll fix the bastards.'

'It was an accident,' is all Jessica will say.

'It's the tar boys, isn't it?' Billy keeps at her.

Jessica turns away to hide her tears just as the hooter sounds to call the tar boys back to sweep the board.

Jack looks down at Jessica and wipes his hand across his mouth. 'Jessie, I'm taking you over to the big house to get you fixed up. Fetch my horse and yours too, we'll ride over now.'

'No, please!' She looks anxiously back at the shearing shed. 'I've gotta get back,' Jessica says, knowing that her being out of the shed is bound to come to the notice of Mike Malloy, especially if Jack's also missing. She'll be dismissed and Joe will be disgraced. 'Please, Jack, I don't want no trouble, it can wait. I'll be right. I've gotta go now.'

'No, hang on!' Jack grabs her wrist. 'There's benzine at the homestead, it should take the tar off. Maybe we should try the engine gas-oil here?'

'Please Jack! I'll lose me job!' Jessica begs.

'Let her go, Jack,' Billy says, 'her hair ain't gunna get any worse if we wait till the day ends. She's right, Mike Malloy'll be out to find her if she doesn't get back.

Don't you worry, Tea Leaf, I'll sort out the lads later.'

Jessica sees that Jack doesn't like Billy taking over like this. 'Billy's right, Jack,' she says urgently. 'Please, I'm late, Jack, it's me job!'

Jack looks a bit miffed. 'Well, you get the horses ready as soon as we break, right?' he says crossly, sitting back on his apple crate and picking up his mug again. 'But wait on a moment, if you go in there like this Mike Malloy will see the stuff all over your shoulders,' he points to her, 'the tar running down.'

Jessica looks more panic-stricken than ever. 'I'll cover it up.'

Jack grabs her by the hand. 'Come with me.'

Inside the dark little shed which houses the donkey engine Jack takes up a gallon can of paraffin. He soaks a bit of rough hessian in it and begins to scrub the tar from Jessica's neck and her collar and over her shoulders. Jessica tries not to wince at the smell and the scrubbing, and finally Jack stops. 'There, that's better! If Mike Malloy asks where you've been tell him I kept you back.'

Jessica nods and runs back to the shed. Her scalp itches from the tar and her skin burns where the paraffin has removed the tar from her neck and shoulders. When she returns to the shed the foreman is nowhere to be seen and she breathes a sigh of relief.

Towards the end of the afternoon she manages to get away for a few minutes to find the stable boy and tell him to saddle Jack's horse and her own and to bring them round ready for when work ends.

The boys watch her all afternoon, giggling each time she passes one of them. At last the hooter for the end of the day goes and Billy, who has stopped shearing five minutes before to clean and oil his clippers, jumps from his station and walks down the board. He grabs a tar pot and stick and then collars all six boys and marches them out of the shed.

The other shearers watch, confused. It's a tar boy's job to do the last sweep and clean up. First in, last out, the lowest works the longest is the rule. The donkey engine comes to a stop, then the wool press does the same and the shed has suddenly quietened down.

'What's up, Billy?' one of the shearers calls, but Billy doesn't answer, roughly pushing the boys ahead of him. The shearers look at each other and then at Jack, who's grabbed hold of Jessica so she doesn't run for her horse. 'A spot of bother with the tars,' Jack says. 'They'll be back in a while, Billy's just sorting it out.' He is holding the shears and, spying a bit of Jessica's tar-covered hair sticking out from under her hat, snips it off and puts it into his pocket.

The men are not happy. Billy and Jack are the youngest shearers in the shed and have no right to be taking such liberties when the boys are needed. But they let it go and turn back to the oiling of their clippers and their preparations to leave. Perhaps they wonder why Jessica is standing with Jack, and not among the tar boys, but minding your own business is the first rule of any shearing shed and Jack is still the boss's son. Jessica is shaking like a leaf and Jack is right to hold her. She's near to panic and she'd have scarpered, running for her horse to get home.

'Come on,' Jack now says, leading her out of the shed. 'They'll think I'm marching you out, like Billy's doing with the others.'

'Please Jack, stop Billy, he's gunna ruin it for me,' Jessica cries.

'Leave Billy be, Tea Leaf, he's old enough and ugly enough to take care of himself. Come on, we've got to fix your hair,' Jack replies.

'No, no, please stop Billy. You said the benzine will fix my hair, that's all that matters. We can do it later. It was a joke, that's all. Just a stupid joke.' Jessica reaches over and pulls at Jack's sleeve. 'Your father said he'd fire me if there was trouble. Jack, please, Joe needs the money I make for the mortgage. You've got to stop Billy before it's too late, before he wrecks everything!' she pleads desperately.

Jack stops, and looking into Jessie's eyes sees the panic there. They've reached the horses tethered to a stump. He unties both reins and hands Jessica hers as he thinks for a moment. 'I'll try,' he says finally, 'though Billy can be a stubborn bastard.' Then, placing his boot in the stirrup, he swings into the saddle. Jessica does the same and they ride to where Billy has collected the six tar boys behind the shearing shed.

The boys stand in front of Billy with their heads bowed. Five are barefoot and only one wears a pair of heavy boots, which are too big for him. They are all dirty and sweating and their top lips have turned to snot runs. When they're running around the shed you wouldn't notice what a bedraggled lot they are. But standing together in the late afternoon sun in their rags and tatters, filthy dirty from the day's work, sniffing and forlorn, they're as pathetic-looking a mob as you'd ever wish to see, Jessica thinks to herself. But she knows too that while her clothes are better, well patched by Hester, she doesn't look much different.

'Righto, here's what's gunna happen,' Billy is saying as Jack and Jessica come riding up.

'Hey, Billy, what say we leave this to Mike Malloy?' Jack calls down to him.

Billy turns and looks up at Jack. 'Nah, it's our business, Jack. They did it to our tar boy, it's ours to fix.'

Jack climbs down from the saddle and tethers his horse to a tall mallee stump behind Billy. Jessica does the same.

'Mate, Jessie doesn't want you to go on with it,' Jack continues. 'She says it was just a joke they played on her.'

The tar boys all look up hopefully. Billy fixes his eyes on Jessica. 'Some joke! Take off yer hat, Jessie.'

Jessica shakes her head.

'Jessie, lift yer hat, that's a bloody order!' Billy shouts.

'Lift it, Tea Leaf,' Jack whispers beside her.

Her hat is stuck firmly to her hair and she tries to remove it, lifting it gingerly, trying not to show the pain it's causing her. She winces and gets one side of the hat free so that it lifts like a hinged lid, just enough for them to see that her scalp and short fair hair is completely covered and matted with tar. Some of the men have come out from the shed to see what's going on, and a couple of them whistle with surprise at this sight. Jessica quickly pulls the side of the hat down again, flushing with embarrassment. 'Please, Billy, there's no harm done,' she pleads.

Billy isn't listening and now he turns to the tar boys. 'You gutless cowards done that to our tar boy and you're gunna have to pay. You're gunna have to fight me or have your heads done same as hers,' Billy says.

'What, all o' us against you?' the biggest among them says, smirking, hardly able to believe his ears. 'All six of us in one go?' It's Flats Sullivan. Flats is not his real name, nobody knows his real name, not even him – he is called Flats because when he was a baby he fell out of his cot and onto the stone floor in the kitchen. It broke his nose and flattened his face out a treat. His dad later said it didn't matter much because he was always fighting and his face would just as likely have ended up that way anyway. Jessica recalls it was Flats who sat on her chest and pinned her arms.

'No, wait on, Billy,' Jack says again. 'Mr Malloy will fine them a day's pay and they'll get the living daylights belted out of them at home.'

'That ain't fair!' one of the tar boys, Fly-speck, yells out.

'Why not?' Jack asks, surprised. 'Would you rather get walloped, or go home with a head full of tar?'

'Shit, yes!' Fly-speck says. 'Me old man will flatten me if I don't bring home me pay!' He points to Billy. 'I'm scared of him, but I'm more scared of me father.'

He looks around at the others. 'Some of them'll get off light, it ain't fair. We all done it the same to her!'

'That's a confession if ever I heard one,' Billy says, smiling at Jack. 'You heard him.'

'We'll fight yiz,' Flats decides suddenly.

Billy turns back to him. 'Wait on, you ain't heard the terms. It's two at a time, one minute by the clock fighting, half a minute rest for me, then I take the next two and so on, till the six of you has learned yer lesson.'

'How many times do we fight?' Fly-speck asks. Though he's the smallest of them all, he's clearly the brains in the group.

'Just the once.'

Fly-speck looks over at Flats and nods.

Jack tries one last time, Jessica egging him on silently. 'Billy, Jessie thinks she'll lose her place in the shed. She says my old man told her any trouble and she's out.'

'Bullshit!' Billy points to the tar boys. 'They've chosen their own punishment. They've admitted they did it, you heard the boy. It's not her that's responsible, it's them lot that has to cop what's coming.'

By now most of the men have come from the shed and they've made a semicircle around the group. There is a hum of approval at Billy's reasoning. Billy is one of them, a grafter, and while Jack is a good lad who can put in a day's work, he's still the boss's boy. The men like to settle things their way. Billy's right – the tar boys have to learn they can't muck about. What's more, it's a fair contest. These are all tough kids and at fourteen years they know how to scrap. The men don't say it, but it's also a bit of amusement before tea.

'So, what's it to be?' Billy asks. 'A bucket of tar over yer miserable heads, or fight me two at a time?'

Jack looks down at Jessica and shrugs, then says quietly so that only she can hear, 'She'll be right, Jessie. I'll talk to my father if it comes up. I'll take care of it – you won't lose your job.'

The tar boys go into a huddle. They break and Flats says again, 'We'll fight ya, Billy.'

Billy digs into his pocket and takes out a battered watch together with his rosary beads and hands both to Jack. 'You're the timekeeper, mate. One minute on, half a minute off.' He points to the tar boys. 'Two of them girlie beaters at a time.' He pulls his shirt over his head and hangs it on the mallee log where the two horses are tethered.

Billy now stands bare-chested with his legs apart facing the tar boys. 'Righto, first two step up,' he says to the six boys, none of whom has removed the rags they wear for shirts. Billy is a magnificent-looking young man, deep-muscled, huge in the chest with a stomach flat and rippled like a washboard.

Flats pushes two of the boys forward, the one wearing boots and another with his head clean-shaved.

Billy grins. 'You should've picked the tar brush, son,' he says, getting a laugh from the crowd.

The men form a circle around the fight. There's fear to be seen in all the tar boys' eyes but they can't back out if they ever hope to make it in a shearing shed. They walk around Billy, Boots to the back of him, the shaven-headed one to the front. Billy slaps the boy in front of him to the side of his head with the flat of his hand, hard enough to give him a thick ear and not much more. The boy jerks his head back as Billy pushes him and the lad loses his balance and falls to the dirt. Billy turns quickly to confront the second boy, but he's not fast enough. The boy takes a vicious kick at Billy and the steel toe-cap of his boot connects with Billy's knee. Billy goes down into the dirt clutching at his knee.

Then all the other boys rush in, kicking and flailing wildly at Billy, their fists and feet landing anywhere they can find. One of them bites a chunk out of his ear. Billy manages to scramble to his feet, but his knee won't hold up. Then three of the tar boys rush at him, collecting him in the midriff, and he careers backwards into the rump of Jack's tethered horse. The frightened beast tries to move away but finds it is pushed hard up against the mallee stump and rears and begins to fall, its hooves lashing out frantically as it tries to keep its balance. Billy lands sprawling in the dirt under Jack's horse as its rear hoof strikes out backwards, collecting Billy's head and cracking his skull open like a pumpkin fallen from a cart. A moment later the horse, still trying to regain its footing, drives a second hoof into Billy's face.

In the confusion that followed, Jessica can remember little of what happened next. Jack, it seemed, pulled her away and she was told much later she was screaming hysterically and he had to slap her across the face several times to make her stop. Even now, four years later, she is sick at the thought of that day. She still carries the guilt of Billy Simon with her. She's told herself a thousand times she wasn't to know what would happen. That she was only trying to save her job so Joe could get her money. But still the guilt lingers.

They bandaged the two sides of Billy's skull together, then wrapped the bandages with baling twine so the sides would hold firm. One of the shearers told Jessica later that the crack down his skull was about half an inch wide, and through it he could see Billy's brain, a throbbing bloody sponge. Then they bandaged his shattered face. His nose was badly broken and all but the very back teeth smashed out of his mouth. When they'd finished with him he looked like one of those Egyptian mummies – all they left showing were two holes for his nose and mouth.

Jack rode all the way to Narrandera with Billy Simon, sitting in the back of the horse cart himself to look after his mate. The trip took nearly fourteen hours and the others who'd gone with Billy, following the cart on horseback, told how Jack never left Billy and twice stopped to change his blood-soaked bandages, doing the dressings himself.

They told how Billy would come round and Jack would talk quietly to him and he would stop moaning at the sound of his mate's voice. Then Jack would roll a smoke and hold it to the crimson opening in the bandage and make him draw back for the small comfort the tobacco might bring him. Jack also poured brandy mixed with a little water down Billy's throat every time he regained consciousness, sitting him up so he wouldn't choke. The men joked that poor Billy was pissed as a newt, feeling no pain, by the time they got him to the doctor at Narrandera.

When Billy came out of the hospital three months later Jack paid all his expenses and took him home, even though he was brain-damaged and the doctor said nothing could be done further, that he'd never be right in the head again. The accident had left a huge, ugly scar that ran the length of Billy's skull to an inch above his left eyebrow, a pinkish track through his black curls. Not that you'd ever see it – the day Billy came home from Narrandera he had his hat pulled down hard over his eyes, and was never after seen without it firmly on his noggin.

Folk soon took to calling him Billy Simple, which was a cruel sort of joke. Before the accident, no bastard would have been game to attempt such a play on Billy Simon's name for fear of having their own features rearranged. Now he was treated as a harmless idiot.

Billy Simple, when he became well enough, was given a job for life as the gardener at Riverview homestead. All of this was Jack's doing, against the wishes of George Thomas, Winifred and Gwen, these last two protesting that it was degrading to have a lunatic wandering around the garden.

Surprisingly, Jack wouldn't have succeeded in his endeavour to help Billy without the support of his mother. In the beginning, she had sided with the others, but when Jack had threatened to leave home and become an itinerant shearer and to take Billy with him, Ada, besotted with her only son, quickly gave in. Later, though, she and her daughters would wreak their revenge on poor, helpless Billy Simple. Jessica has heard Jack's angry tales of his family's mean teasing of Billy, and she certainly knows how nasty those women can be.

Jessica herself has learned over the past four years to dislike the Thomas women almost as much as she dislikes their father. When she'd been forced to eat at the homestead that first year, every dinner she took with them became a torture. The two girls, Winifred and Gwen, delighted in making fun of her.

They'd hold their noses when Jessica entered the kitchen. 'Pooh, you smell of sheep!' they'd exclaim, even though Jessica always took care to wash her face and arms at the pump before entering the house.

They spoke about her in French, which they were learning from their tutor, giggling and hugging each other, overcome with their own amusement. They remarked loudly on her awkward table manners and imitated her holding her knife in her fist and resting its end on the table as she ate. They always sat at the other end of the kitchen table, noting loudly that it was as far from her pong as they could possibly get.

They remarked constantly on her looks, her greasy work clothes and her short cropped hair, and wondered aloud how a woman could sink so low that she'd dress like a man and work in a shearing shed.

Jessica dared not fight back and learned to take her meals in silence, gulping down her food so that she could make her escape. Winifred and Gwen never ceased delighting in taunting her and seemed between them to have an endless capacity to be vindictive. Ada would sometimes come into the kitchen and sit at the table but even then the teasing didn't stop. Jessica soon sensed that while she did not join in, Ada Thomas was secretly very amused by their taunts and carrying on.

'You two really are the limit,' she'd say to her daughters, though there would be a small smile on her lips. 'Leave the poor girl alone.'

Jessica used to beg Joe to let her go without her dinner at the homestead, to take bread and cold mutton with her and eat alone. But Hester would never allow it, saying that keeping the family's relationship with the Thomas girls cordial was a great opportunity for Meg to get closer to young Jack.

'Don't you *ever* show disrespect to them, or answer back – you'll ruin our chances for Meg,' her mother had admonished her, making Joe promise that their young daughter would do nothing to upset Ada, Winifred or Gwen.

As Jessica nears the homestead now she can hear the dogs barking, and grins when she thinks how angry they'll be at being locked up and missing out on the fun. Again, she lets herself feel happy at the thought of a few days without Meg and Hester and their endless pursuit of the Thomas family.

Her mother and sister have turned posh and become

Church of England, taking their example from Mrs
Thomas and her daughters, Winifred and Gwen, which to
Jessica's mind is about the worst thing you could do. They
clutch their prayer books to their bosoms for all to see as
they arrive at St Stephen's in the sulky. As you can't go
clutching a prayer book to your bosom while looking
saintly and, at the same time, hold the reins and talk to
the horse, their new-found piety requires Jessica to drive
them to church of a Sunday. This means she has to sit on
her bum in a hard pew while the Reverend Samuel Mathews, M.A. Oxon., takes an hour of sunlight out of her life
to get through the dreary Sunday sermon. It's a speech
which generally seems to involve the perfidy of mankind,
the futility of life and the need to be good and love thy
neighbour so that you may reap the reward in the here-
after for enduring a miserable life out here in the bush.

As Ada Thomas and her thin-lipped daughters are
their nearest neighbours, Hester and Meg are determined to love their neighbours, even if they should die
in the attempt. Liking, let alone loving, the shrill-voiced
Ada and her daughters, Jessica decides, is going to take
a whole Bible full of Christian charity on their part. If
Jack Thomas isn't to be the ultimate prize, she doubts
whether even Hester and Meg would bother to go the
distance with the three Thomas women.

And if Mrs Thomas and her girls are aware of the plan
to snare their only son, brother and the heir to Riverview
Station, they certainly don't let on. They accept all the
bowing and scraping and smiling as their due, and
include Hester and Meg in their larger tea parties. It is

obvious they don't consider Hester and Meg up to scratch, but this only seems to make the two Bergman women more in awe of the Thomases.

Hester and Meg admire Ada and her girls blindly, in the way poor people often admire the rich, endowing them with character and intelligence they don't possess. Money, Jessica has discovered, is a clever way to conceal stupidity and meanness in people's personalities. Her mother and sister will tolerate no criticism of the three, although Jessica reckons that the more Hester and Meg kowtow to them, the snootier the Thomas women seem to get.

What's more, she thinks that the three Thomas women are just plain-looking, plain stupid and plain snobs. It should be said in fairness that Hester and Meg aren't the only ones who dare not cross Ada Thomas. Nobody in the parish is prepared to speak out against them or put them in their place. This has allowed them to become the arbiters of all that's good or bad in the district and, with Ada's money, the major dispensers of its charity and goodwill. Not that goodwill has a lot going for it in the Riverina, if Ada's an example, Jessica thinks.

Ada Thomas is President of the Women's Committee at St Stephen's and also of the Red Cross Society, formed in Narrandera after the Boer War. At church and charity she wields her power and uses her two daughters as her gossip and information gatherers.

'The Three Must-interferes' is what folks call them behind their backs. Their role, as they see it, is to flush out gossip or sniff out any misdemeanour in the parish and generally to pass judgement on anything or anyone.

As a consequence, the sick, the lame and the down-trodden receive only that portion of charity which Ada Thomas decides they deserve, based on their past conduct, church attendance record and pecking order on the social ladder.

The poorest usually get the least. This, in Ada Thomas's eyes, is as it should be. After all, the working-class poor set the lowest standards, have the least aspirations and, besides, are accustomed to doing without, so they should not be given false hopes of any large entitlement.

If you're a family in need of the church's munificence you make damn sure you scrub the faces of your children and send them off to Sunday School in clean pinnies and patched knickerbockers. And if the brats don't have boots you brush their hair and wash their feet and cut their toenails, because you can be sure that all will be noted by Winifred and Gwen and reported back to Ada.

What's more, if you know what's good for you, you get your own bum into a pew quick smart of a Sunday morning and try to put a penny in the plate. This last observance is in the hands of Ada's two daughters, who've replaced the anonymous black tithe bag with an open plate. They report with clerical accuracy every farthing given and by whom.

Mrs Thomas has let it be known to one and all that she has no charity for godless blasphemers, shirkers and for most of the working-class poor.

'God is not mocked,' she will say after rejecting a name put forward on the church charity list on the basis of infrequent attendance at Sunday morning worship, combined with recent knowledge of a husband seen full as a boot outside the Royal Mail Hotel.

The Thomases are the richest family in the district by far. That is to say, Ada Thomas is, because it was the fortune she brought to the marriage that made her husband George prosper despite his being an ex-riverboat captain without any previous experience on the land. He's still the more unpopular of the two, but she holds the cheque book and that, people say, makes her an even bigger bitch than he is a bastard, though there's little to choose between them.

Even the vicar dares not stand up to Ada Thomas, possessing as he does a flock under his pastoral care with barely a penny between them. His is not a wealthy congregation and his living is a precarious one. Ada Thomas's benevolence forms the major part of the parish income and so Reverend Samuel Mathews, M.A. Oxon., figuratively touches his forelock to the mistress of Riverview. His well-cultivated vowels are used too frequently in her praise when he ought to have been telling her to mind her own business.

If it wasn't for Ada Thomas, the Anglicans would not be any better off than the rest of God's local affiliations. The Catholics look after their own and with the local Irish making up most of the congregation their resources are sorely stretched. The Lutherans are really missionaries who take care of the Aborigines and so are quite unacceptable. The Baptists and Presbyterians don't have any money to speak of. In fact, Jesus is a pauper in all these denominations.

The God-fearing Ada was not amused when, nearly a year after Billy Simon's accident at Riverview Station, a mob of starving Aborigines, trying to escape the terrible drought further up north around the Darling River, turned up at Ada's doorstep begging for sustenance. Ada immediately saw them as the property of the Lutherans and therefore a pestilence sent against the Anglicans by another, inferior denomination.

Ada tried to send them away, but they were either too exhausted or too desperate to move and remained in the yard, pleading for food.

'If we feed the brutes they'll just stay,' she told the cook. 'You're not to give them anything except water. They're like animals – if you show them kindness, we'll never get rid of them.'

The dogs were out with the men on one of the runs and so she couldn't set them onto the blacks camped in the yard. Ada called Billy in from the garden and demanded he fire a charge of birdshot into the air above their heads. This he refused to do, blubbering and clutching his hat over his head while she shouted furiously at him in vain. Then when he'd mumbled and stammered and finally run away to hide, she'd done it herself. But the blacks still wouldn't move and she'd finally lost her temper and fired the small-bore shotgun at the legs of several of the adult men who stood to one side of their gins. The light birdshot peppered them, sending bright rivulets of blood down their dark, stick-thin legs, over their large, broken feet and the cracks in the soles and down into the dust.

That was not the end of it, either. Calling for their horses to be saddled, Mrs Thomas and her two daughters drove the blacks off their land, beating them over the head and shoulders with their riding crops. Long lines of flies queued along the furrows of dried blood on their dust-encrusted legs. The men remained silent, unflinching at the blows from the riding crops, though the gins wailed their misery, carrying and dragging their starving kids with them.

Ada Thomas was fined ten shillings by the police magistrate when he sat at Narrandera a month later. Her defence had been that they were trespassing on her land and were godless creatures and so didn't rate her charity or the Lord's compassion.

'They should have gone to the Lutherans,' she'd said with a toss of her head, followed by a sniff which clearly indicated her opinion of this denomination.

'Be that as it may, Mrs Thomas, may I remind you that in things temporal we don't go around shooting blacks,' the magistrate replied.

'Why not?' Ada Thomas demanded. 'Be *that* as it may, Mr Craddock, we've been doing it for the past hundred years and may I remind *you*, I only used birdshot!'

There was much laughter at this and the magistrate was forced to clear the court, sending the crowd out into Larmer Street where they watched the proceedings through the open bay windows.

The whole town had turned up for the hearing. When the magistrate pronounced the fine, Ada Thomas took a ten-shilling note out of her handbag and in an imperious voice demanded a receipt from the clerk of the court. When he'd written it out and handed it to her she'd looked the magistrate straight in the eye and said, 'This could not have happened if Mr Donaldson had been here. He knew me for a good Christian lady.' She paused before delivering her ultimate judgement of the magistrate. 'God is not mocked, Mr Craddock!'

The police magistrate did not bat an eyelid at the mention of his predecessor. 'Maybe God is not mocked, but I am, Mrs Thomas. You have twice referred to me by name. You will kindly refer to the bench in this court as "Your Worship"!'

Ada Thomas merely sniffed at this rebuke, to a ripple of sympathetic laughter from the open windows. The magistrate had finally had enough. 'The defendant is fined another one pound ten shillings for contempt of this court!' he bellowed. Later the crowd outside the window would quip that being rude to a magistrate was a threefold bigger crime than shooting an Abo.

Jack Thomas had his brand new De Dion motor car waiting outside the courthouse, its engine cranked and ready for a quick getaway when his mother emerged. The large crowd greeted her with cheers, surrounding the handsome vehicle, many of them shouting, 'Good on ya, Mrs Thomas! Australia for the white man!'

Jessica remembers being told how Ada Thomas climbed up into the seat beside Jack and then started to smile and wave at the crowd like bloody Queen Mary at her own coronation, finally departing in a cloud of dust and smoke from young Jack's motor.

The cheering townsfolk, or the men anyway, repaired to the pub across the street to drink the health of a woman who was a fair dinkum hero, who'd done the right thing by decent society. Except, they laughed, she should have used buckshot. If they had their way, Ada Thomas would be given a medal by the governor.

Joe said that blacks were 'useless bastards', but then he'd tell Jessica how he'd worked with some up north, good blokes who'd been hard-working stockmen. 'But that sort are few and far between,' he reckoned. 'They're mostly dirty and drunk and you couldn't trust one as far as you could throw him.'

But when a small group of blacks, drifting down from the same drought along the Darling River as Ada's unfortunate lot, had come to their back door a couple of months after her court case, Joe hadn't turned them away like she had.

Jessica remembers what a pitiful sight they'd been, no more than skin and bone. Their arms and legs were covered in open sores where the flies clustered in swarms. The stomachs of the naked children were distended to the size of small watermelons and their dark eyes seemed too large in their woolly little heads. She could see the shape of their skulls under the tightly stretched skin covering their coal-black faces. Flies crawled at the corners of their eyes and up their nostrils and they seemed too tired to brush them aside. Their limbs were like twigs you could snap with a sharp twist of your thumb and forefinger, and lice swarmed over their heads.

'Poor bastards, all ribs and prick, like a drover's dog,' Joe said.

Jessica recalls how the adults smelled of rotting flesh. The torn, filthy rags they wore may have once been clothing but now concealed very little. They hung in bits and pieces over random parts of their skinny bodies, hardly hiding their private parts.

Meg had come to the kitchen door first and ran screaming for Hester. Hester called to Jessica to bring the shotgun, but Joe came in and stopped his wife from driving them away.

He'd given them a bag of flour for damper and let them have a wether, slaughtering the old sheep for them himself. He allowed them to stay in the bottom paddock which fronted the river and was well wooded and out of sight, warning them not to be seen or he'd have to send them away.

He'd let Jessica use the shotgun to kill a roo for them every other day, or take the small-bore rifle, the .22, and shoot half a dozen rabbits. At this time of the year, though, there was hardly a bite of meat on a rabbit. 'Vermin eating vermin,' Joe would laugh, making a cheap joke out of his own charity. The roos she shot were full of worms but Joe said, 'Blacks don't care, don't take any notice of things like that.'

'You mean people who are starving don't care!' she'd protested.

'Right,' he said, seeing the look in her eyes and not wishing to take the matter any further.

Jessica had gone into their camp every afternoon with strips of clean rags for bandages and a big jar of sulphur ointment Joe had produced for her. He said it was good for horses and he'd often enough used it on himself when he was a boundary rider and he'd come to no harm. She boiled water and cleaned the sores on the children's little arms and legs with a strong permanganate of potash solution before applying Joe's ointment. She tried not to retch at the suppurating flesh that came away on the dressings, often leaving only bone behind. The children hardly ever bawled when she dressed them and they loved the brightly coloured bandages and so were careful to keep them on afterwards.

Joe told her she'd done good, but not to get too concerned, blacks were tough as old boots and had their own bush medicine. He said, 'If they want to die they'll just lay down and be dead on the spot, Jessie, wish themselves dead, and there's nothing yiz can do about it.' But Jessica didn't see them gathering any of their own medicine and none of them seemed to want to lie down and die, so she kept on with the dressings.

After a while one of the gins grew a bit friendly. She was younger than most of the women. Jessica thought she was sixteen, a year older than herself, though it was difficult to tell from her starving body. Her mission name was Mary Simpson and she spoke a little English, learned from the Lutheran Mission station up near the Lachlan Swamps.

Mary was from the local Wiradjuri tribe, and had been taken as a bride by the Wongaibon tribe from the north who made up the rest of her small band. She first approached Jessica to say that some of the gins wanted to use Joe's ointment on themselves as well as on the children. Soon Mary was helping her with the dressings and translating what Jessica told her into their own language.

They were a sad little mob, but in a few days with a bit of tucker in them, they started to smile again. The children seemed to recover first and soon got strong enough to play in the river, which meant they didn't smell quite as bad as before.

One afternoon Mary came up to Jessica with all the kids in tow and they presented her with two yellow-belly and a redfin they'd caught.

'For you,' Mary said shyly. 'They catch for you, Missus Jessie.'

They were starving but still they gave her the three fish, which she knew she couldn't refuse. She thanked them, tears in her eyes. Yellow-belly is a good eating fish and she'd taken them home and cooked them. Hester and Meg turned up their noses but Joe said, apart from tasting a bit muddy this time of year, they were real good.

Hester commanded Jessica not to speak of Joe's kindness. 'You don't breathe a word, you hear? Not to anyone. Folk are terrible tattle-tales – if people hear Joe Bergman is helping blacks it will do your father's reputation no good.' Hester knew well enough that any threat to Joe would keep her younger daughter's trap firmly shut.

But Jessica, even then, knew what her mother really meant. On the basis of the popularity she'd gained over the shooing of the Aborigines off Riverview Station, Ada Thomas was thinking of standing for the position of councillor in the Shire elections, the first woman in the Riverina ever to contemplate such an action. If Joe's kindness to the Aborigines was known then the Bergmans could be seen as nigger lovers, which would do Meg's chances any amount of harm. But, despite all Hester's fears, Ada Thomas lost the election anyway. People may have thought she was a hero but she was still a bossy boots and no one wanted to give her any more power than she already had.

As Jessica arrives at the homestead, she can hear that the dogs have worked themselves up into a howling frenzy. She's locked the three kelpies in the shed so they wouldn't follow her down to the river and get themselves bit to death. Red is gunna be real cranky, Jessica thinks to herself. Red is her dog, the oldest of the three, and he likes to be around her, always on the lookout in case she comes to harm. Red sees Jessica as his responsibility and he doesn't like to be insulted by being shut away when there's something going on.

By way of making up to them, Red in particular, Jessica decides they'll get a bit extra in their bucket of bones and boiled hogget scraps. Maybe she'll toss in a ladle or two of Hester's soup gravy – that, she decides, should cheer 'em up a treat. She can just hear Joe's voice now, scolding her: 'They're working dogs, girlie.

Spoil a dog and it'll never come good again. Sit on its bum under a tree all flaming day!'

But it would just be another of Joe's gloomy predictions. Any deviation from the normal makes Joe uncomfortable and brings out his sense of impending disaster, what Jessica has come to think of as his 'never come trues'. Red and the two other kelpies love to work and if one of them were to lay down on the job you could be damned sure something was seriously wrong with it – distemper, maybe, or a tick or a bite from a snake.

Jessica grins because she's long since called her father's bluff – she knows he's not the cranky old bugger he pretends to be. He's kind enough for anyone's liking, but he just doesn't want to be caught at it.

The Aborigines aren't the only instance where Jessica's caught Joe not practising his dog-eat-dog theory. He'll slaughter a two-tooth and leave the dressed carcass at the back door of someone's place, or do the same with a side of bacon. He'll hear a farmer is taken ill, and he'll turn up to put in a couple of days' ploughing, shearing, harvesting or whatever needs doing.

It's just that you never know what Joe is up to when he is doing good because he never speaks of it. If you catch him at it he'll get stroppy and deny any do-gooding. He'll claim he's sold the two-tooth for good money, or obtained a more than fair price for the bacon, or been paid wages for his labour. Meanwhile, it's as plain as the nose on your face that the people who've received his kindness can no more afford a side of bacon than pay cash for the crown jewels. Yes,

Jessica knows her old man, all right. He can be a real stubborn bugger with a bad temper, but as for dog-eat-dog, Joe never ate another dog in his life.

Jessica thinks over something wise Joe said recently. 'There's talk of war coming,' he told her over smoko one day, 'there's war clouds gathering over Europe. The young fellers will have to head over there if it does come.' Jessica imagines the dark gunpowder-black clouds over the cities and villages, with frightened people in coats and boots and scarves wrapped half around their faces looking up at them as more and more of them gather, until they fill every patch of blue sky. The wind howling and snow beginning to fall, with a terrible kind of darkness beginning to descend.

'When will we know?' asked Jessica, wide-eyed.

'Reckon I'll know more when we get back from town and I've seen the Sydney papers. I reckon Australia will be in it, boots and all. Young bucks being blooded, lots of bullshit flying around about duty to King and Country. Boer War veterans waving the flag and beating the drum, wearing their medals in the pub and telling how they knew A. H. Dufrayer, the hero from Morundah who was awarded the Queen's Scarf – before he got killed, that is,' Joe finished with a laconic twist.

'What's the Queen's Scarf?' she'd wanted to know.

'Well, old Queen Victoria, who must have been near dead herself, knitted four of these scarves to be given to a colonial soldier for outstanding bravery. Bloody useful it must've been in the hot sun of Africa,' Joe said.

'You know, Jessica, I can't see why we should give

England the lives of our young blokes for a quarrel that's got bugger-all to do with us here in Australia,' he sighed. 'But careful what you say – don't tell anyone what I reckon. Could be dangerous. Remember, girlie, to some people around here I'm still a bloody foreigner – Danish is near enough to being German for some folk.'

'What about you, Father? Would you fight?' Jessica had asked.

'You know me, Jessie – I'd fight for Australia, no questions asked, except I'm too old to join up. But loyalty to the Union Jack, or Denmark for that matter, means bugger-all to me. They done nothing for us, 'cept grow rich. The bastards own the banks and most of the good land. Why should we help them, die for those bastards that hold our mortgages and sell our farms out from under us when we can't pay? No bloody chance, eh girlie?'

This is certainly not the feeling of the district, where they're all true blue, sons of England, Rule Britannia marmalade and jam. The local-born are the worst of the lot, Joe reckons, their duty to King George and the British Empire never to be questioned. 'Pax Britannica, there's a laugh,' Joe says, 'buggers can't get into the scrap with the Boche soon enough for their liking.

'The young fellers'll be pushing their ages forward and trying to grow a moustache and the old bastards'll be pushing theirs back, buying every packet of those fancy new Gillette blades they can lay their hands on to shave real close so the recruiting sergeant can't see the grey. They'll be falling over each other to pack a rifle and volunteer to die for King and bloody Country.' Joe pauses and rubs the stubble on his chin. 'I saw it in the Boer War, bullshit baffles brains every time when it comes to joining up and wearing a uniform with brass buttons and a cockade of chook's feathers in your flamin' bush hat!'

If Joe's not joining up, Jessica can't imagine war changing anything very much in her life. Joe staying here is all she cares about. The sun will still come up in the morning, the paddocks will still dry out by early summer, the rains will still be late or never come and the snakes will still dance down by the river.

The dogs are now happily scoffing their feed. There's still enough twilight left to put the hens and the rooster into the chicken run for the night, light the slush lamp, trim the warmer wick and turn the eggs in the hatchery. What's more, there's a good part of a cold leg of lamb and some roast taties Hester has left for her tea, so Jessica won't have to cook for herself either. Things could be a whole lot worse.

Then it suddenly strikes Jessica. Hits her like a smack in the mouth. Bloody hell! If there's a war coming, like Joe says, Jack will join up to fight – he's just the sort to volunteer. Where will that leave Hester and Meg and their precious marriage plans?

CHAPTER THREE

Jessica awakens to the barking of the dogs. The sky is just beginning to lighten and she judges it to be half an hour before sunrise. Perhaps a fox trying to get at the chickens – couldn't be a snake, she thinks, dogs make a different sound around a snake. From their barking, though, they seem to be down near the top paddock, nothing much to worry about.

Though she has lain on top of her narrow cot all night, Jessica's body is wet with perspiration and her cotton nightdress clings to her small breasts and hips. She pours water from a jug into the washbasin and splashes her face and neck, then rinses a washcloth and wipes the night's sleep from her eyes and cleans the inside of her ears. She washed before she slept but the grit is always there, except for the brief periods when there's been rain. She slips off the sweat-soaked garment and stands nude, completely unaware of her strong, shapely legs and flat, hard stomach. She runs her hand absently along her right thigh and her hand pauses briefly, then, as though it has a mind of its own, her fingers trail lightly through the soft hair between her legs.

More and more Jessica feels drawn to enter her

womanhood, to rub it with the soft pads of her fingers. At eleven she had quite accidentally discovered this way of pleasuring herself, and the urge has increased as she's grown older. She now submits to it most nights, her fingers at first absently stroking, and then more urgently rubbing and sliding until she feels a sweet ache and a rising of her blood, followed by a few moments of pleasure which take her breath away. Then comes a wonderful sense of release, a lightness as if she's floating. For a brief moment in time she is complete. Sleep follows almost immediately, as though the two actions have become dependent upon each other.

At first Jessica wondered if what she'd discovered was wicked, and in the months that followed her guilt increased. She knew enough from the schoolyard to know that it is dirty 'down there'. She made an early resolve not to take any chances by mentioning it to her sister Meg, not that they ever talked to each other anyway, although she's often wondered if Meg does it too.

Then one morning, just over a year after she first started exploring, disaster struck. Her monthly bleeding came for the first time. Never having been told about menstruation, Jessica was terrified, thinking the blood was caused by her nightly rubbing, that her finger had worn away something vital inside her and that she must surely bleed to death.

She knew there was no way out and she wouldn't be missed anyhow, so she lay down on her narrow iron cot to die, hoping death would come quickly and painlessly. She did think it rather stupid of herself to cause her own demise just when she'd finished her schooling and was about to become grown up. It was then that she remembered Hester's warning to her when she was little.

Hester made Jessica wear black flannel knickers down to her knees right up until she was twelve. This hideous garment contained a drawstring at the end of each leg and another around her waist, and seemed to possess her body and restrict it from moving freely. When Jessica was still too small to manage them herself Hester would pull the tapes so tightly that they almost stopped the circulation above her knees, and the drawstring around her waist cut deeply into her flesh and was most uncomfortable in the heat, leaving a deep red welt when it was removed at night.

When Jessica had complained to Hester about the tightness of the cords her mother sniffed dismissively. 'It's to keep your little hands away from sin and temptation!' Hester held the young Jessica by the shoulders, and looking directly into her eyes she said sternly, 'The wages of sin is death!'

No more was said about it, but Jessica gathered from the tone of her mother's voice that her hands, against her own wishes, could be quite capable of doing something truly wicked from which Hester was safeguarding her with the dreaded drawstrings.

When, at eleven, Jessica discovered the joy her fingers could give her she did not for one moment associate them with the same hands that would one day lead her to sin and temptation and onwards from there to an untimely death. There was a simple enough explanation for this. Her hands only found their way down there at night when she was wearing a nightgown and when her knickers were neatly folded beside her dress on the stool beside her bed. Plainly, knickers were for use in the daytime, when sin and temptation obviously struck. With a child's logic, Jessica had reasoned she need only be on the alert for these calamities during daylight hours, when she was safely under the protection of Hester's drawstring knickers.

Now, as she lay bleeding to death, her mother's words finally made sense to her. The drawstrings were to stop her hands yielding to temptation and going down there to sin. Hester had obviously known all along that the wages of sin was death by bleeding.

And so, on her deathbed, Jessica had yet another reason for resenting her mother. Why couldn't she have just come out and told her properly, just said it plainly like Joe would have done: 'Jessica, don't rub down there or you'll bleed to death!' She would have understood an instruction like that.

Jessica must have fallen asleep in the process of dying, for Hester entered the room and saw her blood-stained nightdress. Next thing Jessica knew she was briefly back in her mother's affections, held tightly clasped to her ample bosom.

'My little girl has begun her journey to womanhood,' Hester said.

'You mean I'm not gunna die, Mama?' Jessica asked, pushing away in confusion from her mother's large breasts.

'No, Jessica, you're going to grow up to be a fine young lady.'

Jessica had never seen Hester so loving, and she promised God, then and there, never to touch herself again. She told herself she would henceforth imagine invisible drawstrings around her waist and above her knees when she went to bed. She managed to keep her promise to God for an entire week after her first bleeding ended and then her resolve crumbled and the temptations of the flesh became too much to overcome and back came the delicious sin of her fingers.

With the knowledge that she was now a woman and could have children, which is what Hester told her, Jessica knows what she is doing must be wrong and that 'it', for that's what she's called the end result of her exploring hands, might stop her having babies one day.

Jessica's guilt as a child has grown into shame as a young woman. But with it, her desire seems to have increased. When she's lonely or sad, her fingers give her comfort. When Joe is in one of his moods and doesn't talk to her for several days, it's some solace. When she sees Meg dressed up for church, pretty as a picture, and herself, in Hester's borrowed dress, flat in front and ugly, or so she thinks, when she hears some of the women at the church say, 'What a pretty dress, Jessica,' and then turn to Meg and say, 'Don't you look pretty today,' she will secretly dream of being pretty herself and those are nights she does *it*.

Jessica can feel how the other young women envy her sister, with her thick chestnut hair, her alabaster skin and delicate curves. Jessica doesn't envy Meg's looks, but she sometimes weeps secretly in her bed at night because Meg and Hester seem to know exactly what they're doing, where they're going, what it means to be a woman, and all she has is Joe, who keeps doggedly pressing on, expecting nothing good, as if life is a punishment he must endure, just letting everything happen to him, expecting her to be the same.

When Jessica thinks about all these things she sometimes feels resentful and even a bit sorry for herself. She's the ugly duckling who must try to look as if she doesn't care. Her flannel shirt, moleskins and scuffed and broken boots are the symbols of her defiance. But Jessica has never wanted to be a man – she just doesn't want to have to act stupid, to be less than she is. She has observed the ways of the men, the smallholders in the district, how they own the women they marry and treat them badly and beat them when they're drunk.

Meg will marry a rich man and she will be spared the life of a poor farmer's wife but she, Jessica, won't. She'll be expected to become one of those dull-eyed, exhausted women whom men call 'a good little breeder' and have ten or more children and wear herself out caring for them while, at the same time, being a slave to her husband. She will be pregnant or nursing a baby for most of the first twenty years of her married life, or, as happens often enough, she will die in childbirth or simply from being worn out.

But if she can only be a poor farmer's wife, then she would prefer to stay where she is, with the life she has being Joe's partner. All of this wells up in Jessica and leaves her confused – she has only questions and no answers.

Now, at eighteen, she tells herself she isn't going to get a husband who will treat her half decent. Hester has told her that often enough for Jessica to believe her. So, she convinces herself, having babies doesn't matter, you can't have babies if you don't have a husband.

Jessica is aware that most of the marriages in the district are shotgun weddings, but she won't let that happen to her. Often at night, though, alone in bed, she wonders what it would be like to love a man and have him be inside her. Yet the thought that what she's doing with her fingers, that what feels so good, is secretive and sinful disturbs her. She is not like that, she is not bad and has no other secrets but for this one, bad as it is.

Jessica longs to talk to someone about how she feels, to unburden herself, confess that she's done wrong. But she can't imagine anyone she knows who would listen to her without thinking she was a wicked girl who has sinned against God.

When Jessica left school at twelve to help Joe, she'd soon lost contact with girls her own age except to see them at the Narrandera Show or sometimes in church or a woolshed dance. Most are now married with a child at their side and another at the breast, or swelling in their stomach, the first the proverbial shotgun pregnancy and the second the result of their fecundity and a young husband exercising his conjugal rights. At eighteen their thighs are beginning to thicken, shoulders to droop, they have lost the brightness in their eyes, and their expressions are no longer curious. It's this vacant look of the respectable country poor which Jessica dreads might some day be her own fate.

Jessica thought about talking to God, but from what she knows of Him, compliments of the Reverend Mathews, M.A. Oxon., He wouldn't be exactly sympathetic. 'Straight to Hell for you, my girl! No pleasuring of parts unseen before wedlock. Out of my sight!' He'd be like Hester, only worse.

Standing naked in the tiny room, Jessica feels the first prickle of the day's heat. Her right shoulder hurts and she recalls the shotgun blast and smiles to herself – the snakes are another secret, something else she must keep to herself. Though she doesn't feel guilty about that one. What they don't know can't hurt them and she hasn't done anything wrong. She prods at her right shoulder, it feels stiff and aches a bit. She tentatively winds her arm around a couple of times and winces. Not too bad, the bruise isn't showing yet, no more than a bit of swelling, could be worse. She decides she can use the arm well enough – it will loosen up when she's milking.

She takes up the washcloth again and rinses it, then wipes her sweat-covered body all over, not bothering to towel herself dry. The damp cloth feels cool against her skin, but she knows that in the few moments it will take to dry, the rising heat will make her face and neck break out in a thin coat of sweat again.

Jessica doesn't spare a second thought for the weather outside – it's wasted energy thinking about the heat. Like every other day, this one's going to be a scorcher. It's two months before the rains are due, if they come at all. She pours fresh water into a tin mug and scrubs her teeth with some bicarbonate of soda, spitting into the basin and then rinsing her mouth.

Considering the heat she has slept well enough, though she can remember dreaming of clouds. Blood-red clouds. Probably from thinking of what Joe's said about war coming.

The dogs have stopped barking as she pulls on a pair of old cotton bloomers with elastic at the waist and above her knees. Elastic is a new invention which Jessica thinks must surely be one of the best things ever made for women. She pulls on her moleskin trousers and a red flannel shirt, which she carelessly tucks into her waistband, and then buckles her broad leather belt. In her only concession to femininity Jessica reaches for her pinafore hanging from a nail on the wall, slips it around her neck and ties it about her waist. The pinny is a useful garment with its large front pocket, far more practical than the pockets in her moleskins, and so she sees no reason to discard it. She even enjoys the way a new stockman or shearer will look at the rosebud Meg or Hester always embroiders in the corner, not quite knowing what to think of her.

Finally she goes over to the side of her iron cot where she'd kicked off her working boots last night. Holding one boot pinned to the floor with her toes she works her small foot into its worn and scruffy leather upper, then sits herself down on the bed and pulls the second boot onto her left foot.

As part of the routine she uses to get into the day Jessica bends slightly forward and massages her skull vigorously, then rakes the fingers of both hands impatiently through her short fair hair, patting it down. Hair, Jessica discovered as a child, keeps the fair sex in bondage, from which, at fourteen, she decided to make her escape.

When she'd got the job at the shearing shed and had suggested to her mother that she'd like her hair cut short Hester had become hysterical. 'You'll look like a boy!' she'd shouted at her daughter. 'I forbid you! A woman's hair is a gift from the Lord God Himself! What *could* you be thinking of, Jessica?'

But this argument didn't impress Jessica, who'd never really found God to be on her side anyway. Rejecting His gift to womankind she took to her long blonde hair with a pair of scissors, cropping her head like a man's. She'd cut Joe's often enough to know her way around a head of hair and when her snipping was complete she was confident she'd made a passable job of it. Knowing that no matter what happened next it couldn't be put back again, Jessica resolved to take whatever punishment she had coming from her mother. Looking defiant, she'd walked into the kitchen where Hester and Meg were baking oat biscuits.

Meg had been the first to look up as she entered. Bringing her flour-whitened hands to her cheeks, she'd let out a piercing scream. Hester looked up in alarm and then promptly burst into tears.

'Oh my God!' she wailed. 'We've lost her! Lost her for good to the Devil!'

Jessica felt a bit better. Her mother being busy with blubbing meant that she wouldn't think of a particularly nasty punishment on the spot. 'I'm not dead, Mother!' she'd protested.

'Might as well be,' Hester wept. 'You're no daughter of mine any more!'

Meg, recovered from her initial shock, then had a go at Jessica. 'You're a foolish girl and a disgrace to your kind. How dare you do this to us! To *me*!' She shook a floury finger at her sister. 'Just you wait until Father sees what you've done!'

Jessica was saved. By referring her hair to Joe, her sister made it impossible for Hester to interfere and impose her own punishment. Jessica often feels that Meg is more the cranky mother than Hester, and certainly they have no sisterly relationship. Only three years separate them, but it might as well be a whole generation.

At tea that night Joe barely glanced at his youngest daughter and despite Hester and Meg trying to prod him into punishing her, he simply looked up at Jessica and said, 'I reckon it's damned practical for the work she does, that's all. Leave her alone.'

'But it will destroy us, Father,' Meg had howled.

'The only thing that'll destroy us is if the bank doesn't give me an extension on our loan until the heifer sales,' Joe growled in reply. 'I'm telling ya, leave the girlie alone.'

Jessica recalls how she wasn't too upset at Hester's threat that she was 'no daughter of mine'. Since the time when Joe clouted her at the table over the snake incident and her mother abandoned her for the meat dish, there have been a dozen or more such declarations, all followed by a promise of permanent banishment from Hester's affections.

The most recent incident was when she'd come second in her age group at the Narrandera Agricultural Show, working Red, the oldest kelpie, to herd and pen thirty sheep.

'Listen to me, my girl, men don't like a woman who shows them up! A working dog is men's work,' Hester scolded her. 'I give up on you!'

In a strange way, these constant threats have made Jessica realise that in her mother's eyes, she might still hold some hope. One day she might have a long enough run of good behaviour to get back into Hester's good books. Although, until Meg gets hitched to Jack Thomas or, if she fails to hook him, some other eligible young bloke, Jessica isn't sweating on a change of heart from her mother.

If Jessica has never wished to be a boy, she's never really been allowed to be a girl either. She only wants to be accepted as being as capable as those who work with her. It is her misfortune that what she does well is generally seen as a man's work. But she doesn't ask any favours because she's a girl. If she's up to the job, then she wants to be treated as an equal. If she fails, then she's prepared to cop whatever's coming to her and learn from the experience. In her naturally stubborn mind it is a simple enough request. She doesn't want to play at being the modest little woman always putting herself down in front of males. She can do the job well enough. It is what Joe expects from her, and she doesn't know how it could be otherwise if she is to be his partner on the land. But with her green eyes, blonde hair and full sweet mouth, there's not much chance of Jessica pulling off any such grand ambition. The young blokes won't have it – she can't be one of them even if she works as hard and is as good as they are. She's still a girl and therefore she must publicly cop their scorn and privately feed their fantasies.

Jessica, of course, doesn't see any of this. What she has in determination she lacks in vanity. If she thinks about it at all, she sees herself as plain-faced and ordinary-looking, and she supposes she must be ugly. She only coincidentally glances into a mirror, something she regards as almost the sole territory of her sister, who possesses the only mirror in the house. Jessica happily accepts that Meg's been given all the family looks and, in this regard at least, she feels no resentment. God just didn't make her pretty and, since she was twelve, Joe needed her to be outside with him, so that was that. But it doesn't stop her from often feeling hurt and confused and lonely.

What Jessica sees plainly enough is that men regard women as inferior, in a whole separate class from them, one that can't be compared with their own. It's as though some law exists in the minds of males which says she must know her place and accept her inferior lot. If she beats a man at any task which folk consider to be in his masculine domain, then she somehow brings shame upon herself and upon all womankind. She doesn't see the justice in this notion and simply refuses to play the supportive and secondary role demanded of her sex. She doesn't wish to cheer prettily from the sidelines when she can conduct herself as competently in the arena as most young blokes her age.

Jessica sees the way they look at her, the scorn in their eyes, as though she's got no right to be among them and is a disgrace to her own kind. Not only that, but when she competes with blokes she senses the shame *they* feel. She is never praised for the skill she shows against her opponent. Instead *he* is humiliated in front of his mates for having allowed himself to be matched or beaten by a girl. She has not won fair and square, and he has lost because he is inferior to a bloody sheila.

Jessica is aware that there's nothing she can do about it – she lives in a world of men. It may be unfair, but she knows there is no point in whingeing. Even if she did, she tells herself there is nobody to whom she could explain her resentment, and so it's stuff she keeps to herself. If she told Joe how she felt he'd only nod his head, not really listening, or give her one of his dog-eat-dog lectures. He'd tell her she was perfectly right, and not to go banging her head against a brick wall. He'd be likely to say, 'If yiz wants a good husband, girlie,

yiz'll have to learn to act stupid and buckle under.'
Hester and Meg would, of course, agree with this viewpoint – in their minds acting stupid is part of being
smart if you're a female.

'There's more ways than one to skin a cat,' Hester has
warned her often enough in the past. 'You can't shame
a man, Jessica, their pride won't take it. A woman must
be soft as putty on the outside and, on the inside, like
the Rock of Gibraltar.'

When Jack Thomas first got his new De Dion motor
car a few years ago, the first automobile in the district
and his pride and joy, Hester sent off to Sydney for a
pamphlet on the role of the motor car in the modern
society. When it arrived she and Meg conducted a series
of long, boring debates in the kitchen. Was it better to
know nothing about motor cars and let young Jack
carry on about them to Meg's admiring oohs and ahs, or
was it better to ask a lot of pertinent questions to make
him think Meg was the kind of girl he ought to marry
not only for her looks but also for her brains?

In the end they'd settled for the oohs and ahs, deciding that as Jack Thomas had a mother and two sisters
with an opinion on just about everything under the sun,
he wouldn't be too keen to have a bossy boots know-
all for a wife.

Jessica had thought this was pretty damn smart of
them for a change, but then she secretly learnt the pamphlet off by heart. She likes working with Jack up at
Riverview, and he seems to enjoy working beside her.
When he discusses his precious De Dion motor car he's

pleased that she knows what he's on about and has some ideas of her own.

Jessica values this mateship, and tells herself that she's just as good as any of the blokes. Her flannel shirt is as sweat-stained as any ringer's, her moleskins as dirty and worn, her boots as scuffed. She rides as hard and stays as long in the saddle as the men do, and knows her way around cattle and sheep as well as most. She works hard, doesn't whinge, brushes the same flies from her eyes, gets the same dust up her nostrils, eats the same damper and drinks the same billy tea. But still they look at her differently.

What Jessica hates in herself is the feeling, deep down, that they may be right. That she is different, and can never belong to their world. And that men don't try to do the things women do, don't even want to, and so she's being stupid trying to prove she's as good as them when she knows in her heart that in some things, being a woman means she can't ever be the same as them, or be respected for who she is.

For instance, there comes a time when men no longer try to solve their differences sensibly. They simply jump down from their horses or pile out of the pub and try to beat the living daylights out of each other. It's a part of their world she knows she can never enter. A very important part. Nor can she hope to compensate for her useless female fists with her mouth – men hate a sharp tongue when they reckon a blunt fist is the best way to sort out a problem. Then after, when they've beaten the shit out of each other, they shake hands in a sort of ceremony of forgiveness, both of them good mates again. It is this same, stupid male logic she sees in their eyes when they look at her, and Jessica is aware she's helpless against it. She is trapped between two worlds – neither sex will have her as she is, and both seem to want to punish her for being too much of the other. She knows she can't punch their teeth in like Joe or Jack Thomas would if someone should look at them in the way a stockman might sneer at her, or spit to the side of his boots as he turns and walks away.

Jessica admits to herself that Jack Thomas is the one male other than her father who takes her at face value. He doesn't look at her like others do, but treats her with some respect and more or less like an equal. He seems to enjoy competing with her openly. He's 'a real man', Jessica thinks to herself with surprise and then feels angry that if a man were to call her 'a real woman' this would be followed by a sly nod and a wink and knowing smiles all around the camp fire. Not, she's pleased to think, that she will ever qualify in their minds for that role.

Joe, of course, is oblivious to all of this. He's grown accustomed to having Jessica at his side and she knows it seldom occurs to him that she's a woman. She's simply a much needed extra pair of hands, though perhaps a little on the small side – a flyweight, he calls her. Jessica senses that Joe wishes she was a bit stronger so that she could help with the shearing or lift and carry an ironbark cornerpost. He's such a big bugger himself and, at seventy-two, still strong as a bull and thinks everyone else must be the same.

She knows she meets Joe's requirements in most things. In a rare moment, she'd once overheard him tell a shearer that his little girlie could flick a blowfly off the lead bullock's neck with a stockwhip, or post and string a fence quick as look at you. It wasn't exactly true, though she can use a stockwhip well enough and even drive a bullock wagon if she has to. Joe's bragging had made her feel good for about a year after. In fact, it is Joe's confidence in Jessica which forms the basis of her strong resolve. He's a bloody hard taskmaster and she reckons if she can satisfy him, then she ought to be good enough for any other boss around the district.

Joe himself has long since learned that his youngest daughter's pride forbids him to interfere any more than he might if she were his son. He knows Jessica wouldn't think to tell him to go to blazes, but she has a way of looking when she's mad that tells him to watch out. Her chin rests damn nearly on her chest, her green eyes are almost closed with anger, her jaw is clenched and her pretty mouth drained of its colour. It's a look that makes him back off without a single harsh word spoken between them. Joe knows that he can't run the place without her. Jessica is his girlie, right down to the fair colouring and Bergman temper, while Meg, dark and delicate, rightly belongs to her mother and the Heathwood side.

Joe used to worry for Jessica when she was small, knowing she'd copped his stubborn nature and rough ways. But as she grew into a useful and happy child he reckoned that what couldn't be changed in himself, he couldn't expect to change in her. It was best to let her get on with it and keep a close eye on her.

As she's grown into a young woman, Joe's come to accept Jessica as his right-hand man. She's more intelligent than he is, more intelligent than the lot of them, Meg included. She might have left school at twelve but she still reads books whenever she can get her hands on one. Reads them good and fast, too. But, Joe knows, hers isn't the sort of intelligence that wins marks as a young woman. His girlie is much too outspoken and her wilfulness and determination will get her into no end of trouble with men as she grows older. He admires her spirit, though. He knows for sure that there is not an ounce of bad blood in her. With her chopped hair and body flat as a plank she may not be a beauty like her sister, but he wouldn't swap her for a son for all the bloody tea in China, or the coffee in Brazil.

If Joe ever thought about love, then he supposes he loves Jessica. Whatever it is he feels for his youngest daughter he has no such emotion for Meg. He admires Hester for creating in her a young woman such as he could never have aspired to know in his own humble youth. Meg is a definite step up and away from the life of respectable poverty they know with him, while Jessica, despite her cleverness, is more of the same common stock to which Joe knows himself to belong.

Hester is a Heathwood, and they're a family of shop-keepers, indoors people with scrubbed white hands and clean nails. Joe has always accepted that his wife is well bred, from people above his own station in life. Hester has never really taken to the battler's life on the land and he knows well enough that he's not the sort of bloke she would have fancied before her dashing young subaltern went off with the New South Wales Lancers to fight for Mother England in the Anglo-Egyptian Sudan and got himself killed.

Joe wasn't to know that all subalterns are dashing once they are dead. That Auntie Agnes thought Hester's intended was a thorough bounder and up to no good, just the sort of person the Heathwoods should avoid at all costs. Privately she felt his untimely demise had probably saved the family.

Joe had waited until he had something he could call his own before he went looking for a wife. At thirty-five he'd given up his life as a boundary rider and taken up a government allotment along the Murrumbidgee. It had taken him nearly fifteen years to clear the scrub and stock it, build a home and, in a good year, profitably run a smallholding. His land had been hard-won through two droughts, two locust plagues, a mouse plague, a flood and a bushfire, which destroyed his home and the outbuildings and burned his stock alive. Joe Bergman was fifty years old when at last he felt he had enough behind him to take a bride.

After her soldier had died, Hester had got herself stuck behind the counter of her father Henry's haberdashery shop in Narrandera. At thirty-five years old, when she met Joe, she was well past the marriageable age, with slim prospects of finding a man with a decent spread.

All the same, Joe didn't need to be told he was no

great catch. When he'd asked her to be his bride, she'd refused at first, then finally accepted, but only after a great deal of persistence on his part and some unexpected involvement by her Auntie Agnes.

Hester's father, a widower, had been reluctant to let her go and insisted she was needed in the shop and at home to cook and clean. But his sister Agnes, who lived in Whitton, folk said to be away from her brother, and was herself a widow and the mother of two sons who'd both turned out like their father, wastrels and drunkards, had come to Joe's rescue.

Agnes had insisted that her niece still had a few good years left in which to have a family. 'A woman,' she'd said, 'can breed until she's in her mid-forties, there's time for half a dozen if you're quick at it!' She'd pointed out that Joe, even though a foreigner and of a lower class, was a big, strapping man with fair hair and blue eyes, just the sort of new blood the Heathwoods needed. He was known never to touch a drop, and though a bachelor for so long, could never be accused of having hot britches for the women. 'Hester, my dear, Joe Bergman is a good man, rough but decent.' She'd wagged a bony finger at her niece. 'A hard-working and sober husband of humble origins is better than a drunken lord in a grand palace,' she'd proclaimed. When Hester had tried to use her father's welfare as an excuse, Auntie Agnes had countered, saying, 'I'll send your father down to Sydney, to the Easter Show, to find himself a grateful widow who can clean house and work in the shop. They're two a penny in the big smoke.'

When Hester finally accepted Joe's hand in marriage, he was aware she did so without much enthusiasm. For his part, Joe has never complained about her lack of affection. She's been a dutiful wife beyond his expectations, she cooks well and runs a neat home. She is a good little woman in lots of ways. If he has a wound she dresses and binds it for him, and if, as sometimes happens, he gets a bad chest, she prepares a mustard poultice or doses him with a tablespoon of sugar soaked in eucalyptus oil. Though these days it's Jessica who cares for him. Hester washes and mends his clothes and she keeps herself neat and, with it all, gives him a sense of being the head of the family. And she doesn't complain any more than can be expected from someone who has been forced to come down a notch or two in life.

It seems only fair to Joe that Hester should devote most of her time and love to Meg, that she should want a life for her eldest daughter which she must once have imagined for herself. He knows he isn't much chop but he's done the best he can and there's always been food on the table, Hester makes their clothes from good material and they have boots on their feet. It may not be much but it's a damn sight better than most. Hester occasionally even has a little extra to spend on pretty ribbons and a bit of lace for Meg.

Joe sometimes wonders if things would have been different if they'd had a big family like other folk. But they'd started out too late for that. The doctor said it was probably him getting the mumps when he was fifty-five that put a stop to her pregnancies. He would have liked a boy, but there you go, can't have everything. Now he wouldn't change Jessica for a football team of lads built like bullocks. So Hester can enjoy Meg.

Hester constantly refers to Meg's hair as her crowning glory and at night delights in releasing the thick plaits Meg wears coiled about her head, letting them fall to her waist. She takes care to brush it a hundred strokes with an expensive English hairbrush ordered up from Anthony Hordern's in Sydney. Joe hears the two of them still chatting away like a couple of budgerigars long after Jessica has taken to her narrow iron cot and him to the bed out the back. Hester has made it very clear to Joe that she has no further interest in marital relations, as she calls it.

Hester firmly believes that the coming together of a married couple has the singular purpose of bringing forth issue. Having done what was required of her and given her husband two daughters, she doesn't see that she has any further duties to perform in the marital bed, and Joe's shooting blanks has been a stroke of luck for her.

For his part, Joe has spent too many years alone in his life not to know how to seek his own relief and so he lets her be, though he knows other blokes in the same circumstances would think they'd been shafted. Most of the men in the district would climb into the saddle regardless. It would never occur to them to ask permission, or that a wife has a say in the first place. For most it was a man's flamin' right, that's all there was to it. 'A skinful on a Saturdee night, mount the missus and there she goes! Conjugal rights, mate! It's written in the Bible when yiz gets hitched.' Joe has heard it often enough in the shearing sheds and elsewhere. But he leaves Hester alone as part of the price he feels he has to pay for not being her equal. In his seventies, his urges have become a lot easier than perhaps they used to be.

Joe sometimes wakes up to go for a piss in the yard only to find his wife and eldest daughter in the kitchen still chewing the fat as late as ten o'clock at night. It amazes him that after being together from morning till dusk they still find something to talk about. He and Jessica are often together for hours without a word passing between them. Yet Joe knows that Jessie can talk the hind leg off a donkey if she's in the mood or is excited by something new she's seen or learned. He remembers how as a child she never stopped asking questions, wanting to know everything, couldn't be put off. Why, why, why? Until he was nearly out of his mind. So very different the two girls, chalk and cheese.

When the two of them are together, strangers hardly ever know that they're sisters. Although if they were to stop and examine them closely, they would see both have a fullness around the mouth and an identical shape to their lips. This sweetly shaped mouth makes Meg seem a bit exotic, as if she might be foreign, an Italian contessa or a Spanish dancer or something splendid like that.

Jessica is aware that she and Meg share the same-shaped mouth. And while Jessica agrees it looks very pretty on Meg, she is not at all sure that it isn't the shape of her own mouth that creates most of her problems. She secretly bemoans the fact that it cannot be used like a proper mouth, like a mouth that doesn't say things to men before it's opened. No matter what she does with it, it always ends up looking like Meg's mouth. That is to say, it ends up looking pretty and feminine and promising something unspoken when no such promise exists in Jessica's mind.

Meg's mouth goes with her lovely figure. Meg has all the right curves to suit the fashion of the day and they can easily enough be imagined under her tight-waisted dress. Her lips, which she has the habit of keeping just a fraction apart so that she looks slightly breathless, are calculated, along with everything else about her, to drive a young bloke round the twist. On the other hand, Jessica feels her own mouth is just stupid and looks out of place with the rest of her body, which is flat as a pancake all the way down the front.

Hester has long since given up trying to influence Jessica's appearance. Despite the dress she is required to wear to church of a Sunday, which Hester has sewn and embroidered around the collar as prettily as may be, Jessica remains as plain-looking as mustard pickles in a jar.

Hester no longer feels guilty about Jessica and has convinced herself that it's only natural that her duty is to concentrate on Meg, who has all the looks she needs to get the kind of husband she herself missed out on. But she's well aware that any mother who has an eligible boy with a decent inheritance coming to him goes to market knowing prettiness alone is not enough to qualify for her son's hand in matrimony.

Hester knows well enough that there's nothing quite like childbirth to take the bloom off a woman's good looks. Meg must also be seen to look as though she will turn matronly in an appropriate manner after having given birth to the mandatory six or more children, hopefully including a brace of sons thrown in for good measure.

Finally, and almost as important as her capacity to bear healthy children in large numbers, her eldest daughter has all the domestic qualifications needed for a good home-maker. Meg is an excellent cook and her preserves and needlework are always among the best at the Narrandera Agricultural Show and she has twice won a blue ribbon there for the best starched and pressed tablecloth.

All in all, Hester quietly congratulates herself that all of this adds up to a set of marriage qualifications which any future mother-in-law would be anxious to secure for her son.

Using the same rules, she has come to accept that it would be difficult for any potential mother-in-law to imagine how Jessica's narrow-hipped, lean little body could possibly endure a pregnancy without complica-tions. Or that the young lads who might gladly call on Meg would be likely to entertain the idea of walking out with the family leftover. In her mind Hester has consigned Jessica to a spinsterhood she herself has only managed to avoid by the skin of her teeth.

It is one sentiment Joe is forced to share with his

wife. He once sadly remarked, 'Meg is prime stock for the marriage market, but Jessie is gunna be left alone in the saleyards long after every young bloke's climbed back on his horse and gone home.'

It is hardly surprising that Jessica's family haven't noticed that, though still flat in front at eighteen years old, Jessica has a neatly rounded little backside which fits snugly into a pair of moleskins and sits well enough in the saddle for many a young stockman to happily let her take the lead when riding single file.

Nor are they aware that Jack Thomas will most often choose to be Jessica's partner on a cattle drive or when they're branding the ewes from the wethers, castrating or crutching sheep. This fact entirely escapes Joe's notice – like his wife, he's so resigned to the notion that Meg must win young Jack that he could not even conceive of Jessica having a place, no matter how platonic, in the young man's affections. Hester and Meg are none the wiser, as both are unaware of the Thomas boy's peripheral presence in Jessica's life.

Jessica lacks the personal vanity to suppose for one moment that Jack might think of her as anything but a good working partner or even a mate when they attend lectures at the government experimental farm. Her self-esteem requires no more bolstering than this from her future brother-in-law. She continues to enjoy working with Jack, being his firm friend. They both seem to anticipate each other's movements on a horse and together they can drive a large herd through the scrub better than most.

Jessica now hears the currawongs in the river gums – they're always the first to greet the sunrise – and she goes out to the woodpile and gathers an armful of firewood. She returns to the kitchen, builds a fire in the cast-iron stove and sets the kettle to boil. While she waits she chops a turnip, a parsnip, two carrots and several potatoes into the soup pot and adds what's left of last night's lamb bone. Then she empties half a jug of water into it and adds a handful of gelatine crystals to compensate for giving the dogs a generous splash of soup over their feed of bones last night.

Joe would be annoyed that she'd added the gravy to their tucker, but he'll never know, she smiles to herself.

Hester, or perhaps Meg, has set four bread pans of dough to rise overnight on the scrubbed pine kitchen table, covering them with cheesecloth. Jessica removes the cloth and sprinkles a little milk over the top of the risen dough, spreading it evenly over the top of the loaves with the tips of her fingers so the crusts will brown in the baking. Then she returns to the stove and adjusts the flue to heat the oven. In about half an hour it will be hot enough to bake and by the time she gets back from milking the cow the bread will be ready to be taken out of the oven and cooled on the window ledge.

Hester knows that Jessica would rather eat the last of the loaves when it is three days old than go to the trouble of mixing and kneading a batch of dough and baking fresh bread herself. Despite her coldness to her youngest daughter, Hester is a dutiful mother. There's the stockpot bubbling away on the back of the stove, a side of bacon in the cool house and another leg of lamb cooked and ready to eat cold, tea, bread, eggs, milk and yesterday's churned butter – Jessica will want for nothing while they're away.

Jessica stops to listen as the dogs bark again. The same bark as before, though this time a little more urgent. Kelpies are working dogs and don't usually bark at nothing. Jessica's ear is now tuned to the sound as the barking draws closer. Just when she's about to go outside and whistle them in, their barking stops once more. Nevertheless she goes to the cupboard and fetches the shotgun, breaks it and loads both barrels but does not pull the hammers back. She leans the twelve-bore against the wall near the door to the yard. The kettle comes to the boil and Jessica prepares a pot of tea. She likes it strong and black with lots of sugar, the way it's made in a billy on an open fire.

Today is Sunday, though she's buggered if she's going to drive the five miles to church. Joe hardly ever goes to church, though he observes a day of rest more as a matter of habit than piety. He'll usually spend the day stitching and mending harnesses or some such task. Jessica's in charge now and she'll act the same way he does on the Sabbath. For a start, she'll keep well clear of St Stephen's with the ever-present Thomas women ticking off the names of the worshippers.

If Hester asks, she'll say one of the wheels on the sulky is giving a bit of trouble so she decided not to chance it. It's only half a fib, the rear axle does need minor attention. Hester will not allow her to go to church on horseback as she thinks it unladylike and reflects badly on the family.

All of which adds up to a pretty lazy day ahead. She'll milk the jersey cow and leave it in the paddock with its calf. Let the little fellow get his fill for once – she's not going to need the milk or the cream. She'll feed the chooks, give the two horses half a bale of hay and fill their water trough. Then it'll be time to feed the pigs with the cabbages gone to seed in the vegie-plot. She'll take a look at the sheep and then ride down to see if the cows in the paddock nearest the river have got their hopes up yet.

Joe's paid George Thomas for one week's use of his Shorthorn stud bull, Trump Card, which Jack rode over with on Wednesday. But so far the great slack bovine bastard hasn't bothered to climb up the back of a single cow. Joe won't want to pay Mr Thomas if the bull doesn't service half a dozen cows and then there'll be a blue which will leave Hester and Meg at Joe's throat.

George Thomas's temper hasn't improved any since that first time when Joe took Jessica over to Riverview Station. Outside the shearing shed he has a rotten habit of picking on his son and so Jack tries to work separately from his father whenever possible, often calling on Jessica to partner him on musters and other work.

Over the past four years Jessica has taken Joe's advice and stayed well clear of George Thomas. Joe can be a difficult sod, but he's got nothing on old man Thomas, a bloody know-all who thinks every ringer, stockman, shearer and rouseabout is a born malingerer and out to cheat him. By the end of a day's work his face is always crimson as a turkey's wattle and he's fit to burst with anger. As often as not, it's his own boy who has to cop his bad temper. Jessica's watched dozens of times as Jack stands there and takes it while George Thomas abuses him. She sees how the knuckles of Jack's clenched fists whiten as he holds his arms rigidly to his sides while his father humiliates him in front of the stockmen. George Thomas always needs an audience.

Afterwards Jack will move into the bush to be on his own for a bit, away from the scene of his shaming. Jessica will let him go for a while and then follow him, pretending to be gathering wood for the fire, and whistling a bit of a tune so he'll hear her before she comes upon him. Bush rules say she should leave him be, mind her own business, it's every man for himself. But when she comes up to him he never tells her to bugger off and he'll let her sit quietly, chewing on the end of a stalk of kangaroo grass, a few paces away from where he sits.

Jack's no mother's boy who blubs easily, Jessica knows that. If one of the stockmen shows him disrespect he'll climb down from his horse and have a go. Scrap with him right there, where they'll bump against the flanks of their horses and sometimes wrestle in the dust, horses whinnying and shying, clouds of dirt flying everywhere.

The stockmen always come running, not caring who wins, only hoping to see a good stoush. Jack's no pushover and knows how to scrap, but if his opponent gets the better of him, which sometimes happens, Jack'll take his punishment and shake the other bloke's hand afterwards. The men respect him as much as they hate his old man.

The men remember too how it was Jack who took care of Billy Simple after his accident at the shearing shed and they like him for it. Most would have walked away, taking no responsibility. They see the way Jack looks out for Billy, sometimes bringing him down to the shed for some company as he works, talking to him and making sure he eats his tucker.

It's been three years since Billy's accident and the men working at Riverview Station have grown used to seeing him with a watering can or digging in the homestead garden. Those who remember him of old will shout him a greeting and Billy will wave back shyly, though he gets nervous if anyone comes too close. He's grown even taller and now stands at six feet and six inches, a shambling giant of a boy with his scarred face hidden under the brim of his hat and no teeth in his mouth except for the big molars at the back.

Jessica sips her tea and thinks of poor Billy Simple. Since the accident he's somehow got his religion mixed up with his penis, which is a source of amusement for those who didn't know him before. Billy isn't a complete idiot and he can understand simple directions well enough. He'll stand with his head bowed and his hands clasped below his waist, shaking in terror when he's being addressed, especially when it's Ada Thomas. Then he'll look up calmly, no longer shaking, his watery blue eyes focused on whoever's in front of him. He'll cross himself and say, 'Hail Mary, Mother of God!' And give a toothless smile and politely inquire, 'Would you like to see the big cock Jesus gave me?' Then he'll start his shaking again, head bowed, eyes tightly closed, lips mumbling senselessly, his great raw hands with their bitten and broken fingernails clasped together and resting on his chest.

Billy will stay like this until he hears the word 'Amen', which he takes as permission to leave. With his shoulders hunched he'll shamble off, his broken boots shuffling in the dust.

When Jessica works on Riverview Station she always stops over to see Billy in the garden. She'll get boiling water from the cook and make up a billy of tea and take it to him together with a bit of damper soaked in golden syrup that she's brought from home for him.

Billy, seeing her coming, will drop whatever he's doing and jump up and down and laugh like a little boy. Jessica will walk up to him and put the billy and the damper down at her feet. Then the two of them will stand quite still, Billy towering above her. After a few moments he'll reach out shyly and touch Jessica on the cheek with the back of his fingers and then reach down and take her small hand in both his huge fists and hold it for a while.

' 'Owyergoin', Billy, orright?' Jessica will say after a while.

Then he'll release her hand and clasp his own in prayer, and break into his big, gaping smile and say, 'Hail Mary, Mother of God, would you like to see the big cock Jesus gave me?'

The first time he did this, Jessica had blushed and protested, but she soon enough realised that Billy's saying it is an empty threat. Now when he says it she looks stern and says 'Amen' and then, 'Bend down, Billy.'

Billy will come down on his knees and Jessica, first making sure no one is looking, will take a wet cloth and clean his face, wiping the mucus from his nose as any mother might do to a small boy. Then she'll kiss him lightly on the cheek. Billy will rise to his feet and tear off around the vegetable patch and then come panting back to her side like an excited puppy. Whereupon she'll give him the tea and damper, which he'll break off into little bits and push furiously into his mouth, swallowing tea with the bread to soften it so he doesn't have to chew.

Jessica recalls how on one occasion, when she and Jack were earmarking some sheep, they were talking about Billy Simple. On a curious impulse she suddenly asked Jack, 'When Billy talks about his gift from Jesus, has he ever, you know, shown it to you?'

Jack at first didn't understand. 'Shown what to me?'

'You know, what he says Jesus gave him?' Jessica was trying not to giggle.

'Nah.'

'Have you seen it?'

'Yeah, I suppose,' Jack replied, shrugging his shoulders.

'Suppose?'

'Well, I seen him taking a piss lots of times in the old days.'

'Were it, you know,' Jessica paused, 'like he says?'

Jack, she remembers, looked up at her and grinned.

'Yeah, I reckon. A bloody monster!' he'd said, laughing. 'In the shearing quarters when he'd take a piss someone would always say, "Hey, Billy, you should take that thing to Mike Malloy to lock up in the flamin' gun locker!"'

They'd fallen about laughing, as much at Jessica's boldness as at Billy's superior equipment.

Then Jack had suddenly grown serious, and told her how Billy had become the object of horrible taunting by Gwen and Winifred, who took delight in Billy's confusion and terror in their presence.

According to Jack they're getting worse and Ada Thomas, it seems, is no better. Billy works hard in the garden and is as strong as a bull, but 'the papist idiot', as Jack's mother calls him, can do nothing right. 'You can see the map of Ireland all over his face,' she'll say to anyone who'll listen. Jack says she constantly tells Billy off, even beating him over his shoulders with her English blackthorn walking stick. He's often made to repeat a task for no good reason other than to please her.

Once, Jack told Jessica, Ada had spent a day making Billy move a large pile of rocks intended for a bed of succulents, changing her mind each time he'd completed the task and making him move them to a different location again. Jack had come home at sunset to find Billy collapsed over a pile of rocks, the skin stripped from his hands, the flesh of his palms reduced to a bloody pulp, and him shuddering and whimpering in a heap.

Billy had become totally bewildered for weeks after this. Jack would come home at night and find him on his knees mumbling incoherently, stuttering and fumbling at his rosary beads in the tiny garden shed – the home he shared with the garden tools, though scarcely large enough to contain his huge frame.

Since then the very sound of his mistress's shrill voice causes poor Billy to go into a blind panic. Holding his hands over his ears he'll squat on his haunches wherever he happens to be working and rock his body back and forth until she ceases her haranguing.

Billy can manage words well enough if you give him time to get them out. All it takes is a little bit of patience and calmness. Billy responds to calmness and to folks who are gentle with him.

'There's no need to hound him, he works hard and keeps to himself. He loves the garden and has taken naturally to planting things,' Jack has said to Jessica.

'But why, if he's doing a good job in the garden, does your mother give him a hard time?' Jessica asked.

'I reckon she's never forgiven Billy for running away when she ordered him to fire the shotgun at the Aborigines,' Jack replied. 'I bet she thought that him firing at the blacks was a good way to kill two birds with one stone. She could have had Billy arrested for attempted manslaughter and put into the loony-bin on account of it and, at the same time, she'd be rid of the poor starving blacks. I wouldn't put it past her.'

'Poor Billy, can't we do something?'

Jack shook his head. 'Whenever she can, Mother blames Billy for involving her in a court case and for the fine she had to pay. She moans about him causing her to get a criminal record and says that's why she wasn't elected to the district council.'

'But she didn't get enough votes!'

'I know, but of course she doesn't see it that way. She claims the other councillors spread it around that, with her criminal record, she wasn't eligible and to save her the embarrassment, folk shouldn't vote for her.' Jack gave a bitter laugh. 'It's all Billy's fault, you see.'

Jack's tried many times to intervene on Billy's behalf, warning his sisters to stay away from him and begging his mother to leave him alone. But Jack is seldom at the homestead during the day, when all the teasing takes place. He tries to keep an eye on Billy, even thinking once to take him out on the land with him, but Billy became terrified around the horses.

At Riverview, Billy has also suffered the wrath of George Thomas, which drove him into a fresh state of terror where for two days he lay too stupefied to get to his feet, shaking and whimpering, his hand in his mouth.

Jack told Jessica how he found Billy and tried to get him to drink some water, afraid he might die of heat apoplexy. Eventually he had to kneel beside the pile of potato sacks on which Billy lay in his tiny shed, with his hat pulled down as far as it would go over his face, and haul him into a sitting position so he could get him to swallow a mug of water. Jack said how the fear in Billy had caused him to tremble so much that half the water spilled down his front.

Jack spread his hands and shrugged. 'What can I do,

Jessie? He's better off in the garden – at least he's safe from being harmed.'

On her visits to see Billy, Jessica keeps well clear of Ada Thomas and the two girls, afraid of what they might say to Hester and Meg.

Jack respects Jessica for spending time with Billy and Jessica was surprised the first time he'd said so. 'Jessie, he likes you. You and me are all he has. It's sometimes nice to know there's someone who has the time to sit with someone else,' he'd remarked.

Jessica knows he doesn't only mean Billy Simple. She will sit quietly next to Jack when he's gone bush after his old man has roused on him. Then, after a bit, she'll try and cheer him up. Like she'll say, 'Don't let the old man getcha, Jack. One day he'll be that agitated his nose'll blast right off his fat face and he'll have his great hairy arm down yer throat tryin' to fetch it back.' She'll try to make Jack laugh. 'Then, when he can't reach it, he'll have you shitting in the porcelain potty next day looking for his flamin' hooter!'

Jack will sit there, looking down between his parted knees, a twig in his hand, drawing squiggles in the dirt at his feet and she'll see him trying not to smile.

'There it'll be, your old man's nose with the wart on the end, sticking out the top of the rest of what's in the potty, trying its hardest not to sneeze!'

Her teasing will usually get him back to his old laughing self again. Funny that, she wouldn't do the same for any other bloke except perhaps for Joe. Though she couldn't imagine ever teasing her father.

Jessica knows that Joe's relationship with George Thomas hasn't improved at all. George Thomas likes to humiliate a man and make him sing for his supper. She's seen it herself often enough in the four years she's worked on and off at Riverview Station.

'That's the problem with being a poor feller,' Joe once confided to her. 'You can never sort things out man-to-man with a rich bastard like George Thomas. Not the way it ought to be possible between two blokes. Even if he has it coming to him, and you've got every bloody right and a charter from the flamin' King of England. You can't have a go at him, can't square with him, or punch him, can't expect justice when he's done the wrong thing by you, because, as sure as God made little green apples, you're gunna have to go cap in hand to him one of these flamin' days.' He'd paused and watched a couple of bush doves fly overhead, their wings fluting the air. 'Being poor is like the drought: when the rains come and the paddocks are up to a sheep's belly in green grass, remember that the mud is only wet dust waiting to dry out.' That was Joe, ever the gloomy one.

Sooner or later George Thomas has a go at everyone who works for him at Riverview. Although he didn't fire her after Billy's accident. Jessica had been too upset at the time to care whether he did or not, but after a week Mike Malloy had told Joe to fetch her back to the shearing shed. Since then she's stayed out of the owner's way, though she expects that one of these days her turn will come.

She likes to imagine she'll give him some of his own

back, stand toe-to-toe and trade abuse. Show him a real woman doesn't have to take that from any man! Tell him to his face that he may be able to get away with it when it's his son, because the lowest thing a boy can do is hit his father, but she won't put up with his abuse when she's done nothing wrong. She'll go on to say he can yell at the poor stockmen or shearers all he likes – they have to take it on the chin, because they need the money to feed their scrawny kids. But she won't put up with him, he can go to Hell.

Yet she knows, if push came to shove, she probably doesn't have the courage to trade insults with Jack's father. George Thomas is an ex-riverboat captain (Jack says it must have been a slave ship) and he has more blow-hard than a sperm whale and most of it ugly enough to fry the hair off your head.

Folk say he made his fortune carrying stuff up the river when the water was low and the other boats couldn't navigate the shallows. He'd sunk and capsized his boat dozens of times until, shortly after the railway was put through, he'd sunk it one final time, claiming he'd struck a fallen tree and split the bow in two. The boat had conveniently gone down in one of the deep holes in the river so his claim could never be substantiated. He'd collected the insurance from North British & Mercantile, bought himself a fancy horse and rig and walked out a while with Ada Murphy, the only daughter of Jack Murphy of Bindaloo Station. He'd married her for her money and Riverview Station, the property she'd inherited from her grandfather.

Jessica sighs to herself. Now she thinks about it, there isn't much she can do if George Thomas has a go at her. Joe doesn't pay her wages, she eats at his table and shares the good seasons with the bad, the plenty with the nothing. It doesn't occur to either of them there may be any other way. So working on the Thomas property is the main source of Jessica's income. Apart from mustering cattle, the shearing shed goes eight weeks and while most of what she earns there goes to Joe he gives her threepence in the florin, which makes up the bulk of her income. That and a bit of work she can sometimes get from one of the smaller stations that may be shorthanded.

Jessica depends on the few shillings she earns to pay for her moleskins, flannel shirts and boots, all of which, with the exception of her hat, Hester refuses on principle to supply now that she's a grown woman.

'You want to look like a man, *you* pay for it!' her mother insists.

Hester reluctantly accepts, however, that a bonnet isn't practical for the sort of work her youngest daughter does around the farm. She also makes her pinafores, which Jessica wants plain without any flounces, like a carpenter's apron. Meg, thinking she's being funny, always embroiders a pink half-opened rosebud with stem and leaves on the pocket of the apron, no doubt hoping her sister will object. But Jessica wouldn't give her the satisfaction – in fact, she rather likes the little decoration.

With the money she earns from working at Riverview, Jessica is also saving up for a new saddle, which she reckons is going to take her as long as it will take the rosebud on her apron to grow into a rose bush.

While Joe needs the money she earns, Jessica secretly welcomes the opportunity to work at Riverview Station. Often lonely for company of her own age, she looks forward to Jack Thomas being on the horse beside her on a muster. They'll grin at each other every time they ride up close to turn a beast in the right direction, shouting instructions through a haze of grey dust. Then they'll gallop off furiously, hooves kicking up clods of earth behind them, laughing and skylarking all the day long.

The fear of George Thomas turning on her may never be far from her mind, but Jessica reckons it's worth it to work with Jack and do what she loves best. And deep down, she feels pretty sure that if George Thomas really lost his rag with her for no good reason, her father would have a piece of him, no matter how poor they happened to be at the time. Maybe Mr Thomas knows that Joe Bergman has a reputation for being a hard man.

Joe had once shot a man and got off scot-free when the judge in Sydney said it was self-defence. Jessica didn't know the exact details, he'd never told her about it himself, but she thought it had something to do with his settlement. This was Crown land, which had been appropriated by the Great Peter's Run, a vast station belonging to John Peter, and which was said to stretch all the way to the Victorian border.

Joe's government settlement interrupted John Peter's run and so his foreman had taken to knocking down

Joe's fences as soon as they were erected. Joe had re-erected the fences twenty times or more before he'd finally had enough. One bitter winter's morning he'd gone to see John Peter's foreman, a notorious bully named Dutch Miller. As Joe approached the foreman's camp on horseback he'd been challenged and then threatened. The foreman had drawn a gun and claimed he'd kill Joe unless he moved off what he claimed was rightfully John Peter's land. Joe had refused, waving the land certificate which entitled him to two lots of 640 acres in the parish of Ourendumbee.

'I don't give a damn what the paper says, Joe Bergman, that land belongs to John Peter by right of use and we're taking it back,' Dutch Miller shouted. Then he'd fired at Joe, the bullet from his revolver chipping the bottom of Joe's collarbone and travelling to the side of his chest, coming out directly under his left arm. Then Joe finally lost his patience and he calmly raised his Winchester and shot the man, his aim not nearly as careless as the foreman's, the bullet making a neat hole in the centre of his forehead. Or so the story went, anyway. The wound Joe had received left a lovely scar for the judge in Sydney to see, and a hole in Joe's best and only overcoat front and back.

The oven is now ready and Jessica places the four bread tins in it and unhooks the milk pail, ready to milk the cow. She fills a billy with what was left of the water in the kettle to wash the cow's udder and teats and then, carrying the milk pail in one hand and the billy in the other, she steps out into the yard.

She's only gone a few yards from the homestead when the dogs start up again. Jessica stops in her tracks. She is certain now that they are onto something, that the kelpies have disturbed some sort of intruder, a dingo or a fox maybe, probably have it bailed up. She returns to the kitchen, puts the milk pail and the billy on the table and picks up the shotgun. Then, carrying both cans in her right hand to save her sore shoulder, she slings the shotgun over her left shoulder. Jessica leaves again through the kitchen door, heading for the small paddock where they keep the jersey cow and her calf.

When she draws close enough she whistles for the dogs. They stop barking for a moment and then continue. The kelpies are trained to the whistle and when she doesn't see them coming Jessica places the pail and the billy at her feet and works the hammers back on the shotgun. Then she retrieves the cans and walks towards the barking dogs, carrying the shotgun in her right hand so if she needs to move fast she can drop the cans and quickly bring the gun up to her shoulder. She realises that she's forgotten to fit the shoulder pad and hopes it's all a false alarm.

Then she sees the dogs near the cow paddock, standing around the base of a pepper tree, barking up into the branches. Can't be a snake, she thinks. Dogs use a peculiar bark when they're around a snake, a small whine and then a sharp bark and then a whine again and a growl – but the kelpies aren't barking like that now. Jessica whistles to them again and this time they leave the tree and turn, Red leading them, reluctantly padding towards her but turning around every few steps to bark back up at the tree. Jessica puts the pail and the billy down and starts to move forward slowly. Sensing her caution, the dogs turn and rush back to the tree, jumping, their paws scrabbling against its trunk.

Jessica whistles again and the dogs stop barking and immediately go down on all fours, whining and growling their excitement. Then she sees a boot and part of a man's leg hanging from a branch. She's almost reached the tree but stands in open ground – if whoever is up the tree has a rifle she is dead meat. But then, if he is armed, she tries to reason in her growing panic, he could long since have shot the dogs and made his escape.

'Come down!' she calls, 'or I'll bloody fire!'

'Dogs!' she hears a man's terrified voice call from the pepper tree. 'Dogs! Dogs!'

Jessica moves closer with the shotgun now held against her shoulder and pointed up into the pepper tree. 'Get down, they won't hurt you. Get down, or I'll fire!' she commands, her voice sounding braver than she feels.

Then the voice in the tree begins to howl like a small child.

'Billy?' Jessica calls out in surprise. 'Is that you?'

The voice howls even louder and the dogs grow overexcited and start barking again. Jessica whistles them to silence. By this time she stands among them, looking up into the tree where Billy Simple sits howling fit to burst.

Coming out of the bright early morning sunlight into the dark shade under the tree, Jessica can only just make out Billy's huge shape clinging for dear life to a branch with both hands, his cheek against another branch as he wails. It is only after her eyes have adjusted that she sees he is covered in dried blood – it's all over his face and hands and the front of his flannel shirt and all the way down his moleskins.

'Billy, what happened?' Jessica screams. 'Are you hurt? Who hurt you, Billy? Tell me who hurt you!'

Billy stops howling. 'Hail Mary, Mother of God . . .' he begins.

'Billy, Amen, stop that! Tell me what happened!'

Billy tries to smile at her through his tears, a pitiful attempt, his mouth working for words. 'Jessie my friend, eh?'

'Yes Billy, I'm your friend. Now you come down and I'll give you some tea and tucker.'

'No, no, shoot! You shoot Billy, Jessie. Billy bad boy!'

'Billy, stop that nonsense. I can't come up and fetch you, so you come down at once, you hear me, Billy!'

To Jessica's relief Billy Simple starts to untangle himself from the branches of the tree and after a few moments he lets himself drop to the ground, falling to his knees and then rolling in the dust towards her.

The dogs go for him, thinking he is about to attack Jessica. Billy screams and covers his face with his arms and pulls his knees up into his chest to protect himself from the kelpies.

'Stay!' Jessica commands the dogs and lets out a piercing whistle. The dogs draw back. 'Down!' The kelpies lie panting, their pink tongues lolling wetly.

Billy slowly uncurls himself and gets to his feet. It is then that Jessica sees the full extent of the blood on him. It seems to be everywhere, as if he's somehow fallen into a slaughter trough at the abattoir in Hay. His face, neck and arms, as well as his clothing, are dark and stiff with dried blood, yet she can see no cuts or the wetness of a seeping wound anywhere on his body.

'Jesus, Billy, what have you done to yourself?' Jessica asks again.

Billy is now standing in front of Jessica with his head bowed, hands clasped below his waist, shaking like a leaf.

'Billy, it's me, Jessica. Don't be afraid, mate. I won't hurt you. Jessica likes you, Billy, I'm your friend. Remember?'

Billy looks up and then shakes his huge, ugly head several times.

'No more! Jessie don't like Billy no more.' He lowers his head to his chest again and begins to blub, snot bubbles blowing from his flattened nose.

'Billy, that's not true. I'm your friend. Jack and me, we're your best mates. Tell me, Billy, what happened?'

He stops bawling as suddenly as he'd started and looks up, grinning at Jessica. 'Hail Mary –'

'No, Billy, you can say that later. Now tell me why you're covered in blood. Have you killed a beast?' It's now clear to Jessica that, despite the blood, Billy doesn't seem to be hurt.

'No! No!' Billy shakes his head vigorously. 'I kilt 'em, Jessie.' He covers his ears with his hands as though blocking out some sound only he can hear. He rocks, moving his body back and forth. 'No more, no more,' he howls.

Jessica reaches out and grabs his damp bloody sleeve. 'Killed what, Billy? What did you kill?'

Billy stops rocking. 'Three!' he shouts. Then again, 'Three!' Suddenly he gives an excited little hop, like a child impatient to reveal a secret, then, grinning, holds three fingers proudly up to his face.

'Three? You killed three? Three what?' Jessica suddenly feels cold. 'Three *people*?'

Billy nods, still grinning.

'Who, Billy?' Jessica's mouth has gone dry, her tongue sticks to its roof. She swallows hard and tries to wet her mouth, running her tongue round her lips. Her heart is beating furiously as she tries to fight down the horror she feels because she knows who Billy's murdered.

Billy looks slyly down at Jessica, slowly closing his three raised fingers back into his fist. Then, as though he is performing some sort of conjuring trick, he allows a single blood-stained forefinger to shoot up out of his huge hand. 'A-da!' he says triumphantly, pronouncing each syllable carefully, much as a small child might do to please a parent with a newly learned name.

Jessica thinks she is going to be sick and she finds it difficult to look into Billy's bloodshot eyes.

Billy's second finger shoots up. 'Ga-wen.' He pauses and looks at Jessica, as though expecting her to applaud, and then up shoots the third. 'Win-fred!' he pronounces proudly. 'Kilt! Kilt! Kilt!'

'Oh my God, the Thomases! You've murdered them, Billy!'

Billy Simple now senses the distress in Jessica's voice and looks surprised, then doleful, and begins to whimper and then to sob. Soon great tears run down his blood-smeared cheeks. He crosses himself, 'Hail Mary, Mother of God,' he chokes. Then, looking up at Jessica, he smiles through his tears and says, 'Would you like to see the big cock Jesus gave me?'

CHAPTER FOUR

Jessica stands still for a long time, desperately trying to gather her wits. Billy Simple has dropped to his knees in the dust at her feet, hunched over, clutching her ankles with his blood-stained fingers, tears falling onto the scuffed toe-caps of her boots. The kelpies are agitated, but they lie obediently, eyes on their mistress. Red makes sharp little whining sounds, jerking his head upwards, his front paws scratching at the dust, his yellow eyes waiting for her command to attack.

Jessica looks down, horrified, and sees the top of Billy's head as he kneels at her feet. There is the great scar that runs the length of his skull where Jack's horse crushed it. The jagged pinkish-white line, stained dark in parts with dried blood, runs through his matted black hair like a path seen from the top of a hill winding through saltbush and scrub. She has never seen the scar before. Billy's always worn his hat clamped on his head pulled down to his eyeline, even when he sleeps.

Now suddenly Jessica can't hear Billy sobbing at her feet, or the dogs whimpering, or even the carolling of the magpies – the sounds of the morning are no longer present. It is as though the shock has contained her in a giant wave of silence and the world about her has shut down.

The silence is magnified by only one sound, the distant cawing of a crow. Jessica thinks it must be in her imagination. Crows are always there, as much a part of the day as the sunrise. The moment you wake, if you stop to listen for a few moments, you'll hear the mournful cawing of a crow. They say if the last thing you hear before you die is the cawing of a crow, it is the Devil beckoning you to Hell. Church bells are right for weddings, but crows caw at funerals. Dismal bastards.

Unbidden, it comes into Jessica's mind to wonder if the crow has been feeding on the snakes she shot last night. She sees their shapes clearly. In her mind's eye they lie stiffened in death, curled and knotted together, the patterns of their last frantic convulsions plainly marked in the river dust.

Now she sees the snakes and then the tiny black ants swarming where the birdshot has ripped their putty-coloured underscales apart. Where do the ants come from? You never see little sugar ants in the bush until something dies. Meat ants are always there, under strips of bark or stones, running along the black stalks of the saltbush or pouring from neat holes in the dry earth. Joe says a swarm of 'meats' will demolish a dead kangaroo in a week. 'Chew the hind leg off a horse if it stands long enough in one spot,' he jokes. But the little sugar ants appear from nowhere, marching in military precision and then attacking a dead thing in their tens of hundreds of thousands. They'll carry away a dung beetle a thousand times their size, a million little ant shoulders heaving and pushing.

Jessica's panicked, shocked mind continues to wander. Do ants know about snake venom? Would they avoid the pulped mess around the fangs, the flesh contaminated with poison from the burst sacs behind the jaw? The crows seem to know – they'll never touch a snake's head. Foxes, too, and kookaburras. Maybe ants are not affected, or there are so many it don't matter – the first hundred thousand die cleaning up the poisoned area and the rest carry on? Dog-eat-dog.

All around her are images of death, and Jessica can feel the panic growing. It lies like a coiled serpent in her guts, ready to rise up and strike through her throat.

Despite her efforts her mind won't be denied and the sounds of the real world about her begin to come back, growing stronger, intruding into her imagination. They seem to come in a sequence, first Red yelping and the two other dogs whining, then Billy sobbing, followed by the birds chittering in the kangaroo thorn, yellow box and bimble, after them the high-pitched zinging of the cicadas in the red gums by the river and finally the bloody crow again.

Jessica is trembling, her entire body shaking, the strength in her seems to be leaking out through her hands. Try as she may she cannot maintain her grip on the shotgun and it drops from her fingers to the ground beside her right boot. She can't move, can't stoop to pick the gun up. The twelve-bore, with both its hammers pulled back ready to fire, lies no more than six inches from Billy's hands, which still grip her ankles.

As the shotgun clatters to the ground, Billy's sobbing stops abruptly. Then she feels his hold on her ankles loosen. Jessica's teeth are chattering and she can't bend her neck to look downwards. Billy now rises to his feet, all six feet and six inches of him, his chest as broad as a stallion's rump. He towers above Jessica, looking confused, holding the shotgun pointed at her chest, his eyes glazed.

'No, no,' he says, 'Billy not shoot them blacks! No, Missus Thomas. No, no no!' He howls, then sucks his lips tightly inwards, the top covering the bottom, his face flushed.

Oh God, he's going to kill me. He thinks I'm Ada Thomas! The thought forces Jessica to regain her wits a little. 'No, Billy! It's Jessica. Jessica's your friend!' she cries, then takes a deep breath, forcing her panic down. 'Open it, break it open, Billy!' Even in her shocked state Jessica doesn't want him to ease the twin hammers back down to the safety position in case he accidentally triggers one of them. 'Break it, Billy, break the barrels open!'

'Break gun?' Billy looks puzzled, then grins. 'Break gun, Jessie!'

'No, Billy, open it.' She makes a gesture to indicate he should open the gun to expose the cartridges.

Billy turns the shotgun about so that he's now gripping halfway up the barrels, the butt pointing at Jessica and the barrels into his own chest. 'Billy break gun!' he yells joyously. Jessica screams as he swings the shotgun in an arc and smashes the butt against the pepper tree.

There's a huge explosion as the trigger guard smashes against the trunk of the tree and, denting inwards, drives down both triggers, firing the twin barrels straight into the face of a snarling Red, who has leapt towards Billy to defend Jessica. He is dead before his body hits the ground.

The remaining two dogs, shocked by the blast, have fled, yelping and howling for their lives, but now they turn and fall to the ground to watch. Billy Simple, thrown off-balance by the shotgun blast, has tripped on a root and lies sprawling on his back, his head narrowly missing a large protruding rock. Seeing him on his back, the two dogs now rush snarling to the attack.

Billy's arms fold about his face as the two dogs go for him, tearing at the back of his arms, maddened by Red's blood and gore that now covers the front of his flannel shirt, neck and part of his face. One of the kelpies leaves off his arms and tears into his blood-soaked gut.

Billy yowls in pain and his knees shoot up into his belly, then his great arms fling wide, sending the kelpie trying to get at his throat sprawling in the dust. Half rising, with one huge hand he grabs the dog caught between his knees and stomach around the top of its neck. With his fingers and thumb pressing behind the kelpie's jaw, he squeezes down on the dog's larynx. Then, with his free hand gripping the rock beside him, he pulls himself into a sitting position and scrambles awkwardly to his feet. All the while he holds the dog, which has its back legs on the ground and is frantically trying to squirm out of his grip. The first kelpie has come back again and is tearing at Billy's calf, hanging on grimly as Billy tries to shake his leg free. But the kelpie's body weight is too much and the dog has its teeth firmly fixed into his calf muscle. Shouting in agony, Billy brings his free hand to join the other around the second dog's throat and increases the downward pressure.

The helpless dog, eyes popping from its head, hind legs kicking frantically in the dust, tongue turned blue and forced from its mouth, is already near dead when Billy swings it up high above his right shoulder and with a grunt smashes its back down against the trunk of the tree. The kelpie, its spine snapped, goes limp in his hands. Billy flings it several yards away where it thuds down, skidding in a cloud of black dust.

Jessica is unaware she is screaming. Her body is filled with horror. She's paralysed with fright, too panic-stricken to whistle for the remaining kelpie to pull back, though the dog, maddened by fear and the smell of blood, would be unlikely to respond. Billy now bends and grabs the hind legs of the dog, one leg in each fist.

'No, Billy! No!' Jessica screams.

Billy seems not to hear and jerks the snarling kelpie away from his leg and high into the air, then turns it in a wide circle above his head, almost losing his balance in the process, and he dashes it downwards, smashing its skull against the sharp ridge of rock at his feet, splitting its body open from the neck to its hindquarters.

Panting furiously, his chest and stomach wet with fresh blood, the left leg of his moleskins torn from the knee down and with blood running down into his boots, Billy turns to Jessica. He doesn't seem to notice he's still holding the dead kelpie by the hind legs, its mouth and nose dripping blood and its steaming stomach viscera plopping onto the soil at his feet, its tawny brown body still quivering in the death throes.

'Dogs hurt Billy, Jessie,' he pants, then adds in a near whisper, 'sorry, eh.' Billy casts the lifeless kelpie aside. 'Dog hurt me leg, Jessie.'

Jessica falls to her knees, sobbing hysterically, banging the ground with her small fists. Quite how long she remains like this she can't say, nor is she aware that Billy is standing in front of her with his blood-spattered head bowed and his blood-stained hands folded in prayer.

Then Jessica feels herself swept up from the ground and realises she's in Billy Simple's arms and they are walking away from the dogs, towards the homestead. She kicks and screams, but he holds her so tightly pressed to his chest that she is powerless. She can smell the gore of the dead kelpies, their sinew, blood and bone mixed with the rancid sweat and stink of dried human blood on Billy's clothes and body. She feels she's going to vomit and fights to keep from gagging. The right side of her body is sticky from being held against his bloody shirt. Then she realises that she has pissed her trousers. By the time they reach the kitchen door she is whimpering helplessly in his arms.

Billy puts her down gently. 'Billy sorry, Jessie,' he says nervously, wringing his hands, standing in front of Jessica with his head bowed. 'Hail Mary . . .'

'Stop it! Stop it!' Jessica screams. 'Amen, Billy!' Then she bends over and vomits in the yard at her feet.

Billy starts to weep again. He has taken a blood-soaked set of rosary beads from his pocket and is counting them off, head bowed, as his lips mumble, 'Hail Mary, full of grace, the Lord is with Thee . . .'

Jessica remains bent over, her hands clasping her knees. She can feel her wits returning and she straightens up then sniffs. Lifting her pinny to her face, she wipes her eyes and mouth and blows her streaming nose. 'Oh God, help me!' she cries.

Billy stops his mumbled prayer and looks at her. 'Billy likes Jessie, she his friend,' he says, surprised.

'Don't hurt me, Billy! Please don't hurt me!' Jessica's throat grows tight and she begins to sob softly.

Billy looks confused. 'Jessie my friend. Billy don't hurt.' He lifts his head and sniffs deeply, clearing the contents of his nose into the back of his throat, then he knuckles the tears from his own eyes. 'Billy hungry, Jessie.'

'Hungry?' Jessica asks stupidly, not comprehending his meaning.

Billy claps his hands together. 'Hungry, hungry, hungry!'

Jessica slowly becomes aware of the smell of fresh-baked bread coming from the kitchen and thinks that she can buy some time to distract Billy.

'It's the bread, it's burning!' she cries. Then she runs into the kitchen and over to the stove and grabs a cloth, opening the oven door. This simple task steadies her. She's lost all sense of time but sees by the loaves that she's been away no longer than it would have taken her to milk the cow. The loaves stand high and handsome in the bread pans, the brown tops just beginning to turn to a darker burn.

Billy enters the kitchen while she's busy with the bread. 'Bread!' he shouts excitedly.

'It's too hot to eat, Billy,' Jessica says with her back to him. She brings a pan over to the table and up-ends it so that the loaf falls free, resting on its side.

'Bread!' Billy repeats urgently and grabs at the steaming loaf, picking it up in both hands. There is a moment's delay before he drops the loaf onto the kitchen floor. 'Bread hot!' he yells.

Jessica has got herself together a bit, though she's still trembling. She stoops, picks the loaf up with the cloth, and places it back on the table. 'I told you!' she scolds, surprised how strong her voice sounds. Billy looks contrite.

When she'd bent down for the bread she could smell the urine soaking the front of her moleskins. I don't want to die pissing my pants, she suddenly thinks. The absurdity of this thought almost makes her laugh out loud. Pissing my pants is the least of my problems, she thinks. 'I'll make you some real nice tucker, Billy. What would you like, eggs and bacon, as much as you can eat?'

'Billy hungry now!' he cries again.

Jessica looks up at him. His expression is completely harmless – Billy Simple is a little boy who's hungry and nothing more. She tells herself he's forgotten all about the dogs, and his confused mind is now concerned only with the need to eat. If she pulls herself together she'll be all right, if she doesn't think about the deaths, the deaths everywhere. She takes a deep breath and removes the remaining three pans from the stove, tapping them out onto the table. 'Don't touch,' she cautions Billy, more for the reassuring sound of her own voice than for him to take note.

Billy watches her, and then smiles again. 'Soup! Billy want soup!'

'It's not ready, Billy. I put some fresh vegies in, and they won't be cooked yet.' The ordinariness of this carry-on in Hester's kitchen has a calming effect on Jessica. She begins to realise that Billy Simple isn't going to hurt her unless he thinks himself threatened.

'Soup! Soup! Billy hungry, Jessie,' he whines, looking disappointed.

Jessica thinks of the Billy she knew at Riverview and understands that, despite her fear, she must take control of the situation. Billy expects to be told what to do, knows no other way to behave. If she doesn't take charge, he'll grow nervous again. She must dominate him – it's the only way he knows. The reason he's come to her in the first place is because he expects her to take over, to tell him what he must do.

'Billy, you can't sit in the kitchen like that, you're going to have to wash and change your clothes before you can eat. You hear me, Billy? Wash! I'll get you some fresh clobber to wear.'

Joe is not quite as tall as Billy but he's nearly as broad

in the chest and age has thickened his waist, so Jessica decides his clothes ought to fit Billy well enough. Either that or she'll have to strip Billy naked and wash what he's wearing. The thought makes her want to throw up again.

Jessica thinks about what she's going to have to do. She's going to have to take Billy Simple in. Turn him in to the magistrate at Narrandera. Her heart pounds as she realises what will be involved. She knows she can't keep him on the farm. Even if she can trick him, lure him into a room, there's nowhere she can lock him up safely until Joe returns in two days or while she rides for help. Billy would break down the door of the shed the moment her back is turned. Unless he could be persuaded to let her tie his legs and wrists?

Jessica looks at him – she doesn't much like her chances. Right now Billy Simple trusts her. But if she tries to restrain him or push him he'll grow nervous again, and she shudders at the thought of what he might do if he's panicked, as he was with the dogs.

Billy looks down, examining himself as though for the first time. His torn flannel shirt and ripped moleskins are stiff with dried and drying blood. Red's gore, bits of skin and hair and tissue add to the mess. Long crimson runnels of drying blood run the length of both arms down to his wrists and over his hands, disappearing between his fingers. It is as though he has been carelessly tattooed or viciously raked. The torn bottom fifteen inches of the right leg of his moleskins are also fresh-soaked, though already starting to darken as the blood dries. Billy Simple is a fearsome and frightening sight to behold.

'There's a tin tub beside the windlass out the back, go and draw up some water from the well and fill it and take all your clothes off, Billy.' Jessica speaks slowly as if instructing a child. Then she goes over to a shelf and takes a bar of lye soap and hands it to him. 'Get in the tub and wash all over with lots of soap.' Jessica makes a soaping motion in the air above her head. 'And mind you wash your hair. Can you do that for me, Billy?'

Billy nods and grins, holding the bar of soap in his hand. 'Lotsa soap, hair!' he says happily, making a scrubbing motion above his own head.

'And everywhere else.' Jessica makes more circular motions, this time over her body, 'Lots of soap, everywhere. And wash your belt and boots when you're finished.' She tries to smile at him. 'You come back a good clean boy and Jessie will let you have soup and bread, eggs and bacon, all you can stuff into yourself,' she promises him.

Jessica is amazed at the increasing calm she feels. 'Leave your clothes at the well, Billy, I'll bring you some others. Call out when you've finished washing yourself. There's a scrubbing brush in the tub, use it real hard, you hear me now, Billy?' She sees his face has darkened again – he looks panicky. 'What's the matter now, Billy?' she asks.

Billy clasps his hands over the top of his head, sniffling. 'Billy want hat, Jessie. Please!'

Jessica looks at him, his big hands covering his head.

It's as if he's only just realised he hasn't got his hat on. 'You take a bath and wash your hair good, like I said, and I'll bring you a hat. Orright?'

Billy nods, happy again. 'Righto, Jessie.' He leaves carrying the bar of soap in both hands as though it's some precious object. Jessica watches him shambling towards the windlass and sees that he is limping, dragging his right foot along the ground. She remembers the billy and milking pail she's left near where the dead dogs lie. She should fetch them back but right now she doesn't have the courage to go back there.

Jessica feels herself go cold. She has been so calm until now – in shock – that she hasn't thought that Billy might run away. If he does, she thinks, there isn't much she could do except ride around to a few of the surrounding stations and farms and get what men she could find who aren't too Sunday-drunk to saddle up and ride out to track him down.

But she feels sick at the thought of what these men might do if they came upon Billy alone in the bush. If a bunch of drunken larrikins should find him in some lonely gully they wouldn't stop to ask any questions, they'd string Billy Simple up to the nearest branch or shoot him and leave him for the dingoes and the crows.

Jessica quickly crosses the kitchen and walks into the tiny dark parlour where Joe keeps the small .22 lever action repeater. She takes the Winchester from the wall above the mantelpiece and goes over to the dresser and takes a packet of rimfire cartridges from a shelf. Then she feeds eight copper-cased bullets, one by one, into the magazine. The feel of the metal bullets in her hand gives her a little more confidence, though she knows a .22 won't stop Billy if he comes for her unless it's a heart or brain shot. She pulls down the triggering arm and pushes the safety catch on. Jessica returns to the kitchen and puts the rifle into the wood box, covering it with several split logs.

The rifle now hidden, but easy to retrieve if need be, she runs to her bedroom and pours fresh water into the washbasin. Kicking her boots off, Jessica tears the clothes from her back and, standing naked at the basin, scrubs herself furiously. She rubs the sticky blood from her arm and scrubs between her legs and the inside of her thighs where she's wet herself, then, rinsing the washcloth in the basin, she pulls a bucket from under the washstand and stuffs her discarded clothes into it, emptying the basin of soapy water over them. Jessica refills the basin from the jug and rinses the soap from her body. She washes her hair then dumps the soapy water again into the bucket and uses fresh water to rinse her hair. She reaches for a small, rough towel which hangs from the end of the washstand.

All this is done at a frantic pace, Jessica's heart pounding all the while, fearful that Billy Simple might return and discover her naked. By the time she's changed into fresh clothes and tied a new pinny about her waist, she is panting from the effort and the anxiety.

She moves to the back of the house, to Joe's sleep-out. She finds an old flannel shirt and a pair of work-stained moleskins, worn and patched but clean. She takes up

Joe's working hat, which has a hole in the crown. He's gunna be real cranky about losing it, Jessica decides, for she knows it's a toss-up whether a man likes a good worn pair of riding boots or his old, sweat-crusted hat best. She can't remember a time when Joe didn't have this battered and broken old headgear.

Jessica tucks the clothing and hat under her arm and is about to go to Joe's medicine box when she notices a half-used packet of shag tobacco and cigarette papers on the apple box Joe uses for a bedside table. She drops the makings into her apron pocket together with a box of lucifers.

Now, from the small personal medicine box Joe keeps under his bed, she takes out a jar of his famous horse ointment. With Joe's clothes and the yellow sulphur ointment, Jessica returns to the kitchen, placing the stuff on Hester's working stool beside the table.

Since the killing of the dogs, Jessica hasn't thought about Ada, Winifred and Gwen, the three dead Thomas women. She's deliberately shunted them to the back of her mind, knowing that if she starts to brood, to stop and think what Billy has done, the horror of what has happened at Riverview will sap her will and she won't have the strength to continue. Jack, where are you? she thinks, worrying about her friend and what's going to happen when he gets home.

But Billy, for the moment, must be her only concern, all she can cope with.

Jessica still can't get the dogs out of her mind, though. The terror she felt when Billy killed them so quickly and without a thought keeps returning. The sight of the two kelpies arcing in the air, the dull thud and cloud of black dust as Billy discarded the first, as though it were a bag of oats or a slaughtered rabbit.

Joe says death is a part of living in the country and sometimes comes when you least expect it. She loved Red, who was a strong-eyed dog who ran wide. He was a dog, Joe said, that could only ever serve one master and he'd chosen a mistress who was bloody spoiling him rotten. 'Shows what a smart bugger he is,' Joe would sometimes joke when he was in a good mood and the dogs had worked well.

While the other two kelpies were Joe's dogs, both were loose-eyed and not in Red's class. Red was hers only and always a champ. When he nuzzled his wet nose into the palm of her hand she knew it was to tell her he loved her. She knows she'll grieve bitterly for him later. She thinks of his torn and broken body lying in the sun near the pepper tree and her eyes fill with tears. She'll bury him in some special place – it's all she can do for him now.

Joe will be angry at the loss of the dogs. They were animals that grafted for their living and he depended on them to work the cattle and sheep. It will be a long, hard winter without the three of them in the paddocks.

They'll have to buy pups from a good pedigree litter and then go through the long hours, the weeks and months of training it takes to make a good sheep- and cattle-dog. Joe doesn't have that much patience any more and she doubts he's up to the training it takes.

Jessica knows she isn't as good as him with dogs and that they'll never get another like Red. And it all takes time and money, Jessica sighs, money Joe doesn't have.

Jessica tries to think what Joe would do in her place. He's killed a man before, and she wonders would he do the same to Billy Simple? Take the Winchester and go out and put a bullet through Billy's head while he's sitting in the tub happily soaping and scrubbing himself? Is that what she should do? Quick, simple, no questions asked. Bang! You're dead, Billy. All the blood tidily caught in the tub water. God rest your immortal soul, Billy Simple. You ain't gunna be missed by no one 'cept Jack and me.

Jessica has a sudden alarming thought. If she shoots Billy then Meg would be certain to get Jack Thomas. It'd be damn near impossible for him not to marry into the family who avenged the death of his mother and sisters.

Jessica realises Jack will spend the rest of his life carrying the guilt for what Billy has done. She knows him well enough to think he'll blame himself for Billy's actions. First the accident with the horse, then he brought the poor simpleton to work at Riverview. But he couldn't save Billy from human cruelty, and now he'll think it's his fault that his mother and sisters are dead.

None of this, Jessica thinks, is a good enough reason for Jack to have to marry Meg, even though she knows, if she shoots Billy, Jack will see it as his duty. It would be something salvaged from the tragedy. The whole district would applaud such an ending, the triumph of good over evil. Pretty Meg and handsome, decent Jack united in holy matrimony.

She knows it's crazy, but Jessica thinks suddenly that if she brought Meg and Jack together by killing Billy, then Hester would have to be grateful to her.

All she'd be doing, she tells herself, is what is already going to happen. Billy's going to die at the end of a rope. Why shouldn't she kill him now? It would be doing him a favour. It would also bring Meg and Jack together, but this time brought about by her own doing and not the grand plans and schemes of Hester and Meg. One simple little bullet in the back of his head and Hester will forgive her for everything.

For a brief moment Jessica sees herself as a true-blue heroine, applauded by everyone, for once the centre of attention. She can hear the things people would say. 'Yeah, the plain one, she done it, Joe's young 'un. Showed a lot o' guts if you ask me! Make someone a grand little missus that one would, not afraid to work neither.'

All she has to do is kill Billy Simple. Put a bullet in the soft spot where his spine connects with his skull.

In her mind Jessica rehearses the scene a second time. Billy will be sitting in the tin bathtub next to the windlass, scrubbing away, thinking himself a very good boy, trying his best to please her. She will move up quietly, the creaking of the windlass will cover her until she's about twenty feet away. She'll fire the bullet through the back of his head. If he turns and comes for her she'll still have time with the Winchester to put a second shot right between his eyes.

Jessica tells herself again that Billy is going to die any- way, strung up at the end of the hangman's rope. His poor, miserable, unhappy life is as good as over. Her shooting him would spare Billy the cruel treatment that must surely follow his arrest, or the terrible death he would suffer should the lynch mob catch up with him.

Jessica goes to the soup pot and stirs it, then she tastes a small chunk of turnip from the tip of the wooden spoon. It's not fully cooked but it's soft enough for Billy not to know the difference, and the soup will do him good.

She takes a skillet pan from the hook above the stove and drops a generous dob of dripping into it. She puts the skillet on the back plate of the stove to heat up slowly. Then Jessica takes down the leg of bacon hanging in its muslin bag and places it on the butcher's block where she slices an inch-thick slab from the side. She cuts it up into tiny squares so Billy can manage it with no teeth, and soon it's bubbling and sizzling in the pan. It is more than she could eat in a month of Sundays, but she's seen Joe tuck in after a day's shearing, and she supposes Billy will be the same. God knows when he last ate. Then she takes six eggs and puts them into a bowl beside the stove and places a tin spoon and a bowl for the soup on the table, the familiar movements calming her. The bread is still hot to the touch, so using a cloth she lifts a loaf and places it on the window ledge to cool, covering it with cheesecloth to keep the flies away.

If she did shoot Billy, Jessica thinks, she could always claim she was protecting herself and no one would disagree. A young girl alone on a deserted farm with a

madman who has killed three women on the loose.
What's more, when she tells the story of how Billy killed
the dogs, most people would feel she'd had every right to
shoot him. A good working dog is worth its weight in
gold and people have said Red was good enough to
compete at the Sydney Easter Show. He'd won at the
Narrandera Show three times and once at Wagga Wagga.
Everyone knows Joe Bergman has three dogs second to
none in the district and Red the best of them all.

Jessica hears a yell from the yard, 'Jessie, Jessie, Billy
clean boy!' and she puts all these thoughts to the back
of her mind for now. She takes Joe's moleskins and hat,
leaving the faded flannel shirt on the stool together with
the ointment, then she grabs a small towel from behind
the stove and walks out into the yard and towards the
windlass.

'Billy, I'm coming!' she calls. 'Now you sit still, ya
hear? In the tub. And turn yer back to me. Tell me when
you're ready!'

'Jessie come,' Billy calls out almost immediately,
'Billy clean boy!'

Jessica approaches the windlass and sees Billy sitting
in the tub, his broad, strongly muscled back facing her.
She walks up and places Joe's moleskins and hat down
on a log beside the tub.

'There's a pair of moles here, Billy, and a towel and
I've brought you a hat. Shirt's in the kitchen – I want to
dress them cuts and scrapes before you put it on. You
come back when you're done, tucker's near ready.'

'Hat! Hat!' Billy shouts excitedly. Then suddenly he

stands up in the tub and turns to face Jessica. 'Hat, gimme hat!' he pleads, his arms stretched out urgently towards her. Billy's torso and arms are covered in cuts and dark bruises but Jessica's eyes are drawn to his thighs the moment before she shuts them tight. She cannot believe what she's seen hanging between his massive legs.

'Turn around, Billy! Sit in the tub!' Jessica says in a low voice, her eyes still closed.

'Hat, Jessie! Gimme hat!' Billy whimpers.

Jessica's heart is thumping, filling her throat. She turns about so that she has her back to Billy. 'Orright, orright, Billy!' she cries over her shoulder.

'Hat! Hat!' Billy is now sobbing and panting wildly.

Jessica grabs Joe's hat and turns again to face Billy, whose extreme agitation has caused him to have an erection, though he's oblivious of this, his arms stretched out to take the hat, his lips trembling. Jack's right, Jessica thinks, it is a monster. She shuts her eyes again and edges towards the tub, extending Joe's hat to Billy Simple.

Billy snatches the hat from her hand, grunting and snuffling like a pig, then Jessica hears the splash as he subsides into the water. There is a moment's silence as Billy pulls the hat over his head and then, like a little boy addressing his mother, he says, 'Thank you, Jessie. Billy happy now. Look, look, washed good!'

Jessica opens her eyes and tries to keep her voice steady. 'Have you washed your hair, Billy?' she says. She turns her back on him and begins to walk away.

'Billy wash his hair, lotsa soap!' Billy calls out after her.

'Good boy. Now hurry and dry yerself and get dressed, there's plenty of good tucker in the kitchen.'

Billy arrives in the kitchen shortly afterwards, Joe's hat clamped down over his eyes. The dark ends of his hair poking out from underneath the hat are still dripping water from the tub and it runs down his neck and shoulders onto his naked wet torso.

He's done a pretty fair job of washing himself and the bites from the dogs seem to have largely stopped bleeding. He's also washed his boots and belt and there's a puddle where he stands in the wet boots.

'Billy hungry, Jessie!' he pleads.

'Sit, then,' Jessica says, pointing to the table with the soup ladle. She feels like she is in command once again. With Billy seated on Meg's stool Jessica takes Joe's large enamel soup bowl over to the stove and ladles soup into it, then she returns and places the steaming broth down in front of Billy.

'Careful now, it's hot. Use the spoon, blow on it, or it'll burn your tongue.'

Jessica goes to the window, fetches the loaf of fresh bread and breaks it in half. Steam rises from the freshly broken ends. Billy grabs one half and tears at it, wide-eyed with excitement, and he stuffs the warm bread into his mouth, grunting happily, his cheeks blown out so that he can barely chew. 'There's plenty of food, Billy. Take your time, no need to make yourself sick!' Now she breaks six eggs into the bacon fat sizzling in the skillet. 'New bread eaten too fast will give you a gut ache, *indeejestin*!'

Billy eats everything Jessica lays in front of him, polishing off the remains of the egg and bacon fat on his plate with the last of the loaf of bread. When she puts a mug of sweet black tea in front of him, Billy beams up at her, licking his chops.

'We're gunna clean and dress those cuts now, Billy. Drink your tea and be a brave boy while I fix you up.'

Jessica brings a bowl of warm water over and drops a pinch of Condy's crystals into it, turning the water a deep purple. Then she fetches a bottle of iodine and a pile of old rags from Hester's cupboard.

She sponges the numerous cuts and dog bites on Billy's arms and chest with the warm solution and washes the deep gash in his stomach. Then she makes a swab from a piece of rag, soaks it in iodine from the bottle and dabs it over his wounds. She's felt the sting of iodine often enough herself to know how it must be hurting Billy. But he only winces momentarily as the liquid burns white hot. Jessica waits until the iodine has dried over his cuts and then she applies Joe's horse ointment and ties a bandage wherever she can. Billy has a deep, ugly tear in the muscle of his right leg where the kelpie ripped into him. Jessica makes him take off his boot and put his foot on her lap while she rolls up the leg of Joe's moleskins and cleans and dresses the torn flesh before bandaging it. When she's through he looks like a giant scarecrow with bits of coloured rag wrapped all about him.

Jessica takes up Joe's faded red shirt and helps Billy get himself into it. It fits perfectly. Then she brings over the pot of tea, refills Billy's tin mug and ladles three heaped tablespoons of sugar into it and stirs it for him. The room is silent but for the clinking of the spoon against the sides of the mug.

'Now Billy, what are we gunna do with you?' Jessica asks, sitting on the stool beside him.

Billy looks confused then licks his lips. 'Billy stay here, plenty good tucker.'

'No, Billy, you can't stay here, you've done wrong.' Jessica can feel her heart start to pound again as she speaks. She doesn't want to upset Billy, but she doesn't know how else to put it.

'Billy bad boy!' he suddenly bursts out.

'Billy, I'm going to have to take you in. Do you understand?'

'Billy stay with Jessie.'

'Billy, you've done something terrible, you can't stay here.'

Billy looks as though he's about to cry. 'But d-d-d-dogs bite Billy!' he stammers. 'Sorry kilt dogs, Jessie.'

'No, Billy, not the dogs! What you did at Riverview!'

Billy Simple looks as though he's trying to recall something stuck way back in his past. He smiles. 'Ah! Billy break gun! Missus Thomas shot-gun!' Then he says urgently, 'No! no! Billy *not* shoot them blacks.'

Jessica sighs. 'No, Billy, not the shotgun, that was this mornin'. What you did yesterday, or was it in the night? Did you do it last night? You know, what you said you did to Mrs Thomas, Winifred and Gwen at Riverview?' She can't bring herself to be more specific.

Billy smiles again and claps his hands triumphantly. 'Kilt 'em!'

'You killed them? Are you sure, Billy?'

'Kilt, kilt, kilt!' Billy repeats happily. He balls his fist in front of his face and his forefinger shoots up. 'A-da!' He looks at his finger proudly, then the second finger follows, 'Win-fred!' and then he wiggles his thumb, 'Ga-wen!'

'You killed them? All three?'

Billy looks at Jessica and nods his head vigorously. 'One, two, three, Billy caught a flea, flea died, Billy cried, one, two, three!' He recites the nursery rhyme perfectly and then claps his hands.

Billy stops clapping when he sees Jessica isn't responding and hangs his head and then sniffs.

'Billy, why did you come here?' He sniffs again but doesn't look up. 'Look at me, Billy.' He raises his head slowly and looks at Jessica as she asks again, 'Billy, why did you come to Jessie?'

'Billy bad boy!' He looks slyly at Jessica. 'Jessie hide Billy.'

Jessica shakes her head. 'No, Billy, can't be done, mate. They'll be after you, they could be out looking for you already.'

Billy Simple looks over his shoulder as though he expects his pursuers to come through the kitchen doorway at any moment. 'No, no, Jessie hide Billy!' he cries again.

Jessica remains silent for some time, looking down at her hands, then she raises her head and, sighing, looks at Billy. 'Billy, someone will have found Mrs Thomas and the two girls. They'll see you're missing and they'll come after you. Look, if I hide you they'll find you soon enough. And if you run away, they'll run you down, find you in the bush.' Jessica pauses, then adds, 'They won't be good men, Billy, they'll shoot you down like a mad dog.' Jessica's heart skips a beat as she realises what she's just said, but Billy doesn't seem to notice.

Billy crosses himself. 'Hail Mary –'

'No, Billy, don't!'

But this time he ignores her. 'Hail Mary, Mother of God,' he repeats, 'would you like to see the big cock Jesus gave me?'

Jessica can see he's getting upset again and she changes tack. 'Billy, would you like to sleep, have a good kip, eh?'

Billy nods his head slowly as though he's thinking about this idea.

'Did you sleep last night?' Billy shakes his head. 'Where were you all last night, you poor bugger? C'mon then, you can use Joe's bed, it's nice and long, out the back in the sleep-out.'

Billy looks suspiciously at Jessica. 'Men come shoot Billy like mad dog.'

Jessica sighs. 'True enough.' She shrugs her shoulders. 'But if you won't come to Narrandera with me you might as well have a good sleep.' She continues with this peculiar logic, 'It's a bloody sight better than sitting on yer arse shittin' yer britches, waiting for them to come and get ya. Ain't it now, Billy?'

Billy looks up, surprised. 'Narran-dera?'

Jessica remembers that Billy is afraid to ride a horse. 'It's near twelve hours by sulky. They won't think you'd head for Narrandera, they'll expect you to go bush, into emu country,' she says, knowing it's a lie, that he'd be dead of thirst and the sun in a day and a half. Billy would be driven back towards the river if he were on his own without water.

He suddenly removes his hat and drops his head and parts his hair with his hands, exposing the scarred pathway. 'Narran-dera Hos-pit-al fix me 'ead, Jessie.' He removes his hands from his head and looks up at her eagerly. 'Narran-dera good! Jessie take Billy to Narrandera to fix me, eh?' He takes his hat and pulls it back over his head.

Jessica can't believe her luck. 'Yes, Billy, someone there will know what to do with you.'

'Jessie come too!' Billy says in sudden alarm.

Jessica nods her head. 'You won't make it alone, mate.'

She now realises she's been on the edge of panic, worrying that someone may already have discovered the murdered women at Riverview and be heading straight over, Joe's place being the nearest property to the Thomases' station. But she knows that their cook has Saturday afternoon and Sunday off to visit her sister, the cook at North Yanco Station, and won't return to Riverview till this Sunday evening. And she figures it can't be much past nine o'clock, still a little early to expect callers. With Jack and his old man out mustering, there's just a chance there'll be no one at the homestead and the bodies may not yet have been found.

Although if a stable boy comes in to groom the horses or to harness the Thomas sulky for church, he'd be sure to raise the alarm.

Anyone going for help would probably ride to one of the bigger stations to report the murders. Narrandera and Whitton are both too far, a good nine hours on horseback. They might go looking for Jack and old man Thomas in the bush but they'd be lucky to spot them inside a couple of hours, or more if they're working one of the more distant runs. They'd know Joe's the nearest male to Riverview and might sensibly decide to begin recruiting a search party by starting with him.

Jessica reckons it'll take half a day to gather a mob of men to come looking for Billy, maybe even longer. She probably has four hours or a little more lead on them if she and Billy get going soon. If she stays here with Billy and if the mob arrives, probably drunk, they're just as likely to lynch Billy on the spot, string him from the windlass. She can't just sit here and wait for that to happen, and Jessica shudders at the thought of more death. No, she makes up her mind, she doesn't know what she's going to do with Billy, but she's got to get going in the next half-hour.

'Billy, I'll have to go harness the sulky, will you come with me?' Billy nods and goes to stand up but she raises her hand. 'No wait, I'll pack some food for the way first.' She finds a large basket and puts in two of the loaves, adds half a packet of tea and a small tin of sugar, then slices several thick wedges from the leg of bacon and wraps them in a cloth. Finally she makes a nest of straw and puts a dozen eggs carefully into the basket.

The eggs remind Jessica that she hasn't fed the chickens or the pigs and she hastily makes a bucket of meal mash for the pigs and fills an old jam tin with cracked corn for the chooks. It's double rations for both so if she's away tomorrow, as she expects, they'll be hungry but they'll last until she returns. 'Billy, will you go to the well and draw water for the chooks, and then go back and get another couple of buckets for the pigs.'

Billy rises from the stool and Jessica sees he is now limping very badly.

'You orright, mate?' Jessica carries a bottle of kero for the hatcher lamp and, with the cracked corn in one hand and the bucket of mash in the other, she walks towards the door.

'Leg hurts,' Billy groans, limping behind her.

Well, that's one good thing, Jessica thinks, he won't be trying to escape by running for it.

When they return to the kitchen it's obvious to Jessica that Billy's leg is troubling him badly. He is sweating buckets and sits down as they come in. He grabs his leg in both hands, holding it behind the knee so his foot doesn't touch the floor.

'Here, let's have another squiz at your leg,' she says. 'Take off yer boot, mate.'

Billy is reluctant to reach down to his boot, not sure how to go about it without hurting himself more.

'Wait on,' Jessica says and kneels down on the floor

and gently works the broken boot off his foot. Then she pulls up the leg of Joe's moleskins again and sees that the blood has seeped through the bandage and some has run down over Billy's ankles. His heel is sticky with blood and the inside of his boot is full of it.

She cleans up his foot and the boot, then removes the blood-soaked bandage and examines the tear in his calf, which appears to have opened even further. 'It needs to be stitched,' she says, more to herself than to Billy.

'Billy, I'm gunna have to stitch it, or it'll bleed or worse, get infected and make you real crook.' Jessica knows that she's losing time now but she's got no alternative. She has to try to stem the blood by closing the wound. She makes a thick swab of rag and shows Billy how to hold it against his calf.

'I'll be back soon, Billy, just going out the back to get the stuff I need to fix you.'

Billy nods and Jessica goes back to the sleep-out and Joe's medicine box. She opens one of the little drawers in it and takes out the gramophone needle box in which Joe keeps his suturing needles. Then she removes a packet of horsehair from the drawer next to it. She's stitched the dogs several times when they've been caught on a fence and many a calf, and once a bad cut to Joe's arm he got stringing barbed wire. She knows she's not too strong at suturing a wound, Joe's a lot better at it, but Billy's leg is not going to close without a dozen or more stitches.

Jessica finds a scrap of paper and a pencil stub on Joe's apple box and hurriedly writes him a note:

Dear Father,

Billy Simple's gone crazy and murdered Mrs Thomas and the girls. I've taken him to the magistrate at Narrandera, left Sunday morning.

Don't worry about me, I'll be all right.

Jessica.

P.S. I've taken the Winchester.

She places the note inside Joe's medicine box and returns to the kitchen, where she takes the kettle off the hob and sterilises the needle and then swabs the dog bite, wiping away all the blood and sulphur ointment and making sure to clean the wound deep into the muscle fibre. Billy grips both hands tightly above his knee, his eyes closed, tears running silently down his cheeks.

'Sorry, mate, it's gunna get worse before I'm finished with you. You can yell out if you like, there's nobody here but us.' Jessica sutures the wound the way Joe's shown her. By now Billy's swallowing his bottom lip and Jessica, glancing up at him, thinks it's a damn good thing Billy hasn't got any teeth or he'd slice it right off. He's sweating heavily and still gripping his leg with both hands, but he doesn't once cry out.

Jessica knots and then cuts the end of the horsehair. Her work is by no means a thing of beauty and Joe would probably scold her for a messy job, but she figures it will probably hold unless Billy has to run for it. She swabs the stitched wound with iodine and wraps a bandage tightly about it, then sterilises the needle again and puts it back into the little gramophone needle box.

Jessica leaves what remains of the horsehair and the little tin box on the kitchen table. She knows Joe will see the gear on his return and will take it to his medicine box. Joe has a tidy mind and has drilled her since she was a brat about putting things back where they've come from. Jessica knows he'll find her note.

'There you go, put your boot back on, Billy. You'll have to stay here in the kitchen while I harness the sulky, no use opening that up again trying to walk down to the paddock.' Jessica is anxious now – time is running out.

Billy looks frightened. 'D-d-d . . . don't leave me, Jessie.'

'I'm not going nowhere without ya, love.' Jessica smiles at him, then folds her arms in front of her and pretends to rest her forehead on them. 'Good chance to get some shut-eye, what say, eh, Billy?' She points to the table.

Billy obediently folds his arms and places them on the table and rests his head between them, closing his eyes.

'Good boy. Won't be long. You stay there and be good, Billy.'

On her way to the paddock Jessica passes the windlass and sees a crow pecking at Billy's bloody clothes, which are draped over the wall of the well. She shouts and the crow flies off in a clatter of urgent wings, cawing its protest. Bloody vermin, doesn't take them long, Jessica thinks.

The water remains in the tub and Jessica can see what's left of the soap lying on the bottom. Pushing her shirt sleeve up well past her elbows, she reaches down into the scummy water for the soap and places it to dry on the wall of the well, then she retrieves the scrubbing brush floating on the surface and puts it beside the soap.

Her arm's now covered in a film of pink scum and several of Red's hairs stick to her. She'll have to leave poor Red to the crows and the meat ants, she sighs. And tonight there'll be a fox or two to have a good feed off him and the other dogs. It'll be a couple of days before she can bury their bones and what bits of skin and fur remain.

Jessica fills up a bucket of water from the tank and, scooping her left hand into the bucket, she splashes her arm clean and unrolls and buttons her sleeve at the wrist again. She casts about for a stick. Finding a stout twig, she uses it to lift Billy's shirt, now almost dried and beginning to stiffen in the hot morning sun. She drops it gingerly into the tin tub where it floats on the surface of the water. Jessica pushes it down under the water, forcing the air pockets from it with the stick. Then in go Billy's torn moleskins. After this she departs to get the horse, a pony named Napoleon, who'll go all day at five miles an hour if you give him a bit of a spell every now and then and let him poke his nose into a bag of oats.

Back in the kitchen she finds Billy Simple asleep, his head still cupped in his arms. She loads the basket into the back of the sulky and returns to fetch a couple of blankets, which she rolls and ties with a piece of twine.

It's not yet cold enough to damp down the heat of the day but in the early mornings there's just the beginning of a chill in the air. Finally she carries a billy and a canvas water bag she's filled out to the sulky and hangs both on a hook behind the front seat. It's time to go.

She shakes Billy awake. 'Wake up, Billy, got to kick the dust, mate.'

Billy is drugged for want of sleep and he whimpers, protesting, 'No, no, Billy sleep now!'

'Billy, wake up! We've got to get moving, the mob coming after you will be here soon enough.'

Billy rises painfully to his feet. Jessica knows she's got no more than an outside chance of getting Billy all the way to Narrandera in the sulky, especially if the men are out after him now on their horses. As Joe would say, 'Not a good risk, girlie, you're on a hiding to nothing, better give it a miss this time.'

But Jessica knows she can't do that, she's got to try to bring Billy to safety. Along with Jack Thomas, she's Billy's only friend. You don't let a mate down when the going gets rough, no matter what. Joe says it's a rule you can never break. She knows that to do what he's done, poor Billy Simple must have been provoked beyond any possible endurance – she knows he's suffered for so long now in that household. She is aware that he can't ever be forgiven and will die for his crime. Jessica knows this for sure, but she's not going to let a mob of drunken shearers and stockmen string him up, give him a dose of bush justice and have a real good time doing it, then boast to their grandsons one day how they did this noble deed. She feels certain Jack would do the same as her if he were standing in her boots right at this moment. This last thought gives Jessica some comfort.

Jessica watches as Billy limps over to the sulky. He struggles to climb aboard, glancing anxiously at Napoleon. Poor bugger can't even run for it, she thinks. Then she remembers the Winchester in the wood box and races to the kitchen to retrieve it. She can hear Joe's voice chiding her for her carelessness, 'You're getting too bloody cocky, girlie. Remember the poor bastard's mad as a meat axe – if he comes for yiz, shoot him dead!'

Billy sees the gun and pulls back in alarm. 'It's for Joe Blakes, Billy. We may have to camp the night. Don't want you bitten by a mulga, now, do we?' Jessica wonders what else they'll find out there, apart from snakes. If a mob catches up with them, would she stand her ground, use the Winchester? Like standing up to George Thomas? She doesn't know, can't think about it now.

She climbs aboard and sits beside Billy, placing the gun at her feet and taking up the reins. 'Ha, Napoleon!' She raps the reins across the pony's rump and he moves off, happy to be out and about.

Jessica knows she's got the next twelve hours to try to keep Billy Simple alive in the bush, away from a drunken, hostile mob out to get him. Joe wouldn't care for the odds on her succeeding, she thinks. Jessica knows she doesn't much care for them herself.

CHAPTER FIVE

They hug the river, keeping the sulky close to the trees. Jessica knows that anyone coming after them from the open ground will have difficulty picking them up against the darkness of the river gums. They're two hours away from the punt where she and Billy must cross the river if they are to make it to Narrandera.

As the sulky moves along at its steady, slow pace, Jessica tries to think about the mob of horsemen that she's sure will be out after them.

She reckons that it'll take at least four or five hours to get a mob of men together from the various homesteads and stations around, then they'll proceed to Riverview to inspect the three dead women. If they decide to tell the two Thomas men of the tragedy, locating the run where they're working might take another hour at least and the return to Riverview the same. Getting to Joe's place will add yet more time, which means they wouldn't arrive there till late in the afternoon.

After that, drunk or sober, there'll be some good bushmen among them and they're not men to be easily fooled. They'll see the dead dogs, the milk pail and billy abandoned together with the broken shotgun. Then they'll come up to the house and see Billy's discarded clothes floating in the tub beside the windlass, and her own stuffed into a bucket in her bedroom. There'll be blood on everything, evidence of violence everywhere. It wouldn't be too hard to make a decision as to what's happened. Jessica runs the most logical sequence through her mind, trying to think as the men might do.

They'll conclude that there's been a struggle of some sort at the pepper tree and that Billy has slaughtered the dogs. Then, when they go up to the homestead and find Billy's torn rags and her own blood-stained clothes, the most likely conclusion they'll reach will be that he's murdered Jessica as well. But when they can't find her body, they'll change their minds and decide Billy's taken her hostage and that her life is in danger.

The missing sulky will confirm this. After that it won't take them too long to discover the sulky's tracks running along the river front and they'll be on their way in hot pursuit.

Jessica does have one thing in her favour, if it's all going as she expects. If the men get to Joe's in the afternoon, and then spend an hour looking around before they set off for the punt, they won't get to it till sundown, the time when the snakes come out to dance. She knows a good horseman won't take the risk of a snake-bite to his mount, so with any luck the mob will agree that they can't track Billy in the dark and that setting out in the morning is much the better plan of action.

The country on the far side of the river and stretching all the way to the Lachlan is lightly wooded at best and most of it is flat as a pancake, black soil and scrub country where it isn't difficult to track a man down once you're onto him. They'll probably have a black tracker along with them, too.

Jessica reckons they'll assume that Billy is in charge and she, if still alive, is his hostage. Billy, they'll think, has long since lost the skills of the bush and will have trouble finding water or earning his tucker off the land. There is simply no hiding for long in this type of country and once they've picked up his tracks they'll reckon they have a better than even chance of tracking down their quarry before sundown tomorrow.

Most of the men will have come out without rations, eager for the chase and with half a skinful of Sunday grog to cloud their judgement. Some, with the drink already leached out of them in the day's riding, will now want to go home and pick up enough rations for a couple of days. Unless Jack Thomas or his old man has thought to issue rations to the horsemen before they'd set out from Riverview. But it's better not to think that way, Jessica decides.

Jessica thinks she's left the homestead around nine o'clock in the morning, which, after they've negotiated the punt, should put them across the river a little before noon. On the other side of the river they'll take the road to Narrandera and from there, if the track isn't too rutted, they should make pretty good time.

She reckons the journey to Narrandera will take her and Billy around twelve hours in the sulky, allowing for stops every three hours to give the pony the spells he will need. If nothing goes wrong, they could make it to Narrandera just before midnight, although Jessica isn't fool enough not to know that something almost always goes wrong and that no journey in the bush is ever completed according to plan.

The drought has left very little grass about and their wheel tracks in the black soil won't be hard to follow. The mob'll soon enough know that she and Billy have headed for the punt. If they've reached Joe Bergman's place earlier than she's supposed and make it across the river before sundown, then they'll have plenty of time to catch her. No matter what Jessica does, the sulky can't outrun a mob of men on horseback. So she prays silently that she's calculated correctly.

For the first few miles Billy sits nervously in the sulky, watching Napoleon's rump, but after an hour or so he settles down and even seems to have forgotten about the danger they face. Jessica sees no reason to alert him – she realises that, like a small child, he has put his trust in her and is now enjoying their ride. It is as if they're on a day's outing or on their way to a picnic on the river bank. Might as well let the poor bugger have his freedom while he can, she thinks.

Billy loves the birds. The sulky frequently comes across a flock of galahs feeding in the dust, though on God knows what – there must be grass seed waiting for the rain. Billy's eyes grow bright as they approach the feeding birds and he chortles with delight when the rose-breasted galahs rise at the last possible moment in front of the sulky. He claps his hands, pleased as punch when they *schwark* their indignation at being disturbed. Then he does an imitation of their cries, laughing and puffing out his chest, feeling very pleased with himself. Jessica reckons he can do a better than fair imitation of almost every bird call they hear.

'Jessie, Jessie, look,' Billy frequently shouts and then he might point to a sulphur-crested cockatoo sitting high up in a river gum. He'll imitate the raucous sound of the big white bird, and often, to his immense delight, elicit a reply.

He does the same when they see a kookaburra or any of the parrots and rosellas they encounter on the way and he claps and chortles all the while, happy as can be, a small boy with a voice box of tricks showing off in front of her. She is grateful that it's a game he seems never to tire of playing, leaving her to her own dark thoughts. Again she thinks miserably how kind it would be just to kill Billy out here, while he's still happy and free, before anyone gets to him.

The sun is almost directly overhead when they arrive at the punt. Jessica can hardly believe her luck – it is moored on their side of the river. She sees the winch on a small platform built into its side, with the wind-in rope strung back to the far shore and the take-up neatly wound on its drum close to where she stands. Bringing the punt across the river is a tiring task, usually managed by two strong men. She hopes that Billy, with what help she can add, has the strength to wind them over to the other side of the river.

Jessica drives the sulky onto the punt and signals for

Billy to climb down. 'Billy, you'll have to wind us over now,' she says, taking him by the hand and standing him in front of the winch barrel with its large wheel. 'You're a strong lad, Billy, will you show Jessie how you can turn the wheel?'

Billy is delighted at the compliment. 'Billy strong boy, Jessie!' He smiles, rubbing his hands together and then spitting onto each palm.

Jessica releases the drum brake and adds her strength to the wheel as Billy starts to wind the rope in on one barrel while paying it out on the other, grunting as he pulls the punt slowly across the river. It is hard work, and the river, even though turgid and its current slow, catches the side of the punt, pushing it downstream so that Billy and Jessica must fight to keep both the ropes taut to prevent it from slipping sideways. Billy is soon drenched in sweat and near exhausted by his efforts and Jessica thinks her arms must surely fall off. Nearly half an hour passes before they reach the far shore of the Murrumbidgee.

Jessica leads the pony and sulky off the punt and up the embankment and gives Napoleon his nosebag of oats. Then she takes the hand axe, cuts a stout pole from a river gum and returns to the water's edge to jam it into the rope drum so that it cannot release if an attempt is made to pull the punt back to the other side of the river.

It isn't much of a delaying tactic, as all it will require is for a man to swim across and unlock it again, but if as she's hoping their pursuers arrive at sundown they may just decide to leave off until the morning, afraid of the snakes. Even if some of the men have packed rations, they may decide to stay the night and camp some distance away from the river bank to cross at first light, by which time she hopes to have reached Narrandera or to be no more than two or three hours away.

Billy is knackered and sits on the punt. Jessica calls for him to follow her and he climbs slowly to his feet and tries to walk, but the torn muscle in his leg has stiffened and he seems unable to move.

'Come on, Billy, you must try,' Jessica urges him.

He tries to hobble and then hops on one foot towards her. It is at once obvious that he cannot manage the steep incline up the river bank. Jessica returns with the pony and sulky and, after much effort, manages to get Billy up into the seat and now tries to lead the pony up the embankment. But the horse is harnessed for flat country and wears no breastplate, and it cannot pull Billy's added weight up the slope, making but a foot each time and then sliding the full distance back again.

Jessica takes everything she can from the sulky in order to lighten it – the tucker basket, axe, water bag, blankets, billy, skillet, tin plates and mugs, the bag of oats she's brought for the pony and finally the Winchester. She tries again, but no luck. Finally she chops down a cypress pine and lops the branches along the trunk some three or four inches from where they abut so that each short spike will dig into the river bank and act as resistance when the sulky wheels run backwards against the spiked log.

The cypress trunk is heavy and she is already exhausted, but with each small gain up the embankment

Jessica somehow manages to keep sliding it under the sulky wheels. In this manner, almost inch by inch, they make it to the top. It is an hour before they've conquered the slope and the pony is almost spent and will need another spell before they can move on. Jessica is anxious and impatient, but knows they have no choice while Billy, seated in the sulky, is soon enough asleep.

It's well after two in the afternoon when she has reloaded the sulky and they finally get away again. What Jessica had hoped would take them no more than three hours including the river crossing has taken them two hours more. They have at least another ten hours to go before they reach Narrandera and Jessica now knows they won't make it in one haul.

She decides they'll go as far as they can before stopping for the night. When the sun sets there'll be enough moonlight to guide them along the rutted road. But the pony, even with frequent spells, has no more than six hours left in him and will be unable to work any longer without a good night's rest. At the latest, by nine o'clock they'll have to stop and camp for the night.

If the men on horseback get across the river by sundown, they'll catch them anyway and Billy won't see another dawn. But if they do stay the night on the far shore and cross at daylight, then, with a fair amount of luck, she and Billy should be no more than four hours away from Narrandera and the mob won't catch her. It's a lot to ask of Napoleon, but he's a stock pony in his prime, bred tough, and unless he goes lame she knows he'll give her all he's got.

By sundown they are twenty miles from the river crossing and Jessica knows the next two hours will tell if their pursuers have managed to cross the river. Going any further, she tells herself, isn't going to make any difference. She decides to take a spell and boil the billy.

Billy is in a lot of pain as she helps him down from the sulky and allows him to use her shoulder to steady himself as he hops on one leg off the track. She helps him lower himself to the ground with his back resting against the trunk of a boree tree. Jessica makes a fire of dry scrub and boils the billy. Making two strong mugs of sweet black tea, she hands one to him. She adds more twigs and a few dry branches from the boree and allows them to burn down, then puts the skillet on the hot ashes and cooks a thick slice of bacon, which she cuts into tiny squares so Billy can swallow them easily. She hollows out the centre of half a loaf and packs in the bacon pieces and then replaces the bread. It's the only way she can think to prepare a quick meal for this poor creature who has no teeth.

Jessica tries to sound cheerful as she hands the bread and bacon to him. 'There you go, Billy, eat it all up now. I doubt there'll be much more coming your way till mornin', mate. When we make camp tonight, I won't have the strength to cook and you'll have to settle for dry rations, a bit o' bread maybe, eh?'

Billy snatches at the bread and bacon, grunting as he tears at it with his fingers, cramming pieces into his mouth as fast as he can manage, softening the bread with gulps of tea. Then Jessica sits on her haunches and eats a little of the bread and drinks her tea and wonders if this is the last supper for poor Billy Simple.

She is dog-tired and the thought that the mob may have made it across the river makes her want to cry. She tells herself that Billy is her charge and she must deliver him to the police magistrate. She cannot bear the thought of failing, of seeing him gunned down short.

Joe wouldn't say anything and he'd be happy she was alive, but she knows that deep down he would think she'd failed, that she didn't correctly calculate the risks. 'Girlie, they killed him, didn't they? And he could've killed ya, eh, eh? A waste o' time and effort and now them what did the killing'll think things about you and him. Bad things.' Jessica can hear him clear as a bell, even though she reckons he'd never say such a thing to her face.

She thinks about Jack. What will he say about all this? Earlier she felt he would agree she'd done right taking Billy to the police magistrate at Narrandera. But now she's not so sure. If he's among the men when they come, will he be the one to pull the trigger? The mob would expect it. Will Jack put Billy up against a tree and blast what few brains he has left out of his ugly head? Jack's own self-respect may demand that Billy die by his hand.

But how would Jessica react then? Would she try to defend Billy Simple against the mob, against Jack? If she did, she knows it'd be taken real bad by all who heard of it, not just the drunken mob on horseback, but by folk everywhere. Jessica can hear the gossip in her head:

'A woman who defends a murderer must have a reason, don't ya reckon? She's ugly and can't get a man what's normal. Hey, wait a minute, maybe them two . . . ? What's he say all the time about what Jesus give him? Maybe she's been helping herself on the side? Joe's youngest, she ain't like her older sister. Never did like her much. A proper tomboy, and ya can't trust a woman what dresses like a man, can ya? Dirty little bugger!'

Jessica can see their looks, hear the sniggers from the women at St Stephen's or at the agricultural show. Hester and Meg could never again hold their heads up in polite society.

Again she thinks about killing Billy. She could claim he tried to rape her when she was asleep. She could say she was trying to bring him to justice and also to save him from what the men would do to him – that was true enough. Then he'd attacked her, a madman coming at her in the night.

Jessica isn't even too sure what rape is, or how it is done. It is a word she'd first read in the newspapers when she was ten and when she'd asked Hester her mother had said it wasn't something a little girl should know about. When she'd persisted Hester sighed and replied that rape was when a man made a baby with a woman he didn't know from Adam.

The young Jessica simply couldn't imagine why a man would want to do that. Almost all the people she knew had too many children as it was. It was hard enough trying to feed the brats they had with their own wives, let alone the kids of someone they didn't know. But when she'd asked Hester why a man would do that, Hester had gotten real cranky and said that all Jessica needed to know about men was not to let one touch her until she was married and never to talk to a foreigner in a railway station.

As Jessica had never been in a railway station and couldn't remember if she'd ever met a foreigner she'd felt pretty safe from this particular version of rape. When she told Joe what Hester had said and asked him was it true, he'd grunted, plainly embarrassed, then, after a while he'd cleared his throat and replied, 'Yer mother's right, girlie, most men are animals, not just foreigners.' She supposed Joe had to say that because he'd once been a foreigner himself.

Now, at the age of eighteen, Jessica hasn't acquired a lot more knowledge about rape. If men are animals, like Joe says, then they must do it like animals. This thought has preoccupied her greatly. She wonders how a man could rape her if she refuses to go down on all fours in front of him? He'd have to threaten to kill her and she'd have to do it to save her own life. That's what she'll say Billy did, threatened to kill her. He'd be dead and with him being mad and a murderer, there'd be nobody wouldn't take her word for it.

Still and all, she's read about a woman in Sydney who'd been surprised in her bed by a man who'd come through her window one night. She'd kept a knife under her pillow and she'd stabbed him to death in the act of raping her. Jessica has often puzzled about how the woman could stab him with her being on all fours with him behind her and her with her back to him and her hands and knees planted on the mattress. She's concluded that the woman must have done it afterwards. The paper didn't say, just said she'd stabbed him with a kitchen knife.

Jessica now realises that she can't say Billy threatened to rape her. Because it will mean Billy has made her go down on all fours and done *it* to her before she killed him, like the woman in Sydney must have done. Otherwise how can she prove he tried to rape her?

The judge let the woman in Sydney off, but the newspaper didn't say if she'd had the dead man's baby. Jessica doesn't want people thinking she is going to have Billy Simple's baby. That Billy actually did it to her. It would shame Joe something terrible and Hester and Meg could never live such a thing down. Even when she doesn't have the child because nothing happened, people will always say that she *could* have, that he'd done it to her rape or not. They'll point to her and whisper to each other that she'd been raped by a madman and they'll giggle and repeat the thing Billy always said about his gift from Jesus. They'll think, she's had his big thing inside of her. The shame of it might even prevent Meg marrying Jack Thomas, which will cause Hester to banish Jessica to purgatory for a lifetime or even longer. Jessica decides then and there that she definitely can't make rape her reason for killing Billy.

In fact, Jessica knows now that she can't kill Billy Simple in cold blood, come what may. She looks over to where he sits with his back against the boree tree. He's finished his tucker and now holds the empty mug on his lap, as he lies fast asleep with his chin tucked into his shoulder.

He'd never even know if I put a bullet between his eyes, she thinks for the last time. Jessica grins sadly to herself. He is so bloody ugly, but she knows instinctively that he won't harm her, and that he's her responsibility. The poor bugger must have copped so much from those Thomas women over the years to do what he's done.

Jessica has no doubt that Billy will be hanged for what he's done. But it must be done by the law, done fairly and respectable and not by a drunken lynch mob. The least Billy has coming to him after his miserable life is a fair trial. There is terror enough in that, but it isn't as bad as being strung up out here in the bush. Someone ought to speak up on his behalf, say what the Thomas women did to him. It won't help, but at least people will know the murders weren't done in cold blood. They'd know he was provoked real bad. Jessica remembers how fair Billy had been when he dealt with the tar boys the day all this started, four years ago. It's only right that he's treated with some kindness in return, though she knows that before the night is out she may still witness him hanging from the branch of a gum tree or see his big, clumsy body riddled with bullets. Jessica feels the tears starting to well up.

She'd once heard tell of how Ben Hall was gunned down, bullets smashing into him. A terrible picture passes through her mind, it is of Billy lying helpless on the ground looking up at her, his eyes confused. Then of men rushing over to fire point-blank into him, the way they did with Ben Hall, emptying their magazines into him, so they could later claim they'd personally shot him.

Poor bastard can't even make a run for it with that leg of his, she thinks, he'd just stand there facing them. He'd be whimpering, confused, not knowing what was going on, looking over at her, thinking she'd let him down, then looking at them, until the first volley of bullets knocked him down, his chest pumping blood into the warm dust.

The sun goes down quickly out here in the southwest, sinking below the flat horizon like a coin slotting into a money box. Nor does it take the moon long to rise in the eastern sky. By the time they have to move on, a moon two days short of being full is up and the track's easy enough to follow in the moonlight. There's been no sign of the mob, no sound of hooves, and Jessica lets herself hope that they haven't crossed the river tonight.

She can barely think straight, she's so bone-tired. Billy is drifting off to sleep beside her, moaning every once in a while. His injured leg stretched out in front of him is clearly giving him pain.

Jessica inspected it before they'd left their last camp. The horsehair stitches still hold and the wound looks clean enough, though Billy's leg is badly swollen and he'd winced when she'd dabbed fresh iodine over the area of the stitches, even though she'd applied it very gently. She's left the original bandage off to give him some relief. The leg has stiffened and Billy is having great difficulty bending his knee, so she's cut two stout black box saplings the length of his leg and used them as splints, tying one on either side of his damaged leg so that the splints rest on the rail of the sulky's footrest and Billy's leg is stretched rigid out over Napoleon's rump. Under the prevailing circumstances it is the best she can think to do to make the poor bugger feel a mite more comfortable.

The pony seems fresh enough as they continue their journey, and the heat has gone from the air, so Jessica wraps Billy in a blanket and throws one over her own shoulders as well. The surrounding countryside is now ghosted in moonlight, and the only other sounds besides the jangle of Napoleon's harness and the rattle of wheels are the occasional hoot of an owl or the cry of a night-jar. Billy has long since stopped imitating their cries. The further they travel tonight the more confident Jessica grows that the men have not crossed the river.

It is almost midnight when they finally stop for the night. The river, which has been at some distance from them since crossing the punt, has taken a wide loop of several miles and is now only a hundred yards or so from the track. With water for the pony available, Jessica decides here's a good spot to camp for the remainder of the night.

They move to a clump of cypress pines growing from sand dunes near the river, which Joe says are the last traces of what was once a great inland sea. The softer sand makes a good bed for their blankets and is an unstable environment for a snake to make its hole.

Jessica has a lot of trouble getting Billy down from the sulky. And again, once on the ground he finds it impossible to move on his own, so that he has to put his arm about her shoulders to move a few steps. He then holds onto the trunk of a cypress pine while she spreads his blanket for him. He collapses gratefully down on it with his back propped against the trunk of the tree.

'Sorry, Billy, I'm too tired to make you something to eat or even make a brew. Tell you what, how would you like a smoke?' Jessica reaches into her pinny pocket for the makings she took from Joe's bedside and rolls Billy a cigarette. She licks the sticky edge of the cigarette paper and hands him the slim tube of tobacco. Billy brings it to his lips and Jessica lights it for him and goes about the business of setting up for the night.

She unharnesses the pony and lowers the sulky shafts to the ground. Then she reaches for the Winchester and slings it over her left shoulder together with the water bag. A rifle isn't ideal if she should come upon a snake, but she tells herself it's better than nothing, though Joe would disagree. 'If you ain't got a shotgun use a stick or an axe, girlie. You got Buckley's of making a head shot with a rifle, even if it's a repeater.' But Jessica hasn't got a stick and thinks about going back for the axe, but decides bugger it, she's too tired to bother. She keeps a sharp eye out in the bright moonlight, though, as she leads Napoleon down to the river to drink.

On her return she finds that Billy has finished his smoko. His eyes are closed and his lips are moving, and in his hands are his rosary beads, which he pushes along the string awkwardly as he mumbles his prayers. Jessica swallows the lump in her throat as she wonders how it's all going to end for Billy Simple.

She lets the pony have his nosebag of oats and hobbles him for the night. She pours a mug of water for Billy, then refills the water bag and hangs it from its place at the rear of the sulky so that the condensation through the canvas will cool it overnight. Finally she ties the tucker basket to the highest branch she can reach on a cypress pine in case a fox or a dingo comes sniffing around the camp while they're asleep and jumps up onto the sulky to steal what's left of the bacon.

Jessica brings the mug over to Billy, along with their blankets for the night. 'Here, Billy, drink some water,' she commands, interrupting his prayers. Billy opens his eyes as though startled to see her, then he takes the tin mug and drinks greedily, water spilling from the sides of his mouth and running down his chin and neck. Finally he hands the mug back to her.

Jessica sits down beside Billy and wraps the blanket about him. 'Good night, Billy, sleep tight,' she says to him, touching him lightly on the cheek with her free hand and then settling herself under the other blanket, the Winchester next to her on the ground.

Billy's eyes fill suddenly with tears at her touch and he begins to sob quietly, the rosary beads resting in his lap. Jessica wonders to herself how long it's been since someone has wished Billy Simple goodnight. 'You're a good boy, Billy,' she says quietly and, bending, kisses him lightly on the cheek.

Billy looks up at her from under his hat. He sniffs
and then says in a sob, 'Billy *not* a good boy! Billy bad
boy, Jessie. You shoot him tonight, eh!'

Jessica is horrified at this, and her heart goes out to
him. She puts a protective arm around him and Billy
moves close to her – it's probably the first comfort he's
known in years. 'You're all right, Billy,' she says softly
as they lie there in the moonlight by the cypress pines.

'Jessie look after Billy?' he asks, gazing up at her.

'Yes, Billy,' Jessica replies, a lump in her throat.

'Thank you, Jessie,' he croaks, and snuggles against
her.

'Go to sleep now, Billy.' She points to the rosary
beads on his lap. 'You ask God to keep us both safe.'

The sky is the colour of old pewter when she wakes and
Jessica knows at once that it's less than an hour before
sunrise. She rises from her blanket, wiping off the grit
that's blown over her shirt and moleskins during the
night. Stiff and sore from all yesterday's efforts, she walks
slowly over to untie Napoleon and leads him to the river
for a drink. Then she tethers him to a shrub while she
washes her face and arms. She's annoyed with herself for
over-sleeping – they should have been well on their way
at least two hours before sunrise.

On her return she fills Napoleon's nosebag with fresh
oats. With the pony now rested, watered and fed, Jessica
will try to make the remaining four hours of their journey to Narrandera without stopping. She quickly gathers
the few sticks she can find and builds a fire for breakfast.

Then she chops what remains of the bacon into the skillet and waits for the rind fat to grease the pan before breaking eight eggs over it, which she scrambles together. The billy goes on the embers to boil while she hurriedly eats a small portion of the eggs straight from the pan. Jessica adds the last of the bread to the eggs and bacon and she carries the pan over to Billy, then shakes him awake. Placing Billy's breakfast beside him, she helps him to prop himself up against the cypress pine. 'Eat your breakfast, Billy, we've got to get movin'. I'll bring you a cuppa in a shake.'

'Billy gotta piss,' he moans, knuckling the sleep from his eyes. The cuts on the back of his arms where the dogs have bitten him look nasty.

'Can't you do it sitting down? No, I suppose not,' Jessica says, impatient to get under way. 'C'mon, lemme help you up. Don't worry, I'll turn me back.'

Eventually she gets him to his feet and goes over to make the tea, conscious of the loud plopping noise as Billy's hot piss hits the dry dust at his feet. She steals a look at his broad back – the poor lad looks like any normal, healthy bloke from this angle – then she turns back to the tea until the noise has stopped.

'Ready, Jessie,' Billy calls.

With her mug of tea in her hand, Jessica moves over to help him. As she draws closer Billy half turns, calling out, 'All done!' like a small child, and Jessica finds herself staring directly at his gift from Jesus, which hangs, drooping from his open fly, a good eight inches down his trouser leg.

Jessica gasps in surprise then says sharply, 'Put it away, Billy! Put it away at once!'

Billy, alarmed at her unexpected anger, takes a step backwards and with his leg in splints loses his balance and falls sprawling onto his back, his large member plopping against his moleskins.

Jessica, still holding the mug of hot tea, points down in the direction of his open fly, though with her head now averted.

Billy looks confused, then realises what she means and, still on his back, he fumbles desperately, clumsily buttoning himself up.

'All done, Jessie,' he now says.

Jessica looks down warily and, seeing he has success-fully completed the task, says, 'Good boy, Billy.' She places the mug of tea down and puts one foot on either side of Billy's hips. Then, gripping both hands about his wrist, she manages to pull him up into a sitting position. She brings the skillet over to him. 'Eat your breakfast and don't take all day!' she scolds him, in an attempt to cover her embarrassment.

It's almost sunrise before they finally get away and Jessica chides herself again for sleeping in. The men will have crossed the river at dawn, delayed no more than fifteen or twenty minutes by the log she's jammed into the rope drum.

She's still got enough time to get to Narrandera, but Jessica knows that if something goes wrong on the track the mob could still reach her in time to get hold of poor Billy.

Despite the birds calling at sunrise Billy has been strangely quiet and Jessica thinks he might be sulking because of her angry outburst. Billy can't keep anything much in his mind for very long, though, and Jessica expects he'll cheer up after a while. But when he remains silent she stops the sulky so she can take a good look at him. His face is flushed and covered in sweat and he's trembling badly. She puts her hand on his forehead. He is burning up. Billy has a fever and Jessica doesn't need to be told it is probably his leg. She gently pulls up his trouser leg and looks at his calf. Somehow, perhaps when he fell onto his back, he's split the stitches in his leg and the wound is open and festering. The flesh around the stitches has turned shiny and inflamed with the infection that's now spreading up past his knee. Jessica knows Billy is in serious trouble and she must get him to the cottage hospital in Narrandera as soon as possible.

Jessica starts off again, though she knows if the pony is to last the distance she can't make him go too fast. She judges they've been going for nearly an hour and a half now, and as the sun climbs higher it grows unbearably hot. The black flies cluster around Billy's wounds and seem to grow thicker all the time. Eventually Jessica stops and cuts two small branches from a bush for them to use as fly-swats. But they don't help much, and the flies cluster on Napoleon's rump, feeding on his sweat, until it's hard to see the colour of his hide.

When they are two hours down the track, the left wheel, the one on Billy's side of the sulky, begins to wobble. Jessica feels her heart sink, and she pulls up. In all the anxiety of yesterday's events she's entirely forgotten about the faulty axle. Joe had said it'd need to be re-heated in the forge and straightened or it was likely to snap.

She climbs down and walks over to Billy's side and inspects the wheel. The axle has bent alarmingly and she can see a fracture beginning in the metal near where it enters the hub. Jessica is no smithy but she knows at once that the sulky can't make it much further along the road and that they'll be stopped well short of their destination.

It's almost more than she can bear and she begins to weep softly, leaning against the side of the sulky. Nothing is going right; she's at least ten miles from Narrandera, the mob'll be no more than three hours away now, and while she may be able to walk it, Billy can't move a yard. They've even left the scrub plains behind. It's open country here, flat as a table, mostly desert without a tree or a blade of grass to be seen, only an occasional ball of tumbleweed breaking the remorseless flat land.

Out here there is nowhere she can hide Billy and go on foot for help. By the time she returned he'd be a bullet-torn carcass left on the side of the road for carrion or brought into town slung across the back of a horse, like a slaughtered beast.

Joe once told her that after the bushranger Dan Morgan killed six men the government brought in what was known as the Felon's Apprehension Act, whereby anyone could shoot a known felon on sight and, furthermore, if you were found helping such a person to escape you were liable to receive a fifteen-year jail sentence.

Even though it was fifty years ago, Jessica reckons it could still apply to her helping Billy Simple. Joe says they never change laws that are against the poor. Billy is now a known felon all right, having just murdered Ada Thomas and the two girls. You don't get more known than that, do you? Jessica asks herself darkly. What's more, if they come upon them on the track, she can't prove she's taking him to the police magistrate. It's her word against theirs. They're free to shoot Billy down on the spot and they'll soon realise that she isn't his hostage, that she's obviously helping him, so they'll arrest her as well. Fifteen years in the clink and no chance to prove she's innocent.

Joe had gone on to tell her how after they'd shot Morgan they'd severed his head to be given to the scientists in Sydney, his beard was skinned like a possum and tobacco pouches were made from the skin of his penis and scrotum. Even worse than that, afterwards they'd put his headless body on public display outside the town lock-up, where townsfolk queued to be photographed standing beside his decomposing corpse. Panicking now, and working herself into hysterics, Jessica sees all of this happening to poor Billy Simple, with his gift from Jesus being cut off and put on the train to Sydney addressed to the scientists with a note, 'Biggest ever seen in the Riverina'.

'Jessie?' she hears Billy call fitfully from the sulky directly above her, 'Whassa matter?'

'Axle's broke, Billy, we're beat, mate,' Jessica sobs and then grows suddenly furious and takes a kick at the wheel. 'Bastard!' she yells.

Billy is silent for a bit, then he speaks quietly, 'Billy sick, Jessie, you shoot him now, eh?' Jessica looks up to see Billy is still shaking and burning up with the fever.

'We're gunna get you to the doctor, Billy. Remember? We're goin' to the hospital in Narrandera where they fixed your head up good.'

'But Billy no good no more, Jessie.' He points to the Winchester, his voice pitiful. 'Shoot me, Jessie.'

Jessica feels a slow anger growing inside her gut. The bastards are not going to get Billy Simple, she vows to herself. Not now, not ever, fuck 'em!

'It'll be all right, Billy,' she says, looking up at him. 'We're not beaten yet.'

The black flies hum around her head, the fierce sun beats down and Jessica climbs aboard again and sets off, determined to go as far as the cracked axle will take her.

Almost a mile down the track the axle breaks, but by then she's worked out a plan.

Jessica turns to Billy. 'Billy, you're gunna have to sit on the pony, and I'm gunna have to walk you in.'

Billy's teeth are chattering and his shirt is drenched with sweat. 'Horse hurt Billy,' he says plaintively, 'horse hurt Billy's head.'

'It's our only chance, mate. I'm bloody not givin' up now!' Jessica moves to help Billy down from the sulky and he winces and draws away from her.

'Damn you, Billy, help me!' she shouts at him.

Whimpering, Billy tries to get down from the sulky but he loses his balance and falls against Jessica. They both tumble to the ground. Billy rolls away from her, moaning and crying out with the pain.

Jessica lies still – she feels as though she's been run over by a team of horses. After a few moments she realises she hasn't broken any bones. She rises slowly to her feet, too shocked to cry. Blood runs from her cheek and she sees she's grazed her arm, but she doesn't care. Now she has only one thought in her mind, to get Billy Simple into Narrandera. Beat those bastards heading down the track. Hobbling over to Billy, she manages to get him to sit up on the side of the sulky while she unharnesses Napoleon.

'Billy, we're going to take your splint off so you can sit on the pony, you understand?'

Billy makes no reply, his head hangs between his knees and he is sniffling. But he lets Jessica untie the splints and remove them. Jessica then takes her bowie knife and cuts the leg of Joe's moleskins to the thigh so that Billy's badly swollen leg is less restrained.

The infection has spread higher up his leg and Jessica knows that if she doesn't get him into Narrandera on time he'll die of blood poisoning. She's seen it happen before, to a stockman who'd been gored by a beast and couldn't be brought in from the run in time.

'Billy, I know it's going to hurt a lot getting you onto the pony's back, but you gotta try for me.'

Jessica brings the pony around to stand beside Billy. Then she helps him onto his good foot, but he starts to blubber. 'C'mon, Billy,' she says, 'jump up, you gotta try, *please*!'

Billy makes several attempts and fails. Napoleon shifts his rump around, disturbed by all the movement, and Jessica tries to keep him still long enough to let Billy get on him. Each attempt causes him great pain so that he is now bawling like a child. 'Can't, Jessie, can't!' he sobs.

'Damn you, Billy,' Jessica screams at him, losing her patience in her anxiety. Then she takes a deep breath and tries to calm herself. 'Billy, please try, try for me, your friend Jessie. You must try, we have to get going.'

Billy makes one final attempt and this time manages to hang on long enough for Jessica to get her body under him and hold him up so he can get his good foot over the pony's back, pulling himself more or less up by the mane. Jessica thinks her back'll break but she grabs Billy's infected leg and pushes for all she's worth. Billy screams in agony but holds on and finally sits unsteadily astride the horse, weeping and whimpering, great tears splashing down his dirty cheeks.

Jessica collapses at the side of the track, panting. Then she throws up her breakfast. 'Good boy, Billy,' she finally pants, spitting in the dirt, all but spent from the effort. 'Now you hang on. Don't let go, no matter what. Don't let go, Billy!' She is bent over with her hands on her knees, gasping as she tries to regain her breath.

Billy looks down blearily and starts to hiccup, then suddenly he vomits over the pony's flank. His whimpering grows even louder. 'Hang on, Billy!' Jessica yells. 'Never mind that, just bloody hang on, will ya!'

She shortens the reins and, with the Winchester slung over her shoulder, Jessica sets off down the track, leading Billy on the pony. They have about ten miles to go and, by her calculations, two and a half hours to get to Narrandera before they're overtaken.

The black flies swarm around the vomit on the pony's flank and cover half Billy Simple's face where he's dribbled down his chin. Jessica sees none of this. She has set her mind on getting to Narrandera and no bastard is going to stop her now. They'll have to shoot her to make her stop. Joe always said she was too bloody stubborn for her own good.

For years folk would tell how at ten o'clock on the last Monday morning in April 1914 Joe Bergman's girl Jessica came into town leading a stock pony with a half-dead man on its back. Him lying with his arms slung around the horse's neck and his head lolling to one side with a cloud of black flies about it, like the Devil's halo.

They recalled how this slip of a girl, wearing a man's flannel shirt, moleskins and stockman's boots, walked down the centre of the dusty main street in Narrandera, staring ahead of her, ignoring the folk who'd come out into the street. Twice she'd stumbled onto her knees from exhaustion, but she just picked herself up and kept going. There was blood on her arm and face where she'd fallen somewhere out on the track.

They told how she was no more than two hundred yards from the courthouse when a mob of horsemen came galloping into town behind her. Must have been twenty or more, with rifles slung. She'd stopped and turned to face them and unslung her rifle to fire two shots over their heads, bringing them to a halt in a cloud of dust. Then she'd turned, calm as you like, and, taking up the reins, went on her way up the street, looking neither left nor right.

One of the horsemen broke from the pack and came trotting up towards her and she'd turned again with the rifle aimed straight up at him. She'd have fair dinkum shot him right out of the saddle if he'd come any further. The young bloke pulled his horse up and raised his hands in the air. 'Jessie! Jessie, it's me, Jack. Jack Thomas. Don't shoot!' he called down at her. The girl stood and stared at the young horseman, the rifle still pointed at his chest, then, without a word, she lowered the rifle and slung it, then turned back to the pony and continued leading it towards the courthouse.

The young bloke turned his horse in and rode behind the pony with his hand held up, keeping the mob of horsemen behind him at bay.

It was a sight the townsfolk would take to their graves. A lone girl with blood on her arms and face, no more to her than a hundred or so pounds, leading a stock pony with no saddle carrying a huge, lifeless-looking fellow spread across its back, his cut and bloodied arms locked about the horse's neck.

'It's the murderer!' one of the horsemen shouts to the crowd. 'Him on the pony. The Thomas women from Riverview Station, all murdered!'

The young lass has brought the murderer in all by herself. And behind the pony, young Jack Thomas, the son and brother of the murdered women, on a horse keeping back the lynch mob.

And then old man Thomas shouting and cursing his son, coming up to him on his horse. The horse pulling its head back and prancing sideways. The father red as a cockscomb, eyes almost popping out in anger.

Then the young bloke pushing the barrel of his Winchester into his father's fat gut, warning him not to interfere or he'd shoot his balls off. The rest of the mob on horseback armed to the teeth and angry as sin, wanting to get at the murderer and finish him off, do for him right then and there in the main street of Narrandera. Do what they'd come to do.

And Joe Bergman's little girlie walking on, leading the pony, not looking back, not hearing nothing, taking no notice.

By the time Jessica reaches the courthouse a fair-sized crowd has gathered. Somebody must have alerted the police magistrate, Patrick Brown, because he now stands on the courthouse steps beside a fat constable with shiny buttons on his dirty tunic, the last three undone to let his gut breathe out.

Jessica leads the pony right up to the steps, its withers a lather of sweat, nostrils blowing hard. The poor beast is about done in, its nose almost touching the ground, when she relaxes the reins. Jessica looks up at the police magistrate and wearily extends the reins to him. The surprised official takes hold of them, not quite sure what's expected of him next.

'Your Honour, I've brought Billy Simple. He's done a murder and he's hurt bad and needs a doctor.' Jessica collapses at the astonished official's feet, the Winchester clattering to the ground beside her.

Jack Thomas jumps down from his horse and rushes over to Jessica, kneeling beside her. Then he picks her up in his arms and brushes straight past the magistrate and the constable, carrying her up the steps and into the safety of the courthouse. 'Jessie, Jessie, Jessie,' he keeps saying.

BOOK TWO

CHAPTER SIX

The news of the murders is brought into Whitton by young Sam Cully, who has inherited the role of stock and station agent from his father Henry. Sam called in at Riverview on the Sunday evening, planning to spend the night in the shearers' quarters. On the Monday morning he hoped to interest George Thomas in a Shorthorn stud bull from Groongal Station, bought three years back by Mr Ralph Falkiner from a famous stud in Scotland. Sam's heard the rumour around the district that George's present bull, Trump Card, has turned out to be a bit of a joker and is firing blanks.

What Sam found at Riverview was the cook alone, returned from her visit to North Yanco and in a fearful state. Her eyes were red from weeping and upon seeing him she became quite hysterical.

She had returned to find the three Thomas women wrapped in bed linen and hanging in the meat cooler, with a note from Mr Thomas explaining what had happened and instructing her to contact Reverend Mathews at St Stephen's to prepare for their burials. Also, he had asked for someone to go to Darlington Point first thing on Monday to fetch Coffin Nail, the Italian carpenter.

All this the cook told Sam Cully in sobs and sniffs, and Sam obligingly offered to go, eager to spread the news at Whitton on the way.

Coffin Nail, a master cabinet-maker by trade, was originally brought out from Italy to do the interior panelling, fittings and staircase at the McCaughey homestead at North Yanco Station. His real name was Copernicus Di Nallo, but this proved too much of a mouthful for the locals and after he started making coffins in his spare time he quickly became known as Coffin Nail.

After he'd finished the job at North Yanco Station, Coffin Nail decided that he liked the black soil country so much, though Gawd knows why, that he took up a settler's selection, which he named Santa Sophia, after the name of his village in northern Italy. He was never short of work, and developed a nice sideline in fancy carved coffins for the squattocracy and, as Joe puts it, 'for folk what's foolish or wicked enough to take death so seriously they want to invest money in it'. Unwittingly, many a rich Protestant squatter has gone to his eternal rest with the coat of arms of the tiny Catholic village of Santa Sophia carved on the lid of his fancy Tasmanian blackwood coffin.

George Thomas has left instructions, to be given to Coffin Nail, to measure up and make three caskets of pine, and give them the full mahogany varnish so to the uninitiated they will look like expensive Tasmanian blackwood.

On the lid of each must be carved just the first name of the occupant, but at no greater cost than four shillings and sixpence per carving. This is a tender touch that George hopes will distract the mourners' attention from the cheap varnished wood. He has spelt out each name carefully in capital letters so the dago won't get it wrong: 'ADA. GWEN. WINIFRED. @ 4/6d each.'

Then he's instructed that the interior of the coffins must be lined and padded in white Chinese satin, which is three shillings a yard cheaper than silk and readily available at Heathwood's store in Narrandera. Upholstery studs and padding give the interior a prestigious appearance, of course.

As for the exterior of the caskets, these he wants fitted with fancy handles, brass for the girls, silver plate for the mistress of the house. They are to be hired only, George's offer of rent to Coffin Nail being one shilling a day for the brass and two for the silver plate, the handles to be redeemed by the gravedigger for threepence a fixture after the mourners have gone home.

Finally, Coffin Nail is to deliver the caskets to Riverview by Wednesday morning so that visitors may pay their last respects to the dear departed before they start to get on the nose, the funeral to be held the next day.

George Thomas's note sets out to make Coffin Nail aware, in no uncertain terms, that George knows his coffins, their prices and quality and every trick in the mortician's book. The I-tal-yin is in for the very devil of a tongue-lashing and can expect a damn good whipping if he attempts to overcharge the owner of Riverview by so much as a silver sixpence. George is fond of saying that it pays to be precise with bloody foreigners about money. 'Give them half a chance and they'd rob the wax from your ears and sell it back to you as altar candles!'

George Thomas got to be a bit of an expert on coffins during his riverboat days. He always carried at least four of the most fancy kind on board. These included two child's caskets, children being the most likely to suddenly depart from the mortal coil and also subject to gestures of gross sentimentality. George has long ago learned the caskets that conveyed a child to heaven could command an outrageous price on earth.

He'd also stock two basic adult caskets, as well as an assortment of expensive metal handles, locks, crucifixes and other decorations, pictures and paraphernalia, all at prices to be negotiated in the profitable context of grief. George believes that death ought to line the pockets of the living, and that those stricken by sorrow will pay good cash.

To the sorrowing husband, he would tap his knuckle against the hard wooden interior of a coffin and shake his head piously before looking his prospect in the eye. 'Life was hard enough, my friend. She bore you six children in life and never complained, surely a little comfort in death wouldn't go astray.' Then he'd produce the four padded lining boards for the interior of the coffin, white silk for purity studded with purple upholstery studs. 'Purple, the colour of Heaven's majesty,' he'd pronounce grandly, wiping an imaginary tear from his eye. If he sensed a little hesitancy in his prospect he'd point to the coffin and say, 'This is the last carriage taking the dearly departed to the Kingdom of Heaven. We don't want them angels opening the lid to bare boards and austerity now, does we?'

Ridiculous as it may sound, the analogy of coffin turned into heavenly carriage to convey the dead to glory invariably worked. Coffins made George a tidy sum over the years, the coffin lining being the most profitable element. He seldom completed a trip up and down the Murrumbidgee without selling at least one coffin to a sheep station along the river.

Corpses ripen quickly in the hot weather and shouldn't be left lying around. Even in the meat cooler with the cross-breeze from the river playing over them they won't go much beyond five days before they must be gutted and drained of a gallimaufry of fluids. This is the putrefaction, the noxious juices which roil and ferment as they prepare to burst through every available orifice, or build up and erupt in such an internal combustion as to split open the corpses' bloated guts like an overripe melon.

George Thomas can feel little true grief at the loss of his nagging wife and demanding daughters, but publicly he must be seen to pursue the killer with suitable outrage and vengeance, of course.

To George Thomas's credit, or so it seems, before setting out to hunt down Billy Simple he had attended to the bodies of his wife and daughters, carefully removing and pocketing the rings from their fingers and the chains from their necks. He swaddled their battered heads in cotton wool and bandages and then wrapped each in a damp bed sheet before winding them about with wool bale twine. He left enough of the sheet above each of their heads to make loops which he lashed with twine, so that each appeared to wear a linen topknot, to which he tied a ticket with their name. All this he did alone and asked only for the assistance of two of the assembled stockmen to help him hang his wife and two daughters by their loops onto hooks in the meat cooler, where they dangle with their feet only inches from the ground.

Joe, Hester and Meg only hear Sam Cully's news on Tuesday, the morning they are to leave Whitton for the homestead. They hear that the three Thomas women have been murdered, but they know nothing of what's happened to Jessica. As far as they're aware, Jessica doesn't even know of the killings, although Joe is worried for her safety, what with a killer on the loose, and he's keen to get back home.

Hester and Meg profess themselves shocked and manage to shed a few tears when they stop off at a shop to purchase several yards of black crepe for their funeral bonnets.

Later, on the journey home, they exclaim together about the awful calamity. Their eyes are downcast, but secretly both think it might be a lot easier to win Jack Thomas now that Ada is out of the way. Joe notices with a scowl that already there's talk of inviting Jack over for tea after a respectable period of mourning. Soon enough Hester and Meg are worrying about how long such a period might be, and debating what gown Meg should wear when Jack comes over for the first time. In the end they agree on black with two white petticoats and a small clutch of yellow roses at Meg's breast. The black dress is for sorrow, the white petticoats to show a glimmer of hope, and the yellow roses for friendship, of course, all to ensnare Jack Thomas.

Billy Simple's trial takes place in July, just eight weeks after Jessica has delivered him to the police magistrate at Narrandera. There's been good rain in the Riverina the night before, rain from a sky that's carried herringbone clouds for two days but has otherwise been dry-eyed, pale as a blister, for six months.

The dust is settled, the sky clean and blue and there is the smell of hope in the air. Joe says a spot of unexpected rain turns people stupid, makes them think things they oughtn't to, have hope they're not entitled to, make plans only an idiot would contemplate.

Jessica has been summoned, along with the cook from Riverview, to be a Crown witness at the trial.

She talks to Jack before she leaves, and asks him if he'll be going to Wagga Wagga to attend the trial. Jack hesitates then says quietly, 'Jessie, it's really hard – my father's going and, well, you know how we're not on speaking terms. He's such a big mouth, he'll be carrying on a treat to anyone and everyone who'll listen, about justice and hanging the bastard by his balls, and all that sort of thing. I'd be expected to publicly take a side against Billy.' Jack is plainly distressed as he looks at Jessica. 'I can only say this to you and no one else: what Billy did was terrible and it can *never* be forgiven

and I know he's got to hang for his crime . . .' he hesitates, searching for the right words, 'I loved my mother
and sisters, but it *was* them that finally drove Billy
mad – I know it deep down in my heart.' He shrugs,
still upset, unable to communicate his feelings properly.
'I can't help Billy now, I'm . . . I'm not sure I'd even
want to if I could, but I *can* stay away and not be a part
of the old man's gleeful public vengeance.'

Jessica and Joe, who is attending the trial as her chap-
erone, are given two second-class tickets on the train to
Wagga Wagga by the Department of Justice. As well as
accommodation, all found, at Mrs Ma Shannon's
boarding house close to the courthouse. They also
receive a further stipend of eight shillings a day to compensate them for being away from work. This is as
much as Jessica and Joe can earn together working an
eight hour and forty minute shift as shearer and rouseabout in a woolshed, the longest they can work
according to the Shearers' Union.

At first Joe objects. 'I don't take money for sittin' on
me bum,' he tells the clerk of the court.

'Why ever not?' the surprised official asks. 'The
judge does!'

'Dunno about that, it's important work, the court
an' all,' Joe mumbles.

'Well, what about the prime minister? He sits on his
bum all day.'

Joe grins. 'I starts to see your point, sir,' he replies.
'Jessica and me will practise doing bugger-all, hard as
we can.'

But Jessica hasn't been doing nothing – she's found herself frequently in the witness box, where the more she answers the Crown prosecutor's questions the worse it looks for poor Billy Simple. Billy has proved to be too traumatised and confused to speak for himself, and simply cries and sighs when put into the box, so that it is soon decided to refrain from attempting to question him. He is unable to utter a sentence in his own defence, and sits mumbling to himself in the dock.

The Crown prosecutor has mounted a strong case against Billy, and he plays on the sensibilities of the jurors with all the morbid details of the killings.

The time of death has been clearly established as early Saturday evening. The beds were still made up, a pot of burnt stew rested on the wood stove and on the marble sink beside it were six skinned potatoes floating in an enamel dish of water.

It was known furthermore that Billy Simple used to water the vegetable garden in the cool of the evening, and a half-empty watering can was found resting beside a bed of beetroot with Billy's hat lying abandoned on the path a few feet from it.

The bodies of the three Thomas women were found in different parts of the garden where Billy Simple had taken to them with a mattock.

Ada had been struck to the side of her neck, the mattock severing her spine and cutting her throat at the same time. Her head remained connected to her shoulders by a small bridge of muscle.

The girls, who must have attempted to escape, were

each discovered separately. They had been struck by almost identical blows to the back of the head, which split open their skulls. Like their mother, they appeared to have died instantly.

Other than these singular blows and the dark stains of ant-infested blood that seeped into the gritty soil, there was no sign of any further mutilation. Billy Simple killed the three women quickly and cleanly, a fact the Crown prosecutor makes much of in his case, which will count greatly against Billy.

Laying down all the gruesome facts before the jury, the Crown prosecutor, confident to the point of arrogance, then sums up his case against the accused.

'Members of the jury, if the killer were a madman, driven to despair by the three women as has been suggested, he surely would not stop with one blow,' he points out. 'He would be furious, enraged, he would set out to vent his frustration on his hapless victims by mutilating them again and again.' Then in a low voice he adds, 'You must ask yourselves: are we dealing here with a simple-minded man driven to despair and well beyond his mental capacity to think rationally, or is the accused a vengeful killer capable of three vicious and premeditated murders?' He pauses meaningfully before continuing.

'You will recall the witness for the Crown, Miss . . . er . . . Jessica Bergman, how she described to you the killing of the three dogs on her father's property. Was this not another appalling example of a ruthless and efficient killer at work? The dogs were killed with the same lack of emotion as the accused displayed when he ended the lives of his three human victims. The incisive and cold-blooded nature of all of the killings should be given very careful and urgent consideration. You will decide whether you are dealing here with misadventure brought about by a confused and insane mind driven beyond its feeble endurance or with three *deliberate and calculated homicides*. These are the requirements of the law and of justice, are they not?' He pauses again and then raises his voice.

'I believe we have proved beyond reasonable doubt that William D'arcy Simon, better known as Billy Simple, is guilty of murder. Murder without mercy. Cold-blooded and premeditated murder.' The prosecutor's voice rises and he enunciates each of his final words slowly. 'These murders were premeditated and executed in cold blood with almost surgical precision by an unfeeling and callous killer and it is up to you, members of the jury, to decide on this and to give this killer the punishment he deserves.' Then quietly he adds, 'I thank you for your patience, and I rest the case for the prosecution.'

It is masterfully done. At the moment of his conclusion Jessica can see a burning conviction of Billy's guilt in the eyes of every jury member. The Crown prosecutor's words have hanged Billy Simple as effectively as if all twelve jurymen had personally been present at Riverview and looked on as he killed the three Thomas women.

Jessica looks at Billy, who sits slumped in the dock, his scarred head hidden in his hands because he can't wear his hat. He whimpers constantly, a small boy lost among strangers, and Jessica glares at his lawyer, who has not lifted a finger since the trial began.

Richard Runche KC works the circuit courts where King's Counsels are thin on the ground. He depends for his briefs on local solicitors who, in a mutual back-scratching exercise, are themselves appointed by the court. It is an arrangement happily tolerated by the bench.

Runche is an Englishman educated at Cambridge, said to be the prodigal son of an aristocratic family in Hampshire, sent to the colonies with a generous allowance to avoid them any possible embarrassment. His mild manners coupled with his wild intemperance make him a favourite of the circuit judges. He is good company in the evenings and gives them few problems during the day.

He is always the first chosen when the presence of a KC for the defence is required by legal procedure for what is thought to be an open and shut case. Richard Runche's alarming ineptitude has the capacity to conclude a trial several days early, a notion much approved of by a busy and harassed circuit judge. His very appearance for the accused has come to signal a verdict of guilty, and to everyone's mind he's the obvious choice to defend Billy Simple.

Runche's reputation has earned him a couple of colourful nicknames from the local wags. Some say that KC stands for King Claret, while others dream up a nice bit of rhyming slang and Richard Runche becomes Liquid Lunch.

Never was a more suitable name given to a member of the New South Wales Bar. For while he makes some small sense after breakfast, where he restricts himself to two large brandies taken in a tumbler of warm milk, he makes none whatsoever after lunch, when his preferred tipple has consisted of two bottles of a raw-boned claret which contains enough tannin to cure the hide of a Shorthorn bull.

During the trial Jessica has watched while Richard Runche KC has one or two feeble attempts each morning to make a case for the accused. He is seldom stirred to do so in the afternoon, when he frequently nods off with the silent approval of the judge.

Even to someone as naive as Jessica, Billy's trial is proving to be a travesty of justice. She is not allowed to tell the whole sad story of Billy's life, or how the three Thomas women tortured and tormented him for years. After three days of frequent visits to the stand, she hasn't on one single occasion been cross-examined by the defence. Jessica is becoming more and more agitated as she watches Mr Richard Runche snore away Billy's mortal life. And so Jessica goes to Joe for help. After all, Joe was once in Billy's shoes, on a murder charge, and the jury set him free.

'You gotta get Billy's barrister to tell his side of the story,' Joe tells her. 'You can be bloody sure yer not gunna hear it from the Crown prosecutor.' Joe shakes his head. 'But I don't fancy yer chances, girlie.'

'How can I do that?' Jessica cries. 'How can I get the silly old bugger to speak up for Billy? He's pissed all the time!'

Joe shrugs. 'You been through enough, girlie. Let go

206 BRYCE COURTENAY

of it, eh? No good goin' on – Billy ain't gunna get off. He did the murders all right, he'll have to cop it sweet.'

'But it's not fair!' Jessica protests. 'Nobody's telling his side. They tried to get him to answer questions, but he doesn't understand, he can't talk for himself. It wasn't no cold-blooded murder like they're saying!'

'Murders. It were more than one, girlie,' Joe reminds her. 'Listen to me. Billy ain't got a bloody side. The judge ain't gunna waste time pickin' through the details just for the flamin' record. What d'ya expect him to do? He's got three women from the richest family round these parts been murdered by a bloody halfwit! Now you want him to look for mitigating circumstances? Grow up, will yiz? Who gives a shit about Billy's side?' Joe looks at her and she can see he's wild at her. 'And it don't look too good neither, you jumping to his defence. Don't look good for yer mother and Meg.' Joe pauses, staring at his boots, and mutters, 'Me neither. I got a job to worry about. So've you.'

Jessica spends a sleepless night thinking about Billy. Joe is right. Joe is wrong. Fair's fair. Who cares, anyway? What can she do? She's a nobody. The lawyers know what they're doing. Billy is going to hang no matter what. Hester and Meg'd be furious if she made a fuss. Joe is real pissed off with her. He is her father after all, she should obey his wishes. But what will Jack Thomas think if she doesn't put up a fight? Jack, who'd carried her up the courthouse steps at Narrandera, whose face, wet with tears, was the first she saw when she came to, who stayed with her for two days when the doctor put her in the hospital. They say war is only a matter of weeks off being declared. Joe says people will want normal things tidied away. They'll want to get on with killing the Germans.

Jessica thinks she must have dozed off eventually, for she wakes at about six o'clock the next morning, feeling exhausted and sick in the stomach. She's forced to run outside to the dunny, where she throws up violently for nearly half an hour. She's weak from bringing up all Mrs Shannon's mutton stew and is feeling wretched, but she's made up her mind and she's quite decided what she must do.

At half past seven she enters the Albion Hotel, where the drunken lawyer is staying. Nervously she asks the young desk clerk if she may see Mr Richard Runche KC. The clerk seems very young, with not a hair on his chin, and Jessica takes courage at this.

'I'm sorry, Mr Runche don't entertain guests to breakfast,' the clerk replies curtly, taking a good long squiz at her.

Jessica knows none of Meg's cunning ways but she tries to smile at the young man and look helpless, hiding her anger and impatience. 'It's a matter of great urgency, sir,' she says, her large green eyes appealing to him for help. Jessica is wearing a light blue dress, one of three good frocks belonging to Meg which Hester says she must wear to court so the judge knows she comes from decent folk. She's washed and brushed her short blonde hair and she supposes she looks about as pretty as she ever will.

The young clerk nibbles at the end of the pen, and she can see he's trying to decide whether he has the authority to help her.

'Please, sir?' Jessica begs again, tilting her head slightly to one side and pouting her lips the way she's watched Meg do in the company of young blokes. What surprises her is how naturally it all comes – her duplicity requires no effort on her part.

'Hey, aren't you the one, you know, what brought the murderer in on the horse?' he asks suddenly.

Jessica nods, then drops her eyes modestly, deliberately averting her gaze.

'That was very brave,' the young clerk says, frowning down at the ledger, and Jessica notices that while he now holds the pen poised over the ledger, there is no ink-pot anywhere to be seen and the nib is brand new and bone dry. She knows nothing about hotels but she's been around a few young stockmen and ringers in her time and she reckons she's just about got the measure of this bloke.

'Thank you, but I'm sure a big strong bloke like you would have done the same.' She pauses and smiles again, and the reedy young man blushes profusely and looks down at the ledger again.

'I don't think so,' he mumbles, but she can see he's dead pleased.

'No, I mean it,' Jessica lies. 'You can always tell when a bloke's got guts, isn't afraid to do something. It shows in his eyes,' she pauses, 'a sort of faraway, squinty look.' Joe would have said 'when a young bloke's got balls', but she knew she couldn't get away with saying it without him shying at her words.

The young clerk – though Jessica was beginning to seriously doubt this was his true vocation, for he was now nervously cleaning his nails with the nib of the pen – answered shyly, 'It were a brave thing to do, him killing them three women an' all.'

Jessica knows she's won. 'I need to see Mr Runche at once. It's about the murderer. Things he has to know,' she adds darkly.

Just then an older man walks in through a door directly behind the young desk clerk, his beetle-black hair parted down the centre and pasted down on either side of his head, shiny as a sergeant-major's toe-cap. He is short, narrow about the shoulders and hips, and with a head too big for his torso. To complement his hair he sports a black moustache tweaked a good two inches at each end and curved upwards towards his ears, giving him what Jessica supposes is meant to be a fierce look. Looking closely, she sees that he has a soft and slightly dainty manner about him, not in the least frightening. He walks on his toes with his bum tucked in and his chin held high, as though denying his nose the right to smell things.

'That will do, Jimmy Jenkins. Back to your work, chop chop!' he says, clapping his hands twice then holding one hand out for the pen. 'We haven't got all day here, my lad. The banister brass has dirty great fingerprints all over it and the front steps must be swept before the morning train comes in from Sydney. Hurry, hurry, we'll have no idle hands, if you please!'

Once he hands back the pen to the older man, Jimmy Jenkins loses his authority and is suddenly transformed from desk clerk back to hotel rouseabout. He grins sheepishly at Jessica. 'Yes, Mr Snibbs,' he says meekly, lifting the counter bar and stepping to Jessica's side of the foyer.

'And who's this?' the man asks, looking at Jessica with one eyebrow slightly arched.

'She's an old friend, Mr Snibbs,' Jimmy says quickly, 'come to visit me.'

'Cat brought her in from the bush, eh?' Snibbs quips. Then, feigning no further interest, he turns to the ledger, his pen running across the scribbled lines as though searching for some important piece of information.

You'll keep, mate, Jessica thinks. The bastard wouldn't have said that if Joe had been with her.

'Come, miss,' Jimmy Jenkins whispers out of the corner of his mouth.

Jessica follows Jimmy across a square of black and white marble tiles towards the entrance of the dining room. 'Brasses, Jimmy! Brasses, my boy!' Snibbs calls after him.

'Yes, Mr Snibbs, right away, no problems!' Jimmy calls back, touching his finger to the side of his head. Then in a voice meant only for Jessica, he says, 'Bloody old nancy boy', but Jessica has no idea what it means.

Jimmy Jenkins leads her past several of the breakfasting guests and over to the lawyer's table, which is situated in the darkest corner of the large room, behind a magnificent stand of aspidistra and a second, almost as impressive, of cascading fish fern. It is a setting concealed from all the other tables and in the natural gloom created in part by the plants it appears almost like a dark corner of an overgrown garden.

'It is a propinquity,' Richard Runche KC later explains to Jessica, 'that has been created for one by a sympathetic and very decent hotel management. They have thought it most conducive to the amelioration of a severe hangover.' He sighs, wiping his brow with his napkin. 'My dear, I don't know how I should possibly manage without such kind and dear friends.'

Jimmy later tells Jessica, though, that the management's kindness is strictly confined to the till in the club lounge. Richard Runche KC, alias Liquid Lunch, is worth four times the bar takings of any other regular guest and is, to boot, an excellent drunk who always staggers outside to throw up. 'You can't ask no more from a guest than that, now can yiz?' Jimmy whispers proudly to Jessica.

Jessica has never been in a room as large or a public place as grand and she feels more than a little intimidated by the clatter of cutlery, clink of porcelain plates and the rattle of teacups, not to mention all the finely dressed folk around her.

The table occupied by Billy's barrister possesses only one chair. Jessica is not for one moment expecting to be asked to sit down, but there's hardly enough room for her to stand, and she can feel the leaves of the aspidistra pressing into her back. There is certainly no place for Jimmy Jenkins, who is forced to peer through the fish fern, where his face, draped in fronds, looks like that of a monkey in a forest.

It's indicative of Mr Richard Runche's severe hangover that he completely fails to recognise Jessica, even though she has appeared in the witness box, sometimes for extended periods, on six occasions over the past three days.

He squints at her through rheumy eyes, cupping his hand to the edge of his brow to dissuade any ray of light that might think to intrude. Before he can bring himself to speak, Jimmy makes the necessary introductions from the fernery. 'Sir, I have the honour ter introduce . . .' He looks up at Jessica in a panic, having forgotten to ask her name.

'Miss Jessica Bergman,' she answers, smiling down at the lawyer.

'Miss Jessica Bergman, may I introduce yiz to Mr Richard Runche KC, a gennelman most famous around these parts.'

'Yes, yes, don't fuss, boy. I know quite well who I am.' Richard Runche sighs then falls silent. 'Bergman, eh?' he says at last.

'Yes, sir,' Jessica says, her mouth growing dry.

'Bergman . . . Bergman,' he says, turning the name over in his sore, fuzzy head. Then a glint of recognition shows in his bloodshot eyes. 'I say, isn't there a Bergman, young gel, appearing for the prosecution?' Before Jessica can answer he exclaims, 'Yes, by Jove, I believe it's you!' Then just as rapidly he falls into a trough of silence. His elbow rests on the table and he covers his eyes with the palm of his left hand. After a while, he looks up and mutters, shaking his head at her, 'Quite improper, quite, quite.'

'Please, sir, I *have* to see you,' Jessica pleads.

'I don't see people at breakfast, my dear.' The lawyer cups his hand to his eyes again. 'In fact, I can barely see anything. No, no, quite impossible!'

Richard Runche picks up his table napkin in both hands and wipes his thin, bloodless lips. It's intended as a gesture of dismissal, yet his hands shake so badly that Jessica is now more concerned for him than she is afraid.

The only things on the table are a glass of caramel-coloured milk, a half-empty bottle of brandy and a battered pork-pie hat. 'Quite improper!' Runche repeats weakly, glancing about nervously as if hoping someone would rescue him from this determined young woman.

A tall and angular man, who appears somehow to have sharp points to his knees and elbows, he brings to Jessica's mind an illustration she's once seen in a children's book by Washington Irving of a long-legged bird-like character named Ichabod Crane. But at this moment he looks rather frail and crumpled.

Richard Runche KC is also clean-shaven. Jessica wonders why this should be, for if he wakes up with such a bad headache every morning, why would he take the trouble to shave? Exposing the chin to a razor may be all the fashion in the city, but nothing about Mr Runche suggests that he gives a fig for fashion, and with the terrible shake in his hands, shaving would be positively dangerous to attempt.

Sure enough, Jessica now sees that he wears shaving papers stuck to several nasty cuts on his chin, which has the colour, texture and appearance of a plucked chicken's arse.

Nurtured by alcohol, Runche's once-thin nose has long since blossomed and widened and in the process turned a deep rose colour. It is heavily tinctured by a network of scarlet and purple veins knitting its bulbous surface together, as if they alone keep his unnatural-looking proboscis firmly attached to his gaunt and unhappy face.

His salt and pepper eyebrows are thick and scraggly, giving his face its only feature of authority. What remains of his hair seems to have been roughly parted by hand while still wet and lies pasted across his balding skull.

The remainder of Richard Runche KC, is scarcely more prepossessing. He wears a crumpled black linen jacket with a grey worsted waistcoat across which loops a cheap silver fob chain. His soiled white shirt sports a grubby celluloid collar, with the head of a gold stud showing clearly above the greasy knot of a thin black necktie shiny with over-use and frayed at the edges.

Jessica looks down at the dishevelled lawyer and feels only pity, not fear. She is here to fight for her friend and Jack's, Billy Simple. She takes a deep breath and says, 'Sir, if you send me away you will take my pride from me and I shall never again have respect for the law.'

'Pride? Whose pride? What pride? The sort that cometh before a fall, I dare say! I sense it in you, my dear. As for the law? Respect for the law? What non-sense! The law respects only two things – property and money. It will defend both at the cost of truth and justice! Rubbish and codswallop to the law!'

'But . . . but you said just now, about me being quite improper, I mean with the law an' all?'

'The law? No, no, not the law, be blowed to the law. Quite improper to me, I meant, to disturb a gentleman at breakfast. Worse than waylaying him in his bed-chamber!'

This outburst was more than Richard Runche has said in three days in court and he appears exhausted by the effort.

Jessica can feel her temper rising. 'Sir, I'm sorry for interrupting you, but somebody has to take Billy Simple's side. He done wrong and I know he must be punished, that he's gunna be hanged.' Jessica looks appealingly at the lawyer, who, reluctantly, appears to be listening. 'Billy done the killings, but it wasn't like they said in court, it wasn't in cold blood. There was other things not told. Things that only you can tell.' Now Jessica can't hold back her sobs. 'And you ain't! You bloody ain't gunna!'

Runche covers his face with both hands. 'Please, please, I can't abide tears,' he says in a pained voice.

'I'm sorry, sir,' Jessica sobs, struggling to stop her tears. 'But it just ain't right.'

Runche slowly wipes his hands downwards away from his face, and stares at his open palms. 'No, my dear, it is I who must apologise,' he says at last, turning his bloodshot eyes to her.

Jessica looks at him, startled. 'What do you mean, sir?' she stammers.

The lawyer ignores her question and continues. 'I must apologise, for I had forgotten that some people still want the truth for its own sake. Justice, not as vindication, or as revenge, or as material compensation, but as an idea in itself. Isn't that what you're saying, my dear?'

'Billy's got rights too!' Jessica says doggedly, not sure what the lawyer's on about but determined to keep fighting.

'Justice for no other reason than that the scales may be seen to be evenly balanced.' He reaches over for the glass of brandy and milk and, gripping it in both hands, he brings it to his lips and swallows the contents, not pausing until the glass is empty.

The brandy and milk seems to improve his spirits remarkably, and he gestures in Jessica's direction, indicating an invisible chair. 'Do join me, my dear. Would you like a cup of tea? Yes, yes, of course you would. Have you partaken of breakfast?' When he realises no second chair exists, he looks about him and his bemused gaze alights on Jimmy Jenkins, still peeping through the fernery. 'Who the devil are you? Where did you come from? Good God, where are your manners, boy? Fetch this young lady a chair at once,' he demands, waving the boy away with a flick of his hand.

Jimmy brings a chair and shortly afterwards a waiter arrives with a pot of tea. With all the anxieties of the morning, Jessica feels none too well and the weak black tea seems to calm her stomach a little as she tells Richard

Runche all she knows of Billy's earlier life, the years of ridicule and humiliation he suffered at the hands of the three Thomas women.

Runche listens all the while, taking regular sips from his second glass of brandy and milk. When at last she completes her story, he reaches over and pats her hand.

'My dear, I am most grateful to you. When the court commences this morning I shall ask the judge's permission to put you on the stand for cross-examination before I address the jury with my summing-up. His Honour is a very decent chap and I feel sure he'll agree with my opinion, though I'll warrant not without considerable surprise. It has been some time since I have behaved like a barrister, after all!'

Richard Runche is as good as his word and requests the opportunity to cross-examine Miss Jessica Bergman.

The judge is astonished. 'It is highly irregular, Counsel, the prosecution has already completed its summation.'

'Yes, Your Honour, I am aware that it is against precedent and I ask that the prosecution agrees to it on this occasion. Belated, though important, information has been given to me. My request is made in the furtherance of justice.'

'I shall call a ten-minute recess and will see both counsel in my chambers,' the judge now says.

Jessica sits alone trembling, hoping that the prosecution will allow Richard Runche KC to let her onto the stand to help Billy Simple. She stares at her lap, avoiding the hostile gazes of those around her, including George

Thomas. They agree that such a request is highly irregular, the prosecution having already made its final address to the jury.

However, both the judge and the senior counsel for the prosecution secretly hold Runche in such low regard that they feel his attempts will come to nothing. The prosecution agrees to the request without much further ado. The judge consents with the single proviso that the counsel for the defence be as brief as possible. The honourable reason for this, which he does not of course state, is that he wishes to catch the evening train to Sydney so that he can attend the Saturday races at Randwick.

Billy Simple's barrister begins a little haltingly at first, but is soon enough into his stride. In the next hour he shows surprising skill at cross-examination. He is patient and always kind to Jessica without wasting time. Slowly the harsh truth about the Thomas women begins to emerge.

At first Jessica's knees tremble, but under the barrister's gentle questioning she soon grows more confident. The jury hears how Billy was once a gun shearer respected as a young man for his common sense. She tells how he'd gone to her protection and how the accident with the horses had occurred during the fight with the tar boys. Jessica then tells of how, when Jack wasn't around to protect him, the Thomas women would persecute Billy, making him repeat meaningless tasks, running him ragged. She explains how he was made to move a pile of rocks from one place to another endlessly, until there was no skin left on the palms of his hands and he finally

dropped, exhausted, sobbing and helpless, in the dirt.
How Mrs Thomas had tried to make Billy use the shotgun on the starving Aborigines, which Billy knew was
wrong in the eyes of God and so had run away, to be
severely punished later.

At the end of an hour the judge has on three separate
occasions been forced to silence the court as the public
gallery becomes more and more excited by Billy Simple's
story which Jessica recounts. They soon sense that the
truth, hidden from them until now, is being told. Richard
Runche also calls the cook at Riverview to testify and,
being an honest woman, she answers his questions as
best she may. Her answers do nothing but corroborate
Jessica's own story.

After the cross-examination has been completed and
amid the obvious fury of the prosecutor and George
Thomas beside him, the judge calls for a short recess
before allowing Richard Runche to make his final address
to the jury.

In his summing-up, Runche concentrates on the prosecution's insistence that Billy killed the women in cold
blood. He points out that there is no question of Billy's
guilt – that he has already confessed to the crime. What
is to be questioned is the reason for the crime in the first
place, the nature of the killing method and the state of
mind of the accused when it took place. Jessica gave him
some important facts this morning and now, inspired by
his young witness, Runche lays them before the court.

'Let me begin with a hat,' he announces to the members of the jury. He reaches out and picks up his hat,

holding it up to their view. 'A hat not too different from this one. Not a very prepossessing item, would you say, eh?' The jury smiles as they look at the battered and grease-stained hat. 'Yet I love it. Of all the items I possess, this is the one I am least likely to part with until it finally parts with me, by means of natural disintegration.' This brings a titter from the gallery. 'If a man does not possess the comfort of a dog in his life, as Billy Simple did not, then you may be sure his hat will become his best friend. His shelter from the sun and the rain. His decision to leave poor or bad company. His means of polite gesture to the opposite sex, his security in insecure moments.'

All this brings laughter and admiration from the gallery. The judge scowls up at them and tentatively raises his gavel before saying, 'Will you kindly come to the point, Mr Runche?'

'Certainly, Your Honour.' Billy's counsel bows his head to the bench in a gesture of apology and then returns to addressing the jury.

'Billy Simple had such a hat, not too different from this one. But he had more reason to wear a hat than any other man. He carries a painfully ugly and jagged scar across the breadth of his head.' Runche gazes up at the gallery. 'I dare say that some of you up there in the gallery will have seen this terrible deformity during this trial.'

'The defence will restrict his remarks to the jury,' the judge interrupts, increasingly annoyed that his trip to the race meeting is in jeopardy.

Runche turns again to the judge and bows. 'I apologise, Your Honour, for a moment I lost my head.' The
gallery titters at his pun. Holding up the hat again to
the jury, he says, 'But I did not lose my hat! You see,
William Simon, known to you all as Billy Simple, lost
his head on two occasions. He lost it when he killed the
three Thomas ladies, and, as you have heard tell from
my previous witness, lost it four years before that by
having his skull crushed under the hooves of a horse!'

The barrister allows the jury to dwell on this for a
moment before he continues. 'When he returned from
hospital, Billy had a jagged scar that zigzagged across
his head and down to his forehead. He had, in a very
real sense, lost his head. Lost his capacity to think. Lost
his good sense. Lost his ability to be quick and respon-
sive, like you and me.' He grins. 'Well, perhaps not like
me, certainly not after luncheon!' He allows the laughter to die down and bows in anticipation to the judge.
'He lost the capacity to be rational and judgemental
and, as a consequence, he subsequently received the
regrettably apt nickname, Billy Simple.'

Runche pauses here, pacing for a few moments. 'But
even in his saddest moments, during his most dim-
witted times, he knew that he was ashamed of the scar
he wore, he somehow perceived that it was to blame for
his misery, his being outcast. So, I ask you to think carefully, what does he do? He does what any simpleton
would do, probably what those less simple among us
would do, he covers it. He wears a hat, a broken, battered hat, and covers the deeply offensive scar by pulling

his hat down almost to his eyes.' With this the barrister jams his own hat down hard almost over his eyes. At once he looks no longer like the counsel for the defence but like Billy Simple himself. The court gasps. Runche pulls the hat off his head and takes a step towards the jury box and bends slightly forward for emphasis. 'Billy Simple was never – I repeat, *never* in the four whole years he spent working at Riverview Station after the accident – seen without his hat on his head. He slept with it on, he prayed with it on, he bathed with it on and he worked with it on. Billy's hat was his best friend! Billy's hat was a matter of life and death to him! Billy's hat was all that was left of his pride and his dignity! You saw him in the witness box, where he is not allowed to wear a hat. Did you see how, even with his hands man-acled, he tried to cover the scar on his head? How he stood ashamed – not only for what he'd done, he has confessed to that and is repentant – but for the ugly, ter-rible scar that runs across his poor, sad, confused head. Look at him now, members of the jury, where he sits clutching his head, his shame, before you.'

Richard Runche is still for a moment. 'Now I ask you to consider the evidence. You've heard the prosecution say that Billy Simple is a cold-blooded killer. That the murders of his three victims were a result of planning and premeditation. That the mattock with its sharp chopping head was a weapon that would arouse no sus-picion when in the possession of a gardener. That the cold – I think the word used by my learned colleague was "surgical" – that the surgical precision used was the work of an intransigent and cold-hearted murderer. That the murders were premeditated and executed in cold blood with surgical precision by an unfeeling and callous killer. I think those were the final words used by the prosecution, were they not?'

Runche holds the hat aloft and swings it around. 'What of the hat, I ask you? The hat, left next to the half-empty watering can on the pathway. The hat, which had come off Billy Simple's head when he'd been taunted beyond any possible endurance so that he dropped the watering can he was using at his feet. He grabbed the nearest thing he could find, the mattock he had been using in the vegetable patch during the afternoon, losing his hat as he stooped to pick it up. I venture to suggest that the poor soul was so overcome by the tormenting from the three ladies that he did not even pause to retrieve his hat! The hat he always wears! Can you imagine how extreme his state of anxiety must have been for Billy Simple to forget the hat which hides his shame?

'The killing, we have heard, would have taken place in a matter of a few minutes when Billy had finally lost what few senses he had at his command. If he had been the cold-blooded, callous killer he has been made out to be, would he not have returned to retrieve his hat? The one item in his life he couldn't bear to be without?

'Instead he runs panic-stricken away from the scene of the crime. And when his panic had subsided sufficiently, we have heard how he made his way to the Bergman homestead to give himself up to the only friend he knew how to find – Miss Jessica Bergman.

'Did he not plead with her, whimper, beg, until she gave him her father's work hat to cover his head? Is this the way a cold-blooded, callous killer would behave?

'Or is it what we would expect from a simple-minded child in the body of an adult male? Was not the action Billy Simple took, the terrible crime he committed, the result of a nescient mind driven beyond despair by three women who took great amusement from their cruel tormenting?'

The court has by this time grown very still. 'Members of the jury, in the time-honoured manner of British justice, I place the life of Billy Simple in your hands. I ask that you take into consideration the nature of justice itself, which is to balance the scales, to hear both sides, to understand mitigation of circumstance. I ask for your extreme care in deciding this matter. If you should render a verdict of murder you will not be serving the full purpose of the law, which is to deliver a just response after all of the evidence has been taken. I ask now that you deliver your verdict of manslaughter. I ask that William Simon, and those who care about him, if such people there are, know that you have examined both sides and come to your verdict honestly. I thank you for your patience, and I rest my case.'

After no more than an hour of deliberation the jury renders a verdict of murder. Jessica sits stunned, while George Thomas shakes hands with the prosecution. The judge, in delivering his final summary, compliments the jury on having arrived at a just and fair verdict. He then describes the accused as a vicious killer, whereupon he places the silk square on his head, pulls on the white gloves, and pronounces, 'William D'arcy Simon of the Parish of Ourendumbee in the County of Boyd, I sentence you to be hanged by the neck until dead, the sentence to take place at such time and place as his Excellency the Governor of New South Wales shall determine.'

Much to Joe's shame, Jessica, upon hearing the verdict, is seen by all within the court to burst into a torrent of tears. 'No, no, it's not fair!' she shrieks at the jury. 'Billy!' she cries out to the poor wretch, 'I tried! Oh Billy – I've failed you! Forgive me – forgive us all!'

The case is widely reported and in the process Jessica's reputation is destroyed. The *Narrandera Argus* account of the case concludes:

> *It is one thing for a slip of a girl to bring a madman, a killer, to justice and for this Miss Jessica Bergman deserves the highest praise.*
>
> *However, it is quite another thing for this young heroine to turn into a hostile witness and to defend the accused in court and, in the process, to sully the reputations of the respectable dead.*
>
> *In the judge's own words, William Simon, alias Billy Simple, is a vicious, cold-blooded killer. His victims, the three murdered women, were ever of chaste behaviour, well known to most people in Boyd County and throughout the Riverina as personages of the most genteel character to be held in the highest esteem.*

They were, mother and daughters, women almost sainted for their good works, veritable pillars of the church and tireless workers for charity, much admired for their selfless deeds, piety and goodwill towards the sick and the poor.

By seeking to defend William Simon, Miss Bergman has betrayed all that is good in society.

This correspondent cannot help but wonder whether the ordeals suffered by Miss Bergman during the hazardous and dangerous undertaking have not damaged her nerves, her very sanity. This would seem to be the only possible explanation for her aberrant behaviour.

Some of the bolder newspapers, led by the *Sydney Morning Herald*, go so far as to speculate that, in retrospect, such behaviour from a member of the weaker sex was most peculiar in both circumstances – in her over-bold capture of Billy Simple and then her subsequent defence of the convicted murderer while under oath. They, too, suggest that William Simon may not be the only person who is of unsound mind. Or is there, they ask, an entirely different motive for Miss Bergman's apparent affection for the murderer?

CHAPTER SEVEN

Since the incident at Narrandera when Jack defied his father to allow Jessica to deliver Billy Simple to the police magistrate he has grown much closer to the Bergman family. Meg and Hester have welcomed him, though not perhaps with quite the same ardour as they had originally anticipated.

George Thomas has spoken hardly a word to young Jack since their confrontation in the main street and has insisted his son move out of the homestead and into the cottage usually occupied by the foreman of the shearing shed. Jack is expected to cook and fend for himself and he and George are careful to work on separate runs at Riverview Station.

Old man Thomas has also let it be known that by defying him, Jack is no longer considered to be his son. Assuming, with his wife's death, that he is the sole owner of Riverview, George has announced, not without a certain degree of melodrama, that Jack has been disinherited.

This comes as a severe blow to Hester and Meg. George Thomas is known for his stubborn and cantankerous nature as well as his ability never to forget a slight. While he is a loud-mouth, a braggart and a mean bastard, no one doubts that his disinheritance of young Jack is fair dinkum. The Narrandera confrontation when Jack threatened to shoot him was a public humiliation he cannot forgive. Moreover, with young Jack's refusal to back down, it has compounded his determination to disinherit his son.

Hester has had to make new plans for Meg, for she can no longer regard Jack Thomas as the prime candidate for her daughter's hand in marriage. Jack with Riverview Station in his saddlebag is one thing, Jack as a penniless station hand is quite another.

So, while Hester and Meg have remained conscientious in their attentions to young Jack's healthy appetite over the last two months, cooking roast dinners and baking the day prior to his Sunday visit, Meg's petticoats have not been lifted quite as high as she comes down the steps of the homestead to meet him, nor do her pretty hands draw downwards to emphasise her trim waist as they once did at every opportunity. To an astute observer, her eyes are not as charmingly averted, her beautiful smile is employed less often and her maidenly expression is not quite as demure. The abandonment of Jack Thomas has been subtle but determined. With the cooling down of Hester's ardour for Meg's long-term suitor, her eldest daughter has been instructed to start casting her glances elsewhere.

For his part, Jack Thomas has seemed hardly to notice the lessening of Meg's affections. He arrives each Sunday shortly after Hester, Meg and Jessica have attended morning service at St Stephen's. They can hear the whine of his motor car a good ten minutes before he comes up the rutted road with a fearful clatter and clank of rotating parts. Jessica runs out to meet him with her hands to her ears as he pulls up with a final exhilarated roar of the engine followed by fearful backfiring and a cloud of blue smoke.

Though she works alongside him often enough, Jessica feels strangely shy when he arrives. It is as though the neat cotton dress with its wide skirt which emphasises her tiny waist makes her more vulnerable and calls for a different expression of her self.

In moleskins and shirt she might greet him with a casual 'G'day!'. In her Sunday dress with its neat white lace collar she feels obliged to say, 'Good morning, Jack.'

Jack, too, regards his Sunday visit as different. 'Good morning, Jessie,' he says, greeting her as formally in return. But then he shakes her hand and looks down at her with a little smile on his face and hangs onto her hand for a moment longer than necessary. There is a look in his eye which always suggests to Jessica that he wants to say something else. But she lacks the courage to keep her hand in his and pulls away laughing. 'Father will be pouring a stout for you, he won't want it to lose its head of foam.' Jessica finds her heart is always beating a good bit faster after this formal Sunday morning greeting.

She tells herself not to be ridiculous, that what happened in Narrandera was nothing to concern herself about. Jack is her mate and Billy's too, and he'd done what he did to protect her from the mob trying to get to Billy Simple. It was a mate thing, even when he carried her up the steps of the courthouse. His visits to the Narrandera hospital for the next two days while she recovered were also part of his friendship and concern. She dares not think otherwise, and even now that Meg has abandoned her affections for him and Jack is available, Jessica tells herself she is ugly and flat in front and not the sort of person Jack will choose for his wife.

Jack, like Joe, seldom goes to church, but on Sundays he's careful to wear a clean shirt and moleskins, with his boots freshly dubbined, his neck well scrubbed and his face shaved. He wolfs down his food as though he has been starved all week and is careful to extend his appreciation to Hester and Meg, exclaiming loudly and delightedly at the tarts, trifles and cakes they place before him after the Sunday roast.

Like most young blokes his age, Jack isn't a big talker. His conversation is polite and agreeable, but largely restricted to matters of cattle and sheep and the working and efficacy of machinery in the shearing shed. Even these contributions are prodded from him as though with the sharp end of a knitting needle. It is only when Jessica asks him a question on irrigation that he replies spontaneously. He is all for the elaborate system of canals and pump stations planned for the Riverina, some of which are already in place. His enthusiasm for what Joe refers to as 'bloody McCaughey's harebrained scheme' seems to know no bounds.

Joe is too polite to openly show his disdain for this idea, but after Jack's departure he'll have a go at him.

'He don't think practical, you can't take a flamin' river where it don't want to go! The canals will silt up from the dust and the walls will collapse the first rains we get. This is sheep and cattle country when it's good and good for bugger-all when it ain't, nothing's gunna change that. You can't raise regular crops on soil that grows nothin' much 'cept mulga scrub and saltbush. There's talk of growing rice like China and two crops of wheat a year – I should live to see the day.'

Jessica points out that Jack is as good a sheep and cattle man as you can get and Joe admits this is true. 'But them bloody stupid schemes, building canals and pumps, that'll soon enough take care o' the wool cheque and then some! You know how I feel about that bastard George Thomas, but it's probably a good thing he still holds the reins at Riverview, can't let them young blokes muck about too much, 'fore you know it they've blown the lot and they're into the bank for a loan.'

Joe is fond enough of young Jack and reckons he'll come good in the end. 'Give him a few more years of being belted about in the bush, he'll come around.' He has watched the friendship between Jack and Jessica grow and he is grateful to the boy for accepting his younger daughter as a serious worker and for not taking the piss as the other young ringers try to do – until they see her on a horse working cattle or sheep and are forced to show a little respect.

Now, with Jack's diminished future, the friendship between Jessica and Jack seems to Joe to be most fortunate. While he is not as sure as Hester that Jack has his eyes on Jessica, he cannot help hoping they might go on with it. He is seventy-two years old and sees the possibility of the disinherited Jack and Jessica taking over the property from him. If he can knock some of the damn fool ideas out of the young man's head, Joe reckons that Jessica will have found a good man as her partner.

Hester declares herself just as pleased if such an arrangement may be brought about and sets to work on Jessica, urging her to show more amorous attention to Jack. If Jessica and Jack are regarded by the parish as a courting couple then Meg will not be seen as fickle or changing her affections with the downturn of Jack's fortunes.

The story of Jack walking up the steps of the Narrandera courthouse with Jessica in his arms has been romanticised to almost legendary status and the whole county is waiting, wanting to be convinced there is a big romance in the air. If Jessica and Jack can be seen walking out together there won't be a single discordant voice in the community.

All seems to be going well until after the murder trial, when the newspaper talk of Jessica's strange behaviour in the defence of Billy Simple causes tongues to wag aplenty.

'Will that child never cease in her tormenting of us?' Hester howls to Joe. 'We shall never live down the shame.'

'She done what she thought was right,' Joe says in Jessica's defence. 'I admit it were stupid, but it come from the heart.'

'Joe Bergman, you don't understand what she's done to us!' Hester screams at her husband. 'Don't you see, Meg's prospects are forever ruined! How shall we face a decent family with an eligible son when your daughter has shamed our name like this?'

'Don't you talk to me in that voice, Hester,' Joe warns. 'You were quick enough to use Jessie to get Meg off the hook with Jack Thomas once you knew his prospects were ruined. You reckoned he was a good enough catch for Jessie though, didn't ya?'

Hester attempts to calm her voice. 'You were there, you should not have let her see that drunken lawyer. You should have stopped her. For Godsakes, Joe, you must have known the shame it would bring us, her defending the murderer against Ada Thomas and her two girls? Whatever could have possessed the girl? Doesn't she ever stop to think what people will say? How can Jack take her for his wife now she's shown herself to be against his mother and sisters? How will Meg make a decent marriage? How can we ever show our faces in public again?'

To Hester's surprise, Joe laughs. 'You should know better. Since when has anyone been able to change Jessie's mind when it's made up? You and Meg been trying for years to rein her in and she's took no notice. She done what she thought was fair and honest. Never mind what the newspapers say, Jessie done a decent thing.'

'Decent thing! Defending that brute! You call that decent? She's ruined Meg's chances and blown her own forever. You may be sure there'll be no Jack Thomas over for Sunday dinner from now on!'

Joe grins. 'Pity that, best tucker I've eaten in years. I'm not so sure Jessie ever thought she had a chance. Nor does he seem too interested. They ain't exactly lovey-dovey. Like I said before, it were you and Meg that were playing matchmakers, thinking it were a great opportunity to get Meg off the hook with young Jack. Meg, the loving sister, giving up Jack Thomas to brave little Jessie who brought the mad bloke to justice. Christ, yiz make me sick!'

Hester brings her fingers up to her lips, trying to calm down. 'Joe, can't you see, people think Jessica's gone crazy! Wrong in the head. Where does that leave us?'

'Us? Meg, you mean?' Joe laughs again. 'Up shit creek for the time being, I reckon.' Joe lights his pipe and takes a couple of puffs. 'But Jessie's *not* crazy and there's enough folk around here who'll soon enough notice that. It'll sort itself out. Never mind about Meg, she's too pretty to stay on the shelf for too long. Anyway, the pair of yiz is too fussy, perhaps you should settle for less than the landed bloody gentry?'

'That I'll not do, Joe Bergman!' Hester pronounces. 'Meg's not been born to be some scrub farmer's wife. She deserves the best and I'll see she gets it, despite Jessica's every effort to destroy her,' Hester sniffs.

'Good onya, in the meantime, let's just get on with our lives. Jessica's never done nothing to harm Meg, nor would she ever. Meg will survive and Jessie's no worse off but for a bit of idle newspaper gossip. You and Meg have got rid of Jack now he's broke. I dare say the Bergman family will survive the shame,' Joe grins, 'though I can't speak for the Heathwood side.'

Hester is wrong about Jack Thomas who, after the trial is over, turns up as usual for Sunday dinner. The furore caused by the newspapers about Jessica's behaviour at Billy Simple's trial is soon enough forgotten by the local gossips, or more likely tucked away for a rainy day when a bit of malicious tattle might come in useful.

Country folk have their own way of making up their minds about people and, while Jessica has always been thought of as a bit of a tomboy, there's many a settler who'd like a daughter like her around to help him. The rumour of the romance started publicly on the steps of the Narrandera courthouse proves much the superior topic among the tongue-waggers. If Jessica has gone a bit strange there's plenty more in the district to join her. They'll soon enough make up their own minds, thank you very much.

Nor does Jessica's defence of Billy Simple seem to have affected Meg's chances with the better families, who are showing more than their usual cordiality towards Hester and her older daughter. Though Hester has decided to take her husband's advice and lie low for a while, she is much encouraged by their reception at St Stephen's. It is almost as though everyone has breathed a sigh of relief at the passing of the interfering and self-righteous Ada Thomas and her two nosy daughters.

Meg lives to see another day and to find someone befitting her beauty and intelligence, while Jessica – poor, plain Jessie – fulfils the romantic dreams of every lonely, work-worn farmer's wife hungry for a bit of romance and affection. Such is the nature of romantic illusion that Jack's apparent lack of outward affection for Jessica is simply put down by everyone to his grief and the need for an appropriate and seemly period of mourning for his mother and sisters to pass.

Then one Sunday, a few weeks after the drama of the trial has passed, Jack, in a casual remark, tells the Bergman family he has just spent two days with the Thomas family lawyer in Narrandera, where he attended the reading of his mother's last will and testament.

Hester and Meg immediately assume conciliatory expressions. Then Jack announces that Ada Thomas has left the bulk of her considerable fortune to him, as well as the deeds to Riverview Station which, it turns out, had always been in her name.

'You mean you now own Riverview Station?' Hester, the first to recover from Jack's announcement, exclaims.

'Yeah, I suppose that's true,' Jack grins.

Jessica reaches over and grabs his arm. 'You'll be able to do all the things you've talked about,' she says excitedly.

Meg is stunned. Jessica has won the prize she has worked so hard to earn. It is too much to bear and she pushes back her stool and flees, sobbing, from the table.

Jack looks perplexed. 'What's the matter? Did I say something wrong?' he asks bewildered.

Hester is again the first to recover. 'No, no, it's simply her way of showing how pleased she is for you, Jack,' she says hastily. 'She's been terribly upset since your . . . er, father . . .' She does not complete the sentence but takes a deep breath to steady herself, then says, 'Well I can't tell you what a great relief it is to us all to know that your future is secure.' She tries hard to make her smile seem sincere, though Jessica knows her mother well enough to see she's biting back her frustration.

Jack looks relieved. 'That's very nice of you and Meg, Mrs Bergman.' Then he shrugs and gives a short laugh. 'I dunno about my future being secure, though. As you know I'm in the local militia, well they've asked us to join up. I'm going to fight in the war.'

Hester has risen and is halfway out of the room on her way to force Meg to return to the table. 'The war? You're going off to the war?' she says, as though she can't quite comprehend such an idea. 'But there isn't any war?'

'There will be, could be declared any day now.' Jack turns to Joe for confirmation. 'Wouldn't yer reckon, Joe?'

'Yeah,' Joe says flatly. 'It's comin' orright, war clouds gathering over Europe.'

Jessica has remained silent since Jack's last announcement. She has her head bowed and fidgets with her pinny. Jack turns to her. 'I've got an uncle in Sydney who's going to be the colonel of a squadron of the 1st New South Wales Light Horse, he's got me in.' He shakes his head. 'Fancy that, Jessie, I'm going to war on horseback. Don't you wish you could come, mate?'

Jessica looks up slowly, tears running silently down her cheeks. 'You could get killed,' she sniffs, then knuckles the tears from her eyes.

Jack laughs. 'Nah, not me, mate. I'm too ugly and stupid to die.'

'You're not ugly and stupid!' Jessica cries out, then falls silent, blushing furiously.

Joe sees Jessica's dismay and looks over to Jack and inquires, 'How long have you got?'

'What do you mean, Joe?'

'Here. Before you go?'

'A week, then Sydney for ten weeks, then . . .' Jack shrugs. 'I dunno, could be over the pond right off if war is declared.'

Later Jack goes for a walk with Jessica. It has become a habit for them to do so after dinner when they'll stroll down to look at the cows or simply sit under a tree and chat. After what Jack's told them Jessica's mind is racing. She hasn't, as Hester and Meg have done, seen the significance of Jack regaining his inheritance. Her thoughts are consumed by the idea that he will be going away to war and that he will be in danger.

'Jack, can't you wait to be called up? Joe says they'll probably have to call the older blokes first. They won't want the young blokes from the militia going straight away.'

'Nah, Jessie, I've got to do my bit. Australians have always volunteered, it's . . .' he stops to think a moment then continues, 'well, it's the right thing to do, ain't it?'

'But Joe says the Brits haven't done all that much for us. He doesn't see it's our war. It doesn't make sense,' Jessica says slowly, then she looks up at Jack, her eyes damp with tears. 'Jack, I'm gunna miss you something terrible.' A tear now runs down Jessica's cheek and she tries to laugh, brushing it away impatiently with her fist.

Jack reaches out and takes her hand. 'Jessie, I dunno how to say it, mate.'

Jessica looks up at Jack, surprised. 'Say what?'

'Well, nothing's changed since Narrandera. But it's my duty to fight for my country.' He pulls Jessica's hand against his chest. 'I ain't much good at saying things, Jessie, but if I come back will you marry me?'

Jessica bursts into tears, not sure she's heard Jack correct. 'What?' she asks astonished, unable quite to grasp Jack's words. 'Marry? You and me?'

'Yeah, I thought, you know after Narrandera and all that . . .' his voice trails off.

'You don't have to, Jack.'

Jack reaches out and holds her against his chest and pats her clumsily on the back. 'Jessica I can't *now*, not until I come back, I just wanted to . . .' He does not complete the sentence.

Jessica pulls away suddenly and looks at him. 'Oh, Jack, I love you so, I want you, I want your children.'

'Hey, steady, girl,' Jack laughs, then he is suddenly serious. 'Jessie, that's just it, ain't it. I can't marry you until I get back from the war. What if we had a child and I wasn't there, and say I was killed – you'd be a widow and the child would have no father, I couldn't ever do that to you, Jess.' Jack stands awkwardly in front of Jessica. 'Will you wait for me, Tea Leaf?'

Jessica smiles through her tears. 'Only if you'll kiss me now, Jack Thomas.'

Jack takes Jessica in his arms and kisses her and Jessica feels she must surely die if his lips should ever leave hers again.

Jack pushes her away gently. 'Shall we go back and tell your parents we are betrothed?'

Jessica grows suddenly cold. In the excitement of Jack's joining up she had quite forgotten Meg's reaction to his announcement about Ada's fortune and his inheritance of Riverview Station. She now realises she has won the prize and that Hester and Meg will never forgive her. Then as quickly her heart grows cold with fear. Jack might be killed – she might never have him as her own. Then she thinks again of Hester. Her mother will want to make the best of it, she will put pressure on Jack to marry her before he goes away. Hester will not want so rich a prize to slip through her fingers.

'No, Jack, I can't bear to have others think of you as mine until you are returned safely to me. If you will keep your promise, I will keep mine. It must be our secret, our . . .' Jessica wants to say love but is too shy to use the unfamiliar word. 'What began at Narrandera, we'll have again when you get back. Already there are too many tongues wagging. I don't want to live with people talking about me, about us . . . I'll wait and pray for your safety every day you're away, I don't need no ring to remind me of your promise.'

After Jack has departed all hell breaks loose in the Bergman household. Meg has taken to her bed, weeping, with Hester in attendance. The two of them spend all afternoon together while Jessica and Joe go about the usual Sunday chores. Jessica is just back from milking the cow and enters the kitchen carrying a pail of milk when Hester turns to her and takes the pail.

'Sit down, Jessica, I want to talk to you.'

Meg is nowhere to be seen and Jessica supposes she is still in bed. How very glad she is that Jack has not made an announcement.

'Jessica, I want you to listen to me now,' Hester says again and indicates a stool. Jessica realises that her mother must have seen her coming up from the cow paddock and has already placed a mug of tea down on the table for her.

'I ain't done nothing,' Jessica says defensively.

Hester ignores her protest. 'It's about Jack.'

'Jack? What about Jack?' Jessica immediately feels guilty, Hester can't possibly know.

'About him going away in a week. I don't want you to see him again.'

'Huh?' Jessica frowns and looks up at her mother puzzled, 'Why ever not, Mother?' Her heart is beginning to beat faster.

Hester sighs and sits down on the stool beside Jessica. 'You're not a fool, Jessica, and you know there are people who think you and Jack, well, after what happened at the courthouse in Narrandera people think . . .'

'Think what?' Jessica interrupts.

'Think that you'll soon be betrothed.'

Jessica looks down into her lap and bites her bottom lip. She hesitates a moment as she fights back her tears. 'He's going to the war, he may be killed,' she chokes, then looks up tearfully at Hester. 'But why can't I see him, he's my friend?'

Hester takes Jessica's small hand and absently examines her broken nails. 'Because he's not yours – he's Meg's.'

'Meg's? But I thought . . . ?' Jessica is deeply shocked.

'Well you were wrong, my girl. We were just allowing things to quieten down a bit. Meg was being kind to you. I expect Jack was, too.'

'Kind? What do you mean, kind? What things?'

'Well, after you took Billy Simple in to Narrandera, the doctor at the hospital there said you might have a nervous breakdown, what with everything that happened. He said we should be careful not to upset you.'

'What's a nervous breakdown?'

'It's something that sometimes happens when you've had a bad shock, like the business with Billy Simple.'

'What's it got to do with Jack?'

'Well, he told Jack too,' Hester lies. 'Meg and Jack, they were just being kind to you.'

'But Jack . . .' Jessica exclaims, about to explain, but manages to hold her tongue just in time as Hester holds up her hand and interrupts.

'Jessica, stop imagining things! Jack carrying you when you fainted doesn't mean anything. Has Jack even held your hand? Has he ever tried to be alone with you when he comes over?'

'Me and Jack . . .' Jessica bites back the words.

'Well, there you are,' Hester announces. 'All he's been is kind, like the doctor told us, told *him* and us we should be,' Hester lies again.

'But I *haven't* had a nervous breakdown,' Jessica protests.

Hester looks kindly at her youngest daughter, and speaks in a soft, consoling voice. 'We're not at all sure about that, Jessica. What about the sickness? In the mornings? The doctor said you could have nightmares, terrible nightmares, and wake up exhausted and feeling ill. Well, isn't that what's happened?'

'Mother, what are you saying? Are you saying I'm mad?'

Hester's face grows hard. 'The newspapers think your behaviour at the trial of Billy Simple was very strange, Jessica. They say something must have happened to your mind.'

'But you don't believe that!' Jessica cries. 'What I did was only fair!'

Hester's eyes narrow. 'Being fair to a person that's murdered three of our dearest friends is a very strange way to behave, even your father thinks that,' she snaps.

'They were not *my* friends! Besides, Father didn't say that. He said it wouldn't look good me sticking up for Billy Simple. He didn't say not to! He didn't forbid me!'

Hester, suddenly impatient, clicks her tongue and throws her head back, letting go of Jessica's hand. 'I'm sorry, Jessica, things have changed, we can't afford to mollycoddle you any longer. You have to stay away from Jack Thomas, you hear me, that's an order.' She grabs Jessica's wrist and hisses, 'Meg has only got a week to get him to marry her.'

'Marry? Meg? But he's going to the war!' Jessica howls. 'He can't marry anyone.'

'Oh you stupid, stupid girl, he'll be no bloody use to us dead! You just stay away, you hear me? Stay away from Meg's man!'

'He's not her man!' Jessica howls. 'He's mine now, she gave him up, you said so yourself, Mother!'

Hester can bear no more. 'Jessica, leave off, you're not to go near Jack Thomas.'

'But what if he asks me to work at Riverview?' Jessica begs.

'He's off to Sydney in a week, he'll not be needing you. If he does, Joe will tell him you're not well, which is the truth.'

Jessica rises from the stool and, with her hands covering her face, she stumbles out of the kitchen into the yard. Hester watches as she walks slowly down to the cow paddock. She can see from the appearance of her shoulders that her youngest daughter is weeping.

Hester tells herself that Meg is a juicy morsel in any man's eyes, a feast for a young man's natural appetites. She must now take desperate measures if she is to get Jack for her eldest daughter, for Jack is a shy and awkward young man with little or no experience beyond the women he has grown up with. She and Meg have often enough seen Jack's hungry eyes wandering over Meg's bosom and fixing on her trim waist and the still further promise contained in the sweetly curved hips below it. It is time for firm resolve, it's now or never, time for Meg's skirt and petticoats to hit the floor so she can claim what's rightfully hers.

That evening Hester prepares Meg for the onslaught to come. Hester herself knows little of the methods of seduction but she's confident that a pretty girl left alone with a randy young man will find a way. Meg, for her part, is equally determined. She has worked long and hard to win Jack Thomas and she's not going to let him slip through her fingers now. 'We have just a week for him to make you pregnant, my dear,' Hester tells her daughter. 'There is no time to lose.'

'But Mother, what if he doesn't like me? What if he won't, you know, do it?'

Hester looks into the dark eyes of her daughter. 'He'll be thinking with what your father calls his trouser snake, my darling,' she smiles, 'and trouser snakes, I am told,' Hester pauses and giggles, 'are not known for their intelligence!' Both women are hysterical with laughter.

Hester plans carefully. She persuades Joe that she's concerned about Jessica's recurring sickness and that it is time to take her into Wagga Wagga to see old Dr Merrick, the Heathwood family physician. Thirty years earlier the Heathwoods had quarrelled with Dr Lethbridge in Narrandera and they had taken their business to Wagga, despite the inconvenience of two days' travel. Joe, who is genuinely concerned for Jessica, readily agrees and it is arranged for the coming Wednesday. Hester herself makes plans to visit old Mrs Baker, a distant cousin and a widow who is the organist at St Stephen's and is known to be in poor health. Finally, with everything prepared, she sends a note to Jack, giving it to a bullock driver who is passing by Riverview Station.

> *Dear Jack,*
>
> *I have a great favour to ask of you but the opportunity to do so when you were last here did not arise. It is a small conspiracy and so of a confidential nature and I hope you will indulge an old woman but keep the details to yourself.*
>
> *Joe has a bad back which, at the age of seventy-two, isn't getting any better.*
>
> *As you well know he is an exceedingly stubborn and proud man and won't listen to sense, even though Jessie, who has more influence with him than any of us, tries to tell him not to lift heavy things. He still thinks he's a young lad and as strong as a bull.*
>
> *We have recently obtained a wagonload of fence posts, which the timber-getter dumped in the wrong place and these now have to be moved to the north paddock.*
>
> *I am most fearful that if Joe performs this task he may damage himself and, of course, Jessica cannot do it alone.*
>
> *I was wondering if, on Wednesday afternoon (as late as you like), you could come over and help Jessica load the logs onto the small dray and take them to the right location?*
>
> *Joe knows nothing of this and he would kill me if he knew I'd asked you to help him.*

*So if you could possibly drop in, pretending you
have work for Jessica, and, seeing the pile of logs,
ask about them in my presence. I will then explain
about them needing to be moved and then, if you'll
offer to help load them, right there in front of Joe?*

*We can offer you little in return, but would be
delighted if you would stay for tea. I know Jessica
and Meg would like that very much.*

Yours sincerely,

Hester Bergman (Mrs).

It is a crude enough plan but it has the virtue of simplicity and an element of truth. The fence posts do need
to be moved and Joe's back has been troubling him sufficiently for Jessica to persuade him to postpone the task
for several days.

The idea is for Jack to arrive and to be told by Meg
that Jessica has been somewhat unwell for some time. Joe,
unbeknownst to Hester, has that very morning decided to
take her into Wagga to see their family doctor. Furthermore, a message has arrived to say that old Mrs Baker has
taken a turn for the worse and Hester has gone over to be
with her. The combination of events has, regrettably,
made it impossible to get a note over to Riverview Station
in time to cancel Jack's visit. Meg is therefore left behind,
alone in the homestead, but she's made a nice tea and
baked an apple pie and she insists Jack stays to eat as
originally planned by her mother. The rest, as they say in
the classics, should see nature take its course.

There is usually very little movement on the road to Yanco before sun-up and not a lot after. Occasionally a bullock dray makes an early start to avoid the heat of the day and may be seen trudging its weary-looking way to one of the outlying stations. If such is the case on this particular Thursday early morning, its driver will be puzzled to observe Jack Thomas clattering and clanking on his way home to Riverview Station in his motor car.

Jack has slept little, with Meg proving to be a most willing partner, keeping him busy until he cries out from exhaustion. It had proved very awkward when Meg first started to be amorous with Jack who was somewhat taken by surprise. He had moved the logs on his own and had returned to the kitchen, where Meg had put out a bottle of stout for him. She'd bade him sit on a small bench at the table and poured the dark, rich liquid into a glass and placed it in front of him, and then she'd sat next to him, her thigh rubbing against his. He tries now to recall the exact sequence of events, his mind back in the Bergman kitchen.

Jack is unable to move without sliding off the side of the bench. He is nonplussed and brings the glass to his lips to conceal his embarrassment. Now he feels Meg's hand placed boldly on his thigh.

He brings the glass down from his lips and places it back on the table. 'Ah, I don't think we should, er . . . I'm not sure,' he stammers.

Meg laughs. 'It's a present, a going-away present,

just a little kiss, Jack.' She is surprised at her own boldness and at how easily the words come.

'Meg, we're not walking out together,' Jack says
doubtfully.

'But we should be, Jack, I have always wanted you.'

'Wanted me?' Jack looks at her, surprised.

'To walk out with me,' Meg laughs.

'Well, it's not like that, see,' Jack manages, 'I'm sort
of . . . well, Jessie.'

'We both love you, Jack,' Meg says quickly, stopping
him from going any further. 'Don't you want me to say
goodbye to you properly?' Meg rises slightly and kisses
Jack on the cheek. She smells of rosewater and her lips
are soft against his rough, stubbled skin. Her hand now
rests between his legs and Jack knows that she will soon
feel his rising, feel him coming alive. He tries to fight
back the urge that overcomes him.

'Meg, I mustn't.'

'Mustn't what, Jack? Mustn't let me give you a little
farewell kiss, a little present to take to the war?' She
takes Jack's head in both her hands and turns him
towards her and kisses him gently on the lips, her kiss
lingering. Meg is beginning to get excited herself. Suddenly she rises from the table. 'Come, Jack.'

Jack is afraid to rise, afraid his reaction to her kisses
will show through his trousers, but Meg pulls at his
hand. He rises slowly, and Meg turns and kisses him as
he stands. 'Come and get your reward, my brave soldier
going to war,' she coos.

Meg leads Jack into Hester's bedroom which still

contains the marriage bed which Joe has not shared for many years. The linen is freshly starched and the bed wears the prettiest rose and blue coloured quilt Meg herself has appliquéd.

'No, Meg, really,' Jack says, pulling back, 'I can't, please, I mustn't.'

Meg stops and turns to him and her large, dark eyes fill with tears. 'Jack I want to give you this present. I want to give you what I value the most.' She gives a pitiful little sob. 'Now I see I'm not good enough for you. Not good enough for the high and mighty Jack Thomas.' She gives a second little sob and looks up at him. Bending her forefinger, she wipes a single tear from her cheek.

Jack doesn't know what to say. 'Of course you are, Meg. You're beautiful, it's just that me and . . .' His voice trails off.

'It's only a little present. It's all a country girl has got to give. Something only you and I will ever know about, Jack. It can be our secret forever.' Then she adds, 'Poor Jack, don't be concerned, it is only little me saying goodbye. I am so very proud of you, you know, volunteering to fight the Germans.' She bursts into tears and sits on the bed. 'Jack, you may die, you may never come back,' she says in a sad little voice. 'May I not have this at least to remember you by?'

Jack looks down at the distraught Meg. She is achingly beautiful and her snowy breasts heave most enticingly with her distress, for somehow the top four buttons to her blouse have come loose and he can see the warm, firm flesh rising and falling.

He quickly moves over to Meg and puts his hand on her shoulder to comfort her. 'Meg, please . . .' Meg grabs his hand and places it against her eyes so that the wetness of her tears is felt on the back of his hand. Then she kisses his hand and pulls it downward so that it rests on her breast. Jack feels he must surely burst through his moleskins. She places her free hand about Jack's neck and pulls him down to her so that Jack is forced to go onto his knees in front of her. She looks directly into his eyes, her own shining with her sweet tears. 'Do you hate me so much, Jack, that you would humiliate me so?' She sobs and throws herself at him, embracing him, whimpering against his chest.

Jack can contain himself no longer. Her heat is against him and he thinks he must die from his desire to take her.

'No, no, Meg, you are lovely,' he gasps, overcome with the need to tear her dress from her body.

Meg now smiles brilliantly through her tears and then pushes him gently away and rises from the bed. As she stands upright again her skirt mysteriously drops from her waist to the floor and at the same time the last two buttons on her blouse seem to have unfastened so that her breasts now rise high above a straining bodice, half of one nipple showing pink and sublime.

Meg steps neatly out of her skirt as though she hardly notices it's fallen from her waist. It is all done seemingly in one movement whereupon she reaches out and turns the lamp down and then bends over the glass to blow it out. Jack is thus presented with the sight of her pantaloons curving out from her tiny waist and pointing deliciously at him, the cotton material pulled tight and smooth over her derriere, her shapely calf and trim ankles also showing to their very best effect.

Jack senses he has one last opportunity to make his escape, but he knows as well that he will not take it. His earlier resolve has leaked from him like water through a kitchen sieve and he trembles at the knees. 'Oh, God,' he groans, his entire body now filled with desire. Meg is a very pretty thing indeed, well beyond the wildest dreams of most young men and she has driven him way beyond any reason.

With her back to Jack, Meg now removes her blouse and bodice then turns to face him. In the half light her lovely breasts, free of all constraints, are heaving invitingly. Meg smiles. If she is feeling self-conscious standing near naked for the first time in front of a man, she does not show it. She cups her breasts in her hands and lifts them slightly as though she is offering them to him. Jack's mouth is dry and his tongue frantically works around the roof of his mouth, trying to regain its moisture. Now Meg's hands leave her breasts, which drop no more than an inch, firm and round with the nipples pointed upwards. She runs her hands down the smooth curves of her waist and effortlessly slips her pantaloons down over her legs as though her hands have found them in error and they have peeled off her hips and legs as though intended to do so by nature. She steps out of her underwear to finally stand nude in front of Jack.

Meg allows him but a moment to see her beautiful

body before she steps forward and puts her arms about his neck and pulls him towards her. She can feel Jack trembling against her and she senses he is ready and cannot contain himself much longer.

'Oh God, I must have you, Meg,' he groans. 'I must take you now!'

Meg goes onto her tip-toes and kisses him on the mouth.

'Oh Jack, you are so handsome,' she whispers.

Jack's hands go frantically to his belt as Meg begins to unfasten the buttons of his shirt and then pulls it over his head and casts it aside as his trousers drop to his boots. Jack, with his pants now about his ankles, sits on a small stool beside the bed, tugging desperately to remove his boots.

With the moonlight streaming through the window, Meg pulls back the sheets, her beautiful body turned half sideways to Jack. She looks over her shoulder and smiles almost wistfully. 'Come, Jack,' she says softly, 'come and get your going-away present.' Then she slides between the fresh sheets, holding them up to her chin. 'Come now Jack Thomas, my soldier of the King,' Meg giggles. 'Show me how you fire your gun.'

In the early hours of Thursday morning, as Jack sits brooding in the De Dion on the way to Riverview, he knows that the temptation had been too great for him to resist. That Meg was a dish too sweet not to savour. If it should ever happen again, he now tells himself, he will be well able to resist her future advances. But Jack senses that he is deluding himself – he knows his willpower does not possess sufficient strength to refuse a body as tempting or lips so soft. He is well aware that he has been seduced and is not so arrogant nor so stupid as to deny the pleasure he has derived from Meg's body, or even so naive as to tarnish the experience with a fit of conscience.

He has come away in wonderment at the delight of Meg's body and her female ways, but he is also aware he has betrayed Jessica and that his manhood has ridden roughshod over his sensibilities. He knows it's pointless to feel remorse, though his guilt is quite clear to him. Now, with the dawn breaking, he wonders why his thoughts are not singularly of the beautiful Meg, but are instead persistently of Jessica.

Why could it not have been Jessie waiting for me? he thinks. Jack Thomas knows he does not love Jessica less for having spent the night with Meg, nor does he mean to castigate himself for his unfaithfulness. He tells himself he must first return from the war before he can claim his sweet Jessica and be true to her forever. Meg has said it will be their secret, that nobody will ever know. As Jack heads for home in the quickening light, this thought proves a balm for a conscience where the one-eyed snake is king. Hester was right.

Later the same morning, though this time closer to the noon hour, Meg sees Hester's pony trap approaching the house on her return from old Mrs Baker's sickbed. She drops her crocheting and comes running out into the yard to meet her mother.

'Oh Mama,' she cries, as Hester alights, falling into

her mother's arms, 'it was awful at first and I thought I must surely die of shame, but then it was wonderful!' Meg pushes away and holds Hester at arm's length. 'I was very, very good.'

Hester smiles, collecting her bags from the trap. 'Yes, yes, my dear, it is not seemly that you should enjoy yourself, but will you be pregnant? That is the question.'

'Oh, Mama, it will not be for want of trying,' Meg laughs gaily. 'I think I shall make a splendid Mrs Jack Thomas of Riverview Station.'

'Now, now, my dear, there is still much to be done, do not count your chickens before they hatch.'

CHAPTER EIGHT

Jessica's vomiting continues until it can't be ignored, and Joe decides she needs some attention.

Joe and Jessica arrive in Wagga Wagga to see the Heathwood family doctor, an old codger named Nathaniel Merrick who calls a spade a flamin' shovel and is a man who well understands the ways of the bush.

Joe remains on the verandah seated in a wicker chair while Dr Merrick examines Jessica behind a screen in his surgery. After a thorough examination, he allows Jessica to dress while he washes his hands, then goes out and calls Joe into his surgery. The old doctor shows him to a seat in front of a battered-looking desk and then sits behind it in an old captain's chair with a swivel base so that he appears somewhat unstable, rocking from side to side. As if to steady himself, he places his elbows on the surface of the desk and rests his chin on his clasped hands, then leans slightly forward and addresses his attention to Joe.

'Mr Bergman, your daughter tells me she is not married.'

Joe nods his head. 'This is true, doctor.'

The doctor unclasps his fingers and leans backwards

in the chair, which squeaks in protest. He absently reaches forward and picks up his pen from the desk and places it down again.

'Well, I have examined your girlie and she is pregnant,' he announces.

Joe stares at the old physician in disbelief. 'Pregnant? But she's just been a bit crook in the guts, that's all.'

'Ah, a common enough occurrence with pregnancy, Mr Bergman. She is, I estimate, about two and a half months gone, if I'm not very much mistaken.' He looks up cheerily at Joe. 'Not enough to disgrace the lass, eh? Though you'll want to contact the family of the young bloke concerned and make the necessary wedding arrangements.' He pauses then adds, 'Soon as possible, eh? These things are best done sooner than later.'

Dr Merrick notes Joe's look of surprise and leans over and in a conspiratorial voice declares, 'Come now, these things happen. You may count on my discretion in this matter and, when the time comes, I'll issue a birth certificate with a notice attached to say the child is of premature birth.' He pauses and chuckles. 'Two months is about the average shortfall in the district.'

Jessica, now fully clothed, has come to stand to one side in front of the examination screen. The doctor seems oblivious of her presence and speaks to Joe as if she's not there. 'We are, Mr Bergman, famous in this district for hastily rung wedding bells, a tintinnabulation which proves to us once again that the forces of nature are always more powerful than our intellect.' The physician smiles to himself. 'Any doctor around these parts who mentions the word "shotgun" will, I'll vouch, soon enough find his practice starved of customers.'

Dr Nathaniel Merrick now hears a sob from behind him and turns, surprised. It is as though he has entirely forgotten Jessica's presence in the room. 'Oh there you are, Miss Bergman,' he says. 'Come, come, my dear, it is not such a tragedy. Take my word for it, these things generally have a way of turning out quite splendidly in the end.'

'Thank you, doctor,' Joe mumbles and rises and stands awkwardly, his big fists holding his money purse.

'That will be five shillings and sixpence, thank you,' Nathaniel Merrick says crisply.

Joe counts out the silver coins. He has the exact amount, two half-crowns and a sixpenny bit, and places the coins down on the desk.

'You may have a receipt if you wish, though in these circumstances evidence of a doctor's visit can sometimes prove a botheration. What do you think?'

'No, it don't matter, doctor.'

'We'll keep it to ourselves then,' he says, adding kindly, 'until further notice, eh?'

'Yes, thank you, sir.' Joe nods to Jessica to follow him. They cross the small room and Joe allows Jessica to leave the surgery. He pauses with his hand on the doorknob, turning back. 'Are you real sure, Dr Merrick? Are you, I mean, positive, like?'

The old physician removes his eyeglasses and begins to polish them slowly using a clean gauze dressing. He looks up at Joe quizzically. 'As positive as fifty years of practice in my profession can make me, Joe Bergman. Two and a half months, I'll stand by that.' Joe remains at the door a moment longer and seems to hesitate. Noting Joe's worried expression, the old physician looks sternly at him. 'Mr Bergman, is there something you haven't told me? Have you and the girl . . . ? I think you know what I'm trying to say. Can we expect a normal child?'

'Right,' Joe says absently, not understanding the implications of the old doctor's question. 'Right then, doctor, we'll be off.' He closes the door behind him. Jessica is waiting for him outside and follows him to the sulky and climbs up into the seat. Her head is bowed, and she is trying with all her strength not to cry. Without a word or a look to his youngest daughter, Joe climbs aboard, takes the reins and turns the pony for home. They stop briefly at the Oatbank Brewery beside the river on the edge of town where Joe purchases a bottle of brandy. He is not a drinking man normally – two glasses of milk stout of a Sunday with Jack Thomas is about his limit. Feeling her father's shame, and there being nothing she can possibly say that will comfort Joe, Jessica begins to sob.

It is almost four hours before Joe feels able to speak, by which time Jessica has stopped crying. 'Jessie, who done it to you? Who is the father of your bastard?' Joe tries to keep his voice even but his anger comes through and Jessica draws back as though his words alone have the capacity to harm her. She remains silent, staring miserably out at the flat, remorseless landscape, where the saltbush seems to be dancing in the heat.

'Jessie, dammit, speak to me. Who put you up the duff?'

Jessica shakes her head. 'I can't say,' she replies quietly, trying not to cry again.

'Can't say, or won't say? Look at me, girl!' Joe demands.

Jessica does not reply and bites her bottom lip, refusing to look at Joe.

'Can't or won't? Answer me, will ya!' Joe thunders.

'Won't, Father,' Jessica says softly, then gives a small involuntary sob.

With the reins in his right hand, Joe suddenly reaches out and grabs her by the throat, very nearly pushing her from the sulky. 'I'll not take that from you! You tell me now, Jessie!' With his left hand, he pulls Jessica around so that she looks directly at him. His thumb and forefinger are pushing against her windpipe. 'You tell your father, or I'll thrash you, girl!' Joe stares straight down into Jessica's eyes. They are red-rimmed from weeping, but there's something he's seen in them before – Jessica isn't afraid. He knows she's not going to tell him. His fingers close tighter around her slender neck and he begins to shake her as though the information he needs can be forced from her. He realises that Jessica is going blue, her tongue is protruding from her mouth. She claws frantically at his hand, her eyes filled with terror.

Panting, Joe releases her throat and sees the deep scarlet marks his thumb and finger have made on her neck. He's gripped her too hard and he is shocked to think he might have killed her. There'll be bruises to show for it, the marks on her throat clear for weeks. Jessica bends over and coughs violently, clasping at her throat with both hands. Then she leans quickly over the moving sulky and vomits.

Joe pulls to a halt and waits for his daughter to recover, getting down from the sulky and bringing her the canvas water bag hanging from the back. 'Here, drink this,' he says gruffly, the anger gone from his voice.

Jessica rinses her mouth and spits, then takes a sip of water and winces at the pain of swallowing. She hands the water bag back to Joe before wiping her mouth using her pinny, but doesn't once look at her father. Joe is feeling remorse, realising that he's hurt her, but seeing her recovered, his anxiety turns back into fresh anger. 'You'll tell us or you'll be punished, girl, you understand?' he says roughly. 'Your mother will not forgive you ever, you hear? She's a proud woman and you've shamed her terribly. She'll make you answer for this!'

Jessica turns to face him. 'I can't never tell, Father,' she rasps, her voice barely above a whisper.

Joe stands silent, holding the water bag. The doctor's words keep repeating in his head. Two and a half months – exactly the time when Jessica took Billy Simple into Narrandera. Jessica has been fucked by the idiot and now she carries a murderer's child.

Joe clears his throat and looks across the flat land, shimmering in the afternoon heat. Jessica will bring a shame upon the family from which they can never recover. Hester has been right all along, Joe thinks. His youngest daughter is no good, a rotten apple, and now it's too late. She's destroyed them all and no decent family will consider the notion of Meg as a wife for their son and heir. What Jessica's done will haunt them for the rest of their lives. They will be outcast from society. He has been alone before – he knows he can survive. But Hester will be destroyed and so will Meg, their hopes dashed forever. The foreigner's family tainted with his bad blood, that's what they'll think of us, Joe tells himself harshly.

'It's five hours before we get home. By that time you better have the answer or you'll be sorry.' Joe doesn't shout. His voice is cold and Jessica knows it's his stubbornness against hers, his Bergman will against her own. Joe is going back into his darkness. 'You'll tell your mother who it was, or I'll take the stockwhip to you and thrash you to within an inch of your life.'

He walks around the back of the sulky, hanging the water bag back on its hook. Then he climbs in and holds the reins loosely, not yet urging the pony on. 'Jessica, is it . . . ?' He cannot bring himself to say Billy Simple's name.

Jessica is silent for a while, then she turns to Joe, her hand clasped to her throat. 'You can kill me, but I ain't never gunna tell, Father,' she says in a hoarse whisper.

When Jessica and Joe arrive home Jessica sits outside while Joe goes in to tell Hester of Jessica's pregnancy. Jessica already knows that she's reached the final point with Hester, that her mother cannot forgive her. She also knows that her mother's anger will be more to do with how her pregnancy affects Meg's chances than with any humiliation it brings on the family.

Joe comes back outside and brings Jessica in to sit at the kitchen table to face her mother.

'Who is it?' Hester asks in a savage voice. 'Tell me – or your father will give you a belting you'll never forget.'

Jessica does not respond, but stares stubbornly at her boots.

'Is it that vile creature, Billy Simple?' She does not wait for an answer. 'Hanging is too good for him and now he has destroyed us as well.'

Jessica does not answer and Hester continues, 'How could you do this to us? You are possessed by the Devil. You are the Devil's child!' She turns to Joe, seated at the end of the table. 'Jessica's gone quite mad! She cannot be trusted to live with us. She must receive a whipping and then be banished! She must be put away from decent folk.'

Jessica looks up, frightened. She has expected the whipping, but not that she will be cast out from her family. Surely Joe will not allow this to happen? She looks over to where he sits at the end of the table. But Joe has his head bowed and he has his hands in his lap. Jessica's heart sinks – Joe has given up on her.

'Who knows that Jessica is pregnant?' Hester now asks Joe.

'Only the doctor,' Joe grunts.

'Can we trust him to keep quiet?'

Joe shrugs, not looking up at his wife. 'He said it were in confidence. You should bloody know, he's your family doctor.'

Hester sighs, and then suddenly bursts into tears. 'You

wicked, wicked girl, how could you do this to us? How can you think to so utterly destroy us?' she wails, her lips spit-flecked. She points at Jessica, stabbing a bony fore-finger repeatedly into the air. 'You whore! You filthy whore!' she screams. Rising from the table she rushes over to Jessica and beats her fists against her shoulders and head. 'You dirty little slut!'

'Father! Father!' Jessica howls, pulling her arms over her head to protect her from her mother's flailing blows.

But Joe remains silent and Hester stops as abruptly as she has begun. Her daughter has reduced her to using a word which has rarely passed her lips and one she never thought she'd use against either of her daughters. She stands over Jessica, panting, her entire body trembling, and then says slowly, 'We must be rid of it! The filthy thing. That creature's vile thing inside of you! Kill it!'

Jessica starts to cry. 'Mama, I don't want you to kill it. Please don't kill it!' she sobs.

Meg has stepped into the kitchen, and it is quite apparent that she's been listening all the while at the door. 'It'll be mad like its father,' she says.

'You hold your tongue, Meg,' Joe commands.

'Please, Father. It's mine, don't let them kill my baby,' Jessica sobs, her voice barely above a whisper. She looks up at Joe, pleading. 'Please, Father?'

Hester leans over Jessica and shouts, 'You've done enough damage already, you'll do as you're told!'

Joe looks up suddenly and, half rising from his chair, bangs his fist hard down on the table. 'Silence all of you! Not another word from you lot!' he thunders.

Jessica continues to sob, her head buried again in her arms. Hester and Meg, brought to silence, look to Joe, stunned.

'Jessica, your mother's right. If it gets out that you're pregnant to Billy Simple we'll all be destroyed. It will be the end of us as a family. Nobody is ever to know you're in the family way. You hear me, girl? You will not be seen by anyone. You'll not show your face anywhere. You will not leave this house.'

Jessica looks up at Joe again, appealing to him. 'She's not going to kill my baby, then, Father?' Jessica turns to Hester. 'I swear if you try, I'll tell the whole world you done it, you killed my baby!' she howls.

'Ha, she's mad!' Hester snaps, turning her back on Jessica.

'Jessie, go to your room,' Joe commands. 'You stay there until you're called. Meg, you go to yours too, I want to talk to your mother.'

Jessica gets up from the table and walks towards her bedroom. Her nose is running and her eyes are red and swollen from crying all day. She lets out an involuntary sob as she passes Meg, standing with her arms folded, the hint of a cruel smile at the corners of her mouth. 'Now you've gone and done it,' Meg says smugly, so that only Jessica can hear. 'You've got a bastard in your stomach.'

Jessica is too forlorn to answer her and continues past her to her own room. 'You're disgusting, a whore,' Meg hisses after her.

In the kitchen Joe sighs. 'Perhaps it's someone else's,' he says hopefully.

Hester looks up sharply. 'Whose?'

'I dunno – there's other lads she works with at River-view Station.'

'She's had no work at Riverview for months now. Except for going to Wagga for the trial, she's been here working with you.'

'Maybe someone she met at the trial? I wasn't always with her. It were a boarding house where we stayed – other men were about.'

'Joe, the trial was one month ago. She's two and a half months gone!' Hester looks knowingly at her husband. 'He's the only one Jessica's been with alone. It was two and a half months ago she spent the whole night with Billy Simple when she took him to Narrandera. Your daughter's no heroine, Joe, she's a tart, a floosie, call it what you like. I dare say she's been doing it with him for some time. I can't even think about it, it's that horrible. I should have listened when Ada Thomas, God rest her soul, said Jessica was always around the monster when she went over to work at Riverview.'

Joe looks up at his wife. 'That's because they were mates. I don't believe you, Jessie's not like that. Maybe something happened on the way to Narrandera, but it would be only the once.'

Hester sighs. 'Once is quite enough. It doesn't matter if it's once or a dozen times, she's pregnant to a monster, Joe. What will the child be like, have you thought of that?'

'Whoa, wait now, Billy Simple weren't born a wrong 'un. It were the horse kicked him that done his brain in.

He were a strappin' lad, no fool neither – his children will be normal as you and me.'

'Joe, he's a murderer *and* an Irish Catholic. There's bad blood there and that's passed on,' Hester says darkly.

'What about young Jack? It could be him, they're out alone in the bush often enough,' Joe says. 'He's been over here from time to time, brought the bull over once, took it back, that's twice. There were other times. We could tell him Jessica's pregnant. If he'd done it to her he'd say so, he's a decent enough lad. He'd do the right thing.'

'Joe, don't you dare! Nobody must know about this, least of all Jack Thomas. It would ruin Meg's chances.'

Joe looks at her. 'What chances? It's too late now. She's done her dash – he's off to Sydney on Sunday.'

Hester clears her throat and then swallows hard. 'There's news you don't know yet and God knows this is not the time to tell you.' She shrugs her shoulders. 'It's that . . .'

Joe looks up suspiciously. 'What?' he interjects.

'It's Meg. She could be pregnant to Jack Thomas.'

Joe stares at Hester, unable to comprehend.

Hester holds up her hand. 'No, wait – don't say anything, let me explain.'

Joe brings his hands up to cover his face. 'Ohmegawd! What are you saying, woman?'

'Remember how you once said it would be the only way Meg could get him? Well, it happened while you were away. Jack saw the fence posts the timber-getter brought and I happened to mention to him they were in the wrong place and would need to be shifted to the north paddock. He came over on Wednesday, quite unexpected.' Hester tries to look contrite. 'I mentioned your bad back and he offered to load them and move them.' Hester pauses and says, 'I'm sorry Joe, but you could have gotten hurt moving them.'

'That were decent of him,' Joe growls, though plainly unhappy. 'But him knowing I've got a bad back ain't gunna help me. You shoulda known better, Hester. Shearing season's coming up, I need the work at the station.'

'Jack won't be there, Joe. He's off to the war. He's not going to tell George Thomas – they're still not on speaking terms.'

'Anyway, what's the fence posts got to do with him and Meg?' Joe asks.

'Well, I wasn't here Wednesday night. I was called over to see old Mrs Baker – you know, the organist at St Stephen's. She's got a bad heart – you know how she's always going on about it so that nobody takes much notice – but she was took ill and sent for me. I rode over in the sulky and when I got there she was that unwell I decided to stay the night and mind her.'

'So, what yer tellin' me, him and her was alone? Jack and Meg?'

'Well, I wasn't to know that he was coming over, was I?' Hester protests. 'Meg naturally asked him to stay for tea, to thank him for moving the posts.' Hester pauses and shrugs. 'Two young people in love left together all night . . . It's not surprising under the circumstances.'

'You mean Meg saw her big opportunity?'

'She loves him, Joe!'

'Eh? That one only loves herself. She bloody saw her chance and took it, grabbed it with both hands. I'll bet she couldn't get her bloomers down fast enough.'

Hester sighs. 'You're wrong about Meg, but I won't argue with you, Joe Bergman. The fact is, we can't ask Jack about Jessica.'

'Oh, I see, you *do* think he could've done it to Jessie as well?'

'No, Joe, I don't. You know as well as I do whose child Jessica's carrying. It's Billy Simple's. She'd have told us if it was Jack's, if only to spite Meg.'

Joe frowns, thinking. 'I dunno. Jessie's not foolish, she's not that sort of girl.'

'Ha, little do *you* know!' Hester exclaims.

'What do yer mean by that?'

'Nothing,' Hester says, covering up. 'Just that she's a young girl.'

'Bullshit. That's not what you mean. What are you saying about Jessie?' Joe demands.

'Well, she does things.'

'Does things? What sort o' things?'

Hester sighs. 'Joe, it's not something you ought to know about.'

'Jesus! The girl's pregnant to a fucking monster and it's not something I oughta know about?' Joe yells. '*What* bloody things, woman?'

'She fiddles with herself, does unnatural things to herself.'

'What's that supposed ter mean?'

'In places where she ought not.'

Joe looks at his wife, bemused. 'What places?'

Hester sighs. 'Women's places. Places a man hasn't got.'

A look of astonishment appears on Joe's face. 'You mean . . . ? Do women do that?'

'No, Joe, only very wicked ones, dirty buggers.' Hester taps the side of her head. 'Jessica's been doing it a long time.'

'How do you know?'

'I'm her mother. I saw it with my own eyes – she left her bedroom door open, and I saw her!'

'Does Meg do it as well?'

'Of course not! Meg wouldn't. It isn't decent. Meg's a nice clean girl.'

Joe looks suspiciously at his wife. 'You're not making all this up, are you, Hester?'

'I swear it, on my life.'

Joe is silent for a while, then says gruffly, 'It don't mean nothing. Just growing pains.'

'Ha! Joe, it explains everything,' Hester protests, then stabs her finger at Joe's chest. 'Might as well hear it from me, Jessica is a slag. She's been doing filthy things to herself since she was eleven years old. I tell you, it isn't natural and it's what's made her go loony, too!'

'Bullshit! I don't believe she's mad, not for a minute,' Joe protests, but he's out of his depth with such women's talk. Hester senses his confusion and is quick to take advantage.

'Joe, listen to me. Jessica's not well.' Hester taps her head. 'Who knows what she'll do the way she is at the moment? Besides, she doesn't know about Meg and Jack.' Hester sighs. 'What I'm saying is, if Meg is pregnant to Jack he could use the scandal of Jessica's pregnancy to Billy Simple to get out of marrying her. Then where would we be? *Both* Bergman girls pregnant out of wedlock, the one to a murderer and a madman, the other trying to entrap the richest lad in the Riverina before he goes to war? Jack Thomas would have the sympathy of the whole community. They'd urge him not to marry Meg, not to go near the little gold digger. We'd be dirt and people would say we deserve all that's coming to us.' Hester spreads her hands, appealing to her husband. 'Joe, don't you see – it's not just Meg who's involved, it's all of us!'

'Shit, shit, shit! How did all this happen?' Joe says despairingly, then looks up at Hester. 'One night don't guarantee nothing. What if Meg ain't pregnant?'

Hester shrugs. 'We still can't take the chance of telling Jack about Jessica, not in the next three days anyway. Maybe later – he'll be in Sydney for at least ten weeks. We'll know for sure by then.' Hester walks over and takes Joe's hand in a rare pretence at affection. 'Joe, don't you see? It's Jack's child with Meg who needs to be protected. Jessie's carrying Billy Simple's bastard and if that gets out, it's the end of all of us.'

Joe sees the logic in Hester's argument, sees clearly that they've been caught between a rock and a hard place. He brings his hands to his forehead and then wipes them slowly across his face. 'We'll have to decide about Jessie, what to do,' he says wearily.

'Joe, we've got to get rid of it. There's a woman in Wagga I've heard about . . .'

'No!' Joe looks up at his wife sharply. 'No, I won't hear of it, you understand? I've heard of them backyard doings, knitting needles and bits o' fencing wire to hook it out. Come what may, I ain't putting Jessie's life in danger. She's still our daughter.'

Hester sniffs. 'Yours maybe.'

Joe pretends he doesn't hear. 'We'll have to think of something else. We could keep her in the house and when folk ask where she is we could say she's had one o' them nervous breakdowns like the newspapers said.' He glances at Hester hopefully. 'We could admit to that, it's better than the other. They'll soon enough figure out that she's gorn a bit in the head, like. They'll understand that. It's not too unusual anyway, especially her being through what she's been.' Joe stops and seems to be thinking. 'After a while she could get better an' all,' he says, again hopefully.

'True enough,' Hester sniffs and then adds sarcastically, 'and her going loony has put a lot of weight on her at the same time, all of it in front, so she looks just like she's pregnant! Joe, she can't just stay in the house for the next seven months until her baby comes. Even if we manage to keep her hidden, then what? What do we tell people? The stork brought us a brand-new baby? A bastard who looks just like Billy Simple? It come down the chimney one dark and stormy night?'

'She's not getting rid of it, that's all there is to it. You heard what she said, she wants to keep the baby.'

'Joe, she's not right in the head. Don't you see? She's not responsible, not normal. What does Jessica know about babies, eh? I ask you! Would anyone normal who has a murderer's bastard child, a madman's brat in her stomach, want to keep it? I know I wouldn't. Meg wouldn't. No sane woman would! Can you imagine the future for the child? For Jessica herself? People pointing at her and the child, never forgetting where it came from. "There goes mad Jessie with the murderer's bastard child",' Hester mimics. 'Joe, she'd be better off in her grave, and the child with her!'

Joe cannot believe he has heard Hester correctly. *Better off in her grave?* It's all about Meg, ain't it? All about your precious daughter. Not spoiling her chances,' he says coldly.

'It's about us, Joe,' Hester now says urgently, 'all of us!' She is close to tears. 'Meg hasn't let us down, she deserves her chance!'

'Well, if it's about all of us, then we stick together. Jessie is us, she's our daughter. I don't give a fuck about what folk say. I come from nowhere, I'm nothing, nobody, but I won't destroy me own. Jessie's not to be tampered with, you hear me, Hester?'

Hester bursts into tears. 'You won't have to destroy her, she's already done it to herself.' She looks up sob-faced. 'Joe, I beg you. This is Meg's last chance. We've got to hide Jessica, if only for another three weeks, please!'

'Three weeks? Why three weeks?'

'Meg, she's not like Jessie – she's always on time with her monthly. Her bleeding. If she doesn't bleed we'll know she's pregnant.'

'And then what?' Joe asks, still not understanding.

Hester looks fiercely at Joe. He recognises it is the same look she had when she banished him from her bed eighteen years before, a look in her dark eyes that brooks no refusal. 'If she's pregnant we'll take her to Sydney and make Jack Thomas marry her.' She glares defiantly at Joe. 'I'll not have both my daughters branded whores!'

'Oh, Jesus, what will become of us?' Joe says, more to himself than to his wife. Looking up at Hester, he says slowly, 'Woman, I know this is of your making. You and your daughter. I pray that Meg ain't pregnant to Jack Thomas – that what you done isn't forever on our conscience.'

'Then you agree?' Hester demands to know. Joe nods wearily. Hester straightens up and wipes her hands across her apron, now the picture of resolve. 'Joe, Jessica mustn't know about Meg and Jack, not until she sees Meg's pregnant for herself.' Joe nods again. 'And she can't be about when Jack comes over to say good-bye to us – it may give her a chance to speak to him.' Hester looks at Joe, her eyes narrowed. 'Besides, he'll want to know what the marks are on her throat.'

Joe ignores this last remark. 'So? What are you saying, woman?'

'We can say the doctor kept her in hospital in Narrandera. He knows you took her in to see him and that she wasn't well.'

'Nah, he's gotta go to Narrandera to report to the recruiting office and then catch the train to Sydney. He'll want to see her – they've been good mates a long time. She'll just have to stay in her room when he comes over on Sunday.'

'No, Joe, you know how stubborn she is. Even if we lock her in, she's just as likely to scream out, shout to him. The way she is, she could do anything.'

Joe looks down and scratches his head. 'She could go down to the hut, I s'pose. You know the little corrugated-iron humpy down by the creek. Boundary riders used it when this was part of the Great Peter's Run. It's still in good enough nick – nothing but tin and a dirt floor, but the weather don't get in too much.'

Hester looks puzzled. 'You mean lock her up?'

'I could, though there's no door. I guess I could make one. Take a good part of the day, though. It's a mile off – she won't be heard by anyone if she shouts and I'll fetch her back after Jack's gone.' Joe can't believe what he is saying to his wife – that he could do such a thing to Jessica.

Hester is immensely pleased with the idea and claps her hands. 'We'll tell Jack she's had to go to Wagga – something to do with Billy Simple's trial, some paper she has to sign for the court that they didn't tell her about at the time.'

'Nah, won't work. Jack'll be suspicious that I let her go alone, him knowing she isn't well and me having gone with her before.'

'Better still then, you go with her. Stay with her in the

stockman's humpy. With you there to keep an eye on her, she won't try to escape to see him. We're going to need a place where she can hide in the next few months. Can you fix it up a bit? Maybe she'll have to stay longer than a day or two at times.'

And so it is decided. Hester and Meg will be left alone to say goodbye to Jack Thomas when he arrives on Sunday for his last home-cooked dinner. They are to eat early so he has plenty of time to ride into town and arrive before nightfall. Jack has joined the New South Wales Light Horse, his uncle's regiment.

On Sunday morning early, Jessica, distraught that she's not to be allowed to see Jack and bid him farewell, has left with Joe for the old boundary rider's hut. Joe hasn't tried to deceive her, but he's made a deal with her. She won't be sent away from home, won't be banished, if she'll agree not to try to see Jack again.

Joe tells her he wants to make sure the boundary rider's hut is still good for storing winter hay against the rain and she can help him make a door. They'll also look at the fences while they're gone. It's not the usual Sunday work but Jessica knows that he wants her to be well away from the homestead.

Joe hasn't found it easy to convince Jessica to stay away from saying goodbye to Jack. 'Why, Father?' she asks him. 'Is it because I'm pregnant? But Jack doesn't know!' She looks down at her belly. 'He can't see nothing. I'm not gunna tell him – I already gave you my word.'

Joe sighs heavily. 'I trust you, girlie, but your mother don't. She told you herself you couldn't see him.'

'Because of Meg?'

'You know it is, Jessie.'

'But that were just for the last week. To see if Meg could catch him. This is his last day. Father, I may never see Jack again! Can't I just say goodbye? That can't do no harm to Meg.'

'I'm sorry, Jessie. I promised your mother,' Joe says tight-lipped. 'Please? No more, I'm not gunna argue with you. What's done is done.'

Jessica thinks her heart must surely break. How she aches to see Jack just one last time. Just to have him standing in front of her, to touch his hand, feel it clasped in her own. To kiss him no matter how briefly. To breathe him in, remember his smell. Hear him laugh. Rub her hand up his forearm and watch the thick blond hair through the gaps between her fingers. She remembers how she once told him it looked like the wind passing through late summer grass. If she can have just one moment to look into his blue eyes, just long enough so she can remember him, fix his dear face clearly in her mind until he returns to her.

'But he's my friend!' she says desperately. Joe can see she's terribly upset and is fighting to hold back her tears. Jessica hasn't cried since they got back from the doctor, and after that first evening in the kitchen. Or, at least, she hasn't let them see her weep. 'Whatever will Jack think of me if I don't say goodbye, Father?' she pleads one final time.

'We already took care of that, girlie. You and me has had to go to Wagga urgent, some papers to sign about

the trial that was forgotten to do when we was there.'
Joe looks at his daughter, not unkindly. 'He'll understand, Jessie. He'll know it wasn't your fault, that you'd
be there to say goodbye to him if you could.'

'Will you give him a letter from me, then?' Jessica
asks. 'He'll at least expect a letter if I'm supposed to
have gone away. He knows I wouldn't let him go without saying goodbye!'

Joe sees the sense in this. 'Orright,' he says slowly,
knowing he'll have to leave the letter with Hester who
will see to it that it never gets delivered. 'But you must
let me read it first.'

'No!' Jessica says suddenly. Despite all that's happened
she can't believe Joe doesn't trust her. Then, realising
she's over-reacted, she adds, 'I wouldn't read *your* letter,
Father.'

'Then you must promise me you won't tell him about
what's happened to you.'

Jessica looks up at Joe, her clear green eyes showing
she is hurt. 'Father, I already told you, I won't tell him
about my baby. I give you my word.'

Jessica tries to deny the weakness she now sees in Joe.
She's seen it before, though she's always thought the
bond between them was something that couldn't be broken – that, in the end, he'd always take her side. Now
she's no longer certain, no longer sure she can depend on
him. Joe is becoming an old man and, more and more,
giving way to his wife. Hester is now pulling the strings
with most things. Jessica knows Hester will read the letter, so she can't put nothing in it about her love for Jack.

Their love for each other. Nor can she tell him she will wait for him – that no man will ever take his place in her life. She will be forced to write a letter stiff and formal, not revealing her true feelings, simply expressing her friendship. Hester and Meg have her trapped, and Jessica's heart is filled with despair.

It is at that moment, when Jessica promises him that she won't talk to Jack about her child, that Joe too feels total despair – feels he has broken from his youngest daughter forever. He believes Jessica when she says she won't speak to Jack about her child. She's never lied to him. Up to this moment he's still harboured some hope in his heart that Jack may be the father, that the opportunity may all have come about when he and Jessica went for one of their walks after a Sunday dinner. Joe's imagination is limited, but he's told himself that if Meg and Jessica both have a child of Jack's and Jack marries Meg, then Jessica's child will be took care of. He understands that Jack may prefer Jessica. They're long-time mates, of the right age, and so why not, he argues to himself. It'd be natural enough. Gawd knows, the two o' them are well enough suited. But now that Joe knows for certain Jessica won't tell Jack about her baby, it can mean only one thing. She *isn't* carrying his child. Jessica is pregnant to Billy Simple and Hester is right about her.

Hester and Meg cook up a storm for Jack's farewell Sunday dinner. It's a roast leg of lamb and a rump roast of beef, with the sideboard stacked with tarts, pies and cakes enough to feed an army. The homestead smells

deliciously of roasting meat and baking by the time
Jack arrives on horseback around ten o'clock.

It is too early yet to eat and he's barely climbed down
from his horse, tied it to the post rail and given it the
feed bag Joe's left out, when Meg comes tripping down
the front steps wearing a hat. She suggests they go for
a walk before dinner.

'Shouldn't I say g'day to your folks . . . to Jessie?'
Jack asks, surprised.

Meg grasps his arm, a look of concern on her face.
'Oh, Jack, it is such a terrible shame. Jessica and Father
can't be here, they've had to go to Wagga.'

'Wagga? Why'd they do that?' Meg can see Jack is
disappointed.

'The trial, Billy Simple's trial – they forgot to sign some
papers when they were there. He can't be hanged unless
they do,' she adds dramatically. 'They couldn't stay, it was
government orders to be there first thing tomorrow.' Meg
smiles. 'Jessica says to say goodbye, Father also.'

Jack is silent for a while, then looks up slowly at Meg.
'Just goodbye? She didn't leave a letter or anything?'

Meg dances gaily ahead of him then, turning, says,
'Why heavens, no! Jessie doesn't much care for writing.' She walks back to Jack and, reaching up, places
her hands on his shoulders. Standing on tip-toe, she
kisses him on the cheek. Then she takes Jack's hand.
'Come, a walk will do your appetite the world of good.
I've baked all the things you like.'

Jack stops, pulling Meg to a halt. He releases her
hand. 'Meg, about the other night . . .'

'Oh, Jack, it was so lovely, us being alone.'

Jack looks down at his riding boots. 'It's just, well, I don't know what come over me.'

Meg stands in front of him and puts her hands on her hips in a show of pretended exasperation, then she sighs prettily. 'Jack, if you're trying to say you're sorry, please don't. It was my way of saying goodbye.' She pauses, a frown on her pretty face, her lips now formed into a pout. 'You're not angry with me, are you, Jack?'

Jack looks up in alarm. 'Angry? Of course not.'

'And I made you happy, didn't I?'

Jack nods, knowing he is being cleverly led away from what he wants to say. 'It was lovely, Meg, it's just –'

'That you feel you shouldn't have taken advantage,' Meg interrupts. 'Well you should have, Jack, I wanted you to.' She grabs Jack's big hand in both her own and brings it to her lips. 'Jack Thomas, you're the first man I've ever loved and I'll never love another. What happened to us was beautiful.'

Jack feels trapped and can think of nothing to say. 'Meg, you're pretty and all, but the war . . . I'm off to the war. Anything could happen.' Jack scratches his head. 'I, er . . . wouldn't want you to think . . .'

'Think what? That you're obliged to me?'

'Well, yes,' Jack says gratefully, 'it wouldn't be right to make plans, not knowing what the future will hold.' He puts his head to one side. 'It's uncertain times ahead, Meg.'

'Of course I'm not making plans. What plans? I'm not your wife, Jack.' Meg laughs lightly. 'Not your missus with a brat hanging onto her skirt, seeing her old man going off to war.'

Jack gives a wry grin at Meg's description. 'Too right!' He's grasped at Meg's pronouncement like a man drowning. 'It would be wrong to make any commitment. I don't want you to think what happened is, well, like . . . a betrothal.'

Meg gives Jack an indulgent smile. 'These are modern times, Jack. Queen Victoria is long dead.' She tosses her head back. 'But, there you go, you're not married to me and I have no children clutching at my skirt.' Meg loosens the ribbon on her hat sufficiently so that it falls from her head and rests on the back of her shoulders. She squints slightly, adjusting to the bright sunlight. 'What happened between us was so lovely.' Her eyes glisten with sudden tears. 'Oh, Jack, it was the first time for me and I shall cherish it all the days of my life.' She pauses and draws right up to him, staring into Jack's blue eyes, her lips pursed invitingly.

Jack tries hard to conceal his relief that she doesn't expect him to marry her. 'Meg, you're a grand girl, a true sport.'

Meg smiles and draws back. The tears of a moment before seem to have disappeared as quickly as they'd first appeared. Plucking at the sides of her skirt, she does a pretty little curtsy in front of Jack. 'Why thank you, kind sir.' Then straightening, she says, 'Now shall we feed the gallant soldier?'

'But aren't we going for a walk?'

'Never mind that now. We have an array of fine

dishes fit for a general in command waiting for you.' Meg laughs again. 'I confess, Mother and I have been cooking for two days.'

Jack grins, hugely relieved at the outcome. 'Goodo! I'm starving hungry, lemme at it.' He turns towards the homestead steps but Meg pulls him back.

'You have to pay for your dinner, Jack.' Meg puts her hands behind her back and, closing her eyes, tilts her head towards him, her lips slightly parted as she offers them to him.

Jack bends down and kisses her lightly on the cheek. Meg's eyes open wide in alarm. 'No, Jack, I want a kiss from a soldier going to war! A kiss to remember!' Her arms now come out to embrace him and Jack is obliged to receive her into his own. Then he bends and kisses Meg on the mouth. He can feel her warmth against him, she smells of some light perfume and her lips pressed into his seem soft as rose petals. But all he can think of is Jessica. Of kissing and holding sweet, lithe Jessica in his arms.

At dinner Hester and Meg make most of the chatter as Jack tucks into his food. He's never been known for his conversation at the table and it's usually only Jessica who can get him to talk much beyond the usual courtesies. But today he seems unusually bereft of words. The talk outside with Meg seems to have quietened him down completely and Hester realises how much Jessica adds to his presence when they're at the table. Meg thinks it's as if Jack has come to get something off his mind and having done so, has more or less exhausted his daily allotment of words. His responses to the bright words she and Hester banter about are only barely polite, though, thankfully, his lack of words is not matched by a poor appetite and he digs into his food as though he hasn't eaten for a fortnight.

'Best food I've ever had, Mrs Bergman,' he ventures at last. 'I'm full to bursting, like a cow in the lucerne paddock.'

Hester smiles. 'Don't thank me, Jack. Thank Meg, she cooked most of it. A young woman should know how to cook well, don't you think?'

'I'll say!' Jack now turns to Meg. 'Great tucker, Meg. Thank you.'

'And how to take care of a large house,' Hester continues. 'Though with only the four of us and this place only a cottage, she doesn't get much of a chance to show off her homemaking or culinary skills. Joe and Jessie are plain eaters both.'

'Well, I don't suppose I'll eat like that again in a while.' Jack grins and thinks for a moment. 'The two girls couldn't cook for toffee, my mother neither. Come to think of it, Mrs Briggs, our cook, isn't too good either – meat and potatoes and steamed puddin' left for us cold of a Sunday.' Jack grins at the memory. 'Bloody steamed pud, never want to taste another mouthful.'

At the unexpected mention of Ada Thomas and Jack's two sisters, Hester and Meg grow silent. But before they can speak, Jack continues, unaware of the shock he's caused in the two of them. 'I miss the fighting. They were always fighting, shouting at each other.

All three of them. There was always someone crying.'
Jack looks over at Hester. 'You wouldn't think you'd
miss that, would you?'

Hester sighs. 'Such a terrible tragedy, Jack. You poor
boy.'

'Jack, will you have another cuppa?' Meg asks suddenly, hoping to lift the conversation to a brighter note.

Jack shakes his head. 'Mrs Bergman, I know what
I'm going to say I shouldn't. But I'm going off to the
war . . . and who knows? I want to say something
about Jessica and Billy.'

Meg stretches out and touches the back of Jack's
hand. 'There's no need, Jack. You don't have to say
anything.'

'No, no, I want to. I couldn't maybe have said this in
front of Jessica, but now she's not here I can – I must.'

'Do you mean all the talk about what happened at
the courthouse in Narrandera?' Hester asks hurriedly.
'There's no need, Jack. It's idle talk, you know how
country people are. They love a bit of gossip. We
haven't taken it seriously.'

'No, not that, Mrs Bergman. What the newspapers
said after the trial, how Jessica stuck up for Billy. The
newspapers reckon she's had a nervous breakdown, saying she's, well, you know, around the twist. Saying no
one in their right mind could stick up for a murderer
when he's done what Billy did to my mother and sisters.'

'Jessica's been under a great strain, Jack. She's not
been well. Please don't blame her for defending Billy
Simple,' Hester says softly. Then, almost pleading, she

adds, 'Meg is very different to her sister, they're chalk and cheese.'

'Blame her?' Jack looks bewildered. 'I'm not blaming Jessie. What Billy did was wrong. It's terrible sad that he'll hang for it, but I suppose he must. But Jessica did the right thing by him. She told his side in the court.' Jack looks at both of them in turn. 'I know you think I shouldn't be talking like this when it's my mother and sisters he killed.'

'Jack, there's no need,' Meg cries, 'you've been through enough!'

'No, no, I want to go on. I don't want to go into it, you know, the badness of it all. It makes me too sad even to think about what was done to my family. Maybe, when I go to the war it'll help me to forget. But, still and all, Billy *did* have a side and Jessie had the courage to say so.'

'Jack, my daughter's not well, she's . . .'

Jack, normally polite, talks over Hester. 'What Jessie did, knowing she'd be hated and misunderstood by everyone, was very brave and I take my hat off to her.' Jack pauses. Meg sees that he's sweating and he wipes his hand over his face so that it comes away wet and he wipes it on his napkin. 'The three of us were real good mates before what happened to Billy, and she stuck by him right to the last. She gave poor Billy some dignity to take to his grave. It was me who let him down. I admire Jessie more than I can say.' Jack is silent with his head bowed, then he raises it slowly and looks first at Meg and then at Hester. 'That's all I wanted to say, except that I'd like to leave her a note. To say goodbye. Will you let me do that?'

It is more than Jack has said in all the time they have known him.

After Jack has departed Hester tears open the sealed envelope he's given her for Jessica and unfolds the single page within it. Hester is surprised at the very few words on the page. Jack's hand is clear and well formed, the way they teach them at the King's School.

> *Goodbye, Tea Leaf.*
> *See you when I get back.*
> *Yours, ever,*
> *Jack.*

Hester passes the note over to Meg. 'Hmph! We should've told the stupid boy. We should've told him whose bastard she's got in her stomach. That'd fix him proper! It looks like our fight's not over yet, Meg.'

Meg looks up from the letter she holds. Her dark eyes are bright with her hatred, her voice close to tears. 'No, Mama, it's not over yet,' she says fiercely. 'Jack is mine!'

CHAPTER NINE

The date is announced for the hanging of Billy
Simple. He will pay his final debt to society at the
new Long Bay Prison in Sydney on the sixth of August,
1914. The announcement is made just two weeks after
Jack Thomas has commenced training camp. By some
terrible quirk of fate, he will be riding in his passing-out
parade as the trapdoor opens to end Billy Simple's short,
sad life.

On the day Billy Simple's hanging is announced, Jessica takes herself down to the river to weep. She has
written to him on three occasions, hoping that her letters will be read to him, that they will comfort him in his
loneliness. Joe had taken her letters and posted
them – he'd even provided the pen and ink and paper,
although he'd made her promise first that she wouldn't
try to write to Jack Thomas. However, after extracting
her promise, he'd never asked her why she wanted the
paper, though she'd told him it was to write to Billy
Simple. Poor Billy has no one. His family up near the
Lachlan have disowned him. Jessica sees him sitting forlorn in his death cell, not understanding. She has heard
no word since the day he was sentenced in Wagga. She

recalls how Joe had told her that day: 'Best forget him, think of him as already dead, girlie.'

Jessica is now showing enough so that any experienced female eye will observe her condition and she is forced to wear a cotton skirt to accommodate her pregnancy. Joe is spending the days for the most part fixing up the boundary rider's hut, though Jessica, busy on another part of the property, is not aware of this. She is kept close to the homestead and if anyone is seen to approach Hester makes her come indoors immediately and go to her room. If this is not possible, she has to remain out of sight until the visitor has departed. Already there are whispers in the farming community that she has taken leave of her senses. When Hester or Meg are asked about Jessica at St Stephen's they pause briefly and seem strangely hesitant to speak about her, which heightens the suspicions of the stickybeaks.

The shearing season is almost upon them and, as usual, George Thomas has called for the locals to front up at the shearing shed. But Joe has been rejected for the first time in twenty years. For the past three years Jessica's been his rouseabout and together they have managed to get through their quota, though with increasing difficulty as Joe's back has grown worse each season. But now, without her, Joe is simply an old man with rheumatism who is unfortunate enough to have to depend on George Thomas, an employer without sentiment or loyalty. So Joe is given the heave-ho and his days as a shearer at Riverview Station are over.

Joe is also aware that Jessica's involvement with Billy

Simple's capture will have put the kybosh on further work from George Thomas. Without Jessica at his side on the farm, and with no money coming in from the shearing season, Joe is in a state of despair. The drought, except for a little winter rain, has gone on for three years and he has been forced to kill off his lambs. His cattle are four legs and a casement of skin and bone. What sheep are left won't bring enough wool to buy feed for them through another summer of drought – and the mortgage payments on the property are already six months in arrears.

Joe has lapsed into a state of darkness where he can barely speak for the fear that tortures him. He rises in the morning in silence and returns home to stare at his plate for ten minutes before forcing himself to eat what is set before him. Then, after tea in the evenings, with a grunt, he is off to his sleep-out. Jessica, whose room is nearest to the back of the house, can hear him crying out in his sleep.

Joe no longer tolerates her working at his side, nor will he speak to her beyond the basic necessities. Jessica is isolated by her father's private torture and his loss of trust in her, and even more so by Meg and Hester, who have placed her in purgatory ever since Jack Thomas departed for Sydney.

Shortly after sunrise one day in the same week as the date of Billy Simple's hanging is announced, Meg enters the kitchen wide-eyed and sobbing. Hester, who is busy at the stove stirring porridge, puts down her wooden spoon and takes her in her arms.

'What is it, precious?' Hester asks in alarm.

'Mama, my monthly has come!' Meg wails.

Hester holds her daughter in her arms for some time, fussing, patting her back, sharing her grief, for she feels the shock of Meg's news almost as greatly as her daughter.

It has all finally come to an end. Hester's plans to have Jack Thomas for her elder daughter have foundered. Ever since Meg was fourteen years old, they have had their eye on him, and everything that Meg has striven for is so that she will be the mistress of Riverview one day. Even when they thought Jack had been disinherited, Meg had found it difficult to think beyond this prospect. Now, after employing every device at their command, they have finally failed, defeated by nature.

After a while Hester pushes a sobbing Meg away. 'Sit, dearest, I'll make you a nice cuppa,' she says gently. She is suddenly conscious of the porridge burning, so hastens back to the stove and stirs the pot quickly. She reaches for the kettle which sits on the back hob and pours a little water into the stiffening oatmeal, then uses what remains to make a pot of tea.

'Oh God, it's not fair,' Meg cries, banging her fist on the kitchen table. 'That little bitch has got pregnant and I can't.' Hester places a tin mug of hot, sweet tea in front of her daughter. 'It's not fair! It's not fair!' Meg howls.

'Meg, shut up!' Hester says.

Meg looks up in alarm. 'Mama?'

'Shhh! Let me think,' Hester says. 'Bawling isn't going to get us anywhere, girl. Go and wash your face.

Your father and Jessica will be back from the paddocks any moment to get their breakfast. I want you smiling, you hear? Smiling and happy as though nothing has happened.'

'Smiling? Mama, how can I?'

'Meg, go now. If you can't come out cheerful you must remain in your room.'

With Meg and Hester responding to Joe's dark moods, breakfast is increasingly a silent affair. But this morning Meg, being a real little trouper, has rallied and they speak cheerily enough among themselves. Joe, as usual, says little and slops up his porridge, speaking only in monosyllables usually to demand the salt or more milk or butter.

Jessica, who has endured almost three weeks of being shunned, has reached a point when she thinks she must be going mad to be punished so. She has lost her confidence and jumps each time Joe grunts at her or her mother plonks a plate of food in front of her. She grows increasingly nervous at Meg's sly smile and begins to think that her sister takes pleasure from her distress.

Jessica is frightened and lonely and her body seems to be changing. Her breasts have grown larger and her nipples are sore to the touch and have taken to weeping a clear fluid. Thankfully the queasiness and vomiting in the morning have ceased. But she has no one who can share her concerns or comfort her. Her mother has not given her a single word of advice.

Jessica is sure of one thing, though – they will not harm the life that is growing in her. She has never thought seriously that she might bear a child, but now she wants the infant she carries with every breath in her body.

After breakfast Jessica goes off to feed the pigs. Joe is about to leave when Hester asks him to stay and pours him a third cup of tea. She sends Meg away, then pours herself a second cup and sits beside her husband at the table.

'Joe, Meg's had her monthly. She's not pregnant,' Hester announces.

'Well, thank Christ for that,' Joe says, relieved.

'It's a great disappointment.'

'Disappointment my arse. It's justice.' For the first time in two weeks, Joe smiles. 'She's had her come-uppance at bloody last!'

'Joe, listen to me, there's still a way.'

'Bullshit! Maybe now Meg can be put to work, Gawd knows we need the money.'

'Put to work?' Hester says, alarmed. 'Joe, Meg isn't Jessica, she doesn't know about sheep and cattle or how to do things about the place.'

'Mike Malloy at the shearing shed says they're putting up the telegraph at Yanco and they're looking for a lass who can read and speak nice and who knows everyone. He says Meg could be just the ticket.'

'She'll do no such thing,' Hester snorts. 'Meg is a lady. I haven't brought her up to work in the post office.'

Joe looks at Hester wearily. 'I've been rejected at the shed, George Thomas has thrown me out. I'm beaten neck and crop, love. Jessie's not earning neither – that's two wages we've lost, good money too, the best we earn all year. We'll lose the run if I can't meet the bank payments.' Joe covers his face with his hands. 'Oh shit, things couldn't be bloody worse.'

Hester has never seen him like this – never seen him cry. No sound comes from behind his hands and his shoulders shake. She can feel Joe's terrible humiliation. He's not talked about money before, though she knows they've come close enough to disaster several times in the past. Joe has somehow always managed to keep his worries to himself, to keep his pride intact and their little drought-struck island afloat in a sea of debt.

'Joe, I've thought of a way.'

Joe looks up, his eyes angry. 'What bloody way is that? Meg to give crochet lessons to the landed fucking gentry?'

'I don't know, maybe a way to solve everything.'

Joe shrugs. 'Hester, you know nothing about making a quid.'

'Be that as it may, Joe Bergman, I know something about making plans.'

Joe says nothing, cupping his hands around the mug of tea in front of him and staring at the cross-grain in the timber of the table.

'Joe, Jessica doesn't know that Meg's pregnant.'

'Meg ain't pregnant, you just said so.'

'Yes, but Jessica doesn't know she was *supposed* to be. We must tell her that Meg is pregnant and is going to have Jack's child.'

'No! The girl has suffered enough. No, fuck you, Hester, we'll not make it worse for her, you pleased as punch with Meg and poor bloody Jessica in disgrace!'

'Joe, please, mind your language. Listen to me, it's important.' Hester takes a breath. 'Nobody knows *Jessica's* pregnant, do they?'

'The doctor bloody knows.'

'That's just it. Now try to remember, when you saw Dr Merrick did you give him Jessica's name, her Christian name?'

Joe scratches his head, trying to recall. 'No, I just said she was me daughter. You know, "Doctor, I'd like you ter look at me daughter, she's been chucking up her guts in the mornin'." '

'You sure of that? He didn't write anything down?'

'Nah, she said not, when I asked later. She said he took her behind a screen and examined her and asked about the vomiting.' Joe tries to think if there is anything else. 'Yeah, now I remember, he called her "my dear" at first and then "Miss Bergman". That were only the once, when we was talking after, like.'

' "Miss Bergman". He said "Miss Bergman"?' Hester repeats in delight. 'Are you sure?'

'Yeah. I dunno. Maybe he said somethin' behind the screen she forgot to say, but I didn't hear him say nothing 'cept questions to me.'

'All right, then. Joe, you're going to have to go in and see old Dr Merrick and take him a letter from me. Take him in a flitch of your cured bacon as well.'

Hester then explains her plan to Joe, who is at first reluctant to go along with his wife, though after much convincing he agrees. Desperate to save his family, he sees that in her plan there is a chance to do so, though his conscience is sorely tried. Hester sits down to compose a letter to the Heathwood family doctor.

Dr Nathaniel Merrick Esq.
Wagga Wagga

30 July 1914

Dear Dr Merrick,

I trust you are well and in good spirits. Thank you for seeing our daughter Meg and for so very kindly agreeing to keep our untimely news confidential. It is nice to think that in times like these we may turn to the family doctor for compassion and understanding.

You have seen the comings and goings of three generations of the Heathwood family and I hope you will agree we have always conducted ourselves with the utmost respectability in the Narrandera community.

We lead a quiet life here in the country so I don't expect that the townsfolk will come to hear of our most recent misfortune, though it saddens me greatly to think that our daughter has so badly let our little family down. Alas, the problem we face is more than at first it seemed. We have discovered our daughter's affections have been extended over some months to not one, but two young men.

Meg admits to a special regard for one particular lad and I am happy to report that he is from a good

Protestant family and is not entirely without prospects. The other boy is of the other religion and entirely unsuitable and would, we feel quite sure, make for an unhappy future for our daughter.

However, we are now faced with a dilemma which I am sure you will readily understand. While we require a letter from you attesting to Meg's pregnancy, we do not wish you to state its duration.

The lad she has chosen and who seems to return her affections is afraid to approach his father. He, the boy in question, works on a big station and his father may well be able to prove his son was away on one of the bigger runs at the time you state Meg fell pregnant.

It would be best for all concerned if you will see your way to state in your letter simply that Meg is expecting, so that we may use this confirmation to its greatest effect when my husband and I visit the father of the young man.

I would be so very grateful if you will oblige us with this preference, as, at your own suggestion, we are anxious to put right this matter as soon as possible so that the child may be born within wedlock.

I beg you to destroy this letter so that it may not prove a future source of suffering to us should it ever come into the possession of other interested parties.

Yours sincerely,
Hester Bergman (Mrs) nee Heathwood.

Joe leaves in the morning, riding all day, and is ushered into the old doctor's surgery in the late afternoon, carrying the flitch of bacon carefully wrapped in cheesecloth. 'Sit down, Mr Bergman, I had not expected you back so soon,' Nathaniel Merrick invites.

Joe tries to conceal his nervous state. He places the bacon down, leaning it against the desk. 'Doctor, a nice bit o' bacon, Hester thought you might fancy a slice or two for yer breakfast,' Joe begins. Then, lost for further words, he adds quickly, 'Cured with a bit o' redgum honey, like they done in Denmark.'

'Thank you, very kind of you.' Nathaniel Merrick clears his throat. 'What was it you wanted to see me about, Joe?'

Joe immediately feels more comfortable. 'Doctor, you remember my wife, Hester Heathwood?'

The old man hesitates. Joe fears suddenly that he doesn't remember Hester and the letter will come to naught. 'Heathwood, ah yes, an old name around these parts. The Heathwoods have always been with me. There were a few of them, still a few around.'

'Yes, well she gimme this letter to give to you.' Joe takes Hester's letter from his coat pocket and hands it to the doctor.

The physician places the envelope down in front of him, then realises Joe is still standing. 'Sit, Joe, please.'

Joe sits facing the doctor and watches as he fusses with his eyeglasses and then turns his attention to the opening of Hester's letter. He uses a silver and enamel paper-knife and his hands shake something terrible, so that he makes several attempts to insert the knife into the corner of the envelope. Joe notices how very old the physician is. He is feeling old himself and his back hurts from the long ride into town. Not too long for this world, that one, he thinks to himself, immediately feeling a little better.

After a while Nathaniel Merrick looks up and Joe sees that he is amused. 'Well, well, boys will be boys, Joe Bergman. I can't say anything's changed in the fifty years I've been in practice.' He looks up at the ceiling as if he is trying to recall something. 'Oh, yes,' he says, chuckling to himself, and recites:

> 'When apples are red
> and nuts are brown
> skirts come up
> and trousers down!'

The old doctor doesn't look to see if Joe is amused, it's enough that he has remembered the rhyme. 'She's a fine-looking young filly as I recall. Bit narrow in the hips, though – she'll need a midwife when her time comes.'

He places Hester's letter to one side and reaches for a writing tablet before smiling at Joe. 'Happy to oblige, Joe Bergman. There's no sense in making unnecessary trouble for your lass.' He reaches for his pen, briefly rubs his thumb and forefinger across the surface of the steel nib and then further tests its point with his thumb. Then he dips it into the ink-pot and says, 'Meg, was it?'

Joe swallows and nods. 'Meg Charlotte Bergman, doctor.'

The old physician begins to write, then pauses. 'I seem to recall the name "Jessie" when I attended her?'

Joe has been primed by Hester in case this should happen. 'It's what we calls her, you know, her nickname, like.'

The doctor sighs and then continues writing, the steel nib of his pen scratching Joe's lie across the width of the snowy white paper.

Joe is elated, but doesn't show it, careful to keep his face without expression. 'Thank you, doctor. Most grateful for yer help.'

Merrick chuckles. 'I'm too old to make judgements, Joe Bergman. But if I was younger with a more inquisitive mind I'd say your wife is up to something, eh? A very clever letter, worthy of her old aunt.' He thinks for a moment. 'Agnes Heathwood – a fine-looking but most mischievous and interfering woman, always up to something. Clever and complicated as a cat's cradle.'

Joe leaves for home that same evening, crossing the river and continuing on for two hours before making camp for the night to allow his horse to rest. Shortly before dawn he sets out again, knowing that they'll have to set off for Narrandera in a few days to catch the train for Sydney.

They will have to leave Jessica behind to care for the selection and take their chances that no one will see her. Joe wonders to himself how wise it is to tell her about Meg's pregnancy to Jack Thomas, but he can think of no other explanation for their going to Sydney. He's not silly enough to think his youngest daughter has gone ratty in the head. He wonders if he should stay behind and allow Hester and Meg to confront Jack with Dr Merrick's letter.

Joe sighs heavily. Hester will know what to do, and anyway he is too tired these days to think for himself. Lately he's been getting pains in the chest and down his left arm. He finds himself panting after the least exertion. 'I'm losing me wits,' he mutters to himself. 'A man's goin' out backwards.'

Hester and Meg are excited when, on Joe's return, they hear the news. 'There's no time to be lost, we must leave for Sydney in the morning,' Hester declares.

'Who's gunna tell Jessie?' Joe asks.

'You should, Joe,' Hester answers.

Joe looks down, examining his fingernails. 'Nah, I don't think so,' he says softly, though he knows it is weak. 'It's women's business.'

Hester gives a long-suffering sigh, though she is secretly pleased. More and more she is taking charge. 'As usual I have to do the dirty work,' she says mournfully to cover her satisfaction.

At tea that night, Hester breaks her silence to Jessica. 'Jessica, we have some news,' she announces.

Jessica jumps at the sound of her mother's voice directed at her. So surprised is she to hear her name that her eyes glisten with tears of relief. 'Yes, Mama,' she manages in no more than a whisper.

'Your father, Meg and I are going to Sydney tomorrow.'

Jessica wipes away her tears. 'Sydney? But that's where Jack is!'

'Yes, well, as a matter of fact, we're going to see Jack.'

Jessica cannot at first comprehend what her mother is saying. 'But why?' she asks finally.

'Meg is pregnant to him.'

'Pregnant? Meg? To Jack?' Now Jessica simply cannot believe her ears and her hand goes to her heart. 'But how, Mama?'

'Oh you stupid girl! You of all people! *How*!'

Jessica bites her lower lip, her eyes brimming. 'Please, Mama, can I come too?'

Joe, who has his head bowed and seems to be examining his fingernails, now looks up. 'No, girlie. Yiz'll stay here and take care o' things.'

'And stay out of sight,' Hester adds, her voice hard.

Jessica rises from the table, unable to see for the tears that blind her. She brushes roughly past Meg, who draws away from her, pulling her arms up against her breasts as if repulsed by her touch. Jessica runs to her room, where she can contain her emotions no longer and begins to howl.

Her grieving can be heard in the kitchen and Meg looks at her mother and shakes her head.

'Oh, God, will we never be rid of the trouble she causes?' Hester cries.

'Jesus Christ, what have we done?' Joe cries. 'A man ought to be ashamed of hisself.'

Hester turns and admonishes him. 'Joe Bergman, don't you back down now!'

They leave just before sunrise, with the winter morning bitterly cold and the frost white on the ground. Jessica can hear a crow cawing in the cow paddock, though it's still too early for the other birds. There has been a fall of rain overnight, too little to matter much, but the early morning air is sharp and sweet and the dust dampened down under a clear blue sky.

Neither Hester nor Meg speaks to Jessica as they step up into the sulky and cover their knees with a rug. Joe stops to give her instructions, though he knows Jessica can manage on her own well enough and it is only an excuse to speak with his younger daughter.

'It'll be better when we're back, you'll see,' Joe says, touching his daughter's arm. 'There's a lamb fresh slaughtered in the cool house, and after that there's bacon.' He stands awkwardly, looking down at his boots, then says slowly, 'We'll be gone a fortnight, less I hope, certainly no more. Look after yerself then, eh, girlie.'

Jessica's teeth are chattering from the early morning cold and she hugs her chest. 'Father, will you give Jack a message for me?' she asks quietly.

'Now Jessie, you know I can't do that. What have you done? Wrote a letter?'

'No, Father, just a message, for you to tell him.' She looks at Joe, her eyes appealing to him. 'It can't do no harm, Father. Tell him, "Tea Leaf will be here when you get back."'

'Tea Leaf? Tea Leaf will be here when he gets back?' Joe smiles. 'Don't see no harm can come from saying that,' he says, happy to be able to do something for his sad little daughter.

'No Father, tell it exact. "Tea Leaf will be here when *you* get back." '

'Tea Leaf, eh? That what he calls yiz?'

It takes all day to get to Narrandera, where they put up for the night at the home of Hester's ageing father and Dolly, his second wife twenty years his junior. Dolly is the widow Auntie Agnes sent Henry Heathwood down to Sydney to find at the Easter Show. She was to be Hester's replacement behind the counter and in the kitchen, in order that her spinster niece might marry big, silent Joe Bergman.

Dolly is a cheerful soul who now runs the shop with the help of a young female assistant. She makes them feel most welcome and thoroughly at home. Henry Heathwood, always of a morbid disposition and now in his dotage, continues in his cheerless ways. His mind has taken to wandering of late and he no longer works in his haberdashery shop. Instead he spends most days seated in an old wicker chair under the grapevine in the backyard, mumbling to himself and dribbling down his chin. He is too feeble even to follow in the tradition of the Heathwood men. Most of them spent their old age as colourful local identities, which, among the town's middle-class tradesmen, is the euphemism for one of their kind being in a constant state of inebriation.

The express train for Sydney is due to leave at 9.45 a.m. and Joe has only just enough time to get to the recruitment office to obtain the papers he will need in order to visit Jack Thomas at the Victoria Barracks in Sydney.

Dolly packs them a splendid hamper and gives Meg a new bonnet. She proudly claims, 'It came up unadorned from Melbourne and I've titivated it a bit – it's wonderful what a bit of ribbon and a bow or two can do. I made the red velvet roses myself,' she adds proudly. Dolly then tells them she is of a mind to branch into hats as she feels she has a flair for decoration. Meg says she fears it is a little ostentatious with her plain brown dress and its white Chinese lace collar. 'Nonsense, child,' Aunt Dolly insists, 'hats bright as peacock birds are all the rage in Sydney and Melbourne.'

Apart from coming into Sydney by boat as a young boy from Denmark, Joe has only ever visited the town on two other occasions, both towards the end of the last century when old Queen Victoria was still on the throne. His memory is of a busy place, too many people, all of them talking at the same time. Of shoulders bumped in the street without so much as an apologetic grunt. Of smoke-filled pubs with tiled walls and floors, their polished hardwood counters awash with spilled ale and the approach to them three rowdy drinkers deep. And ever more noise, the clatter and clanging of the cable and electric trams, of coaches and traps, sulkies and wagons of every description and every cross-street jammed with people hurrying somewhere, like a colony of ants on the march.

But the Sydney they come into seems to have taken

on a different dimension. They've seen a good many young men on the train wearing the bush on their faces like a weary smile, some dressed in patched trousers and broken stockmen's boots, others neat as squatters' sons at a picnic dance, and all of them coming in to enlist even before there has been an official call to arms. War has not yet been declared but the rumour of its coming has swept through the bush to flush out the young bucks who have been weaned to a rifle and are eager to the fray. Word has it that the city blokes will go first and these young bushmen don't want to miss out on the grand adventure which some of the punters are betting will be over in just a few months.

The whistles of the self-important, black-uniformed, peak-capped conductors, the hiss and spit of steam, the yells and squeals, laughter, babble and shouted commands, quite take their breath away.

'A regular Sodom and Gomorrah and Tower of Babel all at once!' Hester shouts, cupping her hand against Meg's ear. Meg, for her part, stands wide-eyed. She has never seen so many young blokes together and she tries to imagine them in uniform, with a band blaring and them marching off to war, rifle over one shoulder, free arm swinging, their jaws clamped tight with pride. She can feel the pounding of her heart as she observes how the young men look at her in Aunt Dolly's hat. Their eyes hungry, devouring her breasts and trim waist, darting away shyly when she dares a glance at them.

Meg wonders if they can see her for the country bumpkin she is, in her plain brown dress and unfashionable boots, Aunt Dolly's elaborate bonnet perched on top of it all. She looks frantically to see if there are other bonnets like hers, but sees none and thinks the young blokes must be looking at her bonnet and laughing to themselves. But when she looks into their faces she can see the bronze of sun and wind, the natural creases around eyes kept narrow by too much sharp light, and she knows she's among her own kind.

These are country boys from all the bush towns, farms and sheep runs in the land. Australia is sending the very heart and soul of the dry and dusty plains to fight for old Mother England. Tall, gangly, slow-talking country lads, who sit upon a horse and carry a rifle as easily as they use a knife and spoon. These colonial lads are off to sort out the Hun – the Kaiser had better watch out.

The three Bergmans struggle with the two old suitcases and the wicker hamper until they stand clear of the station and hail a hansom cab. 'Oxford Street, mate, how much?' Joe asks, trying not to feel too lost and unimportant.

'Dunno, mate, depends, don't it?'

'Dunno what you mean, mate.'

'Oxford Street goes two, maybe two an' a arf miles.'

'Paddington? We're goin' to Paddington, know where it is?'

The cabby tries not to look insulted. 'Cost you sixpence each and another zack for the luggage,' he says, looking down on them from his high seat, seeing them for what they are.

'How far is it, mate?' Joe now asks.

'Nearest point?' The cabby rubs his chin. 'Arf a mile.'

'Near the barracks, the Victoria Barracks, in Paddington. We got the name of a boardin' house, Mrs O'Shane.'

'About a mile, then,' the cabby points, 'up thataway.'

'You know Mrs O'Shane?' Joe asks in surprise.

'Nah, mate, the flamin' barracks, about a mile,' the cab driver says impatiently.

'Thank you, we'll walk,' Joe says, lifting his hat to the cabby.

'Nah, don't be bloody silly, catch the electric tram. Cost ya a deener the lot o' yiz.' He points to the tram stop. 'Waverley tram goes right past.'

At the boarding house Mrs O'Shane is a big woman with hands and face red as boiled lobster. She seems all heat and fuss, with a voice rough as the sound of a wood rasp. But she remembers Dolly well enough and, it seems, with some favourable feeling, for she shows them a tiny room for Hester and Meg and a bed for Joe in the single men's quarters out the back.

The room isn't clean, but then it isn't dirty either. It has the pungency of human wear and tear but not of cat's piss and fried kippers, the redolent smell of just about every cheap English-speaking boarding house in the world. Hester has brought her own sheets and a thick blanket together with a bottle of eucalyptus oil so the bed bugs and fleas are more or less taken care of. The room is declared tolerable, its two major attractions being a stout door with a good lock and a brass key and furthermore, it is what they can afford.

They are all bone-weary from the train trip through the night, where they sat up all the way in a second-class carriage. Behind the door is a notice which spells out the rules for Mrs O'Shane's establishment.

NO SLEEPING PAST 7 A.M. IN THE ROOMS AND NOT AGAIN UNTIL SIX O'CLOCK IN THE EVENING.

Mrs O' Shane later explains it's to stop double dipping, that is, nightshift and dayshift workers sharing the cost of a room between them.

DURING THE DAY, IF THE OCCUPANTS ARE IN THEIR ROOMS, THE DOORS ARE TO BE KEPT OPEN.

This, she says, is to prevent any hanky-panky and so forth and so on.

UPON LEAVING THE PREMISES THE ROOMS MUST BE LOCKED AND THE KEY HANDED IN TO THE LANDLADY. ALL CARE AND NO RESPONSIBILITY TAKEN. FRONT DOOR WILL BE LOCKED BY TEN O'CLOCK, NO VISITORS ALLOWED AFTER NINE IN THE EVENING.

'I know yiz are respectable folk from the country an' all, but I can't make no exceptions,' Mrs O'Shane explains. 'Them's the rules and it's one in, all in, I 'opes you understand? At night keep yer door locked and yer purse under the pillow and don't open for no one 'cept if you recognise their voice. Don't have eyes in the back

o' me 'ead now, do I?' She looks sternly at Meg. 'No soldiers allowed, no sailors neither. Best to talk to no one,
'less they's introduced by me. Breakfast at seven o'clock
sharp, porridge and tea, no toast. Dinner yer finds yerself outside, cafe on the corner, fish 'n' chips two doors
down. Tea at six o'clock, ternight it's Irish stew or
bangers 'n' mash or savoury mince, take yer choice, rice
pudding to finish, all the tea yiz can drink, no intoxicat-
ing fluids to be brought to the table.' She glares at them,
one eye closed. 'Does I make meself clear?'

It is mid-afternoon by the time they've settled in and
Joe goes off to the barracks a block away to find out
how they might go about contacting young Jack
Thomas. Hester and Meg are off window-shopping in
George Street and Meg finds herself the subject of many
an admiring glance, even though she has chosen to
leave Aunt Dolly's velvet roses, bowed and ribboned
extravaganza in the boarding house and wears her
second-best plain brown bonnet instead.

There are soldiers everywhere and they see several
officers on horseback who look so grand Meg thinks
the younger ones must be captains and the older, with
their curled moustaches, at the very least generals in
command. Eventually they end up in the Botanical Gardens, where they rest on the clipped green grass under
a large Moreton Bay fig. They take off their boots and
share a vanilla ice cream together while they watch the
mallard ducks floating on a small pond covered with
lilac waterlilies.

At tea that night Joe announces that they'll see Jack

Thomas at four o'clock on the following afternoon for an hour by special permission of his squadron commander, Lieutenant Ormington. They're to meet at the main gate of the barracks and Jack is allowed out but must report back by five-fifteen sharp.

'We'll need to bring him back here,' Joe says, 'so we can speak to him private, like.'

'What about the rules, Father? Door open and no soldiers,' Meg says, her heart pounding at the thought of the confrontation to come. There has been no mention of their little conspiracy since the first night. She has planned and waited for Jack Thomas so long that what they're doing now seems almost normal. It is the thought of seeing Jack that makes her nervous – she's seen so many handsome young men in uniform that she hopes he stacks up. She wants her man to be as good as the others.

'We could go by tram to Hyde Park, talk to him in the open?' Hester suggests. 'Best that way, he'll be more at ease.'

Joe grunts, 'Fair enough.'

Hester turns to Meg. The venue for the meeting now decided, she expects she'll have to do most of the talking. Joe is simply not up to it any more. 'Meg, we'll have to ask Mrs O'Shane for the loan of a flat iron. The creases in your blue velvet dress simply won't fall out and we want you to look your very best, my precious.'

Meg is as pretty as a picture when they meet Jack Thomas late the following afternoon and Jack seems pleased to see them.

'G'day, Joe!' he says, extending his hand. Then he

turns to Hester, 'Afternoon, Mrs Bergman,' then he looks at Meg and smiles. 'Hello Meg, what a nice surprise.' He shakes her formally by the hand then glances around hopefully. 'Jessie not here?'

Joe tries to smile naturally. 'She had to take care o' things back home. Lambing season, we've had some rain. Not much, but there's a bit o' green about, and the ewes are dropping.'

Jack shrugs, clearly disappointed. 'It would have been real nice to see her,' he says wistfully.

Meg now turns to Jack. 'Don't I get a kiss then, Jack Thomas?'

Jack looks nervous, knowing the two sentries must see him and perhaps there are others watching. He pecks Meg lightly on the cheek, blushing violently.

'My, Meg, doesn't he look handsome in his uniform,' Hester exclaims, smiling, her head to one side as she looks him over.

Jack pulls at his tunic and tries to grin. 'Never done so much shining in my life, boots 'n' brasses and the curry-comb have become my whole flamin' existence.'

'We've only got an hour,' Hester now says. 'We thought a walk in Hyde Park might be nice?'

'That'll be fine, Mrs Bergman,' Jack says as they set off for the tram stop. 'Be good to see a face that ain't got a cap on its head I have to salute.'

Once into the park Joe buys ice-cream cones for them all and they find a small tree that throws enough shade for them to sit out of the sun, though it's late in the afternoon and the heat is already gone from the winter sun. They seek the shade instinctively rather than from need.

Joe waits until they've finished their ice creams and the girls have given Jack all the local gossip. He has a pain in his chest and he wonders to himself if he can get the words out proper. 'Jack,' he says at last, 'I suppose yer wonderin' why we've come down to the big smoke?'

Jack looks up at Joe. 'Well, yeah, it did cross my mind. What with shearing starting in the shed, I was surprised to see you.'

Joe is happy to be distracted. 'No more shearing, me back's gorn.'

'George, eh?' Jack says knowingly, then, looking serious, adds, 'Joe, there's always a job for you at Riverview. It's my property now, not my old man's. I'll see to it. Is that why you've come down?'

'No, Jack,' Hester says, growing impatient at the small talk. 'We've come to give you some news,' she looks up directly at Jack, meeting his eye, 'good news I hope.' Meg at her side has her hands folded in her lap and her eyes are lowered. 'Jack, Meg is pregnant – she carries your child.'

Hester is the only one who continues to look at Jack, who appears to be completely stunned by the news and gets to his feet without being conscious of having done so. He now stands almost at attention, looking down at them. 'My child,' he says, trying the words on for the first time. After a few moments, 'My child?' he repeats, now looking at Hester. 'Are you sure, Mrs Bergman?'

Hester hands him Dr Merrick's letter and Jack unfolds it and reads it slowly, shaking his head as he reads.

'Oh Jack, I am so happy,' Meg says. Then, scrambling to her feet, she embraces him, placing her head on his chest. Jack, not knowing what else to do, puts his arms about her shoulders.

'Bloody stupid thing to happen,' Joe grunts, 'but can't be stopped now.'

Jack pushes Meg gently away and hands the letter back to Hester. 'Mrs Bergman, I don't know what to say. I mean, the war and everything . . .' He wipes his forehead and grimaces. 'What can I say?'

'You'll marry her, of course. Meg's not to have your bastard child, Jack Thomas.' Hester's voice is grown suddenly hard, her lips drawn tight. She's determined not to take a step backwards.

'Oh, Jack, I love you so,' Meg says, bringing her hands together as though in supplication. 'I do so want your child.' She clutches melodramatically at her stomach. 'I *must* have your child.' She smiles up at Jack, her pretty head to one side. 'It will be a boy, I know it will be a boy as handsome and strong as his father.'

Jack now has his head bowed, his hands behind his back. Without raising his head, he looks at Meg. 'You said it was between us, that nobody'd know.'

Meg's pretty dark eyes take on a distressed look and she pouts defiantly. 'Jack, I didn't know this was going to happen. I just wanted to love you, to say goodbye.' She pauses for a moment. 'Because you see, I do! I love you with all my heart. If you'll marry me I'll be the best wife a man could ever have.' Meg begins to sob softly. 'Oh, Jack, I didn't mean this to happen, honest I didn't.'

Jack looks at Joe, not quite knowing why. Joe is confused and feels ashamed and embarrassed at Meg's outburst. He thinks Jack's a fine-looking, decent young bloke and that he deserves better than his elder daughter. 'Jack, we hope yiz'll do the right thing by Meg,' he says slowly without enthusiasm.

Jack stares down at his polished riding boots. 'I'll have to ask my C.O. – you see, we've got to get permission to marry,' he explains. He looks back up at Joe. 'He'll have to see you all, I guess. Interview you.' Jack seems to hesitate a moment then says, 'I think I told you he's my uncle – not that it counts,' he adds hastily, 'I haven't even met him since I've been down here.'

Colonel Septimus Cunningham-Thomas, Jack's commanding officer and his uncle, is a Sydney barrister in civilian life. He is a tall man with steel-grey hair and a clipped moustache almost matched in size by thick eyebrows turned salt and peppery that give him a most imposing appearance. He and his brother George are chalk and cheese in their looks and stature and George has long since dropped the hyphen from his name so that he won't be disadvantageously compared with his older brother. Jack's commandant is known appropriately enough by his men as Cunning Tom, because little escapes his notice and, in the terminology of the army, it is very difficult to 'put one over him'. In this, he and his brother are similar. He sees the Bergmans without Jack being present and addresses himself to Joe first.

'Mr Bergman, it is my duty to take care of the best interests of the men under me. I am charged by virtue of my commission to be, not only their direct commander in battle, but also their surrogate mother and father.' He purses his lips in a practised and perfunctory manner. 'Though the regimental sergeant-major might quarrel with me about this particular duty.'

He pauses and picks up a paper-knife on the desk behind which he is seated and twiddles it absently. 'I am also obliged to admit to a particular and personal interest in Trooper Jack Thomas. I believe he has mentioned to you that I am his uncle and, of course, I know about the tragic circumstances surrounding the death of his mother and two sisters.' The colonel leans forward slightly as if to emphasise his next statement. 'I want you, in particular, to bear this in mind and to understand that his welfare is of the utmost importance to me as he and his father are . . .' the colonel seems to be searching for a word, '. . . at loggerheads. I have heard what Trooper Thomas has to say and I have decided under the prevailing circumstances to grant him permission to marry your daughter.' He puts down the ivory paper-knife and holds up his forefinger. 'But there is a proviso.' The colonel pauses and now, for the first time, looks at Hester. 'While you seem a decent family and have a letter from your family doctor,' he pauses and glances sternly at Joe, 'which I believe to be genuine, the army nevertheless instructs that I must take due care in these matters.'

He turns to Meg, who blushes violently the moment

his stern eyes come to rest upon her. 'Trooper Thomas admits readily enough to having had sexual congress on a single occasion with your daughter. But it is my experience that one swallow does not make a spring and despite the good doctor's letter to say that she is pregnant, the army manual states that three weeks is not sufficient time to be certain whether this condition is established.'

Jack's C.O. pauses and looks at each of them in turn. 'So it is my duty to instruct Trooper Thomas in his rights under the law. I also remind you that, being a legal man, I have the knowledge to do so and the power as his senior officer to add a legally binding proviso to the marriage contract. I have spoken at length to Trooper Thomas and taken instructions from him, which I admit have benefited from my past knowledge in such matters. Together we have drawn up a document which you will be required to sign before he consents to the marriage.'

Colonel Cunningham-Thomas now pushes his chair slightly backwards, opens a drawer to the desk and takes out a manila folder which is tied with pink legal tape. He places it down in front of him and carefully unties the tape and then opens the binder. 'Before I read it to you I will paraphrase the contents.'

'Paraphrase?' Joe asks.

'Tell you more or less what's in it, though you will read it for yourself before your daughter and, as she is not yet twenty-one years of age, both of you as her legal guardians must sign it.' He gives a wan smile. 'I expect you, like most folk, become confused by legal jargon.'

'Do we get our own copy?' Hester asks, fed up with the colonel's lugubrious tone and high-handed manner. 'We are not ignorant and can read and write well enough.'

Meg gasps audibly at her mother's audacity and Jack's C.O. is barely able to conceal his surprise at Hester's interruption. It is clear from his expression that he is not accustomed to being challenged, particularly by a member of the opposite sex. 'As you wish, madam,' he says abruptly. Closing the folder, he is about to push it across the desk when Joe speaks.

'Please, sir, we'd like yer own words on this matter. I'm not what you'd call an educated man.' Joe glares at Hester, challenging her to contradict him. Hester remains silent and keeps her eyes downcast.

'Very well then, Mr Bergman, it is my experience that these things are generally better explained in layman's terms.' Colonel Cunningham-Thomas clears his throat and taps the now closed binder. 'The document says in effect that while the marriage is a legally binding contract the property rights within it are subject to a very specific set of conditions. Your daughter Meg must comply with these if she is to obtain any material benefit from the nuptial agreement.' The colonel looks at Hester. 'Am I making myself clear to you, Mrs Bergman?'

Hester shoots a glance at Joe. 'Yes, sir,' she says dutifully, feeling her anger growing inside her. She wishes she had the courage of an Ada Thomas to challenge the old fool.

'Good. Then let me continue. If it should prove that

your daughter is *not* pregnant, though legally married, she will forfeit any claims whatsoever to her husband's property in the event that he is killed in action. She cannot benefit in any possible way, whether in property, goods, services or emolument. Do you understand me? I should remind you at this point that a wife cannot testify against her husband in a court of law.'

'Emolument?' Joe asks.

'Money, Mr Bergman. Your daughter will inherit nothing.' Jack's uncle brushes his moustache across the length of his forefinger and sniffs. 'Furthermore, your daughter may not occupy Riverview homestead until the day of the birth of her child, whereupon she may enjoy all its amenities and will be considered to be the mistress of the house, with a monthly stipend to run her domestic affairs until her husband returns to control his property.'

Cunningham-Thomas grips the edge of the desk with both hands and leans slightly backwards and smiles. 'However, it is not all bad news. If Trooper Thomas has a legitimate child by your daughter and he is killed in action, then his entire estate will go to your child.' He looks directly at Meg. 'You will be the child's guardian and oversee the affairs of Riverview Station, which will remain in trust to him or her until he or she reaches the age of twenty-one.' Jack's C.O. pauses and raises one eyebrow ever so slightly. 'I'm sure you'll agree these are most extremely generous terms, Miss Bergman, most generous, eh?' he asks in his patronising voice.

Hester, unable to contain her agitation any longer, asks, 'What if she should have a miscarriage?' Then adds quickly, 'Be pregnant but have a miscarriage? Does she get nothing?' Then she further pronounces melodramatically, 'Is that fair to the girl?' Her expression is now openly hostile. 'The virgin is seduced and left abandoned? The innocent young girl who, through no fault of her own, carried his child, left without a penny to her name?' Hester then adds for good measure, one eyebrow slightly arched, 'Whose reputation and prospects will be ruined if she is deserted by the high and mighty Jack Thomas?' It is a performance worthy of Ada Thomas.

Colonel Cunningham-Thomas is not moved by Hester's dramatic outburst. 'If it should be proved your daughter is *not* pregnant is what I think the document says,' he repeats, one peppery eyebrow slightly raised as a caution to her not to try his patience much further. 'Trooper Thomas has informed me that given normal circumstances he would not choose to marry your daughter Meg, but he does not want the child conceived by him to be without a father,' he pauses a moment for the effect it will have, '– to be a bastard.'

He now picks up the paper-knife again and taps the ivory tip against the edge of the desk and then looks at Hester. 'There is no intention to punish your daughter, Mrs Bergman, but rather to ensure that, as Trooper Thomas himself so aptly put it to me, "The right thing is done by all." He asks that, in the event of a miscarriage or stillborn child, Meg remain with her parents until he returns from the war. He assumes that you will best be able to comfort your daughter in her sorrow at losing a child.

'However, in the event that Trooper Thomas is killed, he has allowed, should the circumstances be as you have just suggested, that your daughter will receive the Riverview homestead with five hundred acres of riverfront land attached to it. This allows for irrigation and, if judiciously worked, will supply a generous living and prove a more than adequate dowry should she decide to remarry. Would you not agree that this is a fair settlement?'

Jack's uncle does not wait for a reply. 'Furthermore, under the same circumstances, that is that your child is stillborn or miscarried and its father is killed in battle, there is a second five hundred acres of irrigation land which is to go to . . .' Cunningham-Thomas opens the folder and flicks through several pages and then allows his finger to run down a page and come to rest, '. . . Ah yes, here it is.' He looks up from the page. 'Miss Jessica Bergman, whom he tells me he had hoped to take as his bride if he returned.'

There is a loud gasp of astonishment from Meg and Hester, though Cunningham-Thomas may have anticipated it, for he seems deliberately to ignore it. 'The disposal of the remaining land under these specific and prevailing circumstances is not of your concern,' he concludes.

The colonel now closes the manila folder and carefully ties it with the pink tape before pushing it over to rest on the desk in front of Joe.

'You'll find there are four copies of the same document. I want you to go away and read it and then, if you agree to the conditions, return with it to me at the same time tomorrow and be prepared to sign each copy. One of the copies will belong to you, and the others will be lodged with Trooper Thomas's legal firm in Narrandera and his bank in Sydney, and I shall retain a copy in my own files. Lieutenant Ormington will be one witness to your signatures and I shall be the other. Do I make myself quite clear?'

'Yes, sir,' Joe says.

'Do we have a say, I mean if we object to something?' Hester asks.

Cunningham-Thomas shakes his head slowly and with just the hint of a smile says, 'If you want the marriage to proceed you will need to sign it as it is.'

'Thank you, sir,' Joe says, rising from his chair, and he indicates that Hester and Meg should follow suit.

'Oh yes, there is one more thing.' Colonel Cunningham-Thomas waits so he has their full attention. 'It is customary for the army to grant the groom twenty-four hours' leave in order to,' he clears his throat, 'consummate the marriage.' He looks directly at Hester. 'Trooper Thomas may marry in the barracks chapel if he wishes, or alternatively at the Registry Office in the city, but he will have to report back to the guard room an hour after the ceremony and will be granted no further leave.'

'You mean they will not be allowed to be together?' Hester exclaims, showing her consternation. In her mind she had always imagined that if they could force Jack into marriage there would be other opportunities afforded him to make Meg pregnant before he left for the war in Europe, or for training.

'That is exactly what I mean, Mrs Bergman.'

'But that's not fair. Isn't my daughter entitled to spend the night with her husband?' Hester ventures.

'As I understand it, the union has already been consummated,' the colonel barks, for a moment showing his anger. 'Not to put too fine a point on it, isn't that why we find ourselves here in the first place?'

'Well it just seems unfair,' Hester mumbles, 'unfair to them both.'

Colonel Cunningham-Thomas regains his composure. 'Trooper Thomas does not feel the same way, Mrs Bergman, and my duty is first and foremost to my men. I shall send his squadron commander, Lieutenant Ormington, along with him as his best man or, if it is to be a civil wedding, as his witness. He will accompany your daughter's husband back to the barracks immediately after the wedding service and the toast to the King and the drinking of the wedding cup is concluded.'

'May we not have him come out for a bit of tea?' Hester persists.

The colonel sighs, his impatience at Hester's constant questioning now obvious. 'No, you may *not*, Mrs Bergman.'

Jack Thomas is waiting outside the colonel's office and walks with them to the barracks gates, where Meg draws him aside and kisses him tearfully. 'I'm sorry, Jack,' she whispers, 'but you won't regret this, I promise you,' she pleads.

'Meg, you know you're the wrong sister, don't yer?'

Jack says, so that only she can hear and then turns away, not wishing her to see his anguish.

Meg brings her hands up to cover her face and begins to sob, so that a grim-faced Hester comes running over to her daughter. She takes Meg's arm and draws her away from where Jack is standing with his back to her. 'There, there, my girl, we're not beaten yet,' she whispers into her daughter's ear. She has already decided the marriage must take place, even though Jack, or rather his bloody interfering uncle, has crushed her every hope for Meg's future.

'He hates me, Mother,' Meg sobs.

'He's going off to the war – we may never have to care if he does or not,' Hester hisses, though in a voice only Meg can hear.

Joe, who has not seen the exchange between Jack and his daughter, finds himself strangely cheered as a result of the interview with Jack's commanding officer. It is as though a huge weight has been lifted from his shoulders. The grant of land, the precious five hundred acres of riverfront for Jessica in the document he carries under his arm, proves that Jack has thought to provide for her in the event of his death. Even though the specific terms and Meg's inability to comply with them make it impossible for Jessica to benefit, it proves to Joe once again that Jack Thomas loves Jessica Bergman, and wanted to marry his little girlie. Perhaps, he thinks to himself, despite her pregnancy to Billy Simple, things may be sorted out when Jack returns from the war, for surely Meg's marriage to Jack cannot now take place?

Joe decides there and then to tell Jack the message Jessica has asked him to deliver.

'Jack, a quick word, mate?' he says, and takes Jack by the arm and draws him aside. 'Son, I've got a message for you,' he says a little above a whisper. 'It's from Jessie. She says to tell you . . .' Joe hesitates. 'I'll say it just how she said it to me, she said, "Father, tell Jack: Tea Leaf will be here when you get back." '

'Oh, God, what have I done?' Jack chokes, clutching at the tunic pocket covering his heart. Joe sees the sudden tears that well in the young soldier's eyes.

CHAPTER TEN

Two days after Meg's wedding and only three hours off the train, Joe turns out of Dolly's yard at Narrandera and heads for home. They'd taken the train overnight and despite Hester's pleas to rest up for the day with Dolly Heathwood, Joe insists on staying only long enough for Dolly to pack them a hamper for the road and to allow him to get the pony and sulky from a nearby stable yard. Shortly after eight o'clock, with the sun already hot enough to chase away the morning chill, they are back on the road home.

Joe has hardly spoken since the wedding and is back into his darkness. The three of them form a cheerless little group, with Meg spending most of the hours since the nuptials sniffing and weeping. Meanwhile Hester grows increasingly bad-tempered with her and not a great deal better disposed to her morose and silent husband.

'For God's sake, daughter, stop your snivelling. Have we not done what we came for? Are you not Mrs Jack Thomas? Buck up, girl!' Hester is no longer able to abide either of them for their lack of gumption.

'But Mama, it has all come to nothing,' Meg wails.

'Nothing? Mistress of Riverview. You call that nothing?' Hester snaps.

'But I'm not! The colonel said . . .' Meg gulps. 'What about the piece of paper he made Father sign?'

'Ha, paper!' Hester says dismissively. 'You've got a gold band on your finger, that's a lot better than a piece of paper.'

'But it means we can't move into Riverview unless I have Jack's child!' Meg looks up at Hester. 'And I *don't* have his child, do I?' Meg looks at her mother, distressed. 'Do I, Mother?'

'Oh do be quiet, Meg,' Hester admonishes her. 'You don't have his child *yet*.'

Meg looks at her mother in astonishment. 'Yet? Whatever do you mean?'

'You heard me the first time, I will not repeat myself.' Hester will comment no further, leaving Joe to his silent misery, and Meg no less weepy than before.

They had not been able to talk in the crowded second-class train carriage. On the long ride to Narrandera, seated on the train's hard wooden seats, Joe and Meg seemed miraculously able to sleep but Hester could, at best, snatch a few minutes' sleep at a time, waking at each jolt and halting of the engine, so that she had ample time to think about the predicament into which they had been placed by Jack's wily uncle.

They had taken the milk train, which stopped at every station throughout the long and wearisome night until time and space seemed to be filled with clickety-clacks, shouts, shunts and the clanking of trucks at lonely sidings.

Sudden shrill whistles, the weary huff and puff of driving steam, the acrid smell of smoke and the sharp, metallic taste of coal dust. Hester was exhausted by the time they came into Narrandera in the early hours of the morning, but she was determined on one thing – that come what may, Jack's commanding officer, the man they called Cunning Tom, was not going to defeat her. As far as she was concerned, her daughter was now Mrs Jack Thomas and that was just the beginning.

Now, on the road home from Narrandera, Hester tries unsuccessfully to engage Joe in conversation. After hours of badgering, Joe begins to make replies beyond a cursory grunt. By now he is numb with fatigue. Hester seems somehow to have recovered and is sharp and clear as ever. She wants Joe to agree to a course of action concerning Meg before they reach home.

She has persisted all the while with a single question until Meg, exhausted by her mother's pestering and Joe's stubborn silence, begs her to stop, putting her hands to her ears. But Hester continues. 'What will you tell Jessica?'

Joe's answer comes at last. 'Nothing. I ain't sayin' nothing, you hear?'

'But you must tell her that Meg is now married to Jack Thomas.'

'Why?'

'Because we'll have to tell folk. It will need to be announced on Sunday at St Stephen's. People will want to know.'

Joe reaches into the pocket of his jacket and produces the folded paper Colonel Cunningham-Thomas has given him. He waves it at Hester. 'What, announce the marriage terms,' he waves the letter again, 'tell them about this, will we? No brat, no marriage, all signed proper by us?' Joe grimaces and slips the contract back inside his jacket.

'Of course not! There's no need. Just that she's married to him, to Jack.' Hester now looks shrewdly at Joe. 'The bank will be impressed – it may help you.'

Joe jerks his head. 'Bullshit.'

Hester looks down and sees that Meg is asleep beside her. She leans over and grabs Joe's arm and in an urgent tone of voice says, 'Don't you see? We have to go on with the pregnancy – people must see Meg getting bigger, growing.'

'And then what?'

'A miscarriage. Joe, you remember what the colonel said when I asked? What's in the contract? A miscarriage is all right – if Jack dies in the war Meg will have the homestead and the five hundred acres of river-front land. Jessica will get the other five hundred. You've said yourself often enough it's the best thousand acres on the Riverina.' Hester pauses then adds, 'All we need is a reliable witness or two.'

Joe looks at Hester, startled. 'Miscarriage? Witnesses? What are you talking about? Meg's not even up the duff.'

'There's ways to make it happen. It's better than nothing, isn't it?'

'No, it ain't better than nothing! Hester, Jack don't love her, don't love Meg. If there's no child, he'll not keep her on as his wife.'

'Ah yes, but if he dies, then what?'

Joe shrugs. 'Meg gets nothing,' he gives a bitter little laugh, 'which is fair enough – she don't deserve a brass razoo anyway!'

'Unless, like I told you, she has a miscarriage *and* he dies.'

'Miscarriage? What miscarriage? The girlie ain't bloody pregnant!'

Hester shakes Joe by the sleeve of his jacket. 'Joe, listen to me. Once when one of the sows miscarried, you said how the unborn piglets looked just like a human foetus.'

'Jesus, how would I bloody know? I've never seen an unborn, whatd'yacallit, human foetus. All I said was it looked like, well, what I *thought* a baby would look like before it was growed a bit.'

'That's precisely it, Joe. That's what I mean. It's worth a try. We've come this far, got her married. A midwife would know a sow's foetus if she saw it, but nobody else is going to be any the wiser. The Reverend Mathews won't know. Neither would Mrs Baker, the organist at St Stephen's. The two of them, they could be our witnesses.

'Joe, look, we could arrange for Mrs Baker to visit and by chance be there when it happens. Her eyes aren't too good and in the poor light with lots of pig's blood around, she'll not want to look too close. The two of them, her and the vicar, neither will want to be poking around counting off fingers and toes.'

'Nah, it's too bloody risky. And what if Jack don't die?'

Hester spreads her hands. 'Then he comes back and we sort things out. Meg's still married to him. He could come back different, happy to have her, who knows?'

'Or he could throw her out on her neck. The contract says he don't owe her a bean.'

'Joe, if we can, you know, make it seem like a miscarriage, just think what it may mean. If Jack is killed, both your daughters will be safe, will be taken care of for life – Jessica in particular, her bastard taken care of. Isn't that worth a shot?'

Joe is silent for a long while and then he says, 'How are you gunna get Reverend Mathews . . . Just how you gunna get him to witness a flamin' miscarriage?'

'I shall go to him and show him the marriage contract and make him swear not to divulge its contents, then throw myself on his mercy. He's very fond of Meg and he'll want what he thinks is fair.'

'What, show him the foetus?'

'I'll have to, won't I? There'll be lots of blood. He won't look too close, he's not the sort. I'll tell him as we have no doctor, he'll *have* to be the witness so the terms of the contract are met.'

'What, and get him to bury it?' Joe laughs suddenly. 'Bury the bloody pig's innards? Give it a Christian burial, "The Lord is my shepherd", organ music, hole in the church yard, coffin an' all?'

Hester shakes her head. 'No Joe, he can't do that anyway – a child has no soul until it's born. We'll get him to say a prayer in church, a blessing, so folk will share our misfortune, know about it. He's done that before. Then we'll bury it somewhere it can't be found. Meg will have fulfilled the terms of the colonel's letter and be able to move into Riverview homestead and act the dutiful wife.'

'God, what has become of us?' Joe sighs. 'Will there be no end to this wickedness?'

'Oh, Mother, do you think it will work?' Meg suddenly exclaims.

Hester turns to Meg, surprised. 'Good Lord, child, I thought you were asleep.'

'Mama, will it work?' Meg pleads.

Hester shrugs. 'It has to work. You got any better ideas?'

'But what if we're caught?'

'Then we'll know we've tried everything we can,' Hester says calmly, 'and you'll be a very poor widow or an unwanted wife, one of the two.'

'But we'll be disgraced if we're found out,' Meg protests.

'We are already disgraced – your sister has seen to that,' Hester snaps. Then, to Meg's surprise, she adds calmly, 'I have some plain white wool from your Aunt Dolly. You're to be seen knitting for your baby whenever there are folk gathered about.'

At the mention of Jessica and the disgrace she has caused them, Joe is once more consumed with guilt. He has conspired to make Jack marry Meg when he's in love with Jessica. Jack will go to war knowing that if he returns he will be trapped into a marriage he doesn't want with a woman he doesn't love. Joe is sensitive enough to know that a young man going to war should carry the memory of his sweetheart to comfort and sustain him. He tries, though with little success, to assuage his own guilt by telling himself that should Jack know that Jessica carries Billy Simple's child he would think quite differently about her. He even imagines Jack might willingly settle for Meg in such circumstances and all would be well in the end.

Joe does not blame Jack for succumbing to Meg's seduction. He can well see attractive Meg offering herself to a young buck naked in the soft moonlight, without demanding a commitment. A scheming whore whose price is his future. She has fooled him by relying on his innate sense of decency, and his company commanding officer, Colonel Cunningham-Thomas, is right to have drawn up the contract. The guilt and frustration grow within him and he feels more and more that he is on Jack's side, on Jessica's as well. But Hester has committed him, implicated him completely in her plot to snare the young owner of Riverview Station for their eldest daughter.

Joe knows he's stuck. But if he simply draws the line and tells Hester they'll take their chances and announce that Meg isn't pregnant, there is the letter from old Doc Merrick to explain and their plan to trap Jack Thomas, all this followed by admitting to Jessica's pregnancy, with the whole bloody countryside taking one simple guess as to who the daddy is and getting it right in one. If Jack returns from the war, Meg will be trapped with a husband who dislikes her and, if he doesn't, she'll have wasted her youth on the duration of the war only to end up a penniless widow. Two daughters, both of whom have destroyed their lives and who, with the money he owes to the bank, soon won't even have a home to go to.

Slowly Hester's idea of faking a miscarriage gains momentum in Joe's mind. After all, if Jack is killed, the chances are that bastard George Thomas will get Riverview Station or, just as bad, some obscure Thomas relations, perhaps even his uncle, the colonel. Didn't he say he was gunna keep a copy of the contract? Besides, Joe thinks, Jack has admitted he loves Jessica. Why shouldn't Jessica, who's always loved Jack selflessly and been his best mate, get something? Christ knows, she's gunna need it with a monster's small child in her arms.

Joe is growing increasingly morbid about his health. With Meg and Hester at Riverview homestead with good irrigation land, and Jessica with her own allotment, they'd be well took care of if he should die. Joe sighs. They've come too far to turn back now. His wife's fierce ambition for Meg has, in the end, proved too strong for him. He's beat, and he must go along with her until the end, whatever it may be. He, who knows nothing of irony, thinks now how Hester's need for respectability for herself and their oldest daughter has caused all of them, except Jessica, to sink lower than a snake's belly.

Joe is disgusted with himself for his weakness and his silence, his attempts to remain uninvolved. He tells himself that he should use his fists on Hester for destroying his pride as a man. On every important occasion she has trapped him, committed him, made him do things which serve her ambition for Meg. Now, by making him aware that not just Meg but his youngest daughter will also be saved if Jack Thomas is killed in action, she has shown him up for the useless bastard he really is. Their future depends on a faked miscarriage and a fine young bloke being killed. Christ, life is a bloody nightmare, a man ought to put a bullet to his own head.

Joe is feeling increasingly weary. His back aches constantly and the dull pains in his chest and left arm come more often now and seem to last longer each day. He knows that keeping the selection for his youngest daughter seems more than he dare ask. It's all too much – the sudden frailty of his body, the never-ending drought and the banks, who would rob him of all he has worked his guts out for.

Always before, Joe's seen hard work as his salvation. Even in the worst times he's managed to scrape through by working in a shearing shed, as a drover, fencing, or as a bush carpenter, even walking behind a stump-jump plough. His powerful body has been there to support him, to work harder than other blokes, if only to pull and push, lift and carry. There has always been someone who will hire Joe Bergman for his strength and the value he puts into a day's hard yakka.

Now these tasks are simply beyond him. Though the heat is less at this time of the year, he tires after the least exertion and often finds himself stooped, gasping, with his hands clasped to his knees. It's for this reason he has made Jessica work away from him – so that she won't try to compensate and do too much in her condition. Joe is sad and confused but he doesn't want Jessica to lose her child. He has seen the fierce, protective look in her eyes. Jessica's child means everything to her and he is determined that, in this one thing, he won't let her down.

Jessica, he realises, will soon be severely slowed down, too heavy with child to help him to keep the rabbit fences up. With no dogs to help her, she'll be unable to bend low enough to crutch and worm the few sheep that remain, or move the cattle to pasture to fatten them in time for the spring sales. That is, always supposing the rains come this season to bring the bitter dust to life.

Joe lies in his cot at night in dread of first light and what the new day may bring. He worries that when the summer heat is upon them again he'll be too exhausted to struggle through the day. He is already six months in arrears with the bank payments and he knows of two small selections like his own that have been repossessed by the bank. Both owned by good blokes, who don't drink that much, work their land well and take pride in their capacity to feed their large families.

He has seen it before – a single cart piled high with a few pitiful sticks of furniture pulled by an old horse the bank couldn't hope to sell. The family walking behind, kids with bare feet and runny noses, husband and wife with their heads bowed, too ashamed to acknowledge his greeting. He's even seen the kids pulling a cart, the bank sometimes not even allowing them a horse to take with them. These are the dispossessed, men robbed of their land, the work of the greedy mongrels in their city clothes and brown derby hats who come in their fancy traps with leather-bound ledgers under their arms. 'Mr Bergman, may I come in? A small matter of the mortgage payments.' A small matter that will destroy his confidence and cause him to whimper and bite his knuckles in his sleep.

Joe knows he could not bear such a humiliation. He thinks bitterly that his only hope lies in the prospect of one of the sows getting the attentions of the ageing boar. He is back in Hester's clutches and she has trapped him once again. These are his thoughts as he approaches the homestead across the flat, dry, dusty saltbush plain.

Jessica has seen them coming ever since the sulky appeared out of the dark line of river gums to regain its outline in the late afternoon sunshine. She's prepared a pot of lamb stew, which has been bubbling away on the stove for three days. Not knowing when they would arrive back, Jessica's had it for her own tea each night, and then topped it up in the morning with vegetables and the last of the lamb Joe slaughtered before he left, which she's par-boiled to make it last longer so they might have a stew with a bit of meat to it.

Jessica well knows how tired they will be after the long trip from Narrandera, though she knows nothing of the wearisome overnight train journey. There is no time to bake bread, and so she quickly mixes flour and water for damper and, at the same time, prepares a batch of scones, before putting the kettle on for tea. They have almost reached the homestead by the time she has adjusted the flue and popped the scones into the oven.

She finds her heart beating harder as she watches the

sulky coming towards the homestead. She's determined she will not cry for fear of what her family have done or may yet do to her. She will weep for Jack when they cannot hear her, but they must never be allowed to know her sadness.

Jessica's baby is kicking in her stomach and, with the sense of the life growing inside her, she's resolved that it won't suffer from any loss of her normally robust health. She knows little about having a child but she has heard the old adage that she must eat for them both. That a healthy baby comes from a well-fed mother and that sadness in pregnancy will make a sad child. She must, Jessica tells herself, follow both these rules with all her strength. The life within her has become everything to her and she has come to believe that she must protect it against the dark forces ranged against her, forces which she sees clearly enough in the form of Hester and Meg. But even Joe has changed and is showing an increasing indifference to her.

Jessica knows that she will have to put up with Hester's unremitting attention to Meg's pregnancy. That she must willingly suffer her mother's scorn and anger at the prospect of the child she carries in her own stomach – the child they think of as her great mortal sin, while regarding Meg's baby as a triumph.

She knows, too, that Joe is no longer on her side. He has given up, suddenly grown old and tired. Her mother has finally beaten Joe, and Jessica can no longer depend on him to help her, or feel his big heavy hand on her shoulder to comfort her.

Joe's silences have become morbid, no longer are they just the silences of a naturally shy man who has spent a near lifetime on his own in the bush. Nor is the darkness which has befallen him the same as the silent thinking that he believes is hard-won from nature, when stillness and observation will slowly evolve to become wisdom. Joe's new silence is born of sadness and desperation and Jessica doesn't know how to comfort him, thinking all the while that she is the major cause of his misery.

Jessica is also aware that she must somehow keep to herself the terrible anger she feels against Meg and Hester, who are trying to steal Jack from her. They know only one Jack, the rich Jack Thomas of Riverview Station. But they do not know the Jack with the smiling blue eyes she has known since she was a brat. The Jack who once snipped a lock of her tar-covered hair so that the men in the shearing shed would not see her fourteen-year-old shame. The Jack who would sit and talk to Billy Simple and make him feel as though he was a man again. The silent Jack, seated in the bush with the shame of his father's humiliation bearing down on him. The Jack of the sly smile when she went to comfort him with a rude joke so that in the end they could laugh about George Thomas and his big brandy nose. The earnest Jack of pipes and canals, donkey engines and irrigation. Jack in his motor car, all clank and roar and backfire and boyish grin. But most of all, the Jack Thomas on horseback kicking up clods of earth, daring her to ride beside him, driving and turning a beast, whooping through the salt-bush and mulga scrub, jumping from his horse to pull down a calf and laughing when he missed and went rolling in the black dust. The Jack Thomas who has always accepted her as an equal, as a mate – yet loved her as a woman, too shy to show the tenderness she could see in his eyes when he looked at her. That is the Jack, the Jack who called her Tea Leaf, whom they could never take away from her. This is the Jack she would wait for until the end of her life.

She tells herself that no good will come from the hate she feels for her mother and sister, but she also knows that there is a part of her that will not forgive them. Jessica is no Christian soul, nor is she taken in by the pious sermons of the Reverend Mathews, M.A. Oxon., and his exhortations to love all creatures great and small. For it's Jessica's observation that it's the small, helpless creatures who always cop the shit.

She comforts herself with the knowledge that now all that matters is her baby, and her need to nourish the fierce and wonderful love for the child that breathes within her. Jessica will make no plans until she can carry this precious and unexpected gift in her arms and suckle it at her small breasts. She will simply do as she is told and stay out of trouble. Gentle Jessica meek and mild, look upon your little child, she laughs to herself.

Stubborn Jessica, with her flat chest, blunt, broken nails, carelessly cropped hair, sweat-stained cotton shirt, dirty moleskins and scuffed boots, will stay out of harm's way. She wants nothing more than to be the mother of her own child, to love and cherish it with every beat of her heart. She will do nothing to endanger its birth. Jessica feels the womanliness in her come to life like a great, surging force, a power she has never felt in herself before, and she knows she will not be broken.

Jessica now goes out to meet them. Joe's face is grey with weariness, Hester ignores her and turns away at her greeting, and in Meg's prim little face her eyes are ringed red from weeping.

'Go in, Father,' Jessica says to Joe, 'leave the pony to me.'

Joe casts her a grateful glance. 'Nice to see yiz, girlie.'

'There's tea made in the pot and the scones will be ready soon,' Jessica says, trying to sound cheerful. 'I've made a stew for tea t'night, not much lamb left in it, though.' Climbing into the sulky, Jessica watches as Joe takes down the two battered suitcases. 'Leave 'em, I'll bring them in,' she says.

Joe glances up at her. For a moment she sees his old scornful look and then his expression crumbles. 'Much obliged, Jessie,' he says softly. 'It's me arm, I've got a crook left arm.' He tries to grin but it comes out more as a grimace and Jessica can feel his pain.

Hester and Meg have gone ahead meanwhile, walking towards the kitchen door. At the door Hester pauses and looks back over her shoulder. 'You'll need to congratulate your sister, girl,' she says loudly. Then, as Jessica turns at the sound of her voice, Hester lifts her eyebrows and tilts her head slightly so that she appears to be looking down her nose. It's an expression Jessica saw often enough on the face of Ada Thomas. 'Meg is now Mrs Jack Thomas of Riverview homestead!' Hester calls.

Jessica turns away from her mother. Her heart is a rush of terrible sadness and anger, an emotional turmoil within her so overwhelming that she is close to fainting. She grips the rail on the sulky to steady herself, feeling the sun-baked metal burn into her palms. Then she grabs the reins and sends the tired pony forward, her back rigid and her head, as her mother must observe it from the back, held high. Hester cannot see that her daughter is biting her bottom lip so hard a trickle of blood now runs down her chin, or that her eyes are so tight-closed that it takes several moments before the first tears squeeze through her soft lashes.

Joe, standing beside the sulky with the two old cardboard and twine-bound suitcases at his feet, witnesses it all. He clutches suddenly at his chest and sinks to his knees and then pitches forward into the dirt.

Joe's 'fit of melancholy', as he calls it, lasts two days, after which he rises from his bed in the sleep-out. Though Hester has fussed somewhat over him, he hasn't allowed either of his daughters to see him. On the morning of the third day he emerges silently and seats himself at the kitchen table for breakfast.

Jessica, returning from milking the cows and feeding the pigs, enters the kitchen. 'Oh, Father!' she cries out in delight and rushes towards Joe tearfully. But he puts up his hands to fend her off.

'Don't fuss, girl,' Hester admonishes, though she has earlier allowed Meg to embrace him, much to Joe's consternation. 'Your father is well. It was some trick of the sun, a fever perhaps.'

Jessica pulls up short, tears now in her eyes. Joe looks well enough, though his hands shake as he dips a spoon into his porridge. Jessica seats herself quietly at the table and Hester places a plate of oatmeal porridge in front of her.

'Jessie, I want you to separate the three sows without piglets and let the boar at them,' Joe says suddenly.

Jessica looks at Joe in surprise. 'But Father, two are too young and could abort or the piglets could die in the cold. Besides, the old sow is well past it – her piglets usually die soon after they're born.'

Joe looks down into his plate of porridge. 'Do as I say, girlie.'

Jessica bows her head. 'Yes, Father.'

Since Joe's collapse, when they helped her to carry him to his bed, Hester and Meg have hardly spoken to Jessica. The incident with Joe which Hester now calls a trick of the sun has postponed Jessica's shock at the news of Meg's wedding, which has not been mentioned since by anyone. Now, sure that Joe will live at least for the moment, Jessica takes herself down to the river to weep for Jack.

Meg's marriage to Jack isn't entirely unexpected. Jessica reckons she'd be pretty stupid if she thought that Meg's going off pregnant to Sydney with Hester to confront Jack would not have resulted in Hester extracting some promise from him. It's only that she loves Jack so very much, that she is quite unable to comprehend how he could agree to marry Meg for the sake of her child. He could have given Meg money, she tells herself, or

offered to care for her child and asked her to wait until
he returns. He'd said himself that he didn't want to go
to war with the responsibility of a wife or a family.

In her emotional confusion Jessica cannot see that
Jack's decency has forced him to legitimise Meg's child,
but only that Jack has deserted her. That he has allowed
Meg to seduce him and that Meg and Hester have once
again cheated her of what she wanted most in all the
world – besides the child in her womb. Jack has been
taken from her and Joe could soon enough be taken as
well, for she had seen him clutch at his heart and she's
not fooled by Hester's sun and fever story. Jessica, who
has often enough been lonely, suddenly knows herself
now to be utterly alone in the world. It is not the same
thing as loneliness and it's a feeling she has never experienced before.

After breakfast she goes down to the pig pen and
separates the two young sows and old Maude, the ageing sow. The old girl has in her time produced numerous
piglets but now seldom becomes a farrowing sow. When
she does, the piglets usually die or are crushed by her
rolling on them. Jessica calls to the sows, who follow
her, grunting loudly, smelling the cabbage leaves in her
hand. She leads them into a small holding pen they use
for breeding when the weather is warmer.

The boar is a cranky old bastard, usually handled by
Joe, and Jessica approaches him with some trepidation.
But he's sighted the three sows and the cabbage leaves
she's placed in their pen. When released from his enclo-
sure he makes straight for them, although, once in, he

seems more interested in feeding his face than in servicing his womenfolk.

With winter well advanced, Jessica can't imagine why Joe wants the sows to breed. It isn't good farming practice – the freezing cold, or a sudden frost in the early mornings, will often enough kill off a litter and, besides, the sows require extra rations to keep up their milk supply.

The household settles down to some semblance of normalcy. In the weeks that follow Joe still works apart from Jessica, and it is obvious from the things that are left undone about the place that he is slowing down considerably.

Joe seems to be working most days down by the creek where the old boundary rider's hut is situated and he mentions that he's decided to try breeding turkeys. This statement is made without explanation when Jessica ventures to ask him what he's doing in a part of the selection where there is normally little work to do. She is surprised at her father's response, for poultry breeding had been one of Jack's so-called harebrained ideas. With the telegraph and the train line coming through in a year or two, the Sydney and Melbourne market will open up, he claimed, and poultry might be the go for smaller properties where labour is the sole responsibility of the family on the land. At one of their Sunday dinners he'd told them all that with irrigation the grain and the green needed for turkeys could be grown, that live poultry in special trucks could easily enough be sent off, bred for the Christmas market when the lambing and calving season was well over. Jessica can't recall that Joe had shown any enthusiasm for Jack's idea at the time and so she is surprised and at the same time hurt that he hasn't invited her to see what he is doing or to share in the task. But she knows well enough to stay away from the section where he works, trying for her part to keep the remainder of the paddocks going as best she can.

A month after she'd let the old boar in with the sows Jessica comes back in from the cow paddock for breakfast one Saturday morning to see Joe emerge from the pig pen with his hands and arms covered in blood up to the elbow and carrying a zinc bucket covered with a piece of hessian.

He stops only long enough to say, 'I'll need yer help after breakfast, girlie.'

'What for, Father? Have you slaughtered old Maude?'

'Nah, the two young 'uns. You'll help me to dress them and make bacon. Scrub out a pickling barrel, will ya?' He continues on his way over to the well to wash, taking the bucket with him.

Jessica is alarmed and confused. The two sows were a pedigree cross, Berkshire and Saddleback, which Joe had selected for his breeding stock after a great deal of care. They'd cost a fair whack, more than Joe could rightly afford, and he'd been that proud of them. She's surprised that he'd let them breed so young and now, for no good reason, he's slaughtered them. It doesn't make sense, Jessica thinks – both were in prime health.

He couldn't want them for ham, as they were not yet old enough to make a good-sized hindquarter.

She goes into breakfast puzzled, but no further explanation is forthcoming from her father. Jessica spends the better part of the day with him and by its end her hands are red and puffed from the near-boiling water used to scrape the hair from the skin, and they hurt from the exposure to the brine and spices in the bacon trough and pickling barrel. Throughout it all Joe remains grimly silent.

After the evening meal Hester and Meg talk about inviting Mrs Baker to Sunday dinner after church the following morning. Jessica is surprised – while Hester sometimes visits the old girl, she's not, by her own admission, all that fond of her. Even by Hester and Meg's standards, Mrs Baker is sanctimonious and, as well, a terrible old whinger and gossip.

'A nice feed of pork chops and a bit of crackling will do the old dear a power of good,' Hester asserts to no one in particular. 'She's poor as a church mouse and eats like a bird. I'm sure that's what mostly ails her.' Then she turns to Joe. 'Will that be all right, Joe?' She doesn't wait for his answer before she concludes, 'Good then, we'll bring her home with us after morning service.' Hester now turns to Jessica. 'You'll need to stay out of the way, Jessica. I don't want Mrs Baker seeing you in your condition. She's a fearful old gossip and the whole world will know in a day. You'll be in your room when we return from St Stephen's and I'll thank you to stay there until your father takes her home later on in the afternoon.'

They are the most words Hester has spoken to her in a week. The previous time her mother had addressed her was to point out that Meg was beginning to show, making her eldest daughter stand up and spread her hands tightly across either side of her stomach so that Jessica might see the slight bulge under the brown bombazine of her sister's dress. 'Such a pretty little bulge,' Hester said, smiling benignly up at Meg.

Jessica does not reply to her mother, but rises slowly, almost painfully, from the table to go to her room. It has been a tiring day. Slaughtering and dressing pork is hard work and Joe seems less able to do his usual share. With all the bending, lifting and carrying, scalding and scraping the bristles from the skin and cutting up the carcasses, Jessica's back also aches something terrible. Besides, her baby has been unusually active and she is sore all over and exhausted. She washes herself carefully and retires gratefully to her cot, glad to spend the afternoon of the following day alone in her own room.

Jessica spends the next morning doing her usual Sunday chores until shortly past noon, when she sees the sulky approaching across the saltbush plain leading from the river, whereupon she dutifully retires to her bedroom.

She is happy enough to accept the enforced rest, as she doesn't much care for Mrs Baker – a dreadful and interfering old gossip who spends most of her waking hours complaining to anyone who will listen about the poor state of her health. This, she will tirelessly explain, has been brought about by a peculiar condition of her heart, which, according to a famous Sydney physician she'd once seen, doesn't throb to a regular cadence like everyone else's. It seems Mrs Baker's heart is known to miss a beat every so often, a condition known as *arrhythmia*. Accordingly, her dicky heart is always on the verge of giving up the ghost. She explains that it is something to do with the way it ticks, which she refers to as her *arithmetic*. She will conclude with a deep and distinctly mournful sigh and declare, 'A body could drop dead this very moment from me arithmetic.'

As long as anyone can remember, the organist at St Stephen's has pronounced to all and sundry that she is living on borrowed time. 'My life is a gift from the Lord, only He knows the day and the hour,' she will say melodramatically. 'I ask only that He take me to Paradise while I am seated at the organ in praise of His precious name.'

And so Jessica had taken a plate of roast pork and potatoes into the bedroom with her and concluded happily that being absent from any dinner table shared by Mrs Baker is no hardship.

Jessica is completely unaware of her mother's true reason for inviting old Mrs Baker, who has been so carefully chosen for her very morbidity. It is Hester's guess that the advent of Meg's faked miscarriage will render the old girl hysterical, so that when she accompanies Joe with the bloody evidence to the vicarage that afternoon she will have a pronounced effect on the Reverend Mathews, M.A. Oxon.

Hester has finally decided that Joe should show

Jack's contract indicating the terms of her marriage to the vicar and then, immediately after, expose the evidence of the miscarriage for him to examine. Joe will reveal it quickly so the vicar may obtain only the briefest glance. Whereupon Mrs Baker will tearfully confirm that she had been present when Meg was took ill, quite out of the blue and not an hour after Sunday dinner. The vicar's lack of anatomical knowledge, coupled with squeamishness and his almost certain reluctance to make a second closer inspection of the evidence, will, Hester anticipates, finalise the matter.

Joe hasn't at first wanted to get involved to this degree, afraid that he will show his nerves and give the game away. 'The more you shake and quaver the better,' Hester replies. 'He'll see it for your grief.' She then points out that no loving mother would leave her poor suffering daughter alone under such trying conditions. Furthermore, she says, with Joe handling the bloody evidence and Mrs Baker whimpering at his side, the Reverend Mathews, M.A. Oxon., is even less likely to embarrass him with a close and careful scrutiny of the gory evidence. It may safely be assumed he will wish only to ply Joe with a deep and abiding sympathy for the terrible tragedy which has befallen their daughter. After all, Hester points out, Meg is the new Mrs Jack Thomas and the reverend can only hope that she proves to be as generous to the church and to himself as was the former incumbent of Riverview Station.

'Never you mind, that one knows which side his bread is buttered on,' Hester concludes.

But, while Hester has been able to influence her husband to conspire with her, she has quite underestimated the calibre of opponent she faces in Colonel Septimus Cunningham-Thomas, Jack's company commander. In what can only be described as a strange coincidence, Hester is handed a letter for Joe from the verger at St Stephen's the very Sunday morning they are to return home with Mrs Baker. This isn't in itself unusual. Folk travelling to Narrandera will collect any mail for people in the district and leave it at the vicarage or bring it to Sunday worship to be handed to the recipients. What is a coincidence are the contents of the letter.

Hester is so preoccupied with the plans for the day that she forgets to give the letter to Joe when she returns with Mrs Baker from morning worship. It is this seemingly innocent oversight that will cost a life, and contribute to a tragedy that will last for the next fifty years.

All goes well at Sunday dinner. Hester and Meg chat happily with Mrs Baker and even listen for the umpteenth time to the story of her dicky heart and its arithmetic. Joe is his usual silent self and Mrs Baker declares the pork quite the best that she has tasted in a good while. After Mrs Baker has had her last piece of crackling, Meg clears the dishes from the table and Joe, with hardly a grunt, leaves the three of them at it and says he's going over to the north paddock. After she's cleared the table and washed the dishes, Meg also excuses herself.

'What's the matter, dearest?' Hester asks, a little surprised.

'It's the pork I think, a bit too rich.' Meg holds her stomach, emphasising the far from impressive bulge under her dress. 'Maybe the baby doesn't care for crackling as much as Mrs Baker,' she says, giving her mother a wan smile.

'You go to your room and rest, my dear, I'll look in a little later,' Hester says, comforting her daughter. 'Perhaps a little water? Take some in with you.'

Meg pours herself a mug of water from the clay pitcher on the table and departs. 'Such a lovely girl,' she hears Mrs Baker say.

It is less than twenty minutes later when Meg reappears. She is sobbing and clutching at her abdomen with part of her skirt bunched in her hands so that the hem is lifted to her knees. Blood runs down her right leg and into the top of her boot. 'Mama, something terrible is happening to me,' she wails.

'Oh my God!' Hester gasps, bringing her hand to her lips. She rises from the table. 'Oh my God, the baby!' she repeats, rushing over to Meg and turning her away from an astonished Mrs Baker. Then, putting her arm around her daughter's shoulder, she leads Meg back into her room.

Old Mrs Baker sits for a moment like a stunned mullet, then she clutches at her heart. 'Oh, my heart!' she screams. 'Water, water!'

Jessica hears the scream and comes running into the kitchen from her room. She is dressed only in her pantaloons, having removed the remainder of her clothes in the privacy of her room to bring her some comfort from the heat and her pregnancy. Mrs Baker, who has her back to Jessica, has risen from the table and has her hands thrown into the air and is stumbling about in a circle, sobbing and gasping and screaming out whenever she can catch her breath.

'What is it?' Jessica cries as Mrs Baker turns to see a young woman near nude and with her pregnant stomach boldly distended.

Mrs Baker cannot believe her eyes, which seem to pop from her head at the sight of Jessica. 'Oh, oh, *help*!' she yells, then she points a trembling finger. 'It's you! Oh Gawd, you're p . . . p . . . pregnant!' she stammers and seems as though she must at any moment faint.

Jessica crosses the room quickly and takes her by the arm. 'Come and sit, Mrs Baker,' she says, steering the old lady to a chair. 'Sit, I'll get you some water. Is it your heart?' she asks as she pours the old girl a mug of water.

'My heart, oh yes my heart,' Mrs Baker says, clutching at her bosom. With the shock of seeing Jessica pregnant and almost naked, she has for the moment forgotten why she became upset in the first instance.

Jessica holds the mug to her lips. 'Drink, Mrs Baker.'

The old woman drinks greedily from the mug, some of the water spilling down her front. Just then Hester walks into the kitchen. 'Jessica!' she shouts. 'Get back to your room at once!'

'Mother, Mrs Baker is unwell,' Jessica protests.

'At once, you hear me! Go!' A fine spray of spittle flies from Hester's mouth as she holds her arms rigid, her hands balled into fists. 'You wicked girl! Look at you! Are you quite mad?' Hester screams at her.

Jessica glances downwards and, suddenly aware of her state of undress, she gasps and places the mug on the table beside Mrs Baker, then turns and flees back to her room.

Hester watches her youngest daughter leave and then turns to the old woman seated at the table. 'Mrs Baker, Meg has had a miscarriage. Will you help me, please?' She speaks calmly enough, though her voice is not without anxiety, and her tone brings the old lady halfway back to her senses. Hester crosses to the stove, where she takes the kettle from the hob and pours boiling water into a small basin and then cools it with water from the clay pitcher. She takes three rough kitchen towels from the line beside the stove and places them over her arm before she picks up the basin. 'Come, you must help me,' she says to Mrs Baker. 'Follow me, please,' she says in a voice which brooks no contradiction.

Mrs Baker enters Meg's darkened room to see Meg spreadeagled on top of the counterpane, clutching her pillow and wailing. The centre of the counterpane between Meg's wide-open legs is soaked with blood, though the bloodied material of her skirt covers her to the knees. At the bottom of the mattress is a blood-soaked towel, wrapped into a small bundle.

'Here, hold this,' Hester instructs, handing the small basin of steaming hot water to the old lady.

'I fear I c . . . c . . . ca . . . can't,' Mrs Baker says tearfully, her teeth chattering.

'You must,' Hester snaps. 'Just hold it.' She now dips one of the towels into the basin and starts to clean up Meg. 'You don't have to look. Close your eyes, just hold the basin close.'

The old woman closes her eyes while Hester works at cleaning up a wailing, sobbing, seemingly hysterical Meg.

'There, there, dearest, it's all come away, you'll be safe now,' she says soothingly to her eldest daughter. 'God in his infinite mercy didn't want you to have this dear child.'

At the mention of God, whom Mrs Baker regards as her own personal territory, she opens her eyes. 'God bless you, my dear,' she manages to say, though whether this is meant for Hester or Meg is not clear. 'The little mite is on its way to Paradise.' These dear sweet words seem to surprise and cheer her up no end and she offers to take the blood-tinged contents of the basin into the kitchen and return with fresh hot water from the kettle.

'Not too hot,' Hester instructs quietly. 'She is so very tender.' She looks up at the old woman, and Mrs Baker gives an involuntary sob as she sees the terrible sadness in Hester's eyes. She turns and hurries as much as she might with the basin in her hands into the kitchen.

When she returns Hester tells her to place the basin on the floor beside where she sits on the bed. In Mrs Baker's absence she has moved a chair to the further-most side of the bed. 'Will you sit, my dear, and hold Meg's hand?' she asks. 'I must go and find her father.'

Mrs Baker moves over to the chair, happy to be able

to do something for Hester and knowing herself calm enough to hold Meg's hand. Hester pauses at the door and speaks to Meg. 'Dearest, I must fetch your father,' she says, as though Meg hasn't heard her words to Mrs Baker.

'Mama, don't go! Please don't go,' Meg wails. 'Send Jessica!'

Hester sighs deeply. 'She's not well, my precious.' Hester now turns to Mrs Baker and in a whisper, as if she is still talking to Meg, says, 'Poor Mrs Baker saw our dear Jessica naked, her mind quite gone.' She looks again at Meg. 'Try to sleep, my dearest, Mama will be back soon.' She leans over and kisses Meg on the forehead. 'Mrs Baker will mind you while I'm gone.'

Hester, free from the homestead and on her way to the cow paddock where Joe will be waiting, is both elated and despairing. Mrs Baker will make a fine witness without her ever having seen the evidence. But, at the same time, she has witnessed Jessica's condition and will now have to be sworn to secrecy. Hester despairs at the thought that she will need to throw herself on the old woman's mercy and beg her not to reveal Jessica's pregnancy. She knows the old lady, despite any assurances she may give, cannot be trusted, for she simply can't help herself. There is nothing much Hester can do about this latest predicament and she is furious at Jessica's behaviour. Once again her youngest daughter has shamed them all.

Joe nods quietly when she tells him all this, though she doesn't tell Joe how she has meant Mrs Baker to believe Jessica has gone strange in the head.

'It would have come out sooner or later,' Joe says philosophically, 'we can't hide the girlie's pregnancy forever.'

It is as they are walking back from the paddock together that Hester remembers the letter. Quite why it would pop into her head at such a moment she cannot think. 'Joe, there is a letter for you – the verger gave it to me this morning.'

Joe goes into Meg's room when they return to the homestead. He feels awkward in front of Mrs Baker, who still clings dutifully to Meg's hand, but it is this very awkwardness which makes the scene all the more convincing.

'I'm sorry, girlie,' he mumbles. 'You get better now, eh.' Then he turns and walks out slowly, followed by Hester who goes to her handbag and gives him the letter.

Joe, who knows himself to be a slow reader, goes to sit at the kitchen table. Tearing open the envelope, he begins to read.

Dear Mr Bergman,

I most sincerely trust you and your good wife are in excellent health, though, as a physician, I hope this is even more the case with your daughter Meg, a fine young woman whom I understand is now married to young Jack Thomas. An admirable family and an excellent choice, if I may say so. As I recall saying to you, these things have a splendid way of working out for the best.

However, I am charged with a most extraordinary duty and all of it in the name of King and Country. I have received a letter from Colonel Septimus Cunningham-Thomas who is, I believe, the colonel in charge of Jack Thomas's battalion and also, I seem to recall, his uncle, on his father's side. In what seems to me to be a highly unnecessary precaution, he asks that in the unlikely event of a miscarriage or stillbirth, Meg is overseen by myself or a midwife of my nomination, and the sad occasion witnessed and certified by either one of us.

I have told him that it is unlikely that I will be in a position to oversee the birth, or, as it may be, miscarriage, but that I will recommend a certain Mrs Colleen O'Sullivan, a woman in whom I have complete trust. She lives in Yanco and while she is of the Church of Rome this should not be held against her as she is thoroughly trustworthy and highly skilled in the modern technique of delivery.

In the sad event of a miscarriage or stillbirth, I, or as it is likely to transpire, Mrs O'Sullivan, may be called as witnesses. In such an instance I regret that you must keep the foetus in your possession for inspection by myself or Mrs O'Sullivan.

I hasten to say that I feel it highly unlikely that such a calamity will befall your daughter. Nevertheless I have written to say that we will comply with the colonel's instructions, as they are in your best interests. I say this because I am led to conclude from his letter that the marriage contract is in some way implicated if Meg's pregnancy is not forthcoming.

I am too old to feel insulted by such a manifest doubt in my ability to determine so obvious a condition of pregnancy, but for the sake of good relations with your son-in-law's military commander, I have agreed for Mrs O'Sullivan to be called as the primary witness if such a tragedy should occur. Upon her evidence I would then certify to the colonel's satisfaction that a miscarriage has in fact taken place or that the child was stillborn.

All this is, of course, entirely unnecessary. Your daughter Meg is to my mind in excellent health and, but for the slimness of her hips, I foresee no complications. She should carry the full nine months and give birth to a healthy child, though I strongly suggest she remains out of the saddle for the last two months of her pregnancy and is required to undertake only light duties.

Please let me know when the birth takes place so that we may adjust the little matter of timing we talked about previously.

My felicitations to your dear wife and daughter.

I remain, yours faithfully,

Nathaniel Merrick (Physician).

Joe rises slowly from the kitchen table and walks over to stand in the doorway of Meg's bedroom. Hester looks up as he reaches the door and he indicates with a jerk of his head that she should follow him. Back in the kitchen, he hands her the letter from Dr Merrick. 'Come outside, we'll talk there,' he mutters.

Hester stands in the yard and reads the letter and then looks up at Joe and sighs.

'What now?' Joe asks, spreading his hands as they begin to walk towards the cow paddock.

Hester hands him back the letter and walks silently for a while, thinking. After a time she looks up at her husband. 'We'll have to do her in.' She shrugs. 'There's simply no other way out, Joe.'

'Do her in? Do who in?' Joe asks, confused.

'Mrs Baker.'

Joe shakes his head, lost for words. He is about to say something when Hester interrupts. 'Joe, can't you see, she now thinks there's been a miscarriage. We can't go denying it happened – pretending Meg is still pregnant.'

'I thought you said you'd speak to her . . . Mrs Baker . . . about Jessica, get her to shut her trap. Ask her to do the same now about the miscarriage.'

Hester brings the tips of her forefingers of both hands to press down on either side of her nose. 'She'll know we're up to something. It may have worked with Jessica – she saw her half naked, to her that would be a sure sign of Jessica's insanity. She will also understand how it has come about after Jessica's trip with Billy Simple.' Hester now looks up. 'But she believes she saw Meg's miscarriage with her own eyes. She won't be able to keep quiet about that.' Hester looks pleadingly at Joe. 'If she asks me why she shouldn't tell about Meg,' what reason will I give her? Will I tell her that we're try-ing to deceive Jack? The old girl was very fond of Ada Thomas – Ada paid her salary for years! She'll see what we're trying to do to Jack.' Hester bows her head and starts to cry softly. 'We're ruined. We will be disgraced, destroyed,' she sobs.

'Yeah, well, it was always asking too much. It was bound to go wrong, come unstuck in the end. Bloody hell, maybe Jack will come back from the war, dump Meg and marry Jessica.'

Hester's head shoots up in alarm and Joe sees the look of hatred on her face. 'Never! You hear, never! Jack belongs to Meg. Jessica's not getting him no matter what.'

'Yeah, well, there you go,' Joe says helplessly, shrug-ging his shoulders once again.

Hester grabs his arm. 'Listen, Joe, only Mrs Baker knows about the miscarriage, no one else. She's got a dicky heart – you've heard her say it often enough, how she could pass over to the other side at any moment – her arithmetic. The whole district knows about it, nobody will be in the least surprised.'

'What are you saying?'

'We'll make an excuse, say you can't take her home, that we'd be most grateful if she'd stay the night. Ask her, as a comfort to me – say you'd be much obliged if she'd stay. She can share my bed. Then, when she's asleep we'll suffocate her with a pillow. She'll not be strong enough to fight us both.'

Joe stops and looks at his wife. 'Hester, we are going mad! This has got to stop.'

'Joe, we have one more chance,' Hester begs. 'One last chance to keep Meg's pregnancy alive.'

'What are you saying, woman? In the end there'll be no child for Meg, and Jack will be free to dump her anyway!'

'Joe, if we can stop Mrs Baker talking so that nobody knows Jessica is pregnant, Meg could have her baby. Jessica's baby!' Hester says all this in a rush, getting it out before Joe can fully react to what she's said. She thinks Joe may hit her and she's prepared for this, lifting her arms up to her face in anticipation.

Instead Joe stops and brings his hands to cover his face. 'As God is my witness, you have gorn stark starin' mad, woman,' he says slowly.

Hester knows she has won – Joe would have hit her otherwise. 'Joe, it's not madness, it's madness the other way. Don't you see? If Jessica keeps her child she will be disgraced, and the child will be persecuted all its life for being Billy Simple's bastard. A monster's child. Jessica will never live it down – there is already some talk that she's mad.'

'Yeah, no doubt started by the two of yiz.'

'Joe, people aren't stupid. They ask why she doesn't come to church any more.'

'And the two of yiz shakes yer heads and looks mournful and they catch on soon enough. Something's not right with Jessica, they tell themselves, which is what yiz two want them to think, ain't it?'

'Well, we can't say she's pregnant, can we?' Hester protests.

'Why not? Get it bloody over with, it's not the end of the world!'

'Joe, if we take Jessica's baby for Meg, it will have a good life as the son or daughter of Jack Thomas. It's an even better idea than the miscarriage.' Hester hesitates, then adds, 'Jessica is still young. She'll recover and be none the worse for the experience. She'd be free to marry or she can run Riverview Station for Meg if Jack doesn't come back. Meg claims Jessica's child for herself and it has a grand future.' Hester looks up, pleading with her husband. 'Can't you see how it would solve everything and be so very good for Jessica as well?'

Hester observes how Joe hesitates. She knows he feels guilty about Jessica, that he feels he's let her down. 'It would be the greatest service you could ever render her, Joe,' she urges. 'Jessica's child will grow up rich and be the master of Riverview Station one day.'

Joe gives a bitter little laugh. 'All we have to do is kill Mrs Baker, hope Jack carks it in the war and steal Jessica's child, is that it?'

'Joe, we'd be giving both the baby and Jessica a decent life. You'd be looking after Jessica's best interests. If Jack doesn't come back from the war, Jessica gets the five hundred acres Jack said she could have.' Hester sees her husband hesitate a second time and she cleverly changes the subject, leaving Joe to ponder what she's promised their youngest daughter.

'Mrs Baker is poorly by her own confession, she could go at any moment!' Hester then adds spitefully, 'Mr Duffy the verger has wanted to play the organ for years. It's her that's kept him out – her waiting for God to take her to Paradise in the middle of "Onward Christian Soldiers"!'

Despite himself Joe laughs, but then falls silent again as they turn to walk back to the homestead. Just before they reach the front door, he sighs. 'I'll ask her to stay overnight,' he says, then closes his eyes tightly and shakes his head in silent denial. 'God have mercy on our souls, woman.'

Mrs Baker is secretly delighted to be asked to stay the night. She feels herself an important part of what's happened and now that she's over her initial shock she relishes the prospect of talking about Meg's tragedy for weeks to come. She has already decided she will do so in a confidential whisper, as though the person she is talking to is the only one privileged to hear the details. And such details! Already her febrile imagination has gone well beyond what she has witnessed. Already details both intimate and sanguinary to titillate the imagination of her wide-eyed listener abound in her mind. She must use them sparingly, like a miser, make them last, and invent others to keep the experience fresh.

Mrs Baker reminds herself happily that the field of rumours concerning Meg is well ploughed and folk have already turned up a fair amount of dirt. They've put two and two together and come up with the conclusion that Meg's marriage to young Jack Thomas is not one of mutual enchantment but more likely one of singular entrapment. The young lad may have been caught with his trousers down but it was her hands that pulled them to his ankles. Now, with Jack's compromised child carried away in a flush of blood, Meg has had her comeuppance and she, Florence Baker, has the whole story of the Bergmans and the Thomases all to herself. She well remembers Ada Thomas's oft-quoted words, 'I am not mocked saith the Lord.'

This is a tragedy Mrs Baker thinks she knows how to play for all it is worth. The last tragedy in Mrs Baker's life was never properly played out, never consummated with public tears, tea and sympathy and then the gift of a permanently tragic demeanour. She still remembers the young merchant marine officer who wooed her and married her all in forty-eight hours and then, to the strains of 'Auld Lang Syne', left her on the wharf and sailed away, never to return, though not listed as deceased. The disgrace of it has kept her silent for fifty-eight years, when a thousand times over she has longed to possess all the trappings of a tragic life, so that she might truly enjoy the substance of sadness.

Now, at last, Mrs Baker has something for herself. Meg's miscarriage can be worked into her conversation in a dozen ways. This is not hearsay or second-hand gossip – she was there, she saw it happen, she has the gory details in her head as fresh as newly baked bread.

Mrs Baker climbs into Hester's bed and snuggles under the goosedown quilt, then she hugs herself in the darkness, for she cannot remember when she has enjoyed such excitement. Hester has read her like a book. Mrs Florence Baker could not be cajoled into silence however hard she tried – it is for this very reason she was chosen to be a witness to the miscarriage.

The moon is the merest crescent in a star-pricked sky and all that may be heard outside is the occasional barking of a fox and the mournful intermittent hoot of a boobook owl near the cow paddock. Beside Hester's bed the Wesclock ticks rapidly. Hester lies awake waiting to go and get Joe, while beside her old Mrs Baker snores without letting up, her arms clasped to her breast. A good sleeper, that one, Hester decides.

Just after one o'clock in the morning she slides carefully from the big double bed and walks quietly through the house to wake Joe out back. Joe is not asleep and he sits up at her first whispered call and climbs from his narrow cot. Together they return to Hester's room, the bedchamber from which Joe has been banished for so long. Hester takes up the pillow. It has already been decided that Joe will pin the old woman to the bed to stop her from thrashing about. He will lie on top of Mrs Baker and pin her arms and clamp her legs together with his own while Hester smothers her, bearing all her weight down on the pillow covering her face.

'Do not bruise her,' Hester cautions Joe in a whisper. Joe nods and Hester counts to three and clamps the pillow over the old woman's face while Joe places his huge body over hers and pushes her shoulders deeply into the mattress.

This is the final step for Joe, the point of no return. He's always thought himself a half-decent man, but now he knows he hasn't the strength to fight his wife, nor the character to save his youngest daughter from Hester's evil.

No more than four or five muffled grunts escape from under the pillow – it is at once clear that Mrs Baker doesn't possess the strength to combat Joe's weight. In a surprisingly short time the old lady gives a convulsive shudder and Joe feels her rigid body suddenly relax under him. Hester keeps the pillow pressed down over Mrs Baker's face for a further minute or so and then lifts it carefully.

Mrs Baker stares pop-eyed back at her, her mouth wide open with her dentures pushed at a weird angle halfway down her throat. 'Get up,' Hester whispers urgently to Joe. 'She's gone.'

Joe lifts himself off Mrs Baker and for some reason he cannot explain he whistles 'Onward Christian Soldiers', in a breath only just audible. It is not that he thinks the incident is humorous – in fact, he is very close to panic – it is just something to clear his mind and keep him from thinking that he's gone completely insane.

'Hush, Joe!' Hester whispers, though he can sense the relief in her voice. With the stupid hymn gone from his lips, Joe tries to push all thought of what they've done from his mind. He watches as Hester fits Mrs Baker's false teeth back into her mouth and tries to think only that what he has done is for Jessica and her unborn child. That Billy Simple's child will have Jack as its father, and will grow up to be one of the high and mighty Thomases. If Jessie has a son he'll be a member of the squattocracy, landed gentry, no less. He'll go to the King's School and eventually be master of Riverview Station. Joe tries to comfort himself with these thoughts as Hester straightens the bed and arranges Mrs Baker's stringy grey hair, unplaited for the night, neatly about the pillow. For all the world she now appears to be an old lady fast asleep. The morning light will show a small cut at the corner of her mouth sustained from her false teeth jarring, though it is too small even to bleed.

Shortly after dawn Joe taps on Jessica's door. 'Get up, girlie.' He waits for her response, then adds, 'Fold and bring your blankets and all your clothes.'

Joe hears Jessica shout, 'Wait on, Father,' and shortly after her head appears from behind the door. 'What for?' she asks him.

'Do as I say, Jessie. All your blankets and clobber. I'm taking you somewhere – be ready in ten minutes, eh?'

Jessica dresses hurriedly and pulls a tattered sheepskin coat over her cotton dress. She folds the three blankets she uses against the cold and places them next to the door. Then she finds an old canvas bag and folds and bundles the two old dresses Hester has let out at the front to accommodate her stomach, her hairbrush and a few odds and ends along with her Sunday boots and two sets of bloomers into it. Two small towels follow and she has just about reached the extent of her personal possessions but for her two books, *Wuthering Heights* and *Oliver Twist*, both battered from having been read a dozen times. She puts them into the bag and looks about her. Then, as an afterthought, she throws in her moleskins and two flannel shirts.

Joe taps on the door shortly afterwards. 'Come, girlie,' is all he says, then, 'bring what you can, I'll take the rest.'

Jessica comes into the yard carrying her canvas bag to see that Joe has the sulky outside with Napoleon already harnessed, his nostrils puffing cold air. Joe follows a few moments later with her blankets, which he tosses into the back of the sulky. Jessica sees that the large wicker hamper has been packed and that there's a spare axe as well.

'Climb in,' Joe commands, then moves over to his side, steps up into the sulky and takes up the reins. 'Haya!' he says to Napoleon, lightly flicking the pony's rump with the take-up from the leather straps.

'Where are we going, Father?' Jessica asks again. 'It's hardly light. Are we going to Narrandera?'

Joe ignores her question and Jessica knows better than to persist. They are headed in the wrong direction and soon leave the rutted path and proceed across open ground towards the creek that runs down the edge of their selection. After about ten minutes Joe reins in the pony. The light is beginning to grow more rapidly now and in the distance Jessica can hear the currawongs beginning to call. It will be half an hour yet to sunrise and the morning is bitterly cold with a low mist hovering above the cow paddock. She pulls the sheepskin coat about her, making sure her stomach is covered and warm.

'Jessie, I want to talk to you,' Joe begins. He is looking downwards as though he's inspecting his broken nails.

'Yes, Father?'

'This morning your mother found Mrs Baker dead in her bed.'

Jessica mistakes Joe's meaning. 'Mother stayed with Mrs Baker last night?'

'No, no, Mrs Baker stayed with us last night, she slept with your mother in the big bed.' Joe looks up briefly. 'She musta died in her sleep, heart attack or somethin'.'

Jessica brings her fingers to her lips. 'Oh my Gawd!' she gasps.

'Yes,' Joe lies, 'it were a terrible shock for your mother.'

'I must go to her,' Jessica cries.

'No!' Joe says quickly. 'No, that's why you must leave.'

'Leave? Leave the house? But why can't I stay in my room like before?'

'There'll be people coming. We'll have to report the death. The house will be full of people, stickybeaks, you mustn't be seen.' Joe now pauses and looks over to where a curtain of mist obscures the trees that grow beside the distant creek. 'Not in your condition, your mother won't allow it,' he says softly, as though the quieter tone of his voice might comfort her.

'Where will you take me? How long will I be away?'

Joe sighs. 'The old boundary rider's hut. I've fixed it some, yiz'll be okay for a few days. Make a fire, it's warm enough with a good fire going. I've chopped and split all the wood, you'll have no need to chop, the hard work's done.' Joe flicks his thumb to indicate the rear of the sulky. 'There's plenty of tucker, you won't starve. Maybe only a few days, eh girlie? Yiz'll come to no harm and I'll be down to see yiz from time to time.'

Jessica is too dumbstruck to speak. Joe takes up the reins again and urges the pony on and they bounce and rattle across the paddock, hitting rabbit holes. Joe has not spoken this much to her in weeks and, at first, she thinks she must be grateful, as his voice has been kind. But then her stubborn nature overcomes her and she grows suddenly angry, fed up to the back teeth. She's tired of the shit she's had to cop from Hester and Meg and Joe's increasing darkness.

'Father, why are you doing this to me? I ain't done nothing Meg 'asn't done! Why does she cop it sweet and I'm in the shit all the time? It's not fair and you know it!' Jessica shouts, tears coming to her eyes. 'It ain't right!'

'Hush, Jessie. Meg's married, you ain't, that's all.'

'*Married*? She and Hester shanghaied Jack. You know it as well as I do, they trapped him into getting her pregnant! She dropped her bloomers for him!'

'There's no crime in that, Jessie. Some folk would say it were bloody clever of your sister. Jack was the big catch. You can't say she hasn't been working at it a good while.'

'And I'm the stupid one 'cause I didn't do the same? What about when she didn't want him no more and she give him to me and then took him back when he was gunna be rich again? Was that fair?'

Joe rubs the stubble on his chin. 'You should have took your chance when yer got it, Jessie, like your sister.'

'But Father, Jack said he couldn't have a wife and children, him going off to war an' all. It ain't fair, not responsible, he said.'

'Fair? Nothing's fair in love and war, Jessie.' Joe now looks up at Jessica and shrugs. 'You was already pregnant to Billy Simple anyway. That wouldn't have been fair to Jack neither, would it?'

'I didn't say it were Billy Simple's. I never said that,' Jessica protests.

'You didn't say whose it was.' Joe pauses and looks directly at Jessica. 'Whose is it, girlie?' he demands.

Jessica folds her arms across her chest. 'I can't say, Father. I swore on my child's life I'd never tell nobody, never, unless it's the man I marry. He'd have to know.'

Joe looks at Jessica and she can see he is close to tears. Joe close to tears is almost more than she can bear. 'Jessie, I need to know. You must tell me, it could make all the difference.'

Jessica feels her heart must surely break. 'Father, I can't. I swore on my baby's life.'

Joe turns away and looks into the misty distance. The sun is just coming up over the river and the first rays are warm on the back of their necks. 'Please, Father – I can't,' she sobs.

Joe turns and Jessica can see his face is set hard. 'Well, it's a bastard and it's not welcome. You'll stay out of the way until it's born and then we'll see what we will see.'

Jessica looks tearfully at Joe but her eyes are now set as hard as her father's. 'Tell Mother she won't take my child away from me. I'll kill her if she tries.'

Joe has seen his youngest daughter stubborn before, although he's never seen the expression she now wears. But he's felt it, he instinctively knows it must be the same expression he carried on the day he killed the foreman of the Great Peter's Run. He knows for certain Jessica means what she says. His daughter never tries anything on. It's just the same as he felt when he was aiming for the foreman's head and not some soft wound that would leave him harmless but alive. Jessica could kill her mother if Hester meddles with her child.

Joe is suddenly overcome with the frustration and the lies of the last three weeks and his temper rises. He wants to smash his huge fist into someone's face – not Jessica's, he loves her, but someone's. His huge fist closes and draws back and all he can see in front of him is her distended stomach, the madman's bastard child growing in her stomach. His fist begins to move in an arc and Jessica screams, for she can see where it will land. Then, at the last moment, Joe's fist flies open and he desperately grabs at the tattered sheepskin coat and begins to shake Jessica. 'You'll stay away from your mother . . . *and* your sister, you hear me, Jessie.' Joe now pulls her into him so that his face is almost up against her own, and Jessica can smell his rancid morning breath. 'If you don't, I swear I'll flay the madman's bastard right out of yiz!'

He finally lets go of Jessica, who slumps into a heap

with her head cupped into her hands. Joe yanks on the reins and shouts furiously at Napoleon to move on.

It is some time before they get to the tin shack. The hut is well known to Jessica, for it has stood there throughout her childhood. Joe has now added a door to it, and a bit of a chimney, which looks slightly ridiculous as it sticks out of the corrugated-iron roof at a curious angle. Beside the door is a stack of split logs as high as the roof line and continuing all the way along one side of the hut – it is enough firewood to last the remainder of the winter. Joe climbs down from the sulky and removes the hamper and places it outside the door, not venturing into the hut. Then he adds a sack of flour, a frying pan, a kettle and a pot as well as a cast-iron camp oven. 'Git yer blankets and stuff,' he now says through clenched teeth.

Jessica has wiped away her tears – crying in front of Joe makes her ashamed. She removes the blankets and the canvas bag and enters the hut alone. It is several moments before her eyes adjust to the dark interior. Inside Joe has built a cot which contains a hessian mattress stuffed tight with straw. He has also constructed a small table and chair and a couple of shelves. Later she will find nails hammered into the back of the door for hanging her clothes. In addition Joe has built a small hearth with its ridiculous chimney to carry away the smoke. If Joe built it, it will work, Jessica thinks to herself. The hut is so small there is barely space for her to move about, but with a fire going it will warm nicely. How Joe, with his huge, clumsy frame, could have managed the work he has done in the interior Jessica cannot imagine.

She shivers suddenly, for the winter sun has not yet reached the hut and it is bitterly cold inside. Jessica sees that Joe has prepared kindling on the hearth and stacked several small logs for the fire. A hurricane lamp hangs from a post beside the hearth and she supposes there must be a bottle of kerosene somewhere about, so she won't be alone in the dark.

Joe's head appears suddenly at the door and he holds the four-ten shotgun which he now props against the crude door-frame. 'For the snakes,' he says, dropping a small canvas bag to the ground beside the gun. 'There's ten cartridges, I'll bring more soon.'

Jessica comes to the door of the hut and then moves outside just as Joe climbs back into the sulky. 'You're not to come near the house, Jessie. Stay away, ya hear? I'll come by from time to time and bring yer rations, once a week, maybe a bit more.' Then, without bidding her farewell, Joe moves away.

Jessica picks up the shotgun and breaks it. The lighter four-ten is much easier for her to manage than the twelve-bore. She knows its range well enough, no more than fifty feet. She quickly slips two cartridges into the barrel, locks it and cocks the hammers. Joe is only just within range for the pellets to reach him with some fury left in them. Jessica fires the first barrel at his back – she knows the pellets will do no more than sting him, real bad she hopes, make him aware of her defiance. She lets him have the second barrel straight off and has the satisfaction of seeing his hat fly from his head to land spinning in a clump of saltbush. 'Bastards!' she shouts. 'Bloody mongrel bastards, yiz can all get fucked!'

Joe lifts one hand in acknowledgement but he doesn't turn or stop to retrieve his hat. He doesn't want Jessica to see his pride at her rebellion. His neck, peppered with birdshot, stings furiously and he is hard put not to grab at it. He can feel several warm trickles of blood running down the back of his neck. But Joe hasn't felt better in weeks. 'That's my girlie,' he grins to himself. 'Don't let the bastards get yiz down.'

CHAPTER ELEVEN

On Thursday 6 August 1914, news reaches Australia that war is declared against Germany and Billy Simple's hanging takes place on the dawn of the same day. The war against Kaiser Bill is announced on all the news vendors' posters for the *Sydney Morning Herald* in letters five inches high.

**GREAT BRITAIN
DECLARES WAR
ON GERMANY!**

There is no need for any other details as few are surprised by the announcement. The news is the result of months of posturing and three days of ultimatum by Britain to Germany.

On Monday 3 August, Germany declares war on Russia. On Tuesday 4 August, Britain issues an ultimatum to the German High Command following their invasion of Belgium and Luxembourg.

On Wednesday 5 August, by 12.30 a.m. Greenwich Mean Time, Germany has failed to respond to the British initiative and war is declared on Germany.

Telegrams are sent out by the War Office to the

dominions to arrive at 12.30 p.m. in Australia, too late
for the newspapers, so that the nation has to wait until
the following morning, 6 August, to learn that it is officially at war.

The *Herald* is high on rhetoric and filled with earnest
injunctions for every able-bodied man to do his duty to
King and Country in the war to end all wars.

Though nobody seems able to give a sensible reason
why Australia, or anyone else for that matter, should go
to war, this doesn't cut any mustard with the prevailing
sentiment. The Australian public is overwhelmingly in
favour of getting involved in the fray, going to the aid
of the mother country whatever the reason.

In the heat and fervour of the moment the nation
seems more than happy to sacrifice the flower of its
youth willy-nilly, in what will later seem the silliest of
quarrels between a bunch of old men. It will result in
the loss of countless young lives.

The hostilities all began with the assassination in
Sarajevo of the Archduke Ferdinand of Austria, the heir
to the throne of the Austro-Hungarian Empire. In itself,
his death is no sound reason for even the most junior
cabinet minister to get out of bed and put on his slippers
to read the telegram telling of the Archduke's murder.
But the assassination comes after months of squabbling
and quibbling between the major nations, Germany,
Russia, France and Great Britain. There is by now so
much confusion, cross-accusation and name-calling that
the almost comic death of a minor prince seems as good
a reason as any to fight each other. It's simply the spark

needed to set the dry tinder of failed diplomacy alight. The entire matter is not unlike two schoolboys calling each other names and threatening each other in the playground, until eventually they are required to fight or be declared humbugs.

All this has been said by the more sober news columns in the weeks leading up to the declaration of war. But now, the sheer stupidity of the warring factions is forgotten. The call to arms takes on an urgency and there is a feeling of elation and adventure in the air. Australia will join the mother country to show the Hun who's the boss and no bloody mucking about. Old men tweak their moustaches and polish their medals in anticipation and young boys think of the grand adventure to come. The government has agreed to supply twenty thousand fully equipped fighting men and there is a veritable stampede to get to the recruitment centres in time to enlist before the quota is exceeded.

A poster appears on hoardings all over Sydney and Melbourne – and soon in every small dusty town and church hall in the land – showing a grandly moustached General Kitchener, scowling under a stiff-brimmed cap, his forefinger pointed directly outwards. 'Your Country Needs You!' the poster proclaims. And so starts the first day of the greatest slaughter of men in the history of human warfare.

Factory workers, clerks, shop assistants, hat-maker apprentices, stable hands and dock workers walk off the job and line up, jostling each other for places in the long queues outside the recruitment centres. In the country, stockmen, rouseabouts, bullock drivers, shearers and ploughmen make for the nearest country town to join up, walking from the scrub farms and the sheep runs, others simply leaving the mobs they're driving to the older men.

Their mood is infectious and they call out 'Cooee!' to their mates, urging them to come along to join what a popular recruitment poster calls 'The grand picnic in Europe'. In three days the shutters come down, the government can take no more volunteers. Australia has answered the call of Mother England.

Inside the same day's newspaper, on the right-hand column on page nineteen, the sub-editor's clever little headline 'Simple Simon meets the hangman' announces the execution, at dawn that very morning at His Majesty's Prison, Long Bay, of William D'arcy Simon, late of Lachlan River and Yanco. The briefest details follow, only sufficient for a reader seeking some relief from the high-blown rhetoric of war, to know that justice has been served in society's other little battle against people who kill people for no apparent reason.

Poor Billy Simple, he hasn't even got the timing of his execution right. On any other day a hanging would make the news headlines, but today he rates no more than half a column in the deep interior of the famous Sydney newspaper.

Jessica has risen before dawn on this same morning. It is bitterly cold in the little tin hut and as she prepares to light a fire she realises she hasn't brought in any wood the previous night. She goes outside, to see that the moon is still up and that its silver glow makes the frost on the paddock look like winter snow, an enchantment of pure white under a full moon on the bitter morning of Billy's death.

Her teeth chatter and her fingers grow numb as she removes the topmost logs to find dry wood beneath them. She wants to be wide awake when they hang Billy, to be sitting thinking of him when they release the trapdoor and poor Billy's worries are finally over. Jessica's quite certain that if she thinks about Billy hard enough he'll somehow know he's not alone. Jessica isn't aware yet that war has been declared and so she doesn't know that Jack, too, is being taken away from her, destined to sail with the very first contingent of the 1st Australian Light Horse Brigade. They will be sent to Britain where they will undergo further training.

Jessica has been in the tin hut now for two weeks. Joe, who visits her every three days to bring her rations, has not mentioned when she can return to the homestead. She has asked him on two previous occasions but he has simply replied, 'Not yet.' Now she's vowed not to ask him again.

Joe has brought a milking cow and calf over to provide her with milk and, except for the bitter cold at night, she is reasonably comfortable. Jessica's relationship with her father during the past couple of months has grown steadily worse and, if the truth be known, she's grateful to be away from the lot of them.

Where the hut is located has always been one of her favourite places on the selection, situated on the banks of a creek where the water flows most of the year. It's still too cold for mosquitoes and the frost has killed most of the fly larvae, so surroundings are close to idyllic. Jessica knows that the conditions will deteriorate in the summer, but she expects to be back in the homestead by the time the warm weather comes.

Joe has brought her the newspapers a couple of times and she is busy re-reading each of her books yet again. Joe's also carted in several rolls of chicken wire and instructed her to build a turkey run. 'Keep you busy, no point in sittin' around moping,' he says. Jessica is increasingly heavy with child and, though she enjoys the work, her progress is slow. Carting her big belly about causes her to tire easily.

The next three months pass without Joe once suggesting that it's time to come home. The turkey run at the back of the hut is completed though no turkeys are in evidence. Jessica reluctantly accepts that she will remain in the tin hut until the birth of the baby, a prospect which frightens her enormously.

'Who's gunna help me give birth?' she asks Joe.

'Your mother,' he answers brusquely, 'she's been reading up on it.'

'Can't I have the midwife, like Dr Merrick said? You know what he said about my hips an' all?'

'Nah, you'll be orright, your mother's a sensible woman.'

'But she doesn't know nothing about delivering babies,' Jessica protests.

'Why not? She's had the two of yiz!' Joe answers implacably.

'Father, we can't keep it a secret forever. Folks will know soon enough.'

'Don't worry your head about that. You never know what could happen, girlie.'

'Could happen?' Jessica becomes at once suspicious but won't say so. Instead she says, 'What? That it's not born alive?' She sticks out her belly and pats it. 'It's alive orright, it's gunna kick its way out if I'm any judge,' she says, trying to sound confident.

'Let's just wait and see. No use telling the whole flamin' world until we know for sure.'

Jessica now looks anxiously at Joe and says, 'Father, you won't take my child away and put it in one of them orphanages?'

'No, Jessie, it's your child, it stays in the family,' Joe says somewhat guiltily. 'There's been enough trouble at home, what with the death of Mrs Baker. Don't want no more, do we?' he says, trying to reassure Jessica.

In fact, the death of Mrs Baker has caused little comment and it isn't more than a couple of Sundays before the folk at St Stephen's are congratulating themselves on having found a much better organist in the verger.

Nor has Mrs Baker's death been a surprise. Everyone knew about her crook heart, her arithmetic, and secretly most of them would have dearly loved to see the old girl topple from her stool, taken off to meet her Maker in the middle of a hymn as she'd always wanted. Nevertheless, things settle down very nicely with the verger, a man of sound heart who puts a great deal more enthusiasm and vigour into the makings of a hymn.

The church folk soon stop asking Hester or Meg about Jessica. Some even openly admire their fortitude in the matter, for being so unfailingly cheerful when it must be very difficult to care for someone who has gone round the twist.

There is much favourable comment that Meg will make a very good Mrs Jack Thomas. The vicar, with an eye to the future, is especially anxious to stay on the right side of the pair of them. He is as nice as pie when they come to church and never fails to ask about the state of Meg's pregnancy, which is becoming increasingly apparent, likewise her constant knitting of tiny booties and matinee jackets. Hester has it in mind to ask the vicar to Sunday dinner quite soon after the birth of Jessica's baby, or – as the world will know it to be – Meg's baby. Her excuse will be that they want to discuss the christening.

It's mid-afternoon, a Friday in late November. Suddenly Jessica hears a woman's voice calling out, and she comes to the door of the hut.

'Hello, missus Jessie, you remember me?'

'It's Mary, ain't it?' Jessica says, squinting against the bright afternoon light before stepping out of the hut.

Four years have passed since the ragged bunch of starving blacks turned up at the kitchen door and Joe allowed them to stay. But Jessica immediately recognises the Aboriginal woman she had befriended among the little mob of blacks when she was fifteen years old.

'Your memory good one, missus,' Mary Simpson laughs. 'You remember me?'

'Same as if it were yesterday. 'Owyergoin', Mary?'

'I heard about you,' Mary says quietly.

'Heard? About me?' Jessica asks, surprised.

Mary points to Jessica's stomach. 'That. You gunna have a baby, your people kicked you out.' Her English has improved over the years and she now speaks with confidence.

'But nobody's supposed to know!'

'Bush talk, missus. Blackfella know, we watch over you.' Mary doesn't explain any further.

'Jessie. Call me Jessie,' Jessica grins, pleased to have the unexpected company. 'You're older than me, it should be me calls *you* missus.'

Mary grins too. 'You gunna need help, Jessie?'

Jessica looks forlornly down at her belly. 'I dunno, I've never had one before, but my mother's supposed to know what to do.'

Mary can hear the doubt in Jessica's voice and sniffs, rubbing her hand across her flat nose. 'Your mum, eh? She done it before, then?'

Jessica shakes her head. 'No, I don't think so. The doctor says there ain't much room, me hips is too small.'

Mary places her head to one side, examining Jessica's hips expertly. 'First baby always like that,' she says reassuringly. She points to her own somewhat broader hips, then laughs softly. 'After number one, the buggers jump out like a frog in yer hands, no worries.' She stops talking for a moment and looks kindly at Jessica. 'Never mind hips, that baby find a way for bloody sure. It don't want to stay in there more than it must.'

Jessica suddenly feels safe and happy for the first time in months. 'Mary, come inside, I've got soup and a bit o' damper.' She then adds, smiling, 'Ain't much room though, me with me big stomach an' all.'

Mary moves across to the doorway and pokes her head into the tiny hut. Jessica has lit the hurricane lamp and the interior is bathed in warm light, a fire crackles on the hearth under a pot and she can smell the hot soup. 'You made it nice,' she says after a while.

Jessica nods. 'It's bloody cold at night, though, lemme tell ya.'

'It's a real good humpy,' Mary concludes, bringing her head back out of the door.

'You going to stay for some soup? I've got two plates but we'll have to share the spoon.'

Mary shakes her head. 'It's your tucker. I just come to see you orright.' She smiles at Jessica and points to her stomach. 'Your baby look pretty right. Got three of me own now, also two died. Girls, no boys, boys is trouble.'

'I'd like a boy,' Jessica laughs. 'Joe, that's me dad, he always wanted a boy.'

'You better pray God gives you a girl, Jessie, boy's no bloody good,' Mary repeats.

'Will you come again, Mary? Come and see me?'

Mary smiles. 'You good to me and my mob, missus Jessie. My memory good. I don't forget what you done.' She looks about her. The sun is beginning to set and the creek is a silver ribbon with the river gums bathed in a soft golden light. The birds are settling early for the night, making the usual fuss high up in the branches.

Mary now points to the creek. 'I make you a fish trap. There's yellow-belly in there for sure, I show you how to catch the buggers. Good tucker, yellow-belly.'

'Yeah, I remember,' Jessica says.

'You have good memory, Jessie. One of them boys caught you that fish, he's dead now.'

'Oh. I'm so sorry, Mary,' Jessica exclaims.

'TB,' Mary says, 'cough hisself to death.'

'Come any time you like, you hear, any time,' Jessica pleads with the black woman.

Mary takes a step towards Jessica and pats her on the stomach. 'This women's things, I help you, eh Jessie?'

'Oh, yes please, Mary.' Jessica smiles, and the Aboriginal woman can see she's close to tears.

'Don't you worry, you'll be good,' Mary says smiling. 'You got a nice one in there, Jessie.'

And so a friendship begins between Jessica Bergman and Mary Simpson that is to last for many years. The Aboriginal woman comes almost every day towards the end of Jessica's pregnancy. She shows her how she must squat when the baby comes and makes her practise, the two of them laughing their heads off when at first Jessica falls over and tumbles in the dust. But after a while, as Mary instructs her in the tribal ways of giving birth, Jessica becomes accustomed to it and finds it more comfortable to squat. It feels more and more natural as her hips begin to expand with the baby pressing downwards.

'I'll be with you, Jessie, don't worry about nothing, you hear? It ain't so hard, just listen when I talk, do what I say.' Mary pats her on the shoulder, comforting her.

'You gunna be real good and I give you stuff after to make you better, bush medicine.' She laughs. 'Women's stuff the aunties know about.'

Jessica hasn't told Joe about Mary's visits, so when he arrives one morning happy with the news that it's time for her to come home he is surprised at her reaction.

'Jessie, your mother and I, we'd like you home for Christmas.'

'What, for Christmas dinner?'

'Nah, by Christmas. You're to stay on – the baby's due soon.'

'I ain't coming,' Jessica says defiantly.

Joe's been aware of Jessica's increasing independence, but he's still taken aback by her answer. 'What you saying, girlie?' he asks. 'What you mean, yer not coming?'

Jessica places her hands on her hips, her legs are spaced wide and her baby is sticking out like a stolen pumpkin concealed under her dress. Joe knows the look of old – it's Bergman versus Bergman and he doesn't know if he's got the upper hand any more.

'No!' Jessica says defiantly. 'You can't make me.'

'I'm asking nicely, girlie,' Joe threatens. 'I don't want to have to fetch ya, tie ya up and drag ya back.'

'If you do I'll tell the whole world about my baby.'

Joe shrugs and gives a bitter laugh. 'You know something, girlie? Them two have done such a good job on you to the folk in the district that they won't believe you. They all think you've gone loony, them at the church. All your mother would say is that you're not well, that you're making it up, that you're hysterical about Meg having a child and they'd believe her right off.' Joe pauses. 'They know Meg's expecting, Hester has made a big thing of it. They'll just think her baby's come early, that's all.'

'Come early? But she's still got this big stomach stickin' out?' Jessica says scornfully, disappointed at Joe's stupidity. 'What's she gunna do? Have its twin two months later?'

Joe sighs, but his heart beats rapidly as he's damn nearly spilled the beans. 'That ain't a problem beyond your mother. She'd find a way, you know that, girlie,' Joe growls. He wants to get off the subject fast in case Jessica twigs to what's going to happen. 'Jessica, I ain't asking, I'm telling ya, yer to be home for Christmas and then yer stayin' on, ya hear me?'

Jessica's eyes narrow as she looks at Joe and she can feel the anger welling up in her chest. 'You've let me stay out here four and a half months, in the freezin' cold and now in the heat. In the spring, with the snakes breeding and cranky as hell, you left me alone. One day I shot ten, all of them near enough to the door. What was you hoping for? That one would get me? Jessie dead to a mulga?

'You brought me rations twice a week like a bloody swaggie, sometimes you didn't even talk to me! It was what Hester and Meg wanted, that was good enough by you. Now they want me back. Can't let it happen in a tin hut, can we – it ain't Christian. Can't leave me to have my baby alone, or folk might hear about it.' Jessica tries to fight back her tears, but a single sob escapes like a hiccup. 'You've taken Hester's side against me. I dunno what I've done to you, Father. I've always loved you,' she cries.

Joe starts to protest. 'No,' Jessica raises her hand, 'let me go on.' She is suddenly calm again. 'Hester pushed Meg into Jack's arms so she'd get pregnant to him – planned it every step, I reckon. Meg ain't got the imagination to do it without her. Now she's Mrs Jack Thomas and a bloody heroine knitting baby booties.' Jessica pauses. 'But me? What *I* done, that's dirty, that's a disgrace. Meg's a lady, so it's all right for her to trap Jack into a marriage he don't want, but Jessica's a slut! And you? You go along with it, you take their side, like I done something terrible and Meg done something glorious.'

Jessica takes a deep breath, her chest heaving with her anger. 'Now you tell me I've got to come home because that's what Hester wants.' Jessica draws breath again then continues, 'Well let me tell you something, that's *not* what she wants. She wants my baby dead. That's what *she* wants! If I come home to have my baby she'll kill it – it won't draw ten breaths before she puts a pillow over its face. Poor mad Jessie, the Lord took her baby in child-birth. The Lord giveth and the Lord taketh away.' Jessica points her finger at Joe, not caring what he thinks. 'You won't kill my baby, Father. I'm not bloody coming home for Christmas, so fuck you, fuck the lot of yiz!'

Joe can't believe what he's hearing. He's confused, but he knows what Jessica is saying must seem right to her, must seem logical. In fact, he's glad she's said it, got it off her chest and had the guts to stand up to Hester, to him, to all of them. But he tells himself she doesn't know what's at stake. That if he lets her keep her baby they'll all be destroyed, her included. If he wants to save Jessie, save his little girlie, Hester must get her baby for Meg to claim as her own.

'Jessie, I swear on my life your baby will live. We won't let it die, come what may. If it's healthy born, it will live, I swear to you on me life. I'll be in the room, I'll hold your hand.'

Jessica can't believe what her father has just said, that he'll be in the room to watch out for her. She senses that Joe is no longer trying to threaten her and that he knows what she's said about Hester is true. That, for all his weakness, in this one important thing she should trust him again. But she's been hurt too badly by Joe's neglect of her and doesn't know if she can or even wants to believe him now.

'Father, I don't want to have my baby at home. I'll come for Christmas dinner, but then, you've got to promise, you'll bring me back here. Mother can come here if she wants, when it's time, as long as you come too.' Jessica waves her hand, indicating the tin hut. 'She reckons this is good enough for me, putting me out here so I won't embarrass her. Well, if it's good enough for me, then it's good enough for my baby. It won't be the first or the last baby born in the bush. I'll take me chances.'

Jessica is a bit shocked that she's had the guts to talk to Joe in this manner, but she knows she's not talking for herself, she's talking for her child. She'd ten times rather trust her child to Mary Simpson than to Hester, even if Hester didn't hate her. The fact that Joe says Hester won't let her have a midwife shows her mother doesn't give a bugger about Jessica's child. Mary cares, Mary will always look after her.

Jessica knows she wouldn't think like this without Mary Simpson being in her life. She'd be too terrified left alone to have her baby. But now she's all right, she's got a friend, someone who cares, who'll take care of her when her time comes. Jessica doesn't want to belong to her family any longer, even to Joe, whom she loves despite his betrayal. The new life breathing within her tells her she can't depend on Joe any more, even if he's holding her hand in childbirth. The little black lady with the shy smile, skinny legs and spreading hips who's taught her to squat in preparation for childbirth is her true sister, better than her kith or kin.

'Righto,' Joe says, 'come home for Christmas and I'll talk to your mother about the other.'

'No, Father, talk to her first. I want your word on it.'

Joe sighs wearily. He is seated on a log outside the tin hut with his hands covering his face. Jessica looks down at him. He's wearing the hat he had on the day she shot it off his head and it landed in the saltbush – he came and retrieved it later that day. It was once his best hat, but he'd been forced to wear it for every day because she gave his work hat to Billy Simple. But now it's lost its shape a bit and is peppered with holes from the bird-shot. Jessica reckons she's done Joe a big favour and made his best hat into a work hat with just two blasts of the shotgun when it would've took him a year of sweat and mucking about to achieve the same result. That hat, she decides, always looked crook on Joe – too new, the nap brushed by Hester the moment they got home from somewhere then put away in a box from Heathwood's Haberdashery. Now it looks perfectly natural, like it's been around a fair while.

Joe draws his hands slowly down over his chin. 'We done wrong by you, Jessie, I admit it. But it's for your own good. You don't understand yet, and I don't blame yiz for going crook on us, but one day you'll see the reason we done what we done. Your mother's acted right and proper. I know you think it's only for Meg, but that ain't true, she's done her best for you too.'

Jessica looks at her father scornfully. 'Bullshit,' she says. 'I'm sorry, Father, but I don't believe you.'

Joe looks despairingly up at his youngest daughter, chastened by what she's said to him. 'Honest, girlie, your mother's only done what she thinks is right for us all.' Then he shrugs his shoulders and gives a deep sigh, bringing his big hands to rest on his knees and looking down into the dirt just like Jack would do after his father had a go at him and he'd crept away to hide. Without looking up, Joe beseeches her, 'How am I gunna make you believe that, eh?'

'You can't,' Jessica says simply, 'I don't believe nothing she says any more.'

Jessica suddenly wants to cry, for she can see Joe honestly thinks that Hester is doing the right thing. Joe is going along with his wife because he reckons, in the end, it will be best for Jessica and her baby. Hester has defeated Joe so completely that he is no longer capable of standing up to her. Joe is finished. 'Bergmans nil, Heathwoods ten!' That's how Jack would have said it. He was always turning things into teams. 'Heifers three, jackaroos one,' he'd laugh after a mob of heifers got away from them in the scrub. 'Ten nil to the Heathwoods, put down your glasses. It's a walkover, a right thrashing!' he'd have said, grinning.

Not a day has passed when she hasn't thought of Jack and longed to hear word from him. Her first question every time Joe comes to the hut is, 'Have you heard from Jack?' Joe always says no, though she senses this is because Hester's told him to. Joe is not a good liar and he hesitates too long before he answers her. Once he'd said that Jack's regiment hadn't gone to Britain but to Egypt to guard the Suez Canal, but then hurriedly added that he'd read this in the newspaper.

Jessica tries to imagine Jack in Egypt, a place she'd learned about in Bible lessons at Sunday School. Him sitting on his horse near the pyramids with date palms, and camels passing by, Arabs in their long, white robes seated astride them like the three wise men on Christmas cards. The sand looking like a yellow sea with waves, only not moving, carved by the desert wind and stretching to the other side of sunset.

She wonders if Jack will wear a burnous, so the sand don't get into his eyes and up his nose. She'd seen a postcard once of just such a scene, but without the Suez Canal, which she thinks of as like the Yanco irrigation channel, but dug in the desert and a bit bigger of course, so as to accommodate giant ships. Pity it can't be fresh water, she thinks, then Jack would see the desert bloom, like he's always said will happen in the Riverina.

Jessica feels in her heart that Jack *has* written to her and that Hester's kept his letter, or letters, back from her. It's just another reason why she doesn't want her family any longer. She'll wait for Jack and even if she can't have him, there'll never be anyone else, Tea Leaf will always love him.

'Jessica, how am I gunna convince you that your mother will let you come back here after Christmas dinner?' Joe now asks.

Jessica sees her father's problem immediately – nothing Hester can say or do will make her trust her mother. Jessica has a sudden idea, and grins. 'We could have it here,' she says. 'A picnic on Christmas Day, Christmas dinner beside the stream,' she points towards the place, 'under that big river gum. I'll clear a space.'

Joe looks doubtful. 'She'll want the turkey hot, like always, she won't want to serve dinner on a cold plate.'

Jessica laughs harshly. 'It's always what she wants, ain't it, never what anyone else wants? If she wants to help with the birth, she's gunna have to come here anyway. May as well kill two birds with one stone.'

Joe rises wearily to his feet. 'I'll tell her you're not comin' home, not comin' for Christmas dinner neither, but you'll have a picnic here, that's all.' He looks at Jessica. 'Best I can do, girlie. I can't tell your mother nothing no more,' Joe confesses.

On the morning of Christmas Eve, Jessica decides she'll spend the day clearing around the big red river gum in preparation for the next day. Joe has brought back the news that Hester has agreed to come over and bring Christmas dinner – cold turkey and her special pudding. Jessica feels both triumphant and frightened. She hasn't seen her mother and sister for five months and she doesn't know how she'll react when they arrive.

Meg's baby, she thinks, will be nearly as big as her own by now. Jack's child in her sister's stomach – she doesn't know if she'll be able to contain her tears, or even her anger. The child Jack didn't want to have, in case he was killed, is sitting snug as a bug in a rug inside Meg's tummy. In the stomach of Mrs Jack Thomas. Jessica thinks bitterly to herself that her beloved Jack has ended up with the child he doesn't want, inside the wife he doesn't want, and all because of her mother and sister wanting to get their greedy hands on his fortune.

Jessica decides she must make a large clearing in case of snakes. They'll need to be able to spread the rug Hester brings so that there's lots of cleared ground around it. Snakes don't see or hear too well and with so many about, one could quite easily drop in on them. She'll keep the shotgun and the axe nearby and Joe carries the Winchester in the sulky at all times.

Jessica plans to start early, before sun-up so as to beat the worst of the heat. But as she comes out of her hut not long after first light, she finds Mary waiting for her.

'Good morning, Mary, you've come early,' Jessica greets her.

'Sorry, Jessie, but I can't come this afternoon. They's having a Christmas party for the blackfellas' kids up the Lutheran Mission and me two young 'uns wants to go and some of the others from the mob also. I'm the Mission girlie, see, so I gotta take 'em.'

'Can you stay for a cuppa?' Jessica asks.

'No, ta Jessie, I got to go.' Mary tilts her head to one side and examines Jessica. 'It's getting pretty close, that baby,' she laughs, and puts her small black hand on Jessica's stomach. Then she bends and puts her ear to the side of her tummy, still keeping her hand on it. 'Strewth, could be your Christmas present from Santy Claus.' She laughs again, then she straightens up and wishes Jessica a merry Christmas, putting her hand into the pocket of her pinny and taking out a brown paper packet. 'For your baby, Jessie.' She smiles shyly, then says, 'The mob got a bit o' money together. They not forget you, Jessie. Us aunties, we gone into Narrandera and bought it in the Chink shop,' Mary explains proudly.

Jessica opens the packet and pulls out a tiny baby's dress in oyster-coloured Chinese silk with cherry blossoms embroidered on the front. 'It's for a girl,' Mary announces. 'Boys go bad, you're gunna have a girl, Jessie.'

'Oh Mary, it's lovely,' Jessica exclaims, holding the tiny dress up. She kisses Mary. 'Thank you, thank you,' she cries and bursts into tears. 'Mary, you are so kind to me,' Jessica sobs. Mary embraces her and takes her into her arms, though she can hardly manage to do so for the size of Jessica's baby sticking out in front.

'That baby coming soon – crying, that's always the

sign,' the little Aboriginal woman declares, then adds, 'You do them squatting, you hear, Jessie? Much as you can. I come back tonight after Santy Claus seen the kids at the Mission.'

After Mary has departed Jessica starts on the clearing. The sun won't be long in coming but she thinks the shade of the river gum will protect her from the worst of it for a while. She finds that she's panting after the least effort. But almost two hours later, with the sun well up, the heat haze shimmering in the north paddock so that the old man saltbush is a green glassy smudge, she has all but completed the task. There remains just one large boulder, large only because of her present state and Jessica knows better than to try to lift it. Joe can do it when he comes tomorrow, she thinks. Then she changes her mind – she wouldn't have left it for him before, so why now? She won't leave a job half done. She decides to cut a stout sapling and use it as a crowbar to move the rock so she doesn't have to use much of her own strength.

Jessica cuts an ironbark pole about four inches in diameter and six feet long and sharpens one end to a wedge shape so it will slip easily under the rock. Her efforts prove successful enough and she tumbles the rock towards the edge of the clearing, using the leverage of the pole. She needs only to move it another couple of feet when it lands after a roll in a small hollow. It's jammed and she has difficulty slipping the wedged tip of the pole in under it. After a bit of a struggle she gets the wedge halfway in – enough, she hopes, to allow her to move the rock out of the indentation and onwards. Jessica pushes her end of the pole downwards, but it isn't secured well enough under the rock and springs loose. She stumbles and pitches forward onto the hard ground, breaking her fall with her hands and rolling on her side.

Jessica lies perfectly still, panting, not wanting to move, her heart beating furiously, waiting to see where she hurts. But after a few moments she realises she hasn't hurt herself or her baby and slowly struggles to bring herself up onto her hands and knees. The pole lies within reach and she grabs it up and pushes it into the ground in front of her and, with both hands grasping the stake, pulls herself up. Jessica is almost standing when she feels a terrible cramping pain in her back.

Jessica is panting hard and she puts her hand on her stomach. Maybe it was simply a pain from doing too much, she tells herself. But now another comes. Mary has told her to expect labour pains – 'They come slow and you think it's nothing much, just the baby kicking or something like that. But you got to listen, wait for them. After a few hours they keeps comin' faster, time's getting near, you got to get ready 'cause that baby wanting to break out of jail.'

Jessica comforts herself that the pains will keep coming for some hours, that Mary will be back to look after her by the time they come closer together. She decides to go into the hut and rest and try to get everything ready. She's got an enamel basin and there's a fire laid with the kettle filled, so all Mary's got to do is boil the water. She's got an old sheet and three old towels: one for the birth mat, one for cleaning the baby and one for swaddling it. There's a sharp knife for cutting the umbilical cord and a bit of cat gut to tie it. There's also plenty of swabs made by the two of them from one of her dresses, boiled clean and dried in the sun on a hot stone and then stacked up tidy on the tiny table. The hurricane lamp is filled with kerosene with its wick trimmed in case they have to work at night. Jessica can't teach Mary how to stitch her if she needs it, so she hasn't asked Joe for his horsehair and needle, though he's brought a jar of Condy's crystals, petroleum jelly and a tin of boracic powder.

Jessica barely makes it to the hut before another contraction comes, but it's not too bad, she thinks to herself again – it must have taken about five minutes to get to the door from the clearing. But she just makes it to the bed before she has another. She manages to kick off her boots and even to remove her bloomers. The labour pains are now no more than two minutes apart, though she has no way of timing them as she doesn't have a clock. She is already wet with perspiration and her dress is soaked and clinging to her body. The hut is a veritable furnace, with the noon sun beating down on the tin roof.

'Oh, Gawd, let me last until Mary comes,' Jessica prays. She manages to get herself onto Joe's rough wooden bed and she feels woozy, but thinks it must be from the heat. She's put a mug of water on the table and now she reaches for it and brings it to her mouth, spilling half of it down her dress.

The pains are coming more frequently now, every

minute or so, and Jessica knows her baby is very near. She feels she will faint from the suffocating heat and some deep instinct tells her she must get out of the hut, go to the creek under the trees and get her legs into the water. The creek still runs quite quickly and there is a shallow pool under the river gum where Mary has set a fish trap. Jessica knows it comes up no further than her knees. She remembers that Mary has told her how the women of some Aboriginal tribes give birth in a creek, which keeps the child safe 'cause it doesn't come out the womb breathing proper. She can hear Mary's voice in her head, 'They pull it out the water and give it a whack on the bum to make it cry, fill its lungs with air. Some of the aunties say it's the best way, but the Wiradjuri, we don't do it.'

Jessica struggles from the bed, the pain now gripping her like a vice so that she howls out, but she makes it to the door where she's left the pole. Using it to support her, she moves towards the creek, screaming and howling. She can feel the baby coming, pushing down, the contractions increasing and becoming so powerful that she knows she's got to squat soon. She reaches the side of the creek and starts to squat, pulling her skirt up above her waist. The part of the embankment where she squats gives way suddenly and the sand bank crumbles into the water. Jessica cannot maintain her balance and she tumbles headlong into the stream.

Jessica thinks her whole body will split apart from the pain she feels, but she struggles to regain her feet, splashing furiously in the water, gasping and thrashing about. She feels the sandy bottom under the soles of her feet and this gives her a little security, though she is still too panic-stricken to know that the water has cooled her and given her a buoyancy she desperately needs. She reaches for the creek bank and knows at once that she hasn't the strength to pull herself up.

Jessica feels as though something has exploded within her as her waters break and flow away into the stream. She's utterly helpless and all she can do is squat down in the water, bear down and let the pain come. She feels her vagina stretching, the contractions coming faster, and her body seems to be tearing open as her baby's head starts to come through and they increase in power again. Her heart beats even faster and she screams suddenly so that a flock of galahs in the paddock across the creek rise in fright, their high-pitched splintered screeching *chirra-chirra* filling the air. There is nothing Jessica can do to stop the baby coming now. 'Push down, push, yiz gotta push hard,' Mary's voice says in her head. 'I can't!' she cries aloud, as though Mary is present. 'Oh Mary, help meeee!' she screams as the terrible pain overcomes her.

The water around Jessica is bloody, but it clears quickly with the flow of the stream and then is almost immediately bloody again. She looks down and sees that her baby is halfway out of her body. Instinctively she reaches down and takes it by the shoulders and pulls. Just at the very moment she's quite sure she must die from the pain, suddenly she is holding her little baby. It is out and she lifts it out of the water with the umbilical cord still attached. The water has washed some of the blood from the tiny body. Jessica holds it in one hand and spanks its bottom. The baby gives a tiny sneeze then screws up its eyes and yowls, taking in its first lungful of glorious air.

Sitting back in the stream, Jessica rests her baby on her stomach with its head against her heart, and laughs and weeps and laughs again, and sniffs and sobs and laughs in what becomes an ecstatic giggle. One hand trails in the cool water that reaches up to her thighs. She takes her hand from the stream and moves the baby slightly to one side. She has given birth to a boy. The boy Joe always wanted – a boy she will call Joey, after him.

After a while Jessica gathers enough strength to cup her hands into the water and wash her baby, splashing its head and tiny body until it is clean all over, the almost brick-red colour of the newly born.

Jessica stays in the stream, too weak to move. She's lucky that she is shaded by the leaves of the big river gum overhead. She knows she's got to cut the umbilical cord quickly and get rid of the placenta, as Mary told her it can create infection. She has no knife and worries that she might have to bite it through. But then she searches the bottom of the creek around where she is sitting and, after pulling out several small stones, finds one with a sharp edge. She's already asked Mary if cutting the cord would hurt her baby or herself. 'That cord it dead when the baby come out, it don't work no more, it don't hurt to cut,' Mary replied. 'What about the blood?' Jessica remembers asking. 'No blood, Jessie, blood don't come no more in that string.'

The umbilical cord, once her baby's life line, floats in the clear water at her waist, the knotted blue and red veins and arteries showing clearly through the almost translucent tube. Using the sharp stone, Jessica takes a deep breath and saws at the thick cord as near to her baby's navel as she dares to go and after some time it is cut through and, together with the placenta, floats off downstream for the yellow-bellies and yabbies to feed on. Everything has to find a way to live, she thinks, watching it go.

Though they're still in the shade of the giant river gum, Jessica grows concerned about her baby's head in this heat. She tears off the short sleeve of her summer dress and, with it, fashions a little cap for the tiny infant's crown.

After crying for a few minutes her baby sleeps, his thumb stuck in his mouth. Jessica is too frightened to remove his hand, though she's worried that it might stop him breathing. But her child seems perfectly content, his breathing even, his little chest rising and falling against her breasts, which have ached for two months as they prepared to produce the milk her child will need.

The sun beats down and Jessica remains in the creek, bathing and cooling her infant from time to time, splashing water over his body and head. Jessica tries to stand, but she is still too weak. She prays that Mary will come before sundown, before the mosquitoes begin to swarm, as she and her baby will be helpless against them. Just after sundown, in the gathering dusk, the swarm gathers above the creek, blackening the warm, thick air, their whine enough to pierce the eardrums. If they come for her they will easily kill her newborn infant in a matter of hours. They will sting it until it dies of the trauma, its tiny body blackened by thousands and thousands of mosquitoes until it appears to be covered by a dark, softly vibrating fur. She knows if Mary doesn't come very soon she must somehow get into the hut and under the mosquito net.

At five o'clock, an hour before sundown and seven hours after Jessica's child is born, Mary arrives at the hut. Jessica, still seated in the water, holds up her baby. 'See, Mary, see what Santy Claus sent me,' she shouts, and then begins to bawl her heart out.

Mary works all night, going back to the Aboriginal camp and returning with bush medicine for Jessica. She has tied the umbilical cord and generally tidied her up. At Jessica's insistence she bathes the baby in a light solution of permanganate of potash. After this, she powders Jessica in her most tender places with boracic powder. But for the deeper, internal birth injuries she applies her own bush medicine.

'Jessie, you had a good one that birth. When I tell the aunties they gunna say whitefella woman she done good going in the water. Where you learn that?'

Jessica looks astonished. '*You* told me, Mary.'

Mary is surprised, not remembering the conversation. 'Me? I never did!' she exclaims, 'I only heard it once before, not from the Wiradjuri. Some tribe I heard up north, they done that.'

Mary stays with Jessica all night, giving the baby

boiled cool water into which she has mixed a little sugar, feeding it into his rose-petal lips by wetting her finger and pushing it into the infant's mouth so he won't dehydrate in the heat. Then she puts him to suck on Jessica's breast for her colostrum. She will have to wait two days for her milk to come and the baby will be sustained by the thick, creamy substance that exudes from her nipples. 'Them little buggers know it's there somewheres,' Mary laughs. 'If they keep sucking the milk's gunna come, but that stuff you got, that real good tucker for him. It's good you let him suck, learn the ways,' Mary explains, then shows Jessica how to gently stroke her baby's cheek to turn its head in towards her so that, with a touch of the nipples to its pursed lips, her child will begin to suck. She is almost as happy about Jessica's baby as its mother is.

The little Aboriginal woman watches over Jessica while she sleeps and at one stage warms up a lamb stew and wakes Jessica and makes her eat. Later she gives her a mug of milk and another of water. Then she eats some of the stew herself.

Towards morning, sitting on the floor beside Jessica's crude timber bed, Mary falls asleep and it is well into the morning, an hour after sunrise, when they both wake up to the baby's mewling.

Mary puts it back onto Jessica's breast. Having slept a few hours, Jessica feels the first tremendous joy of motherhood, the sense of having something in her life which is entirely her own. As the tiny infant sucks at her sticky paps she has never felt more complete and thinks she must burst with happiness. Her child is well formed – ten fingers and ten toes, and everything where God intended to put it. Jessica has a perfect baby with a tuft of reddish-blond hair fine as spun silk.

Mary leaves after she's cooked porridge for Jessica and made tea. She wants to stay, but is afraid that if she remains much longer Joe might arrive at the hut. Or, worse, Hester and Meg may decide to make a day of it and come early.

'This the best Christmas present you can get, Jessie,' Mary says, handing Jessica her baby when she's eaten some breakfast. 'I come back tonight, your old people be gone back home.'

'No, wait,' Jessica cries, 'we've got to dress him. You've got to tell the aunties what he looks like in his dress.'

Together they dress little Joey in his Chinese dress. 'He gunna poop on it, spoil it,' Mary laughs.

'I just want you to see it before you go. I'll take it off and put it back on just before they come.'

'He looks beautiful, eh?' Mary says. 'Pity he's a boy, he make a nice girl in that pretty dress.'

Mary takes her leave and walks towards the creek, watched by Jessica holding her baby. She turns just before she enters the shallow water to wade to the far side. 'Jessie, don't let them mongrels take your baby!' she shouts. Then she swings around and splashes through the shallow water and up a slight embankment to disappear into the dark green mulga and bush on the other bank.

'Mary, I love you!' Jessica calls after her, surprised at

the strange look on the Aborigine's face as she shouted
her warning. Why would Mary look at her like that?
The black people know things, but Joe has given his
word her baby will be safe and she knows he won't go
back on it, no matter what Hester wants.

Joe arrives in the sulky with Hester and Meg just
after midday. Jessica is seated in the shade with her
back against the big river gum and hears them coming
some way off. Earlier she made a brush broom and
swept the clearing again. The offending rock still lies at
its edge, though she wonders why she'd bothered with
it at all – there's plenty of room for a picnic blanket and
clear ground beyond in case of snakes.

She places her baby, dressed in his little Chinese out-
fit, snugly in a pillowcase. Now he lies in a carefully
made towelling nest between two above-ground roots of
the big gum tree. Jessica's cut some of the mosquito net
and fashioned a little tent over him to keep the black
flies away. Little Joey sleeps to the sound of the creek
water gurgling over rock.

At the approach of her family Jessica takes the still
sleeping baby from the pillowcase and lifts him into her
arms, clutching him against her breast. Then she stands
in the centre of the clearing and waits for them to arrive.
She's washed her face and brushed her hair and put on
a clean cotton dress and her best Sunday boots. And
she's wearing one of the special pinnies Hester made for
her with Meg's rosebud embroidered on the large front
pocket. Mary's bush medicine has helped her no end,
and while she is still pretty tender, she feels strong and

well rested. Jessica knows she will make a very good mother for young Joey Bergman who, unconcerned about being moved, sleeps contentedly in her arms with his thumb in his mouth.

Joe pulls the sulky to a halt outside the hut, not seeing her at first. Hester and Meg are both carrying parasols and are dolled up to the nines in their Sunday best, though Jessica can't imagine why when it's so bloody hot. As Meg steps down from the sulky, Jessica sees immediately that her stomach has grown, though she expected it to be a lot bigger. They now all stand in the bright sunlight and are temporarily blinded, not able to see her in the shade of the big river gum until she calls out.

'Oh, there you are,' Hester says, turning in the direction of Jessica's voice. 'Merry Christmas, my dear.' Hester's voice has already taken on a more imperious tone and Jessica realises she's getting ready to be the second mistress of Riverview homestead. Poor bloody Jack – not only Meg but also Hester to contend with.

Joe unharnesses Napoleon and leads the pony to the creek to drink while Hester and Meg walk towards Jessica with their parasols held high, picking their way daintily along the creek bank. Neither of them is looking over to where she stands. Jessica wonders briefly if they feel any guilt for leaving her to fend for herself in the tin hut. Indeed, how would her precious sister feel if it were done to her? But she refuses to be angry, to spoil her news and her special Christmas present to Joe.

The baby suddenly cries out and it is Meg who looks

up first, for she and her mother have reached the clearing and are now only a few feet from where Jessica
stands.

'Eeeeek!' is the only sound that comes from Meg's
mouth as she clutches at her chest in astonishment.

Hester looks up. 'Oh my God!' she gasps. 'Oh, oh,
what have you done, girl?' she exclaims, taken completely by surprise.

'Why, Mother, I've had my baby.' Jessica turns the
tiny infant's face so that her mother can see it more
clearly. 'See.' Then she says, 'It's a boy. His name is
gunna be Joey, Joey Bergman.'

'Take that ridiculous thing off him, he's not Chinese!
Where on earth did you get it, child?'

At that moment Joe has come up so Jessica doesn't
have to explain. Her father's big shambling shape is trying to run, for he's heard the baby cry out as well.
'Jessie, what in Gawd's name!' he bellows.

Jessica now holds her son up for Joe to see. 'It's a
boy, Father,' she says happily as Joe reaches the picnic
clearing.

'Oh my God,' Hester says again, bringing two fingers up to her lips.

'I've made a place for the picnic,' Jessica now says,
for neither Hester nor Meg ventures forward to take a
closer look at the baby and Joe's expression is a mixture
of utter confusion and just dawning delight.

'You done it yourself, girlie – all by yerself?' He shakes
his head, not yet fully comprehending. 'Jesus Christ,
I take me hat off to yiz, Jessie.' Joe turns suddenly to

Hester and Meg, his expression defiant. 'The girl's got more guts and character than the lot of us put together!' He turns back to Jessica. 'It's time to come home, Jessie – you can look after the little bloke better at the homestead.'

It's clear from the way he says this that Joe has decided Jessica can keep her baby, come what may. He's seen the look on her face, her love for her child, and he's not prepared to steal it away from her whatever may become of them as a family. 'I'm proud of yiz, Jessie, dead proud that you're me daughter, proud to have the young bloke as me grandchild just the way he is.'

Jessica looks directly at Joe and he sees the stubborn Bergman look he knows so well. 'I'm not coming home, Father.' She turns and looks at her sister. 'Not till Meg has her own child and she and Mother move to River-view.' She points to the tin hut. 'That's my home. You all sent me there and that's where I'll stay put. It's where my son were born, and I'll not leave it until Meg's left for Riverview Station.'

Meg drops her parasol, bringing both hands to her face and stumbling towards the river gum. She stands with her forehead pressed against the smooth, grey bark and bursts into tears, banging both her fists against the tree. 'No, no!' she screams.

Hester, totally taken aback, vents her frustration at Joe. 'Now look what you've done!' she shouts, then drops her parasol and goes over to the sobbing Meg, placing her hand on her daughter's shoulder, trying to comfort her.

Meg jerks her shoulder away, rejecting her mother's embrace. 'It's not fair! It's not fair! Father said he'd do it!' she howls. She turns her face from the tree and looks tearfully at Joe. 'You said!' she screams and then turns back and sobs uncontrollably with her forehead once again hard against the trunk of the tree.

After Meg's anguished appeal to Joe, Jessica looks anxiously at him, puzzled. But Joe still wears this big grin on his gob – his pride in her is unconfined. Jessica knows suddenly that Joe still loves her and is back on her side at last.

She moves over to stand in front of her father and offers him her baby. Joe hesitates, then accepts the tiny bundle awkwardly, holding it cupped in his big hands and away from his body, not knowing what to do and terrified he might drop it.

'It's the boy you always wanted, Father – merry Christmas,' Jessica says softly, then she grins and reaches out and, with the tip of her forefinger, lightly touches the crown of her baby's head. 'See his hair, Father. He's a Bergman, not a Heathwood, and he's bloody perfect.'

Jessica undresses her baby and puts him back into his pillowcase. The picnic that follows is a strained affair with very little Christmas good cheer. Hester tries to cover up for Meg who sniffs throughout, her eyes fixed on her lap never once looking up, and refusing to eat anything. 'She's worried about her own child,' Hester explains to Jessica. 'Especially now that yours is so healthy. It's only natural she'd be concerned.'

'It's me what had the narrow hips,' Jessica says, trying

hard to conceal her pride. 'Meg is made to have babies, you've said it yourself, lots of times.'

Hester sighs. 'It's a difficult time, that's all. It's her nerves, what with Jack gone overseas.'

Jessica looks at Hester anxiously. 'Have you had a letter? I mean, has Meg? Has Jack written to say where he is?'

Joe turns his head away so Jessica can't see his expression. Without knowing he's doing it, he clears his throat, and Jessica knows for certain that Jack's written to her.

Hester sniffs. 'We've had no news except what's in the newspaper. That's a good part of what ails your sister. Your father says sometimes the army won't let troops write home for fear they'll give away vital information.' She turns to Joe. 'Isn't that true, Joe?'

'Yeah, right,' he says and Jessica hears the lack of conviction in his voice. Joe, like herself, is a poor liar. Keep things straight, girlie, can't get into no trouble that way, he's always told her. Now she wonders what's going on in her father's mind, for Jessica senses that Joe is not taking his own advice and is ashamed. She concludes it can only mean that she's got a letter from Jack and Hester is concealing it from her. Jessica has been alone now for so long that she can much more clearly pick up the meanings in Hester's voice, and Joe has never been much good at concealing things from her.

Both Hester and Meg have declined to hold the baby, Hester protesting that he might dirty their dresses while Meg simply shakes her head and blows her nose.

Joe, on the other hand, has got the knack of holding

the young bloke, as he has taken to calling Jessica's baby, and he can't get enough. Halfway through the picnic the baby begins to cry and a look of panic crosses Joe's face. 'Shit, what now?' he says anxiously. Jessica laughs and takes the child from him and places the infant on her lap and then, turning her back to Joe, she opens the buttons of her summer dress. Exposing her breast, she allows the child to suckle.

'Oh dear me!' Hester protests. 'Not in front of your father, child!'

'Wait on, she has her back to me,' Joe says.

'Back or front, it's not to be done in public. It's disgusting that she should feed it in front of you!'

'Oh bullshit,' Joe growls. 'How else she gunna feed it? It's natural, ain't it?'

'For ignorant folk, perhaps,' Hester snorts.

Jessica gets to her feet somewhat painfully. She's still sore and bruised, and sitting in one position on the picnic blanket has stiffened her limbs. She waddles slowly, awkwardly, to the edge of the creek with her back to her family. Looking over the blur of scrub on the far side, her eyes fill with tears. 'Why won't them two even hold my baby? He's done nothing wrong,' she sobs. She looks down at the tiny face sucking at her breast.

Jessica is dead tired when at about five o'clock her family take their leave. Meg has pulled herself together a little and she turns to Jessica just before climbing into the sulky. 'I'm sorry . . . it's just . . .' she mumbles. 'Your baby . . . it's nice,' she says without completing her previous sentence.

JESSICA 415

'Don't worry, you'll soon have your own,' Jessica comforts her. To her surprise, Meg bursts into a fresh flood of tears and has to be helped up into the sulky by Hester, who, in her fussing around Meg, forgets to wish Jessica goodbye.

Joe looks down from the sulky at his youngest daughter. 'I'm sorry, girlie, it weren't much of a Christmas dinner. The tucker was good, the company pretty ordinary except for you and the young bloke. I'll come and see you termorra. I'll bring me medicine box – you should have it here for the baby, in case.' He hesitates, then says, 'I'm that proud of you both, girlie.'

Jessica thinks it's a strange thing that Joe wants to bring the medicine box – he's already brought her all the medicine he has. Still, he's never had a grandchild before. Maybe it's just his way of saying she should take good care of baby Joey.

They have not been gone more than five minutes or so when Mary appears. 'Happy Christmas, Jessie! How yer Christmas present goin', he pooped his nice dress yet?' she shouts happily, waving to Jessica as she wades across the shallow part of the creek so the hem of her dress doesn't get wet.

Mary has been waiting for two hours on the far bank, watching Jessica's family. She's seen Jessica come to the edge of the creek to feed her baby and sensed that she was crying.

Her stick legs shine black as ebony after splashing through the water as she comes up to Jessie and immediately reaches out and takes the baby into her arms. 'You tired, Jessie? Too much cranky folks to visit, eh?' She points to the apple box Joe has left at the door of the hut filled with the leftovers. 'Lotsa tucker,' she observes, then goes over to the box and, holding the baby against her shoulder she pokes about, ignoring the turkey, until she finds half a Christmas pudding on a chipped enamel plate. Mary breaks off a piece and pops it into her mouth. 'Christmas pudding! We called it "Once a year tucker" when I was a kid at the Lutheran Mission up Lachlan River way.'

'Oh Mary, it was horrible,' Jessica cries. 'My mum and sister, they didn't touch him, even once!'

'They's got no heart, Jessie. Some folks got no heart for babies,' Mary says, trying to comfort Jessica. Holding the baby cradled in one arm, she takes Jessica by the elbow. 'Too hot in there,' she says, nodding at the hut. 'We go in the creek to cool down and then you sleep, you hear?'

Mary steers Jessica to the banks of the creek and then walks splashing ahead until the water is up to her waist. 'Come, Jessie,' she calls, 'we bathe your baby.'

Jessica follows Mary into the creek and laughs, her skirt floating in the water as she comes up to her. The cool water has already rejuvenated her. 'Here, take him,' Mary says, handing Jessica the baby. Then she takes off her dress and squeezes out the wet skirt, balls it up and throws it to land with a wet slap onto the bank of the creek. Standing naked with the water to her waist, she takes the baby from Jessica again. 'Jessie, take off your dress,' Mary instructs. Jessica unties her pinny and slips her head through the straps and squeezes the water from the bottom half and throws it onto the creek bank. Then she pulls her dress over her head and does the same with it. The first few inches of her bloomers show above the water-line. Mary points to Jessica's waist, taking charge. 'You want to wash with your clothes on?' Then she grins, her nice white teeth showing in her calm face. 'I seen it all before, remember?'

Jessica blushes, but she laughs and takes off her bloomers and squeezes them out and sends them flying onto the creek bank, where they land spread out on a small bush. 'They dry nice there,' Mary giggles. 'Come, I show you how to wash your baby.'

They stay in the creek, happy and laughing, until the sun begins to set. 'We go now, Jessie eh, mozzies soon and them snakes come soon.' Mary points to the sky. 'Tonight it's big fella moon, they come and do their corroboree for sure.'

'I just want to sleep, Mary,' Jessica sighs. 'It's been a long day.'

Meg continues to sniff and sob most of the way home while Hester and Joe do not talk to each other. It has been one of the most difficult days of Hester's life, for she senses strongly that Joe is going to go back on his word. After everything they've been through, it seems that all is about to be lost. She wants to scream for the frustration she feels. She's always hoped that Jessica's child could be taken from her at birth, so that she would never hold it or get to know it. With a bit of luck they could have said it was stillborn and later refused to show it to her, said they'd buried it right off, when she asked. It would've been easy enough to fake a grave, then a few days later they could have announced a premature birth to Meg. Now Hester knows Jessica will never give up her child even if it should cost her her life.

Upon returning home, Meg goes straight to her room and Hester sets about making Joe his tea, a bit of egg and bacon. Joe is surprisingly hungry after the big Christmas picnic where he'd been the only one to tuck in, relishing the food. Hester senses he has changed, and the blackness is not there any more. Somehow the birth of Jessica's baby has changed him, given him an appetite for life again.

After wiping his plate with a piece of bread, Joe asks for another cup of tea. Then he sits back and crosses his legs, the steaming mug of tea in front of him on the kitchen table. 'Well, that were a turn around for the books, eh, Hester?' he says calmly.

'What was?' Hester asks, knowing full well what he means.

'The baby. The young bloke, Joey.' He grins.

Hester turns around suddenly. 'Joe, you can't change your mind! Nothing's changed.'

Joe shakes his head. 'No, Hester, we're not going through with it,' he says firmly, bracing himself for what's to come.

'Joe, can't you see she's mad? She refused to come home when you asked her. She wants to stay in that tin hut and keep the baby there! How long do you think it will last? It'll be dead in a week – a snake will get it, or a tick or a scorpion, and it will die.'

'Ha, it's a damn sight safer in the bush than with the two of yiz. The girlie's gunna make a real good little mother,' Joe nods his head in the direction of Meg's room, 'not like that little viper.'

Hester cannot contain herself a moment longer. 'You bloody fool, can't you see what you're doing? You're ruining us all. Not just me and Meg, the lot of us, you and Jessica as well!'

'Hester, mind yer mouth,' Joe warns her.

But Hester is too angry to listen. 'No, you mind yours! You listen to me, Joe Bergman, you always were an ignorant bastard. You've never amounted to anything and you never will. That slut and her baby are the same, a chip off the same stupid Bergman block. You're bad blood – you couldn't even make a son! The bank is going to take this place and we'll be out on the road without a penny, with your mad bitch daughter clutching her bastard child! Well, I won't have it, you hear! I won't let you ruin us! Damn you, Joe, I hate you! I've always hated you and your foreign ways!'

Joe rises slowly from his chair, his huge fists balled. All the hard years have built up to this one moment, his anger grown stronger, more furious, because he knows some of what Hester says is right. All the loneliness and frustration he's felt over the years in this bloody terrible land boils up in him. The endless disappointment, things never turning out right, the drought and the roiling floods, the big blows that flatten everything, the bushfires that destroy the simple dreams and leave only smoke and the ashes of hope in their wake, the rabbit, locust and mice plagues. He's had a bellyful, enough of the bloody flies, the heat and the pestilence, the pale, remorseless, mocking sky, the constant worries with them mongrels from the bank, each shearing season having to crawl up George Thomas's fat arse for a job in his shed.

Joe has never so much as lifted a finger to his wife, never belted her like other blokes. But now he knows he's going to kill her, kill the Heathwood bitch, wring her scrawny neck. Press his broad thumbs into her windpipe until the life leaves her and her evil tongue protrudes from her mouth.

Joe's head seems to fill with dark blood as he moves towards Hester. He feels himself choking, gasping for air. The pain in his chest smashes down on him like a huge, angry, roaring thing he can't define beyond the noise it makes in his ears. Joe collapses to his knees and pitches forward. He is dead before his head hits the kitchen floor.

Hester stands frozen. Joe has almost reached her and now lies stone-dead at her feet. She had seen his eyes and knew he was coming for her. Her anger turns to ice, then nothing, then surprised relief. She feels no sorrow – it is as though an impediment has gone from her life. Now at last she can make the decisions and, for once, get them right. Then she begins to shake, the shock of her husband's death reaching her consciousness. She shouts for Meg and then starts to weep, the tears a part of the numbness she feels. Joe, such a big

man when he was alive, now seems suddenly small, vulnerable, a crumpled shape lying on the kitchen floor.
'Meg!' she calls. 'Meg, come quickly!'

Meg comes into the kitchen. She is in her nightdress,
though it is not yet seven o'clock. She gasps as she sees
Joe lying on the floor, then she screams and screams,
overcome by hysteria. 'Stop it! Stop it!' Hester shouts,
glad to have her daughter at the centre of her stunned
concentration. She runs over and starts to shake Meg
violently. 'Stop it, you hear! Stop it!' Meg sinks to the
floor and starts to sob. 'Your father's collapsed, I think
he's dead,' Hester says, trying to keep her voice level.

With the courage she's gained from Meg's presence,
Hester kneels down beside Joe and feels his pulse. She'd
learned this years before at St John's Ambulance Asso-
ciation classes in Narrandera not long after the Boer
War. Joe shows no pulse, but Hester has little confidence in her ability and so she opens his flannel shirt
and puts her hand over his heart. His mouth is slightly
open and his eyes stare at her in what appears to be a
look of astonishment, as though he cannot himself
believe he is dead.

'He's dead, Meg. Your father's dead,' Hester pronounces, surprised at the calmness she feels. If Joe is
dead, then she is in charge.

It is just after sunrise the following morning when Hester pulls up in the sulky outside Jessica's hut. Jessica is
already up and has made a cup of tea and is stirring the
oatmeal porridge, adding warm milk from the cow she's

not long since milked. She is looking forward to the day and Joe's visit and wants her father to see her baby wearing a nappy. Mary has dismissed the idea with a pronounced sniff. 'That nappy, that whitefella stuff, Jessie. Baby shit, you clean him, why you want to carry it round in that cloth?' Jessica has nevertheless cut six squares from the old towel she had intended to use as a birth mat and fashioned two pins from Joe's chicken wire to hold the nappy in place. She means to practise putting a nappy on baby Joey before her father arrives.

She's slightly annoyed and disappointed when she hears the sulky, as Joe usually arrives later in the morning. Jessica takes the porridge pot off the hearth and goes outside. Shocked to see her mother at the reins of the sulky, she asks instinctively, 'Mother, what's wrong?'

Hester looks down from the sulky at her youngest daughter. 'Your father's dead, you must come home, girl,' she announces without sentiment.

Jessica stands still in the morning sunlight, unable to comprehend what her mother has just told her. She can hear the water running over stones in the creek and the soft *phlurrrrr* of air escaping from the pony's nostrils. Somewhere she hears the carolling of a magpie and the sound of cicadas stinging the air. The sun feels warm on her cheek.

'His heart gave in, just after tea last night,' Hester now says. 'He'd want you at his funeral, Jessica. You can't let him down.'

'No!' Jessica says slowly. 'No, Mother, I won't come.'

To Jessica's astonishment, Hester starts to cry. Jessica

has rarely seen her mother in tears before. 'But you must, Jessie,' she weeps. 'You're in charge now, darling. Meg and I can't cope with the selection.' She looks up despairingly. 'The bank had been to see Joe! We'll all be ruined!' Hester sniffs. 'We can't manage without you, my dear.'

'Bullshit!' Jessica can't believe she's said it.

'What?' Hester asks, looking down at her tearfully.

'Mother, as soon as Meg's child is born you're going over to Riverview homestead. You and Meg will be jake – you couldn't give a bugger about the selection.'

Hester does not deny this. Instead, she wipes her eyes on her handkerchief and sighs deeply. 'Jessica, the bank will foreclose on the property now your father's dead, unless you come and we convince them you can take over. Your father always intended for you to have the selection. If we can only hang on until Meg's baby is born I'm sure, what with the war and the security of Meg being Mrs Jack Thomas, they'll let you extend the overdraft.' Hester now looks appealingly at Jessica, wiping her eyes again and sighing. 'I know you think I haven't been a good mother, that I've always favoured your sister, and in some respects that's true. But I know it would be Joe's dearest wish that you and your child be safe and secure. He would have wanted you to have the property. And when we leave for Riverview, it will all be yours. You must come to the funeral, so folk can see you are well again.'

'*Again*? What, that I'm not mad?' Jessica now says, trying hard not to show the triumph in her voice. She would dearly like to refuse her mother, but she knows

Hester's right – she must take care of her child. If the property can be saved it will be Joey's future. She has thought long and hard about the small section of river-front they possess, and although it's not much – this creek and a hundred yards of river – both could be used for irrigation, although Joe would never listen to her.

'What about my baby?' she now asks.

Hester pulls back slightly, aware that Jessica could be persuaded to come to Joe's funeral. She knows better than to appear contrite. 'Your father was right, these things pass with time. Now that Meg's married to Jack and will soon have a child to give him when he comes back from the war, I dare say we'll manage to cope, to live with the shame you've caused.'

'You mean if me and my son stay away from River-view? Well, don't you worry, Mother, we will,' Jessica says bitterly.

'Please, Jessica? Bring your baby and come with me now. There is much to be done.' It is the same old Hester, back in control.

Jessica thinks hard. 'Mother,' she announces, 'I want a piece of paper to say Joe's left the place to me and my baby.'

'Yes, of course, my dear,' Hester smiles, 'as soon as we get home.'

'No, now!' Jessica says. 'I've got pen and paper.'

Hester hesitates. 'Really, we must hurry, dear. Can't it wait?' she says trying to soothe Jessica.

'It won't take long,' Jessica counters. 'I'll make you a cuppa while you write it out.'

Jessica makes Hester sit at the table and brings her a pen and ink and a sheet of paper, both of which have been supplied by Joe.

Jessica wants to crawl away on her own and bawl her heart out for Joe, but she doesn't want her dry-eyed mother to have the satisfaction of seeing her grieve.

PROPERTY SETTLEMENT

With concern to the last will and testament of Joseph Karl Bergman, deceased on 25 December 1914.

I, Hester Bergman, wife of the late Joseph Karl Bergman, believe myself to be the sole beneficiary of all my husband's worldly goods, property and possessions, which consist of his selection, as well as all that stands upon it, including his livestock.

I hereby, in the presence of witnesses, agree that such property as comes into my possession as a consequence of my husband's death I freely pass over to my daughter, Jessica Margaret Bergman. I also promise to make no further claims on such property at a future date and agree in the event of Jessica's death that the property shall become the sole possession of her child, Joey Bergman.

Signed: Hester Maude Bergman
Witnesses:

Hester looks up from the small table where she has been writing. 'Meg can witness it when we get home.'

'I don't think she's allowed,' Jessica says. 'Besides, Joe says you always get two independent witnesses.'

'The Reverend Mathews, then,' Hester suggests. 'He can sign it after the funeral.'

'Wait,' Jessica says and walks out of the little hut and stands on the bank of the creek. She brings her fingers to her lips and whistles and a few moments later Mary appears, emerging from the bush.

'Mary, come on over!' Jessica shouts.

Hester is more than surprised to see the Aboriginal woman. There is barely room for the three of them and Hester sniffs as Jessica introduces her to Mary Simpson. 'Pleased, I'm sure,' she says with her lips pursed, but refuses to accept Mary's outstretched hand.

'Hello, missus,' Mary says, smiling, ignoring the snub. 'Nice baby, eh?'

'Mary, can you write your name?' Jessica now asks.

Mary nods, not speaking but still smiling. It is plain she's not intimidated by Hester.

'Where does she sign?' Jessica asks her mother.

Hester silently points to a place under her own signature and hands the pen to Jessica, who dips the pen into the ink-pot and gives it to Mary. Hester shifts out of the way to make room for Mary to sign and she is forced to sit on the bed where Jessica's baby sleeps contentedly. She looks down at the sleeping infant. 'He's a fine boy,' she says, trying to smile.

Mary writes her name carefully and Jessica sees that the letters are well formed and all sloped in a nice copperplate script. Mary notices her looking and grins. 'It's them Lutherans,' she explains, 'the buggers teach us how to write our names so we can sign for gubberment rations.'

Joe's funeral is to take place two days later at St Stephen's. Meg and Hester spend most of the time baking for the wake to be held in the church hall afterwards.

Jessica, who is determined not to show her grief for Joe's passing, lasts until they arrive at the homestead and she goes to the back of the house, to the sleep-out where her father lies, dressed in his Sunday suit with his arms folded, his big hands clasped over his chest.

It is his hair that finally causes her to break down. Despite being married to Joe for twenty-two years, Hester has parted his hair on the wrong side. It is such a little thing, yet it says everything about their relationship, and Jessica weeps for her father – for Joe the foreigner who never quite got the hang of his new land, who'd come from the green grass of Denmark to the black soil plains of south-western New South Wales. Stubborn, silent Joe, who tried so hard but never had any luck. She weeps for more than an hour and then rises, thinking she must go to her baby. It is then that she remembers Joe's curious promise to bring his medicine box over to the tin hut.

Jessica goes to the familiar box and opens the top drawer. It seems the same as ever – the horsehair and the stitching needles, a packet of safety razor blades and a small pair of pliers for pulling the needle through a beast's stubborn skin, everything neatly in its place. She opens the second little drawer and inside are two letters addressed to her in Jack's handwriting.

It is at this moment that she hears Meg's voice shouting for her to come quickly because the baby is crying, and she hurriedly conceals the letters in the pocket of her pinny. Jessica goes into the kitchen, where a worried Meg is trying to soothe the baby.

'He's probably hungry,' Jessica says, trying to sound matter-of-fact. She takes the baby into her bedroom and, closing the door, allows him to nuzzle at her breast. His hungry little mouth clasps around her nipple and begins to suck furiously and Jessica is suddenly aware that her milk has arrived. Not much, but young Joey seems to know the difference and now pulls frantically at her swollen nipple.

'Oh Joey, I love you so much,' Jessica sobs. 'Joe would have loved you so.'

Jessica then takes the two letters out of her pinny and looks at the date on the stamps, to see which is the first. One carries an Australian stamp and the other is Egyptian. She tears open the first and begins to read.

S.S. Star of Victoria

28 October 1914

My dearest Jessie,

We are away at last but not yet bound for England as the convoy has to assemble in the King George Sound at Albany in Western Australia. They don't tell us much so there isn't much more I can say. We have been joined by the New Zealanders.

I am writing this on board ship. Lots of the men have been seasick but, touch wood, I've been okay. The horses are coming on another ship, the Clan

MacCorquodale, *and I worry about them, although they are stout horses and should be right.*

About your sister, Meg. It has all been a terrible mistake and I want to say sorry to you. I am very ashamed of what happened and that I made her pregnant. She is my wife now so I can't say anything more. But you know how I feel in my heart about you and I always will. There is only one Tea Leaf and I shall take her into the war with me. If you can manage to write could you send me a photograph of yourself. I beg you to forgive me, Jessie.

Your loving friend,
Jack.

Jessica tearfully folds the first letter and then, pumping her left breast the way Mary has shown her, she is surprised to see a spray of milk issue from the nipple. Her breast is sore and tight and it is an immediate relief when she puts Joey onto it. She waits until he is suckling contentedly before she opens the second letter.

Cpl. J. Thomas – No LHNSW 8760
Mena Camp – Egypt

10 December 1914

My dearest Jessica,
I hope you received my last letter. And now for the news. Instead of going to England we were

off-loaded in the Port of Alexandria in Egypt. We then went by train to Cairo and marched to a place called Mena where the pyramids are. And guess what? Near the pyramids is a whole stand of eucalypt! Imagine that, a bit of Australia waiting to welcome us. They are bigger than I expected – I mean the pyramids. We climbed the Great Pyramid to put our names on one of the higher blocks and, you wouldn't credit it, there were names there of soldiers from the Napoleonic Wars who'd done the same. Just imagine that.

We arrived here to find that the British High Command hadn't sent us enough tents – only about half of what was needed and it will take two weeks for the others to arrive. So some of us bivouac in the open, with our horses. It's a bit like being out on a run at home, and the lads from the country don't seem to mind as we're used to sleeping under the stars. The horses are in good shape. I quite like the desert, it reminds me a bit of home, which means it reminds me of you.

They don't tell us much, but the rumour is that we're going to be trained here and then sent on to Europe to fight. But another rumour says Turkey is going to join the Germans and we'll stay here and guard the Suez Canal. I hope the first and not the second, eh?

Please write to me, Jessie. Have you had a photograph taken yet? I don't want to forget your dear, sweet face.

*I know you will not show this letter to your sis-
ter, and you'll think me cruel, but will you tell me
when she has the baby? I will write then and do
my duty by her.*

*I am well and think constantly of my little Tea
Leaf. Please write to me!*

    Yours lovingly,

    Jack.

Jessica cries softly. She has lost Jack to Meg in marriage
but she hasn't lost his heart. She vows he will always
stay in her own heart, the only man she'll ever love, no
matter what. Jessica looks down at her child sucking
away for all he's worth. 'We're not alone, Joey. Jack
loves me, and he'll love you too when he gets back,
you'll see,' she promises softly.

On the day of the funeral Hester persuades Jessica to
leave her baby with Meg, though, at first, Jessica is reluctant to do so.

'Why can't I take my baby?' she asks.

Hester is uncharacteristically patient with her. 'Jessica, you know why. People have come to think things
about you. We must show them that you are well.'

'What things? That I'm mad?'

Hester sighs. 'We've discussed it before, child, at the
tin hut.'

'I don't have to go,' Jessica says defiantly. 'I've said
goodbye to Father my own way.'

'Yes you do, dear,' Hester insists, 'if only to show
people that you are well. Besides, Reverend Mathews

has to witness the paper, the deeds to the land, remember?' Hester has a sudden inspiration. 'If the bank is going to let us carry on, they'll have to know you're well again, that the silly rumours are baseless. They won't let you have the place otherwise.' Hester smiles. 'Who better than the vicar to vouch for you?'

'We could do it after – after the funeral. The vicar could come here.'

'My dear, people *must* see you there. See you being your normal old self, know that the rumours about your health are quite untrue.' Hester purses her lips and pulls her head back. 'But if they see you with a baby!' She pauses, then continues, 'Well! All the tongues will be wagging, won't they? And you *know* what they'll all be thinking.'

'But they're gunna know sooner or later!' Jessica protests. 'We can't keep my baby hidden forever.'

Hester is suddenly stern-faced. 'Jessica, it's your father's funeral. We won't make a mockery of it. Surely you can understand that much, child? This is simply not the time to show your baby.' Then, as if to mollify her youngest daughter, she adds in a softer tone, 'With Meg so far gone, it's not seemly for her to be seen in public, so it will be easy to explain her absence. We'll simply tell folk she's feeling a bit poorly, what with her pregnancy and your father's death, and they'll understand immediately. She can look after Joey for you.'

Jessica cannot deny that Meg is capable of caring for her baby. Since she's returned to the homestead, Meg has done a complete about turn and has taken every opportunity to hold the infant and care for him. At first a little apprehensive, she now dotes on Jessica's child. Despite the sadness of Joe's death, Meg has been cheerful and busy and ever so helpful, asking to look after Joey whenever she's given the least opportunity.

And so, finally, Jessica agrees to accompany her mother alone to the funeral.

Despite his silent and often morose character, Joe was popular in the district and there is a big turn-out at the funeral. Hardly a person present cannot testify to some past kindness received from him. They greet Jessica with surprise and delight, for most of them associate her with Joe and are pleased to see her again, offering her their condolences almost as often as they address them to Hester.

Hester has ordered the plainest pine casket from Coffin Nail, the Italian carpenter turned funeral director, knowing Joe wouldn't want the fuss or the waste of money. Five of the local shearers and Mike Malloy, the foreman at Riverview shearing shed, carry his coffin into the church. The congregation sing 'Abide With Me', which they like a lot and sing with gusto as they all know the tune. This is followed by 'Onward Christian Soldiers', another favourite and now grown even more popular because of the war. Hester's heart pounds briefly as she recalls Joe humming the tune after they'd done in old Mrs Baker. In both hymns the verger proves a tremendous success, thumping away at the ageing organ with great enthusiasm.

The vicar then gives his eulogy to the dearly departed.

He's done his research well and the congregation are soon nodding their heads, quietly agreeing that folk didn't come any better than Joe Bergman.

The organ starts up again, this time sonorous and funereal in its tone, and the coffin-bearers lead the way out of the church to the small fenced graveyard at the side of St Stephen's.

Joe is going to join Mrs Baker, the little congregation's most recent contribution to the heavenly hosts. This is also the resting place of Ada, Winifred and Gwen Thomas, who lie in their Chinese-silk-lined, now handleless, fake mahogany coffins, with their names carved on the lid, just in case St Peter doesn't know who they are when they arrive at the gates of Paradise.

It is at the graveside that the vicar waits to begin the famous 'dust to dust' and 'ashes to ashes' part of the funeral oration. Jessica smiles quietly to herself, remembering how Joe once remarked, after a funeral they'd attended, that God must have been speaking specifically about the black soil country when he made up that dust to dust and ashes to ashes bit. 'That's the whole flamin' story o' the plains, everything turns to dust or bloody ashes.'

'The Lord giveth and the Lord taketh away,' Jessica now hears the Reverend Mathews pronounce in his most pontifical style. But then he suddenly departs from the known text. Instead, he stops and spreads his arms wide in a benevolent gesture, looking at the people gathered around the graveside.

'How apt this is,' he says smiling. 'The Lord has taken

away our brother, Joe Bergman, but he has, in return, given us a new life born on Christmas Day, the day the infant Jesus, our Saviour, was born to save the world from sin. A new life to replace the one He hath taken away.' He pauses and looks about him. 'You will, on this sad occasion, have missed the charming presence of Hester Bergman's eldest daughter, Mrs Meg Thomas. This, I am pleased to announce, is because Meg has given birth, on Christmas Day, to a son for Jack and a grand-child for Joe, just hours after he departed so tragically from this mortal coil.' Pleased with this opportune observation, the Reverend Mathews, M.A. Oxon., smiles beatifically. 'The Lord giveth and the Lord taketh away, blessed is the Lord,' he intones.

'*No!*' Jessica screams. '*No!*' She turns to Hester and starts to beat at her with her fists. 'You can't, you can't take my baby!'

Hester tries frantically to back away, but Jessica, still screaming, follows her and, swinging wildly, she knocks Hester's hat off her head. Then she grabs her mother by the hair and scratches at her face and eyes. 'I'll kill you! I'll kill you!' she screams.

Hester keeps moving backwards, her arms held across her face as she attempts to avoid Jessica's blows. She stumbles, then trips and tumbles backwards onto the ground. Jessica, her teeth bared, hurls herself on top of Hester and continues to flail at her with her fists. 'My baby! You've took my baby!'

Suddenly male hands come from everywhere, pulling Jessica away from her mother, lifting her away. Jessica fights like a wildcat, kicking out and struggling frantically as they grapple to subdue her.

'No! Nooooooo! She's stolen my baby! *My baaaaby!*' she screams. Finally she is restrained, though it takes four men to hold onto her and then to carry her bodily off to the manse, still screaming hysterically.

Hester is helped to her feet. Her face is scratched and a streak of grey hair, torn from one side of her bun, falls across her left eye. She covers her face with her hands and begins to sob as the vicar drops his prayer book and runs to comfort her, the skirts of his white cassock whipping about his ankles. Several of the women present gather around the distraught Hester, two of them trying to dust her skirt and shoulders while another picks up her hat. Two others hold her steady, tut-tutting and commiserating, the shock at what they've just witnessed clearly written over their concerned faces.

Hester slowly brings her hands down from her anguished face and tears stream from her eyes. She looks directly at the vicar. 'We thought she was better, that our darling Jessie had got better again,' she sobs.

BOOK THREE

Jessica spent the next four years, from 1 January 1915 to 1 December 1918, at the Hospital for the Insane at Callan Park in Sydney.

The records for the institution show a J. M. Bergman listed as an in-patient during this period. Although the patient's gender is not initially given, it is evident from the Christmas manifest, which records that on three separate occasions, the Christmases of 1915, 1916 and 1917, the patient received a new green smock and a pair of black boots, the standard uniform for female inmates at Callan Park.

Several other events over this period can be determined from public and private records.

Joseph Thomas, the first-born son of Meg and Jack Thomas of Riverview Station, was christened on Sunday, 9 February 1915 by the Reverend Mathews, M.A. Oxon., at St Stephen's Church, Yanco.

On the occasion of his christening Joseph was given a sterling silver christening cup, with a Hardy Brothers, Sydney, hallmark and inscribed 'Joseph Thomas – God's precious gift to us – from his maternal grandmother, Mrs Hester Bergman, nee Heathwood'.

On 5 April 1915, Meg Thomas and her mother Hester took up residence at Riverview homestead. They seem to have given almost immediate notice to the incumbent, George Thomas, to leave the large sheep station, though this may have been done on the instructions of Jack Thomas. There is a final withdrawal of funds in the name of G. A. Thomas for the amount of £15,000 shown on 1 May 1915, whereupon the account in the same name at the Narrandera branch of the Bank of New South Wales was closed. George

Thomas is last heard of selling shares in a gold strike in the Northern Territory in a reef named King Solomon's Mines.

The Riverview Station records show that ten days later, on 10 May 1915, two months before the commencement of the shearing season that year, Mr Mike Malloy was appointed as manager.

The mortgage, owned by the Bank of New South Wales, covering Selection Nos. 41 & 42 (1280 acres) and Tubbo No. 1 (340 acres) in the Parish of Ourendumbee in the County of Boyd, registered in the name of the late Joseph Bergman, was paid off on 21 January 1918 by Mrs Meg Thomas, and the acreage transferred to Riverview Station.

Sergeant Jack Thomas was killed in the Battle of Magdhaba fought on 23 December 1916 in the Northern Sinai Desert near the Mediterranean coastal town of El Arish. The attack on the Turks by elements of the 1st Light Horse was led by Major-General Harry Chauvel. The attack commenced at daybreak after No. 1 Squadron of the Australian Flying Corps, flying low over the village of Magdhaba (which was being used by the enemy as a base), established the Turkish dispositions. What followed was a hard-fought battle resulting in a significant victory against a stubborn and courageous enemy. Three hundred Turks were killed with only twenty-two dead on the British side, Sergeant Jack Thomas among them. Jack died of his wounds in a military hospital at El Arish in the early hours of Christmas Eve.

Jack Thomas's entire estate (with the exception of a gold hunter watch, misplaced after his death) passed into the hands of his son, Joseph 'Joey' Thomas, to be held in trust *for him by his mother, Meg Charlotte Thomas, and the second trustee, Major-General Septimus Cunningham-Thomas, until he reached the age of twenty-one. The mention of the gold hunter watch seems a curious notation in an estate valued at £280,000. It is assumed to have been a family heirloom taken from Jack's bedside after he died.*

CHAPTER TWELVE

Jessica sits outside her tin hut just before sundown, before the mosquitoes come, and thinks about the morning. Rusty, her new kelpie, lies at her feet, his tongue lolling in the heat even though he's just been sent into the creek to cool down. She can smell his wetness, his doggy smell. Any moment now the rabbits will come to the creek to drink, crushing together and jostling each other, fifty of them all trying to get to the water in one spot though there's the whole creek bank to choose from. Jessica thinks that the rabbits can't be all that high up on the animal intelligence scale. She loads the twelve-bore shotgun – she can, if she's careful, get ten of the buggers, maybe a few more to make up the hundred pelts she needs to fill her quota for the hat factory in Sydney. She'll just have enough time before nightfall to skin them and stretch the pelts over wire U-frames.

The turkeys are making their usual racket in the run out back – they must know they're getting a feed of corn tonight. If they weren't turkeys and so dumb, they'd sense this wasn't good news for the lot that's been separated to go to the rail siding tomorrow at dawn.

Joe always said there's nothing more stupid than a

chook unless it's a turkey. He used to say 'gobble-gobble' was the exact right sound for them, grub pecked up into their flamin' beaks and squirted out their bums without a single thought in between, that's your basic turkey. Chooks, Joe'd say, seem to have a bit of nous – not much, mind, but a bit. Hens have something going for them. They'll scratch and when they've laid an egg, they'll cackle proud as all get-out, tell the world what they've just gone and done. Then they'll get broody and mind their eggs. They take real good care of their chicks when they hatch, and hide them under their wings if there's a goshawk about, and make a terrible racket if a snake comes into the coop. What's more, cocks crow and strut and fight each other and sometimes even mind their hens, herding them together when there's danger about.

But turkeys are a different kettle of fish altogether. They're bloody useless buggers – they lose their chicks, or stand on them, or peck them in the head till they die. They'll let a hawk take as many chicks as it likes, or they'll walk right up to a fox and look him in the eye, usually for the last time before they kiss their life good-bye. They'll even die of thirst when there's water twenty feet away, but mostly they'll panic. They panic over the slightest thing, gobble-gobbling hysterically and scattering to the four winds. 'You can't teach a turkey nothing it don't already know and that's bugger-all anyway,' Joe would say to Jessica when she was a little kid. 'There's nothing about a turkey you can like until it's been plucked and the stuffing's steaming in its bum.'

It's a full moon tonight and, as usual, not a cloud in the sky. Jessica will be up at four o'clock and on the road to Yanco Siding to arrive with her turkeys not long after sun-up. She rubs the sole of her scuffed boot behind Rusty's ear. 'Not much of a job for a sheep-dog, is it mate?' she says fondly to him. She wonders whether Rusty senses that he was bred for better things – whether he knows that herding Solly Goldberg's fattened Christmas turkeys to the railway siding is a bit of an insult.

But, Jessica thinks, the kelpie does it willingly enough. When you come to think of it, sheep aren't exactly the most intelligent animals anyway and this dog's never been trained to work sheep, never been introduced to a sheep. Turkeys are all he knows – they're his sheep – so perhaps Rusty takes pride in being the best turkey-dog in the Riverina, maybe in the whole world. It's a compliment really, as sheep are positively docile compared to turkeys. A turkey panic needs great skill to bring it to order and Rusty is just the dog to do it. It may be an undignified way for a sheep-dog to make a living but nobody's told him so, and he's got his work cut out to keep a flock in line. Not too many sheep-dogs could do what he does. What's more, if ever he meets another sheep-dog Rusty doesn't back down – no, he's got a ton of courage, so he's still got all his pride going for him.

Rusty seems happy enough, Jessica thinks. She's a pretty good mistress who loves him, he has plenty of rabbit meat to eat and a big flock of turkeys to mind. Kelpies like to keep busy and this one's on the go most of the day, watching that the silly buggers don't get lost in the saltbush or the mulga scrub and keeping an eye out for the odd fox lurking about or the sparrow-hawks and kites ready to have a go at the chicks.

Jessica doesn't keep her turkeys in the run all the time but lets them out during the day to run free over the ten acres she owns. So even Rusty loses a few during the course of a year but it's worth it – Jessica's turkeys have a flavour to the meat that has made her famous in one small part of the world, in Goldberg's Kosher Butchery in Hall Street, Bondi Beach, in Sydney. Mr Solly Goldberg orders fifteen turkeys a week, year in year out, and fifty at a time for *Hanukkah*, which he once explained to her was, 'Like Jewish Christmas without no Jesus or Christmas trees, my dear.'

This solid business contact with Solly Goldberg all began in Callan Park, where his son Moishe, a Sydney lawyer, was sent because of his dark moods and after he'd made several incompetent attempts to top himself. Dark moods were something Jessica understood very well, having spent a lifetime with Joe, and she soon made friends with the strange, shy, pencil-thin Jewish boy whose trousers always looked about to fall down.

Jessica would sit with Moishe, talking quietly to him during his dark times until his confidence slowly returned. In return Moishe Goldberg would read to her. He had a lovely, gentle voice and a great passion for literature.

Jessica didn't pretend to understand everything he read to her. In fact, for the first year of their acquaintance she understood very little. But Moishe, when he wasn't in one of his dark moods, was an excellent teacher and he would explain to her that writers weren't only involved with telling stories but were also interested in ideas. 'We humans have become a superior species because we have been given the gift of speech and with it the gift of imagination. We have the ability to think,' he once told her.

It had never occurred to Jessica that the major purpose of thinking was to arrive at a better solution than the one which already existed. If she'd ever thought about it, which she hadn't, she felt that, like most people, the knowledge she needed already existed and that it was her own ignorance that prevented her from finding the proper solution.

Everything, Jessica assumed, was already known and decided upon and if she came up with a viewpoint which contradicted the one held by conventional wisdom, then *she* must be wrong and ignorant.

But Moishe didn't see things in quite the same way. He held that most of what we believed in was wrong. That the world could be a better place without so many fixed ideas, that humans were like sheep allowing themselves to be led by the dog who barks the loudest and bites the hardest. He told Jessica that all this was about to end, that a couple of really big-time thinkers called Marx and Engels had finally found the answer to the misery and oppression of the working classes.

Moishe would excitedly read to her from the works of these men, outlining the doctrine called Commu-nism – the first political movement, he explained, ever to represent the common people. The workers of the world, 'the proletariat', as they seemed to be called, were about to unite to overthrow the capitalist system and bring justice to society.

'People just like you and me, Jessie,' Moishe would say. 'It's a system of government that delivers the common people from the clutches of the greedy capitalists and the privileged classes. Imagine, no more wars, no more killing – man's inhumanity to his fellow man will stop, Jessie.' Grabbing her impatiently by the shoulder as though he wished to shake the sense of it into her, he'd continue, 'Greed and disregard for the welfare of the worker is what drives the capitalist world. Generosity and goodwill towards people like you and me is the Communist manifesto! Jessie, we can't have another war like this one again. There must be a revolution in Australia, just like the one that's coming in Russia.'

Moishe's enthusiasm for Communism knew no bounds and his greatest disappointment occurred when he finally realised that Jessica failed to share his vision or even to understand it.

Jessica kept reminding herself that Moishe was mad – otherwise why was he at Callan Park? While she didn't believe for one moment that she was crazy, she wasn't silly enough to assume that everyone in the place was similarly wronged. Quite clearly the place was full of loonies, and Moishe, when his dark moods descended upon him, was one of them. Jessica was a country girl with no real experience of being exploited by the ruling classes beyond the greed of George Thomas, who'd never been thought of as a member of the ruling classes so much as a mongrel in his very own right.

Jessica had been brought up by Joe to believe that life was meant to be a huge bloody struggle. And, except for the bank, which he never thought of in human terms anyway, it wasn't man's inhumanity to man that made life miserable. It was nature that supplied most of the toil, disadvantage and heartbreak.

Therefore she was pretty lukewarm over Moishe's enthusiasm for Communism, a doctrine she believed had no chance of working, out in the bush. Especially when Moishe spoke to her about the concept of the collective farm, where everyone worked the land for the mutual benefit of all of the people.

'This bloke Karl Marx, does he come from the bush?' she once asked Moishe.

'No, he was born in Trier and educated in Bonn and Berlin,' Moishe replied, showing off the depth of his knowledge.

'That the big smoke?'

'What, Berlin? It's the capital of Germany.'

'Yeah, thought so,' Jessica sniffed.

'What's that supposed to mean?' Moishe asked.

'Well, this Marx bloke, he ain't never put his theory to country folk, that's for sure.'

'Why ever not?'

'Well, mate, you can't get two blokes to agree on bloody nothing in the bush, except maybe that the government don't know its arse from its elbow. They'd think this bloke Marx was talkin' out the back of his head.'

But Moishe, a lad from the city, didn't care to have a country bumpkin like Jessica contradicting him. 'It is precisely by harnessing the vast discontent felt by the Russian workers towards the Tsar that Communism will succeed,' he protested. 'It is the same here – a movement that will be led by the masses, by the proletariat, the people on the land and in the factories. We must begin with the overthrow of the landed gentry and the capitalists, and often enough they're the same people,' Moishe explained patiently, though Jessica could sense his frustration with her.

The only landed gentry Jessica could think of was Jack Thomas, the man she loved, and George Thomas, whom everyone agreed to hate. But the idea of overthrowing Riverview Station and turning it into a collective sheep station was just plain silly.

'Bullshit, Moishe,' Jessica said.

The idea of rising up against George Thomas or any of the other squattocracy simply didn't make sense. George was a liar and a cheat but you already knew that, so you made a deal and you kept to it. It was never totally fair or unfair neither, just George Thomas wanting to show you who was the boss. But once you shook hands, the both of you made it work. It was all part of what happened in the bush, Jessica thought, and by no means the worst part.

On two occasions, however, she and Joe had attended a hastily convened meeting behind the shearing shed at Riverview. The stop-work had been called by Joe Blundell, the shop steward for the Shearers'

Union. The first time had been to have a bit of a whinge about the time allowed for a smoko. Another time he went on about whether, when the wool was damp, they should reduce the number of sheep shorn to qualify for the higher pay rate.

But on the way home after both meetings, Joe said it wasn't to be took too serious. The idea of a strike over working conditions never occurred to them on River-view Station. There were sheds that were worse and some better but that was life. There was talk that in some stations the Shearers' Union got a bit cranky and threatened the boss. But in Joe's book you worked hard, you got paid and you kept your trap shut. Joe was right, nothing ever came of those Shearers' Union meetings. George Thomas just told Joe Blundell to get stuffed, and that as far as he was concerned they could collect their pay-packet and piss off the lot of them, because there was enough local labour around to fill the shearing shed twice over. As Joe said, a good union man becomes scab labour as soon as the brats start to starve. Everyone knew this was true, so they shut their gobs and took home a wage that was half decent by local standards.

But Moishe would say to her in an exasperated voice, 'Jessie, don't you see, Australia rides on the sheep's back. If the common people hope to own the wealth of the land, the golden fleece, they must overthrow those who exploit them. Surely you can see that?'

But Jessica never could see it and she considered Moishe's greatest gift to her wasn't his belief in the brotherhood of man, but the fact that he taught her how to *really* read, not only for pleasure, but to search for meaning and to ask questions. It was something she would continue to do for the remainder of her life.

Jessica also learned that a mental hospital is an even harder place to survive in than the bush. Avoiding being beaten up or raped by the ward attendants was a constant preoccupation. She would watch as female patients who resisted the advances of the brutes in charge of the wards were given 'the jacket' or, in the winter, 'the wetpack'. They were put into strait-jackets and either marched off to solitary or hosed down with cold water and left to freeze in a cell. It was said to be a treatment to calm them down, but she could see the fear in their eyes when they came out of treatment. Most often it was an experience which caused them to sink even deeper into their misery, confusion and despair. Some caught pneumonia and died, others developed bronchitis. So a lot of the female inmates capitulated, allowing themselves to be used by the ward attendants rather than face time in isolation in the jacket or the wetpack.

Survival became Jessica's singular purpose. She soon learned that a broken heart was of little use in a mental institution and that if she hoped to survive she must keep her grieving to herself. Jessica began to ingratiate herself with the female staff and became useful in a hundred ways. This ensured that she would be left alone, yet come under the protection of the matron, who helped to keep her safe against the groping paws and thrusting thighs of the male ward attendants. Pretty soon they gave up thinking of her as a patient and she was allowed to wander freely within the grounds without being watched over.

Jessica seemed to have an uncanny knack for calming the most agitated of inmates. In time her presence in the wards was welcomed and sometimes even regarded as necessary. Silence, or the sounds we make to comfort a small child, she soon discovered, was the best cure. She would sit with a patient for hours, simply holding a trembling hand, sometimes making soothing noises, sometimes singing softly and rocking them, often enough saying nothing but allowing them to feel her warmth. After a lifetime with Joe, Jessica was an expert at silence and at providing company without seeming threatening.

The patients learned to consider Jessie as someone their confused minds could relate to. She didn't shout at or hector them, she didn't beat or threaten them, or try to make them do things they didn't want to, or were afraid of. She'd just sit and hold their hands or read to them, the gentle rhythm of her voice seeming to calm them, even when they were incapable of understanding the meaning of her stories. When an agitation in one of the wards broke out, 'Call Jessie!' became a common cry among those ward attendants who didn't enjoy the business of beating a patient into submission.

Jessica was by nature a kind person, but she was no angel of mercy. In everything she did, from the moment she was wakened by the ward bell at six o'clock in the morning to the eight p.m. bell which signalled the lock-up and silence for the night, she worked to gain her release from the institution. She was using Joe's rules – work hard, keep your trap shut. Do more than the other bloke, don't whinge, keep your head down and it'll turn out all right in the end. If she showed no signs of being a loony, she reckoned, then sooner or later they'd have to let her go.

Jessica's one thought in life was to return to her child. The pain she felt for her lost baby she mostly kept to herself, but she would weep for Joey in the lonely, dark hours after midnight. Her sobbing was drowned in the cacophony of moans and sudden screams and the endless weeping and nightmares of the harmlessly insane.

Slowly, through an ocean of tears, Jessica's hatred for her mother and sister grew and her resolve to avenge herself became a hard, tight wad of bitterness wrapped around her heart. If she gave the impression of being serene and saintly, in truth Jessica was becoming an avenging angel who thought of nothing else but her freedom and the reclaiming of her child.

Jessica had been admitted to the Callan Park lunatic asylum based on the evidence presented in a report by Hester and the Reverend Mathews and prepared in the presence of the police magistrate at Narrandera.

The day after Joe's funeral, Jessica's wrists were tied with tent-rope and she was taken from the manse to the Narrandera police lock-up and kept in a cell for three days while the papers needed to have her committed were sent up from Sydney. Thereafter she was handcuffed and placed on the train and escorted to Sydney by a cheerful young police constable named Tommy Holbrook, a cheeky young lad who had gone to school with Jessica. The moment the train was out of sight of Narrandera station he'd removed her handcuffs. 'She'll be right, Jessie,' he'd said, comforting her.

Upon arrival at Callan Park, Jessica received a cursory examination by an ageing, overworked, unshaven and exhausted physician in a dirty white coat trying to cope with the shortage of medical staff over the Christmas period. He was doing his best, with the help of generous libations of Tolley's brandy taken from a bottle in the bottom drawer of his desk.

His questions were peremptory and his impatience soon apparent. Jessica, who was still in shock, simply stared at the wall while he interrogated her in a voice devoid of enthusiasm. It was plain enough to see that he had long since lost any sense of compassion for his patients. Unable to get her to respond, the harassed doctor turned to Tommy Holbrook. 'How did the patient behave coming to Sydney? Was she violent? Hysterical? Constantly weeping? Did she shout out or scream? Curse the other passengers?' he asked, holding the nib end of his fountain pen upwards and repeatedly tapping the cap fixed at the other end of the stem on the surface of his desk. Perhaps this was intended to intimidate Tommy or was merely a sign of the doctor's frustration – whatever, it escaped the young country constable's notice.

Tommy Holbrook shrugged. 'She didn't say nothing all the way, sir. Nice an' quiet and mostly slept.

Didn't need no handcuffs neither. If you want my opinion, sir, if Jessie Bergman's a loony, then I'm the Police Superintendent.'

The doctor sighed. 'Medical science is greatly obliged to you for your diagnosis, constable.' Then, turning back to Jessica, he announced, 'Miss Bergman, if you refuse to talk to me I will be forced to make a decision based only on this.' He picked up the report from Narrandera by its corner, lifted it and then let it fall from his fingers back onto the desk. Then he reached down into the open drawer for the brandy bottle and, leaning back, withdrew the cork. 'Well, what will it be?'

'They stole my baby,' Jessica said in a voice barely above a whisper. 'They stole my little baby.' Then she brought her hands up to cover her face and started to sob uncontrollably.

The doctor watched Jessica for a few moments. He took a generous sip from the bottle, sighed, then corked it and replaced it in the drawer. Looking over at the young constable, he pointed to a chair against the wall. 'Bring her a chair, constable,' he commanded.

When Tommy had placed a chair in front of the doctor's desk, the physician instructed, 'Sit down, Miss Bergman.' Then he looked at her, hard-faced. 'I have no time to waste and you, I assure you, will have lots of time for tears later, so I'd be obliged if you'd spare me from them now.' Then without further ado he began to write.

The Hospital for the Insane
Callan Park

* Medical Report*

Patient Name: Jessica Margaret Bergman

Sex: Female

Age: 19

Examined by: Dr J. C. Warwick – Admitting
Physician

Date: 1 January 1915

Comments: *The patient appears from the report
submitted by her mother and the local Anglican
minister (report included) to be suffering from an
acute delusional psychosis, as well as an advanced
state of hysteria. She believes that the child born
to her sister is her own.*

*This delusion may have been triggered by the
death of her father on the same day as the birth of
her sister's child. It is understood the patient was
very close to her father.*

*The patient has shown a tendency to violence and
needed to be physically restrained when she attacked
her mother at the funeral of her father, accusing her
of stealing her baby. Her sister was known by her
church community to be pregnant for the appropriate time leading up to the birth of her child.*

The patient is said to have suffered a nervous

condition for several months prior to the birth of
her sister's child, a condition that was diagnosed
by a doctor at Narrandera Hospital. The state-
ment submitted by her mother refers to this in her
own words as 'a bit of a nervous breakdown, but
we thought she'd got better'.

It would appear that the patient comes from a
good, working-class home with a caring mother
and sister, both respected members of their local
church congregation. They agreed to commit her
only after she had made frequent threats to kill the
mother and sister and it was feared she might harm
the infant.

I have been unable to communicate with the
patient to ascertain her point of view (if any), as
she is so preoccupied with her delusions. I recom-
mend she be committed for treatment pending a
further examination by the Medical Supervisor.

Signed: *J. C. Warwick, MBS.*

At the completion of his report Dr Warwick looked up
again. 'Miss Bergman, my recommendation is subject
to verification by the Medical Supervisor, who will not
be returning from his Christmas holidays until January
10. Do you have anything to say?'

'About what, sir?' Tommy Holbrook asked, speaking for Jessica.

The doctor sighed. 'I am recommending that you be
committed to this institution,' he replied, as if the

question had come from Jessica and not the young police constable. 'Do you have anywhere to stay until you return for a second examination?'

Jessica appeared to be very frightened but gave no other indication that she understood the question. The doctor turned to Tommy Holbrook. 'Constable, does she have anywhere to stay here in Sydney?'

'No, sir, I don't think so. We come down in the train and come straight on here.'

'Very well, Miss Bergman, you may stay in one of our minimum-security wards until your committal is confirmed.' He reached over and picked up a small brass bell and rang it. A sullen-looking nurse of indeterminate age appeared at the door. 'She's to be placed in a low-security ward until further notice,' the weary physician instructed, scribbling an admission slip and handing it to the woman.

'Come,' the nurse said, taking Jessica roughly by the elbow and escorting her to the door. 'We'll have no crying here, stop it at once!' And so life in a mental asylum began for Jessica.

Tommy Holbrook took a step towards Jessica then stopped. 'Don't let the mongrels beat ya, Jessie. You come home soon, ya hear?' he called after her.

Dr Warwick looked up and in a desultory tone said, 'Constable, in the time between now and your becoming the police superintendent, it might be as well to keep your opinions of those of us who labour in this parlous institution to yourself.'

'Yes, sir. Certainly, sir,' were the last words Jessica

would hear spoken by someone from home for almost four years.

Jessica never received a second examination, and she was never officially declared insane. The system simply took over and she became an inmate, an anonymous set of digits, Number 4281, which gave her no rights and no freedom and, because of her insanity, was regarded as attached to a name without a personality of its own.

Jessica soon learned that her only hope of returning to the outside world was to be examined by three outside doctors appointed to the governing board. Each would be required to see her separately, a task which no one in the wards could remember ever having been undertaken. The three-member examining board only visited the hospital twice yearly and when they did, they enjoyed a splendid lunch given by the Medical Supervisor which invariably terminated in the late afternoon after brandy and cigars and with a great deal of *bonhomie* from all concerned. They left promptly at four o'clock, usually too inebriated to walk in a straight line.

Jessica also learned that there was a further catch to this impossible scenario for escape. No such examination could be held until her family or someone of equal responsibility first agreed to take her under their supervision for a probationary period of six months after her release from the asylum.

In her first year at the institution Jessica wrote to Hester and Meg on seven separate occasions to beg them to meet these conditions – to give her a chance to prove her sanity, promising in return not to make trouble.

She received no reply. Hester and Meg had utterly deserted her.

She then wrote to old Dr Merrick, explaining her circumstances and begging him, as an act of mercy, to come to Sydney to identify her as the patient he had found to be pregnant. But the letter was returned unopened with the notation on the front of the envelope by the Postmaster at Wagga Wagga: *Addressee deceased.*

Under Jessica's gentle care and friendship, Moishe Goldberg made such splendid progress that after a year, and with the importuning of the Chief Rabbi of Sydney who somehow arranged for the three gentlemen doctors to assess him, he was allowed to leave, and placed into the care of his family. The impossible had happened and Jessica comforted herself with the notion that if it could happen once then it could happen again.

Moishe Goldberg had been away from Callan Park barely a week when he arrived back to visit Jessica with an armload of books. As it turned out, the books were simply an excuse to visit her. They'd gone for a walk within the high walls of the institution and Moishe had halted under one of the English oaks in the park, the pride and joy of the hospital, which was described in a government report concerning the lunatic asylum as 'A garden of pleasure, a bit of Old England in a faraway land'.

'Jessie,' Moishe said suddenly and clumsily, 'marry me.'

Jessica was completely taken aback. She had never contemplated the likelihood of a proposal from the young

Jew. Moishe had once told her he couldn't marry until after the revolution, after the overthrow of the capitalists. This decision had not evolved from a discussion concerning his feelings towards her, but was simply a statement he'd made in the course of some conversation. 'A man going to war does not leave a wife behind to mourn him should he die,' he'd declared rather melodramatically at the time, reminding her of Jack.

'What do you mean?' she asked now, touching her chest. 'Me marry *you*?'

Moishe nodded, increasingly embarrassed.

'Why?' she asked, too surprised to be tactful.

'Jessie, just think, it could be your way out of here! Besides, I now know I love you.' Moishe raked his bony fingers down his face. 'I've been gone a week and I've not slept a wink for thinking of you.'

Despite the knowledge that marriage to Moishe Goldberg might eventually lead to her freedom, Jessica refused his compassionate offer. She was smart enough to know that whatever had happened between herself and Moishe, he'd never be completely cured of his dark moods and she didn't want another Joe in her life. Besides, she didn't love Moishe Goldberg. Jack Thomas, she told herself, was the only man she would ever love. She would find another way to gain her freedom.

In her imagination Jessica could see Joe shaking his head. 'Jessie, yer too bloody stubborn, get the hell out of there, girlie! Yiz can always bugger off from that Jewboy!'

Moishe's father, Solly Goldberg, a butcher of kosher poultry with a nice sideline in German sausage, had been overjoyed at the news of Jessica's rejection of his son's proposal of marriage.

However, he was also a man of conscience and felt he owed a debt to Jessica for the return of his prodigal son to the bosom of the family. And so he decided to come out to Callan Park to thank her, not only for her care and kindness to Moishe but also for rejecting his son's hand in marriage.

Bondi Beach to Rozelle is a long way to come on a hot Sunday and Solly Goldberg was a big man, sufficiently rotund so that his arms were only just long enough for his hands to clasp about his middle. He took the electric tram into the city from Bondi Beach and then the omnibus from the Town Hall out to Callan Park, lugging a large basket loaded with several bottles of lemonade and crammed with Jewish delicacies which Moishe's mother had prepared for Jessica.

Solly Goldberg was plainly not accustomed to any activity which required self-locomotion and by the time he arrived at the asylum he was huffing and puffing like a sawmill engine.

Jessica had been waiting out the front for him, having been informed of his proposed visit by Moishe who, despite her rejection of him, still came to see her each week. She didn't quite know what to expect. While Moishe spoke often enough of his father, he'd never taken the trouble to describe him. Jessica supposed he might look somewhat like Moishe, who was tall and almost thin enough, he often joked, to slide through the brass letter slot in a door.

Therefore it was somewhat of a surprise when a huge bear of a man with a red and profusely sweating face lumbered up the path leading to the main entrance of the asylum. Seated at the back of his bald head, he wore a brown derby hat – which Jessica was later to discover covered a skull cap – though without a single hair on his head she could never understand how either managed to stay on Solly's cranium. He was making heavy work of his progress and when he eventually reached her he stood for a moment, panting. 'Miss Bergman, my compliments,' the huge man said breathlessly. Jessica noticed that the coarse cotton shirt under his jacket was so wet with the effort of his journey that it clung to the surface of his expansive stomach and clearly showed the outline of his navel. The *tzittzit* – the tassels hanging from his waist, which he later explained to her were the fringes of his prayer shawl, that he wore inside his shirt – dripped with perspiration.

'Mr Goldberg?' Jessica asked tentatively.

'Solly Goldberg, kosher butcher,' Moishe's father announced. Then, placing the basket at his feet, he wiped his hand on the backside of his ample trousers before extending it to Jessica.

'Nice ter meetcha, Mr Goldberg,' Jessica replied nervously, her hand lost in his huge, clammy paw.

Solly Goldberg took a step backwards and, with his head tilted slightly, he appraised Jessica. 'So pretty,' he said, 'but too thin! If you were a chicken I send you to the fat farm.' He had a merry laugh and Jessica's nervousness began to disappear. 'Come, Miss Bergman, we make a picnic. I talk, you eat.'

Jessica helped Solly Goldberg to spread a picnic rug under one of the English oak trees in the asylum grounds. He set about the task of attending to her appetite. With a sweep of the hand he indicated the large basket. 'Miss Bergman, everything we have here, compliments Mrs Goldberg. Eat, my dear, tomorrow maybe comes a pogrom, who knows?'

Jessica, who hadn't seen as much delicious food in over a year, could scarcely believe her eyes.

'Eat, eat, there's no shame, only if I go back, Mrs Goldberg finds maybe something in the basket, then shame!' Solly Goldberg clapped his hands and rolled his eyes in dismay, mimicking his wife's voice. 'So tell me, Solly, your *shiksa* girlfriend, she don't like my strudel?'

But eventually, despite Solly's exhortations to 'Eat, eat, my dear!' Jessica could not manage another morsel.

'Okey-dokey, first we eat and now we talk,' Moishe's father declared, rubbing his hands together in anticipation. 'Maybe a little more lemonade, Miss Bergman? For the throat?'

Jessica laughed, shaking her head. 'I'm full as a goog, Mr Goldberg. Couldn't manage another crumb.'

Solly shook his head sadly. 'Tush! Such a no appetite, maybe you should be a bird, a sparrow no less.'

He hadn't partaken of any of the food himself, content to watch Jessica eat alone, but now he started to dispose of what was left in the interests of not making Mrs Goldberg angry. Jessica had left at least three-quarters of the contents of the basket. After eating steadily for twenty minutes, describing to Jessica between mouthfuls how each delicacy was cooked by his wife, Solly indicated the empty basket and, producing a large bandanna, he wiped his mouth carefully then declared happily, 'I pray every day I die first – without Mrs Goldberg's cooking, to be alive would be a big disappointment.'

'My mother is a good cook, but she couldn't hold a candle to your wife, Mr Goldberg.'

Solly looked pleased. He'd placed his back against the oak tree and stretched his fat legs straight out in front of him, his big butcher's hands resting comfortably upon his stomach. 'Miss Bergman, what you've done to Moishe, it can't be paid back. He is an entire different boychick. But also, I got to thank you for saving my business.'

Jessica looked puzzled. 'Saving your business?'

Solly spread his large hands. 'I ask you, who's heard a kosher butcher his boy is married to a *shiksa*?'

'A *shiksa*? You said that word before.'

'A gentile, my dear. Moishe is a Communist. He tells me it don't matter no more – religion is dead, God is finish. Communism is coming next, a Jew can marry a gentile, who cares!'

Jessica laughed. 'Religion is the opiate of the people?'

Solly looked up, surprised. 'He said it to you also? Maybe he told you as well that Mr Marx is a Jew, but now dead, a German and the son of a rabbi already, so what's the problem, it's not the end of the world? "Moishe," I tell him, "maybe not for you it's the end of the world, to be a Jew is not a religion, it is a pain in the *tukis*!" You know what is a *tukis*, Miss Bergman? In English, if you'll excuse I say it, to be a Jew is a pain in the bum!' He shrugged his shoulders. 'So I say to him, to the boychick, the Communist, "But understand, it's God's pain in the bum and when God scratches his *tukis*, a Jew knows he's somebody chosen by God special and must keep the faith. So tell me, Mr *Shlemiel*, Moishe Goldberg, whose pain in the *tukis* is a Communist? Let me tell you something for nothing, my boy, I'm a butcher, what do I know from Communist? What I know is a chicken is Jewish or gentile, you can't have both in one butcher shop. I wish it could be so, I could make a lot of money." Then I say to him, "Moishe, *Communist kish mit in hinten*!" You know what means that, Miss Bergman? Of course not. It means, Communist can kiss my bum!' Solly Goldberg shook with laughter and clapped his hands, overjoyed to have Jessica laughing with him.

'I never thought of a chicken having a religion. A chicken being Jewish,' Jessica said at last.

'You better believe! A chicken ain't Jewish, I'm out of business! But if a chicken is also a Communist, I'm out of business double. How long you think I'm going to be a kosher butcher I tell people they should eat Communist?'

Jessica laughed again. 'About as long as you'd be a kosher butcher in Bondi if Moishe married me?'

Solly Goldberg clasped his plump hands to his chest. 'You got it, Miss Bergman, kosher chickens and gentile chickens, they can't be in the same shop and Communist chickens, they got no profit.' He pauses and smiles at Jessica. 'But what you done for my boy Moishe, how can I thank you?'

Jessica smiled back at him. 'He done a lot for me too, Mr Goldberg. He taught me to read books.'

Solly looked down at his hands, suddenly silent. Then he spoke quietly, not looking up. 'I've come to ask, my dear. You could maybe turn convert? Become a Jew?' He looked up tentatively to see if the thought offended her, but seeing Jessica smile he continued, 'We could talk to the rabbi, you could take Jew lessons.' He spread his big hands. 'Why not?' He smiled suddenly. 'It's not so hard to be a pain in the *tukis*.' He looked about him and made a sweeping gesture with his right hand, taking in the handsome sandstone buildings about them. 'You already done your fair share of suffering, in this terrible place. If you don't mind my saying, already you're practically Jewish, my dear.'

'That's just it, Mr Goldberg, I'm in the Hospital for the Insane,' Jessica reminded him, laughing and liking Moishe's father immensely.

'So?'

'Well, I'm supposed to be crazy. You know, in the loony-bin?'

Solly Goldberg seemed unimpressed with this line of reasoning. He spread his hands and shrugged his shoulders. 'So? Who's crazy, who ain't? Most my customers, they crazy. You should see how they look at my chickens. A kosher chicken is already blessed one hundred per cent, but in the shop comes a Mrs Chicken Shopper to buy one my nice kosher chickens.

' "You got a nice chicken for me today, Mr Goldberg?" she asks.

' "Not today, *every day* I got a nice chicken," I say to this Mrs Chicken Shopper.

' "That one!" She show me a chicken. It's a nice chicken, hanging quiet and content in the shop. I take it down. "A beautiful chicken," I say and give it her.

' "Ha!" she says. She takes it up, pulls the legs away – already she is hating this chicken, she smell its *tukis*, puts her finger inside, pulls out the giblets, looks down the neck, shake to see if something I don't know what comes out. Push a finger here, there, everywhere she pokes. If that chicken is alive, believe you me, it's dead already from cruelty to chickens. Then she point to another chicken she ain't never touched. "I take that one, Mr Goldberg. This chicken you give me is a disgrace, you ought to be ashamed yourself!" '

Solly Goldberg was an excellent mimic and it had been a long time since Jessica had laughed so heartily, thrown her pretty head back and laughed. Solly rolled his eyes. 'You think that's crazy? From chicken shoppers I got lotsa stories much worse. And from buying a turkey, you wouldn't believe.' He stopped, struck by a sudden thought, bringing his hands up to his face. 'Oh mine God! That the qualification! To be Jewish you got to be crazy.' He tilted his head to one side as though he was examining Jessica. 'Believe me, you could make already a first-class Jew in no time, my dear.'

Jessica declined Solly's invitation to take Jewish lessons but thanked him for the honour. 'I weren't much good at being a Christian, Solly, I don't suppose I'd be much good at being Jewish neither.'

Solly laughed, accepting her decision. 'Being good at being a Jew is impossible, my dear. If you come even close it's a miracle from God.'

A friendship had been struck between Jessica and the kosher butcher from Bondi that would last a lifetime. Solly Goldberg visited Jessica once a month for the next two years and always came alone. 'The boychick don't know about picnics, only books and Communist chickens,' he'd say as if to excuse Moishe's absence. But Jessica knew Solly wanted to come alone and she was greatly flattered that he would make a trip so obviously arduous for someone of his stature.

Moishe, however, never failed to visit Jessica once a week to bring her books and talk to her and often one of the books might have a white feather stuck in it.

When Jessica first asked him about the feathers, thinking it was simply a bookmark made from one of Solly Goldberg's kosher chook feathers, Moishe laughed. 'Women come up to me in the street or on the tram and hand them to me,' he'd said.

'But why?' Jessica asked, curious.

'It's to tell me I'm a coward for not joining up to fight in the war.' He'd smiled quietly. 'I'm keeping myself for the revolution. When the workers rise up, Jessie,' he paused and looked up over the summer trees, 'now that will be a battle worth fighting in.'

'But you told me they wouldn't take you because you had flat feet, Moishe Goldberg!' Jessica laughingly accused him.

'Yeah, that too,' Moishe laughed, embarrassed at being exposed, 'and the bottom of lemonade bottles for specs. But that was *before* I became a Communist, before I'd read Marx and Engels. I wouldn't join up now, not blinkin' likely.'

Jessica hadn't told Moishe about Jack, the man she loved with all her heart, who had joined up the moment he could with just as much fervour and belief in the British Empire and all that it stood for as Moishe felt about his silly Communist revolution.

Jessica thought about these two young men who, together with Billy Simple, had so affected and influenced her life.

Moishe Goldberg, the Semite, pale as first light with a blueish tinge to his chin no matter how closely he shaved, his dark obsidian eyes made large as a possum's by the lenses of impossibly thick spectacles. Moishe, thin as a rake with bones which seemed to rattle about in his clothes, too timid even to touch her, his fine mind filled with theory, revolution and failure, determined to save a working class with whom he had nothing in common.

Jack Thomas, solid, muscle-hard, blue-eyed and tanned by a merciless sun, his hair the colour of ripened wheat, the sum of a hundred generations of Celtic and Anglo-Saxon blood. His mind always on the soil, unimaginative, except perhaps for his precious irrigation canals. Fascinated by the internal combustion engine and the role of mechanicals on the sheep station, yet the finest of horsemen. But he too was vulnerable, as she'd seen often enough when his father had a go at him. Jack, who would come home and take up where he'd left off, never questioning his entitlement. 'A real good bloke for an owner, fair dinkum,' folk would be bound to say about him. 'Married the Bergman girl, the pretty one.'

Both were men with dreams of a world that was a fair and honest place, though each had a vastly different image of what this should be. Both decent men, down to their bootlaces, except that Moishe's were usually undone and Jack wore riding boots with elastic sides. It was Jewish and gentile chickens all over again, Jessica thought wryly.

She greatly enjoyed Moishe's weekly visits, but if the truth be known, they were not anticipated as enthusiastically as Solly's monthly picnics, which had become known as 'Compliments Mrs Goldberg'. Solly would leave her at four o'clock in the afternoon when the gates closed. 'I see you next month, my dear,' he'd say, 'same time, same place, compliments Mrs Goldberg.'

The visits of Solly, with his big basket filled with his wife's culinary love for him, with his stories of the doings in his kosher butcher shop and his life as a child in Poland, became the high point in every long, tedious and always frightening month.

Solly was not only an entertainer, he had the rare ability to be a good listener as well and he grew to love Jessica's stories of the bush. At first she'd been too shy, thinking he was only trying to be polite. But

Solly persisted and one day Jessica said, 'I'm no good at stories, Mr Goldberg, but I could do you a poem me father taught me when I was a young 'un.' She hesitated a moment. 'It's a bit rude, though.'

'A poem? I like that, Miss Bergman.'

The Black Soil Plains

'The herring clouds are stretching
Across the black soil plains.
It's more than folk dare hope for
As they pray for summer rains.

'Six years of drought and hardship,
The dams and rivers dry.
The bank owns a second mortgage
And our sheep and cattle die.

' "Lord, fill our creeks and rivers,
Let pastures green our lands,
Squeeze the moisture from the heavens
With Your ever loving hands."

'God looked down and saw our suffering
And a miracle came to pass.
His tears dropped down from heaven
Just enough to wipe my arse.'

Jessica ended the poem and Solly clapped and chortled.

'I always thought that was the end of the poem until one day a shearer told it to me proper,' Jessica then said. 'Would you like to hear how the rest of it goes?'

'More? I got more? Certainly, with pleasure, my dear.'

Jessica repeated the last verse and corrected the final line, then added another verse.

> *'God looked down and saw our suffering*
> *And a miracle came to pass.*
> *His tears dropped down from heaven*
> *Just enough to rinse my glass.*
> *'So, let's drink to pluck and courage*
> *To the folk on the black soil plains*
> *Who bury their dead on the highest ground*
> *To protect them from the rains!'*

Solly Goldberg clapped again. 'But not so good as the first, I think your father has got it better, eh?'

Solly constantly tried to encourage Jessica to speak about her life and soon she too could tell a story or two to entertain him. Solly would urge her on when she lost her confidence, digging out the facts and the colour of an idea or experience by constant questioning. His interest was always apparent, never wavering, so that Jessica was encouraged to continue, knowing that what she had to say was genuinely interesting to him. Under his skilful guidance she began to understand the way a good tale is constructed and how to bring the characters within it to life.

'Jessica,' he would say, 'listen for the voices. When you hear their voices then also you know the story.' Over a period of three 'Compliments Mrs Goldberg' picnics, Jessica told Solly the story of Billy Simple, ending it where she left him in front of the Narrandera court-house, though without mentioning Jack Thomas's presence in the story at its very end, how he'd picked her up and carried her into the courthouse. Her love for Jack was a secret she would never share. It was as though his memory was fixed in time and that even by talking of him she might disturb the very core of her love.

When Jessica came to the end of the final episode of Billy Simple's journey into captivity, Solly remained silent for a long time, while tears ran down his huge, round face. He'd taken his large bandanna from his trouser pocket and wiped his eyes, then used it to blow his rubbery nose several times, furiously pushing it about within the folds of the large handkerchief, buying time so that he might control his emotion.

Finally he'd looked up at Jessica. 'Miss Bergman, you could have been a wonderful Jew,' he sighed, then shrugged his shoulders. 'So who cares? Already you a wonderful human being.'

Solly demanded ever more stories from her and so Jessica told him about Billy Simple's trial. Between his visits she thought about what she'd tell Solly on his next trip, and she began to realise the true value of what Joe had taught her.

All the years of Joe's silences, when they would be working together and he would be quiet, thinking and observing, sometimes leaving her to complete a task while he followed a bird call or a trail of migrating ants, now came back to Jessica. They provided the colour she needed to satisfy Solly Goldberg's stringent demands for a good yarn. Those occasions with Joe were quite different from his darknesses, his moods of terrible despair. These were the silences where he watched and took time to enchant Jessica with what he'd seen and what he supposed it might mean.

Joe, she realised, translated for Jessica over their years together what he thought was the nature of things on the land and elsewhere. The habits built into a fox's behaviour, the manner in which a bird builds its nest to defeat a predatory snake that can twist and curl from the end of a branch to enter a nest at any angle. The different calls of a bird and what they might signal and the various gestures of a kangaroo looking out for the safety of his females. The way of an emu with its chicks, the peculiar way a rabbit twitches its nose when it senses danger, and how the leaves of the eucalypt constantly change their angle to the sun's rays so that they maintain a constant temperature and survive the drought. Joe would kick at a cow pat and announce that summer would bring a plague of black flies (mind you, Jessica never thought this was much of a prophecy, the summer always brought a plague of black flies). He'd point to the sort of rock most likely to conceal a scorpion beneath it, and he knew why a snake could move up the surface of a seemingly vertical rock.

Now, as she recalled the images of her childhood and Joe's careful tuition, Jessica realised that she too had developed an acute sense of observation and a detailed recollection of events. She began to understand that Solly Goldberg was mining what was already within her and that in his own way, he was trying to restore her hope and renew her self-confidence.

Solly would encourage Jessica to hear the voices in her stories, but she now understood that Joe had taught her to see the pictures as well, to recall movement and colour, to note gesture as well as intonation, to see what differed from the commonplace and to seek the meaning within everything. 'Girlie, everything means something in nature. Everything has a purpose in the bush. While people waste time and energy feeling sorry for themselves, the rest are out there trying to find a feed.'

Joe had not been educated by book-learning like Moishe, nor was he a gregarious storyteller and man of the world like Solly Goldberg, but her father had used his eyes and his patience to seek the truth in things. And in this respect he was more than a match for both Solly and Moishe. But what Solly added was that he gave Jessica back a sense of her own worth.

Jessica would later understand that Moishe, with his books and his earnest talk which she only half understood at the time, taught her to question authority and to beware of those restricting notions that passed for conventional wisdom in society. But it was Solly Goldberg, the custodian of merriment, who taught her to laugh again, and who gave her the courage to fight and not to give up hope. He encouraged her to speak out and not to be afraid of making a fool of herself. The big bear of a butcher who waddled like a penguin and sweated like a working dog was the only one who kept

Jessica sane while she fought to survive the horrors of the mental asylum.

It was while telling Solly the story of Billy Simple's trial that Jessica had a truly inspired idea. She was recounting the incident when she had gone to see 'Liquid Lunch', the barrister who was appointed by the Crown to defend Billy Simple. She was explaining to Solly how she'd confronted him at breakfast in his hotel to beg him to help Billy, when it suddenly struck her that she should write to him – write a letter to Richard Runche KC and beg him to help her! The more Jessica thought about this idea the more appealing it seemed. At the end of Billy's trial Richard Runche had presented his case with great eloquence, so why couldn't he do the same for her? Her hope was that in the period since Billy Simple's trial the lawyer hadn't gone down for the count to the claret bottle – while her fear was that he might have forgotten her.

At the conclusion of the story of Billy Simple's trial, Solly Goldberg looked at Jessica and said, 'So Moishe tells me you have asked him to go to Long Bay Prison, to find where is the grave of Mr Simple?'

'Oh, Mr Goldberg, I'd like so much to see it!' Jessica exclaimed, then she announced, 'When I get out I'm gunna get him a gravestone.'

Solly remained silent, not looking at Jessica.

'What's the matter?' Jessica asked, thinking she must have said something to upset him. 'Don't Jews have gravestones?'

Solly looked up slowly. 'My dear, there is no grave.'

'But there must be! They must have buried him somewhere!'

'You know what is a no-person, Miss Bergman?'

'No.'

'When a man is a murderer he is made a no-person, he got no coffin, he got no grave.'

'That's silly – he must have.'

'They make for him a shroud and they take up the paving-stone in the jail and dig a hole.' He paused. 'You know what is quicklime?' Jessica nodded. 'They put in this hole the body and pour over quicklime, then they put back the paving-stone.' Solly looked at her, forcing himself to continue. 'There is no more Billy Simple. They don't put a name by his grave, they don't tell where is his grave, not even his family, he is a no-person – gone, finish, kaput.'

Jessica remained for some time with her head bowed, quietly sobbing. 'I am so sorry. I am so sorry,' Solly kept saying. 'Moishe, he don't want to tell you.'

Finally Jessica looked up. 'I'll make him a gravestone anyway, a cross, by the creek back home, under the big river gum. Yellow-belly swim there and it's quiet, it don't have to have his body underneath. Billy will know it's there for him – that we done it for him, Jack and me.'

Solly looked pleased at this notion. 'So why not? I got a Mr Gravestone Chicken Shopper, a good man don't poke the chickens, don't look down the *tukis*, I ask him nice to make for you this gravestone.' Then he grinned. 'Mind, I don't know how he goes *mit* Jesus crosses.'

'Would you? Would you really?' Jessica cried. 'When I get out I'll save up the money.'

'So we make an arrangement.'

'An arrangement?' Jessica looked doubtful. 'You mean you'll lend me the money?' She shook her head vigorously. 'Nah, I couldn't. What if something happened and I couldn't pay yiz back?'

Solly Goldberg smiled. 'An arrangement is not a lend, Miss Bergman. We make an arrangement to give back what we owe you.'

'You don't owe me nothing, Mr Goldberg.'

'Maybe *you* don't think so, but Mrs Goldberg she don't agree. She owes you her *boychick*, Moishe the Communist, no less.' He paused and smiled at Jessica. 'Not lend, my dear, *give*, compliments Mrs Goldberg! You must tell me the words we put on the Jesus cross.'

Jessica burst into tears and hugged Solly Goldberg. Later she would realise that it was the first time she had touched another human being in a loving way since she'd embraced Mary Simpson after the birth of her baby.

When Moishe next visited Jessica she asked him to make inquiries as to the whereabouts of Richard Runche KC, and then she'd waited impatiently all week for him to return.

Moishe had little trouble tracing the infamous circuit court barrister, who was still to be found in Wagga scrounging the odd brief from the Crown and between times slowly drowning in cheap claret. When he came back to Jessica with this news, Moishe had also brought along pen and ink, a tablet of blue paper with a matching envelope which he'd correctly addressed and to which he'd affixed a postage stamp of the right denomination.

'Will you help me, Moishe? I ain't too good at writing stuff,' Jessica asked him.

'You write what you want, Jessie. Write it in your own words, and I'll fix it up for you,' Moishe counselled.

Jessica spent the following week painstakingly writing a letter to Richard Runche KC and Moishe corrected her spelling and punctuation. He possessed a beautiful copperplate hand and Jessica wanted him to write the letter, thinking it would impress the barrister no end. But Moishe was wise enough to know that it would be more meaningful to the barrister in Jessica's somewhat childish script and with her own heartfelt words. To this end he had conscientiously kept her letter intact. Jessica wrote several versions until she had one that contained no crossings out. She mailed it with great hope in her heart, kissing the letter several times before dropping it into the pillar box at the porter's gate. It was a letter which had cost her many tears, and many long nights in thinking over all that had happened to her.

> *The Hospital for the Insane*
> *Callan Park*
> *Sydney*
>
> *6 October 1918*

Dear Mr Runche KC,
*   You have probably forgotten who I am, so maybe I should remind you. I was the young girl*

*who saw you one morning at breakfast in your
hotel at your table behind the ferns, and asked
you to help Billy Simple the murderer. You probably remember him by his real name, William
D'arcy Simon. He was the one who killed Mrs
Ada Thomas and her two daughters at Riverview
Station. You proved it wasn't done in cold blood,
which is what the prosecution wanted the jury to
think, though the judge and the jury wouldn't listen and gave him the death sentence.*

Do you remember me now?

*I was very proud because you gave Billy his
dignity so he could die with his head held up
high.*

*Now I am in trouble, which will take quite a
long time to explain to you, so I hope you will
forgive me and not think I am wasting your val-
uable time.*

*What I'm going to say may seem a bit loony,
especially when you see the address above, but I
have been put in here against my wishes by my
mother and sister because of my baby.*

*I will begin at the beginning. After Billy's trial I
fell pregnant and my parents didn't want to know
because I wouldn't tell them who the father was.
They kept me locked away so nobody knew. When
people asked, they said I was sick with a nervous
breakdown, and that I must have quiet and rest
and see nobody.*

Then my sister, Meg, wanted to marry Jack

Thomas, the son of Mrs Thomas who was murdered, and she tricked him into marrying her before he went off to the war, saying she was pregnant by him. But it turned out she wasn't.

I've since worked out what must have happened. Jack Thomas must have said that if Meg had a son, he would inherit Riverview if Jack died in the war. So she pretended she was pregnant, stuffing things under her dress so it would look like a baby was growing inside her. My mother was also in on it, and everyone who saw Meg at St Stephen's every Sunday thought she was pregnant. She even knitted things for the baby she wasn't having.

Then I had my baby on Christmas Eve and my father, Joe Bergman (you might remember him), had a heart attack and died the next day. And at the funeral at St Stephen's my mother made the vicar announce to one and all that Meg had given birth to a boy, saying that my baby was Meg's and that Meg gave birth prematurely on Christmas Day due to the shock of my father's sudden death.

This was when I made my wrong move, Mr Runche. I screamed and screamed and attacked my mother in front of everyone who'd come to the funeral. So they restrained me and my mother said it was because of my nervous breakdown. When my hysterics wouldn't come good I was taken to the lock-up at Narrandera and my mother and the vicar – his name is Reverend

*Mathews, M.A. Oxon. – swore in a statement
that I was suffering from a nervous breakdown
and was having delusions.*

*My mother said in the report that the baby
wasn't mine and I had gone over the edge with
jealousy about my sister having a baby and not
me. The vicar said he knew Meg was pregnant and
that I was not well. They both signed the paper to
commit me, saying they were afraid I would
attack the baby.*

*So they brought me here to Callan Park in Syd-
ney, but they didn't give me a proper examination,
only one doctor saw me. His name is Dr Warwick,
who was drinking brandy when he examined me
on New Year's Day. I didn't have the strength to
answer any of his questions, but I told him they'd
stolen my baby. I could see he didn't believe me
and later I thought I should have asked him to
examine me so he could see I was telling the truth.
But I didn't know then that you could tell if
someone's just had a baby.*

*So Dr Warwick took the decision to commit me
just because of the report. He said I had to have a
second examination by the Medical Supervisor,
but that I had to wait till he came back from the
Christmas holidays. I never did see him and I am
still waiting after three years for that examination.*

*I am hoping that you can help me in my terrible
situation. I am desperate and definitely not insane!
I have never been put in a wetpack or restrained in*

*a strait-jacket or locked up in solitary since coming
here. The Ward Matron says if I am insane then
she is the Queen of Sheba, but she says she can't do
nothing for my situation and only takes orders
from her superiors. I have been lost in the red tape,
she says.*

*Please, Mr Runche, could you write to the
authorities to look into my case? I know I am not
important and just a poor girl from the bush and I
don't even have any money to pay you. But I know
you have a good heart and are the best at asking
questions because I saw what you did for Billy
Simple and how you spoke up for him against
the odds.*

Hoping to hear from you soon.
Yours faithfully,
Jessica Bergman.

Nearly two weeks passed and, while Jessica had not
expected a quick reply from the barrister, she was beginning to despair that Richard Runche KC had ignored
her letter. It was therefore with some surprise when she
was summoned to the reception parlour, to see the barrister seated in one of the old leather club chairs. In the
big scuffed chair he appeared to be even shabbier than
she could recall.

He was wearing the same dark, worn-out suit, greasy
tie with stained celluloid collar and white shirt much in
need of laundering. His skin was pale, with the exception of his nose which had blossomed even more with

blueish-looking veins, his eyes were red-rimmed and rheumy and his thin hair stood every which way, as though he'd just awakened after a restless night and not attended to his *toilette*. Which was quite true, of course. Richard Runche KC was nursing a fearful hangover as usual and had slept seated in a second-class carriage most of the way from Wagga.

The scruffy barrister sat with his legs together, quiet as a tally clerk waiting to be interviewed, with his battered hat resting on his lap. But he seemed to recognise Jessica the moment he saw her approaching and rose to his feet, his hat rolling from his lap to the floor.

Jessica hastened to retrieve it, though Liquid Lunch seemed not to notice and moved forward with his hand extended so that, as Jessica bent down to pick up his hat her head banged into his stomach. 'Oh, dear, have I messed up things already?' he said, concerned. Then, when Jessica rose and their eyes met, he smiled. 'Ah, there you are. How very nice to see you again, my dear Miss Bergman.'

Jessica smiled and thanked him most sincerely for coming and then suggested they go for a walk in the grounds. In greeting Richard Runche she realised how much confidence she'd gained from her friendship with Solly Goldberg.

'Walk?' The barrister seemed surprised at the idea, but then added quickly, 'Can't say I do much walking these days. Damned good idea, though.' She handed him his hat. 'Ah, where did that come from?' he asked, again surprised, then in a slightly more earnest voice inquired, 'I don't suppose there's a pub nearby, give the walk a solid purpose, eh?'

'I'm not allowed to leave the grounds, sir,' Jessica apologised.

'No, no, quite,' Richard Runche agreed. 'Pity though, you look as though a small tincture of Bombay gin might do you the world of good, young lady.' He sniffed and looked about him, taking in the drab green walls and polished wooden floor. 'Miserable sort of place, eh?'

Once outside, her guest placed his hat back on his head and, blinking uncertainly in the sharp light, took Jessica's arm. 'Now, you must tell me everything, young lady.' He stopped suddenly and pointed to the trees. 'Good God, those are not English oaks, are they? Yes, by Jove, they are – how very remarkable!'

Jessica led him to the nearest park bench situated under a large shady oak tree and they settled down to talk. For the hour that followed Richard Runche questioned Jessica closely, as he wanted to know every possible detail. Jessica agreed that she would tell him everything but the name of the father of her child.

'You do realise, Jessica – I may call you Jessica, may I?'

'Yes, sir.'

'Well then, Jessica, you do realise that your refusal to say who the father is puts serious doubts on your claim. You say you gave birth to a child but you will not name the father. Does that not seem to substantiate the story your mother has given the authorities, to support the notion of an imagined child?'

'Please sir, Mr Runche, I swore I'd never tell nobody and I never will.' Richard Runche was about to remember the stubborn streak in Jessica.

He then made her tell him about the circumstances of the birth, urging her to leave nothing out. As she talked she could sense the barrister found it difficult to imagine that she'd given birth to her child sitting in the creek up to her waist in water. 'Good gracious, are you sure?' was all he'd said at the conclusion of her story about the birth of her son, Joey.

'You can ask Mary, Mary Simpson – she saw me straight after, when she come from the Lutheran Church Christmas party for her kids,' Jessica protested.

'Mary Simpson? She witnessed the birth?'

'She come just after and took care of me.'

'Can I speak to this Mary Simpson? How do I contact her?' the barrister asked.

'She's Aboriginal, from the Wiradjuri tribe. You could find her easy enough, they're the local blacks.'

'Aboriginal?'

'Yes, she's my friend, she knows I had the baby. She'll tell you straight off, swear it on a stack of Bibles.'

Richard Runche sat back and brought his hands together, bringing the tips of his fingers to his lips, making a small whistling sound. 'My dear Jessica, the word of an Aboriginal woman against two white women – against your mother and sister – would be unlikely to succeed in court. So far, we have no case.'

'But it's true, I swear it's true!' Jessica cried. 'You must see that, you must believe me, Mr Runche, sir!'

488 BRYCE COURTENAY

The barrister sighed. 'Let me review what you've just told me, Jessica. Let me show you how a judge might see it.' He cleared his throat and began to enunciate, ticking the various points off on the fingers of his left hand. 'You say you were pregnant to a man you won't name. The doctor who pronounced you pregnant is deceased and appears to have kept no records. The woman who can verify that you had a child while sitting waist-deep in water is an Aborigine of no fixed address. A tribal woman, whose testimony may not even be acceptable in a court of law and whose word is unlikely to be taken against that of your mother and sister. Your father, whom you say took you to the doctor who pronounced you pregnant and who saw your child on Christmas Day, is dead.' He changed hands, ticking off the remaining points on the fingers of his right hand. 'The congregation of St Stephen's church is, I imagine, prepared to swear to your sister's pregnancy, backed up by the vicar, the Reverend Mathews, a man of God. Furthermore, you were witnessed to have protested after the announcement by the vicar of the birth of what was, as the congregation had every right to assume, the expected and slightly premature outcome of your sister's pregnancy. You claimed the newborn child belonged to you and proceeded, in front of a hundred or more witnesses, to physically attack your mother on the sad occasion of your father's funeral.' He paused, again pressing the bridge of his nose between his forefinger and thumb. 'And, not to put too fine a point on it, my dear, you reside at present in a lunatic asylum.' Richard

Runche looked sternly at Jessica. 'Do I make myself clear?'

Jessica began to sob softly. 'Please, Mr Runche, I'm not mad. They stole my child! They took Joey away from me!'

Richard Runche KC sighed. 'No, Jessica, I don't think you are mad.' He sighed again, more quietly. 'Though God knows, looking at the evidence, you don't appear to have a leg to stand on.' He reached out and put his hand on Jessica's shoulder. 'But we may have one thing going for us. The paper your mother signed making the farm over to you and your child is signed by this Mary Simpson – and your mother, of course – and that may establish the veracity of the black woman's testimony. Where might this document be, do you have it with you?'

'No, it was left with my things, in my room, when I went to the funeral.'

'Ah, I see,' he sighed. 'Well, I don't suppose it's still there.'

'Not bloody likely,' Jessica sniffed.

Runche frowned. 'So there it is, my dear. Even the document in your mother's handwriting signing your father's property over to you can't be found.' He spread his hands and shrugged, saying nothing.

'Mary signed it, she'll say so.'

The lawyer ignored this remark, having already dismissed the black woman's testimony. 'Think, my dear, there must be something – a little thing, perhaps ever so small, one thing we can use that will at least cast doubt on your mother and sister's version of the truth.'

Jessica looked up at the barrister, shaking her head. 'They took my baby and now I can't prove otherwise,' she choked.

Runche was beginning to wonder what he'd let himself in for. His head throbbed from a hangover that no less than half a dozen glasses of claret could hope to fix. It was way past pub time, his mouth was dry and he could feel the shakes coming on. 'Think, my dear. In my experience there is always *something*, something we might use.'

Jessica lowered her face into her cupped hands, trying to think. She remained like this for a minute or more. Then she looked up slowly, hopefully. 'The Chinese dress. The aunties bought it for me, for my baby.'

'The Chinese dress? Whatever do you mean by that, Jessica?'

'When Hester come an' told me about Joe dying, I brought the baby home with me, but I was that upset I forgot the Chinese dress. It's under the straw mattress of my bed in the tin hut,' Jessica said excitedly.

'You must forgive me, I still don't understand.'

Jessica told Richard Runche about the shopping expedition to the Chinese shop in Narrandera by the aunties to buy her child a birth dress, a gift from the Wiradjuri tribe.

'The court can't say they're all lying, can it? You couldn't make up a thing like that, could you?' she begged.

'Hmm, perhaps not. This Mary Simpson, could she take me to your hut?'

Jessica nodded, whereupon the weary barrister rose from the park bench. 'Very well, my dear. We'll leave it like that for the time being. I shall be in touch.' Richard Runche KC extended his hand and Jessica could see it was trembling. 'And now I must find the nearest pub,' he said, shaking her hand.

'Thank you, sir. Thank you very much.'

He ran his tongue over his cracked lips. 'Don't thank me yet, Jessica, we've a long way to go before you're out of this miserable place.' Then he turned and walked towards the wrought-iron gates, pausing to talk briefly to the porter, who Jessica saw point left, down the road.

Jessica watched as Liquid Lunch crossed Balmain Road and turned left towards the Macarthur Arms. She felt as though she had been run over by a steamroller. She sat quietly in the dark shade of the oak tree and wondered what would become of her. She wished she was dead, like Jack, and that she lay next to him. Then she began to wonder for the thousandth time why, when he had been alive, he hadn't written to her in the asylum.

She'd written to him every month for two years but had never received a reply. Had Hester or Meg – or both of them – written to him to tell him she'd gone crazy? Surely he would be able to tell from her letters that this was not so? She'd always sent them to the right place – Moishe had seen to this, tracking Jack's regiment wherever it went. He'd missed out on Gallipoli and stayed in Egypt, she knew that much. She also knew in her heart that he was alive. Moishe had seen to that detail, too, diligently going through the postings in the daily newspapers by the Defence Department of those killed in action. Not only had Moishe seen to it that Jessica had pen and paper to write with but he'd also paid for the stamps to Egypt.

Dear, sweet Moishe had never asked her about Jack. He'd waited patiently for her to tell him and when she hadn't she supposed he'd considered Jack was the reason why she'd rejected his hand in marriage. It was a fair enough assumption because, of course, it was true – she could love no other man, come what may.

But then in the third week of January 1917 on a Thursday, when Moishe wasn't expected to visit, he arrived to see Jessica and gave her the sad news that Jack was dead. He had died of his wounds sustained in a cavalry charge against the Turks at a place called Magdhaba in Egypt on Christmas Eve, on Joey's second birthday.

Jessica had been inconsolable for several weeks, eating almost nothing and remaining silent for days on end, until she had been threatened with the jacket. Then she'd taken to mourning for Jack after midnight, when the ward was locked and when the moans and the cries and the weeping of the inmates cancelled each other out.

But still, while she mourned for him every day, Jessica could never understand why Jack hadn't given her the benefit of the doubt. It could only have been because of something Meg or Hester had written to him about her, something so horrible it prevented him from writing to her ever again. Jessica couldn't imagine what it could be. Perhaps that she'd tried to kill Meg's baby, his son? Jessica couldn't have told him about Joey.

Now, she thought, even if she'd changed her mind and he were still alive and she'd decided to write to Jack and tell him what had happened, Richard Runche KC had just demonstrated to her how unlikely her story would have sounded even to him, and how easily Meg could have refuted it. Jack would have concluded that Hester and Meg were right and that she *had* gone mad.

Jessica sat alone and wept in the late afternoon sun. She wept for Jack in his windswept grave of desert sand and hoped that they'd buried him in the grove of eucalypts he'd seen near the pyramids. She wept for her own lost son. For herself. 'Maybe I am going mad, *am* mad!' she sobbed softly. Passers-by took no notice of the slim, sad girl in the loony-bin smock and ugly black boots seated under an English oak. People in the grounds of a mental asylum weeping to themselves were a common enough sight. Misery was the stock in trade of such a place. Mad people don't do a lot of laughing.

CHAPTER THIRTEEN

On 1 December 1918, twenty days after the end of the war, Jessica is released from Callan Park into the custody of Mr Richard Runche KC. She is given a cheap cotton calico dress and allowed to keep her bloomers and boots and then she's handed a large manila envelope, which she can't even think about opening for the moment.

Jessica and Richard Runche take the omnibus to Central Station, whereupon the barrister escorts Jessica to platform ten and buys them both a ticket. Runche hands Jessica the ticket and looks at her, slightly shame-faced. 'If you'll excuse me, my dear, I'll just have a tot or two before the train goes. Would you care to accompany me? A drink might do you some good,' he says.

Jessica shakes her head. 'Thank you, Mr Runche, I've never tasted strong drink. Can I just wait here?'

The lawyer looks somewhat relieved. 'This is the correct platform, my dear, and the train departs at nine tonight.' He fishes into his trouser pockets and finds a shilling, then points to the main concourse. 'The tea room is over there, almost directly opposite this platform, should you be feeling a trifle peckish.'

At first Jessica is reluctant to take his money, but the lawyer persists. 'It's a long journey, all night on the train, so you'll need to take some refreshment, Jessica.'

Jessica watches as he walks away, and thinks that even from the back Richard Runche looks frail. The jacket he wears is too short, and the seat of his trousers is shiny, the trousers hanging loosely in folds, their cuffs rumpled and concertinaed about the ankles. His shoes are badly scuffed and down at heel and need a good blacking. His being slightly stooped and wearing an ill-fitting jacket makes one shoulder appear a little higher than the other. Even at a distance the dishevelled lawyer gives the impression of uncertainty and disrepair. He carries a small, battered leather suitcase, barely large enough to contain much more than his shaving soap, razor and one or two small personal items, though Jessica is sure these would not include a spare shirt, underwear or socks.

Jessica sits on the platform for a while, clutching the brown envelope and watching people in the distance as they walk along the concourse. She feels strange in the unfamiliar surroundings, as though she has been transported to another world where she doesn't belong.

For four years her life has been conducted behind high stone walls where the buildings and every tree surrounding them were familiar to her, the witches' broomsticks of the oak trees in winter and the dark shade of their generous leaves in summer.

Jessica needs time to adjust to this new sense of space as well as the number of people that seem to fill it. Everything looks different and unfamiliar, and after the quiet of the lunatic asylum the peripheral noise is deafening. She does not notice the austerity brought about by the war or the shabby clothes most people wear. All she sees is the rush and bustle of city life and the urgent faces of people, all of whom seem to have somewhere to go and with no time to waste. She longs suddenly to be back in the bush, the never-changing bush, where she can belong again.

The railway clock strikes six – three hours to go before the train is due to leave for the west. Jessica glances down uncertainly at the brown envelope on her lap, still lacking the courage to open it. It bulges slightly and looks quite intimidating and strange, belonging to a world she has yet to become accustomed to.

In the mental asylum suppertime was five o'clock and her stomach has grown accustomed to receiving food at this hour. But she decides to sit a while longer while she tries to summon sufficient courage to walk across the platform onto the concourse and then to enter the railway tea room.

Eventually Jessica gets to her feet, but she can feel her knees trembling as she walks towards the brightly lit tea room. At the doorway she peeps in and is alarmed to find it is filled with people chatting and eating, the hum of human voices mixed with the clatter and din of cutlery on china. The large room is fuggy with pipe smoke and the smell of cooking and she draws back, afraid to enter. At the asylum meals were taken in silence and inmates were not allowed to smoke. Jessica has become so used to eating her food in a solitary manner that the railway tea room now seems to her to be filled with mad people. Diners snorting and snuffling, feeding faces with snouts like pigs – a scene more from a dream than reality – and she shrinks back in fear.

'What's the matter, lovey? "*Teleee-graph!*" You 'fraid to go in? "*Teleee-graph!*" Don't blame ya. "*Teleee-graph!*" Them snotty waitresses, "*Teleee-graph!*" full of their own importance, them lot. "*Teleee-graph!*"'

Jessica turns to see the small woman, perhaps in her sixties or a little older, who has spoken to her. She wears a faded green dust-coat which reaches to her ankles and a pair of ancient bedroom slippers with the toenail of her left foot cutting through the dirty felt. A battered leather satchel hangs across her shoulder and flaps against her bony hip and under her arm she carries a bundle of evening newspapers.

'G'day,' Jessica says quietly, not quite knowing if she's expected to answer the old woman.

'Kiosk, lovey, over the end. "*Teleee-graph!*" Do a nice pie or a cornish pasty, "*Teleee-graph!*" cuppa tea and a sticky bun. "*Teleee-graph!*"' The woman is pointing towards the end of the main concourse. 'Skinny Dredge, he's the boss, tell him Myra, "*Teleee-graph!*" sent youse.'

'Thank you,' Jessica says, looking to where the little newspaper seller is pointing.

'Got a penny?' the woman now asks.

Jessica shakes her head and says ingenuously, 'I've only got a shilling.' She opens her hand to reveal the coin Richard Runche has given her.

The newspaper seller quickly counts out eleven pence in change and gives it to Jessica, taking the shilling and handing her a newspaper. 'Ta, lovey,' she says moving away, '*Teleee-graph!*'

Jessica takes a deep breath and then walks over to the kiosk, which isn't too crowded. A large silver urn dominates the rear counter, just like the one they used at Callan Park with a little glass tube set into the side to show how much water there remains in it. It is such a small thing, but its familiar presence gives Jessica confidence. A blackboard with a chalked menu is fixed against the back wall and announces, amongst other items, that a pie and a cup of tea is sixpence and a sticky bun threepence. Jessica doesn't introduce herself with the compliments of Myra, but manages to order both a pie and a bun with a cup of tea. The very act of carrying out this simple task makes her nervous and she stutters slightly.

'Milk, sugar?' the man – presumably Skinny Dredge – asks, placing the steaming mug of tea on the counter. Jessica is too confused to answer. 'How many?' the man asks irritably again, but Jessica doesn't understand. 'C'mon miss, I ain't got all day, you want sugar, how many?' Jessica now realises that she's expected to drink the tea on the spot and that she can't, as she'd hoped, wrap the pie and bun in the newspaper and take the lot back to the bench on the platform to eat in seclusion.

She is suddenly terrified at the idea of eating with other people milling about her. Flustered, she leaves the steaming mug of tea on the counter and quickly wraps the bun and pie in the newspaper and, with the manila envelope clasped under her arm, she flees back to the isolation of the platform. 'Hey, yer tea! Ya forgot yer tea, miss,' she hears Skinny Dredge calling after her.

When she's eaten her first meal out of captivity, Jessica feels strong enough to open the big, brown threatening envelope. She tears it open very slowly, removing only a sliver from across one end of the envelope, watching as the thin strip of paper curls over her thumb, frightened about what the envelope might contain.

Jessica gasps as she peers inside and sees what appears to be at least two dozen letters. Her mouth goes dry and her heart begins to pound. She quickly pulls one of the letters out and sees that it is stamped *Australian Comforts Fund* and is dated and addressed to her in a handwriting she doesn't recognise. She pulls out a second and it, too, has the same stamp and date, and is also addressed to her, though in yet another person's handwriting.

Jessica up-ends the contents of the envelope onto her lap and sees they've all been treated in the same way. When she begins to sort the envelopes she finds they cover a span of two years, from 1915 to 1917, and that there are twenty-seven letters in all.

She is not to know that letters from soldiers overseas were censored by the army and then sent back to Australia in bulk, where they were given to the Comforts Fund by the Post Office to address and send on. Jessica's hands tremble as she opens the first letter and when she sees that it is in Jack's boyish hand, she promptly bursts into tears.

Jessica reads between sobs for an hour and it soon becomes apparent that Jack has not forsaken her and that he always loved her. After reading each letter, Jessica folds it and pushes it back into its envelope and returns it to the larger manila one. She is about to open Jack's last letter when she hears a shout.

'Miss Bergman, we come!' Jessica looks up to see Solly and Moishe Goldberg hurrying down the platform towards her. She brushes away her tears, anxious that they not see she's been crying, that her eyes don't betray her.

Moishe arrives twenty feet ahead of his father. 'We come, Jessie!' He smiles. 'I'm sorry we didn't come to Callan Park. It's Shabbat, we may not ride on the Sabbath.'

Jessica grins, happy that her friends have come to see her off. 'I knew it was a Saturday, that you couldn't come.' She looks up at Moishe, her expression concerned. 'Did you break a Jewish rule to come or something?'

Just then Solly Goldberg arrives, red-faced and puffing and in his usual lather of sweat. He carries the familiar wicker basket, which he now places at his feet. 'Compliments Mrs Goldberg!' he announces breathlessly and then straightens up and spreads his hands to take in Jessica. 'Such wonderful news, you out that place, a miracle from God, no less!'

'Oh, I am so happy we got here in time, Jessie, that we haven't missed you,' Moishe says in a rare display of emotion.

'How did you know? I mean, I didn't even know the train times myself,' Jessica asks.

Moishe grins and shrugs his shoulders. 'You know me, Mr Check-everything-twice-over. I looked up the train timetable and just prayed the nine p.m. train was the right one. It's the only one that leaves overnight for the west and goes all the way to Narrandera. I was going to come anyway, but Sabbath ends at sunset,' he turns to acknowledge Solly Goldberg, 'so my father could also come.'

'For a Communist, a clever boychick,' Solly says happily.

At eight o'clock the conductor appears, looking important in his uniform. By now the platform has become quite crowded and he walks along opening the carriage doors so that the passengers may climb aboard, even though the train's not due to leave for an hour. Moishe climbs aboard and finds a second-class compartment with a seat by a window and Solly Goldberg hands up the 'Compliments Mrs Goldberg' basket. Moishe places it on the seat next to the window, reserving it for Jessica.

'But your beautiful picnic basket?' Jessica cries. 'I won't be able to give it back.'

'Tush!' Solly exclaims. 'A keepsake. Miss Bergman, my dear, we miss you. The boychick and me, also Mrs Goldberg.' He fishes for his bandanna and wipes at the corner of his eye. 'So much we miss you, my dear.'

Jessica looks at Solly and then at Moishe, and tears begin to roll slowly down her cheeks. 'Oh dear, I've cried too much already and now I'm gunna cry again.'

In an attempt to cheer her up Solly Goldberg suddenly declares, 'So now we got a plan.'

Jessica looks up and sniffs. 'A plan?'

'Turkeys!'

Jessica looks over to Moishe for an explanation. 'He wants you to breed turkeys, kosher turkeys for the shop. I told him you had ten acres. You know, like you told me, by the creek?'

Astonished, Jessica turns to Solly Goldberg. 'But how? How will I get them to you?'

Moishe laughs. 'Me again. I've worked out you're only a few miles from the railway line, if you can manage to get the turkeys to Yanco Siding. To be kosher they must arrive alive here in Sydney, so they can be killed by the Shoshet according to the Jewish faith. We've worked out we can make a couple of wood and wire crates for you,' he stretches his arms wide, 'big ones that you can use to send us your turkeys once a week and we'll send back the empty crates. It's only an overnight trip and the experts say that with enough water the turkeys should arrive hale and hearty. I've written to the Hawkesbury Agricultural College for the know-how,' he explains enthusiastically, then adds, 'we'll pay the rail charges, of course.'

'But will it be profitable? I mean, the turkeys comin' all that way?'

Solly Goldberg has remained silent while his son explains the plan to Jessica. Now he says, 'Miss Bergman, you make for me a nice turkey, we make money – we got a nice business.'

'Turkeys, eh?' Jessica muses, not altogether displeased by the notion. 'Joe said turkeys are the dumbest things there is.'

Solly shrugs his shoulders. 'So? We don't tell them what happens, they think maybe they come to make a holiday by the seaside.' He laughs at his own joke, his jowls wobbling in unison with his great belly.

'Mr Goldberg, I owe you and Moishe so much!'

'Owe? Tush, we are your friends. From friends you don't owe.' He looks over at Moishe and then back at Jessica. 'Miss Bergman, you give me back my boychick, it is me who owes you! Believe me, I know what I am saying.'

Moishe kicks one boot with the toe-cap of the other, not looking up. 'He's right, Jessie, without you I'd never have got out of there.'

'Exact!' Solly exclaims. 'Listen to the Communist, he's right, Miss Bergman.'

It is almost time to go and Jessica now enters the carriage and a moment later appears at the window of the compartment. She moves the hamper along the seat, using it to reserve a place for Richard Runche, who has not as yet reappeared. Jessica keeps glancing anxiously towards the platform gate. 'Mr Runche, he's gunna be late,' she finally says, concerned. 'Maybe I should fetch him?'

'Fetch him? Where is he?' Moishe asks.

'In the pub.'

'What, here in the station?'

Jessica nods, a little uncertain. 'I think so.'

'I'll go fetch him,' Moishe volunteers. He has taken several steps towards the platform gate, when he stops and turns. 'How will I recognise him?'

'He's got a mushed-up brown hat and he drinks claret,' Jessica says.

Moishe looks doubtful but turns and continues on his way. 'His name's Runche, like lunch,' Jessica calls after him.

As soon as his son is out of earshot Solly takes two five-pound notes from his pocket. 'Miss Bergman, I want you should buy turkeys.' He hesitates for a moment, then adds, 'For the business.'

'No, I can't take it, Mr Goldberg. I dunno what's waiting for me when I get back – not much I expect,' Jessica protests.

'Take, take, no matter what's waiting a little money can't do no harm.'

But Jessica knows she can't take the money. The stubborn Bergman pride won't let her do it. Sadly Solly seems to sense she won't be persuaded and he puts the notes back in his pocket.

'Miss Bergman, I tell you a story. When I come here from Poland, we all Jews, we come they call it "cattle class" all together below decks on that small ship. Believe me, it's not so good. I got no money, nothing, not even two shillings. I'm a butcher by trade, I got a set knives. Beautiful knives. Without that knives, you understand, I got no trade. I don't speak English, only Yiddish and German and maybe some Hebrew for *shul*.

'A friend, a Jew, he tells me, "Come, Solomon, I take

you to the abattoirs on Glebe Island, they got jobs."
But the shop steward of the union say, "Sorry, you got
no English, no job, mate." We go to the boss. I say to
my friend, "Tell this boss, he show me a carcass, I show
him I can do this job good, I don't need English to cut
meat."

'The boss he say, "Righto, Jewboy," and he give me
a pig.' Solly Goldberg smiles and shrugs his shoulders.
'What can I do? I can't cut up for him this pig, I'm a
Jew. "A cow," I say to my friend, "ask him a cow or
a sheep."

' "Jew!" that boss say. "If you don't cut a pig no
work for you. It's home on the pig's back here, mate!"
All the men they are laughing. A big joke, the Jew don't
cut a pig. Then when we leaving some of them, some of
those men they come. "Bloody Jewboy, you want to
take our jobs, eh?" They beat me and my friend, also
they steal my knives. "Teach you a bloody lesson,
Jew!"

' "We go to the police," my friend says.

' "The police? What for? You *meshugganah*!" I say.
"You think the police they will do something?"

' "They got here fair go," he say.

' "Fair go?" I don't know what is this "fair go".
I know only in Poland a poor Jew don't go to the
police. So we go to that police station, but my friend is
wrong, they ain't got no "fair go". The sergeant he say
to my friend, "Tell your friend this is union business,
not police business." '

Solly looks at Jessica and spreads his hands. 'What

can I do?' He laughs suddenly. 'In the cell in this police station we can see is a man standing. He is listening to my friend. We go to leave. "Hey, mate!" he shouts, this man. "You! Jewboy! C'me 'ere!" Jew is already a word I understand good in English. I look him, this man.' Solly makes a beckoning motion with his right hand, ' "C'me 'ere," he says. "Come 'ere, Jew." My friend and me we look first the sergeant, then we go to the man. The man he asks the sergeant some paper and pencil. Then he write something, I don't know what it is. He fold the paper and he say, "Fair go, mate. Give this to Bill O'Grady at the abattoir." '

Solly Goldberg laughs, fingering his fat nose. 'My nose they have breaking, my side they kick, my lip is cut and my teeth is bleeding inside my mouth. What is this "fair go"? Why we go back that place? That abattoir *kish mit in hinten*, I say to my friend.'

Jessica laughs. 'That abattoir can kiss my bum,' she translates, remembering.

Solly smiles, delighted that Jessica has remembered, then he continues. ' "We got fair go," my friend says. So, we go back the abattoir and ask they call please Mr Bill O'Grady. He come outside. "Don't youse bastards know when yer beaten?" he says. I give him the paper. He reads and shakes his head. Then he throws down the paper on the floor. "Shit, wait on," he says. He go back inside the abattoir. I pick up the paper on the floor. He comes back, maybe two, three minutes, he's got my leather bag, inside is my knives. "Garn, piss off!" he say. "We don't want no Jews and dagoes workin' here on the Island." '

Solly Goldberg takes out a battered wallet and from it he removes a piece of yellowing paper and hands it to Jessica. She unfolds it carefully and can barely make out the words in faded pencil.

Fair go, mate, give the Jewboy back his tools.
                                          Johnny Murphy.

Jessica smiles, nodding her head, and hands the note back to Solly, who now says, 'Soon I am getting work also. From cutting chickens! To cut a chicken is not so important, but my life, it begins already again. I marry one day Mrs Goldberg, we got the boychick, we got the kosher butcher shop.' Solly spreads his hands again. 'What can I say? God is good.' Then he takes the two five-pound notes out of his pocket and offers them to Jessica again. 'Miss Bergman, now you got "fair go" also. Today I pay back Mr Johnny Murphy.'

Jessica's hands shake as she takes the two fivers and stuffs them into the envelope with Jack's letters. Then she leans out of the carriage window and kisses Solly. 'I love you so, Mr Goldberg.'

Solly rubs his cheek where Jessica has kissed him, a rueful smile on his great melon-face. 'Maybe also you can do me a big favour, Miss Bergman,' he says shyly. 'Maybe, now we do business, you can call me Solly?'

'And you call me Jessie,' Jessica whispers, her eyes brimming again.

'We got a business, Jessie,' Solly says, smiling hugely, then he extends his great bear paw. Jessie takes it into her own small hand and they shake, business partners no less.

'I won't let yiz down, Solly. I swear it.'

There is a shrill blast from the conductor's whistle. 'All aboard what's goin' aboard!' he shouts and blows his whistle again. Jessica looks anxiously at the platform gate, just in time to see Moishe with his arm around Richard Runche KC who, from the way he appears to be leaning on the young man for support, is somewhat the worse for wear. Moishe holds the barrister's battered suitcase in his free hand and is trying to run, though Runche's legs flop like a rag doll's, two steps behind and seemingly only barely able to connect with the surface of the platform. In the lawyer's coat pocket, bobbing dangerously up and down, is a bottle of claret.

Jessica gasps, holding her hand to her mouth as Moishe staggers to the carriage, dropping the suitcase at Solly's feet as he passes. The train starts to move away and Moishe hardly has time to open the carriage door and push the top part of his burden onto the train. He begins to run alongside the departing train, feeding the remaining half of the barrister piecemeal onto the carriage. Finally, some twenty yards down the platform, Moishe manages to get Runche's feet onto the train and to shut the carriage door.

Jessica, stuck at the carriage window and unable to go to Moishe's immediate aid, is trying hard not to laugh.

Meanwhile, Solly has picked up the lawyer's suitcase and handed it to Jessica. Then, as if he has suddenly remembered something, he starts to dig frantically into his jacket pockets, attempting at the same time to keep up with the moving train. At last he finds what he is looking for and he thrusts a piece of folded paper at Jessica. 'Compliments Mrs Goldberg,' he shouts, 'take quick, Jessie!'

Jessica reaches out of the compartment window and takes the piece of paper from Solly and absently thrusts it into the manila envelope. 'Goodbye, Moishe!' she shouts. 'Goodbye, Solly, I love you both!'

Moishe looks up, panting furiously. He lifts one hand from his knee and waves weakly, unable to speak, while Solly has his hands on his hips, also trying to catch his breath.

Jessica watches into the fading light until they appear as two tiny figures on the brightly lit platform, the one round as a ball and the other thin as a school pencil.

The train takes a slight bend in the maze of criss-crossing silver tracks leading out of Central Station and the Goldbergs are finally lost to her sight. Jessica gets up to help her drunken travelling companion to his feet and safely into the compartment.

The train is well into the night and a million stars are pinned to the blanket of darkness as Jessica watches out of the compartment window. Richard Runche is slumped asleep beside her, though thankfully not snoring.

He has woken several times for a few moments and each time he's looked blearily at Jessica and touched his battered derby. 'Unconscionable, my dear, must apologise, shocking, shocking,' he mumbles, reaching for the bottle in his jacket pocket, uncorking it clumsily and taking a long swig. 'Hair of the dog, m'dear,' he says.

Re-corking the bottle, he replaces it into his jacket pocket and, almost immediately, slips back into a drunken slumber.

The carriage is in darkness and the other four passengers are attempting to sleep, so that Jessica is unable to read the final letter from Jack. She has her feet placed on the 'Compliments Mrs Goldberg' basket, which has been moved to the floor, but decides she should wait until breakfast before opening it, hoping to share its contents with her badly hungover companion.

The light from the passageway falls across the lawyer's face and Jessica looks at him kindly. He was true to his word and, after visiting Jessica in the asylum that day, he set out to find Mary Simpson, finally locating her in an Aboriginal camp near Yanco. Mary took him to the tin hut where, just as Jessica had said, they found the tiny Chinese silk dress under the straw mattress – the dress the aunties had given Jessica for her baby. After talking to Mary, who fully corroborated what Jessica had told him, Richard Runche KC was soon convinced that Jessica's story was true in every aspect and that Meg's so-called son – Joseph 'Joey' Thomas, the heir to Riverview Station – is indeed Jessica's child.

However, Runche was too much of a realist to believe that he could win the child back for its true mother in a court of law. The Chinese dress was, at best, circumstantial evidence and could easily enough be construed as yet another example of Jessica's delusions. The word of an Aboriginal woman who claimed to have been present shortly after the birth of the child would not be taken against that of Hester Bergman and her daughter, Meg Thomas.

Furthermore, he told himself, even if he did make a reasonable case for the child, a judge, deciding in the final sense what was advantageous for the boy, would be unlikely to give custody to the true mother.

Joseph 'Joey' Thomas, the judge would conclude, is likely to enjoy every possible advantage as the child of Meg Thomas and little or none under the care of Jessica, a woman who had just spent a period of nearly four years in a mental asylum.

The barrister decided he had only one thing going for him. He had to confront Hester and Meg and threaten them with the prospect of a claim on the property by George Thomas and any other family members he might be able to dig up. He'd tell the two women outright that he would inform the Thomas relatives that a serious doubt existed as to the true parentage of the child, that Jack's son and heir was not from his own loins. Furthermore, he'd say that he has reliable witnesses who are prepared to testify to this fact and that in his experience, the news of a fortune to be divided would bring the familial wolves howling to the door.

However, this meant that, in return for what concessions he could wring from Meg Thomas for Jessica, she in turn must give up all claims to her child. Richard Runche KC reasoned that, harsh as this outcome might seem, it was a better solution than leaving his client to rot in an asylum where she'd have no hope of being reunited with her child anyway.

And so he rides out to Riverview Station on his hired horse to confront Meg and Hester. He had spent the past three nights in Jessica's hut and he looks even more derelict than usual. He sets out after a breakfast of half a bottle of claret and a tin of sardines and arrives at the Thomas homestead around mid-morning.

It is Hester who first comes to the door. She takes one look at the forlorn-looking little man standing in front of her and it is obvious she doesn't much like what she sees.

'If you want work, see the foreman at the office. If you want something to eat, go round the back and ask the cook,' she instructs bluntly, beginning to turn away.

Richard Runche raises his battered derby. 'Ah, a moment please, madam?' Hester turns haughtily. 'You must be Mrs Bergman, Mrs Hester Bergman?'

Hester looks surprised. 'Yes?' she replies, her voice a little more cautious as she notes Runche's cultured tone.

'How do you do, madam? May I introduce myself? Richard Runche. You may well have heard of me?'

'I really don't think so, Mr Runche,' Hester sniffs.

'I met your youngest daughter Jessica at the William D'arcy Simon trial.'

'Who?'

'Oh yes, how careless of me. You would probably know him locally by the sobriquet Billy Simple. I was the counsel for the poor lad's defence.'

'Fat lot of good you did him,' Hester snorts, her

confidence now fully restored. Joe had told her about the drunken barrister Jessie had been to see on the idiot's behalf. 'If you want my daughter Jessie, she doesn't live here, she's in Sydney.'

'Well, yes, I am aware of that. I have come to see your other daughter, Mrs Meg Thomas. Is she in?' Runche now asks brightly, ignoring Hester's snub.

Just then Meg comes to the door. 'Who is it, Mother?'

'This is William D'arcy Simon's lawyer,' Hester says tartly.

'Who?'

'Billy Simple, madam. May I introduce myself? My name is Runche – Richard Runche.'

Meg smiles inwardly. She recalls the name, not only from Jessica and Joe, but from the newspapers reporting the trial which had, on several occasions, mentioned the notorious Liquid Lunch, the incompetent barrister in charge of Billy Simple's defence.

'How do you do, Mr Runche,' Meg replies, glancing knowingly at Hester.

'Do you think I might come in? I've taken the liberty of giving my horse to your stable boy to mind.'

Meg nods and she and Hester step aside to let Richard Runche pass through to the large, cool enclosed verandah which contains a wicker setting, four chairs and a small table. A large marmalade cat is asleep on one of the chairs. Richard Runche removes his hat and looks about him. He indicates the chairs. 'Shall we sit here?' he asks.

'Mother, could you ask Martha to bring us some tea,' Meg says. 'Yes, sit down, Mr Lunch.'

514 B R Y C E   C O U R T E N A Y

'Runche. Ah, tea, yes, how jolly,' the lawyer cries. Settling himself into the chair next to the cat, he reaches over and strokes the back of the animal's ear. 'Ah, a marmalade cat, quite the best ratters.'

Both women ignore the remark and Hester turns to her daughter. 'Meg, wait until I return,' she commands.

Meg looks annoyed. 'Mother, I'm quite capable of . . .'

'Oh, yes, we shall wait, I'd like to talk to both of you,' Richard Runche says, smiling at a grim-faced Hester.

When Martha, a fresh-faced country girl, brings the tea and a plate of biscuits Hester pours a cup for each of them. Handing a cup to Meg and Runche, she takes up her own and sits back, resting her cup and saucer comfortably on her lap. She tries to look unconcerned. 'Well then, Mr Runche, what is it you wish to see my daughter about?'

'Both of you, really. I'd like to talk with you about the boy Joseph "Joey" Thomas.'

The barrister can see the sudden anxiety in the eyes of both women and Hester hurriedly places her cup and saucer on the wicker table.

'And what about the boy?' she asks sharply.

Runche deliberately ignores her and turns to Meg. 'There is some doubt that the boy is your legitimate son, Mrs Thomas. I need to talk with you.'

Hester rises from her chair. 'I think you should leave, Mr Runche.' She points to the door. 'Right now!'

'I don't think that would be in your daughter's ultimate interest, madam,' Runche says softly, not in the least intimidated by Hester's imperious command.

'Just who do you think you are, barging in on us like this without so much as a by-your-leave and making these horrible claims?' Hester shouts again.

'Calm down, Mother,' Meg says in a surprisingly composed voice. She turns back to the lawyer. 'What are you trying to say, Mr Runche?'

Richard Runche KC looks surprised. 'Why, I'm not sure I can put it any more precisely than I just have, madam.' He pauses and looks at Hester, then back to Meg. 'Do you wish me to repeat what I have just said?'

'Take no notice, Meg, the man's quite mad. I'll call two of the boys from the stable.'

'You've seen Jessie, haven't you?' Meg says, still ignoring her mother.

'Yes, that I have,' Runche agrees.

'And you know she's . . . she's in the lunatic asylum?'

'In Callan Park, yes.'

'Well, that's why. She has delusions – she *thinks* I've stolen her baby.'

'Oh, but you *have*, my dear,' Richard Runche replies, smiling.

'He's mad! Look at him, he's a mess. Are you trying to threaten us, Mr Runche?' Hester shouts. 'Because if you are, you're going to be very, very sorry you ever came snooping around here!'

'Mother, do sit down!' Meg cries. She turns to Richard Runche. 'Mr Runche, I don't think you quite understand – my sister is insane. She's been committed!'

'Ah, glad you brought that up.' Richard Runche

turns to Hester. 'I believe it was you, Mrs Bergman, who signed the committal papers?'

'I had no choice, she attacked me.'

'She?'

'Jessica.'

'And why would Jessica do that?'

'She was hysterical, she said . . . I mean, she deluded herself that Meg had stolen her child.'

'Ah, there we are, right back to the very reason why I've come to see you and your daughter, madam.'

Meg's bottom lip suddenly starts to quiver. 'Can you imagine how sad that makes us, Mr Runche? Joey is my child, I love him more dearly than my life. Oh, how very much I wish I could share him with Jessie, with his auntie,' she sobs softly.

Hester is suddenly aware that she's not taken Richard Runche seriously enough and that Meg sees the threat posed by the dirty man in front of them much more clearly than she has. She curses herself inwardly for having lost her touch. Meg, so far, is handling the situation far better than she. Hester resumes her seat and silently takes up her cup of tea.

'Ah, I'm so glad you feel this way about your sister, Mrs Thomas. I believe she has written to you both on several occasions – seven to be precise – to beg you to agree to her release. You did not respond to any of those letters. Why is that?'

'I imagine that should be obvious,' Hester says, her voice now greatly mollified. 'We were naturally afraid she might harm the child, harm Meg's baby.'

'I believe she told you in the letters that she would first have to be declared sane by three separate doctors, experts. And that only after they had all agreed did she need your permission and custodial care for a period of six months. Doesn't that suggest that the baby would have been quite safe?'

'Yes, well, Mother and I agreed we couldn't take the chance,' Meg sniffs tearfully.

'The doctors might be wrong,' Hester says, then bites her lip, knowing what Runche will say next.

'Doctors wrong? Three separate doctors? Experts in their field? Does it not occur to you that the *one* doctor who Jessica told you examined her in the first place might have been wrong?' He looks at Hester. 'Yet you were perfectly willing to allow *him* to commit her, to sign the papers involved, despite the fact that Jessica told you in her letters that he'd been drinking and was clearly overworked. One drunken, overworked doctor is right to commit Jessica but three sober experts may be wrong? Is that it?

'You never once inquired after Jessica's welfare, in fact you made no attempt whatsoever to contact her. You were quite happy to allow her to rot forever in that ghastly place. Is this really the act of a loving mother and a caring sister who laments the absence of a kind and loving aunt for the baby she claims as her own?'

Hester's tea cup rattles as she places it down on the table again. 'I think you've said quite enough, Mr Runche. We shall contact our own lawyer.' She raises one eyebrow slightly. 'Perhaps you know of Major-

General Septimus Cunningham-Thomas, who is also a noted Sydney barrister?'

Richard Runche leans back and chuckles. 'A fine advocate, madam. None better in both war and peace. Perhaps we can show him this?' The barrister puts his hand into his jacket pocket and withdraws the little Chinese silk baby dress.

Both women give an involuntary gasp. 'Ah, you've seen it before. Pretty little dress, isn't it? Mary Simpson liked it when she gave it to Jessica for her child. I believe some sixteen of what she refers to as "aunties" went shopping for this little dress.'

'So?' Meg turns to Hester. 'Mother and I have never seen that dress.'

'All the better, my dear. The testimony from Mary Simpson and her aunties will then bear out the truth that, *unbeknownst* to you, the dress was bought for Jessica's baby.'

'They're blacks, the court would take no notice, not against the word of two white women,' Hester snorts. 'It's their word against ours.'

'A very sound point, Mrs Bergman. I admit, the courts are somewhat biased against our indigenous people.' He pauses. 'But I don't think Mr George Thomas, your late husband's father, will see it quite your way. And I dare say there will be others. There is nothing like a questionable will attached to a large inheritance to bring relatives out of the woodwork. In my experience, where money is concerned, families have a nasty habit of . . . well, turning thoroughly horrid to each other.'

'You don't know what was in Jack's will, Mr Runche.'

'Oh, but I do, madam. The will has been published for probate. I am aware that a great deal of money and property is held in trust for the son of the late Jack Thomas. I imagine your late husband's uncle, Major-General Septimus Cunningham-Thomas, will be a very interested party should it be suggested that Joseph "Joey" Thomas is not legitimately his nephew's son. What do you think?'

Meg suddenly rises and brings her hands up to her face and flees from the verandah sobbing, leaving Hester with Richard Runche. Meg's previous confidence has dissolved and she has reverted to her old panicky self. Hester is back in control, though now she is more cautious with the scruffy man seated in the wicker chair, nibbling on an oatmeal biscuit.

'What is it you want, Mr Runche?' she asks.

'A very sensible question, Mrs Bergman, and the answer may well be less than you might suppose.'

'I must warn you, Mr Runche, that we will fight for my daughter's child, if it costs us every penny we've got.' Hester can't help herself and she realises once again that she has overstepped the mark with this sharp man, who seems to know what she is thinking.

'Well then we are agreed, madam. I too shall fight for your daughter Jessica's child with all the sensibility at my command.' He pauses and his voice grows hard. 'Unless we stop this nonsense.' He shrugs and then in a perfectly modulated voice says, 'Please, madam, no more empty threats. I think we should sit down and talk sensibly, don't you?'

'Mr Runche, Joey is the light of our lives. Please, I beg you, if some terrible miscarriage of justice should take place and you are skilful enough to take Meg's precious child from her, how do you imagine the boy will fare in Jessica's care? Do you for one moment think she can give him the advantages he will enjoy as my eldest daughter's rightful child?'

'Mrs Bergman, I am a bachelor, but I do know that Jessica is a young woman of outstanding character. She would love her child and care for it with all her heart and soul. While the boy may not enjoy the privileges your daughter Meg may bestow on him, I do have some experience of a privileged upbringing without love and I can tell you that a mother's love is a fortune far greater than any other. Do not for one moment suppose that Jessica would disadvantage the boy in this regard.'

'Yes, well, we shall never find out,' Hester says crisply. 'He is not her child and we have a birth certificate to prove it.'

'Oh dear, I see that you persist, madam. And I have a little silk dress and the evidence of seventeen people.'

'Aboriginals, itinerant blacks,' Hester snaps.

Richard Runche KC smiles and in a soft, reasonable voice says, 'Well, let me tell you how I might go about the case, Mrs Bergman. That is, of course, if the Thomas family don't pre-empt me, with Uncle Septimus and your daughter's late husband's father, George Thomas, leading the charge.

'I will attempt, of course, to present all the salient facts, much as I have done to you today. I will go about discrediting your character and that of your eldest daughter. We have seen from your response to Jessica's seven letters how easy this might be to do.'

'Oh, but we shall deny that we ever received any letters,' Hester says smugly.

'Then you are unaware that it is standard practice for a copy to be made of every letter sent from a lunatic asylum?' the lawyer lies. Pausing meaningfully, he then continues, 'I am sure we will find other instances as well, all of which indicate a cruel indifference to your younger daughter's suffering.' He now holds up the little silk dress. 'I would use this and the evidence of the aunties and of Mary Simpson.'

'It's all hearsay,' Hester interjects. 'Sticks and stones . . .'

'Ah, sticks and stones may break my bones, but words can never harm me,' Runche says, completing the childish quote. 'You are a clever and determined woman, Mrs Bergman, but there's one thing you can't do, and it has indeed got something to do with bones. In the hands of any competent physician it can be quite easily determined whether a woman has given birth to a child or not. The physiological differences to the opening of the womb and the size of the pelvis, the cervix and . . . er, other parts of the female anatomy, are readily apparent between women who have given birth and those who have not. I would, of course, obtain a court order, then choose *three* eminent surgeons, not one drunken and overworked one, to examine Mrs Thomas and Jessica and then to give the court their findings. Do you understand what I am saying?'

Hester is silent for some time, then she looks up. 'As you can see, Mr Runche, my daughter Meg is a woman of a most nervous disposition. The effects of such an examination – though I have no doubt they would prove our case – would, I believe, do her a great deal of harm. Perhaps we may discuss how such an examination might be avoided?'

'Very sensible, Mrs Bergman. Very sensible indeed. Let us begin with the business of getting Jessica out of Callan Park and, furthermore, how we might provide for her in the future.'

'Mr Runche, do you give me your solemn word that you will not attempt to take the child away from my daughter Meg?'

'My word? Certainly. I shall *also* try to persuade your younger daughter not to seek litigation. All I can say, madam, is that I would personally not help her in this endeavour. Perhaps, if you are generous in your settlement, I may be able to get Jessica to agree to sign an agreement to this effect. Though she can be very stubborn, as I imagine you know.'

'And you must also ensure that, with any arrangement we might conclude, there is no suggestion that Joey has ever had any mother other than my daughter Meg. We will not allow his name to appear in any agreement and possibly at some future time become the subject of rumour or speculation.'

'I can do that, certainly, Mrs Bergman,' Richard Runche replies, 'but I must point out that it is not in your interest. I cannot frame a clause protecting you unless I stipulate what it is you are protected against. In this case, the concession you require is that your daughter Jessica does not take legal action against you to attempt to regain possession of her child.'

'Not her child! Meg's child!' Hester snaps.

'So, now we see the problem, don't we?' Richard Runche KC explains. 'The child is disputed.'

'What will you do, then? We simply *must* have such an agreement. The boy's name mustn't appear.'

'Ah, we will refer to the lad as "the child in question".'

'The child in question?'

'That's right, Mrs Bergman, that way there is no suggestion of whose child it may be.' The lawyer pauses. The roof of his mouth and his tongue are bone-dry and he badly needs a drink. 'It's the only way I can think to phrase it so that it would be acceptable to Jessica. Though perhaps you'd like to engage Mr Cunningham-Thomas, who may find another solution to protect your interests?'

'No, that seems in order,' Hester says, not looking at Runche. Then she adds fiercely, 'And Jessica must never be allowed to see the child.'

'What do you mean by that – she is not allowed access to the boy?'

'Exactly. We don't want her mooning about, demanding to see him.'

'Oh? Do I not recall Mrs Thomas lamenting that . . .

let me see, what were her words? Ah yes. "How very much I wish I could share him with Jessie, with his auntie," wasn't that how she put it?'

'Yes, well, we can't have it. I've . . . Meg's put her foot down about that.'

'Very well then, Mrs Bergman, let us proceed with the documentation. I shall, of course, require Mrs Thomas's signature and so I think perhaps she ought to be here too, don't you?'

It is mid-afternoon, and many further cups of tea and corned beef sandwiches later, before Richard Runche KC completes the documentation and obtains the signatures needed to free Jessica.

He has wrung several concessions out of Meg, including the deed to 'Warralang', ten acres of freehold land, which comprises two allotments on either side of Yanco Creek and encompasses the boundary rider's hut where Jessica gave birth to Joey. In addition, she will be granted the permanent use of the old Bergman homestead for the remainder of her life, or, if it is sold or pulled down as no longer habitable, she will be entitled to a similar domicile anywhere she chooses to have it erected.

Hester points out that the Bergman homestead is two miles from what will become Jessica's land.

'A short ride away. It is, after all, her family home,' Richard Runche argues.

Jessica will be granted a yearly income of one hundred pounds sterling until her death. In addition, she will receive a horse and new saddle every five years, a pony and cart and, as further livestock, immediate allocation of a dozen brood hens and two roosters. She is entitled to a dog from a pedigree kelpie kennel, a small-bore rifle and a shotgun with one hundred rounds for each every year, plus three hundred yards of fine rabbit-proof fencing and such farming tools as she might require up to a cost of seventy-five pounds and a further twenty pounds for the same purpose each year.

Meg Thomas agrees to undertake to engage the services of Richard Runche KC at the normal *per diem* rate of a Sydney barrister in order to conduct Jessica's release from Callan Park. Finally, both Hester and Meg will agree to her release and will sign her probationary papers and implement the probationary conditions they require.

'She will not want to stay with us,' Meg now suggests.

'She will not have to, your old home is provided. You will simply sign the documentation,' Richard Runche says. He is also at pains to point out that, of course, if any one of the three examining physicians should find Jessica to be insane then she will have to remain at Callan Park. But if not, she will be paid a bonus of one hundred pounds for every year she has been 'mistakenly' incarcerated.

In return for agreeing to all of these conditions, Runche explains that Jessica will undertake not to attempt to make any claim in a court of law concerning the parenthood of 'the child in question'. She will effectively not be able to see the child and will allow Meg the undisputed claim to be the natural mother of Joseph

'Joey' Thomas, born on Christmas Day in the year of Our Lord, 1914.

It is the best deal Richard Runche believes he can make under the circumstances. He comes away from Riverview Station not knowing if he can persuade Jessica that she has almost no hope of ever regaining her child. If she refuses to sign the agreement, the alternative is the likelihood that she will spend the remainder of her life incarcerated behind the high stone walls of a lunatic asylum.

On the train to Narrandera, Jessica sleeps fitfully, more wakeful than asleep. She has sold out her child for her own freedom and she must now convince herself that it is in Joey's best interests. Her child, living as her sister Meg's, will enjoy every advantage, and Meg will love and cherish him the way Jessica herself would have done. For nearly two weeks she wrestled with the decision, resisting the barrister's arguments. She couldn't deny that they were sensible but the prospect of losing her child forever nearly destroyed her and several times she made the decision to remain where she was rather than betray Joey in her heart. Jessica cries herself to sleep every night for the month it takes Richard Runche KC to put her case for release to the authorities.

It is Solly Goldberg who comes to her rescue. He visits the asylum for their monthly picnic and finds Jessica in a terribly distressed state. When he asks her what is wrong, Jessica finds herself, for the first time, unable to confide in her friend.

Solly Goldberg remains silent for a long time, then he sighs and begins to talk softly. 'Sometimes, Miss Bergman, we cry. That is good, to cry is good. Sometimes we laugh, and that is better, to laugh is wonderful. Sometimes also we are silent, to be silent is necessary, my dear. But mostly we talk. To talk is to be a human. To be a proper person. To share our *tsuris*, our troubles, all what is our pain. If we don't talk, if we keep the pain inside, we die a little – every day we die a little, until one day the pain is gone. You know why goes the pain, Miss Bergman? I tell you. With the pain goes also the tears and the laughter. When we have no pain we lose everything, only the silence remains. When there is only silence, then you are finish, *kaput*. That is what it means to be mad.' He reaches out and puts his hand on Jessica's shoulder. 'We Jews, we have a saying, "To live and talk is the best revenge."'

Jessica starts to cry and Solly Goldberg moves over and takes her in his arms, rocking her. 'Talk, my dear, tell your Uncle Solly.' So Jessica tells him how she has been forced to give up her child in return for her own freedom.

Richard Runche KC has spent the whole month securing Jessica's release. It's a process that would normally have taken a great deal longer if it were not for the fact that Jessica had never received her second examination by the Medical Supervisor and, furthermore, that the war is all but over and there are a great many disturbed soldier-patients on their way home, needing hospitalisation.

The barrister successfully argues that Jessica did not

undergo the correct admission procedure, which means that she does not require the individual examinations by three physicians to secure her release. Only the completion of the original and neglected examination by the Medical Supervisor is needed.

At the conclusion of Jessica's examination the Medical Supervisor remarks, 'I only wish that my own daughter was as level-headed, sensible and sane as you are, Miss Bergman. I wish you well.' Then, in what can only be construed as an understatement of astronomical proportions, he adds, 'I apologise for any inconvenience to you.'

As Jessica has no history of delusions, hallucinations, delirium, stupor, violence, hysterics, depression, suicidal tendencies or any other mental symptoms, and no record of anything but the most minor punishments while at Callan Park, her release becomes a mere formality, held up only by the usual government red tape.

Jessica finally signs the agreement with Meg, though she's refused to accept any money from her sister. 'They can't buy me off! No flamin' way! The horse and chooks and the tools and things, that's fair enough, Joe would've left those for me. But I'm not takin' their thirty pieces of silver! I can make me own way – I don't need their money.'

Richard Runche KC tries to argue with her, but he is becoming accustomed to the Bergman stubbornness. Finally he is forced to capitulate. 'Very well, my dear. Pity though, it would buy an awful lot of claret,' he jokes, then adds, 'I assure you I shall have no such crisis of conscience with my fee to your sister, my dear.'

Jessica embraces him. He smells a bit like overripe cheese, stale tobacco and spilt wine all mixed together, though she's smelled worse in the shearing shed. 'I can't never repay you, Mr Runche. I owe you me freedom, me life!'

'You have shown yourself to be a very courageous young woman, Jessica. That is sufficient payment. Besides, I haven't found the necessity to be properly drunk for nearly six weeks.'

'You done it all,' Jessica persists. 'Without you I'd never have got out. You knew I couldn't pay – you done it out of the goodness of your heart.'

Richard Runche KC throws back his head and laughs heartily. 'Steady on, old girl. In the interests of the truth, I must remind you that it has been several years since I have been as well paid in return for my humble services.'

Now in the pale dawn light on the train, Jessica watches Richard Runche KC as he sleeps. She ponders how it is that the only people who have helped her in the nearly five years since she'd taken Billy Simple into captivity have been loners, outcasts like herself. A skinny-legged Aboriginal lady, her dear, sweet, loving Mary Simpson; a kosher butcher, his Communist son and his generous-hearted, invisible wife. And a drunken English lawyer, the black sheep of his family sent out to the colonies to get him out of the way.

Jessica reaches over and touches the sleeping barrister lightly. 'Thanks, mate,' she whispers. Then she thinks how he could use a damn good scrub in the tub next to the windlass. Jessica tries to imagine the barrister with his clothes off, the way she'd once seen Billy Simple standing in the tub, and she is forced to giggle even before her imagination has his trousers below his knees.

Jessica waits until it's light enough to read and she takes out Jack's last letter and opens it carefully, determined that she won't cry.

> Sgt Jack Thomas
> New South Wales Light Horse
> El Arish
> Northern Sinai Desert
> Egypt
>
> 22 December 1916

My darling Jessica,

I get your letters every month and I don't know what I should do without them. They are of the greatest comfort to me and are always cheerful. But, as I have said before, you never mention whether you've received mine.

I cannot help feeling that you have been terribly wronged. Something dreadful has happened to put you in that place, why will you not tell me?

I dare not mention my concern for you to your sister Meg. She sends me letters every month about the antics of young Joey, who seems to be growing into a fine young lad. But she never writes of you, despite the fact that in every letter to her I beg her to send you my best wishes and I ask after your welfare.

I find it difficult to think that I have a son to Meg, when it is you I love. Oh, Jessie, I worry so much that it may have been what happened with me and Meg that has put you into that dreadful place. If so, I shall never forgive myself, and when I return I will use every influence I can to get you out.

I think of you every day my dear, sweet Tea Leaf. In the morning first thing and last thing at night. And, if I have a few moments to myself during the day, thoughts of you occupy them as well.

I know I have said all this before in my other letters and I shouldn't go on like this. It is coming up to Christmas and we'll have 24 hours' leave if the bloody Turks don't decide to send us their Christmas greetings via mortar shell.

El Arish is no place to spend Christmas Day. The town seems to have a mangy, starving dog for every one of its inhabitants, who also seem to closely resemble their dogs in appearance and in nature. The Gyppos are a poor lot – both physical and otherwise – and natural thieves and cowards, quite different to the Turks.

I am writing this by lantern light in my tent and the moon outside is the tiniest crescent, merely a silver sliver in a star-pricked sky (that's me going all poetical). It's surprising how dark it can get in the desert and yet, with a full moon, how light. So light that if it were a full moon tonight I would be sitting writing this letter outside, enjoying the breeze that comes up around eight o'clock. Can you remember? The moon is sometimes bright like it is on a summer night at home. 'You can read a newspaper by its light,' folk would always say, though I never saw anyone who did.

The dark nights here are the worst because they are used by the Turk to move up into position for an attack, or we do the same to them. We're moving out tonight, just before midnight (2300 hrs), to take up positions outside a heavily fortified Arab village called Magdhaba. We are going in under cover of darkness, to give them hell at first light. We are the Aussies who form the 1st Australian Light Horse Brigade led by Major-General Harry Chauvel, a good enough bloke and trusted by the men.

So don't worry, I shall probably come to no harm as usual. Desert warfare is a lot to do about nothing much. We ride for long stretches and it's terribly hot and we seldom get a potshot at the enemy, nor him at us, thank God!

Tomorrow, though, it may be different, as we are attacking a well-held Turk position, so I reckon they'll stand and fight. Johnny Turk is no coward and you have to respect him in a stand-up stoush.

Jessie, I've never said this before, but I've been out here two years and sometimes I get a bit jumpy. If something should happen to me I want you to know that I love you. I want you to have my gold watch and chain. I've left instructions with my troop commander to send it to the post office at Narrandera with orders to them to keep the package there until you, <u>and only you</u>, should claim it.

I don't want it sent to where you are now, in case you don't receive my letters. Someone will come and see you in Sydney and tell you about it, just in case you don't get this letter and are still in that awful place.

The watch is a family heirloom and all I've got that's personal, a part of me, so I want you to have it, you know, in case something happens. Inside is the date it was made, 1816, exactly one hundred years ago. The gold chain and fob was given to my great-grandfather by the Lord Mayor of Cardiff in 1819 for something or other, I forget what, probably not for bravery!

I'm sorry about all this morbid stuff – it's the desert, it gets under your skin after a while. I'll probably cheer up over Christmas with a few beers under my belt. Though they'll most likely be warm, only the officers get ice.

I know this will be much too late for Christmas, but I shall spend the entire day thinking about you. Look after yourself and if you're still there when the war is over, me and some of my mates will break down the walls and rescue you.

I love you, Tea Leaf, with all my heart, and will be thinking of you as we go into battle.
Jack.

P.S. They've gone and made me a sergeant – they must be scraping the barrel! J.

Jessica, still holding Jack's last letter to her breast, watches the morning light grow stronger through her tears. The countryside rushing by outside her compartment window is beginning to look familiar. It's flat now, black soil country, her country, the old man saltbush dark in the still uncertain light. This is the hard land Jack will never return to, the sheep country he so loved.

She sighs and brushes away her tears, then folds Jack's letter carefully and slips it into its envelope and then back into the bigger one. In doing so, Jessica sees the edge of the note Solly Goldberg handed to her just as the train was departing from Central. She fishes it out and opens it and sees that it is a consignment note from the New South Wales Railways.

For delivery to Yanco Siding, Riverina
on 7 December 1918.
One only granite headstone,
straw-packed in wooden packing case.
To await collection by
Miss Jessica Bergman.

Richard Runche KC wants to see Jessica as far as Narrandera but she has insisted he leave her at Wagga Wagga.
She has written to Auntie Dolly Heathwood, who replied
with a cheerful letter, inviting her to stay as long as she
wishes. She informs Jessica that old Henry Heathwood
finally fell out of his chair under the grapevine and died
of a stroke and says she would very much enjoy Jessica's
company as, for some reason or other, Hester and Meg
never call in when they are in town. Dolly also hopes that
now that the war is over, she can obtain some bright ribbon and braid to make a few cheerful hats. 'How tired
I am of black straw hats!' she writes.

Jessica plans to stay only long enough to buy the horse
and saddle promised to her in Meg's agreement and to
order the hens, two cockerels and some farm tools. She
will also inquire about the availability of turkeys. With
this done, she's anxious to get out of town. She craves
the isolation of the bush and wants only to return to the
Bergman homestead, which, Richard Runche informs
her, has stood empty ever since Hester and Meg left to
take up residence at Riverview.

Moishe, unbeknownst to Jessica, has also written to
the Narrandera Town Library and arranged for books
to be sent to Yanco Siding every month for Jessica to
collect. He has also sent a postal order to cover the cost
of sending them up the line, plus a donation to the
library to sweeten the arrangement.

Under Moishe's gentle tutelage, books have become
an important part of Jessica's life and reading regularly
is the one thing she knows she will greatly miss.

It is now fully light outside and the other passengers are beginning to stir. The conductor passes shouting, 'Wakey, wakey! Next stop Wagga Wagga, one hour to go, half an hour stop!'

Jessica has some trouble waking Richard Runche but after several attempts he groans softly and rubs his eyes. He looks simply awful and Jessica opens the 'Compliments Mrs Goldberg' and finds a large bottle of Solly's ever-present lemonade and, just as thoughtfully, a bottle opener. She uncaps the lemonade and hands the bottle to the dishevelled lawyer. Richard Runche takes the bottle gratefully and swallows a good third of the contents, then he hands it back to her and gets shakily to his feet. 'If you'll excuse me, my dear,' he says and staggers from the compartment – presumably, Jessica thinks, to visit the toilet at the end of the carriage.

The wicker basket is crammed with enough food for at least eight people and Jessica now invites her fellow passengers to tuck in. There is a grocer and his wife named Bert and Maisie Jones from Wagga Wagga, two cheerful young city lads of about sixteen from Sydney who introduce themselves simply as Macka and Spike, both going to Merribee Station to work as rouseabouts, and an itinerant shearer and his Aboriginal wife, Arthur and Grace Wilkins, who are eventually headed up Lachlan River way, but are stopping off at Wagga for a while to see Grace's auntie who is sick.

The shearer's wife has the flattest nose Jessica has ever seen except perhaps for Flats Sullivan, one of the tar boys at the Riverview shearing shed who'd had a go at her hair with the Stockholm tar pot when Billy Simple got himself hurt nearly to death. The day he fought the tar boys and got himself kicked in the head by Jack's horse.

Bert Jones, urged on by Maisie, pays for eight cups of tea from the passing tea trolley and Jessica finds herself the centre of attention as Mrs Goldberg's basket supplies an excellent early breakfast for them all. Though she finds it difficult to accept the compliments flying around, it's nice to be someone again. She sets aside a little of everything for the return of Richard Runche, who finally gets back to the compartment looking pale as a ghost and Jessica imagines that whatever was contained in his stomach – mostly claret, she supposes – is now staining the gravel between the tracks a mile or two back.

The barrister nibbles in a dispirited way on a kosher chicken leg and then partakes of a small piece of kugelhopf cake while swallowing a little more lemonade. But he refuses any further attempts by Jessica to feed him. His tea has grown cold and Jessica throws the contents of the cup out of the window, much to the chagrin of Bert Jones, who sees tuppence wasted. 'Waste not, want not, cold tea's better than no tea,' he grumbles to his wife, still begrudging his earlier munificence. Jessica hands over what's left of the food to the two boys. Since his return to the compartment, Richard Runche has made no attempt to speak, other than to nod at each of his fellow passengers when Jessica shyly introduces them.

The train pulls into Wagga Wagga station and Jessica prepares to bid Richard Runche KC farewell. She has done enough crying since leaving the asylum. Besides, the company at breakfast were the kind of country folk she knows and understands and they have left her feeling ebullient and even optimistic.

In fact, Jessica finds herself hugely cheered up by what has amounted to her first real contact – of her own bidding – with strangers for four years. She is happy that she has been able to share Mrs Goldberg's generosity among her fellow passengers and she begins to feel, for the first time in a long while, that there is a possibility that she may once more qualify as a legitimate member of the human race. Solly was right, she thinks: to live and talk is the best revenge.

Jessica now follows the barrister along the corridor leading to the platform. Stepping down from the train, she hands him his battered suitcase. It is only then that she realises that Richard Runche has tried to shave when he'd earlier left the compartment. Despite the clumps of white stubble on his chin where the cut-throat razor has missed, and several cuts where his hand had slipped, he has remained an English gentleman to the very last.

'Mr Runche, will you be all right?' she asks. Jessica senses that he is not too keen to remain with her on the platform now that he's home, knowing that 'the hair of the second dog' is only a couple of minutes away from him, at the nearest pub.

'Splendid, my dear Jessica. Thank you for taking care of me.'

Jessica laughs. 'I am free again, thanks to you.'

Runche shrugs. 'I'm sorry, Jessica, that I couldn't

return your boy to you. That would take more skill than I have at my disposal and more money than I dare say we shall, either of us, ever possess.' He pauses and looks down at his scuffed boots, his thumb and forefinger pressed to his temple. 'By the way, my dear, if ever you *should* want to challenge for the return of your child in a court of law, just remember that the term "the child in question" is not a legal one – it is an abstract term and means nothing. In the hands of a good barrister, your agreement could be put aside. In law, my dear, you cannot agree on something you have not first clearly defined and identified.'

Despite her determination not to cry, tears now well in Jessica's eyes. 'You're the greatest lawyer in the world, Mr Richard Runche KC. I owe you everything.'

The lawyer wearily lifts his old derby. 'Miss Bergman, I shall always be available as your counsel when I'm needed.' He grins weakly and Jessica imagines that his head is throbbing something terrible. 'Do not thank me, my dear, it has been a most profitable adventure and has earned me my board and claret for six months.' His bloodshot eyes look into hers for a moment. 'I shall go now, proud to have been reacquainted with you, my dear. You are, Jessica, a remarkable young woman.'

Jessica watches as he shambles away, his concertina trousers brushing the surface of the platform, sending tiny puffs of dust up around his ankles. She thinks how much she has grown to love the drunken old lawyer.

'Mr Runche, I'll never forget yiz, as long as I shall live,' she shouts after him.

Richard Runche stops and half turns, looking over his shoulder, then he lifts his hand and waves briefly and is gone, disappearing into the departing crowd.

Jessica climbs back into the carriage and returns to her compartment where she now sits alone, the rest of her life in front of her.

CHAPTER FOURTEEN

In Narrandera, Jessica purchases a horse and saddle with a pair of leather saddlebags and inquires about obtaining turkey chicks, a turkey cock and, as well, a kerosene-fuelled hatchery. She buys a pony and cart from Tommy Grimlisk and bargains hard, remembering Joe saying that he was the best blacksmith in town but that he had a tendency to chew a bit hard on the end of the pencil when he was writing out a bill.

She arranges for her chickens to be brought out and hires a young lad to load all the essential farm tools into the pony cart, including a couple of hurricane lanterns, a four-gallon tin of kerosene, a sack of cracked corn and another of flour. He's to follow her out in a couple of days, taking his time and making sure to spell the pony as often as it needs to keep him comfortable with the load. He'll also bring the Winchester .22 repeater which has to come up from a gunsmith in Sydney. Jessica reckons she can live on rabbits for a while and also buys a shotgun and cartridges to take with her, as well as a small hand axe, two blankets, a packet of candles, two pairs of moleskins, three flannel shirts and a new Akubra bush hat. But she reckons her loony-bin boots will last her a while yet.

Jessica shops where Joe always went when he could afford it and she follows the instruction of Richard Runche KC, which is not to penny-pinch, but to buy only the best and to charge everything to the Riverview Station account. Most of what she needs comes from Cully's Stock & Station Agents and F. C. Garner, the best general store in town.

When she isn't out fixing up the things she'll need, Jessica spends the time in Dolly Heathwood's cheerful company. Dolly's first task is to buy Jessica two pretty new dresses, some underwear and the first pair of shoes she has ever owned, urging her to throw away the 'disgusting' boots issued to her at Callan Park. Jessica refuses – they're well broken in and she reckons they'll be just the trick in the bush back home.

Ever since Jessica's arrival, Dolly has persistently begged Jessica to remain in Narrandera and to work with her in the haberdashery store. 'People will be wanting the gayest hats now that the war is over and we shall have such fun making them,' she enthuses. 'You're clever with your hands and I shan't last forever. Besides, there's always been a Heathwood in the shop.'

'I'm *not* a Heathwood!' Jessica protests.

Dolly is shocked by the vehemence of Jessica's outburst. 'You've had such a hard time, dearest. You could live with me and have a secure future – the business will do well now that we can get supplies. Do say yes, Jessie,' she urges.

Dolly looks terribly disappointed when Jessica thanks her but declines. 'I have to go home, it's where I belong.'

'Home? To Riverview?' Dolly sniffs. 'Your mother and sister? You'll find they've changed. It's the money. Money changes people and, in my experience, it's seldom for the better.'

'Nah, to our old place. I've got ten acres of me own now.'

'It's not much land, Jessie, and it's dry. What will you do?'

'Turkeys. Breed turkeys,' Jessica announces. 'The creek runs through, so there's always water.'

'Turkeys?' Dolly looks confused. 'Good heavens, whatever for?'

Jessica tries to explain her plans to Dolly but realises they don't sound very practical. Without Solly Goldberg's enthusiasm to back her, putting turkeys on the train to Sydney sounds like a daft idea. 'They eat a lot of turkeys at Christmas time in Sydney,' she says lamely, not wanting to confuse Auntie Dolly any further with a detailed explanation of the whole Goldberg kosher chicken business and now this madness, this turkey business.

'Well, just remember, dearest, there'll always be a place for you here with me,' Dolly says smiling, then she adds kindly, 'pity it isn't America. They eat a lot of turkeys over there on what they call "Thanksgiving".'

It turns out Jessica's auntie is an avid reader of the new sixpenny true romance novels coming out from America. She refers to them as 'Yankee-pankees'.

'Aren't I awful? Can't resist them, my dear,' Dolly confesses, then confides that the books are sent to her in plain brown envelopes from Myer's Emporium in Melbourne.

'Of course, I mustn't be caught reading them – that would never do!' She lowers her voice, 'Very *risqué*,' then she throws back her head and laughs. 'Only in bed with the curtains closed. Ooh, lovely!'

Jessica mentions shyly that she's done a fair bit of reading herself while she's been away and so Dolly promptly invites the town librarian, Miss Amy French, to afternoon tea under the grapevine. 'You'll like her, Jessie, she wears cheerful hats and doesn't care much what folk think,' she confides.

It is from Miss French that Jessica learns that Mr Fix-it, nosy-parker, Moishe Goldberg, has already arranged for her to be sent books. 'Such a charming let-ter from your Mr Goldberg, my dear, with a postal order included. Very generous, I must say. I shall not let you down. We have some of the classics on his list and I shall see you get the others.' Miss French pauses, breaking off another small piece of canary cake and popping it into her mouth. 'Though only one each month,' she says, swallowing, 'and you must be patient, dear, we are not a big library and the town council seems to think books are a luxury we can't afford.' She turns to Dolly. 'Would you believe it, my dear, I ran into old McPherson in the street on Tuesday last.

' "Miss French, a word if you please," he says, call-ing me over like some lackey. He's just come out of the pub and his breath smells of whisky.

' "Good afternoon, Mayor," I say.

' "Miss French, I've got word from reliable sources that you're buying too many books." '

The stout librarian pulls her head back and sniffs. 'I mean, he's a wool and skin buyer, the nerve of the man! "Is there such a thing as too many books in a library, Mr McPherson?" I ask him.

' "Books are not all they're cracked up to be," he says to me.

' "Oh?" I say. "Why is that, Mr McPherson?"

'He wags his finger. "You be careful, Miss French, now the war is over we don't want no foreign ideas coming in and corrupting the minds of the young. We'll have none of them *risky* novels, ya hear."

' "I think the word is *risqué*, Mr Mayor," I say to him.

' "Yeah, whatever, none of them," he says.'

All three women laugh and Dolly casts a sly glance over at Jessica, who immediately translates her look into words – what would Miss French say if she knew about the Yankee-pankees, eh?

After three days of shopping, Jessica's ready to leave. She leaves Narrandera just after dawn on the fourth morning. Dolly has crammed one of her saddlebags with food and the other contains the bare essentials Jessica will need when she arrives back at the Bergman homestead. Matches, candles, shotgun cartridges, a five-pound sack of flour, a quarter-side of bacon, plate, knife, fork, spoon and mug. She has two billies hanging from the straps as well. It's all she'll need until the pony and cart arrive with her other supplies.

Jessica arrives back home just before sunset. The horse she bought has made light work of the journey, despite the extra burden he carries, and she's pleased she can still pick a good working horse when she sees one. She thinks how Jack would have approved.

She dismounts wearily and ties the reins to the hitching post outside the kitchen door. Every bone in her body aches from the ride, after not having been in the saddle for so long. But she's happy to be home and not to have to go bush for the night.

Jessica recalls that the last time she spent the night in the bush was with poor Billy Simple nearly five years back. Then, in a curious twist of memory, she remembers that the pony she'd used to get Billy Simple to Narrandera was named Napoleon. Considering her aching bones, she decides on the spot to call her new horse Bonaparte. She grins to herself at the little joke she's made, knowing Richard Runche KC would think it was clever, while Solly Goldberg would be likely to clap his large hands together and exclaim, 'Exact, my dear!' Moishe would smile quietly and be glad that she was learning things from the books he'd brought for her.

The house appears deserted in the fading light, which is hardly surprising. And it *looks* miserable, old and deserted and unloved, and Jessica can't believe how small it seems. The windlass, though, is still turning and there's plenty of water. To her surprise a lone tomato vine grows up the side of the water tank and sports a display of ripe, red fruit. Other than this single splash of scarlet, everything seems to be grey, the colour of dry dust. The yard around the house is baked iron-hard in the sun and Hester's rose garden is dead, dry thorny branches protruding from the dun-coloured earth. Apart from the rabbit fencing, there is no sign of where the vegetable garden once stood. Jessica walks stiffly, trying to ease the pain in her muscles. The chicken run is empty but still carries the unmistakable whiff of chicken shit. There are feathers gathered up in the corners where the wind has piled up the dust, and tiny white leg-feathers cling stubbornly to the chicken wire. The pig pen leans to one side – several of its planks have fallen to the ground, and its corrugated-iron roof has collapsed on one side.

Jessica begins to cry softly, the memories flooding back. She is afraid to go into the homestead, not sure what she'll find and knowing that if it's empty and cleaned out it will be even worse.

'There's no time to blub, girl,' she tells herself sternly, knuckling the tears from her eyes. The sun is setting and she has to water and stable the horse and have a wash at the well herself. She'll chop wood in the morning as she's too tired and sore to boil the billy right now anyway.

Jessica unstraps the saddlebags and unsaddles Bonaparte and leaves the gear outside the kitchen door together with the shotgun and bed-roll. Then she takes the horse to the windlass and picks three ripe tomatoes there. At the well, she rinses the dust off the smooth red, polished skins and then eats them while she allows Bonaparte to drink his fill. The fleshy fruit is sharp and tart and then sweet at the centre and Jessica relishes the clean taste. She draws a bucket and washes her face and arms, leaving the rest of her toilette until the morning. Then she leads Bonaparte to the stable, hangs up the harness and gives him his feed of oats.

As Jessica walks up to the homestead she can hear the cacophony of the birds settling in, deciding their nightly pecking order on the eucalypt branches down at the river bank. Tonight it's the currawongs that seem to be getting the better of the nocturnal bickering and she wonders how bad the snakes have been this year.

Jessica realises how, of all the sounds of the bush, it is the bird life at sunset that she has missed the most, this squawking and carry-on to announce the end of the hot day and the beginning of the night. More than anything, it is the sound of coming home, of a hard day's work completed with weary legs and arms. Joe riding at her side, the soft *plurrrrr* of their horses and the clink of harness buckles, the dark stains on their shirts and the smell of sweat, the anticipation of a wash at the well, yellow lantern light in the kitchen window, cooking smells and the soft look of the bush in the gathering dusk.

Jessica enters the homestead through the kitchen door. The sun has almost set and the room is already in deep, dark shadow. She sees that the kitchen table remains, and the old iron stove. To her surprise the cast-iron kettle rests in its usual place on the rear hob. Otherwise the room is empty. The kitchen smells slightly rancid, as though the grease of a thousand meals has been allowed to leak back out of the woodwork to permeate the neglect. Every surface is covered in dust and there are bird droppings on the table – most likely an owl, Jessica thinks, come in after mice. She looks up to see the kitchen window is half open, hanging on one hinge, the glass darkened with wind-battered dirt.

Jessica begins to explore the empty house and sees that the parlour has been stripped and only the worn linoleum remains on the floor. In the sleep-out Joe's long wooden cot remains, though the mattress has been removed. Meg's room is empty, the floorboards creak and the candles cast long shadows to make the space around it seem hollow. In Hester's room the cast-iron bed remains, a thing of broken springs and black arms and legs, a dark spider's skeleton in a dead room. Jessica leaves her own bedroom until last, not wishing to feel the same terrible sense of emptiness, the loneliness of things lost forever, of lives disappeared. Her family, with its laughter and quarrels, secret smiles, despair and sometimes even hope, all turned into this emptiness, into nothing.

Finally she turns the knob of her door and opens it inwards. The candles flicker in the draught caused by the door opening, then flare again to light the interior. Jessica gasps. Her room is intact, completely untouched. Though covered in dust, nothing seems to have been removed. It is, as much as the candlelight can show, just as she remembers it when she left.

Jessica steps into the room and goes straight to the bed and lifts the mattress, disturbing a small cloud of dust in the process. Jack's two letters taken from Joe's medicine box after his death are missing from where she'd left them under the mattress. She lets the mattress fall back and it is only then that she sees what lies on the bed. Laid out carefully the length and breadth of the small cot are Billy Simple's blood-stained clothes, the stains now brown patches in the fabric of his torn shirt and moleskins.

Jessica screams and, dropping the candles, she runs from the room, stumbling through the house in the dark until she reaches the kitchen and then staggers, sobbing, into the yard where she falls to her knees, her hands covering her face in despair.

When she eventually looks up the house is already ablaze, the flames sucking greedily at the dry timber. Jessica rushes into the kitchen, which is rapidly filling with smoke, rescues her saddle and then returns for her saddlebags, the two billy cans and her shotgun, barely escaping a wall of flame that rushes down the narrow corridor towards her.

Once outside Jessica struggles to get her things far enough away from the house so that they are safe from the flames. Then she sits, shocked and distraught, on her saddle in the dirt, and watches the homestead burn.

The roof is the first thing to collapse, the corrugated iron twisting and buckling in the heat before glowing red-hot and falling down into the innards of the house in a shower of fiery sparks. Soon the clapboard walls fall one by one, collapsing inwards, so that the flames appear to cease for a moment before the inferno gains momentum and roars on.

In less than an hour all that remains is a heap of charred and smouldering timber with small fires still licking independently in half a dozen places. Only Hester's bed remains upright, standing defiant in the smoking ruins. The bed from which Joe was banished to the sleepout after his children were born, where Meg seduced Jack and where, unbeknownst to Jessica, old Mrs Baker was murdered, now stands like Hester herself – hard, unforgiving, unrepentant and determined to survive.

A near-full moon has risen in the east across the saltbush plains and it is light enough to see the lazy curls of acrid smoke rising upwards from the charred remains of the homestead. Jessica thinks of the words in Jack's last letter when he described the full moon in the desert.

Can you remember? The moon is sometimes bright like it is on a summer night at home. 'You can read a newspaper by its light,' folk would always say, though I never saw anyone who did.

Jessica thinks also of Joe's funeral and the 'ashes to ashes, dust to dust' words intoned over his grave by the Reverend Mathews, M.A. Oxon. And then Joe's own prophetic interpretation of the Biblical sentiment, 'That's the whole flamin' story o' the plains, everything turns to dust or bloody ashes.'

Jessica opens her bed-roll and wraps herself in a blanket and, with her head resting against the saddle, she prepares to go to sleep. Tomorrow she'll move down to the tin hut and start her new life as a supplier of plump turkeys to Solly Goldberg, Kosher Butchery, Hall Street,

Bondi Beach. '*Chickens – second to none! Turkeys – the very best!*'

Jessica is almost asleep when she has a sudden impulse. She decides that, in the morning, even before she goes to the boundary rider's hut, she'll ride to Yanco Siding and hire a man with a cart to bring Billy Simple's gravestone back to Warralang, the ten acres she owns beside the creek. Though it's black soil country, Jessica has now named the place 'Redlands' after Red, her beloved kelpie who was shot by Billy Simple when he tried to defend her.

On the afternoon following the fire, Jessica returns to the burnt-down homestead from Yanco Siding, where she's arranged for Solly Goldberg's beautiful gift to be brought to Redlands. Finding a slightly cracked glass preserving jar near the windlass, she washes it clean and then walks among the still-warm ashes until she locates what remains of her cot. Jessica tells herself she has come to rid herself of the terrible curse her mother had placed on her by arranging Billy Simple's bloody garments on her bed. Jessica is certain now her mother was mad, for she must have kept Billy Simple's garments after finding them in the tub beside the windlass after Hester, Joe and Meg had returned from the reading of Agnes's will in Whitton – the incident of the famous silver tea service.

Using a twig to poke among the debris, Jessica collects almost half a jarful of tiny burnt scraps that were Billy Simple's shirt and moleskins. She thinks to herself that some of the now invisible blood soaked into the material is Billy's own and he has paid the ultimate price for his sins. It is time to bury them together with his virtues.

And so she'd buried the preserving jar with the tiny scraps of burnt cotton under the gravestone. In her mind, she restored Billy Simple from being a non-person buried in quicklime to the real person who had once been her and Jack's good mate.

From that day on, Jessica truly believed in her heart that there was more of the true spirit of Billy Simple lying under the beautiful old river gum, with the quiet stream flowing by, than ever there could be in the chalky remains beneath the hard, anonymous flagstones of Long Bay Prison.

Now almost five years have passed since the Bergman homestead burnt down and tomorrow, before she and Rusty drive the turkeys to the railway, Jessica must put flowers on Billy's grave. It will be 6 August 1923, nine years since the day war was declared in Europe and since Billy's short life ended at dawn. The first of the wattle is already out and in the morning before they leave she'll pick a bunch of the brilliant yellow blossom for Billy's grave.

Jessica watches as the rabbits come down to drink, bunching together and pushing each other as though the only spot along the broad creek bank is the yard of pebbles selected by those who have arrived first. She feeds a single cartridge into the right-hand barrel of the twelve-bore and pulls back the hammer. Rusty now stands beside her, his tongue lolling, his ears pricked up, waiting expectantly for the sound of the shotgun blast.

When it comes, he rushes forward, barking and splashing through the shallows to stand on the furthermost bank even before the echo of the shotgun has fully died down. He sniffs at the dead rabbits, pushing at four or five with his nose as though to make sure they're dead, barking his head off all the while. One of the rabbits tries to crawl away and Rusty quickly snaps it up and crosses over the stream to where Jessica sits. He drops it at her feet, and Jessica reaches down for the rabbit and snaps its neck, putting it out of its misery. Rusty then returns across the creek until eventually nine dead rabbits lie at her feet. Jessica pats him on the head. 'For a sheep-dog who herds turkeys yiz a bloody good retriever, Rusty dog,' she laughs.

Jessica reaches over for her hunting knife and, picking up a plump rabbit, she cuts around the fur at the extremity of the back and front legs then draws the knife up the inside of the back legs, making an incision to the top of the inside haunch. Then she pulls the pelt over the remainder of the body up to the rabbit's head, and quickly cuts around the neck and pulls the entire pelt over the head, clean as a whistle. The whole process takes her less than a minute and she lays the pelt aside and gives the rabbit to Rusty, who trots off happily to take his dinner under a nearby saltbush.

In less than ten minutes Jessica has skinned all the

rabbits and stretched each of the pelts across a wire U-frame. Then she takes them to the turkey run behind the hut, where she hangs them high up on the chicken wire to dry out.

Jessica returns to the hut and cuts up three of the rabbits for the stew pot. It is nearly spring and the late winter rain has put a good topping of grass on the plains, so that the rabbits are nice and plump. She puts another aside for Rusty's dinner the following day. The remaining rabbits she prepares to throw into the creek where the crayfish, redfin and yellow-belly will clean them up a treat or, if any should wash onto the bank further down, a fox or a crow will make a welcome meal of it. It is her contribution to Joe's world of 'everything lives off something else' – a free feed for which some creature, fish, fowl or four-legged animal, won't have to work too hard.

Usually Jessica waits an hour or so before disposing of the surplus rabbit meat. Often enough, one or two of the aunties from the nearby Aboriginal camp – some of Mary Simpson's mob – will hear the shotgun blast at sunset and come on over and get the rabbits Jessica doesn't need.

Jessica wakes at dawn to the sound of roosters crowing and makes a fire outside the hut. While the billy boils she washes at the creek and then, with Rusty by her side, she walks over to a wattle tree near the bank and cuts a large sprig of the brilliant yellow blossom. She returns with it and puts it down for later, when she will go to Billy's grave. Now she pours boiling water

from the billy into a pot and stirs in three or four handfuls of oats and puts the pot back on the embers. With
the remaining water in the billy she makes tea. Jessica
watches the oats impatiently, stirring the pot frequently
as she sips at the mug of sweet, dark tea. When the oatmeal is set she eats quickly, straight from the pot,
blowing frequently at the hot porridge on her spoon.
After only a few spoonfuls she puts the remaining porridge into Rusty's dish and mixes a little of last night's
cold rabbit stew in with it. Rusty is smart enough to
know that it's too hot to eat and he settles down beside
his dish, whining with impatience. 'Be careful, ya'll
burn yer tongue,' Jessica says absently as she fills a jam
jar with water for the wattle blossom.

The birds are already calling out in the river gums,
their morning song well under way, and Jessica stops and
watches briefly as a grey heron glides down to land on a
rock near the far bank of the creek. This morning the
kookaburras are winning the contest, which they usually
do. The turkeys, of course, are having their say, gobbling
away nineteen to the dozen, expecting to be let out of the
run, but the river birds are more than a match for them.

Carrying the jar of wattle blossom and a damp cloth,
Jessica walks the short distance to Billy Simple's grave.
She has 'buried' him between the smooth white folds of
two large surface roots belonging to the giant river
gum, placing the cross exactly where she'd once put her
baby on Christmas morning 1914, when her family had
arrived to find she'd given birth to Joey.

For Jessica this is a sacred spot. Not only is it the site

of Billy Simple's gravestone, but for her it has come to symbolise Jack's death as well. At the end of the day she often comes to sit under the tree beside the gravestone to think of Jack and to read his faded letters.

Jessica places the jar to one side and begins to wipe the face of the cross with the damp cloth. On every occasion she does this she thinks of Solly Goldberg who, so many years ago now, out of the goodness of his heart, commissioned the fine cross of polished grey granite just to please her.

How wonderful he has been to her over the years, taking her turkeys and even giving them a name, so that a 'Redlands Turkey' is known amongst the Jewish community in Sydney as the very best there is. It is a turkey with a unique flavour that, curiously, needs no salt. Jessica once explained to Solly in a letter that this came about because the birds constantly pecked at saltbush.

In his very next letter to her Solly wrote, 'So let me tell you the wonderful news, my dear. Now I am selling turkeys "salted by Mother Nature". You like it? For this, Mrs Turkey Shopper must pay one shilling more!'

Jessica wipes the side and the back of the granite cross and then places the jar of wattle down in front of it. She pulls back slightly to admire her handiwork and then, with her finger, she traces the inscription across the arms and down the centre to its base while quietly reciting the Lord's Prayer.

+
William D'arcy Simon
'Billy Simple'
A great
mate
to
Jack
and
Jessica
R.I.P.
* 1892–1914 *

Finally she reaches to the back of the cross, to the plinth where her finger finds the small inscription written in Yiddish: *Mit'n Best'n Vinchen By Mrs Goldberg*, which she knows in English means 'Compliments Mrs Goldberg'.

It takes a good part of the day to herd the turkeys to the siding and get them into their wire packing cages and to feed, water and settle them down. Jessica collects her library book sent up the line by Miss French and leaves the one she must return and then she goes to visit Joe's grave at St Stephen's. By two o'clock she must be outside the schoolyard in the hope that she might catch a glimpse of young Joey, who has grown into a robust and noisy eight-year-old. The child has blue eyes and fair hair and it's not too hard to see he's a Bergman.

On the days she sees him, Jessica nearly chokes with her love for her son as she watches him get onto his pony and start out for home with two other boys. Sometimes he'll look at her and once he'd ridden up and squinted up at her. 'Why are you dressed like a man, missus?' he'd asked.

Confronted suddenly by the small boy, she couldn't think of anything to say. 'Hello, Joey,' Jessica said shyly. 'Do you like school?'

'I know who you are,' Joey said suddenly, 'you're the turkey lady! My mum says I'm not to talk to you ever!' Then he'd turned his pony about and, laughing, cantered off to join his friends.

Jessica waits outside the school religiously every week after she's sent off her turkeys and visited Joe's grave, but she is never again to talk to her son while he remains at the school. Whenever she appears, the schoolmistress, casting dark looks in Jessica's direction, escorts Joey to the gate and sees him on his way.

However, she can still observe him closely every week. If he has a cut or a bandage Jessica wonders how he's hurt himself and once, when he'd broken his arm, she'd gone nearly crazy worrying about him, despite telling herself repeatedly that it was pretty common boy's stuff and that the arm would come to no harm.

Another time, when there had been a measles epidemic and half the school was away, Joey had not been seen for two weeks and a frantic Jessica determined that if he was not back in the following week, she'd ride out to Riverview to confront Hester and Meg. But the next time she arrived he'd turned up looking no worse for the experience.

On several occasions the same schoolmistress gathers

her courage and, after seeing Joey to the gate, comes
over to remonstrate with Jessica, telling her to please go
away, implying that Mrs Thomas had sent word that she
was not welcome at the school. Though on each such
occasion Jessica sent her off with a flea in her ear, pointing out that she was standing in public property *outside*
the schoolyard and that Meg, far as she knew, didn't
own the school.

On the afternoon of the anniversary of Billy Simple's
death and after she visits the school, Jessica takes the
pony cart into Yanco to collect her mail, go to the bank
and do her shopping. She usually arrives back at Redlands just before sunset. While she finds it a pleasant
enough excursion into town and enjoys the brief con-
versations with the shopkeepers and the bank teller,
she's always grateful when she reaches the creek.

Hester and Meg have assumed the role previously
held by Ada Thomas and her two daughters and have
become the local bullies. Their presence in the district
means that the townsfolk treat Jessica with caution.
Jessica is seen as a woman who lives on her own in
what amounts to not much more than a blackfella's
humpy. It is not at all the sort of thing an Anglican
woman should do.

The local rumour has it that Jessica has plenty of
money in the bank and could easily afford better. While
this isn't true, Solly Goldberg does send her a little more
money for her turkeys than she needs to spend. After
four years of selling him turkeys she's got a bob or two
to spare, but Jessica is by no means well-off or able to

afford a better house. Besides, she is terrified of the respectability a properly built home would mean.

Jessica tells herself that with the trappings of conformity – and there is none better than a new house – she would have to become respectable. This idea, in a community where the pecking order is dominated by her sister and her mother, terrifies her.

Memories in the bush are long, too, and Jessica's attack on her mother at Joe's funeral has never been quite forgotten. There cannot be anyone in the district who doesn't know she's spent time in the loony-bin, Jessica reckons – she can see this all in people's eyes as she passes them on the footpath.

What's more, Jessica has a reputation for going around with the blacks, of being seen from time to time with Aboriginal women. It's not long before the tattle-tales in the district begin to suggest that where there are black women there are also black men. Eyes roll knowingly at afternoon tea parties, allowing the listeners to form their own grubby conclusions as they nibble on lamingtons and dainty sandwiches.

Not long after Jessica had returned and moved into the hut at Yanco Creek, the Reverend Mathews, M.A. Oxon., called by one morning to pay his respects. Jessica had promptly sent him packing. 'Bugger off, yer old hypocrite, or yiz'll get a blast of birdshot up yer sanctimonious arse!' she'd yelled at him.

'Sanctimonious' was a word she'd learned from Moishe Goldberg, who'd once used it to describe the Presbyterian chaplain who came to Callan Park. Jessica hadn't imagined that she would ever have the opportunity to use such a long and elegant-sounding word in its correct context.

'Sanctimonious bastard!' she'd repeated, just to hear the sound of the word again, as the clergyman's horse and trap did an about face and charged off, sending the chooks helter-skelter in a flurry of feathers and setting the turkeys to gobbling overtime.

Jessica senses the silent antipathy towards her and keeps to herself – more and more she is becoming a loner. Even at Christmas time, when she rides the twelve hours into Narrandera to visit Dolly, she finds herself, after only a few hours in Dolly's loquacious company, anxious to get back to the quiet of Redlands and to the company of Rusty and the comfort of a good book.

Jessica does not think of herself as reclusive and is certainly not lonely. Mary Simpson has remained her friend and spends a lot of time with Jessica when she's about. The little Aboriginal woman with her tribe of kids isn't always around, though, as Mary disappears sometimes for weeks at a time. She calls it 'goin' walkabout', but on her return, when she's closely questioned by Jessica, it invariably turns out there was some bloke involved, and not always an Aboriginal neither. Jessica will sigh and ask, 'Has he got you in the family way, Mary?'

Mary will shake her head and frown. 'Men, they's pigs, Jessie. All they thinks of is grog and nookie.'

'Mary, you've got four kids, not counting them that's grown and gorn away. Four kids to four different blokes, you've got to learn to bloody say no!'

Mary laughs ruefully. 'That ain't our way, Jessie. Aboriginal woman can't say no to her man.'

Jessica grows angry. 'Her husband, yes! But you ain't married to these blokes, these bloody no-hopers – some of them ain't even blackfellas! Your real husband buggered off after your second baby. You've got a kid every colour of the bloody rainbow, there's not a full-blood among 'em. It's bullshit, Mary, you've gotta stop! You're thirty years old, you don't want to have any more flamin' babies. How's you gunna bring up decent what you've got already?'

'I loves them, Jessie, they're good kids. It's the blokes what's bad bastards, not them kids.'

'And it's you with your legs open that's just as bad,' Jessica snorts.

When Mary goes walkabout, leaving her kids with the aunties, while she goes to the Warangesda Aboriginal Settlement, or Grong Grong or the sandhills, Jessica sees they're supplied with ample rabbit meat and flour for damper. It's how the aunties have learned to come when they hear the shotgun blast. Often, when she's in town, she'll buy clothes for them and for the other little ragamuffins who seem to breed like flies in the black fellas' camp. Jessica loves Mary's children and they adore her. With some of the other little snot-noses they often come over to the creek to swim and she'll make a great big pot of rabbit stew and give them handfuls of sugar or boiled lollies she's bought in town as a special treat. And so Jessica has earned the reputation of 'hangin' about with the bloody blacks'.

Jessica arrives back at Redlands in the late afternoon on the anniversary of Billy Simple's death to find her friend Mary waiting for her. Mary turns to greet her and Jessica sees that she's been sobbing.

'What's wrong, Mary?' she asks, but the little Aboriginal woman doesn't say. Jessica isn't too concerned – Mary often comes around for a bit of a blub, usually after having been beaten by some worthless bastard, the father of one of her kids arriving in the camp drunk as a skunk. 'Wait on, I'll be there in a tick, just let me remove this saddle and bridle and let the pony have a drink.' Jessica carries the saddle and bridle and puts them under the lean-to, allowing the pony to take himself to the water. She then turns to the disconsolate Mary.

'Some bloke, is it? Been to Warangesda again, has ya?' she asks.

Mary is sitting on a rock beside the creek and she turns to look at Jessica. 'They took my kids,' she says, sniffing.

'Who? Who took your kids?'

'The whitefellas. They made me sign a paper, then they took them.'

'Mary, you can read – what did the paper say?' Jessica runs over and takes Mary in her arms.

'They wouldn't let me read it,' Mary sobs. 'They said it were the law and the paper were from the gubberment!' Mary now begins to howl, and it is a keening Jessica has only heard once before, when one of the Aboriginal elders died and the aunties had started up with this strange, high-pitched lamentation.

'Shush! Mary, they ain't dead,' Jessica scolds her friend, though she does this more to contain her own panic than to stop Mary wailing. 'If they were took, they can be took back.'

Mary stops her wailing suddenly and pulls away from Jessica's arms, shaking her dark head vigorously. 'Nah! They said I couldn't never get them back, Jessie! They said they's from the Aborigines' Protection Board, and it's the law o' the land. They brought a big truck and put me kids in the back and drove away! There were other kids in there also, took from Warangesda and Grong Grong!'

Jessica tries to comfort Mary. 'I know a man, you know the one I told you about, who helped me? He's a clever lawyer – it's him what got me outa the loony-bin. You never mind a thing, Mary, we'll go see him in Wagga, you hear me?'

Three days later Jessica and Mary arrive by train in Wagga to see Richard Runche KC. Before she left Jessica arranged for the aunties to feed and water the turkeys and the chickens and to give Rusty his tucker. She's wearing the shoes and one of the pretty dresses Dolly bought for her and she's given the other to Mary to wear, though her friend's once skinny shape has expanded a bit from her constant childbearing and a diet consisting of too much white flour, sugar and bread.

Over the years Jessica has continued to correspond with the barrister, but in the last two years he has replied spasmodically and the few letters she's received are increasingly illegible and scratchy. 'The grape is taking its toll, my dear, the circuit court has little use for me these days,' he'd confided in the last one she'd received several months back.

Jessica and Mary go directly to the Albion, the hotel where she'd first met Richard Runche at breakfast. She'd been sending her letters here and so is confident of finding him. To her surprise Jimmy Jenkins, the young lad who helped on that first day, is lording it behind the desk and it's clear from his manner that he's become the boss cocky of the desk. In the last nine years he's grown quite plump and is beginning to lose his hair. He wears a black suit with a white shirt, celluloid collar and black tie and sports a watch chain across his little pot-belly. Seeing the two women walking in, one of them being a black, Jimmy's expression becomes alarmed.

'Yes?' he inquires, his voice not in the least accommodating. Nothing about the two women standing in front of him suggests the need for respect.

'Hello, Jimmy Jenkins, remember me?' Jessica says brightly.

Jimmy looks at Jessica and then pulls his head back in surprise. 'My God, it's you! From that trial!' He appears to be thinking, snapping his fingers. 'Jessie!' he says at last.

Jessica smiles shyly. 'Same rotten egg,' she jokes, then turns and touches Mary Simpson on the shoulder. 'This is Mary, my best friend.'

''Owyagoin',' Mary says softly, not presuming to raise her eyes to look at the man before her.

Jimmy Jenkins gives her the briefest nod. Jessica in his

hotel is one thing, but the Aboriginal woman is quite another.

Jessica touches Mary on the arm. 'Mr Jenkins here is an old friend who done me a great favour once.' She smiles at him. 'He's a real good bloke.'

Jimmy Jenkins proves to be as vulnerable to flattery as ever and his demeanour immediately softens. 'Nice to see you, Jessica, I've never forgot you.'

'That's nice, me neither – see how I remembered your name right off?'

'What brings you here?' Jimmy Jenkins now asks. 'You're from down Narrandera way, ain't you?'

Jessica nods. She can see that despite his friendly tone he's growing increasingly anxious and keeps looking about him. Same old Jimmy Jenkins, she thinks, still shit-scared of the management. Mary's continued presence in the hotel lobby is obviously upsetting him. 'We've come to see Mr Runche again,' she announces.

A look of relief crosses Jimmy's face. 'Oh, he don't live here any more, Jessie.'

Jessica looks up, surprised. 'But I send him letters here.'

'Yeah, that's right, but we pass them on. He lives down at Ma Shannon's now.'

'Mrs Shannon? At the boarding house?'

'Yeah, that's right,' Jimmy says.

Jessica turns to Mary. 'That's where we stayed last time, me old man and me. It's very nice,' she explains.

'Well, it ain't really a boarding house now, more a doss-house for down-an'-outers. They even take . . .'

Jimmy stops, realising just in time what he was about to say.

'Abos?' Jessica says it for him.

'Well, yes,' he says embarrassed, not looking at Mary.

'Good, then maybe we can get a room there,' Jessica says tartly. 'Jimmy Jenkins, you always was a bloody snob. Come, Mary, let's go.'

They have almost reached the door when Jimmy Jenkins shouts, 'Better take a bottle with you!'

They take his advice and buy a bottle on their way out. Richard Runche has always been the worse for wear, or at least he has ever since Jessica has known him. But she is not prepared for what they find when fat old gin-swilling Ma Shannon takes them to his room.

'Help yerself,' she says. 'Buggered if I'm goin' in. If he's dead gi's a hoy.'

Jessica turns the doorknob and half opens the door and looks in. 'Jesus!' she exclaims. Richard Runche KC lies on an iron cot on a filthy mattress, his eyes closed, knees drawn up to his chest. He is fully clothed but without his shoes, and his suit is clearly in tatters, his pale feet are sticking out of the ends of his dirty trousers. The buttons on his fly are missing or open. Jessica can't see which, but the gap reveals a pathetic little purple acorn curled into its pubic nest. Runche's greasy jacket is ripped, the lapels frayed at the edge, and his once white shirt, which sports no collar, is almost black.

They enter the tiny room, which smells of shit, stale

sick and grog. Runche groans and sucks at his gums and every few moments shouts out, as though in fear. Whatever is going on inside his grog-soaked brain is obviously not doing him a lot of good.

Both women look about them, their fingers held to their noses. Jessica sees that the single window is shut tight so that the atmosphere is fetid and you could cut the air with an axe. Several blowflies buzz around, bumping against the uncovered dirty window-pane. It is light enough, though, and the rod and rings above the window testify that curtains once hung there. The barrister, groaning, now pulls a filthy pillow over his head against the intrusion of the sharp mid-morning light.

Against the wall to the side of the window stands a dresser made of several four-gallon paraffin tins resting on their sides with one end cut out and the edges hammered flat. Scraps of clothing, empty bottles and nondescript bits and pieces are stuffed into each of its apertures. Beside the bed stands a battered old chair with its cane seat broken inwards, as though a giant has farted and blown the plaited cane asunder. The remainder of the room is filled with law books lying higgledy-piggledy or piled in little heaps among the empty claret bottles and old newspapers.

'Oh me Gawd!' Mary exclaims, bringing her hands up to her face. 'This the whitefella gunna bring me kids back?'

Jessica moves over to the window and after some effort she manages to push it open, though the hinges creak where they've rusted up. 'It'll be orright, Mary,' she says, though she knows she's trying to convince herself as much as she is her friend.

'Nah, missus, that fella he got the DTs. He's gorn, finish.'

Jessica turns on Mary. 'Don't you go Abo on me, ya hear, Mary Simpson, I ain't yer flamin' *missus*!' she says furiously. 'He'll be orright, I'm tellin' yer, I've seen him before, same as this!'

'I'm sorry, Jessie,' Mary says looking down at Richard Runche KC. 'It's just I seen his kind before.' She points to the pathetic shivering form on the bed. 'This ain't new stuff for black people.'

Jessica looks contrite. 'I'm sorry, too, Mary, I didn't mean to shout at yiz, it's me nerves an' all.' She spreads her hands. 'Bloody hell, what're we gunna do?'

'Go home,' Mary says promptly, shrugging one shoulder. 'Can't help that bugger.'

'Go home? What, and leave him like this?'

'Ten minutes ago we didn't know he were like this,' Mary points out.

'So? What's that supposed to mean?'

Mary sighs. 'We close the door and we think who we was ten minutes back. We's Jessie and Mary, remember? And we ain't done nothing wrong to nobody and we's minding our own business trying to get back me kids.' She pauses and takes a breath. 'So we catch the train and go back home.'

'And you never see your kids again! Is that it?'

'Jessie, he's fucked!' Mary cries suddenly. 'He ain't

gunna get me kids back. That poor bastard, he's got snakes and spiders in his head, eh!'

Jessica's jaw sets, the Bergman stubbornness comes upon her, settles down on a rock in her head like the grey heron that comes to the creek of a morning. She shakes her head slowly. 'Nah, I'm not leavin' him, Mary. You can go if yer like, you've got yer train ticket.'

Mary sighs again. 'Jessie, it's bloody hopeless, I seen this a hundred times. When they come out, their brain's gorn, all they can do is dribble and shit their trousers!' She points at the figure on the bed once more. 'One day he like this and he drowns in his own vomit, that the most lucky day for everyone!'

'Yeah, well, okay, but I've got to try.' Jessica looks at Mary. 'He's me friend. Wasn't for him I'd still be in the loony-bin!'

Mary shrugs. 'You're gunna be sorry, Jessica. Don't say I didn't told yer.' She takes a deep breath. 'Righto then, we got to get him awake and to make 'im throw up. You think that fat old woman will lend us a bucket or a big dish?'

'I'll go ask her,' Jessica volunteers, pleased that Mary's going to stay with her.

She returns with a bucket a few minutes later to find that Mary is seated on the side of the iron cot and has the still semi-conscious Runche held in a sitting position on the bed while she massages his neck and the back of his skull. 'He's got nits and I think he's shit hisself,' she announces calmly as Jessica enters. ''Ere, Jessie, hold the bucket on his lap and watch out for your hands.'

Moments later the poor barrister gives a pronounced shudder and half opens his eyes, then he begins to gag and Mary grips him tightly by the back of the neck. His eyes open a little wider and begin to roll in his head and a moment later Mary pushes his face hard down over the bucket and Richard Runche KC empties his stomach into it.

Both women remain silent until finally the poor man seems to have emptied out. 'Take the bucket, give us the bottle,' Mary now says to Jessica.

'What, the claret?'

'Yeah, the bottle we brought him. Be better if it was brandy.'

Jessica takes the bucket and opens the door and places it outside the room. Then she takes from her basket the bottle of claret they'd purchased at Jimmy Jenkins's suggestion. 'Shit, we forgot the corkscrew,' she cries.

Mary laughs and pulls the lawyer back into a sitting position, and her hand goes to the side pocket of his tattered suit jacket. 'Abracadabra!' she says, producing a corkscrew out of the pocket and handing it to Jessica. 'Corkscrew's the one thing they never lose, that and their flamin' thirst,' she says grinning.

At the sound of the cork being drawn from the claret bottle, Runche's eyes pop open and his lips start to smack together. Jessica hands the bottle to Mary. 'Should we, y'know, give him more grog?' she asks, unsure.

'Only way we's gunna get him onto his feet,' Mary says, in a matter-of-fact voice. 'He's all the time drunk anyway, can't do without it no more – grog's what keeps him goin'.' She feeds a little claret into the lawyer's mouth. He closes his eyes and swallows the ruby liquid greedily, then his tongue spreads against his top lip, begging for more, his eyes open again, though no more than a slit. Mary waves the bottle almost within range of his mouth, teasing him with it, and Runche tries to follow the moving claret bottle with his head, his lips now beating frantically together like those of a goldfish in a bowl. Suddenly she grips him behind his scrawny neck and begins to shake him, her thumb digging hard into the flesh under his jaw, her other hand holding the bottle up in front of him. 'No more till yiz speaks to us,' Mary commands.

Richard Runche KC winces. 'Ouch!' he groans.

Mary releases her grip and Runche rubs his eyes like a small child waking and gazes about him. He looks directly at Jessica and she can see the confusion in his eyes. She sees also that he doesn't know who she is.

'It's Jessica, Mr Runche, your friend. Remember me?'

Richard Runche's eyes remain vacant, not comprehending.

'Oh Gawd, his mind's gorn!' Jessica exclaims in alarm, bringing both hands up to cover her mouth.

'I tol' ya,' Mary says quietly.

Just then the barrister's eyes seem to clear. 'Jessica, my dear,' he whispers softly.

CHAPTER FIFTEEN

It is a bright spring morning in late September 1923. Richard Runche KC sits outside Jessica's hut at Redlands, sipping at a mug of sweet black tea. Seven weeks have passed since she and Mary rescued him from Ma Shannon's boarding house. While he still has the shakes, his first thought upon waking is no longer his need for a drink. He is wearing a new pair of moleskins and a flannel shirt, one of two Jessica has purchased for him in Narrandera. His old suit was so completely in tatters that it had to be discarded and burnt, his shirt disintegrating when an attempt was made to wash it.

When Jessica and Mary first brought him to the hut, Runche was in such a fearful mess that they thought he might die. The Englishman lay on Jessica's cot for almost two weeks in a dreadful state of agitation, shivering and shaking, possessed by what Mary refers to as 'them DTs'.

Jessica would sit on the edge of the bed and try to give him a little broth or weak sweet tea, though at first he'd vomit up everything, until she wondered what it was that kept him alive. Mary, who came over from the camp each morning to give her a hand, wasn't overly hopeful of his chances and urged Jessica to give him a little brandy in his tea.

'He can't come off the grog, his brain's pickled. He needs the drink to stay alive,' Mary said.

'Well, I ain't gunna give him no more grog and that's that,' Jessica announced firmly. 'We haven't got any and I ain't getting any.' She turned to face Mary. 'He were as good as dead when we found him and it's the drink that done it. Giving him more won't help!'

'Well that's all I know,' Mary explained. 'They can't do without it when they like this.' She sighed. 'It's them DTs.'

'Mary, the blackfellas you seen, did they die when they was took off the grog?'

'Can't take 'em off, Jessie, I just tol' you.'

'Yes, but did you see any of them die?' Jessica insisted.

'Plenty.'

'From getting no grog?'

'Nah, from the grog. Like I said, you can't take it away from them.' Mary shrugged. 'Don't matter, I s'pose, them's good as dead anyway.'

'Well we're gunna try, that's all,' Jessica said. 'If the old bugger's gunna die like yer said, we might as well kill him trying to make him better.'

For those first two weeks Richard Runche spent most of his time thrashing about in his cot, howling out obscenities or screaming for help, sometimes crying out for his nanny, like a small boy afraid of the dark. Sometimes it got so bad that Jessica and Mary would need to rope him to the wooden bed to keep him from hurting himself.

Jessica felt it was like being back in the asylum. She would sit with him for hours, calming him and wiping his brow with a cool, damp cloth. She'd virtually have to carry him outside to relieve himself, though with the little he ate, such excursions were thankfully not too frequent. With the sun beating down on the tin roof, combined with his fever, the lawyer seemed to burn up all the moisture in his bladder. Jessica was flat out trying to keep him from further dehydration. How grateful she was that the summer was not yet fully upon them, when the heat in the tin hut became unbearable.

But gradually, a little bit each day, she could see her patient getting stronger and his nightmares less frequent. Now, seven weeks later, Richard Runche KC is back on his feet and, while the shakes seem like they're here to stay, is able to get up and about for a few hours each day.

Jessica has extended the lean-to and built a rough wooden bed under it where she slept while her patient was recovering. But now she's returned to the interior of the hut and the barrister is ensconced in the lean-to.

It's now time for Richard Runche KC to earn his keep. This morning Mary is coming over and they're going to confront him with the problem of her missing children.

'He gunna use them books?' Mary asks.

Jessica nods. She had paid Ma Shannon the rent Runche owed when she and Mary came to collect him and together they got a large box and packed all the Englishman's things, along with his law books. Then they hired a cart to transport them to the train. With the sick and semi-conscious Richard Runche KC in tow they'd returned to Redlands.

To house the books, Jessica built three rough timber shelves along the outside wall supporting the lean-to. The green and red leather covers were, for the most part, in a state of disrepair and the gold-embossed lettering on the binding had faded. Some books even had their handsome spines ripped off to expose the glued and stitched linen membrane beneath. But, despite this, and their unprepossessing environment, they looked grand stacked along the shelves. In Jessica's opinion they gave her humble hut a sense of dignity, and she liked to imagine it as a place of importance, a little library in the bush. Mary, who was a good hand with a needle and thread, made a cover from a grain sack to fit over the three bookshelves so that later in the summer, when the paddocks dried up and the air was thick with dust, the books would be protected.

During the weeks it took for Richard Runche KC to dry out, Jessica and Mary had come to think of the books as containing the secret knowledge they needed to return the little black woman's children to her. It was the books which would bring them justice, they decided, with the barrister being the key to unlocking their enormous power.

Jessica seats the still-fragile Richard Runche under the big river gum not far from Billy Simple's gravestone and where she'd built a small bush table and two crude benches. With the water's edge close by it is a cool and comfortable place even on a hot day. Then, with Richard

Runche KC seated, she and Mary tell him the story of Mary's stolen children.

'We want Mary's kids back, Mr Runche. They can't just take them like that. Just come in and put them in a truck and drive off, it ain't right!'

He is silent for a few moments. 'I'm afraid they can, my dear. That is, they can with Aboriginal children.'

'But why? They're people same as us, and the government can't just walk in and steal *our* white babies.'

'Well, perhaps not, unless it can be proved they are being abused or neglected.'

'My children's not neglected!' Mary protests. 'They got good clothes, plenty tucker and they don't have snot runnin' out their noses.'

The little lawyer looks down, examining his fingernails. 'I wish it were as easy as that, my dear. Diligence as a parent is not the criterion – any police constable or child welfare officer can decide whether they're neglected.'

Mary's voice is suddenly bitter. 'Just 'cause we's blackfellas, eh?'

Richard Runche KC nods, then says, 'I'm afraid so, Mary. There's a lot of high-blown rhetoric about the rights of the Aboriginal people, but when it comes down to it, as the Yankees say, it doesn't amount to a hill of beans.' He brings his fist up to his lips and clears his throat. 'There isn't much in the law that looks after your interests when it comes either to property or personal rights.'

Mary turns and points in the direction of the bookshelves. 'You mean them books ain't gunna get me back me kids? Yiz not gunna find out how to get me kids back outa them books?' she repeats, then looks at Jessica and says, 'Shit, Jessie and me, we nearly broke our backs bringing them back.'

'Oh, they'll be useful all right, nothing like a precedent or two to confuse a judge or a police magistrate,' Richard Runche KC says reassuringly. 'Though I'm quite well versed in this part of the law,' he explains. 'When I first arrived in this country in 1890 there was quite a to-do in the papers about a wild race of half-castes growing up in New South Wales. It was then that the Aborigines' Protection Board introduced the notion that the children should be "de-socialised" as Aborigines and "re-socialised" as whites – "assimilation" was what it was being termed at the time. The idea of separating children from their parents was so abhorrent to me that I took some interest in the whole affair. It was not so different from the disenfranchising of the American Red Indians, and I confess I thought it might be an area of the law where I might profitably practise.' He looked up and shrugged. 'Well, it wasn't and then things changed for me,' he said, not explaining any further, though both women knew he meant his drinking. 'We must obtain a copy of the Aborigines' Protection Act. We'll need to know it backwards if we are to proceed.'

'Where would we get one o' them?' Jessica asks. 'Is it a book?'

'Why, the nearest courthouse will have it, I should think, or a police station. It will be a government pamphlet, a guide to the law for police magistrates and the like,' Runche said.

'I'll ride into Yanco termorra and get one,' Jessica promptly responds.

'It may not be quite as easy as that, my dear. You'll not be thanked for asking for it and it might well be withheld.'

'Why?' Jessica asks.

'Well, it's a tricky business at the moment. You see, the Aborigines live on well over a hundred reserves in New South Wales, all of which have been officially set aside for them by past governments. You could say the government has "deeded" them this land, though this viewpoint has always struck me as odd – after all, it was theirs in the first place.'

'Do yer mean like Warangesda, Grong Grong and Sandy Hill?' Mary asks.

'Well, yes, and a great many government stations and missions and reserves like them.'

'Well, why they chasin' the blackfella out them places?' Mary asks. 'If it ours, why can't we stay? We ain't done nuthin' wrong!'

'Ah, well there's the rub. It's good land and now the government wants it back.'

'What for?' Jessica asks.

'Returned soldiers. They want to give the land to the returning troops, divide it into farm settlements.'

'But that's not fair!' Jessica protests.

'No, my dear, it isn't, it isn't even strictly legal,' he says, then glances up at Mary. 'And that, Mary, is where your children come in.'

Both women look at him, puzzled. 'How come, Mr Runche?' Mary asks at last.

Richard Runche KC smiles gently. 'I mean no offence by this question, Mary, but how many of your children are unadulterated?'

Mary shrugs. 'They all adulteried, sir. Me old man, the one I was married to, he buggered off after the first two kids. The two that's already grow'd up. I ain't never married again.'

Richard Runche chuckles despite himself. 'No, no, that's not what I mean, my dear. Serves me right, silly word. Let me begin again. How many are full-bloods?'

'You mean no whitefella somewhere in 'em?'

'Yes.'

Mary shrugs. 'All me girls got whitefella somewhere in 'em.'

'How many full-blood Aboriginal children are there in your camp, Mary?'

'Not many that I knows of.' Mary taps her finger lightly to her chest. 'Me neither, I'm black enough, but me grandad were an Irishman.' She tries to think. 'Some of the old people, the elders maybe, but most of the full-bloods in the Wiradjuri people they long dead, not many left in these parts, I reckon.' She glances at Jessica and smiles. 'Jessie says me kids, they every colour of the rainbow.'

'Well that's precisely it, it's the genetics you see, my dear.'

'What's genetics, please?' Jessica asks.

'What you look like, the colour of your skin, eyes, hair – it's all in your blood, your genes.'

'Oh, you mean like Mary's black and I'm white?'

'With brown eyes and blue eyes, yes, that's the general idea.'

'And when you mixes them two up you gets me kids,' Mary says.

'Exactly, my dear. Now the government of the day happens to think genetics will solve the problem of your people. It seems that, unlike other black races – for instance the negroes in Africa – the Aboriginal people do not "throw back".' He is aware the words mean nothing to either of them. 'What this means is that the colour can be bred out of them quite quickly, and a dark child will not crop up at some future time into a family of white children. If the Aboriginal people can be made to persist with white partners, then their offspring will eventually become white. I am told two or three generations is all it takes.'

Mary turns to Jessica. 'Like Polly.' She looks at the barrister. 'Polly, she the colour of yellawood honey.'

Jessica frowns, looking at Richard Runche. 'I don't understand. What's this genetics got to do with taking Mary's kids?'

'Well the idea is to take part-Aboriginal children from their mothers – Mary's yellowwood-honey child is a perfect example. She'll be able to assimilate and her children will be even lighter skinned.' He pauses before continuing. 'By the way, eight out of every ten children removed are female. They're taken from their families and made wards of the State.'

'That explains what they done!' Mary cries suddenly.

'They never took no boys from the camp. Just me four kids.' Mary looks at him and explains. 'All me kids, they girls.'

'Well, there you have it, my dear. The usual procedure is to place the girls into institutions if foster homes cannot be found. The idea is that they will be taught and reared as if they were white children. At age fourteen, they are required to leave the institution and are placed as servants in white homes, where, alas, it is not unusual for them to become pregnant.'

Mary gives a bitter little smile, no more than a twist to her full mouth. 'To a whitefella. The boss or his son, most likely, it happens all the time – but they don't want their son to marry her, no way, mate. Don't marry the nigger, no bloody chance o' that happenin'!'

'Well now, whether that's the official idea, I can't say,' he ventures, a little disturbed by Mary's outburst. 'But it is *certainly* the government's intention that they mix in the white community with, I dare say, every chance that they will find a white male in or out of wedlock. Hence, I suspect, the preponderance of females removed from their families.'

'And soon there's no black women left in the tribe!' Mary exclaims. She turns to Jessica. 'The gubberment wants to make me kids white and miserable.' Tears begin to run down her dark cheeks and she sniffs, swallowing hard. She tries to wipe her tears away using the ball of her thumb, smudging them all over her pretty face.

Jessica brings her arms about her. 'Mary, we're gunna get your kids back.' She looks up fiercely at him.

'Mr Runche is gunna get them back, ain't ya, Mr Runche?'

He clears his throat. 'Well, my dears, it could be awkward, most awkward. What is being attempted by the government amounts to killing the Aborigines off, and the powers that be don't take kindly to being reminded of this.'

'What, all the blacks?' Jessica now asks. She's still holding her arms about Mary, who is sobbing and again attempting to brush away her tears, comforted by her friend's attention and love.

'Well, you could be excused for thinking that they're trying to eliminate a race of people,' Richard Runche says. 'The idea is to push all the children born of mixed race – the half-castes, the quadroons and octoroons – off the reserves, marginalise them as well as remove their children from their families so they cannot grow up to be Aborigines. The half-castes will be kicked out and the full-bloods will then be pushed onto marginal land, the general consensus being that they are dying out anyway. A nudge is as good as a push, if you know what I mean?'

He leans back and spreads his hands wide. 'In this way the existing native people's reserves can be resumed for soldier settlements. So you see, my dears, with the mixed-blood adults pushed to the edges of the towns to live in beaten tin, plank and sacking humpies, generally under the most extreme living conditions, and with few or no opportunities for employment, they become totally dependent on government rations.'

Mary nods her head in agreement. 'That's us fair dinkum, we can't get no jobs and it's rations what keeps us alive.'

Richard Runche KC brings up his hands in a gesture of futility. 'When a people lose their self-esteem, their pride, when they come to depend on government hand-outs, they are apt to become drunks and layabouts.' He gives a little self-deprecating laugh. 'Not that drunken-ness is a peculiar condition of the Aboriginal people. But, as happened with my own health, soon enough these people become prone to tuberculosis and bronchial infections or, for that matter, any epidemic which may be about. Moreover, as soon as they have children the government pounces, announcing that the children are neglected or in danger of moral corruption, et cetera, and so they remove them.'

'That what the policeman said. He said I weren't able to take care of me kids 'cause I was Aboriginal,' Mary says.

'The idea that the Aboriginal people are irresponsi-ble and can't take care of their children is, of course, now a self-fulfilling prophecy. The black people are reduced to extreme poverty and the cycle of turning black into white has begun. The children are brought up to white man's ways. Their languages and traditions are not passed on and eventually die out.'

Sensing that his listeners may not fully understand the line of his argument, he pauses to give an example. 'We white people are who we are as a result of thousands of years of language and tradition, which make us behave

in unique and intimate ways between ourselves. When
we destroy a language we effectively undermine the culture it belongs to. Language is the very soul of a culture.
A people's collective imagination, their myths and stories, their place on earth, their continuity, that thing
which gives them a soul and makes them different and
wonderful, comes from their language. Make no mistake, my dears, what this government is doing to the
Aboriginal people is a policy which clearly amounts to
an attempt at wiping them out. It is a deliberate and
planned attempt to destroy a race.'

Mary looks up. 'Me grandma told me they tried it
before, I mean gettin' rid o' us. She said it didn't work
too good, but still lots of blackfellas died. In her time the
white folk give the blacks poison in their flour and also
they poison the drinkin' water and shot blacks down
like we was dingoes. She tol' me the whitefella, they
called it "goin' duck shootin'". That's what she said,
"duck shootin'". There was men who put notches on
their guns, "duck notches" she says they called them –
blackfella don't duck so they becomes a notch on a gun!'

Jessica looks at the barrister, whose face is pale and
drawn, and she can see that he too is upset. 'Don't
Mary's people have *any* rights?' she asks sadly.

'When it comes to removing children from their
mothers, very few, my dear. Mind you, there was a time
when black people could resort to the courts for justice.
But in 1915 the Aborigines' Protection Board complained to the parliament that the courts were
obstructing the work of the Board.' He brings his hand

to his brow. 'Let me see if I can remember the honourable gentleman's words. I recall memorising them at the time because they were a measure of the arrogance and disregard for the love and care of a parent for a child that can only be described as breathtakingly callous.' He looks up, remembering. 'Oh yes, what he said went somewhat like this: "... *it is very difficult to prove neglect; if the Aboriginal child happens to be decently clad or apparently looked after, it is very difficult to show that the half-caste or Aboriginal child is actually in a neglected condition, and therefore it is impossible to succeed in the court.*" Those were the words of the minister at the time – I'm sure I have it almost exactly,' he says, pleased with himself.

Mary claps her hands excitedly. 'Me kids are the same as what you just said – they's dressed good and is healthy and I loves them. Like that bloke, that minister, say, them on the Abo Board, they can't prove nothin'. The court gunna give me back me kids!'

Jessica looks across at Richard Runche hopefully, but the barrister shakes his head sadly. 'Perfidy, my dear – there is no greater example than a government determined to have its own way. In the same year – that is, 1915 – the government passed the Aborigines' Protection Amendment Act which gave the Board total power to separate children from their families without having to establish in court that they may be neglected.' He lifts his finger to emphasise his point. 'Now *anyone* – the manager of an Aboriginal station, any employee of the Board, or a policeman of ordinary rank – need only write in the committal notice, as the reason to take control of a child, the simple words, "*For being Aboriginal*". The parent has no further say in the matter, and the Board henceforth has absolute power and discretion over the child or children. In effect, they become the prisoners or even the slaves of the State, of the government.'

'Does that mean Mary can't do nothing about her kids?' Jessica cries in alarm.

'No, not quite. The government must be seen to have a conscience, my dear. Mary can still appeal to the court as a parent, but she must actually sue the Board for the return of her children. She can't stop them being taken and she must sue for their return, where she might or might not win.'

'Has any Aborigine done it and won?' Jessica now asks.

'Not to my knowledge, my dear. It is a most difficult situation.'

Jessica gives a bitter laugh. 'Joe would say she's on a hiding to nothing.'

'Precisely, my dear. Difficult, if not impossible, that is, for an Aborigine, who is not given the same rights as an Australian citizen, to mount a court case. If Mary was a white woman she might be entitled to free legal representation, but as an Aborigine she would be hard put to find a lawyer who would even take the case.' Richard Runche spreads his hands apologetically. 'It's an expensive business and well beyond the means of virtually any Aboriginal parent. It is true to say that the Amendment Act simply allows the Board to steal children away from their parents. It is essentially an act of deliberate and, one is forced to conclude, purposely legislated cruelty.'

Jessica barely hears this final part of his explanation. Her mind is already preoccupied with the business of getting Mary's children back. 'How much?' she asks him.

Richard Runche looks puzzled. 'How much? Oh, you mean to take the case to court?' He rubs his chin. 'Well, we can expect the Aborigines' Protection Board to vigorously oppose it with the full backing of the government.' He sighs, thinking for a moment. 'My dear, it could go on for some time, months, even a year. But then, of course, if we could find a lawyer who'd do it for nothing and with me acting as his brief – his barrister –' he smiles at Mary, 'we could considerably reduce the outgoing expenditure.'

'I have some money, my turkey money! Nearly a hundred pounds,' Jessica exclaims, then she brings her hands to her lips. 'And a lawyer, I know a lawyer, Mr Moishe Goldberg!'

Richard Runche KC grins and, unable to resist the pun, says, 'Well then, my dear, let's talk turkey.'

Jessica and Mary embrace, both of them bursting into tears, their chins resting on each other's shoulder. 'It'll be orright, you'll see,' Jessica sobs to her friend. 'They can't keep your rainbow kids away from you, Mary.'

Then she jumps up and goes over and kisses Richard Runche. 'We're gunna beat the bastards! You'll see, you can do it, Mr Runche!'

'Oh dear, I feel quite faint, I really must lie down,'

the barrister says, colouring furiously. 'If you'll excuse me, ladies?' He gently untangles himself from Jessica's embrace and rises a little unsteadily to his feet. 'The last lady who embraced me was also you, Jessica. I shall never forget that moment.'

'We'll buy yiz a new suit an' all,' Jessica laughs.

Richard Runche turns to depart when he sees Mary still seated at the table, her eyes averted. He knows suddenly with absolute certainty that she would never have the courage to thank him in the same way Jessica has just done – that she is thinking that he would object to being embraced and kissed by a black woman. The Englishman leans over the table and takes Mary's hand, bringing it to his lips. 'We shall do everything we can, my dear. I'm getting to be an old man with few of my wits remaining, but what few you and Jessica have so nobly salvaged are entirely at your disposal, Mary Simpson.'

It is now almost two months later on a hot summer morning in late November of the same year, 1923. Jessica, Mary and Richard Runche KC, perspiring in a new serge suit, are standing together outside the Narrandera courthouse. Moishe Goldberg is inside, going over some procedural details for the hearing with the clerk of the court.

Ever since Jessica wrote to him in Sydney, enclosing with her own letter a brief from Richard Runche, Moishe has been going full steam ahead. *At long last something to get my teeth into*, he's written back to Jessica. *Perhaps this will be my revolution? The first thing is to locate the whereabouts of Mary Simpson's children – can your friend describe them for me? I want to know everything, any scars or distinguishing features are important: eyes, hair, approximate height, dates of birth, birth certificates, if any. I confess, the Aborigines – the few I've seen – all look alike to me, I could be easily fooled. Do Mary's girls have more than one name? Are they all called Simpson, or have they taken the names of their respective fathers?* Moishe's list of questions seems endless and Richard Runche, who remembers meeting Moishe when he was visiting Jessica at Callan Park, is suitably impressed.

'A lawyer who cares about details, how very nice. A good case is built on details, minutiae, and sometimes the smallest things can be the turning point. He's just the man for me, as my poor mind is like a sieve these days,' Runche says.

'Moishe likes to know everything. He's a proper old stickybeak,' Jessica laughs.

'Stickier the better, my dear. We are about to hit the proverbial bureaucratic brick wall with a thump.'

Moishe has written to the Aborigines' Protection Board and the Child Welfare Department, requesting to know where Mary's children have been taken. Both authorities reply that the information is not available to the public or to the children's family. They give no reasons.

The appearance in court this morning is so that they might obtain a court order to issue to both bodies to supply Moishe with the information he needs. It is the first step in the first court case ever attempted by an

Aboriginal parent to get her children back. If Mary Simpson eventually wins, she will make legal history. Richard Runche knows that, at best, their chances are slim to non-existent and he wonders if his health will see him through to its conclusion. This morning, however, he will not be needed as Moishe is entitled to make the plea.

The little party is called into the court and the clerk asks them all to be upstanding while Mr John Sneddon assumes his place at the bench. He is a man of medium height who has a remarkable resemblance to King George, a likeness which he appears to have taken the trouble to emphasise by trimming his sandy beard and combing his thinning hair in precisely the same manner as the monarch. The only notable difference is that he wears pince-nez, a small pair of gold-rimmed glasses pinched onto the bridge of his nose. The clerk now reads out the business of the court, then announces the court is in session and asks the two lawyers to front the bench.

Mr Bruce McDonald, a local attorney, is representing both the Aborigines' Protection Board and the Child Welfare Department, while Moishe Goldberg introduces himself as the lawyer from Sydney for the applicant, Mrs Mary Simpson.

McDonald is a much-admired local who is also President of the Mechanics Institute and Chairman of the School Board. He is a large man of sanguineous complexion, bald for the most part with bushy white eyebrows and a naturally belligerent look – what Miss French the librarian calls 'his bull in a china shop look'.

He has a countryman's gut which spills over a broad belt holding up the trousers of his grey worsted suit. He has already loosened his collar and pulled down his black tie to the second button of his white shirt. On his feet are a pair of unpolished cattleman's boots and it is as if he wishes to give the impression that he is more a man of the land than of the law. Compared to the diminutive and still pencil-slim Moishe, he is an imposing presence in the courtroom.

'Mr *Goldberg*, up from *Sydney*, is it?' Magistrate Sneddon says, taking very little care to disguise his sarcasm, though whether his remark relates to Moishe's surname or the place he hails from, it is not quite clear. McDonald does not see the magistrate's question as ambiguous and it earns a sly grin from the country lawyer.

'Oh dear,' Runche whispers to Jessica, 'I think we may have a couple of "bush brothers" on our hands.'

Moishe appears not to notice, his expression remaining deadpan and his voice, when he replies, contains not a hint of anxiety. 'Yes, Your Worship, I am from Sydney and I am also a Jew,' he says quietly.

Richard Runche smiles, and his admiration for the young Sydney lawyer increases further. Moishe is a wary fish and has not risen to the magistrate's crudely baited hook.

'Well then, Mr Goldberg, having successfully established where you are from and what you are, we will treat this occasion as an open inquiry. You and our colleague here, Mr McDonald, may proceed in an informal manner, provided you apply the normal courtesies due to each other and address all your questions through the bench. I shall decide when to interrupt or call you to order. Perhaps you would like to begin, Mr Goldberg from Sydney.'

'Thank you, Your Worship, my request is simple enough. I wish to locate the whereabouts of four young girls, the daughters of Mrs Mary Simpson, who have been forcibly removed from their family and placed into an institution under the jurisdiction of the Aborigines' Protection Board.'

'Aborigine, eh?' the magistrate asks.

'Well, yes, that is the children's race, not their gender.'

Police Magistrate John Sneddon looks up sternly. 'Mr Goldberg, if we are to proceed in an orderly fashion I must ask you to kindly refrain from using your Semite wit. The question was simple enough, are these children Aborigines?'

'Certainly, Your Worship, they are Aborigines of mixed blood. My point is that, despite the apparent simplicity of the request on behalf of my client, Mrs Simpson, every attempt to obtain the whereabouts of her children from this government instrumentality has been refused. I have received nothing but obfuscation.'

Bruce McDonald lumbers to his feet. 'Your Worship, I object. The law does not require us to state where an Aboriginal child has been taken to. It is my clients' duty to protect these native children. We do not encourage the continuance of the bad influences these half-caste children have been subjected to by allowing visits from their degenerate parents. Our intention is to raise them up so that they may adopt the tenets of Christianity and grow into decent and civilised human beings.'

The magistrate looks at Moishe. 'Well, Mr Goldberg, what do you say to that?'

'Your Worship, as I have pointed out, I am not a Christian, yet I believe myself capable of being a decent human being, hopefully also a civilised one.' Moishe turns to McDonald. 'I ask my learned colleague, is he saying that the one condition is contingent on the other? Are there no decent human beings beyond those who embrace the Christian faith?'

Bruce McDonald half rises. 'That is not what I wished to imply, Your Worship, merely that the children were being protected from harmful outside influences.'

The magistrate looks sternly at Moishe. 'That is not what Mr McDonald wished to imply, Mr Goldberg. You will refrain from making implications of this nature. You are a Jew and he is a Christian and, as far as I know, the native people are heathen animists. However, I should remind you that ours is a predominantly Christian society and it is not surprising that the State would wish the children under its jurisdiction to benefit from the teachings of Jesus Christ our Lord.'

'Oh dear, a Baptist on the bench,' Runche whispers to Jessica. 'I hope he has a conscience.'

Moishe hesitates, and appears to be thinking, gripping his bottom lip between his fingers, his eyes fixed on the floor. 'With the greatest respect, Your Worship, I confess I remain confused. Are you explaining my learned colleague's viewpoint and that of the government? Or are you instructing me to accept that the conversion to Christianity of my client's children is a legitimate reason why she should not be told their whereabouts?'

Richard Runche is filled with admiration for Moishe Goldberg but he is also aware that the young lawyer is not winning the confidence of the country magistrate. Baiting a magistrate or a judge seldom leads to glory in a courtroom. He will have to talk to the young Sydney lawyer. It is no surprise to him therefore when John Sneddon brings down his gavel. 'I must remind you that this is my court, Mr Goldberg, and it is I who do the cross-examination. We will proceed without further cheap asides to the bench or I shall be obliged to terminate this hearing.'

Moishe bows respectfully to Sneddon. 'Your Worship, my original point is that decency, while being common in the Christian faith, may also be found elsewhere. My client, I submit, is a decent and caring mother who has had her children removed from her care without there being any suggestion that she cannot ensure their welfare. I should also point out that she is herself a Christian, raised on a Lutheran Mission, and that she professes herself and her children to be members of that faith.'

Bruce McDonald rises reluctantly to his feet, though he gives the distinct impression that the task is onerous and that he would much rather conduct his side of the case from the comfort of his chair. 'Your Worship, I refer

you to the Aborigines' Protection Amendment Act of
1915 wherein it states that the Aborigines' Protection
Board does not need to prove neglect by a parent in order
to remove the children from a native family. That is the
law and we, the Board and Child Welfare, work within
the letter of the law in this and in every other case.'

Moishe gets to his feet. 'Your Worship, is my learned
colleague saying that despite Mrs Simpson's being both
decent and Christian and well able to care for her children, the law has the right to take them from her and,
furthermore, to prevent her from knowing where they
are?'

The magistrate turns to Bruce McDonald, who sighs
and shakes his head before undertaking the obviously
tedious task of coming to his feet again. It is apparent
from his manner he cannot believe his opponent's sly
inferences. 'The reason why parents are not notified of
the whereabouts of their children is quite simple,' he
growls. 'These children are neither Aboriginal nor are
they white. They are half-castes, or quadroons, or even
octoroons who have the misfortune of being born into
an environment which lacks the advantages of a higher
civilisation such as our own. By removing them from
these primitive influences we are giving them and their
children and their children's children the opportunity to
recover from this unfortunate beginning in life, for
which they are not responsible.' He looks at the magistrate and then at Moishe Goldberg. 'They have as much
right to be white as you or I, so why should they be
condemned to be black? We do not want, nor will we

allow, their natural parents to influence them in their choice. We will allow them to grow up independent of any influence their parents may exert so that, when the time comes, they can make up their own minds. I have not the slightest doubt that they will wish to assimilate with the white population, and that is also what the government wants. When the time comes for them to choose, you may be quite sure they will choose to be added to and counted on the white side of the ledger.'

Jessica looks fearfully at Richard Runche. McDonald, having failed in one area of defence, is now cleverly exploiting another – the concept of white supremacy which has been written into the law by the amendment he had referred to earlier.

Richard Runche scribbles a note and hands it to Jessica: *A contemptible but nevertheless, in the climate of this court and country, a powerful argument. McDonald is no fool – Moishe will need to watch his step.*

'Your Worship, my learned colleague Mr McDonald began by saying that my client's children are being saved from neglect and moral degradation by being embraced by Christianity and taught decency and morality while being incarcerated in a government orphanage. However, now he appears to be saying that they have the right to choose whether they wish to be superior or inferior, white or black. Is this correct?'

The magistrate looks over at McDonald who, with a dismissive wave of his hand, says, 'That is correct, Your Worship.'

'That is correct, Mr Goldberg,' the magistrate repeats.

'Thank you, Your Worship. In effect, my learned colleague is saying that by removing them from the care
and love of their natural mother and placing them in an
institution we give them the right to choose to be white?
By forbidding them to use their original language and
alienating them from their roots we give them the right
to choose to be white? By teaching them that to be
Aboriginal is to be inferior, dirty, primitive, something
they ought to be ashamed of, we give them the right to
choose to be white? By removing them from the love of
their decent and Christian mother we give them the
right to choose to be white? Your Worship, my client's
oldest child is seven and her youngest eighteen months.
Does my learned colleague *honestly* believe they will, at
the age of eighteen, when they cease to be wards of the
State, be placed in an ideal position to make the decision
whether they wish to be white or black?'

'Will you answer please, Mr McDonald,' John Sneddon the magistrate instructs.

Bruce McDonald gives a slow, confident smile. 'Yes,
I do believe this will be the case. Ours is a great humanitarian service, Your Worship. It is our duty to remove
these half-caste children from the baneful influence of
their parents.'

'You have heard your learned colleague's reply, Mr
Goldberg. Do you wish to continue?'

'Yes, thank you, Your Worship. I should like to explore
my learned colleague's reply a little further. Is it a humanitarian service to both the child and the mother to rob a
mother of her child? How humanitarian is it to place the

child in an institution, or in a foster home, or let it out for adoption, without proving first that the mother is incapable or unfit to rear the child in a decent and presumably Christian manner? Is it humanitarian to take a girl child at fourteen and place her into indentured labour with a white employer, with no rights of refusal, so that she is, in effect, a slave or, at the very least, a prisoner?

'Are children under such conditions capable of choosing whether they wish to be regarded as white or black? I ask you, Your Worship: Katie, the eighteen-month-old; Dulcie, the three-year-old; Sarah, who is five, and the seven-year-old, Polly – how will they make a comparison between the culture they have left and the misery they have had to endure for the better part of their childhood?

'May I, Your Worship, suggest that it is hardly a Christian and decent way to treat a small child, whether such behaviour is condoned by an individual or a State. Does this court truly believe that *any* child of eighteen months, or three, five or seven years, is better served in life by being removed from its mother? *Any* child, regardless of its colour or creed. Your child, my child, my learned colleague's child, *every* child needs the warmth and love, care and comfort of its mother to grow into a decent and responsible human being.'

McDonald raises his hand and waves the air in front of his face as though he is diverting a bad smell. 'Objection, Your Worship!' The courtroom is hot and he is perspiring and uncomfortable in his heavy suit. He comes to his feet slowly. 'Your Worship, it is *precisely* because the mother does not care for her child that the child is removed from her custody – the neglect does not have to be proved, it is *assumed*. We *know* these mothers are not capable of caring for, or loving, their children. It is simply not in the half-caste child's interest to remain with the mother. It *is* an act of humanity, decency and, dare I say it, of Christian charity!' He sits down and folds his arms, glaring at Moishe.

Moishe addresses the bench. 'Your Worship, may I have the court's permission to address my learned colleague directly?'

'Do you mean by that, that you wish to cross-examine him? No, Mr Goldberg, you may not, you must address all your questions through the bench,' the magistrate now says.

Bruce McDonald fans himself with his notes. 'I have no objection to being cross-examined, Your Worship,' he says, giving the magistrate a slow, country-boy grin that falls just short of a wink.

'Well I have, Mr McDonald, every objection! Please proceed, Mr Goldberg,' the magistrate snaps.

Richard Runche leans over to Mary and whispers, 'Oh, well done, I think our lad is impressing him.'

'Very well, Your Worship,' Moishe now continues. 'May I ask my learned colleague whether a child is removed from its mother's care by the Aborigines' Protection Board *or* Welfare when it is born into a full-blood Aboriginal family?'

'Your Worship, the Board is not concerned with the removal of full-blood children from their families and will only do so if it can be satisfactorily proved that the child is abused or neglected,' McDonald states.

'Thank you. So I take it that what my learned colleague is saying is that, under normal circumstances, the full-blood Aboriginal mother is thought to be quite capable of rearing her young, provided always that the child is also a full-blood and that the mother's habits are sober and her mind is clear?'

'Is that what you mean, Mr McDonald?' Sneddon asks.

'Near enough, Your Worship,' the big lawyer replies in a relaxed voice.

'So then it must be your opinion that the moment the infant is born a half-caste, quadroon or octoroon, this same mother loses her capacity for motherhood and becomes neglectful of her duties to the immediate detriment of her child?'

McDonald has been caught napping and he looks up, a little startled, then immediately assumes his 'bull in a china shop' expression. 'Your Worship, that is *not* what I said. I object strongly to this line of questioning.'

'Ah, it is a paraphrase, Mr McDonald, and a very good one I might add,' the magistrate replies. 'Your objection is overruled.' He turns to Moishe. 'You may continue your line of questioning, Mr Goldberg.'

Richard Runche smiles to himself. He was right, Moishe has made a breakthrough with the beak.

'Thank you, Your Worship. If, then, we are to follow this line of thinking, and if a full-blood woman has intercourse with a white man or half-caste, quadroon or octoroon and, as a result, gives birth to a mixed-blood child, she must, by virtue of my learned colleague's previous statements, be pronounced an unfit mother by the Aborigines' Protection Board.'

'Do you follow this argument, Mr McDonald?' John Sneddon now asks.

'Yes, yes,' the lawyer says impatiently. 'It is not yet beyond my humble grasp, Your Worship.'

'Well then, let me recapitulate,' Moishe says evenly. 'If a good mother is turned into a bad one by having a mixed-blood child, then it can only mean one thing: the mother has become genetically corrupted by the white genes which have been introduced to create the child. It is the *white* blood now flowing in her child's veins that mysteriously makes her an unsuitable parent. I ask, does this genetic misadventure change her during her pregnancy into an uncaring and unloving mother? Has the half-caste child she now carries somehow poisoned her heart and mind? Let us now suppose her mixed-blood child is a girl, will she, too, carry this infection causing disaffection for her children? Will it make her into an uncaring mother as well? Are we saying all white mothers are, by the physiological nature of their blood, negligent and uncaring?'

The magistrate brings down his gavel hard. 'Mr Goldberg, now you have gone too far!'

Moishe is surprisingly unfazed and speaks quietly. 'I entirely agree with you, Your Worship. My argument is, of course, a nonsense. But no more so than the supposition that the mothers of half-castes, quadroons and octoroons must lose their children on the entirely unproven assumption that their offspring are placed in moral danger by remaining with them. The real truth I suggest is that my learned colleague is saying that *all* Aboriginal mothers with mixed-blood children are by definition negligent and uncaring. That is as much a non-sense as saying that *all* white mothers are by definition negligent and uncaring. The idea that the Aborigines' Protection Board and the Child Welfare Department can take such an arbitrary course without having to supply the slightest evidence to substantiate their decision is an indictment against them and the higher institution which has allowed such a state of affairs to come about.'

The magistrate's head jerks up suddenly and his pince-nez falls onto the surface of the bench. 'Are you impugning the parliament of this State, Mr Goldberg?' He shakes his fingers at Moishe. 'Because if you are, this court takes immediate exception to your remarks and you will be placed in contempt!' John Sneddon picks up his pince-nez and clips the spectacles back onto the bridge of his nose. 'Counsel for the supplicant will with-draw that last remark,' he says, bristling with formality.

'Thank you, Your Worship, I most humbly withdraw my remark.' Moishe now pauses and looks around him at the few people sitting in the court. 'The government of a democratic nation rules with the permission of a majority of its people. Therefore we must conclude that the state of affairs which I have just outlined must meet with the approval of that majority. May I suggest, Your Worship, that when a society punishes its mothers and children in this way it cannot be regarded as a just and fair one. Nor can it, with honesty, be regarded as a Christian society based on the principles of decency, and morality . . . or was it charity?'

Oh, what a marvellous barrister he will one day make, Richard Runche KC thinks to himself.

Moishe now continues, 'The courts of this land are here to seek justice for the individual and, as well, to punish those who offend against the people. The Aboriginal Australian is one group within this democratic nation, the very first group to settle on this land we have so recently called Australia. I submit that we are offending them greatly, and that they are entitled, like any other group, to justice from the courts of their own country. Your Worship, I most humbly beseech this court to allow my client, Mrs Mary Simpson, to be permitted to know where her children have been taken and, furthermore, that she be allowed to visit them. Her children have committed no crime and nor has she. To deny her the right to see them amounts to the most callous disregard for a mother's love for her children. I know that it is not within the jurisdiction of this court to return the four little girls to their mother at this time, or I would ask for this to take place as well. Thank you for your patience, Your Worship.'

Moishe sits down abruptly and Richard Runche reaches over Jessica's lap and clasps Mary's hand, squeezing it briefly, then he looks at Jessica and smiles. 'Bravo! We have our lawyer,' he whispers.

'Have we won?' Jessica whispers back anxiously, holding tightly onto Mary's hand.

'Mr McDonald, have you anything you wish to say before I give my verdict?' John Sneddon asks.

Bruce McDonald wipes his brow with a bright green handkerchief and rises slowly to his feet. 'Yes, Your Worship, I do, I do indeed.' He pauses and looks around the court, taking his time. Then he begins. 'We have heard a great deal of verbal tap-dancing from my learned colleague, most of it a heap of cow cake . . . or, if you like, the masculine aphorism for the same substance.' He rocks a few moments on his feet, seemingly enjoying his own wit and looking about him for approbation. 'Perhaps this has something to do with my learned colleague's origins?' He pauses, then adds quickly, 'I mean, of course, that he comes from the city and has no contact with the blacks. On the other hand, well, I'm a country boy, born and bred in the Riverina. We like to keep things simple out here in the bush. Is it against the law or lawful? Simple stuff. Country bumpkin honesty. No fancy footwork, no shadow-boxing. No smoke and mirrors, only the truth plain as daylight.' He pauses again before continuing. 'Well now, put into bush terms, simple terms, the actions taken by my clients are within their absolute right under the law.' His voice rises suddenly and he bangs his fist into the flat of his hand. 'My clients are acting with the express permission of the law of the land!' He lowers his voice an octave. 'We are not compelled by law to tell Aboriginal parents the whereabouts of their children. I think I have demonstrated that there are good and sufficient reasons for not doing so. In this case, and in *every* other case concerning Aboriginal children taken from their parents, the law has been overwhelmingly on our side. We have its permission to act as we see fit, pure and simple.' He turns and glares at Moishe Goldberg. 'And I submit that, despite the sentimental hogwash from my city colleague, the law remains the law and my clients intend to keep it shining, untarnished by the sentimental ranting of city folks who know nothing about the black people. I ask that you find for my clients, Your Worship.' Whereupon he sits down, perspiring copiously and wiping his tomato complexion with the already damp handkerchief.

The police magistrate brings his gavel down, indicating that he wishes to address the two lawyers and that they should be upstanding. It is obvious to both of them that he has allowed the open discussion in his court to go too far. They both know that if Moishe Goldberg is to continue it must end with a public indictment of government policy. The young Sydney lawyer's arguments must inevitably go to prove that the Aborigines' Protection Amendment Act of 1915 is a policy predicated on overt racism and that it has been expressly designed as the major element in the wiping out of the Aboriginal people.

If he is to avert a legal disaster in his court, Mr John Sneddon, the police magistrate, must now swiftly bring the proceedings to a close.

Moishe Goldberg has plainly got the better of his opponent, and it remains only to be seen whether the police magistrate will slip through the hole in the legal fence McDonald has made for him in his final speech, or have the courage to make a decision of conscience in Mary's favour.

'I have heard both your arguments and I have studied the Amendment Act of 1915 and nowhere does it say that the law expressly forbids the parents of a mixed-blood child to visit it in an institution. I submit to you, Mr McDonald, that this is simply the declared policy of the two government departments you represent.' The police magistrate looks over his pince-nez at Bruce McDonald. 'I have therefore decided to make my decision in favour of the applicant. I find for Mrs Mary Simpson. Furthermore, I direct that the Child Welfare Department as well as the Aborigines' Protection Board immediately inform her of the whereabouts of her four children and that they grant her, together with any other members of her family, permission to visit the Simpson children once a month for a period of one hour.

'Finally, I would like to add a personal observation off the record. It is that, if we can make this same accommodation for felons in His Majesty's prisons, then we ought to be able to allow an innocent child to see its natural mother for a similar period of time without fear that the child's mind will thereby become corrupted.' With this, Magistrate Sneddon brings down his gavel. 'This court is adjourned.'

Jessica hugs Mary and then Richard Runche KC. 'We've won, we've won!' she cries, clasping a sobbing Mary to her breast. 'We're gunna get your kids back, Mary, you'll see!'

CHAPTER SIXTEEN

It's almost a year since Mary was granted permission to see her children, Sarah and Polly, who have been placed into the Cootamundra Girls' Home. During this time Moishe Goldberg has been harassing the Child Welfare Department to reveal the whereabouts of her three-year-old, Dulcie, and the baby, Katie, both of whom are light-skinned and were put into foster homes almost immediately after they arrived at the institution. The Child Welfare Department, however, refuses to reveal the names or whereabouts of the foster families, saying only that as the children are so young the families who have taken them think of themselves more as adoptive than foster parents.

Mary was inconsolable when she arrived with Jessica at the notorious Girls' Home to find that two of her children were missing.

'Where's the baby and little Dulcie?' she asked Polly moments after she'd tearfully embraced her two children.

'Mama, they took them,' Polly said, distressed. 'They said they couldn't stay with us 'cause they almost white, they said plenty white families wanted kids like them two.'

'Don't worry, we'll find them,' Jessica comforted her friend. 'Moishe says they can't be adopted, only fostered.'

But after a year even Moishe has become despondent about ever finding Mary's two little ones and, in preparing the case for the restoration, he has been forced to eliminate the names of the two youngest, fearing it will complicate the case to the point where it stands very little chance of reaching a decision.

In the ensuing period it has become essential to prove that Mary is of good character and a Christian woman with some education, for it is obvious that the Aborigines' Protection Board will try to discredit her in court, in an attempt to prove that she is an unfit mother.

Moishe writes to Jessica suggesting that she test Mary's ability to read and write. *If she can read a simple document and understand it, this will be sufficient for our needs*, he writes. *I have come to understand that literacy is relatively unusual in an Aboriginal woman of her age. Perhaps you can give Mary a test using the newspaper.*

Jessica knows Mary can write her signature in a nice sloping hand and she's confident that her friend will easily pass such a test until she actually tackles her with the task.

Mary shakes her head. 'Jessie, I were taught on the Lutheran Mission to sign me name, that's all. That was the first thing we done, even before the alphabet. They said, "Your name is a picture and you must draw it over and over until you can do it by heart. If you can't draw the picture, you can't be a person. If you don't learn it good, your family can't get no gubberment rations. It's your fault if they don't get no tucker." So we learned that one thing real good, to draw the exact picture of our names. I can do it in me sleep, nice and smooth like people who can write proper.'

'You never talk about the Lutheran Mission, Mary. Why is that?'

'Yeah, well, not much to say about that place, Jessie.'

'But there was a school there, wasn't there?'

Mary is silent for a moment. 'I was born in that stinking, rotten gubberment Mission. It was called the Lachlan River Mission, I dunno why they called it a Mission, God didn't live in that place. I was one of thirteen children and me father worked for rations, for no pay. There was no work, so they divided the work up, me father worked one day a week and for that he gets gubberment rations. He took me along so I could sign for him, *Chicka Simpson*. That was the second picture I learned, to sign his name. You got rations of a Friday. It would be an all-in go, thirteen kids and everyone else who wants a feed – you know that's the Aboriginal way, to share. By Sunday there would be no tucker, so you'd starve till Wednesday.' Mary looks up at Jessica. 'And I mean starve. I don't mean miss a meal, I mean miss three days' meals. Your guts'd be growling for want of food. Then Wednesdays I got to walk through the bush three miles to work at a slaughter yard, scrubbing the mess from the floors. They didn't give me no pay neither. My reward was I was allowed to take all the guts home in a fifty-pound flour bag. It wasn't for me, it was for everyone at the Mission, us kids and everyone. It was a matter of survival. That was before that big drought and when I was married to a Wongai-bon man. We was starvin' and went walkabout with that mob. We come down this way to your place and your old man give us tucker and says we can camp here.' Mary smiles at her friend. 'Jessie, that were the best day of me life, the day I met you.'

Jessica takes Mary's hand and holds it against her cheek. 'We're best friends, Mary, ain't we? I'll teach yiz to read and write, if you like. I wasn't too good meself until Moishe took me in hand when I was in the loony-bin.'

Mary laughs. 'I reckon it might be too late, me brain's fair gone, what with all me worries and havin' them kids lost to me. I didn't have much schoolin' then. They advertised for a manager for the Mission and the shit-carter in Hillston applied for the job. The gubberment give it to him, and his wife become the schoolteacher 'cause there was more pay in it for them. She couldn't read nor write, and always had a headache. There was no schoolin', just a schoolteacher who didn't know how to write her name on the blackboard of that little tin schoolroom. It was a big laugh, because I taught her how to draw her name, same as the missionary taught us. Make it a picture and learn the picture. She was that proud when she could do it. That was our fat teacher, Mrs Lily Murphy, our fat slug teacher, drawin' pay and eatin' good food.'

Despite Mary's earlier protests Jessica, and sometimes Richard Runche, teach her how to read and write. She proves to be a good pupil and over the period of a year has mastered enough reading and writing techniques to pass Moishe's test easy as pie.

Soon after the magistrate's hearing at Narrandera, Moishe issued a writ against the Aborigines' Protection Board, accusing them of conspiring to remove Mary's four children and demanding that they be returned to her.

In the ensuing year the Aborigines' Protection Board tried every tactic in the book to frustrate Moishe's attempts to bring the case to court. But Moishe Goldberg, Mr Detail himself, has met their every challenge and in the process learned a great deal about the Cootamundra Domestic Training Home for Aboriginal Girls and the plight of the half-caste children within it.

A few months after Jessica and Mary visit the two girls in the home, Moishe discovers that the education they receive is of a most desultory nature. Education at the institution is not considered important beyond religious instruction. The girls are destined to become domestic servants and their schooling consists of work that will lead to them taking up a situation in a white home where reading and writing have no possible benefit and are genuinely thought to have no relevance to their lives.

Moishe also learns that Aboriginal children from government institutions are entitled to attend the local school and so he requests that Polly and Sarah Simpson be allowed to go to the government primary school in the town. He wants them to have an education, and his thinking is also that it might give the children an opportunity to be away from the influence of the home for a while each weekday.

However, he receives a letter from the Aborigines' Protection Board stating that while this is indeed official policy it is subject to the approval of the parents of white pupils and that this approval has recently been withdrawn from the appropriate school in Cootamundra.

Moishe, who won't take no for an answer, persists, demanding to know why they can't attend the local school. Finally, unable to get any satisfaction from the Department of Education, he visits Cootamundra himself and interviews the schoolmaster, Mr Fred Burrows.

Burrows proves almost as reluctant to give any information to Moishe as the school authorities in Sydney, but he admits that the school had previously included several Aboriginal children.

'They were removed at the insistence of the white parents. I'm afraid there is nothing I can do about it,' he says, tight-lipped.

'Nothing?'

'Nothing,' the schoolmaster replies, leaning back on his chair and tapping his desk with the end of a pencil.

'Did they give a reason?'

'They don't have to, Mr Goldberg, being Aboriginal is sufficient reason.'

'Do you not find such a concept abhorrent?'

'Mr Goldberg, I have to teach in this town. I'm not a policeman, I'm a schoolmaster. It's all right for you city people to come to the bush with all your fancy demands, but you don't know anything about the blacks. Take it from me, they're just not the same as us.'

'Where have I heard that before, Mr Burrows?'
Moishe muses.

The schoolmaster sighs. 'You really don't have any
idea, do you?'

'What is that supposed to mean, Mr Burrows?'

Burrows sighs heavily and, leaning forward, he
opens the top drawer to his desk. After a few moments
he produces what appears to be a letter written on
cheap lined yellow stationery.

'This is a letter from a man born in this town, a parent of two of the children at this school. He is well liked
and respected, a local businessman and on the town
council, so you can see he carries a fair amount of clout
around these parts.'

Moishe takes the letter and begins to read. He will
later have Richard Runche present the letter in court as
part of their case.

Mr C. Fern
Member, Legislative Assembly
Sydney, New South Wales

Dear Mr Fern,

*I object to the blacks assoiating with the chil-
dren of the whites, especially my own Whom I
am going to with draw Should the blacks be
allowed to continue their attendance at the Above
School.*

*My reassons are, Principle first, Second I con-
tend morraly mentaly and Phisickelly the Blacks*

are not fit to assoiate in the Play ground especially
with children of from 6 to 8 years of adge, as little
children continualy in the company of Blacks
acquire to the ways and moodes of the Aborignies.

I think it is very hard that us out back Should be
put on a level with the Blacks by the Government.

The smell in the School House from the Blacks
in this hot climate is objectionable.

Yours truly,
A. Stevenson.

Moishe looks up from his reading. 'May I make a copy of this letter, please?'

The schoolmaster shrugs. 'Don't see why not. It was sent to the local member who sent it on – it wasn't marked confidential.'

Moishe holds up the letter. 'And so on the evidence of this one letter you removed the Aboriginal children from your school?' he says.

'No, there was also a medical problem.'

'A medical problem? What, with the Aboriginal children?'

Burrows grows suddenly frustrated and rises from behind his desk. 'Mr Goldberg, I am not at liberty to discuss the matter. You will need to write to the Department of Education in Sydney.'

So Moishe does just this and some weeks later he receives a copy of a report written by the principal medical officer of the School Medical Service.

To the Under Secretary
Department of Education

24 June 1923

I visited the Cootamundra Primary School on the 22nd Inst., and inquired into the alleged outbreak of venereal disease among the scholars. It was alleged that one of the school children, named Arthur Simmonds, age 6, had contracted gonorrhoea. That he had been infected through using the school water closet, which had previously been infected by one of the Aboriginal children attending the school. (There are three Aboriginal children attending the school at present.) Some weight was given to the allegations, owing to the known fact that three Aboriginal boys had contracted gonorrhoea in March last. These boys, however, have not attended the Cootamundra Primary School for, at least, twelve months.

I had a meeting with the (white) parents (about 30), at which the matter was freely discussed. The parents were then invited to have their children examined, and 45 children were presented by their parents for that purpose. Arthur S—, age 6, and his brother Tom, age 8, were found to be suffering from well-marked gonorrhoea. This diagnosis I confirmed by bacteriological examination. The other 43 children examined were found free from gonorrhoea, although a fair proportion was found suffering from other conditions of the privates needing attention. These conditions were pointed out and explained to the parents.

Mr Simmonds, father of the two boys suffering from the disease, stated 'the younger boy, Arthur, contracted it first, but he hadn't been at school for nine or ten weeks previous to developing the gonorrhoea'. As the incubation period of gonorrhoea is about five to ten days, and the boy had not been to school for nine or ten weeks previous to developing the disease, the school could not have been the causal agent. Those parents I met appeared now to be quite satisfied that the school could not be looked upon as a source of infection. Many stated 'they would send their children back to school'.

The feeling against allowing Aboriginal children to attend the school appeared to be very acute. I was asked if this could not be stopped, or, short of that, could not these children be made to occupy a separate department of the school. I promised to place the matter before you on my return to Sydney.

Signed

Principal Medical Officer – School Medical Service.

Following up on the report, Moishe discovers that the Simmonds children in question were white and could not have caught gonorrhoea at the school. They could only have contracted the venereal disease either from a member of the family or from someone else involving them in an act of sexual congress. In fact, no one had caught the disease at school. The Simmonds children were excluded along with all Aboriginal children but, unlike the Aboriginal children (who did not have gonorrhoea and who were *never readmitted*), the Simmonds children returned to the school when they recovered from the disease.

However, despite his persistence, all Moishe's efforts with the Department of Education to have Polly and Sarah, now that she had turned six, admitted to the school fail. The girls are condemned to receiving no education of any value within the Cootamundra Domestic Training Home for Aboriginal Girls.

Life in the Cootamundra Girls' Home is a harsh existence. The staff who supervise the children are poorly paid and, for the most part, ignorant, uncaring and cruel. There is nothing more desperate than the lower orders of whites given the opportunity to persecute those they believe to be inferior to themselves. Mary is encouraged by Richard Runche and Moishe Goldberg, on her monthly visits to the home, to obtain details of the conditions within the institution from Polly, so that Runche may use them in the forthcoming court case.

Polly is an intelligent and observant child whose spirit has not yet been broken. But she and Sarah suffer greatly at the hands of the staff, who deeply resent the fact that Mary is allowed to visit her children. The two girls are constantly threatened by the matron to 'keep your gobs shut' and warned that if they tell their mother anything bad about the place they'll be severely punished for telling lies. As a reminder the staff wash out the girls' mouths with soap before every visit by their mother.

But Mary speaks to her children in the Wiradjuri language and usually comes away with a much better insight into the institution, which Richard Runche encourages her to recall on her return to Redlands. He implores her to tell him every detail and suggests new areas of questioning for her next visit. Slowly they build up a comprehensive file on the institution, though of course it is one seen through the eyes of an eight-year-old and can easily be discredited in court, so the Englishman makes Mary repeat questions, often two months later, checking Polly's answers for their consistency.

The food is deplorable – bread and jam and porridge with a cup of tea for breakfast, bread and jam at midday and invariably stew at night. Although the girls say they are always hungry, they are by no means starved and Mary admits that the food appears to be more plentiful than it was back home in the Aboriginal camp.

The children are subject to the usual adult bullying, with the matron having her favourites and then 'the girls she come down on all the time, like me and Sarah', as Polly explains. The children attend school within the institution for two hours each day and this is of such a desultory nature that by the time they leave the institution at fourteen they have seldom passed the stage of the first reader. It is rare that the girls can read at all, and their writing is limited to spelling out their names.

Work takes up the major part of their day and it is mandatory even for the tiny tots. 'Idle hands get up to mischief' is a slogan written in capital letters at the top of the blackboard. In effect, the children do the majority of the labour at the institution – in the kitchens, the laundry, the vegetable gardens, scrubbing and polishing floors, mending clothes, ironing, sweeping, cleaning and emptying the chamber-pots, transporting the garbage and digging the latrines. Discipline is harsh and arbitrary and the most popular method of punishment is to be flogged with a wet rope. But the children's worst nightmare is being locked in the old hospital morgue all night.

The day starts at six a.m., when the old bell in the courtyard is rung for prayers, and ends the same way at eight p.m., six days a week. On Sundays the work is less though the time is taken up with church service, Catholic in the morning and Lutheran in the early evening, with compulsory attendance at both. Religion is thought to be the central core of the girls' assimilation into white society and it is made quite clear to them all that the Lord Jesus is a white man who came to earth to save their dark, black souls. They are taught that life is about good and evil, that there are black thoughts which are wicked and white thoughts that are good. They are told that the black thoughts come from their Aboriginality and the white ones are from the European blood they are fortunate enough to possess. To be black is to be evil and to be white is to be good. They must spend the remainder of their lives combating the blackness within them and nurturing their white purity.

There is no heating in the dormitories during winter

and with only one threadbare blanket per bed the children suffer terribly from the cold. Many can barely walk to the cold showers during winter from the chilblains which so badly affect their feet. All this is thought to be character-forming and small children are severely punished if they double up their blankets by sharing a bed and hugging each other for warmth. Polly tells her mother how she'd waited one bitterly cold night until there was nobody about and she'd taken Sarah's blanket and put it over her own, then taken her sister into her bed to keep her warm.

They'd fallen asleep in each other's arms and had been discovered by the matron in the morning and given a sound flogging. 'You're wicked and it's the Devil part in you, the sinful black part. Go down on your knees at once and ask God for forgiveness!' She'd made them take all their clothes off and kneel naked in front of her to beg God for forgiveness. After this she'd made Polly hold her still-naked, shivering little sister while the matron flogged her with the wet rope. Then she'd doubled the punishment for Polly, whose idea the bed-sharing had been.

'Mama, why is it the Devil part in us? What did we do wrong?' Polly asks Mary on her next visit. 'Are black people wicked and don't know it?'

Mary clasps both her children to her. 'You did nothing wrong – blackfella love God the same as the whitefella. You done good keeping Sarah warm, it the right thing to do.'

'No, mama, you're *wrong*, it *was* wicked – all the

other kids said what we done was wicked, sharing beds is wicked!' Polly says tearfully, now totally confused.

Mary tries to caution her children against believing the things that are said about black people, but Polly will have none of it and Sarah now looks more to her sister than to Mary for the truth in her small, hard life.

'Mama, they tell us all the time, every day, that we mustn't go near black people. Black people is dirty, dirty, dirty, they says.' Polly stops and then asks, 'Mama, don't you want us no more?'

Mary urgently grabs her children and hugs them. 'Mama wants you both with all me heart, my darlin'. We fighting to get you outa this place and back home with your mama.'

Polly looks doubtful. 'They say our people don't want us, they're just dirty and don't want anything to do with us.'

The tears run down Mary's dark cheeks. 'My darlin', you mustn't believe them, your mama loves you and Sarah and Dulcie and baby Katie. The black people love their children, it break their hearts to have them took away, stole from them. You know your mama loves you!'

'We're not allowed to say we love our mother! Millie done that and they killed her.' Then Polly realises what she's said and her eyes grow big and she brings her little hand up to cover her mouth.

Mary looks up in alarm. 'Who killed who, Polly?' she asks slowly.

Polly says in the Wiradjuri language, 'We're not allowed to tell, I'll get into trouble. They'll kill me and

Sarah if we say – that's what the big girls says, to shut our gobs.'

'Who was killed? Who's this Millie? You must tell Mama, Polly.'

'Millie Carter, from Grong Grong, she was at school there with me. She was took with us when they came.'

'Banjo Carter's little girl? I seen her here once when I visited, she waved to me. I told her dad when I got back that I seen her. They killed Millie?'

Polly nods. 'They said she had asthma.'

'What happened to her? Tell me, Polly, tell your mama,' Mary says fiercely.

Polly looks at her sister and then about her, and Mary sees that their eyes are fearful as Polly recounts the story to her mother, keeping her voice down almost to a whisper. 'Millie shouted when we was standing in line for our dinner, she shouted that her mama loves her. She was at the back of the line where those who are the most black must stand. They get everything last – the whitest first and the blackest last – and so when it come her turn there was nothing left, no tucker. That's when she said it.'

'Said what, Polly?'

'Millie said, "Me mother's a blackfella and she loves me!" She shouted it out.'

'Then what?'

Little Sarah, who has been listening silently, now volunteers, 'They said she was very, very wicked, Mama.'

'Yes, and that it's the Devil's talk, and a pack of lies and she must be punished,' Polly continues. 'They took her and tied her to the bell-post out in the courtyard and they flogged her. We could hear her crying and screaming when we was in the dormitory in bed, but we wasn't allowed to look out the window. In the morning she was still there tied up and they found her dead.'

Mary holds Polly by the shoulders. 'Polly, are you sure?'

The two children nod vehemently, their bottom lips tucked under the top. 'We looked out the window early, all us kids,' Polly says. 'We got up before the bell and they was cutting her down and Mr Phillips was pushing her chest with both his hands. The matron was there and Mrs Roberts, the schoolteacher, too. Then he shakes his head and they took her away by her shoulders and legs, Matron and Mrs Roberts, and Millie's arm was dragging on the ground.'

Mary recounts this appalling story to Jessica and Richard Runche when she returns home. They are both deeply shocked but the old barrister clasps Mary's hand and says, 'Though a shocking and terrible story, it could be our salvation, my dear. We must attempt to verify it. If we can substantiate the facts, it might well be pivotal to getting your children returned to you.'

'How come?' Jessica asks.

'Well, my dear, if we can prove that the children are in mortal danger where they are incarcerated, then we have a good chance of proving negligence against the Aborigines' Protection Board – in effect, against the State itself. We will need to get Moishe onto it right away.'

The case of Mary Simpson versus the State is finally convened in the district court at Wagga Wagga on Monday, 14 September 1925. The case attracts very little attention as Aboriginal affairs are of no concern to the white population in the cities and country folk, for the most part, don't have much sympathy for the blacks being kicked off the land or for their dirty, snotty-nosed children being taken away from them. The soldier-settlers have earned their free farms at Gallipoli and Ypres and Paschendale, folk reckon, while the bloody Abos sit on their backsides, breed like flies and draw government rations paid for by the taxes of the hard-working white man.

The case takes place in front of Justice Tom Blackall, a recent appointment to the circuit court and formerly a barrister in Wollongong, of whom not much is known among the country people.

He has a very small head, with a sharp, down-turned nose and dark beady eyes. His skin is of a sallow, waxy complexion with a permanent five o'clock shadow despite his cheeks being closely shaved. His wig seems too new and overly brushed and is much too large for his head. He is tall and extremely thin with a hunched back and an angularity that makes his limbs seem more bone than flesh. Gathered up as he is in his black robes, he looks for all the world like Mr Micawber of story-book fame.

Those who know and care about such things might conclude that a 'touch of the tar brush' might well have lurked somewhere in his distant past. This is not seen as a good sign by Richard Runche, who confesses to Moishe that it often makes them more racist, a sort of backhanded compensation for their appearance.

Moishe shrugs. 'If I looked the way I do and had a touch of the gentile in me, it wouldn't make me an anti-Semite.'

'You're quite right, I'm getting grumpy in my old age,' Runche confesses. 'Although, in my experience, a tincture of colour seems to reserve for itself an especially volatile emotion in the would-be Caucasian.'

The judge calls the two barristers into his chambers to discuss the procedure and to explain his manner of conducting himself in court. Shortly afterwards, to a gallery consisting only of Mary and Jessica, the case begins with Richard Runche's opening remarks.

'Your Honour, I intend to show that my client, Mrs Mary Simpson, has been deeply prejudiced against by the Aborigines' Protection Board of the State of New South Wales. With your permission, Your Honour, I shall in future refer to my learned colleague's client simply as "the Board" or simply "Board"?'

'Permission granted,' the judge says.

'Furthermore, I shall set out to prove that my client's four children have been unjustifiably removed from her care and made wards of the State.

'In the process I hope to prove that the previously mentioned Board has been guilty of gross negligence to the point of endangering the lives of at least two of Mrs Simpson's children.

'I intend also to ask that the court direct the Board to

reveal the whereabouts of Mrs Simpson's two other children, who have been placed into foster homes. Despite a court order stating that she is entitled to visit them, and frequent requests by her solicitor, the Board has continually refused to tell my client the names of the foster families and their places of residence.

'Finally I intend to ask that the two Simpson children at present incarcerated in the Cootamundra Domestic Training Home for Aboriginal Girls be released back into the custody of their mother. And in a separate deposition, I propose to ask that this court direct that the two youngest Simpson children also be returned to her care. I thank you, Your Honour.'

The judge turns to the senior counsel representing the Aborigines' Protection Board. He is the well-known Sydney barrister and racing identity Francis Codlington and assisting him in preparing his case is none other than the redoubtable Narrandera lawyer Bruce McDonald.

Codlington is a big man, broad around the girth and well over six feet in height. He wears a perfectly tailored London suit of blue serge designed with a narrow white pin-stripe and a silk cravat over spotless white linen. He sports a pair of white spats covering the insteps of his highly polished boots, which completes the ensemble but for a red carnation in his buttonhole. At the exposed end of his personage is a shock of shining white hair which serves to nicely offset his immaculate spats at the other end. Immediately below his hirsute glory resides a pair of dark, extremely bushy eyebrows and, further down still, a bristling moustache which appears to have been blacked to match his eyebrows. Codlington gives the impression of a man of altogether superior status and seen as he is beside his crumpled English opponent in his cheap country-shop suit smelling of mothballs, he has an awesome presence.

The stark comparison between the two senior counsel is almost comical, but Francis Codlington and Richard Runche do enjoy a single feature in common – their noses both testify to a more than passing fondness for the bottle. Though again the comparison seems odious – the most likely tipple for a gentleman of the Sydney barrister's standing is the finest malt whisky and not the cheap claret Runche's enforced sobriety has caused him to forsake.

Francis Codlington rises to outline the case for the defendant. 'Your Honour, in the parlance of horse-racing, I hope to show that this case is essentially a one-horse race.' He turns to indicate the seated Bruce McDonald. 'My assistant, Mr McDonald, has had the privilege of hearing out the arguments of my learned colleague's own assistant, Mr Goldberg, in the police magistrate's court in the town of Narrandera.' Codlington now turns to look directly at the seated Richard Runche. He smiles and then says, 'We are extremely confident that the law of the land will survive the onslaught of the *dark* forces which may be ranged against it.'

Codlington obviously enjoys his ambiguous emphasis on the word 'dark' and, still wearing the shadow of his previous smile, he turns back to the judge. 'It is my intention to prove that my client has always acted strictly within the letter of the law and that Mrs Simpson's children have been treated no differently from thousands of Aboriginal children, all of whom have been saved from neglect and hardship by being removed from the parlous influences of their wayward and ignorant parents. We anticipate no surprises here, Your Honour. The law remains, I am thankful to say, quite clear on these matters.' Codlington, every inch a man in control, nods at the judge and sits down.

Judge Blackall thanks Codlington and turns to Runche. 'Senior counsel for the plaintiff may proceed to state their case.'

Richard Runche, wearing a borrowed wig and gown, both somewhat the worse for wear, rises and addresses the court. 'Your Honour, I am delighted to hear that my learned colleague intends to keep the law safe from an onslaught at the hands of the dark forces which threaten to undermine it. However, in my experience, justice is best served when good men seek constantly to challenge the law, to ensure that it leads to a just and fair outcome. I am sure my learned colleague would agree with me that throughout the twisted history of the law there have been unjust as well as just laws, and that it is these unjust laws which history will later refer to as the workings of dark forces within the land. As for the clever ambiguity suggested by my learned colleague with his play on the word "dark" to mean the Aboriginal people, how pleasing it would be if the dark people of this land represented any kind of force to oppose the injustices to which they and their children are subjected by the laws of this government.'

The judge brings down his gavel. 'That is enough! Both counsel will henceforth refrain from ambiguity, innuendo or any play on words. You will not trivialise my court in this manner, do you understand me?' He turns to the clerk of the court. 'You will strike counsel's opening remarks from the records, Mr Hanson.'

Richard Runche bows towards the bench. 'Yes, thank you, Your Honour.'

Francis Codlington shows a reluctance to come to his feet, but now he half rises and nods his acknowledgement to the bench. It is obvious his intention is to dominate the proceedings and in the process attempt to intimidate the inexperienced judge.

'The counsel for the defence will recognise me and address me as "Your Honour" when he is spoken to from the bench,' Judge Blackall now says sharply.

Codlington rises again, this time a little further into an upright position. 'Er . . . yes, Your Honour.' The supercilious smile appears once more on his face.

'The senior counsel for the plaintiff, Mrs Simpson, may proceed,' the judge instructs.

Runche grins inwardly – he has made his point and is even pleased that he hasn't succeeded with the judge because this shows him that Blackall remains firmly in control. He clears his throat and speaks.

'Your Honour, as I had previously stated in my opening address I would like to prove to this court that my client, Mrs Mary Simpson, is a woman who has always

632 B R Y C E   C O U R T E N A Y

taken care of her four children as a responsible and caring mother. I intend to use the major criteria set out by the Child Welfare Department of New South Wales for the creation of a ward of the State. The child, or children, must be deemed to be neglected and the indications of neglect used by the Department are as follows: The child must be certified by a physician to be undernourished as a consequence of the extreme poverty or deliberate neglect of the parent, or parents. The parent, or parents, must be seen to have neglected the child's safety. The parent must be seen to have deprived the child of the education and of those medical services commonly available to children of this State. The parent must be of unsound mind and mentally incapable of taking care of the child. Finally the child must be found to have been physically and/or sexually abused by one or both of its parents or others, so that its welfare is endangered in both a physical and moral sense.

'I put it to you, Your Honour, that none of these circumstances may be said to prevail in connection with my client and her relationship with her children. On the contrary, I will now submit for the perusal of the court documents to testify to Mrs Simpson's past care and concern for her children.'

Moishe hands Runche the first three documents, from the schoolmistress Mrs Mavis Cross of Grong Grong Infants and Primary School. They are the children's end-of-year school reports. 'Please note that these documents relate to the two older children, Sarah and Polly Simpson,' Runche begins. 'They show that both children were in the top bracket of their class. Polly is noted as having been absent from school for just four days in two years up until the time she was removed by the Board. In the case of Sarah, who spent her first year in school prior to also being forcibly removed, she was absent for a total of two days with a severe cold. I should point out that the children would walk six miles either way to attend this school. Their report cards also state that they were always clean, neatly dressed and well behaved. The next document I submit is from the School Medical Service and against both children's names the examining medical officer has placed the words *In good health*. I also submit a written testimony from their schoolmistress, which states that the children were never seen to bear bruises or marks on their bodies that indicated any form of physical abuse. If I may read just one paragraph from her statement . . .' The barrister takes the letter handed to him from Moishe and begins to read.

'Dear Mr Goldberg,

'You have asked me if the two children Polly and Sarah Simpson showed signs of physical neglect or abuse. I can only answer by saying that I pay particular note to such indications, which are lamentably common among the children at this school and, I should say, are shared in an equal proportion between the white and Aboriginal children. Polly and Sarah have always exhibited excellent health and while it is not common for Aboriginal children to be plump, I have never seen

any sign that the Simpson children were either
hungry or bore the marks of abuse. I shall miss
them both in my classroom.

'*I remain, yours faithfully,*'

Richard Runche looks up. 'Signed, Mrs Mavis Cross, Grong Grong Infants and Primary School.'

He pauses and then says, 'I now ask my assistant, Mr Goldberg, to place these documents before this court as evidence of my client's capacity to act as a responsible and caring mother to her children.' The barrister watches as Moishe delivers the documents to the clerk of the court. 'Oh yes, with your permission, Your Honour, I feel that in order to set the record straight I must also point out that my learned colleague in his opening address referred to Aboriginal parents as ignorant. My client Mrs Simpson can both read and write, a skill not possessed by a great many white women in the lower social orders beneath which we, as a society, so cheerfully place the Aboriginals.'

'I object, Your Honour. It was a generalisation and I did not intend to single out a particular Aboriginal person, rare as she might be among her people.'

'I shall ignore my learned colleague's last remark,' Runche says, then adds, 'though I must point out that most racist dogma is based on generalisations.'

'Nevertheless, the counsel for the defence must withdraw his last remark and his objection is denied,' the judge rules.

Codlington is clearly not happy with the proceedings

and shakes his head in silent denial. He now rises. 'I withdraw my remark, Your Honour, and with the court's permission I wish at this point to question Mrs Mary Simpson. My assistant has already notified the court of this intention.'

'Very well, I ask that Mrs Mary Simpson take the witness stand.'

Mary is obviously nervous as she takes the oath – Francis Codlington is a very large whitefella and she doesn't come to much past his well-conditioned waist. 'You are Mrs Mary Simpson, the mother of . . .' Codlington glances down at the paper he holds in his hand, 'Polly, Sarah, Dulcie and Katie Simpson?'

'I am,' Mary replies in a tiny voice.

'Speak up, Mrs Simpson, the judge needs to hear your answers,' Francis Codlington suddenly barks, causing Mary to jump. A look of fear crosses her face.

'There is no cause for alarm, Mrs Simpson. Just answer my questions with a simple "yes" or "no" and speak out clearly. I shall repeat the question. Are you the mother of Polly, Sarah, Dulcie and Kate Simpson?'

'Katie,' Mary says in a slightly louder voice.

'I beg your pardon, what did you say?'

'I said Katie. Me baby's name is Katie, not Kate, and I couldn't say yes when you said it wrong.'

'Katie Simpson?'

'Yes.'

'I put it to you that Simpson is not their rightful surname. That each of them has a different father and therefore a different surname. Is this so?'

Mary swallows hard then replies, 'Yes, sir.'

'Then you have lied to this court about the surnames of your children?'

Richard Runche jumps to his feet. 'Objection, Your Honour. It is customary among the Aboriginal community these days when children are born out of wedlock for them to take the surname of the mother.'

'Objection sustained,' the judge rules.

Codlington bows towards the English barrister. 'I thank my learned colleague for so deftly bringing me to my central conclusion.' He turns back to Mary. 'Mrs Simpson, I have no further questions, you may step down.'

Francis Codlington turns to Judge Blackall. 'Your Honour, we have heard of the saintly nature of my learned colleague's client from his own lips. However, I put it to this court that no woman who has four children to four separate fathers out of wedlock can be regarded as either moral or responsible and certainly cannot be admired for her virtues. I further put it to you that if Mrs Simpson is not a prostitute she falls short of this definition only by virtue of the fact that she has received no payment for her services.' Codlington pauses briefly and then says as an aside, 'And even this has yet to be proved.'

Jessica, seated in the gallery, gasps and brings her hands to cover her face. 'Oh, the miserable bastard,' she says to herself, hating the huge, imperious barrister.

'Objection, Your Honour!' Richard Runche is on his feet again. 'If all the children born out of wedlock, be they white, half-caste, quadroon, octoroon or full-blood Aborigine, were to be discounted in this State, the juvenile population would decrease sufficiently for there to be a population crisis. Government statistics show that there are an estimated five thousand children born illegitimately every year, and I dare say this figure is conservative.' Richard Runche throws his hands in the air. 'Are we to classify all of these mothers as harlots? What is being judged in this court is not the sexual proclivities of my client, but simply her ability to act as a caring and responsible mother. I put it to you that there has not been a single complaint about Mrs Simpson's behaviour in the community in which she lives. She has never been arrested for a crime or named as a prostitute and I challenge my learned colleague to find a single instance when my client has accepted money in exchange for sexual favours. That she is indubitably a good mother has, I submit, been clearly demonstrated by the evidence submitted in this court by people who know her or her children sufficiently well to make a clear judgement.'

'The objection is sustained. Does the counsel for the defence have anything further to say on this matter?' the judge now asks Codlington.

Codlington clears his throat. He is clearly not happy about finding himself more than well matched by a country barrister with a reputation for being a drunken has-been. 'Not at this time, Your Honour, except to say that my client, the Aborigines' Protection Board, is highly experienced in the notion of what constitutes a neglected child and they saw fit to remove all four of the Simpson children.' He stops and looks at Richard Runche. 'Does that not suggest that they had good reason to do so?'

Runche turns to Moishe Goldberg who, without comment, hands him a document. 'Your Honour, I have here a copy of the committal notice for the four children. I now submit it as evidence for the court's perusal. The reason given in this notice for removing my client's children is written down as,' he pauses and pretends to read, ' "*For being Aboriginal*". Does this suggest a lengthy and thorough investigation into the children's welfare or their mother's neglect of them?'

The judge returns his attention to Francis Codlington who, in the hot courtroom, has grown increasingly red in the face and reminds Jessica of Beetroot, the largest of her turkey cocks. 'Does counsel for the defence have anything further to say on the issue of Mrs Simpson's ability to care for her children?'

'No, Your Honour, though we reserve the right to return to it when we argue the meaning of the law in regard to the removal of mixed-blood children.'

'Very well.' The judge now addresses Richard Runche. 'Do you wish to continue to explore the issue of the mother's competence, or do you propose to move on?'

'Your Honour, as long as we have the right to reply when my learned colleague invokes the law in regard to my client's suitability as a mother or the removal of her children by the Board, I am happy to move on.'

'Permission granted,' Judge Blackall says. 'Counsel may continue to state his case for the plaintiff.'

'Your Honour, my next statement is in relation to the safety of my client's two eldest children. I charge that the State and its instrumentality, the Aborigines' Protection Board, has conspired to place my client's eldest children in a position where clearly their lives are in danger. I shall prove that the Board is not competent to protect the children under its care and I shall ask for them to be returned to their mother. I shall call as my first witness Mr Banjo Carter of the Grong Grong Aboriginal community.'

Banjo Carter is a small man, very black, almost certainly a full-blood. He is neatly dressed in a clean flannel shirt and moleskins and wears a pair of stockman's boots which, though well worn, have received a liberal dose of dubbin. His hair is heavily greased back against his skull, though it threatens to spring away at any moment, and he looks thoroughly uncomfortable as he is sworn in.

'Mr Carter, thank you for coming. I shall keep you only as long as I have to. Can you tell the judge what happened to your daughter Millie?'

'She was took by the authorities.'

'Under what circumstances, Mr Carter?'

'In the schoolroom of Mrs Cross, sir. They just came and took Millie and said she had to come with them. Then the police sergeant at Grong Grong come around and said we had to sign a paper, that they'd took Millie and we had to sign for her. He said it was the law and to read the paper. I told him I didn't learn no reading, Gladys, me wife, neither. He said, "Never you mind, just sign." So I signed me name, I learned that in the shearin' shed.'

'Can you tell us what happened next?'

'Nothing, we didn't hear no bloody thing, not where they took her – bugger-all. And then Mary Simpson come to see us, she said she'd seen Millie in Cootamundra, that she was in the same place as her two girls. We was happy just knowing they haven't took her too far and that one day her mother and me, we might see her again.'

'Is the woman, Mary Simpson, present in this court, Mr Carter?'

'Yeah, that her over there,' Carter says, pointing directly at Mary.

Moishe hands Richard Runche a photograph and Runche continues. 'Mr Carter, I have here a photograph taken of the pupils at the Grong Grong Infants and Primary School. Will you please identify your daughter Millie among the children.' The lanky barrister hands the photograph over to Carter, who immediately points out his daughter. 'Ain't too hard, she's the blackest one,' he says, grinning sadly.

Runche hands the photograph back to Moishe. 'Can you tell us when next you heard of Millie?' he asks Carter.

'Mary, Mrs Simpson, she come over to tell us Millie's dead.'

'Dead?'

'Yes, she said that she was flogged and left tied up to a post all night and in the mornin' she was found dead.'

Banjo Carter can't go on and he sniffs back his tears. 'Millie were a good little girlie,' he chokes.

'Mr Carter, I shan't keep you much longer, but it is important that you tell the court what happened next.'

Banjo Carter sniffs and straightens up. 'Mary, Mrs Simpson, she brought a lawyer,' Banjo points to Moishe, 'him. He come and seen Gladys and me and says we got to go to the police and make a statement of a suspicion of murder. We done that like he said and the sergeant says he'll look into it, they'll get onto the Coota police right off. I said to him, "Sergeant, you remember me daughter Millie, the one you took from the school?" He shakes his head. "Banjo, I've took that many black kids you can't expect me to remember them all. I just drives them to the train and hands them over, mate."'

'Can you tell me what happened next, please, Mr Carter?'

'Yeah well, three months ago the sergeant calls me and Gladys and says he's got a report from the police at Coota. "Banjo, they've left no stone unturned, mate," he says. "They done a big investigation and there's even a letter from the Aborigine Board." "What's it say?" I ask. "Yiz'll have to read it to us."' Banjo Carter, now grown more accustomed to his surroundings, is relaxed and, like many people who have to rely on their memories, it is obvious he has a good head for detail. 'Well, it was a long report orright, full of stuff they done and who they seen and lots of inquiries into, and sworn affy davies.'

'Affy davies?' the judge asks.

'Affidavits, Your Honour,' Runche explains. 'Please will you continue, Mr Carter.'

'Yeah well, in the end it don't amount to much. The police report said that there was no record of a Millie Carter being in the Coota Girls' Home. Then he reads the letter from the Aborigines' Protection Board and it says the same. "There you go, Banjo," the sergeant says. "Your daughter's gorn walkabout, she must have escaped from the train." "Sergeant," I says, "she were seven years old!" ' Tears now run down the Aboriginal stockman's dark cheeks.

'Your Honour, this is the letter received by Mr Carter from the Board. With your permission, I would like to read it.'

'Permission granted,' the judge says.

'I shall submit it as evidence so I will skip the formal appendages. The main text of the letter is brief and to the point.

'*Dear Sgt McClymont,*

'*I am charged with the task of informing you that we have no records which show that Millie, the daughter of Banjo and Gladys Carter, ever came under the jurisdiction of this Board.*

'*Furthermore, we have examined the register of the Cootamundra Domestic Training Home for Aboriginal Girls and they similarly have no records of any trainee by the name of Millie Carter having entered the home, nor is there any member of the staff who can identify the girl in*

*the photograph submitted to us by the Coota-
mundra police.*

'*I am writing to you out of a sense of the obli-
gation to all Aboriginal children by the Board and
ask you to convey our sincerest hopes for the
recovery of the Carter girl.*

'*However, I regret we cannot help you further
in this matter.*

'*Yours faithfully,*

'*Nathaniel Rose*

'*Registrar.*'

Francis Codlington rises from his chair. His impatience
is obvious as he brushes his hand through his mop of
white hair. 'Your Honour, I am hard put to know where
all this is leading. Perhaps my learned colleague will
come to the point? With the greatest respect, what does
Mr Carter's missing child have to do with this case?'

'If you will give me just a little longer I think it might
become clear, Your Honour,' Richard Runche says. Then
he turns to Banjo Carter. 'Mr Carter, will you tell us what
happened next? Let me remind you, you were with the
police sergeant. Where was this, Grong Grong?'

'Yessir, at the police station. The sergeant says, "There
you go, Banjo, no point in making trouble, mate. Your
little daughter's gorn and nobody's to blame. The case is
closed, the police have closed their investigation." He
gives me back me photograph,' Banjo points to the letter
Richard Runche still holds, 'and I ask him for that letter
from the Abo Board, he give me that too.'

'Thank you, Mr Carter.' Richard Runche turns to the judge. 'Your Honour, I submit this letter for the court's perusal and I would like to call to the witness box Mr Joshua Phillips.'

Joshua Phillips is almost the direct opposite in appearance to Banjo Carter, though both are small. He is a man in his mid-thirties with a weasel-like face and a pink scalp covered with thin wisps of straw-coloured hair lying flat against his skin. His eyes are red-rimmed and of a distinctly watery blue and his face has a strangely scorched appearance, as though he works in a blast furnace. His eyes dart about the courtroom to see if there is anyone he recognises and he pulls nervously at the lobe of his right ear every few seconds. He finally sees Moishe Goldberg and smiles nervously.

Joshua Phillips takes the oath with great solemnity and has to be reminded to return the Bible to the clerk of the court.

'Mr Phillips, what is your occupation?' Runche asks.

'I work in a bakery, sir.'

'And prior to your present position what did you do?'

'I was odd-job man at the Girls' Home in Cootamundra, sir.'

'The Girls' Home?'

'For the Aboriginal girls,' Phillips replies, tugging on the lobe of his ear.

'Ah, the Cootamundra Domestic Training Home for Aboriginal Girls?'

'Yes sir, that was the one.'

'Mr Phillips, did you, while you were at the home, ever come across a young girl of about seven or eight years of age named Millie Carter?'

'I can't rightly say, sir, they all looked the same to me. They wasn't allowed to speak to us, nor us to them,' he explains.

'Think carefully, Mr Phillips, a very dark little girl, she could easily have been mistaken for a full-blood.'

Phillips shakes his head. 'I can't say, sir.'

'Well then, let me ask you another question. On the morning of the fifth of June, shortly before five o'clock, were you called to the courtyard of the Girls' Home where there had been some sort of an accident?'

Joshua Phillips's eyes grow suddenly bigger. 'It weren't no accident, she was tied up to the bell-post.'

'Who was?'

'This little black girl.'

'And what did you do?'

'Well, the matron said I was to cut her down.'

'Was there anyone else present?'

'Yes, sir, the schoolteacher, Mrs Roberts.'

'What did you do then?'

'Well I untied the ropes round her ankles and wrists that was tied to the post and I, you know, tried to pump her chest like.' Joshua Phillips looks at the judge and then back at Runche. 'I were a stretcher-bearer in the war, sir.'

'And to what effect, Mr Phillips?'

'I beg pardon, sir?'

'Did your efforts to revive the young girl help?'

'No, sir, she was well dead.'

'Objection, Your Honour!' Codlington shouts. His face is puce with rage and he shakes his finger at Richard Runche KC. 'I must ask why you didn't report all this to the police. It is against the law not to do so!' he shouts at the alarmed Phillips.

Judge Blackall brings down his gavel. 'The counsel for the defence will please sit down. You may cross-examine this witness at a later time if you wish.'

'Your Honour, in the interests of the truth, I would be happy for Mr Phillips to answer my learned colleague's question,' Runche says.

'Very well, you may answer, Mr Phillips,' the judge says wearily.

'Well, sir, they didn't ask me. I were dismissed three weeks later from the Girls' Home by the matron, she said it were on instruction from the Board in Sydney. There wasn't no police come to see me at the bakery.'

'Thank you, Mr Phillips. Now let us continue,' Runche says. 'When you were trying to revive this young girl would you not have been in a good position to study her face?'

'I'll never forget it as long as I live,' Phillips replies sombrely.

'Ah, then maybe you can help us, Mr Phillips. I have here a photograph of a group of schoolchildren. Perhaps you can identify the young girl in it.' Moishe hands the photograph to Runche who, in turn, hands it to Joshua Phillips.

Phillips studies the photograph. 'I can't rightly say,

sir,' he says, giving an involuntary tug to his earlobe.

'Mr Phillips, can you read?'

'Yes, sir, I can manage well enough with the newspaper and all.'

Runche turns to Moishe. 'Do you have half a crown, Mr Goldberg?'

Moishe digs into the pocket of his trousers and produces a half-crown piece. Richard Runche KC hands it to Joshua Phillips. 'Mr Phillips, can you read the inscription around the rim on this coin?'

Joshua Phillips squints, holding the coin close. 'Me eyes, they ain't what they used to be – it was the war, sir.'

Moishe, who as usual has thought of everything, hands Richard Runche a large magnifying glass. The barrister passes it to Joshua Phillips. 'Try it now.'

Joshua Phillips holds the magnifying glass to the silver coin. 'George V Rex. 1916 Australia,' he announces.

'Good, now look at the photograph through the magnifying glass, Mr Phillips.'

'The dark girl, she's the one! She had this one tooth missing and that mark on her face, the side of her nose, like a burn. That's her, orright.'

'Are you certain, Mr Phillips?'

'Yeah, I reckon, that's the closest I ever got to a blackfella.' He takes another look through the magnifying glass. 'Yeah, that's her, no risk.'

'Thank you, Mr Phillips, you may step down,' Richard Runche says, 'unless my learned colleague wishes to cross-examine the witness?'

The judge turns to Francis Codlington. 'Do you wish to cross-examine the witness?' he asks.

'No, Your Honour, not at this time.'

'Very well, the senior counsel for the plaintiff will proceed,' Blackall says. Richard Runche has been expecting the judge to pull him up and ask where his questions are leading. But now he senses that Blackall has a keen interest in the evidence unfolding and is giving him a little rope, although whether it's to hang himself or to prove his point, Runche is not yet sure.

'Your Honour, I wish to call Mrs Margaret Roberts to the stand.'

Francis Codlington comes to his feet. 'Your Honour, I must insist that my learned colleague comes to the point. What have the two witnesses he has summoned to the stand – and the one he is about to put under oath – got to do with Mrs Simpson's capacity as a mother, and my client's rights to remove her children from her care?'

The judge looks down Micawber-like at the big barrister. 'I suspect the counsel for the defence is about to find out.' He turns to Richard Runche. 'The counsel for the plaintiff will make clear to the court what he hopes to prove in relation to the question just asked by counsel for the defence. I must say, I am myself somewhat mystified – I appear to be trying an entirely different case, involving a young girl named Millie Carter.'

'Your Honour, I crave your indulgence. What I hope to prove is that the Aborigines' Protection Board is not responsible and cannot be trusted to protect my client's children and that they are therefore far better off under the protection and care of their mother. My next witness will, I hope, further amplify the fact that the Board cannot be trusted with the young lives under its jurisdiction and that it is prepared to act in a duplicitous and conspiratorial way to conceal its incompetence.'

Francis Codlington has become almost apoplectic in his appearance and he is barely able to find the voice to say, 'Your Honour, we wish to ask for an adjournment so that we may study the evidence presented by the counsel for the plaintiff.'

'Adjournment? What sort of an adjournment? I am prepared to give you one hour to be added to your luncheon recess.'

'Thank you, Your Honour. We have come to this court to argue a point of law and now we are confronted with a line of inquiry which we believe to be inappropriate. Our fervent request is for the case to be reconvened at a later date.'

'Inappropriate or inconvenient? This is the first case of this nature to come to the courts. I hope it won't be the last. No, I am not prepared to postpone this hearing. As I understand it, there have been several months of delay caused by your deliberate efforts to prevent it coming before the bench. I see nothing in this case which requires further preparation on your part. You will have ample opportunity to cross-examine the witnesses.'

'Your Honour, I should like to consult with my instructing lawyer.'

'Very well, I shall adjourn this court for lunch. We shall reconvene at two o'clock.'

'What does it all mean?' Jessica asks Moishe and Runche. She is holding onto Mary's hand and they are seated on a park bench munching corned beef sandwiches and drinking lemonade. Richard Runche looks longingly at the pub across the street. He hasn't had a drink for almost two years now, yet what he refers to as the 'clarion call of claret' still sounds cleanly and clearly in his ears.

Moishe grins, nodding towards Runche. 'The old man has caught them flat-footed. They had thought to argue the case on a point of law, to stonewall it.'

'Stonewall?' Mary asks.

'Whatever we say, whatever we prove, they would point to the law of the land. Keep to the one point, that the law allows them to remove mixed-blood children from their families for their own good without necessarily having to prove anything, that's stonewalling,' Moishe says.

'And now?' Jessica asks.

'Well, we're going on an issue of incompetence – an inability, if you like, to carry out the law. If the law allows that it may take mixed-blood children from their parents the assumption must be that it is for the ultimate good of the children. That the children are better off than they might be if left with their own parents. We have set out to prove that this is not the case, and the suspected murder of Millie Carter and the implication that the police inquiry was plainly aborted has, well . . .' Moishe tries to think of a suitable word, 'set the cat among the pigeons.'

'But can we do that? I mean, with Millie Carter? You heard what Mr Codlington said – what's it got to do with Mary's kids?'

Runche grins. 'Get away with it? I don't know, my dear. It depends very much on the judge. It is clear that there is a case for a miscarriage of justice with regard to Millie Carter, but whether it can be married to our case remains to be seen. We are still in a most tenuous situation. Fraught, most fraught.'

The court is reconvened and the judge turns to Richard Runche KC. 'The counsel for Mrs Mary Simpson will explain more clearly why he believes the plaintiff's children are placed in a situation which is likely to endanger their lives. He must do so to my satisfaction or I shall discontinue this line of questioning, which I should point out remains only just within the parameters of this case.'

Knowing himself to be on a warning, Runche decides to take a slightly different tack and not to pursue the Millie Carter murder any further by calling Mrs Roberts to the witness stand. He begins slowly.

'Your Honour, how strong yet fragile is the human condition. We can take starvation and hardship and all manner of physical pain and we may still recover, but if it is done to our heads and our hearts, that cannot be repaired. If we are loved we can endure. If we are hated we will soon perish in spirit. It is when we are young that the love will nourish and the hate will most effectively destroy,

'Man's greatest wickedness is the abuse and malevolent manipulation of the young, innocent mind. The child, in particular the orphan or institutionalised child, has no means at its disposal to resist, nor does it possess sufficient maturity to question the authority or to discover the truth for itself. Children are in no position to argue, they have no one of equal status to contradict the authority of the voices railed against them, and they are subject to arbitrary punishment if they show the slightest resistance to the lies and half-truths inculcated in their tender young minds. These children are the true victims of our white supremacist society. Millie Carter is believed to have shouted out, "Me mother's a black-fella and she loves me!" And for this, for this cry in the wilderness, this child crying out in pain, she was lashed to a bell-post and flogged and left all night to be found dead in the morning. For God's sake!

'Do we honestly believe that children can recover from such an experience? That every child in that Girls' Home will not believe that the same could happen to them? That they won't be filled with terror so that their minds are forever numbed? Your Honour, my client, Mrs Simpson, loves her children and wishes them to grow up as decent and caring human beings. The Aborigines' Protection Board has placed them in a position of terror and anxiety where they believe their very lives are threatened.

'No democratic government, no matter how callous, can stand by and allow this to happen, to condone the control of children through fear, no matter how rigorously the statutes which control the right to steal children from their mothers are written into the law of the land.

'As long as there are good men and women on this earth, as long as freedom prevails in our land, we will be judged on how we regard our children. How we treat those who cannot defend themselves. A child is not a half-caste, or a quadroon or an octoroon, or white or black, it is a small heart that can be made to trust and love or one that can be made to beat in terror and fear. Colour or breed or race doesn't change this. *We* do. We control this love or we create the fear.

'I ask this court to release my client's children from this bondage of terror. Your Honour, I don't believe it is necessary to bring yet another witness to the stand to prove what I believe has already been proved. The authority entrusted by the government to undertake the task of caring for half-caste children is patently unable to adequately undertake for their welfare.' Runche pauses and looks about him. 'I rest my case, Your Honour.'

The judge turns to Francis Codlington. 'I now ask the counsel for the defence to make its reply.'

Codlington paces the court grim-faced, then he looks up. 'Your Honour, what a shame that my learned colleague did not make his concluding speech in front of a jury. Why, I confess myself almost in tears, such mawkish sentimentality is wasted on so few of us. I do not propose to bring any witnesses into this court. I do not even propose to cross-question those witnesses my learned colleague has produced in an attempt to confuse the matter in hand with quite another. However, the law of this land remains inviolable, aloof from the cheapening of emotions. It is the will of the majority of the people and it is the wise counsel of the elders of our land – those men who have been chosen by us to carry out our wishes. I shall put my trust in it and only it.'

Codlington pauses. 'I am appalled by my learned colleague's imputation that it is the wish of our people to persecute the children of this glorious land, whether they be white, black or brindle. It is precisely because we care about our children that we do not wish them to be harmed by an environment of drunkenness, malnutrition, sexual and physical abuse. The law will not tolerate this happening to our children regardless of their colour.

'Now, it is common knowledge that for the most part the half-caste children of this land live in squalor, with disease and malnutrition their constant companions. Their parents do not have the sensibilities the white race enjoy and are quite devoid of responsibility. If we allow their children to come under their influence we will end with a race of wild people who put us all in danger. The half-breed has a dozen children to the single child of the full-blood and the handful of children in a white family. They simply breed like flies without regard for how they will feed the fruit of their pernicious loins. If we allow them to remain on the outskirts of society, on the fringes of our towns and cities, we will soon be overrun by this tide of human vermin. We must find a solution and this we have done.

'The solution is a fair and honest one – it is even a

generous one. We will take their children, these mis-
begotten children, and assimilate them into the white
society. In this way we will give them every opportunity
to succeed in life and we will have the satisfaction of
knowing that they have been well fed, housed and educated at our expense in the hope that they will adopt
Christian ways and live decent and honest lives. That
they will marry white men and women and, in the long
run, breed a race of people as white as any on God's
glorious earth.

'Do we honestly believe that we can afford the process
of selecting these children by giving their mothers and
fathers – that is, if the father may even be found – the
benefit of the doubt? What shall we do – examine the
parents and if they obtain a pass-mark allow them to
keep their children? It is far better to spread a wide net
and to gather in a few innocents while bagging a majority of the guilty. The law is not infallible, it will make
mistakes, but are they not affordable in the light of the
splendid consequences planned for the mixed-blood children of this land?'

Codlington turns to Justice Blackall. 'Your Honour,
I rest my case and put my trust in the laws of this land.
They have made the British people the greatest on earth
and it is a marvel that we are prepared to share the
bounty of our civilisation with people of a lesser one so
that their children might benefit.'

Codlington seems well pleased with himself. Runche
has not interrupted with a host of pernicious objections
so that the flow of his oratory and, he tells himself, his

damned fine common sense have been allowed to prevail. The day in court, which on several occasions looked blighted and where he has been wrong-footed by a man whose reputation as a drunk is only slightly less notorious than his reputation for incompetence, has been rescued by his own acuity. Codlington believes that, by relying on the solid foundations of the law and his belief and trust in the system, he has once again got himself out of the deep water into the murmuring shallows.

Justice Blackall gives notice that he will give his verdict at half past four and retires to his chambers.

Jessica is a bundle of nerves and Mary remains silent. There is too much resting on the outcome for her even to hope and she sits on the park bench outside the courthouse in a state of numbness.

Moishe wonders if they have got it all wrong. Maybe they should have fought the case along similar lines to the magistrate's hearing at Narrandera, he worries. The logic he had used there was irrefutable and he had felt at the time that had the magistrate possessed the power to release Mary's children he would have done so. Codlington's stonewalling had been impressive and Moishe knows that it was an accurate summation of the prevailing opinion of white Australians. Had they taken a wrong turn in trying to prove that the government institution, with the power of the law behind it, was abusing its power? Governments are not prone to censure their own instrumentalities, he knows only too well, and especially if the work of those instrumentalities is approved by a majority of the people.

Runche for his part feels weary and he would sell his soul for a bottle of claret. He has been preoccupied with the case for nearly two years and he has lost the vanity that makes a barrister believe he can win against the odds. It has only been Jessica's burning desire for justice that has kept him going. He's always known that they'd only get one chance, that they would make history or disappear entirely. Runche now tells himself that David very seldom triumphs against Goliath and that they've probably used the wrong tactic – that they should have brought the case of Millie Carter to trial and by winning it perhaps exposed the Aborigines' Protection Board more effectively and thereafter petitioned for a change in the law. How tired he is, how weary of it all – his bones ache, his mind is empty and he thinks only of the oblivion promised in a bottle of cheap claret.

The court is reconvened at half past four to hear Justice Blackall read his verdict. He is careful to sum up both cases and it is clear to Moishe and Runche that the judge has clearly seen what it is they have attempted to do. Jessica and Mary are lost in the tedium of his words until finally he brings down his gavel.

'I have made my decision in favour of the plaintiff, Mrs Mary Simpson. I instruct that her two children, Polly and Sarah, at present under the jurisdiction of the Aborigines' Protection Board and in the care of the Cootamundra Domestic Training Home for Aboriginal Girls, be returned to their mother. I am quite sure in my mind that Mrs Simpson's two girls stand a better chance of living fulfilled and useful lives without the State controlling their destinies. I direct that the whereabouts of Mrs Simpson's two youngest daughters be made known to her and that she be allowed to make the decision as to whether they will be returned to her or will remain with their foster parents.' Justice Blackall pauses. 'We are responsible for the administration of the laws of the land, but we seldom question whether the laws of the land are responsible. It is not sufficient that we accept every law without equivocation simply because we are its custodians. We of the law are accustomed to arguing the smallest points of jurisprudence while often neglecting to see its glaring deficiencies. The law must be based on the charitable behaviour of people rather than making people behave according to the law. Laws should be based on natural justice and not on punitive reaction, on enlightenment and not on our fear. As a judge I am charged to uphold it. As a human being I have only this last to say.' Justice Blackall looks about him. 'As long as history shall prevail, the love of a mother for her child cannot be replaced by an institution which will give the child a full belly and an empty heart.' Justice Blackall brings down his gavel. 'This court is now in recess.'

Richard Runche turns to Jessica, takes her hand and, squeezing it, he says, 'Jessica Bergman, my dear, you have made history.'

Jessica turns tearfully and hugs Mary, though inwardly she mourns for her own lost child, for her precious Joey. 'We've done it, Mary, we've done it!' she sobs.

THE FINAL CHAPTER

The year is 1929 and the New York Stock Exchange has collapsed and plunged the world into the beginning of the Great Depression.

It is also the year that Richard Runche KC doesn't wake up one cloudless morning in mid-March. The old man is usually up at dawn for a wash by the side of the creek, whereupon it is his habit to light the fire outside the hut and put the billy on to boil. He'd make a mug of strong, dark tea sweetened with honey, just the way Jessica likes it, and then he'd wake her up.

Jessica wakes this bright day to find the light too sharp for the hour she usually rises. The hut is stifling with the sun baking down onto the tin roof. She lies for a moment feeling confused, curious that Runche hasn't woken her with her usual cup of tea. She dresses hurriedly and comes outside to find the lanky Englishman lying in his bed under the lean-to on his back with his hands folded across his chest and his legs stuck straight out. He looks for all the world like an ageing knight laid out in a great medieval cathedral. Jessica reaches down and touches his calm face and knows the instant she does that he is dead.

Mary arrives later in the morning and, taking turns to dig the grave, Jessica and Mary bury Richard Runche next to Billy Simple's gravestone and not far from one of Runche's beloved beehives.

The barrister born into the English nobility, whose ancestors, since the time of the crusades, have lain in the same quiet churchyard in the village of Cerne Abbas in Dorset, now lies forever beside a quiet stream under the shade of a giant river gum. Here is no green and pleasant ancestral grave, no murmuring brook or dark shade of oak. This is a landscape beautiful only to those who know that beauty must be hard-won in the mind and the eye as well as in the heart. It is a harsh, new beauty with very little antecedent poetry to till and seed the white man's imagination. A landscape that must be viewed with an Aboriginal eye to see its colours and patterns and cunning shifts in perspective. The white-fella eye is still a long, long way from seeing this land's dreaming and the whitefella's heart is not yet fully opened to the high and ancient antipodean sky.

Jessica and Mary stand over the Englishman's grave and say the Lord's Prayer. Both cry a little, but not for long – they loved the old man too much for a bout of rag-sodden weeping. 'Don't cry for me when I'm gone, my dears, I should hate that,' he once said as they sat around the fire one night.

'Don't worry, we won't,' Jessica had replied cheekily. 'I'll be cranky as hell – who's gunna bring me tea in the mornin'?'

Mary had laughed. 'First thing that's gunna happen,

we're gettin' rid o' them flamin' beehives of yours. I been stung that often I couldn't count that high, even with all the education you give me.'

Now as they sit at the rough wooden table, weary from digging Runche's grave and saying their farewells, Jessica sips a cup of tea. 'Well, I know he died happy. He told me once that getting me outa the loony-bin, and getting back Polly and Sarah from Cootamundra, and fighting for Millie Carter and seeing the matron sent to prison for murdering her were the only good things he reckoned he'd ever done.'

'He didn't take no credit for it neither,' Mary says. 'He always said it was you give him the chance to be decent for once in his life.'

'He was always decent, there wasn't a bad bone in his body. He was born decent and he died decent,' Jessica murmurs sadly.

Mary laughs. 'And givin' up the grog – that was another good thing he did.'

Jessica smiles, remembering. 'Not that we gave the old bugger a chance to get back onto the sauce again. Even Rusty would have stopped him going into a pub if he'd tried.'

'I never seen that done before. I never seen a drunk that's as far gone as him, that's got them DTs, who give up drinkin'. When we brought him back from Wagga, I truly thought you was mad. I was sure we was bringing back a dead whitefella we'd only have to take the trouble to bury.' Mary seems to be thinking. 'And he was right about Dulcie and Katie.'

Jessica looks up, surprised. 'I've never heard you say that before.'

'Well I should have told him so,' Mary says regretfully.

Jessica thinks back to the time after the court case when they'd won, and the judge had ordered the Aborigines' Protection Board to return Mary's children. It had taken another year before the Board finally gave them the name of the foster parents with whom the baby Katie and little Dulcie had been placed. She remembers how they'd arrived at a nice house in Gosford belonging to Kevin and Doreen Blake, a childless couple who'd fostered Mary's two youngest children. What they'd found were two happy, healthy children clinging to the skirts of a pretty white lady who was very close to tears. Dulcie and Katie were dressed in charming little white dresses with yellow socks pulled up to their chubby knees and little patent leather shoes and they both wore a bright yellow ribbon in their hair.

Jessica recalls how Mary rushed up to them and how the two children had backed away from her, their eyes fearful, for of course neither of them recognised the strange dark woman coming at them with her arms wide open. What a crying match that had been. The two girls were howling and clinging to their white foster mother, who was also howling and clasping them tightly. Then Mary had started bawling, not knowing what to do, and even Kevin Blake sniffed into his handkerchief, about as useful as tits on a bull.

Richard Runche, who'd brought the papers with him to reclaim Mary's children, sat them all down and talked things out quietly with them. It was obvious that the Blakes loved Dulcie and Katie as if they were their own and that they were truly broken-hearted at the prospect of losing them. The barrister had finally taken Mary outside into the garden, where they remained talking for nearly an hour while the sobbing continued inside the house. When they returned, a still-sobbing Mary agreed that Kevin and Doreen Blake could keep her two youngest and that they had her permission to formally adopt them. Mary had never yet confided in Jessica what Richard Runche had said to her to make her change her mind.

'Mary, it ain't none of my business, but what did the old bloke say to you, you know, about Dulcie and Katie, when he took you into the garden that time?'

Mary looks up from her mug of tea. 'That a tough day, Jessie. We talked a lot there in that lovely garden and then the old bloke said something that I couldn't find no answer to. He said, "Mary, you can't give more love than they've already got."' Sudden tears well in Mary's eyes as she remembers. 'He was right, Jessie. Whitefella love is the same as blackfella love. Me kids were loved, that's all a mother can ask for.'

At first, after the death of Richard Runche, Jessica finds it difficult to settle down. The old bloke had become part of her life and he'd always been cheerful and busy enough with his beloved bees. The honey from his eight hives is now a Solly Goldberg delicacy and Jessica would send it out in a ten-gallon milk can

along with her turkeys and Solly would bottle and
label it.

REDLANDS RIVER GUM HONEY
'By gum, it's good!'

After his death Jessica gives the hives to Mary, who now
has a small income from the turkeys and bees, even though
the Great Depression is beginning to bite savagely and
times are hard with thousands of Australian families
thrown out of work. There are men on the roads again,
carrying their swags and looking for a day's or a week's
work in return for their tucker and a little tobacco.

And even Solly has had to reduce his weekly order
for turkeys. 'Never mind my dear, we manage. A kosher
turkey is blessed by God.' Jessica has very few personal
needs and her greatest use for money is saving up to put
young Polly Simpson through teachers' training college
at Wagga Wagga when she's old enough.

Young Joey has been sent to the King's School in
Parramatta and Jessica feels fortunate if she can just
catch a glimpse of him on horseback during the school
holidays. He has grown into a tall fourteen-year-old
and takes after his grandfather in looks. He is a big-
boned boy, a little clumsy-looking, with a mop of blond
hair and ice-blue eyes.

The future owner of Riverview Station has for the
past four years competed with boys of his own age at
the Narrandera Show, and Jessica leaves Mary to tend
the turkeys and stays with Auntie Dolly so that she
might attend every event he competes in. Hester and

Meg no longer accept Jessica as family – her friendship with Mary has seen to that – so that they look through her as though she no longer exists.

Joey is too heavy in the saddle and lacks the natural balance needed to be a good horseman, and he always finishes well down in the field. Jessica is finally forced to admit he is a bad loser, for he seems to sulk if he doesn't win. He'll hand his horse to a stable boy and stomp away to be comforted by Meg and Hester, who make no end of a fuss of him.

Back home Jessica tends to bore Mary endlessly with all the details. 'The boy's mollycoddled because Jack's not there to see he grows up proper. He's soft, you can see it – soft in the saddle, lazy, and he doesn't respect the horse. Sniffy too, he don't talk to the other lads much and I ain't seen him rub down his mount once. It's Meg and Hester, them two's made a sissy outa him. Jack would never have stood it. He'd soon have knocked that sort o' nonsense outa him, his grandpa woulda too. Joe wouldn't let him get away with that sort of rot. One day he's got to run Riverview and he's gotta start earnin' his respect now. Country folk've got long memories and Meg and Hester ought to be ashamed of what they're doing to my boy.'

Mary knows this kind of talk will be on for a week after Jessica's return from Narrandera and she has learned to make all the right women's noises without taking too much notice. She knows Jessica hopes that her boy will grow up to be like Jack or if he can't be like Jack, at least like Joe – both hard men. Jessica often wonders aloud to Mary what Joey would be like in a fight. 'Too soft and slow and he'd go bawlin' to Meg or his granny,' she reckons.

It's early October and there have been good rains, though with the Depression the bottom has fallen out of wool prices. Jessica can almost hear Joe looking down from heaven and saying, 'That's right, good rains for the first time in ten years and we have to shoot the lambs and it ain't worth clippin' and balin' the flamin' wool. God hates this bloody country!'

The rains and the early summer heat have brought out the snakes. Snakes seem to know when there's a good season about to come, with plenty of rodents for their young. Jessica is losing more than half a dozen turkey chicks a day and she is forced to keep them inside the run. She's also losing several hens who are too stupid to look where they scratch in the saltbush, and with so many snakes about, Rusty shows her several dead birds each day. The only good thing that can be said is that the wattle and red gum blossom are in profusion and Mary's hives are brimming with the best honey the women can remember getting.

'Good thing Solly's order is down. At this rate I reckon it's gunna be hard to give him the birds he wants, come Hanukkah.'

'What's Hanukkah?' Mary asks.

'It's Jewish Christmas, well sort of, without Jesus,' Jessica says.

'And they eat turkey like us?' Mary laughs. 'Until I know you, Jessie, I never tasted turkey in my whole life. At the Mission all they give us Christmas mornin' was cold mutton with maggots.'

'Nah,' Jessica explains. 'They don't eat turkey at Hanukkah, well not especially anyway. Moishe tells me Solly has a notice in his shop for the Mrs Turkey Shoppers. *To try a little turkey for Hanukkah don't make you Christian. It delicious, it kosher, so why not? God bless!* But Moishe reckons that Solly goes gentile at Christmas and he's got a nice little arrangement with Hannan's Butcher Shop in Rose Bay to sell the turkeys to the rich Eastern Suburbs matrons.'

Jessica sighs and says, 'But this year I don't suppose there's going to be a whole lot of turkey on the table for most folk, what with the snakes and the Depression. I might as well shut the hatchery down and save the kerosene and grain.'

These are the things which occupy Jessica's mind into late October and the coming of summer. It is a really hot morning, the first of the summer blinders. Jessica has let everything except the turkey chicks out of the run and Rusty is busy seeing they stay bunched up in the nearest paddock. Mary has gone up to Wagga to see Polly and Sarah and Jessica is smoking a hive to fill Solly's weekly order for honey. The order for turkeys is still way down but Solly can't get enough Redlands 'By gum, it's good!' honey.

Jessica hears Rusty growl and then give a short, sharp bark. She is holding a full honeycomb, which she's just removed from the frame. 'Oh shit,' she says in alarm and drops the frame and runs to the hut for the shotgun.

Her hands are sticky with honey as she breaks the twin barrels and feeds two birdshot cartridges into them. Rusty is still whining and barking as she comes out of the hut and Jessica is cursing her sticky hands. She runs over to the nearest paddock just in time to see the kelpie emerging from under an old man saltbush.

'Rusty, come here boy,' she calls and the dog turns and comes towards her. At ten feet she can see the two scarlet cuts on his nose. 'Oh Jesus, no!' Jessica screams, frozen to the spot, and the kelpie goes down on his front legs. Rusty gets up and tries to reach her but falls again. His eyes are still bright but he seems to have lost his sense of direction. He gets up and walks sideways, but falls over and tries once more to stand up. Jessica sees with horror the thin line of white foam around his mouth. Rusty makes one last desperate effort to reach his mistress, and gives a pathetic little whine as though he is trying to apologise to her for being so stupid. Then he collapses at her feet.

Jessica's first concern is for her beloved Rusty. She puts the shotgun down and bends her knees to lift him and then cradles him in her arms and starts to carry him towards the hut. The kelpie is heavy and she can feel his heart racing against the inside of her arm. Her hands are sticky against his soft, warm fur and as she holds him, Jessica knows only one snake can have this effect on a dog. She is positive Rusty's been bitten by a king brown. His entire body is now vibrating with the effects of the deadly venom. In her mind Jessica hears Joe's words all those years back when she was just a brat. 'A

dog's got maybe ten minutes, a big man maybe an hour.'
She remembers how he'd looked at her, measuring her
weight in his head, and said, 'Half an hour, you
wouldn't go beyond that, a mulga's a real bastard.' Joe
liked to get things right – he always called a king brown
a mulga, though it didn't sound nearly as dangerous.

Now Jessica puts Rusty down on the table near Billy
Simple's gravestone. She knows there is nothing she can
do to save him, so she runs to the hut and fetches a blanket to cover him. Then she washes her hands quickly
and comes to sit beside him, stroking the kelpie's head
and holding his soft ear in her hand, crying and waiting
for her best mate to die.

'You were the only turkey-dog in the world, Rusty,
and the best friend a whitefella ever had. I love you and
I'm gunna miss you somethin' terrible,' she says, then
Jessica feels his brave heart stop. With one last convulsive jerk, his legs stiffen and he dies.

Rusty, who had come to her as a puppy, a little
squirming bundle of red colour and curiosity. When
she'd come back from the loony-bin he'd been her best
mate from the very first. He'd never whined and every
morning of his life he'd be waiting faithfully for her
outside the hut just to tell her that she was the best missus a dog could have. Rusty, the champion turkey-dog
of the whole world, was dead, bitten by a fucking king
brown when he was trying to save some stupid turkey
hen. Jessica pulls the blanket over his head. 'There's too
many people I love buried around here,' she sobs.

Then her breast is suddenly filled with rage. Nothing

is allowed to live in this godforsaken land, and nothing ever dies naturally. The land, the dust and heat and floods and drought, everything living off everything else, death and destruction everywhere. Nothing is safe from this monstrous land. For the first time in her life Jessica knows what Joe meant all those years ago, feels the bitterness he felt, shares his hatred and the bitter-sweet love for this miserable strip of earth.

Jessica rises, fuming, and in her mind she's marked the spot where Rusty emerged from the bush. Snakes don't move around much in the heat and the king brown always marks its territory. She walks over to the shotgun lying on the ground – the barrel is already too hot to touch from lying in the fierce heat. She pulls back the hammers and then approaches the thicket of saltbush and wattle. Now she sees why there'd be a snake in there. A small clump of rock is hidden by the bushes – it's an ideal place for rodents, and a bloody snake would know that.

Jessica pushes the branches aside, stepping very carefully through the bush. Snakes are almost blind and deaf but if there's one there it will feel her vibrations as she approaches. A king brown, knowing it has a safe place like an outcrop of rock, will stay put and lie in wait rather than risk coming out into open ground.

Jessica stands still, waiting until her eyes have grown used to the deep shade under the saltbush, not moving the shotgun held at her waist. She can fire from the hip if she has to – it will throw her back but at least she wouldn't miss the bastard. Then she sees it – it's a king brown all right, a real big bastard. It lies curled with its ugly head raised, forked tongue testing the air, knowing she is there and measuring the distance between them. She is close enough to see its obsidian eyes, dark as sudden death.

Jessica doesn't panic as she slowly raises the shotgun to her shoulder, pushing the branches aside with the barrel so that she has a clear shot at the serpent's head. She feels her hand pull back the trigger, then the rending of the air from the explosion and then the snake lashing at the branches as its head explodes when the birdshot smashes it to a pulp. 'You bastard! You bastard, I've got you!' Jessica screams, then in her fury she lets the second barrel go, the birdshot at close range ripping the already dead snake apart.

Suddenly she hears Joe's words loud and clear in her head while the sound of the second shot echoes across the creek to the paddock beyond. 'A big brown'll hunt you down, stalk you all the way home. If it's cranky there'll be no stopping it. If you've shot one of the mongrels always keep a fresh shot up the spout for its mate, girlie.'

The second snake strikes high, catching her in the neck. She never even saw it, the mate, its deadly partner which has come after her.

Jessica makes it back to the hut and thinks about saddling the horse and trying to get to Riverview Station, which is an hour's ride away. The bite is just under her jaw and there is no way she can hope to put a tourniquet on it. She is already feeling dizzy and nauseous.

Now she's having trouble with her eyes, starting to see double. She knows she has no chance – she's got half an hour at the most – and she won't be able to stay in the saddle if she tries to ride to Meg and Hester and her beloved Joey.

Jessica pulls the little brass key from around her neck and removes a small box from the shelf above her bed and unlocks it. Inside is a gold hunter watch and a bundle of letters neatly tied. Even with her vision becoming steadily more blurry, Jessica seems to know precisely which letter she wants.

She places the letter and the watch on the table, drags off her boots and strips off her moleskins and flannel shirt and steps out of her bloomers. Naked, she leaves the hut, staggers over to the creek and wades into the water up to her waist and stands beside the same submerged rock she'd pushed against when she'd given birth to Joey fifteen years ago. Jessica washes herself carefully, conserving her strength, her every movement slow and deliberate. She can hear the water running over the rock and a group of rose-breasted galahs quarrelling in the paddock and the cicadas in the gum trees stinging the air with the pitch of their noise. Somehow she makes her way back into the hut. Her body is still hard and young and she still doesn't know how attractive it is. There hasn't been anyone around to tell her that at thirty-three years of age she has become a very beautiful woman.

Jessica dries herself slowly and then puts on one of Auntie Dolly's pretty dresses, the ones she'd been given after she'd left the loony-bin. She feels very dizzy as she attempts to button up her good shoes but manages to complete the task. Then she unfolds a clean pinny – it's one she has kept all these years with Meg's rosebud embroidered in the corner of the pocket. She slips it over her head and ties it behind her back. Her movements are growing slower and her arms are heavy with fatigue as she picks up the watch and letter and puts them in her pocket. Jessica then walks shakily into the blinding sun, though she feels cold and seems to walk as if in a dream.

She reaches the outside table where Rusty lies and slips her arms under his body. His dead weight is almost too much for her but she summons the last of her strength and, lifting him, she places him down in front of Billy's gravestone.

Rusty's head is on his paws as though he is asleep in the shade of the old river gum. Jessica sits down slowly with her back against the rear of the gravestone, against the lettering which says in Yiddish, *Compliments Mrs Goldberg*. She discovered two years ago that there had never been a Mrs Goldberg – that in fact Solly did all the baking, as Moishe's mother had died in childbirth. She gives a weak smile at this thought.

Jessica has only enough strength to reach into her pinny and to open the back of the gold hunter Jack had left her as he lay dying.

Then she takes the letter from her pocket and unfolds it, placing it on her lap with the beautiful old antique watch on top of it so the letter won't blow away. Her eyelids feel leaden and she closes her eyes. 'I loved you, Jack,' she whispers. 'I always did and I always will.'

Mary finds Jessica with her back resting against Billy Simple's gravestone. From a distance Jessica looks as though she is asleep, so Mary does not shout out to her.

It's only when she draws closer that she sees Jessica is dead with Rusty lying beside her, resting together as Mary had seen the two of them so often. 'Good mates, them two,' she murmurs, tears springing to her eyes.

She kneels beside her friend and takes the watch from her lap. Pasted against the open lid is a small curl of blonde hair, which seems to be stuck against the lid with a tiny lump of tar. Scratched into the gold above it in crude letters, as though etched with the blade of a penknife, are the words *I love you, Tea Leaf*.

Mary picks up the letter and sees that it is in Jessica's handwriting. She begins to read.

6 August 1914

My darling Jack,
    Today the war clouds over Europe finally broke and they have taken you from me to fight in the war. I know that you will be brave but my heart breaks for fear that I may never see you again. I am writing this letter to you, though I shall never send it. If you come back to me I shall kiss your sweet

lips and feel your strong body against mine and tell you what it says. If you do not return, you will never know that I carry your child.

My strongest wish is that I may give you a son as handsome and as brave as his father. A boy who you may teach to be a man as loving and gentle as you are.

I shall never love again, for I shall never again feel as I did when you loved me in Narrandera. When you carried me in your arms and stayed by my bed for two days while they made me stay in hospital. I will never forget how on the third night you came to the window. There was a moon, I remember, not quite full, and you came to the window and threw a pebble onto my bed to wake me. 'Come, Jessie,' you said. 'Come and walk in the moonlight with me.'

And then later we made love under a big old gum, with the wind in the high leaves sounding like the waves against the shore I've only dreamt of, those leaves rustling in the wind high up in the gum tree. Your body was so beautiful and when you were inside me, the pleasure was almost unbearable and I thought I must surely die. Oh Jack, I loved you so very much.

I can feel our child, it kicks inside me. I know it will be a boy for already the kicks are rough and wild. With every kick I think of you, my dear, sweet, beautiful Jack.

Stay safe, dear Jack. Stay brave and true. You

*are forgiven for Meg, for she has nothing of you
and I have everything. I have your child.*
    I love you, Jack. I always did and I always will.
    Tea Leaf.

Mary looks up from her letter at the sound of wailing.
Then she sees them, the black people. They are wading
through the creek. The aunties and the old men and the
gins with babies on their breasts. They're splashing
through the shallows and beginning to wail, to cry in
the way that women cry when the greatest has gone
away from them.

At first there are only a few, but as the hours pass
more and more come. By evening there are hundreds,
more black people than Mary knew there could possibly
be in the district. They come continuously for two days
from Lachlan River, Nyngan, Wagga Wagga, Wilcannia
and all the camps and settlements across the black soil
plains and further still. West and north, east and south
from the Victorian border, they come, and they don't
know why. And then they know, they've come to take
Jessica into her dreaming.

ALSO BY

BRYCE COURTENAY

THE POWER OF ONE

First with your head and then with your heart . . .

So says Hoppie Groenewald, boxing champion, to a seven-year-old boy who dreams of being the welterweight champion of the world. For the young Peekay, it is a piece of advice he will carry with him throughout his life.

Born in a South Africa divided by racism and hatred, this one small boy will come to lead all the tribes of Africa. Through enduring friendships with Hymie and Gideon, Peekay gains the strength he needs to win out. And in a final conflict with his childhood enemy, the Judge, Peekay will fight to the death for justice . . .

Bryce Courtenay's classic bestseller is a story of the triumph of the human spirit – a spellbinding tale for all ages

TANDIA

Tandia was overwrought, sitting in the front row of the boxing ring, before the fight began between the man she loved the most and the man she hated the most in the world.

Tandia is a child of all Africa: half Indian, half African, beautiful and intelligent, she is only sixteen when she is first brutalised by the police. Her fear of the white man leads her to join the black resistance movement, where she trains as a terrorist.

Joining her in the fight for justice is the one white man Tandia can trust, the welterweight champion of the world, Peekay. Now the man she loves most must fight their common enemy in order to save both their lives.

A compelling story of good and evil from Australia's most popular storyteller, Bryce Courtenay

THE POTATO FACTORY

Always leave a little salt on the bread . . .

Ikey Solomon's favourite saying is also his way of doing business. And in the business of thieving in thriving nine-teenth-century London, he's very successful indeed. Ikey's partner in crime is his mistress, the forthright Mary Abacus, until misfortune befalls them. They are parted and each must make the harsh journey separately to the convict settlement in Van Diemen's Land.

In the backstreets and dives of Hobart Town, Mary learns the art of brewing and builds The Potato Factory, where she plans a new future. But her ambitions are threatened by Ikey's wife, Hannah, her old enemy. The two women raise their separate families, one legitimate and the other bastard. As each woman sets out to destroy the other, the families are brought to the brink of disaster.

A thrilling tale of Australia's beginnings, told by master storyteller Bryce Courtenay

TOMMO & HAWK

Brutally kidnapped and separated in childhood, Tommo and Hawk are reunited at the age of fifteen in Hobart Town. Together, they escape their troubled pasts and set off on a journey into manhood. From whale hunting in the Pacific to the Maori wars of New Zealand, from the Rocks in Sydney to the miners' riots at the goldfields, Tommo and Hawk must learn each other's strengths and weaknesses in order to survive.

Along the way, Hawk meets the outrageous Maggie Pye, who brings love and laughter into his life. But the demons of Tommo's past return to haunt the brothers. With Tommo at his side, Hawk takes on a fight against all odds to save what they cherish most. In the final confrontation between good and evil, three magpie feathers become the symbol of Tommo and Hawk's rites of passage.

An epic tale of adventure and romance from Australia's bestselling author, Bryce Courtenay

SOLOMON'S SONG

The rivalry between our two families has gone on for two generations – must we take it into a third?

This is the story of two families – branches of the Solomons – transported to an alien land, both of whom eventually grow rich and powerful but who, through three generations, never for one moment relinquish their hatred for each other. It is also the story of our country from the beginning until we came of age as a nation.